Tom Sawyer Abroad

Mark Twain

A WATERMILL CLASSIC

Contents of this edition copyright © 1983 by Watermill Press

Printed in the United States of America.

ISBN 0-89375-712-8

Contents

Chapter 1

Tom Seeks New Adventures

Do you reckon Tom Sawyer was satisfied after all them adventures? I mean the adventures we had down the river, and the time we set Jim free and Tom got shot in the leg. No, he wasn't. It only just p'isoned him for more. That was all the effect it had. You see, when we three came back up the river in glory, as you may say, from that long travel, and the village received us with a torch-light procession and speeches, and everybody hurrah'd and shouted, it made us heroes, and that was what Tom Sawyer had always been hankering to be.

For a while he *was* satisfied. Everybody made much of him, and he tilted up his nose and stepped around the town as though he owned it. Some called him Tom Sawyer the Traveler, and that just swelled him up fit to bust. You see he laid over me and Jim considerable, because we only went down the river on a raft and came back by the steamboat, but Tom went by the steamboat both ways. The boys envied me and Jim a good deal, but land! they just knuckled to the dirt before TOM.

Well, I don't know; maybe he might have been satisfied if it hadn't been for old Nat Parsons, which was postmaster, and powerful long and slim, and king o' good-hearted and silly, and bald-headed, on account of his age, and about the talkiest old cretur I ever see. For as much as thirty years he'd been the only man in the village that had a reputation—I mean a reputation for being a traveler, and of course he was mortal proud of it, and it was reckoned that in the course of that thirty years he had told about that journey over a million times and enjoyed it every time. And now comes along a boy not quite fifteen, and sets everybody admiring and gawking over *his* travels, and it just give the poor old man the high strikes. It made him sick to listen to Tom, and to hear the people say "My land!" "Did you ever!" "My goodness sakes alive!" and all such things, but he couldn't pull away from it, any more than a fly that's got its hind legs fast in the molasses. And always when Tom come to a rest, the poor old cretur would chip in on *his* same old travels and work them for all they were worth; but they were pretty faded, and didn't go for much, and it was pitiful to see. And then Tom would take another innings, and then the old man again—and so on, and so on, for an hour and more, each trying to beat out the other.

You see, Parsons' travels happened like this: When he first got to be postmaster and was green in the business, there come a letter for somebody he didn't know, and there wasn't any such person in the village. Well, he didn't know what to do, nor how to act, and there the letter stayed, and stayed, week in and week out, till the bare sight of it gave him a conniption. The postage wasn't paid on it, and that was another thing to worry about. There wasn't any way to collect that ten cents, and he reckoned the gov'ment would hold him responsible for it and maybe turn him out besides, when they found he hadn't collected it. Well, at last he couldn't stand it any longer. He couldn't sleep nights, he couldn't eat, he was thinned down to a shadder, yet he dasn't ask anybody's advice, for the very person he asked for advice might go back on him and let the gov'ment know about the letter. He had the letter buried under the floor, but that did no good; if he happened to see a person standing over the place it'd give him the cold shivers, and loaded him up with suspicions, and he would sit up that night till the town was still and dark, and then he would sneak there and get it out and bury it in another place. Of course, people got to avoiding him and shaking their heads and whispering, because, the way he was looking and acting, they judged he had killed somebody or done something terrible, they didn't know what, and if he had been a stranger they would've lynched him.

Well, as I was saying, it got so he couldn't stand it any longer; so he made up his mind to pull out for Washington, and just go to the President of the United States and make a clean breast of the whole thing, not keeping back an atom, and then fetch the letter out and lay it before the whole gov'ment, and say, ''Now, there she is—do with me what you're a mind to; though as heaven is my judge I am an innocent man and not deserving of the full penalties of the law and leaving behind me a family that must starve and yet hadn't a thing to do with it, which is the whole truth and I can swear to it.''

So he did it. He had a little wee bit of steamboating, and some stage-coaching, but all the rest of the way was horseback, and it took him three weeks to get to Washington. He saw lots of land and lots of villages and four cities. He was gone 'most eight weeks, and there never was such a proud man in the village as he when he got back. His travels made him the greatest man in all that region, and the most talked about; and people came from as much as thirty miles back in the country, and from over the Illinois bottoms, too, just to look at him—and there they'd stand and gawk, and he'd gabble. You never see anything like it.

Well, there wasn't any way now to settle which was the greatest traveler; some said it was Nat, some said it was Tom. Everybody allowed that Nat had seen the most longitude, but they had to give in that whatever Tom was short in longitude he made up in latitude and climate. It was about a stand-off; so both of them had to whoop up their dangerous adventures, and try to get ahead *that* way. That bullet-wound in Tom's leg was a tough thing for Nat Parsons to buck against, but he bucked the best he could; and at a disadvantage, too, for Tom didn't set still as he'd orter done, to be fair, but always got up and sauntered around and worked his limp while Nat was painting up the adventure that *he* had in Washington; for Tom never let go that limp when his leg got well, but practiced it nights at home, and kept it good as new right along.

Nat's adventure was like this; I don't know how true it is: maybe he got it out of a paper, or somewhere, but I will say this for him, that he *did* know how to tell it. He could make anybody's flesh crawl, and he'd turn pale and hold his breath when he told it, and sometimes women and girls got so faint they couldn't stick it out. Well, it was this way, as near as I can remember:

He come a-loping into Washington, and put up his horse and shoved out to the President's house with his letter, and they told him the President was up to the Capitol, and just going to start for Philadelphia—not a minute to lose if he wanted to catch him. Nat 'most dropped, it made him so sick. His horse was put up, and he didn't know what *to* do. But just then along comes a Negro driving an old ramshackly hack, and he sees his chance. He rushes out and shouts: "A half a dollar if you git me to the Capitol in half an hour, and a quarter extra if you do it in twenty minutes!"

"Done!" says the driver.

Nat he jumped in and slammed the door, and away they went a-ripping and a-tearing over the roughest road a body ever see, and the racket of it was something awful. Nat passed his arms through the loops and hung on for life and death, but pretty soon the hack hit a rock and flew up in the air, and the bottom fell out, and when it come down Nat's feet was on the ground, and he sees he was in the most desperate danger if he couldn't keep up with the hack. He was horrible scared, but he laid into his work for all he was worth, and hung tight to the arm-loops and made his legs fairly fly. He yelled and shouted to the driver to stop, and so did the crowds along the street, for they could see his legs spinning along under the coach, and his head and shoulders bobbing inside through the windows, and he was in awful danger; but the more they all shouted the more the driver whooped and yelled and lashed the horses and shouted, "Don't you fret, I's gwine to git you dah in time, boss; I's gwine to do it, sho'!" for you see he thought they were all hurrying him up, and, of course, he couldn't hear anything for the racket he was making. And so they went ripping along, and everybody just petrified to see it; and when they got to the Capitol at last it was the quickest trip that ever was made, and everybody said so. The horse laid down, and Nat dropped, all tuckered out, and he was all dust and rags and barefooted; but he was in time and just in time, and caught the President and give him the letter, and everything was all right, and the President give him a free pardon on the spot, and Nat give the driver two extra quarters instead of one, because he could see that if he hadn't had the hack he wouldn't 'a' got there in time, nor anywhere near it.

It *was* a powerful good adventure, and Tom Sawyer had to work his bullet-wound mighty lively to hold his own against it.

Well, by and by Tom's glory got to paling down gradu'ly, on account of other things turning up for the people to talk about—first a horse-race, and on top of that a house afire, and on top of that the circus, and on top of that the eclipse; and that started a revival, same as it always does, and by that time there wasn't any more talk about Tom, so to speak, and you never see a person so sick and disgusted.

Pretty soon he got to worrying and fretting right along day in and day out, and when I asked him what *was* he in such a state about, he said it 'most broke his heart to think how time was slipping away, and him getting older and older, and no wars breaking out and no way of making a name for himself that he could see. Now that is the way boys is always thinking, but he was the first one I ever heard come out and say it.

So then he set to work to get up a plan to make him celebrated; and pretty soon he struck it, and offered to take me and Jim in. Tom Sawyer was always free and generous that way. There's a-plenty of boys that's mighty good and friendly when *you've* got a good thing, but when a good thing happens to come their way they don't say a word to you, and try to hog it all. That warn't ever Tom Sawyer's way, I can say that for him. There's plenty of boys that will come hankering and graveling around you when you've got an apple and beg the core off of you; but when they've got one, and you beg for the core and remind them how you give them a core one time, they say thank you 'most to death, but there ain't a-going to be no core. But I notice they always git come-up-with; all you got to do is to wait.

Well, we went out in the woods on the hill, and Tom told us what it was. It was a crusade.

"What's a crusade?" I says.

He looked scornful, the way he's always done when he was ashamed of a person, and says:

"Huck Finn, do you mean to tell me you don't know what a crusade is?"

"No," says I, "I don't. And I don't care to, nuther. I've lived till now and done without it, and had my health, too. But as soon as you tell me, I'll know, and that's soon enough. I don't see any use in finding out things and clogging up my head with them when I mayn't ever have any occasion to use 'em. There was Lance Williams, he learned how to talk Choctaw here till one come and dug his grave for him. Now, then, what's a crusade? But I can tell you one thing before you begin; if it's a patent-right, there's no money in it. Bill Thompson he—"

"Patent-right!" says he. "I never see such an idiot. Why, a crusade is a kind of war."

I thought he must be losing his mind. But no, he was in real earnest, and went right on, perfectly ca'm.

"A crusade is a war to recover the Holy Land from the paynim."

"Which Holy Land?"

"Why, *the* Holy Land—there ain't but one."

"What do *we* want of it?"

"Why, can't you understand? It's in the hands of the paynim, and it's our duty to take it away from them."

"How did we come to let them git hold of it?"

"We didn't come to let them git hold of it. They always had it."

"Why, Tom, then it must belong to them, don't it?"

"Why, of course it does. Who said it didn't?"

I studied over it, but couldn't seem to git at the right of it, no way. I says:

"It's too many for me, Tom Sawyer. If I had a farm and it was mine, and another person wanted it, would it be right for him to—"

"Oh, shucks! you don't know enough to come in when it rains, Huck Finn. It ain't a farm, it's entirely different. You see, it's like this. They own the land, just the mere land, and that's all they *do* own; but it was our folks, our Jews and Christians, that made it holy, and so they haven't any business to be there defiling it. It's a shame, and we ought not to stand it a minute. We ought to march against them and take it away from them."

"Why, it does seem to me it's the most mixed-up thing I ever see! Now, if I had a farm and another person—"

"Don't I tell you it hasn't got anything to do with farming? Farming is business, just common low-down business: that's all it is, it's all you can say for it; but this is higher, this is religious, and totally different."

"Religious to go and take the land away from people that owns it?"

"Certainly; it's always been considered so."

Jim he shook his head, and says:

"Mars Tom, I reckon dey's a mistake about it somers—dey mos' sholy is. I's religious myself, en I knows plenty religious people, but I hain't run across none dat acts like dat.''

It made Tom hot, and he says:

"Well, it's enough to make a body sick, such mulletheaded ignorance! If either of you'd read anything about history, you'd know that Richard Cur de Loon, and the Pope, and Godfrey de Bulleyn, and lot more of the most noble-hearted and pious people in the world, hacked and hammered at the paynims for more than two hundred years trying to take their land away from them, and swum neck-deep in blood the whole time— and yet here's a couple of sap-headed country yahoos out in the backwoods of Missouri setting themselves up to know more about the rights and wrongs of it than they did! Talk about cheek!''

Well, of course, that put a more different light on it, and me and Jim felt pretty cheap and ignorant, and wished we hadn't been quite so chipper. I couldn't say nothing, and Jim he couldn't for a while; then he says:

"Well, den, I reckon it's all right; beca'se ef dey didn't know, dey ain't no use for po' ignorant folks like us to be trying to know; en so, ef it's our duty, we got to go en tackle it en do de bes' we can. Same time, I feel as sorry for dem paynims as Mars Tom. De hard part gwine to be to kill folks dat a body hain't been 'quainted wid and dat hain't done him no harm. Dat's it, you see. Ef we wus to go 'mongst 'em, jist we three, en say we's hungry, en ast 'em for a bite to eat, why, maybe dey's jist like yuther people. Don't you reckon dey is? Why, *dey'd* give it, I know dey would, en den—''

"Then what?''

"Well, Mars Tom, my idea is like dis. It ain't no use, we *can't* kill dem po' strangers dat ain't doin' us no harm, till we've had practice—I knows it perfectly well, Mars Tom—'deed I knows it perfectly well. But ef we takes a' ax or two, jist you en me en Huck, en slips acrost de river tonight arter de moon's gone down, en kills dat sick fam'ly dat's over on the Sny, en burns dey house down, en—"

"Oh, you make me tired!" says Tom. "I don't want to argue any more with people like you and Huck Finn, that's always wandering from the subject, and ain't got any more sense than to try to reason out a thing that's pure theology by the laws that protect real estate!"

Now that's just where Tom Sawyer warn't fair. Jim didn't mean no harm, and I didn't mean no harm. We knowed well enough that he was right and we was wrong, and all we was after was to get at the *how* of it, and that was all; and the only reason he couldn't explain it so we could understand it was because we was ignorant—yes, and pretty dull, too, I ain't denying that; but, land! that ain't no crime, I should think.

But he wouldn't hear no more about it—just said if we had tackled the thing in the proper spirit, he would 'a' raised a couple of thousand knights and put them in steel armor from head to heel, and made me a lieutenant and Jim a sutler, and took the command himself and brushed the whole paynim outfit into the sea like flies and come back across the world in a glory like sunset. But he said we didn't know enough to take the chance when we had it, and he wouldn't ever offer it again. And he didn't. When he once got set, you couldn't budge him.

But I didn't care much. I am peaceable, and don't get up rows with people that ain't doing nothing to me. I allowed if the paynim was satisfied I was, and we would let it stand at that.

Now Tom he got all that notion out of Walter Scott's book, which he was always reading. And it *was* a wild notion, because in my opinion he never could've raised the men, and if he did, as like as not he would've got licked. I took the book and read all about it, and as near as I could make it out, most of the folks that shook farming to go crusading had a mighty rocky time of it.

Chapter 2
The Balloon Ascension

Well, Tom got up one thing after another, but they all had tender spots about em' somewheres, and he had to shove 'em aside. So at last he was about in despair. Then the St. Louis papers begun to talk a good deal about the balloon that was going to sail to Europe, and Tom sort of thought he wanted to go down and see what it looked like, but couldn't make up his mind. But the papers went on talking, and so he allowed that maybe if he didn't go he mightn't ever have another chance to see a balloon; and next, he found out that Nat Parsons was going down to see it, and that decided him, of course. He wasn't going to have Nat Parsons coming back bragging about seeing the balloon, and him having to listen to it and keep quiet. So he wanted me and Jim to go too, and we went.

It was a noble big balloon, and had wings and fans and all sorts of things, and wasn't like any balloon you see in pictures. It was away out toward the edge of town, in a vacant lot, corner of Twelfth Street; and there was a big crowd around it, making fun of it, and making fun of the man—a lean pale feller with that soft kind of moonlight in his eyes, you know—and they kept saying it wouldn't go. It made him hot to hear them, and he would turn on them and shake his fist and say they was animals and blind, but someday they would find they had stood face to face with one of the men that lifts up nations and makes civilizations, and was too dull to know it; and right here on this spot their own children and grandchildren would build a monument to him that would outlast a thousand years, but his name would outlast the monument. And then the crowd would burst out in a laugh again, and yell at him, and ask him what his name was before he was married, and what he would take to not do it, and what was his sister's cat's grand-mother's name, and all the things that a crowd says when they've got hold of a feller that they see they can plague. Well, some things they said *was* funny—yes, and mighty witty too, I ain't denying that—but all the same it warn't fair nor brave, all them people pitching on one, and they so glib and sharp, and him without any gift of talk to answer back with. But, good land! what did he want to sass back for? You see, it couldn't do him no good, and it was just nuts for them. They *had* him, you know. But that was his way. I reckon he couldn't help it; he was made so, I judge. He was a good enough sort of cretur, and hadn't no harm in him, and was just a genius, as the papers said, which wasn't his fault. We can't all be sound: we've got to be the way we're made. As near as I can make out, geniuses think they know it all, and so they won't take people's advice, but always go their own way, which makes everybody forsake them and despise them, and that is perfectly natural. If they was humbler, and listened and tried to learn, it would be better for them.

The part the professor was in was like a boat, and was big and roomy, and had watertight lockers around the inside to keep all sorts of things in, and a body could sit on them, and make beds on them, too. We went aboard, and there was twenty people there, snooping around and examining, and old Nat Parsons was there, too. The professor kept fussing around getting ready, and the people went ashore, drifting out one at a time, and old Nat he was the last. Of course it wouldn't do to let him go out behind *us*. We mustn't budge till he was gone, so we could be last ourselves.

But he was gone now, so it was time for us to follow. I heard a big shout, and turned around— the city was dropping from under us like a shot! It made me sick all through, I was so scared. Jim turned gray and couldn't say a word, and Tom didn't say nothing, but looked excited. The city went on dropping down, and down, and down; but we didn't seem to be doing nothing but just hang in the air and stand still. The houses got smaller and smaller, and the city pulled itself together, closer and closer, and the men and wagons got to looking like ants and bugs crawling around, and the streets like threads and cracks; and then it all kind of melted together, and there wasn't any city anymore: it was only a big scar on

15

the earth, and it seemed to me a body could see up the river and down the river about a thousand miles, though of course it wasn't so much. By and by the earth was a ball—just a round ball, of a dull color, with shiny stripes wriggling and winding around over it, which was rivers. The Widder Douglas always told me the earth was round like a ball, but I never took any stock in a lot of them superstitions o' hers, and of course I paid no attention to that one, because I could see myself that the world was the shape of a plate, and flat. I used to go up the hill, and take a look around and prove it for myself, because I reckon the best way to get a sure thing on a fact is to go and examine for yourself, and not take anybody's say-so. But I had to give in now that the widder was right. That is, she was right as to the rest of the world, but she warn't right about the part our village is in; that part is the shape of a plate, and flat, I take my oath!

The professor had been quiet all this time, as if he was asleep; but he broke loose now, and he was mighty bitter. He says something like this:

"Idiots! They said it wouldn't go; and they wanted to examine it, and spy around and get the secret of it out of me. Nobody knows what makes it move but me; and it's a new power—a new power, and a thousand times the strongest in the earth! Steam's foolishness to it! They said I couldn't go to Europe. To Europe! Why, there's power aboard to last five years, and food for three months. They are fools! What do they know about it? Yes, and they said my airship was flimsy. Why, she's good for fifty years! I can sail the skies all my life if I want to, and steer where I please, though they laughed at that, and said I couldn't. Couldn't steer! Come here, boy; we'll see. You press these buttons as I tell you.''

He made Tom steer the ship all about and every which way, and learnt him the whole thing in nearly no time; and Tom said it was perfectly easy. He made him fetch the ship down 'most to the earth, and had him spin her along so close to the Illinois prairies that a body could talk to the farmers, and hear everything they said perfectly plain; and he flung out printed bills to them that told about the balloon, and said it was going to Europe. Tom got so he could steer straight for a tree till he got nearly to it, and then dart up and skin right along over the top of it. Yes, and he showed Tom how to land her; and he done it first-rate, too, and set he down in the prairies as soft as wool. But the minute we started to skip out the professor says, "No, you don't!" and shot her up in the air again. It was awful. I begun to beg and so did Jim; but it only give his temper a rise, and he begun to rage around and look wild out of his eyes, and I was scared of him.

Well, then he got on to his troubles again, and mourned and grumbled about the way he was treated, and couldn't seem to git over it, and especially people's saying his ship was flimsy. He scoffed at that, and at their saying she warn't simple and would be always getting out of order. Get out of order! That graveled him; he said that she couldn't any more get out of order than the solar sister.

He got worse and worse, and I never see a person take on so. It give me the cold shivers to see him, and so it did Jim. By and by he got to yelling and screaming, and then he swore the world shouldn't ever have his secret at all now, it had treated him so mean. He said he would sail his balloon around the globe just to show what he could do, and then he would sink it in the sea, and sink us all along with it, too. Well, it was the aw-fulest fix to be in, and here was night coming on!

He gave us something to eat, and made us go to the other end of the boat, and he laid down on a locker, where he could boss all the works, and put his old pepper-box revolver under his head, and said if anybody come fooling around there trying to land her, he would kill him.

We set scrunched up together, and thought considerable, but didn't say much—only just a word once in a while when a body had to say something or bust, we was *so* scared and worried. The night dragged along slow and lonesome. We was pretty low down, and the moonshine made everything soft and pretty, and the farmhouses looked snug and homeful, and we could hear the farm sounds, and wished we could be down there; but laws! we just slipped along over them like a ghost, and never left a track.

Away in the night, when all the sounds was late sounds, and the air had a late feel, and a late smell, too—about a two-o'clock feel, as near as I could make out—Tom said the professor was so quiet this time he must be asleep, and we'd better—

"Better what?" I says in a whisper, and feeling sick all over, because I knowed what he was thinking about.

"Better slip back there and tie him, and land the ship," he says.

I says: "No, sir! Don't you budge, Tom Sawyer."

And Jim—well, Jim was o' gasping, he was so scared. He says:

"Oh, Mars Tom, *don't!* Ef you teches him, we's gone—we's gone sho'! I ain't gwine anear him, not for nothin' in dis worl'. Mars Tom, he's plumb crazy."

Tom whispers and says: "That's *why* we've got to do something. If he wasn't crazy I wouldn't give shucks to be anywhere but here; you couldn't hire me to get out—now that I've got used to this balloon and over the scare of being cut loose from solid ground—if he was in his right mind. But it's no good politics, sailing around like this with a person that's out of his head, and says he's going round the world and then drown us all. We've *got* to do something, I tell you, and do it before he wakes up, too, or we mayn't ever get another chance. Come!"

But it made us turn cold and creepy just to think of it, and we said we wouldn't budge. So Tom was for slipping back there by himself to see if he couldn't get at the steering-gear and land the ship. We begged and begged him not to, but it warn't no use; so he got down on his hands and knees, and begun to crawl an inch at a time, we a-holding our breath and watching. After he got to the middle of the boat he crept slower than ever, and it did seem like years to me. But at last we see him get to the professor's head, and sort of raise up soft and look a good spell in his face and listen. Then we see him begin to inch along again toward the professor's feet where the steering-buttons was. Well, he got there all safe, and was reaching slow and steady toward the buttons, but he knocked down something that made a noise, and we see him slump down flat an' soft in the bottom, and lay still. The professor stirred, and says, "What's that?" But everybody kept dead still and quiet, and he begun to mutter and mumble and nestle, like a person that's going to wake up, and I thought I was going to die, I was so worried and scared.

Then a cloud slid over the moon, and I 'most cried, I was so glad. She buried herself deeper and deeper into the cloud, and it got so dark we couldn't see Tom. Then it began to sprinkle rain, and we could hear the professor fussing at his ropes and things and abusing the weather. We was afraid every minute he would touch Tom, and then we would be goners, and no help; but Tom was already on his way back, and when we felt his hands on our knees my breath stopped sudden, and my heart fell down 'mongst my other works, because I couldn't tell in the dark but it might be the professor, which I thought it *was*.

Dear! I was so glad to have him back that I was just as near happy as a person could be that was up in the air that way with a deranged man. You can't land a balloon in the dark, and so I hoped it would keep on raining, for I didn't want Tom to go meddling anymore and make us so awful uncomfortable. Well, I got my wish.

It drizzled along the rest of the night, which wasn't long, though it did seem so; and at daybreak it cleared, and the world looked mighty soft and gray and pretty, and the forests and fields so good to see again, and the horses and cattle standing sober and thinking. Next, the sun come a-blazing up gay and splendid, and then we began to feel rusty and stretchy, and first we knowed we was all asleep.

Chapter 3
Tom Explains

We went to sleep about four o'clock, and woke up about eight. The professor was setting back there at his end, looking glum. He pitched us some breakfast, but he told us not to come abaft the midship compass. That was about the middle of the boat. Well, when you are sharp-set, and you eat and satisfy yourself, everything looks pretty different from what it done before. It makes a body feel pretty near comfortable, even when he is up in a balloon with a genius. We got to talking together.

There was one thing that kept bothering me, and by and by I says:

"Tom, didn't we start east?"

"Yes."

"How fast have we been going?"

"Well, you heard what the professor said when he was raging round. Sometimes, he said, we was making fifty miles an hour, sometimes ninety, sometimes a hundred; said that with a gale to help he could make three hundred any time, and said if he wanted the gale, and wanted it blowing the right direction, he only had to go up higher or down lower to find it.''

"Well, then, it's just as I reckoned. The professor lied.''

"Why?''

"Because if we was going so fast we ought to be past Illinois, oughtn't we?''

"Certainly.''

"Well, we ain't.''

"What's the reason we ain't?''

"I know by the color. We're right over Illinois yet. And you can see for yourself that Indiana ain't in sight.''

"I wonder what's the matter with you, Huck. You know by the *color?*''

"Yes, of course I do.''

"What's the color got to do with it?''

"It's got everything to do with it. Illinois is green, Indiana is pink. You show me any pink down here, if you can. No, sir; it's green.''

"Indiana *pink?* Why, what a lie!''

"It ain't no lie; I've seen it on the map, and it's pink.''

You never seen a person so aggravated and disgusted. He says:

"Well, if I was such a numskull as you, Huck Finn, I would jump over. Seen it on the map! Huck Finn, did you reckon the states was the same color out-of-doors as they are on the map?''

"Tom Sawyer, what's a map for? Ain't it to learn you facts?''

"Of course."

"Well, then, how's it going to do that if it tells lies? That's what I want to know."

"Shucks, you muggins! It don't tell lies."

"It don't, don't it?"

"No, it don't."

"All right, then; if it don't, there ain't no two states the same color. You git around *that*, if you can, Tom Sawyer."

He see I had him, and Jim see it too; and I tell you, I felt pretty good, for Tom Sawyer was always a hard person to get ahead of. Jim slapped his leg and says:

"I tell *you!* dat's smart, dat's right down smart. Ain't no use, Mars Tom; he got you *dis* time, sho'!" He slapped his leg again, and says, "My *lan'*, but it was a smart one!"

I never felt so good in my life; and yet I didn't know I was saying anything much till it was out. I was just mooning along, perfectly careless, and not expecting anything was going to happen, and never *thinking* of such a thing at all, when, all of a sudden, out it came. Why, it was just as much a surprise to me as it was to any of them. It was just the same way it is when a person is munching along on a hunk of corn-pone, and not thinking about anything, and all of a sudden bites into a di'mond. Now all that *he* knows first off is that it's some kind of gravel he's bit into; but he don't find out it's a di'mond till he gits it out and brushes off the sand and crumbs and one thing or another, and has a look at it, and then he's surprised and glad—yes, and proud too; though when you come to look the thing straight in the eye, he ain't entitled to as much credit as he would 'a' been if he'd been *hunting* di'monds. You can see the difference easy if you think it over. You see, an accident, that way, ain't fairly as big a thing as a thing that's done a-purpose. Anybody could find that di'mond in that corn-pone; but mind you, it's got to be somebody that's got *that kind of a corn-pone*. That's where that feller's credit comes in, you see; and that's where mine comes in. I don't claim no great things—I don't reckon I could 'a' done it again—but I done it that time; that's all I claim. And I hadn't no more idea I could do such a thing, and warn't any more thinking about it or trying to, than you be this minute. Why, I was just as ca'am, a body couldn't be any ca'mer, and yet, all of a sudden, out it come. I've often thought of that time, and I can remember just the way everything looked, same as if it was only last week. I can see it all: beautiful rolling country with woods and fields and lakes for hundreds and hundreds of miles all around, and towns and villages scattered everywheres under us, here and there and yonder; and the professor mooning over a chart on his little table, and Tom's cap flopping in the rigging where it was hung up to dry. And one thing in particular was a bird right alongside, not ten foot off, going our way and trying to keep up, but losing ground all the time; and a railroad-train doing the same thing down there, sliding among the trees and farms, and pouring out a long cloud of black smoke and now and then a little puff of white; and when the white was gone so long you had almost forgot it, you would hear a little faint toot, and that was the whistle. And we left the bird and the train both behind, '*way* behind, and done it easy, too.

But Tom he was huffy, and said me and Jim was a couple of ignorant blatherskites, and then he says:

"Suppose there's a brown calf and a big brown dog, and an artist is making a picture of them. What is the *main* thing that that artist has got to do? He has got to paint them so you can tell them apart the minute you look at them, hain't he? Of course. Well, then, do you want him to go and paint *both* of them brown? Certainly you don't. He paints one of them blue, and then you can't make no mistake. It's just the same with the maps. That's why they make every state a different color; it ain't to deceive you, it's to keep you from deceiving youself."

But I couldn't see no argument about that, and neither could Jim. Jim shook his head, and says:

"Why, Mars Tom, if you knowed what chuckleheads dem painters is, you'd wait a long time before you'd fetch one er *dem* in to back up a fac'. I's gwine to tell you, den you kin see for you'self. I see one of 'em a-paintin' away, one day, down in ole Hank Wilson's back lot, en I went down to see, en he was paintin' dat old bridle cow wid de near horn gone—you knows de one I means. En I ast him what he's paintin' her for, en he say when he git her painted, de picture's wuth a hundred dollars. Mars Tom, he could 'a' got de cow fer fifteen, en I *tole* him so. Well, sah, if you'll b'lieve me, he jes' shuck his head, dat painter did, en went on a-dobbin'. Bless you, Mars Tom, *dey* don't know nothin'."

Tom lost his temper. I notice a person 'most always does that's got laid out in an argument. He told us to shut up, and maybe we'd feel better. Then he see a town clock away off down yonder, and he took up the glass and looked at it, and then looked at his silver turnip, and then at the clock, and then at the turnip again, and says:

"That's funny! That clock's near about an hour fast."

So he put up his turnip. Then he see another clock, and took a look, and it was an hour fast, too. That puzzled him.

"That's a mighty curious thing," he says. "I don't understand it."

Then he took the glass and hunted up another clock, and sure enough it was an hour fast, too. Then his eyes began to spread and his breath to come out kinder gaspy like, and he says:

"Ger-reat Scott, it's the *longitude!*"

I says, considerably scared:

"Well, what's been and gone and happened now?"

"Why, the thing that's happened is that this old bladder has slid over Illinois and Indiana and Ohio like nothing, and this is the east end of Pennsylvania or New York, or somewheres around there."

"Tom Sawyer, you don't mean it!"

"Yes, I do, and it's dead sure. We've covered about fifteen degrees of longitude since we left St. Louis yesterday afternoon, and them clocks are *right*. We've come close on to eight hundred miles."

I didn't believe it, but it made the cold streaks

27

trickle down my back just the same. In my experience I knowed it wouldn't take much short of two weeks to do it down the Mississippi on a raft.

Jim was working his mind and studying. Pretty soon he says:

"Mars Tom, did you say dem clocks uz right?"

"Yes, they're right."

"Ain' yo watch right, too?"

"She's right for St. Louis, but she's an hour wrong for here."

"Mars Tom, is you tryin' to let on dat de time ain't de *same* everywheres?"

"No, it ain't the same everywheres, by a long shot."

Jim looked distressed, and says:

"It grieves me to hear you talk like dat, Mars Tom; I's right down ashamed to hear you talk like dat, arter de way you's been raised. Yassir, it'd break yo' Aunt Polly's heart to hear you."

Tom was astonished. He looked Jim over wondering, and didn't say nothing, and Jim went on:

"Mars Tom, who put de people out yonder in St. Louis? De Lord done it. Who put de people here whar we is? De Lord done it. Ain' dey bofe his children? 'Cose dey is. *Well,* den! is he gwine to *scriminate* 'twixt 'em?"

"Scriminate! I never heard such ignorance. There ain't no discriminating about it. When he makes you and some more of his children black, and makes the rest of us white, what do you call that?"

Jim see the p'int. He was stuck. He couldn't answer. Tom says:

"He does discriminate, you see, when he wants to; but this case *here* ain't no discrimination of his, it's man's. The Lord made the day, and he made the night; but he didn't invent the hours, and he didn't distribute them around. Man did that."

"Mars Tom, is dat so? Man done it?"

"Certainly."

"Who tole him he could?"

"Nobody. He never asked."

Jim studied a minute, and says:

"Well, dat do beat me. I wouldn't 'a' tuck no such resk. But some people ain't scared o' nothin'. Dey bangs right ahead; *dey* don't care what happens. So den dey's allays an hour's diff'unce everywhah, Mars Tom?"

"An hour? No! It's four minutes different for every degree of longitude, you know. Fifteen of 'em's an hour, thirty of 'em's two hours, and so on. When it's one o'clock Tuesday morning in England, it's eight o'clock the night before in New York."

Jim moved a little way along the locker, and you could see he was insulted. He kept shaking his head and muttering, and so I slid along to him and patted him on the leg, and petted him up, and got him over the worst of his feelings, and then he says:

"Mars Tom talkin' sich talk as dat! Choosday in one place en Monday in t'other, bofe in the same day! Huck, dis ain't no place to joke—up here what we is. Two days in one day! How you gwine to get two days inter one day? Can't git two hours inter one hour, kin you? Can't git two men

29

inter one skin, kin you? Can't git two gallons of whiskey inter a one-gallon jug, kin you? No, sir, 'twould strain de jug. Yes, en even den you couldn't, *I* don't believe. Why, looky here, Huck, s'posen de Choosday was New Year's— now den! is you gwine to tell me it's dis year in one place en las' year in t'other, bofe in de identical same minute? It's de beatenest rubbage! I can't stan' it—I can't stan' to hear tell 'bout it.'' Then he begun to shiver and turn gray, and Tom says:

"*Now* what's the matter? What's the trouble?''

Jim could hardly speak, but he says:

"Mars Tom, you ain't jokin', en it's *so?*''

"No, I'm not, and it *is* so.''

Jim shivered again, and says:

"Den dat Monday could be de las' day, en dey wouldn't be no las' day in England, en de dead wouldn't be called. We mustn't go over dah, Mars Tom. Please git him to turn back; I wants to be whah—''

All of a sudden we see something, and all jumped up, and forgot everything and begun to gaze. Tom says:

"Ain't that the—'' He catched his breath, then says: "It *is*, sure as you live! It's the ocean!''

That made me and Jim catch out breath, too. Then we all stood petrified but happy, for none of us had ever seen an ocean, or ever expected to. Tom kept muttering:

"Atlantic Ocean—Atlantic. Land, don't it sound great! And that's *it*—and *we* are looking at it—we! Why, it's just too splendid to believe!''

Then we see a big bank of black smoke; and

when we got nearer, it was a city—and a monster she was, too, with a thick fringe of ships around one edge; and we wondered if it was New York, and begun to jaw and dispute about it, and, first we knowed, it slid from under us and went flying behind, and here we was, out over the very ocean itself, and going like a cyclone. Then we woke up, I tell you!

We made a break aft and raised a wail, and begun to beg the professor to turn back and land us, but he jerked out his pistol and motioned us back, and we went, but nobody will ever know how bad we felt.

The land was gone, all but a little streak, like a snake, away off on the edge of the water, and down under us was just ocean, ocean, ocean—millions of miles of it, heaving and pitching and squirming, and white sprays blowing from the wave-tops, and only a few ships in sight, wallowing around and laying over, first on one side and then on t'other, and sticking their bows under and then their sterns; and before long there warn't no ships at all, and we had the sky and the whole ocean to ourselves, and the roomiest place I ever see and the lonesomest.

Chapter 4

Storm

And it got lonesomer and lonesomer. There was the big sky up there, empty and awful deep; and the ocean down there without a thing on it but just the waves. All around us was a ring, where the sky and the water come together; yes, a monstrous big ring it was, and we right in the dead center of it—plumb in the center. We was racing along like a prairie-fire, but it never made any difference, we couldn't seem to git past that center no way. I couldn't see that we ever gained an inch on that ring. It made a body feel creepy, it was so curious and unaccountable.

Well, everything was so awful still that we got to talking in a very low voice, and kept on getting creepier and lonesomer and less and less talky, till at last the talk ran dry altogether, and we just set there and "thunk," as Jim calls it, and never said a word the longest time.

The professor never stirred till the sun was

overhead; then he stood up and put a kind of tri-angle to his eye, and Tom said it was a sextant and he was taking the sun to see whereabouts the balloon was. Then he ciphered a little and looked in a book, and then he begun to carry on again. He said lots of wild things, and, among others, he said he would keep up this hundred-mile gait till the middle of tomorrow afternoon, and then he'd land in London.

We said we would be humbly thankful.

He was turning away, but he whirled around when we said that, and give us a long look of his blackest kind—one of the maliciousest and suspiciousest looks I ever see. Then he says:

"You want to leave me. Don't try to deny it."

We didn't know what to say, so we held in and didn't say nothing at all.

He went aft and set down, but he couldn't seem to git that thing out of his mind. Every now and then he would rip out something about it, and try to make us answer him, but we dasn't.

It got lonesomer and lonesomer right along, and it did seem to me I couldn't stand it. It was still worse when night begun to come on. By and by Tom pinched me and whispers:

"Look!"

I took a glance aft, and see the professor taking a whet out of a bottle. I didn't like the looks of that. By and by he took another drink, and pretty soon he begun to sing. It was dark now, and getting black and stormy. He went on singing, wilder and wilder, and the thunder begun to mutter, and the wind to wheeze and moan among the ropes, and altogether it was awful. It got so black we couldn't see him anymore, and wished we couldn't hear him, but we could. The he got still; but he warn't still ten minutes till we got suspicious, and wished he would start up his noise again, so we could tell where he was. By and by there was a flash of lightning, and we see him start to get up, but he staggered and fell down. We heard him scream out in the dark:

"They don't want to go to England. All right, I'll change the course. They want to leave me. I know they do. Well, they shall—and *now!*"

I 'most died when he said that. Then he was still again—still so long I couldn't bear it, and it did seem to me the lightning wouldn't *ever* come again. But at last there was a blessed flash, and there he was, on his hands and knees crawling, and nor four feet from us. My, but his eyes was terrible! He made a lunge for Tom, and says, "Overboard *you* go!" but it was already pitch-dark again, and I couldn't see whether he got him or not, and Tom didn't make a sound.

There was another long, horrible wait; then there was a flash, and I see Tom's head sink down outside the boat and disappear. He was on the rope-ladder that dangled down in the air from the gunnel. The professor let off a shout and jumped for him, and straight off it was pitch-dark again, and Jim groaned out, "Po' Mars Tom, he's a goner!" and made a jump for the professor, but the professor warn't there.

Then we heard a couple of terrible screams, and then another not so loud, and then another that was 'way below, and you could only *just* hear it; and I heard Jim say, "Po' Mars Tom!"

Then it was awful still, and I reckon a person could 'a' counted four thousand before the next flash come. When it come I see Jim on his knees, with his arms on the locker and his face buried in them, and he was crying. Before I could look over the edge it was all dark again, and I was glad, because I didn't want to see. But when the next flash come, I was watching, and down there I see somebody a-swinging in the wind on the ladder, and it was Tom!

"Come up!" I shouts. "Come up, Tom!"

His voice was so weak, and the wind roared so, I couldn't make out what he said, but I thought he asked was the professor up there. I shouts:

"No, he's down in the ocean! Come up! Can we help you?"

Of course, all this in the dark.

"Huck, who is you hollerin' at?"

"I'm hollerin' at Tom."

"Oh, Huck, how kin you act so, when you know po' Mars Tom—" Then he let off an awful scream, and flung his head and his arms back and let off another one, because there was a white glare just then, and he had raised up his face just in time to see Tom's, as white as snow, rise above the gunnel and look him right in the eye. He thought it was Tom's ghost, you see.

Tom clumb aboard, and when Jim found it *was* him, and not his ghost, he hugged him, and called him all sorts of loving names, and carried on like he was gone crazy, he was so glad. Says I:

"What did you wait for, Tom? Why didn't you come up at first?"

"I dasn't, Huck. I knowed somebody plunged

down past me, but I didn't know who it was in the dark. It could 'a' been you, it could 'a' been Jim."

That was the way with Tom Sawyer—always sound. He warn't coming up till he knowed where the professor was.

The storm let go about this time with all its might; and it was dreadful the way the thunder boomed and tore, and the lightning glared out, and the wind sung and screamed in the rigging, and the rain come down. One second you couldn't see your hand before you, and the next you could count the threads in your coatsleeve, and see a whole wide desert of waves pitching and tossing through a kind of veil of rain. A storm like that is the loveliest thing there is, but it ain't at its best when you are up in the sky and lost, and it's wet and lonesome, and there's just been a death in the family.

We set there huddled up in the bow, and talked low about the poor professor; and everybody was sorry for him, and sorry the world had made fun of him, and treated him so harsh, when he was doing the best he could, and hadn't a friend nor nobody to encourage him and keep him from brooding his mind away and going deranged. There was plenty of clothes and blankets and everything at the other end, but we thought we'd ruther take the rain than go meddling back there.

Chapter 5

Land

We tried to make some plans, but we couldn't come to no agreement. Me and Jim was for turning around and going back home, but Tom allowed that by the time daylight come, so we could see our way, we would be so far toward England that we might as well go there, and come back in a ship, and have the glory of saying we done it.

About midnight the storm quit and the moon come out and lit up the ocean, and we begun to feel comfortable and drowsy; so we stretched out on the lockers and went to sleep, and never woke up again till sun-up. The sea was sparkling like di'monds, and it was nice weather, and pretty soon our things was all dry again.

We went aft to find some breakfast, and the first thing we noticed was that there was a dim light burning in a compass back there under a hood. Then Tom was disturbed. He says:

"You know what that means, easy enough. It

means that somebody has got to stay on watch and steer this thing the same as he would a ship, or she'll wander around and go wherever the wind wants her to."

"Well," I says, "what's she been doing since —er—since we had the accident?"

"Wandering," he says, kinder troubled— "wandering, without any doubt. She's in a wind now that's blowing her south of east. We don't know how long that's been going on, either."

So then he p'inted her east, and said he would hold her there till we rousted out the breakfast. The professor had laid in everything a body could want; he couldn't 'a' been better fixed. There wasn't no milk for the coffee, but there was water and everything else you could want, and a charcoal stove and the fixings for it, and pipes and cigars and matches; and wine and liquor, which warn't in our line; and books, and maps, and charts, and an accordion; and furs, and blankets, and no end of rubbish, like brass beads and brass jewelry, which Tom said was a sure sign that he had an idea of visiting among savages. There was money, too. Yes, the professor was well enough fixed.

After breakfast Tom learned me and Jim how to steer, and divided us all up into four-hour watches, turn and turn about; and when his watch was out I took his place, and he got out the professor's papers and pens and wrote a letter home to his Aunt Polly, telling her everything that had happened to us, and dated it *"In the Welkin, approaching England,"* and folded it together and stuck it fast with a red wafer, and directed it, and wrote above the direction, in big writing, *"From Tom Sawyer, the Erronort,"* and

said it would stump old Nat Parsons, the postmaster, when it come along in the mail. I says:

"Tom Sawyer, this ain't no welkin; it's a balloon."

"Well, now, who *said* it was a welkin, smarty?"

"You've wrote it on the letter, anyway."

"What of it? That don't mean that the balloon's
the welkin."

"Oh, I thought it did. Well, then, what is a
welkin?"

I see in a minute he was stuck. He raked and
scraped around in his mind, but he couldn't find
nothing, so he had to say:

"*I* don't know, and nobody don't know. It's
just a word, and it's a mighty good word, too.
There ain't many that lays over it. I don't believe
there's *any* that does."

"Shucks!" I says. "But what does it *mean?*—
that's the p'int."

"*I* don't know what it means, I tell you. It's a
word that people uses for—for—well, it's orna-
mental. They don't put ruffles on a shirt to keep a
person warm, do they?"

"Course they don't."

"But they put them *on*, don't they?"

"Yes."

"All right, then; that letter I wrote is a shirt, and
the welkin's the ruffle on it."

I judged that that would gravel Jim, and it did.

"No, Mars Tom, it ain't no use to talk like dat;
en, moreover, it's sinful. You knows a letter ain't
no shirt, en dey ain't no ruffles on it, nuther. Dey
ain't no place to put 'em on; you can't put 'em on,
and dey wouldn't stay ef you did."

"Oh, *do* shut up, and wait till something's started that you know something about."

"Why, Mars Tom, sholy you can't mean to say I don't know about shirts, when, goodness knows, I's toted home de washin' ever sence—"

"I tell you, this hasn't got anything to *do* with shirts. I only—"

"Why, Mars Tom, you said yo'self dat a letter—"

"Do you want to drive me crazy? Keep still. I only used it as a metaphor."

That word kinder bricked us up for a minute.

The Jim says—rather timid, because he see Tom was getting pretty tetchy:

"Mars Tom, what is a metaphor?"

"A metaphor's a—well, it's a—a—a metaphor's an illustration." He see *that* didn't git home, so he tried again. "When I say birds of a feather flocks together, it's a metaphorical way of saying—"

"But dey *don't*, Mars Tom. No, sir, 'deed dey don't. Dey ain't no feathers dat's more alike den a bluebird en a jaybird, but ef you waits till you catches 'dem birds together, you'll—"

"Oh, give us a rest! You can't get the simplest little thing through your thick skull. Now don't bother me anymore."

Jim was satisfied to stop. He was dreadful pleased with himself for catching Tom out. The minute Tom begun to talk at birds I judged he was a goner, because Jim knowed more about birds than both of us put together. You see, he had killed hundreds and hundreds of them, and that's the way to find out about birds. That's the way people does that writes books about birds, and loves them so that they'll go hungry and tired and take any amount of trouble to find a new bird and kill it. Their name is ornithologers, and I could have been an ornithologer myself, because I always loved birds and creatures; and I started out to learn how to be one, and I see a bird setting on a limb of a high tree, singing with its head tilted back and its mouth open, and before I thought I fired, and his song stopped and he fell straight down from the limb, all limp like a rag, and his body was warm in my hand, and his head rolled about this way and that, like his neck was broke, and there was a little white skin over his eyes, and one little drop of blood on the side of his head; and, laws! I couldn't see nothing more for the tears; and I hain't never murdered no creature since that warn't doing me no harm, and I ain't going to.

But I was aggravated about that welkin. I wanted to know. I got the subject up again, and then Tom explained, the best he could. He said when a person made a big speech the newspapers said the shouts of the people made the welkin ring. He said they always said that, but none of them ever told what it was, so he allowed it just meant outdoors and up high. Well, that seemed sensible enough, so I was satisfied, and said so.

That pleased Tom and put him in a good humor again, and he says:

"Well, it's all right, then; and we'll let bygones be bygones. I don't know for certain what a welkin is, but when we land in London we'll make it ring, anyway, and don't you forget it."

He said an erronort was a person who sailed

around in balloons; and said it was a mighty sight finer to be Tom Sawyer the Erronort than to be Tom Sawyer the Traveler, and we would be heard of all round the world, if we pulled through all right, and so he wouldn't give shucks to be a traveler now.

Toward the middle of the afternoon we got everything ready to land, and we felt pretty good, too, and proud; and we kept watching with the glasses, like Columbus discovering America. But we couldn't see nothing but ocean. The afternoon wasted out and the sun shut down, and still there warn't no land anywheres. We wondered what was the matter, but reckoned it would come out all right, so we went on steering east, but went up on a higher level so we wouldn't hit any steeples or mountains in the dark.

It was my watch till midnight, and then it was Jim's; but Tom stayed up, because he said ship-captains done that when they was making the land, and didn't stand no regular watch.

Well, when daylight come, Jim give a shout, and we jumped up and looked over, and there was the land sure enough—land all around, as far as you could see, and perfectly level and yaller. We didn't know how long we'd been over it. There warn't no trees, nor hills, nor rocks, nor towns, and Tom and Jim had took it for the sea. They took it for the sea in a dead ca'm; but we was so high up, anyway, that if it had been the sea and rough, it would 'a' looked smooth, all the same, in the night, that way.

We was all in a powerful excitement now, and grabbed the glasses and hunted everywheres for London, but couldn't find hair nor hide of it, nor any other settlement—nor any sign of a lake or a river, either. Tom was clean beat. He said it warn't his notion of England; he thought England looked like America, and always had that idea. So he said we better have breakfast, and then drop down and inquire the quickest way to London. We cut the breakfast pretty short, we was so impatient. As we slanted along down, the weather began to moderate, and pretty soon we shed our furs. But it kept *on* moderating, and in a precious little while it was 'most too moderate. We was close down now, and just blistering!

We settled down to within thirty foot of the land that is, it was land if sand is land; for this wasn't anything but pure sand. Tom and me clumb down the ladder and took a run to stretch our legs, and if felt amazing good—that is, the stretching did, but the sand scorched our feet like hot embers. Next, we see somebody coming, and started to meet him; but we heard Jim shout, and looked around and he was fairly dancing, and making signs, and yelling. We couldn't make out what he said, but we was scared anyway, and begun to heel it back to the balloon. When we got close enough, we understood the words, and they made me sick:

"Run! Run fo' yo' life! Hit's a lion; I kin see him thoo de glass! Run, boys; do please heel it de bes' you kin. He's bu'sted outen de menagerie, en dey ain't nobody to stop him!"

It made Tom fly, but it took the stiffening all out of my legs. I could only just gasp along the way you do in a dream when there's a ghost gaining on you.

Tom got to the ladder and shinned up it a piece

and waited for me; and as soon as I got a foothold on it he shouted to Jim to soar away. But Jim had clean lost his head, and said he had forgot how. So Tom shinned along up and told me to follow; but the lion was arriving, fetching a most ghastly roar with every lope, and my legs shook so I dasn't try to take one of them out of the rounds for fear the other would give way under me.

But Tom was aboard by this time, and he started the balloon up a little, and stopped it again as soon as the end of the ladder was ten or twelve feet above ground. And there was the lion, a-riping around under me, and roaring and springing up in the air at the ladder, and only missing it about a quarter of an inch, it seemed to me. It was delicious to be out of his reach, perfectly delicious, and made me feel good and thankful all up one side; but I was hanging there helpless and couldn't climb, and that made me feel perfectly wretched and miserable all down the other. It is most seldom that a person feels so mixed like that; and it is not to be recommended, either.

Tom asked me what he'd better do, but I didn't know. He asked me if I could hold on whilst he sailed away to a safe place and left the lion behind. I said I could if he didn't go no higher than he was now; but if he went higher I would lose my head and fall, sure. So he said, "Take a good grip," and he started.

"Don't go so fast," I shouted. "It makes my head swim."

He had started like a lightning express. He slowed down, and we glided over the sand slower, but still in a kind of sickening way; for it *is* uncomfortable to see things sliding and gliding under you like that, and not a sound.

But pretty soon there was plenty of sound, for the lion was catching up. His noise fetched others. You could see them coming on the lope from every direction, and pretty soon there was a couple of dozen of them under me, jumping up at the ladder and snarling and snapping at each other; and so we went skimming along over the sand, and these fellers doing what they could to help us to not forget the occasion; and then some other beasts come, without an invite, and they started a regular riot down there.

We see this plan was a mistake. We couldn't ever git away from them at this gait, and I couldn't hold on forever. So Tom took a think, and struck another idea. That was, to kill a lion with the pepper-box revolver, and then sail away while the others stopped to fight over the carcass. So he stopped the balloon still, and done it, and then we sailed off while the fuss was going on, and come down a quarter of a mile off, and they helped me aboard; but by the time we was out of reach again, that gang was on hand once more. And when they see we was really gone and they couldn't get us, they sat down on their hams and looked up at us so kind of disappointed that it was as much as a person could do not to see *their* side of the matter.

Chapter 6

It's a Caravan

I was so weak that the only thing I wanted was a chance to lay down, so I made straight for my locker-bunk, and stretched myself out there. But a body couldn't get back his strength in no such oven as that, so Tom give the command to soar, and Jim started her aloft.

We had to go up a mile before we struck comfortable weather where it was breezy and pleasant and just right, and pretty soon I was all straight again. Tom had been settling quiet and thinking; but now he jumps up and says:

"I bet you a thousand to one *I* know where we are. We're in the great Sahara, as sure as guns!"

He was so excited he couldn't hold still; but I wasn't. I says:

"Well, then, where's the Great Sahara? In England or in Scotland?"

"'Tain't in either; it's in Africa."

Jim's eyes bugged out, and he begun to stare

46

down with no end of interest, because that was where his originals come from; but I didn't more than half believe it. I couldn't, you know; it seemed too awful far away for us to have traveled.

But Tom was full of discovery, as he called it, and said the lions and the sand meant the Great Desert, sure. He said he could 'a' found out, before we sighted land, that we was crowding the land somewheres, if he had thought of one thing; and when we asked him what, he said:

"These clocks. They're chronometers. You always read about them in sea-voyages. One of them is keeping Grinnage time, and the other is keeping St. Louis time, like my watch. When we left St. Louis it was four in the afternoon by my watch and this clock, and it was ten at night by this Grinnage clock. Well, at this time of the year the sun sets about seven o'clock. Now I noticed the time yesterday evening when the sun went down, and it was half-past five o'clock by the Grinnage clock, and half-past eleven A.M. by my watch and the other clock. You see, the sun rose and set by my watch in St. Louis, and the Grinnage clock was six hours fast; but we've come so far east that it comes within less than half an hour of setting by the Grinnage clock now, and I'm away out—more than four hours and a half out. You see, that meant that we was closing up on the longitude of Ireland, and would strike it before long if we was p'inted right—which we wasn't. No, sir, we've been a-wandering—wandering 'way down south of east, and it's my opinion we are in Africa. Look at this map. You see how the shoulder of Africa sticks out to the west. Think how fast we've traveled; if we had gone straight east we would be long past England by this time. You watch for noon, all of you, and we'll stand up, and when we can't cast a shadow we'll find that this Grinnage clock is coming mighty close to marking twelve. Yes, sir, *I* think we're in Africa; and it's just bully.''

Jim was gazing down with the glass. He shook his head and says:

''Mars Tom. I reckon dey's a mistake somers. I haint' seen no Negroes yit.''

''That's nothing; they don't live in the desert. What is that, 'way off yonder? Gimme a glass.''

He took a long look, and said it was like a black string stretched across the sand, but he couldn't guess what it was.

''Well,'' I says, ''I reckon maybe you've got a chance now to find out whereabouts this balloon is, because as like as not that is one of these lines here, that's on the map, that you call meridians of longitude, and we can drop down and look at its number, and—''

''Oh, shucks, Huck Finn, I never see such a lunkhead as you. Did you s'pose there's meridians of longitude on the earth?''

''Tom Sawyer, they're set down on the map, and you know it perfectly well, and here they are, and you can see for yourself.''

''Of course they're on the map, but that's nothing; there ain't any on the *ground.*''

''Tom, do you know that to be so?''

''Certainly I do.''

''Well, then, that map's a liar again. I never see such a liar as that map.''

He fired up at that, and I was ready for him, and Jim was warming his opinion, too, and next minute we'd 'a' broke loose on another argument, if Tom hadn't dropped the glass and began to clap his hands like a maniac and sing out:

"Camels!—Camels!"

So I grabbed a glass and Jim, too, and took a look, but I was disappointed, and says:

"Camels your granny; they're spiders."

"Spiders in a desert, you shad? Spiders walking in a procession? You don't ever reflect, Huck Finn, and I reckon you really haven't got anything to reflect *with*. Don't you know we're as much as a mile up in the air, and that that string of crawlers is two or three miles away? Spiders, good land! Spiders as big as a cow? Perhaps you'd like to go down and milk one of 'em. But they're camels, just the same. It's a caravan, that's what it is, and it's a mile long."

"Well, then, let's go down and look at it. I don't believe in it, and ain't going to till I see it and know it."

"All right," he says, and give the command: "Lower away."

As we come slanting down into the hot weather, we could see that it was camels, sure enough, plodding along, an everlasting string of them, with bales strapped to them, and several hundred men in long white robes, and a thing like a shawl bound over their heads and hanging down with tassels and fringes; and some of the men had long guns and some hadn't, and some was riding and some was walking. And the weather—well, it was just roasting. And how slow they did creep along!

We swooped down now, all of a sudden, and stopped about a hundred yards over their heads.

The men all set up a yell, and some of them fell flat on their stomachs, some begun to fire their guns at us, and the rest broke and scampered every which way, and so did the camels.

We see that we was making trouble, so we went up again about a mile, to the cool weather, and watched them from there. It took them an hour to get together and form the procession again; then they started along, but we could see by the glasses that they wasn't paying much attention to anything but us. We poked along, looking down at them with the glasses, and by and by we see a big sand mound, and something like a man laying on top of the mound that raised his head up every now and then, and seemed to be watching the caravan or us, we didn't know which. As the caravan got nearer, he sneaked down on the other side and rushed to the other men and horses—for that is what they was—and we see them mount in a hurry; and next, here they come, like a house afire, some with lances and some with long guns, and all of them yelling the best they could.

They come a-tearing down onto the caravan, and the next minute both sides crashed together and was all mixed up, and there was such another popping of guns as you never heard, and the air got so full of smoke you could only catch glimpses of them struggling together. There must 'a' been six hundred men in that battle, and it was terrible to see. Then they broke up into gangs and groups, fighting tooth and nail, and scurrying and scampering around, laying into each other like everything; and whenever the smoke cleared a little you could see dead and wounded people and camels scattered far and wide and all about, and camels racing off in every direction.

At last the robbers see they couldn't win, so their chief sounded a signal, and all that was left of them broke away and went scampering across the plain. The last man to go snatched up a child and carried it off in front of him on his horse, and a woman run screaming and begging after him, and followed him away off across the plain till she was separated a long ways from her people; but it warn't no use, and she had to give it up, and we see her sink down on the sand and cover her face with her hands. Then Tom took the hellum, and started for that yahoo, and we come a-whizzing down and made a swoop, and knocked him out of the saddle, the child and all; and he was jarred considerable, but the child wasn't hurt, but laid there working its hands and legs in the air like a tumble-bug that's on its back and can't turn over. The man went strugger- ing off to overtake his horse, and didn't know what had hit him, for we was three or four hundred yards up in the air by this time.

We judged the woman would go and get the child now; but she didn't. We could see her, through the glass, still setting there, with her head bowed down on her knees; so of course she hadn't seen the performance, and thought her child was clean gone with the man. She was nearly a half a mile from her people, so we thought we might go down to the child, which was about a quarter of a mile beyond her, and snake it to her before the caravan people could git to us to do us any harm;

and besides, we reckoned they had enough business on their hands for one while, anyway, with the wounded. We thought we'd chance it, and we did. We swooped down and stopped, and Jim shinned down the ladder and fetched up the kid, which was a nice fat little thing, and a noble good humor, too, considering it was just out of a battle and tumbled off a horse; and then we started for the mother, and stopped back of her and tolerable near by, and Jim slipped down and crept up easy, and when he was close back of her the child goo-goo'd, the way a child does, and she heard it, and whirled and fetched a shriek of joy, and made a jump for the kid and snatched it and hugged it, and dropped it and hugged Jim, and then snatched off a gold chain and hung it around Jim's neck, and hugged him again, and jerked up the child again, a-sobbing and glorifying all the time; and Jim he shoved for the ladder and up it, and in a minute we was back up in the sky and the woman was staring up, with the back of her head between her shoulders and the child with its arms locked around her neck. And there she stood, as long as we was in sight a-sailing away in the sky.

Chapter 7

Tom Respects the Flea

"Noon!" says Tom and so it was. His shadder was just a blot around his feet. We looked, and the Grinnage clock was so close to twelve the difference didn't amount to nothing. So Tom said London was right north of us or right south of us, one or t'other, and he reckoned by the weather and the sand and the camels it was north; and a good many miles north, too; as many as from New York to the City of Mexico, he guessed.

Jim said he reckoned a balloon was a good deal the fastest thing in the world, unless it might be some kind of birds—a wild pigeon, maybe, or a railroad.

But Tom said he had read about railroads in England going nearly a hundred miles an hour for a little ways, and there never was a bird in the world that could do that—except one, and that was a flea.

"A flea? Why, Mars Tom, in de fust place he

ain't a bird strickly speakin'—

"He ain't a bird, eh? Well, then, what is he?"

"I don't rightly know, Mars Tom, but I speck he's only jist a' animal. No, I reckon dat won't do, nuther, he ain't big enough for a' animal. He mus' be a bug. Yassir, dat's what he is, he's a bug."

"I bet he ain't, but let it go. What's your second place?"

"Well, in de second place, birds is creturs dat goes a long ways, but a flea don't."

"He don't, don't he? Come, now, what *is* a long distance, if you know?"

"Why, it's miles, and lots of 'em—anybody knows dat."

"Can't a man walk miles?"

"Yassir, he kin."

"As many as a railroad?"

"Yassir, if you gave him time."

"Can't a flea?"

"Well—I s'pose so—ef you gives him heaps of time."

"Now you begin to see, don't you, that *distance* ain't the thing to judge by, at all; it's the time it takes to go the distance *in* that *counts,* ain't it?"

"Well, hit do look sorter so, but I wouldn't 'a' b'lieved it, Mars Tom."

"It's a matter of *proportion,* that's what it is; and when you come to gauge a thing's speed by its size, where's your bird and your railroad 'longside of a flea? The fastest man can't run more than about ten miles in an hour—not much over ten thousand times his own length. But all the books says any common ordinary third-class flea can jump a hundred and fifty times his own length; yes, and he can make five jumps a second, too— seven hundred and fifty time his own length, in one little second—for he don't fool away time stopping and starting—he does them both at the same time; you'll see, if you try to put your finger on him. Now that's a common, ordinary, third-class flea's gait; but you take an Eyetalian *first*-class, that's been the pet of nobility all his life, and hasn't ever knowed what want or sickness or exposure was, and he can jump more than three hundred times his own length, and keep it up all day, five such jumps every second, which is fifteen hundred times his own length. Well, suppose a man could go fifteen hundred times his own length in a second—say, a mile and a half. It's ninety miles a minute; it's considerable more than five thousand miles an hour. Where's your man *now*?—yes, and your bird, and your railroad, and your balloon? Laws, they don't amount to shucks 'longside of a flea. A flea is just a comet b'iled down small.''

Jim was a good deal astonished, and so was I. Jim said:

''Is dem figgers jist edjackly true, en no jokin' en no lies, Mars Tom?''

''Yes, they are; they're perfectly true.''

''Well, den, honey, a body's got to respec' a flea. I ain't had no respec' for um befo', sca'sely, but dey ain't no gittin' roun' it, dey do deserve it, dat's certain.''

''Well, I bet they do. They've got ever so much more sense, and brains, and brightness, in propor- tion to their size, than any other cretur in the world. A person can learn them 'most anything; and they learn it quicker than any other cretur, too. They've been learnt to haul little carriages in harness, and go this way and that way and t'other way according to their orders; yes, and to march and drill like soldiers, doing it as exact, according to orders, as soldiers does it. They've been learnt to do all sorts of hard and troublesome things. S'pose you could cultivate a flea up to size of a man, and keep his natural smartness a-growing and a-growing right along up, bigger and bigger, and keener and keener, in the same proportion—where'd the human race be, do you reckon? That flea would be President of the United States, and you couldn't any more prevent it than you prevent lightning.''

''My lan', Mars Tom, I never knowed dey was so much *to* de beas'. No, sir, I never had no idea of it, and dat's de fac'.''

''There's more to him, by a long sight, then there is to any other cretur, man or beast, in proportion to size. He's the interestingest of them all. People have so much to say about an ant's strength, and an elephant's, and a locomotive's. Shucks, they don't begin with a flea. He can lift two or three hundred times his own weight. And none of them can come anywhere near it. And, moreover, he has got notions of his own, and is very particular, and you can't fool him; his instinct, or his judgement, or whatever it is, is perfectly sound and clear, and don't ever make a mistake. People think all humans are alike to a flea. It ain't so. There's folks they won't go near, hungry or not hungry, and I'm one of them. I never had one of them on me in my life.''

''Mars Tom!''

"It's so; I ain't joking."

"Well, sah, I hain't ever heard de likes o' dat befo'."

Jim couldn't believe it, and I couldn't; so we had to drop down to the sand and git a supply and see. Tom was right. They went for me and Jim by the thousand, but not one of them lit on Tom. There warn't no explaining it, but there it was and there warn't no getting around it. He said it had always been just so, and he'd just as soon be where there was a million of them as not; they'd never touch him nor bother him.

We went up to the cold weather to freeze 'em out, and stayed a little spell, and then came back to the comfortable weather and went lazying along twenty or twenty-five miles an hour, the way we'd been doing for the last few hours. The reason was that the longer we was in that solemn, peaceful desert, the more the hurry and fuss got kind of soothed down in us, and the more happier and contented and satisfied we got to feeling, and the more we got to liking the desert, and then loving it. So we had cramped the speed down, as I was saying, and was having a most noble good lazy time, sometimes watching through the glasses, sometimes stretched out on the lockers reading, sometimes taking a nap.

It didn't seem like we was the same lot that was in such a state to find land and git ashore, but it was. But we had got over that—clean over it. We was used to the balloon now and not afraid anymore, and didn't want to be anywheres else. Why, it seemed just like home; it 'most seemed as if I had been born and raised in it, and Jim and

Tom said the same. And always I had had hateful
people around me, a-nagging at me, and pestering of me, and scolding, and finding fault, and
fussing and bothering, and sticking to me, and
keeping after me, and making me do this, and
making me do that and t'other, and always select-
ing out the things I didn't want to do, and then
giving me Sam Hill because I shirked and done
something else, and just aggravating the life out
of a body all the time; but up here in the sky it was
so still and sunshiny and lovely, and plenty to eat,
and plenty of sleep, and strange things to see, and
no nagging and no pestering, and no good
people, and just holiday all the time. Land, I
warn't in no hurry to git out and buck at civilization again. Now, one of the worst things about
civilization is that anybody that gits a letter with
trouble in it comes and tells you all about it and
makes you feel bad, and the newspaper fetches
you the troubles of everybody all over the world,
and keeps you downhearted and dismal 'most all
the time, and it's such a heavy load for a person. I
hate them newspapers; and I hate letters; and if I
had my way I wouldn't allow nobody to load his
troubles onto other folks he ain't acquainted with,
on t'other side of the world, that way. Well, up in
a balloon there ain't any of that, and it's the dar-
lingest place there is.

We had supper, and that night was one of the
prettiest nights I ever see. The moon made it just
like daylight, only a heap softer; and once we see
a lion standing all alone by himself, just all alone
on the earth, it seemed like, and his shadder laid
on the sand by him like a puddle of ink. That's the

kind of moonlight to have.

Mainly we laid on our backs and talked; we didn't want to go to sleep. Tom said we was right in the midst of the *Arabian Nights* now. He said it was right along that one of the cutest things in that book happened; so we looked down and watched while he told about it, because there ain't anything that is so interesting to look at as a place that a book has talked about. It was a tale about a camel-driver that had lost his camel, and he came along the desert and met a man, and says:

"Have you run across a stray camel today?"

And the man says:

"Was he blind in his left eye?"

"Yes."

"Had he lost an upper front tooth?"

"Yes."

"Was his off hind leg lame?"

"Yes."

"Was he loaded with millet-seed on one side and honey on the other?"

"Yes, but you needn't go into no more details —that's the one, and I'm in a hurry. Where did you see him?"

"I hain't seen him at all," the man says.

"Hain't seen him at all? How can you describe him so close, then?"

"Because when a person knows how to use his eyes, everything has got a meaning to it; but most people's eyes ain't any good to them. I know he was lame in his off hind leg because he had favored that foot and trod light on it, and his track showed it. I knowed he was blind in his left side because he only nibbled grass on the right side of the trail. I knowed he had lost an upper front tooth because where he bit into the sod his teeth-print showed it. The millet-seed sifted out on one side—the ants told me that; the honey leaked all about your camel, but I hain't seen him.''

Jim says:

"Go on, Mars Tom, hit's a mighty good tale, and powerful interestin'.''

"That's all,'' Tom says.

"All?'' says Jim, astonished. "What 'come o' de camel?''

"I don't know.''

"Mars Tom, don't de tale say?''

"No.''

Jim puzzled a minute, then he says:

"Well! Ef dat ain't de beatenes' tale ever *I* struck. Jist gits to the place whah de intrust is gittin' red-hot, en down she breaks. Why, Mars Tom, dey ain't no *sense* in a tale dat acts like dat. Hain't you got no *idea* whether de man got de camel back er not?''

"No I haven't.''

I see myself there warn't no sense in the tale, to chop square off that way before it come to anything, but I warn't going to say so, because I could see Tom was souring up pretty fast over the way it flatted out and the way Jim had popped onto the weak place in it, and I don't think it's fair for everybody to pile into a feller when he's down. But Tom he whirls on me and says:

"What do *you* think of the tale?''

Of course, then, I had to come out and make a clean breast and say it did seem to me, too, same as it did to Jim, that as long as the tale stopped square in the middle and never got no place, it really warn't worth the trouble of telling.

Tom's chin dropped on his breast, and 'stead of being mad, as I reckoned he'd be, to hear me scoff at his tale that way, he seemed to be only sad; and he says:

"Some people can see, and some can't—just as the man said. Let alone a camel, if a cyclone had gone by, *you* duffers wouldn't 'a' noticed the tracks."

I don't know what he meant by that, and he didn't say; it was just one of his irrulevances, I reckon—he was full of them, sometimes, when he was in a close place and couldn't see no other way out—but I didn't mind. We'd spotted the soft place in that tale sharp enough, he couldn't git away from that little fact. It graveled him like the nation, too, I reckon, much as he tried not to let on.

Chapter 8

The Disappearing Lake

We had an early breakfast in the morning, and set
looking down on the desert, and the weather was
ever so bammy and lovely, although we warn't
high up. You have to come down lower and lower
after sundown in the desert, because it cools off so
fast; and so by the time it is getting toward dawn,
you are skimming along only a little ways above
the sand.

We was watching the shadder of the balloon
slide along the ground, and now and then gazing
off across the desert to see if anything was stirring, and then down on the shadder again, when
all of a sudden almost right under us we see a lot
of men and camels laying scattered about, perfectly quiet, like they was asleep.

We shut off the power, and backed up and stood
over them, and then we see that they was all dead.
It give us the cold shivers. And it made us hush
down, too, and talk low, like people at a funeral.

We dropped down slow and stopped, and me and Tom clumb down and went among them. There were men, and women, and children. They was dried by the sun, and dark and shriveled and leathery, like the pictures of mummies you see in books. And yet they looked just as human, you wouldn't 'a' believed it; just like they was asleep.

Some of the people and animals was partly covered with sand, but most of them not, for the sand was thin there, and the bed was gravel and hard. Most of the clothes had rotted away; and when you took hold of a rag, it tore with a touch, like spider-web. Tom reckoned they had been there for years.

Some of the men had rusty guns by them, some had swords on and had shawl belts with long, silver-mounted pistols stuck in them. All the camels had their loads on yet, but the packs had busted or rotted and split the freight out on the ground. We didn't reckon the swords was any good to the dead people anymore, so we took one apiece, and some pistols. We took a small box, too, because it was so handsome and inlaid so fine; and then we wanted to bury the people; but there warn't no way to do it that we could think of, nothing to do it with but sand, and that would blow away again, of course.

Then we mounted high and sailed away, and pretty soon that black spot on the sand was out of sight, and we wouldn't ever see them poor people again in this world. We wondered, and reasoned, and tried to guess how they come to be there, and how it all happened to them, but we couldn't make it out. First we thought maybe they got lost, and wandered around and about till their food and water give out and they starved to death; but Tom said no wild animals nor vultures hadn't meddled with them, and so that guess wouldn't do. So at last we give it up, and judged we wouldn't think about it no more, because it made us lowspirited.

Then we opened the box, and it had gems and jewels in it, quite a pile, and some little veils of the kind the dead women had on, with fringes made out of curious gold money that we warn't acquainted with. We wondered if we better go and try to find them again, and give it back; but Tom thought it over and said no, it was a country that was full of robbers, and they would come and steal it; and then the sin would be on us for putting the temptation in their way. So we went on; but I wished we had took all they had, so there wouldn't 'a' been no temptation at all left.

We had had two hours of the blazing weather down there, and was dreadful thirsty when we got aboard again. We went straight for the water, but it was spoiled and bitter, besides being pretty near hot enough to scald your mouth. We couldn't drink it. It was Mississippi River water, and the best in the world, and we stirred up the mud in it to see if that would help, but no, the mud wasn't any better than the water.

Well, we hadn't been so very, very thirsty before, while we was interested in the people, but we was now, and as soon as we found we couldn't have a drink, we was more than thirty-five times as thirsty as we was a quarter of a minute before. Why, in a little while we wanted to hold our mouths open and pant like a dog.

Tom said to keep a sharp lookout, all around, everywheres, because we'd got to find an oasis or there warn't no telling what would happen. So we done it. We kept the glasses gliding around all the time, till our arms got so tired we couldn't hold them anymore. Two hours—three hours—just gazing and gazing, and nothing but sand, sand, *sand* and you could see the quivering heat-shimmer playing over it. Dear, dear, a body don't know what real misery is till he is thirsty all the way through and is certain he ain't ever going to come to any water anymore. At last I couldn't stand it to look around on them baking plains; I laid down on the locker, and give it up.

But by and by Tom raised a whoop, and there she was! A lake, wide and shiny, with pa'am trees leaning over it asleep, and their shadders in the water just as soft and delicate as ever you see. I never see anything look so good. It was a long ways off, but that warn't anything to us; we just slapped on a hundred-mile gait, and calculated to be there in seven mintues; but she stayed the same old distance away, all the time we couldn't seem to gain on her; yes, sir, just as far, and shiny, and like a dream; but we couldn't get no nearer; and at last, all of a sudden, she was gone!

Tom's eyes took a spread, and he says:

"Boys, it was a *my*ridge!" Said it like he was glad. I didn't see nothing to be glad about. I says:

"Maybe. I don't care nothing about its name, the thing I want to know is, what's become of it?"

Jim was trembling all over, and so scared he couldn't speak, but he wanted to ask that question himself if he could 'a' done it. Tom says:

"What's *become* of it? Why, you see yourself it's gone."

He looked me over and says:

"Well, now, Huck Finn, where *would* it go to! Don't you know what a myridge is?"

"No, I don't. What is it?"

"It ain't anything but imagination. There ain't anything *to* it."

It warmed me up to hear him talk like that, and I says:

"What's the use you talking that kind of stuff, Tom Sawyer? Didn't I see the lake?"

"Yes—you think you did."

"I don't think nothing about it, I *did* see it."

"I tell you you *didn't* see it either—because it warn't there to see."

It astonished Jim to hear him talk so, and he broke in and says, kind of pleading and distressed:

"Mars Tom, *please* don't say sich things in sich an awful time as dis. You ain't only reskin' yo' own self, but you's reskin' us—same way like Anna Nias en Siffira. De lake *wus* dah—I seen it jis' as plain as I sees you en Huck dis minute."

I says:

"Why, he seen it himself! He was the very one that seen it first. *Now*, then!"

"Yes, Mars Tom, hit's so—you can't deny it. We all seen it, en dat *prove* it was dah."

"Proves it! *How* does it prove it?"

"Same way it does in de courts en everywheres, Mars Tom. One pusson might be drunk, or dreamy, or suthin', en he could be mistaken; en two might, maybe; but I tell you, sah, when three sees a thing, drunk or sober, it's *so*. Dey ain't no gittin' aroun' dat, en you knows it, Mars Tom.''

"I don't know nothing of the kind. There used to be forty thousand million people that seen the sun move from one side of the sky to the other every day. Did that prove that the sun *done* it?''

"'Course it did. En besides, dey warn't no 'casion to prove it. A body 'at's got any sense ain't gwine to doubt it. Dah she is now—a-sailin' thoo de sky, like she allays done.''

Tom turned on me, then, and says:

"What do *you* say—is the sun standing still?''

"Tom Sawyer, what's the use to ask such a jackass question? Anybody that ain't blind can see it don't stand still.''

"Well,'' he said, "I'm lost in the sky with no company but a passel of low-down animals that don't know no more than the head boss of a university did three or four hundred years ago.''

It warn't fair play, and I let him know it. I says:

"Throwin' mud ain't arguin', Tom Sawyer.''

"Oh, my goodness, oh, my goodness gracious, dah's de lake ag'in!'' yelled Jim, just then. "*Now*, Mars Tom, what you gwine to say?''

Yes, sir, there was the lake again, away yonder across the desert, perfectly plain, trees and all, just the same as it was before. I says:

"I reckon you're satisfied now, Tom Sawyer.''

But he says, perfectly ca'm:

"Yes, satisfied there ain't no lake there.''

Jim says:

"*Don't* talk so, Mars Tom—it sk'yers me to hear you. It's so hot, en you's so thirsty, dat you ain't in yo' right mine, Mars Tom. Oh, but don't

she look good! 'clah I doan' know how I's gwine
to wait tell we gits dah, I's *so* thirsty.''

"Well, you'll have to wait; and it won't do you
no good, either, because there ain't no lake there,
I tell you."

I says:

"Jim, don't take your eye off of it, and I won't
either."

"'Deed I won't; en bless you, honey, I
couldn't ef I wanted to."

We went a-tearing along toward it, piling the
miles behind us like nothing, but never gaining
an inch on it—and all of a sudden it was gone
again! Jim staggered, and 'most fell down. When
he got his breath he says, gasping like a fish:

"Mars Tom, hit's a *ghos'*, dat's what it is, en I
hopes to goodness we ain't gwine to see it no mo'.
Dey's *been* a lake, en suthin's happened, en de
lake's dead, en we's seen its ghos', we's seen it
twiste, en dat's proof. De desert's ha'nted, it's
ha'nted, sho'; oh, Mars Tom, let's git outen it;
I'd ruther die den have de night ketch us in it
ag'in en de ghos' er dat lake come a-mournin'
aroun' us en we asleep en doan' know de danger
we's in.''

"Ghost, you gander! It ain't anything but air
and heat and thirstiness pasted together by a person's imagination. If I—gimme the glass!''

He grabbed it and begun to gaze off to the right.

"It's a flock of birds,'' he says. "It's getting
toward sundown, and they're making a beeline
across our track for somewheres. They mean business—maybe they're going for food or water, or
both. Let her go to starboard!—Port your hellum!
Hard down! There—ease up—steady as you go.''

We shut down some of the power, so as not to out-speed them, and took out after them. We went skimming along a quarter of a mile behind them, and when we had followed them an hour and a half and was getting pretty discouraged, and was thirsty clean to unendurableness, Tom says:

"Take the glass, one of you, and see what that is, away ahead of the birds."

Jim got the first glimpse, and slumped down on the locker sick. He was 'most crying, and says:

"She's dah ag'in, Mars Tom, she's dah ag'in, en I knows I's gwine to die, 'case when a body sees a ghos' de third time, dat's what it means. I wisht I'd never come in dis balloon, dat I does."

He wouldn't look no more, and what he said made me afraid, too, because I knowed it was true, for that has always been the way with ghosts; so then I wouldn't look anymore, either. Both of us begged Tom to turn off and go some other way but he wouldn't, and said we was ignorant superstitious blatherskites. Yes, and he'll git come-up-with, one of these days, I says to myself, insulting ghosts that way. They'll stand it for a while, maybe, but they won't stand it always, for anybody that knows about ghosts knows how easy they are hurt, and how revengeful they are.

So we was all quiet and still, Jim and me being scared, and Tom busy. By and by Tom fetched the balloon to a standstill, and says:

"*Now* get up and look, you sapheads."

We done it, and there was the sure-enough water right under us!—clear, and blue, and cool, and deep, and wavy with the breeze, the loveliest sight that ever was. And all about it was grassy banks, and flowers, and shady groves of big trees, looped together with vines, and all looking so peaceful and comfortable—enough to make a body cry, it was so beautiful.

Jim *did* cry, and rip and dance and carry on, he was so thankful and out of his mind for joy. It was my watch, so I had to stay by the works, but Tom and Jim clumb down and drank a barrel apiece, and fetched me up a lot, and I've tasted a many a good thing in my life, but nothing that ever begun with that water.

Then they went down and had a swim, and then Tom came up and spelled me, and me and Jim had a swim, and then Jim spelled Tom, and me and Tom had a footrace and a boxing-mill, and I don't reckon I ever had such a good time in my life. It warn't so very hot, because it was close on to evening, and we hadn't any clothes on, anyway. Clothes is well enough in school, and in towns, and at balls, too, but there ain't no sense in them when there ain't no civilization nor other kinds of bothers and fussiness around.

"Lions a-comin'!—lions! Quick, Mars Tom! Jump for yo' life, Huck!"

Oh, and didn't we! We never stopped for clothes, but waltzed up the ladder just so. Jim lost his head straight off—he always done it whenever he got excited and scared; and so now, 'stead of just easing the ladder up from the ground a little, so the animals couldn't reach it, he turned on a raft of power, and we went whizzing up and was dangling in the sky before he got his wits together and seen what a foolish thing he was doing. Then he stopped her, but he had clean forgot what to do next; so there we was, so high that the lions looked like pups, and we was drifting off in the wind.

But Tom he shinned up and went for the works and begun to slant her down, and back toward the lake, where the animals was gathering like a camp-meeting, and I judged he had lost *his* head, too; for he knowed I was too scared to climb, and did he want to dump me among the tigers and things?

But no, his head was level; he knowed what he was about. He swooped down to within thirty or forty feet of the lake and stopped right over the center, and sung out:

"Leggo, and drop!"

I done it, and shot down, feet first, and seemed to go about a mile toward the bottom; and when I come up, he says:

"Now lay on your back and 'float till you're rested and got your pluck back, then I'll dip the ladder in the water and you can climb aboard."

I done it. Now that was ever so smart in Tom, because if he had started off somewheres else to drop down on the sand, the menagerie would 'a' come along, too, and might 'a' kept us hunting a safe place till I got tuckered out and fell.

And all this time the lions and tigers was sorting out the clothes, and trying to divide them up so there would be some for all, but there was a misunderstanding about it somewheres, on account of some of them trying to hog more than their share; so there was another insurrection, and you never see anything like it in the world.

There must 'a' been fifty of them, all mixed up together, snorting and roaring and snapping and biting and tearing, legs and tails in the air, and you couldn't tell which was which, and the sand and fur a-flying. And when they got done, some was dead, and some was limping off crippled, and the rest was setting around on the battlefield, some of them licking their sore places and the others looking up at us and seemed to be kind of inviting us to come down and have some fun, but which we didn't want any.

As for the clothes, they warn't any, anymore. Every last rag of them was inside of the animals; and not agreeing with them very well, I don't reckon, for there was considerable many brass buttons on them, and there was knives in the pockets, too, and smoking-tobacco, and nails and chalk and marbles and fishhooks and things. But I wasn't caring. All that was bothering me was that all we had now was the professor's clothes, a big enough assortment, but not suitable to go into company with, if we came across any, because the britches was as long as tunnels, and the coats and things according. Still, there was everything a tailor needed, and Jim was a kind of jack-legged tailor, and he allowed he could soon trim a suit or two down for us that would answer.

Chapter 9
Tom Discourses on the Desert

Still, we thought we would drop down there a minute, but on another errand. Most of the professor's cargo of food was put in cans, in the new way that somebody had just invented; the rest was fresh. When you fetch Mississippi beefsteak to the Great Sahara, you want to be particular and stay in the coolish weather. So we reckoned we would drop into the lion market and see how we could make out there.

We hauled in the ladder and dropped down till we were above the reach of the animals, then we let down a rope with a slip-knot in it and hauled up a dead lion, a small tender one, then yanked up a cub tiger. We had to keep the congregation off with the revolver, or they would 'a' took a hand in the proceedings and helped.

We carved off a supply from both, and saved the skins, and hove the rest overboard. Then we baited some of the professor's hooks with the fresh meat and went a-fishing. We stood over the lake just a convenient distance above the water, and catched a lot of the nicest fish you ever see. It was a most amazing good supper we had: lion steak, tiger steak, fresh fish, and hot corn-pone. I don't want nothing better than that.

We had some fruit to finish off with. We got it out of the top of a monstrous tree. It was a very slim tree that hadn't a branch on it from the bottom plumb to the top, and there it bursted out like a feather duster. It was a pa'm tree, of course; anybody knows a pa'm tree the minute he sees it, by the pictures. We went for coconuts in this one, but there warn't none. There was only big loose branches of things like oversized grapes, and Tom allowed they was dates, because he said they answered the description in the *Arabian Nights* and the other books. Of course they mightn't be, and they might be poison; so we had to wait a spell, and watch and see if the birds et them. They done it; so we done it, too, and they was most amazing good.

By this time monstrous big birds begun to come and settle on the dead animals. They was plucky creturs; they would tackle one end of a lion that was being gnawed at the other end by another lion. If the lion drove the bird away, it didn't do no good; he was back again the minute the lion was busy.

The big birds come out of every part of the sky —you could make them out with the glass while they was still so far away you couldn't see them with your naked eye. Tom said the birds didn't find out the meat was there by the smell; they had to find it out by seeing it. Oh, but ain't that an eye for you! Tom said at the distance of five mile a patch of dead lions couldn't look any bigger than a person's fingernail, and he couldn't imagine how the birds could notice sich a little thing so far off.

It was strange and unnatural to see lion eat lion, and we thought maybe they warn't kin. But Jim said that didn't make no difference. He said a hog was fond of her own children, and so was a spider, and reckoned maybe a lion was pretty near as unprincipled, though maybe not quite. He thought likely a lion wouldn't eat his own father, if he knowed which was him, but reckoned he would eat his brother-in-law if he was uncommon hungry, and eat his mother-in-law any time. But *reckoning* don't settle nothing. You can reckon till the cows come home, but that don't fetch you no decision. So we give it up and let it drop.

Generally it was very still in the desert nights, but this time there was music. A lot of other animals come to dinner; sneaking yelpers that Tom allowed was jackals, and roach-backed ones that he said was hyenas; and all the whole biling of them kept up a racket all the time. They made a picture in the moonlight that was more different than any picture I ever see. We had a line out and made fast to the top of a tree and didn't stand no watch, but all turned in and slept; but I was up two or three times to look down at the animals and hear the music. It was like having a front seat at a menagerie for nothing, which I hadn't ever had before, and so it seemed foolish to sleep and not make the most of it; I mightn't ever have such a chance again.

We went a-fishing again in the early dawn, and then lazied around all day in the deep shade on an island, taking turn to watch and see that none of the animals come a-snooping around there after erronorts for dinner. We was going to leave the next day, but couldn't, it was too lovely.

The day after, when we rose up toward the sky and sailed off eastward, we looked back and watched that place till it warn't nothing but just a speck in the desert, and I tell you it was like saying good-bye to a friend that you ain't never going to see anymore.

Jim was thinking to himself, and at last he says:

"Mars Tom, we's mos' to de end er de desert now, I speck."

"Why?"

"Well, hit stan' to reason we is. You knows how long we's been a-skimmin' over it. Mus' be mos' out o' san'. Hit's a wonder to me dat it's hilt out as long as it has."

"Shucks, there's plenty sand, you needn't worry."

"Oh, I ain't a-worryin', Mars Tom, only wondering', dat's all. De Lord's got plenty san', I ain't' doubtin' dat; but nemmine, He ain't gwine to *was 'e* it jist on dat account; en I allows dat dis desert's plenty big enough now, jist de way she is, en you can't spread her out no mo' 'dout was'in' san'."

"Oh, go 'long! we ain't much more than fairly *started* across the desert yet. The United States is pretty big country, ain't it? Ain't it, Huck?"

"Yes," I says, "there ain't no bigger one, I don't reckon."

"Well," he says, "this desert is about the

shape of the United States, and if you was to lay it down on top of the United States, it would cover the land of the free out of sight like a blanket. There'd be a little corner sticking out, up at Maine and away up northwest, and Florida sticking out like a turtle's tail, and that's all. We've took California away from the Mexicans two or three years ago, so that part of the Pacific coast is ours now, and if you laid the Great Sahara down with her edge on the Pacific, she would cover the United States and stick out past New York six hundred miles into the Atlantic Ocean."

I says:

"Good land! have you got the documents for that, Tom Sawyer?"

"Yes, they're right here, and I've been studying them. You can look for yourself. From New York to the Pacific is 2,600 miles. From one end of the Great Desert to the other is 3,200. The United States contains 3,600,000 square miles, the desert contains 4,162,000. With the desert's bulk you could cover up every last inch of the United States, and in under, where the edges projected out, you could tuck England, Scotland, Ireland, France, Denmark, and all Germany. Yes, sir, you could hide the home of the brave and all them countries clean out of sight under the Great Sahara, and you would still have 2,000 square miles of sand left."

"Well," I says, "it clean beats me. Why, Tom, it shows that the Lord took as much pains makin' this desert as makin' the United States and all them other countries."

Jim says: "Huck, dat don' stan' to reason. I

reckon dis desert wa'n't made at all. Now you take a look at it like dis—you look at it, and see ef I's right. What's a desert good for? 'Tain't good for nuthin'. Dey ain't no way to make it pay. Hain't dat so, Huck?''

"Yes, I reckon."

"Hain't it so, Mars Tom?"

"I guess so. Go on."

"Ef a thing ain't good, it's made in vain, ain't it?"

"Yes."

"*Now*, den! Do de Lord make anything in vain? You answer me dat."

"Well—no, He don't."

"Den how come He make a desert?"

"Well, go on. How *did* He come to make it?"

"Mars Tom, *I* b'lieve it uz jes like when you's buildin' a house; dey's allays a lot o' truck en rubbish lef' over. What does you do wid it? Doan' you take en k'yart it off en dump it into a ole vacant back lot? 'Course. Now, den it's my opinion hit was jest like dat—dat de Great Sahara warn't made at all, she jes' *happen*'."

I said it was a real good argument, and I believed it was the best one Jim ever made. Tom he said the same, but said the trouble about arguments is, ain't nothing but *theories* after all, and theories don't prove nothing, they only give you a place to rest on a spell, when you are tuckered out butting around and around trying to find out something there ain't no way *to* find out. And he says:

"There's another trouble about theories: there's always a hole in them somewheres, sure, if you look close enough. It's just so with this one of Jim's. Look what billions and billions of stars there is. How does it come that there was just exactly enough star-stuff, and none left over? How does it come there ain't no sandpile up there?''

But Jim was fixed for him and says:

''What's de Milky Way?—dat's what *I* want to know. What's de Milky Way? Answer me dat!''

In my opinion it was just a sockdologer. It's only an opinion, it's only *my* opinion and others may think different; but I said it then and I stand to it now—it was a sockdologer. And moreover, besides, it landed Tom Sawyer. He couldn't say a word. He had that stunned look of a person that's been shot in the back with a kag of nails. All he said was, as for people like me and Jim, he'd just as soon have intellectual intercourse with a catfish. But anybody can say that—and notice they always do when somebody has fetched them a lifter. Tom Sawyer was tired of that end of the subject.

So we got back to talking about the size of the desert again, and the more we compared it with this and that and t'other thing, the more nobler and bigger and grander it got to look right along. And so, hunting among the figgers, Tom found, by and by, that it was just the same size as the Empire of China. Then he showed us the spread the Empire of China made on the map, and the room she took up in the world. Well, it was wonderful to think of, and I says:

''Why, I've heard talk about the desert plenty of times, but *I* never knowed before how important she was.''

Then Tom says:

"Important! Sahara important! That's just the way with some people. If a thing's big, it's important. That's all the sense they've got. All they can see is *size*. Why, look at England. It's the most important country in the world; and yet you could put it in China's vest-pocket; and not only that, but you'd have the dicken's own time to find it again the next time you wanted it. And look at Russia. It spreads all around and everywhere, and yet ain't no more important in this world than Rhode Island is, and hasn't got half as much in it that's worth saving."

Away off now we see a little hill, a-standing up just on the edge of the world. Tom broke off his talk, and reached for a glass very much excited, and took a look, and says:

"That's it—it's the one I've been looking for, sure. If I'm right, it's the one the dervish took the man into and showed him all the treasures."

So we began to gaze, and he begun to tell about it out of the *Arabian Nights*.

Chapter 10
The Treasure-Hill

Tom said it happened like this:

A dervish was stumping it along through the desert, on foot, one blazing hot day, and had come a thousand miles and was pretty poor, and hungry, and ornery and tired, and along about where we are now he ran across a camel-driver with a hundred camels, and asked him for some a'ms. But the camel-driver he asked to be excused. The dervish said:

"Don't you own these camels?"

"Yes, they're mine."

"Are you in debt?"

"Who—me? No."

"Well, a man who owns a hundred camels and ain't in debt is rich—and not only rich, but very rich. Ain't it so?"

The camel-driver owned up that it was so. Then the dervish says:

"God has made you rich, and He has made

me poor. He had His reasons, and they are wise, blessed be His name. But He was willed that His rich shall help the poor, and you have turned away from me, your brother, in my need, and He will remember this, and you will lose by it."

That made the camel-driver feel shaky, but all the same he was born hoggish after money and didn't like to let go a cent; so he begun to whine and explain, and said times was hard, and although he had took a full freight down to Balsora and got a fat rate for it, he couldn't git no return freight, so he warn't making no great things out of his trip. So the dervish starts along again, and says:

"All right, if you want to take the risk; but I reckon you have made a mistake this time, and missed the chance."

Of course the camel-driver wanted to know what kind of a chance he had missed, because maybe there was money in it; so he ran after the dervish, and begged him so hard and earnest to take pity on him that at last the dervish gave in, and says:

"Do you see that hill yonder? Well, in that hill is all the treasures of the earth, and I was looking around for a man with a particular good kind heart and a noble, generous disposition, because if I could find just that man, I've got a kind of a salve I could put in his eyes and he could see the treasures and get them out."

So then the camel-driver was in a sweat; and he cried, and begged, and took on, and went down on his knees, and said he was just that kind of man, and said he could fetch a thousand people that would say he warn't ever described so exact before.

"Well, then," says the dervish. "All right. If we load the hundred camels, can I have half of them?"

The driver was so glad he couldn't hardly hold in, and says:

"Now you're shouting."

So they shook hands on the bargain, and the dervish got out his box and rubbed the salve on the driver's eye, and the hill opened and he went in, and there, sure enough, was piles and piles of gold and jewels sparkling like all the stars in the heaven had fell down.

So him and the dervish laid into it, and they loaded every camel till he couldn't carry no more; then they said good-bye, and each of them started off with his fifty. But pretty soon the camel-driver came and overtook the dervish and says:

"You ain't in society, you know, and you don't really need all you've got. Won't you be good, and let me have ten of your camels?"

"Well," the dervish says, "I don't know but what you say is reasonable enough."

So he done it, and they separated, and the dervish started off again with his forty. But pretty soon here comes the camel-driver bawling after him again, and whines and slobbers around and begs another ten off him, saying thirty camel-loads of treasures was enough to see a dervish through, because they live very simple, you know, and don't keep house, but board around and give their note.

But that warn't the end yet. The ornery hound kept coming and coming till he had begged back all the camels and had the whole hundred. Then he was satisfied, and ever so grateful, and said he wouldn't ever forget the dervish as long as he lived, and nobody hadn't been so good to him before, and liberal. So they shook hands good-bye, and separated and started off again.

But do you know, it warn't ten minutes till the camel-driver was unsatisfied again—he was the low-downest reptyle in seven countries—and he came a-running again. And this time the thing he wanted was the dervish to rub some of the salve on his other eye.

"Why?" said the dervish.

"Oh, you know," says the driver.

"Know what?"

"Well, you can't fool me," says the driver. "You're trying to keep back something from me, you know it mighty well. You know, I reckon, that if I had salve on the other eye. I could see a lot more things that's valuable. Come—please put it on."

The dervish says:

"I wasn't keeping anything back from you. I don't mind telling you what would happen if I put it on. You'd never see again. You'd be stone-blind the rest of your days."

But do you know that beat wouldn't believe him. No, he begged and begged, and whined and cried, till at last the dervish opened his box and told him to put it on, if he wanted to. So the man done it, and, sure enough, he was blind as a bat in a minute.

Then the dervish laughed at him and mocked at him and made fun of him; and says:

"Good-bye—a man that's blind hain't got no use for jewelry."

And he cleared out with the hundred camels, and left that man to wander around poor and miserable and friendless the rest of his days in the desert.

Jim said he'd bet it was a lesson to him.

"Yes," Tom says, "and like a considerable many lessons a body gets. They ain't no account, because the thing don't ever happen the same way again—and can't. The time Hen Scovil fell down the chimbly and crippled his back for life, everybody said it would be a lesson to him. What kind of a lesson? How was he going to use it? He couldn't climb chimblies no more, and he hadn't no more backs to break."

"All de same, Mars Tom, dey *is* sich a thing as learnin' by expe'ence. De Good Book say de burnt chile shun de fire."

"Well, I ain't denying that a thing's a lesson if it's a thing that can happen twice just the same way. There's lots of such things, and *they* educate a person, that's what Uncle Abner always said; but there's forty *million* lots of the other kind—the kind that don't happen the same way twice—and they ain't no real use, they ain't no more instructive than the small-pox. When you've got it, it ain't no good to find out you ought to been vaccinated, and it ain't no good to git vaccinated afterward, because the smallpox don't come but once. But, on the other hand, Uncle Abner said that the person that had took a bull by the tail once had learnt sixty or seventy times as much as a person that hadn't, and said a person that started in to carry a cat home by the tail was gitting knowledge that was always going to be useful to him, and warn't ever going to grow dim or doubtful. But I can tell you, Jim, Uncle Abner was down on them people that's all the time trying to dig a lesson out of everything that happens, no matter whether—''

But Jim was asleep. Tom looked kind of ashamed, because you know a person always feels bad when he is talking uncommon fine and thinks the other person is admiring, and that other person goes to sleep that way. Of course he oughtn't to go to sleep, because it's shabby; but the finer a person talks the certainer it is to make you sleep, and so when you come to look at it, it ain't nobody's fault in particular; both of them's to blame.

Jim began to snore—soft and blubbery at first, then a long rasp, then a stronger one, then a half a dozen horrible ones, like the last water sucking down the plug-hole of a bathtub, then the same with more power to it, and some big coughs and snorts flung in, the way a cow does that is choking to death; and when the person has got to that point he is at his level best, and can wake up a man that is in the next block with a dipperful of loddanum in him, but can't wake himself up although all that awful noise of his'n ain't but three inches from his own ears. And that is the curiousest thing in the world, seems to me. But you rake a match to light the candle, and that little bit of a noise will fetch him. I wish I knowed what was the reason of that, but there don't seem to be no way to find out. Now there was Jim alarming the whole desert, and yanking the animals out, for miles and miles around, to see what in the nation was going on up there; there warn't nobody nor nothing that was as close to the noise as *he* was, and yet he was the only cretur that wasn't disturbed by it. We yelled at him and whooped at him, it never done no good; but the first time there come a little wee noise that wasn't of a usual kind, it woke him up. No, sir, I've thought it all over, and so has Tom, and there ain't no way to find out why a snorer can't hear himself snore.

Jim said he hadn't been asleep; he just shut his eyes so he could listen better.

Tom said nobody warn't accusing him.

That made him look like he wished he hadn't said anything. And he wanted to git away from the subject, I reckon, because he begun to abuse the camel-driver, just the way a person does when he has got catched in something and wants to take it out on somebody else. He let into the camel-driver the hardest he knowed how, and I had to agree with him; and he praised up the dervish the highest he could, and I had to agree with him there, too. But Tom says:

"I ain't so sure. You call that dervish so dreadful liberal and good and unselfish, but I don't quite see it. He didn't hunt up another poor dervish, did he? No, he didn't. If he was so unselfish, why didn't he go in there himself and take a pocketful of jewels and go along and be satisfied? No, sir, the person he was hunting for was a man with a hundred camels. He wanted to get away with all the treasure he could."

"Why, Mars Tom, he was willin' to divide, fair and square; he only struck for fifty camels."

"Because he knowed how he was going to git all of them by and by."

"Mars Tom, he *tole* de man de truck would make him bline."

"Yes, because he knowed the man's character. It was just the kind of man he was hunting for—a man that never believes anybody's word or anybody's honorableness, because he ain't got none of his own. I reckon there's lots of people like that dervish. They swindle, right and left, but they always make the other person *seem* to swindle himself. They keep inside of the letter of the law all the time, and there ain't no way to git hold of them. *They* don't put the salve on—oh, no, that would be sin; but they know how to fool *you* into putting it on, then it's you that blinds yourself. I reckon the dervish and the camel-driver was just a pair—a fine, smart, brainy rascal, and a dull, coarse, ignorant one, but both of them rascals, just the same."

"Mars Tom, does you reckon dey's any o' dat kind o' salve in de worl' now?"

"Yes, Uncle Abner says there is. He says they've got it in New York, and they put it on the country people's eyes and shows them all the railroads in the world, and they go in and git them, and then when they rub the salve on the other eye the other man bids them good-bye and goes off with their railroads. Here's the treasure-hill now. Lower away!''

We landed, but it warn't as interesting as I thought it was going to be, because we couldn't find the place where they went in to git the treasure. Still, it was plenty interesting enough, just to see the mere hill itself where such a wonderful thing happened. Jim said he wouldn't 'a' missed it for three dollars, and I felt the same way.

And to me and Jim, as wonderful a thing as any was the way Tom could come into a strange big country like this and go straight and find a little hump like that and tell it in a minute from a million other humps that was almost just like it, and nothing to help him but only his own learning and his own natural smartness. We talked it over together, but couldn't make out how he done it. He had the best head on him I ever see; and all he lacked was age to make a name for himself equal to Captain Kidd or George Washington. I bet you it would 'a' crowded either of *them* to find that hill, with all their gifts, but it warn't nothing to Tom Sawyer; he went across the Sahara and put his finger on it as easy as pie.

We found a pond of saltwater close by and scraped up a raft of salt around the edges, and loaded up the lion's skin and the tiger's so as they would keep till Jim could tan them.

Chapter 11
The Sandstorm

We went a-fooling along for a day or two, and then just as the moon was touching the ground on the other side of the desert, we see a string of little black figgers moving across its big silver face. You could see them as plain as if they was painted on the moon with ink. It was another caravan. We cooled down our speed and tagged along after it, just to have company, though it warn't going our way. It was a rattler, that caravan, and a most bully sight to look at next morning when the sun came a-streaming across the desert and flung the long shadders of the camels on the gold sand like a thousand grand-daddy-long-legs marching in procession. We never went very near it, because we knowed better now than to act like that and scare people's camels and break up their caravans. It was the gayest outfit you ever see, for rich clothes and nobby style. Some of the chiefs rode on dromedaries, the first we ever see, and very tall, and they go plunging along like they was on stilts, and they rock the man that is on them pretty violent and churn up his dinner considerable, I bet you, but they make noble good time, and a camel ain't nowheres with them for speed.

The caravan camped during the middle part of the day, and then started again about the middle of the afternoon. Before long the sun began to look very curious. First it kind of turned to brass, and then copper, and after that it began to look like a blood-red ball, and the air got hot and close, and pretty soon all the sky in the west darkened up and looked thick and foggy, but fiery and dreadful—like it looks through a piece of red glass, you know. We looked down and see a big confusion going on in the caravan, and a rushing every which way like they was scared; and then they all flopped down in the sand and laid there perfectly still.

Pretty soon we see something coming that stood up like an amazing wide wall, and reached from the desert up into the sky and hid the sun, and it was coming like the nation, too. Then a little faint breeze struck us, and then it came harder, and grains of sand begun to sift against our faces and sting like fire, and Tom sung out:

"It's a sandstorm—turn your backs to it!"

We done it; and in another minute it was blowing a gale, and the sand beat against us by the shovelful, and the air was so thick with it we couldn't see a thing. In five minutes the boat was level full, and we was setting on the lockers buried up to the chin in sand, and only our heads out and could hardly breathe.

Then the storm thinned, and we see that monstrous wall go a-sailing off across the desert, awful to look at, I tell you. We dug ourselves out and looked down, and where the caravan was before there wasn't anything but just the sand ocean now, and still and quiet. All them people and camels was smothered and dead and buried—buried under ten foot of sand, we reckoned, and Tom allowed it might be years before the wind uncovered them, and all that time their friends wouldn't ever know what become of that caravan. Tom said:

"*Now* we know what happened to the people we got the swords and pistols from."

Yes, sir, that was just it. It was as plain as day now. They got buried in the sandstorm, and the wild animals couldn't get at them, and the wind never uncovered them again until they was dried to leather and warn't fit to eat. It seemed to me we had felt as sorry for them people as a person could for anybody, and as mournful, too, but we was mistaken; the last caravan's death went harder with us, a good deal harder. You see, the others was total strangers, and we never got to feeling acquainted with them at all, except, maybe, a little with the man that was watching the girl, but it was different with the last caravan. We was huvvering around them the whole night and 'most a whole day, and had got to feeling real friendly with them, and acquainted. I have found out that there ain't no surer way to find out whether you like people or hate people than to travel with them. Just so with these. We kind of liked them from the start, and traveling with them, the more we got used to their ways, the better and better we like them, and the gladder and gladder we was that we run across them. We had come to know some of them so well that we called them by name when we was talking about them, and soon got so familiar and sociable that we even dropped the Miss and Mister and just called their plain names without any handle, and it did not seem unpolite, but just the right thing. Of course, it wasn't their own names, but names we give them. There was Mr. Elexander Robinson and Miss Adeline Robinson, and Colonel Jacob McDougal and Miss Harryet McDougal, and Judge Jeremiah Butler and young Bushrod Butler, and these was big chiefs mostly that wore splendid great turbans and simmeters, and dressed like the Grand Mogul, and their families. But as soon as we come to know them good, and like them very much, it warn't Mister, nor Judge, nor nothing, anymore, but only Elleck, and Addy, and Jake, and Hattie, and Jerry, and Buck, and so on.

And you know the more you join in with people in their joys and their sorrows, the more nearer and dearer they come to be to you. Now we warn't cold and indifferent, the way most travelers is, we was right down friendly and sociable, and took a chance in everything that was going, and the caravan could depend on us to be on hand every time, it didn't make no difference what it was.

When they camped, we camped right over them, ten or twelve feet up in the air. When they et a meal, we et ourn, and it made it ever so much homeliker to have their company. When they had a wedding that night, and Buck and Addy got married, we got ourselves up in the very starchiest of the professor's duds for the blowout, and when they danced we jined in and shook a foot up there.

But it is sorrow and trouble that brings you the nearest, and it was a funeral that done it with us. It was next morning, just in the still of dawn. We didn't know the diseased, and he warn't in our set, but that never made no difference; he belonged to the caravan, and that was enough, and there warn't no more sincere tears shed over him than the ones we dripped on him from up there eleven hundred foot on high.

Yes, parting with this caravan was much more bitterer than it was to part with them others, which was comparative strangers, and been dead so long, anyway. We had knowed these in their lives, and was fond of them, too, and now to have death snatch them from right before our faces while we was looking, and leave us so lonesome and friendless in the middle of that big desert, it did hurt so, and we wished we mightn't ever make any more friends on that voyage if we was going to lose them again like that.

We couldn't keep from talking about them, and they was all the time coming up in our memory, and looking just the way they looked when we was all alive and happy together. We could see the line marching, and the shiny spearheads a-winking in the sun; we could see the dromedaries and the funeral; and more oftener than anything lumbering along; we could see the wedding and the funeral; and more oftener than anything else we could see them praying, because they don't allow nothing to prevent that; whenever the call come, several times a day, they would stop right there, and stand up and face to the east, and lift back their heads, and spread out their arms and begin, and four or five times they would go down on their knees, and then fall forward and touch their forehead to the ground.

Well, it warn't good to go on talking about them, lovely as they was in their life, and dear to us in their life and death both, because it didn't do no good, and made us too downhearted. Jim allowed he was going to live as good a life as he could, so he could see them again in a better world; and Tom kept still and didn't tell him they was Mohammedans; it warn't no use to disappoint him, he was feeling bad enough just as it was.

When we woke up next morning we was feeling a little cheerfuler, and had had a most powerful good sleep, because sand is the comfortablest bed there is, and I don't see why people that can afford it don't have it more. And it's terrible good ballast, too; I never see the balloon so steady before.

Tom allowed we had twenty tons of it, and wondered what we better do with it; it was good sand, and it did't seem good sense to throw it away. Jim says:

"Mars Tom, can't we tote it back home en sell it? How long'll it take?"

"Depends on the way we go."

"Well, sah, she's wuth a quarter of a dollar a load at home, en I reckon we's got as much as twenty loads, hain't we? How much would dat be?"

"Five dollars."

"By jings, Mars Tom, le's shove for home right on de spot! Hit's more'n a dollar en a half apiece, hain't it?"

"Yes."

"Well, ef dat ain't makin' money de easiest ever *I* struck! She jes' rained in—never cos' us a lick o' work. Le's mosey right along, Mars Tom."

But Tom was thinking and ciphering away so busy and excited he never heard him. Pretty soon he says:

"Five dollars—sho! Look here, this sand's worth—worth—why, it's worth no end of money."

"How is dat, Mars Tom? Go on, honey, go on!"

"Well, the minute people knows it's genuwyne sand from the genuwyne Desert of Sahara, they'll just be in a perfect state of mind to git hold of some of it to keep on the whatnot in a vial with a label on it for curiosity. All we got to do is to put it up in vials and float around all over the United States and peddle them out at ten cents apiece. We've got all of ten thousand dollars' worth of sand in this boat."

Me and Jim went all to pieces with joy, and

begun to shout whoopjamboreehoo, and Tom says:

"And we can keep on coming back and fetching sand, and coming back and fetching more sand, and just keep it a-going till we've carted this whole desert over there and sold it out; and there ain't ever going to be any opposition, either, because we'll take out a patent."

"My goodness," I says, "we'll be as rich as Creosote, won't we, Tom?"

"Yes—Creesus, you mean. Why, that dervish was hunting in that hill of treasures of the earth, and didn't know he was walking over the real ones for a thousand miles. He was blinder than he made the driver."

"Mars Tom, how much is we gwyne to be worth?"

"Well, I don't know yet. It's got to be ciphered, and it ain't the easiest job to do, either, because it's over four million square miles of sand at ten cents a vial."

Jim was awful excited, but this faded it out considerable, and he shook his head and says:

"Mars Tom, we can't 'ford all dem vials—a king couldn't. We better not try to take de whole desert, Mars Tom, de vials gwyne to bust us, sho'."

Tom's excitement died out, too, now, and I reckoned it was on account of the vials, but it wasn't. He set there thinking, and got bluer and bluer, and at last he says:

"Boys, it won't work; we got to give it up."

"Why, Tom?"

"On account of the duties."

I couldn't make nothing out of that; neither could Jim. I says:

"What *is* our duty, Tom? Because if we can't git around it, why can't we just *do* it? People often has to."

But he says:

"Oh, it ain't that kind of duty. The kind I mean is a tax. Whenever you strike a frontier— that's the border of a country, you know—you find a custom-house there, and the gov'ment officers comes and rummages among your things and charges a big tax, which they call a duty because it's their duty to bust you if they can, and if you don't pay the duty they'll hog your sand. They call it confiscating, but don't deceive nobody, it's just hogging, and that's all it is. Now if we try to carry this sand home the way we're pointed now, we got to climb fences till we git tired—just frontier after frontier—Egypt, Arabia, Hindustan, and so on, and they'll all whack on a duty, and so you see, easy enough, we *can't* go *that* road."

"Why, Tom," I says, "we can sail right over their old frontiers; how are *they* going to stop us?"

He looked sorrowful at me, and says, very grave:

"Huck Finn, do you think that would be honest?"

I hate them kind of interruptions. I never said nothing, and he went on:

"Well, we're shut off the other way, too. If we go back the way we've come, there's the New York custom-house, and that is worse than all of them put together, on account of the kind of cargo we've got.''

"Why?''

"Well, they can't raise Sahara sand in America, of course, and when they can't raise a thing there, the duty is fourteen hundred thousand percent on it if you try to fetch it in from where they do raise it.''

"There ain't no sense in that, Tom Sawyer.''

"Who said there *was*? What do you talk to me like that for, Huck Finn? You wait till I say a thing's got sense in it before you go to accusing me of saying it.''

"All right, consider me crying about it, and sorry. Go on.''

Jim says:

"Mars Tom, do dey jam dat duty onto everything we can't raise in America, en don't make no 'stinction 'twixt' anything?''

"Yes, that's what they do.''

"Mars Tom, ain't de blessin' o' de Lord de mos' valuable thing dey is?''

"Yes, it is.''

"Don't de preacher stan' up in de pulpit en call it down on de people?''

"Yes.''

"Whah do it come from?''

"From heaven.''

"Yassir! you's jes' right, 'deed you is, honey—it come from heaven, en dat's a foreign country. *Now*, den! do dey put a tax on dat blessin'?''

"No, they don't.''

" 'Course dey don't; en so it stan' to reason

dat you's mistaken, Mars Tom. Dey wouldn't put de tax on po' truck like san', dat everybody ain't 'bleeged to have, en leave it off'n de bes' thing dey is, which nobody can't git along widout.''

Tom Sawyer was stumped; he see Jim had got him where he couldn't budge. He tried to wiggle out by saying they had *forgot* to put on that tax, but they'd be sure to remember about it, next season of Congress, and then they'd put it on, but that was a poor lame come-off, and he knowed it. He said there warn't nothing foreign that warn't taxed but just that one, and so they couldn't be consistent without taxing it, and to be consistent was the first law of politics. So he stuck to it that they'd left it out unintentional and would be certain to do their best to fix it before they got caught and laughed at.

But I didn't feel no more interest in such things, as long as we couldn't git our sand through, and it made me low-spirited, and Jim the same. Tom he tried to cheer us up by saying he would think up another speculation for us that would be just as good as this one and better, but it didn't do no good; we didn't believe there was any as big as this. It was mighty hard; such a little while ago we was so rich, and could 'a' bought a country and started a kingdom and been celebrated and happy, and now we was so poor and ornery again, and had our sand left on our hands. The sand was looking so lovely before, just like gold and di'monds, and the feel of it was so soft and so silky and nice, but now I couldn't bear the sight of it, it made me sick to look at it, and I knowed I wouldn't ever feel comfortable again till we got shut of it, and I didn't have it there no more to remind us of what we had been and what we had got degraded down to. The others was feeling the same way about it that I was. I knowed it, because they cheered up so, the minute I says le's throw this truck overboard.

Well, it was going to be work, you know, and pretty solid work, too; so Tom he divided it up according to fairness and strength. He said me and him would clear out a fifth apiece of the sand, and Jim three-fifths. Jim he didn't quite like the agreement. He says:

"'Course I's de stronges', en I's willin' to do a share accordin', but jings you's kinder pilin' it into ole Jim, Mars Tom, hain't you?"

"Well, I didn't think so, Jim, but you try your hand at fixing it, and let's see."

So Jim reckoned it wouldn't be no more than fair if me and Tom done a *tenth* apiece. Tom he turned his back to git room and be private, and then he smole a smile that spread around and covered the whole Sahara to the westward, back to the Atlantic edge of it where we come from. Then he turned around again and said it was a good enough arrangement, and we was satisfied if Jim was. Jim said he was.

So then Tom measured off our two-tenths in the bow and left the rest for Jim, and it surprised Jim a good deal to see how much difference there was and what a raging lot of sand his share came to, and said he was powerful glad now that he spoke up in time and got the first arrangement altered, for he said that even the way it was now, there was more sand than enjoyment in his end of the contract, he believed.

Then we laid into it. It was mighty hot work, and tough; so hot we had to move up into cooler weather or we couldn't 'a' stood it. Me and Tom took turn about, and one worked while t'other rested, but there warn't nobody to spell poor old Jim, and he made all that part of Africa damp, he sweated so. We couldn't work good, we was so full of laugh, and Jim he kept fretting and wanting to know what tickled us so, and we had to keep making things up to account for it, and they was pretty poor inventions, but they done well enough, Jim didn't see through them. At last when we got done we was 'most dead, but not with work but with laughing. By and by Jim was 'most dead, too, but it was with work; then we took turns and spelled him, and he was as thankful as he could be, and would set on the gunnel and swab the sweat, and heave and pant, and say how good we was to a poor old man, and he wouldn't ever forgit us. He was always the gratefulest man I ever see, for any little thing you done for him.

Chapter 12

Jim Standing Siege

The next few meals was pretty sandy, but that
don't make no difference when you are hungry;
and when you ain't it ain't no satisfaction to eat,
anyway, and so a little grit in the meat ain't no
particular drawback, as far as I can see.

Then we struck the east end of the desert at
last, sailing on the northeast course. Away off
on the edge of the sand, in a soft pinky light, we
see three little sharp roofs like tents, and Tom
says:

"It's the pyramids of Egypt."

It made my heart fairly jumpy. You see, I
had seen a many and a many picture of them,
and heard tell of them a hundred times, and yet
to come on them all of a sudden, that way, and
find they was *real*, 'stead of imaginations, 'most
knocked the breath out of me with surprise. It's
a curious thing, that the more you hear about a
grand and big and bully thing or person, the

more it kind of dreamies out, as you may say, and gets to be a big dim wavy figger made out of moonshine and nothing solid to it. It's just so with George Washington, and the same with them pyramids.

And moreover, besides the thing they always said about them seemed to me to be stretchers. There was a feller come to the Sunday-school once, and had a picture of them, and made a speech, and said the biggest pyramid covered thirteen acres, and was 'most five hundred foot high, just a steep mountain, all built out of hunks of stone as big as a bureau, and laid up in perfectly regular layers, like stair-steps. Thirteen acres, you see, for just one building; it's a farm. If it hadn't been in Sunday-school I would 'a' judged it was a lie; and outside I was certain of it. And he said there was a hole in the pyramid, and you go there with candles, and go ever so far up a long slanting tunnel, and come to a large room in the stomach of that stone mountain, and there you would find a big stone chest with a king in it, four thousand years old. I said to myself, then, if that ain't a lie I will eat the king if they will fetch him, for even Methusalem warn't that old, and nobody claims it.

As we come a little nearer we see the yaller sand come to an end in a long straight edge like a blanket, and onto it was joined, edge to edge, a wide country of bright green, with a snaky stripe crooking through it, and Tom said it was the Nile. It made my heart jump again, for the Nile was another thing that wasn't real to me. Now I can tell you one thing which is dead certain; if you will fool along over three thousand miles of yaller sand, all glimmering with heat so that it makes your eyes water to look at it, and you've been a considerable part of a week doing it, the green country will look so like home and heaven to you that it will make your eyes water *again*.

It was just so with me, and the same with Jim.

And when Jim got so he could believe it *was* the land of Egypt he was looking at, he wouldn't enter it standing up, but got down on his knees and took off his hat, because he said it wasn't fitten' for a humble poor man to come any other way where such men had been as Moses and Joseph and Pharoah and the other prophets. He was a Presbyterian, and had a most deep respect for Moses, which was a Presbyterian, too, he said. He was all stirred up, and says:

"Hit's de lan' of Egypt, de lan' of Egypt, en I's 'lowed to look at it wid my own eyes! En dah's de river dat was turn' to blood, en I's looking at de very same groun' whah de plagues was, en de lice, en de frogs, en de locus', en de hail, en whah dey marked de door-pos', en de angel o' de Lord come by in de darkness o' de night en slew de fust-born in all de lan' o' Egypt. Ole Jim ain't worthy to see dis day!"

And then he just broke down and cried, he was so thankful. So between him and Tom there was talk enough, Jim being excited because the land was so full of history—Joseph and his brethren, Moses in the bulrushes, Jacob coming down into Egypt to buy corn, the silver cup in the sack, and all them interesting things; and Tom just as excited too, because the land was so full of history that was in *his* line, about Noureddin, and Bedreddin, and such like monstrous giants, that made Jim's wool rise, and a raft of other *Arabian Nights* folks, which the half of them never done the things they let on they done, I didn't believe.

Then we struck a disappointment, for one of them early morning fogs started up, and it warn't no use to sail over the top of it, because we would go by Egypt sure, so we judged it was best to set her compass straight for the place where the pyramids was gitting blurred and blotted out, and then drop low and skin along pretty close to the ground and keep a sharp lookout. Tom took the hellum, I stood by to let go the anchor, and Jim he straddled the bow to dig through the fog with his eyes and watch out for danger ahead. We went along a steady gait, but not very fast, and the fog got solider and solider, so solid that Jim looked dim and ragged and smoky through it. It was awful still, and we talked low and was anxious. Now and then Jim would say:

"Highst her a p'int, Mars Tom, highst her!" and up she would skip, a foot or two, and we would slide right over a flat-roofed mud cabin, with people that had been asleep on it just beginning to turn out and gap and stretch; and once when a feller was clear up on his hind legs so he could gap and stretch better, we took him a blip in the back and knocked him off. By and by, after about an hour, and everything dead still and we a-straining our ears for sounds and holding our breath, the fog thinned a little, very sudden, and Jim sung out in an awful scare:

"Oh, ford e lan's sake, set her back, Mars

Tom, here's de biggest giant outen de *'Rabian Nights* a-comin' for us!'' and he went over backwards in the boat.

Tom slammed on the back-action, and as we slowed to a standstill a man's face as big as our house at home looked in over the gunnel, same as a house looks out of its windows, and I laid down and died. I must 'a' been clear dead and gone for as much as a minute or more; then I come to, and Tom had hitched a boat-hook onto the lower lip of the giant and was holding the balloon steady with it whilst he canted his head back and got a good long look up at that awful face.

Jim was on his knees with his hands clasped, gazing up at the thing in a begging way, and working his lips, but not getting anything out. I took only just a glimpse, and was fading out again, but Tom says:

"He ain't alive, you fools; it's the Sphinx!"

I never see Tom look so little and like a fly; but that was because the giant's head was so big and awful. Awful, yes, so it was, but not dreadful anymore, because you could see it was a noble face, and kind of sad, and not thinking about you, but other things and larger. It was stone, reddish stone, and its nose and ears battered, and that gave it an abused look, and you felt sorrier for it for that.

We stood off a piece, and sailed around it and over it, and it was just grand. It was a man's head, or maybe a woman's, on a tiger's body a hundred and twenty-five foot long, and there was a dear little temple between its front paws. All but the head used to be under the sand, for hundreds of years, maybe thousands, but they had just lately dug the sand away and found that little temple. It took a power of sand to bury that cretur; 'most as much as it would to bury a steamboat, I reckon.

We landed Jim on top of the head, with an American flag to protect him, it being a foreign land; then we sailed off to this and that and t'other distance, to git what Tom called effects and perspectives and proportions, and Jim he done the best he could, striking all the different kinds of attitudes and positions he could study up, but standing on his head and working his legs the way a frog does was the best. The further we got away, the littler Jim got, and the grander the Sphinx got, till at last it was only a clothespin on a dome, as you might say. That's the way perspective brings out the correct proportions, Tom said; he said Julus Cesar's soldiers didn't know how big he was, they was too close to him.

Then we sailed off further and further, till we couldn't see Jim at all anymore, and then that great figger was at its noblest, a-gazing out over the Nile Valley so still and solemn and lonesome, and all the little shabby huts and things that was scattered about it clean disappeared and gone, and nothing around it now but a soft wide spread of yeller velvet, which was the sand.

That was the right place to stop, and we done it. We set there a-looking and a-thinking for a half an hour, nobody a-saying anything, for it made us feel quiet and kind of solemn to remember it had been looking over that valley just that same way, and thinking its awful thoughts all to itself for thousands of years, and nobody can't find out what they are to this day.

At last I took up the glasses and see some little black things a-capering around on that velvet carpet, and some more a-climbing up the cretur's back, and then I see two or three wee puffs of white smoke, and told Tom to look. He done it, and says:

"They're bugs. No—hold on; they—why, I believe they're men. Yes, it's men—men and horses both. They're hauling a long ladder up onto the Sphinx's back—now ain't that odd? And they're trying to lean it up a—there's some more puffs of smoke—it's guns! Huck, they're after Jim."

We clapped on the power, went for them a-biling. We was there in no time, and come a-whizzing down amongst them, and they broke and scattered every which way, and some that was climbing the ladders after Jim let go all holts and fell. We soared up and found him laying on top of the head panting and most tuckered out, partly from howling for help and partly from scare. He had been standing a siege a long time—a week, *he* said, but it warn't so, it only just seemed so to him because they was crowding him so. They had shot at him, and rained the bullets all around him, but he warn't hit, and when they found he wouldn't stand up and the bullets couldn't git at him when he was laying down, they went for the ladder, and then he knowed it was all up with him if we didn't come pretty quick. Tom was very indignant, and asked him why he didn't show the flag and command them to *git*, in the name of the United States. Jim said he done it, but they never paid no attention. Tom said he would have this thing looked into at Washington, and says:

"You'll see that they'll have to apologize for insulting the flag, and pay indemnity, too, on top of it, even if they git off *that* easy."

Jim says:

"What is an indemnity, Mars Tom?"

"It's cash, that's what it is."

"Who gits it, Mars Tom?"

"Why, *we* do."

"En who gits de apology?"

"The United States. Or, we can take which-ever we please. We can take the apology, if we want to, and let the gov'ment take the money."

"How much money will it be, Mars Tom?"

"Well, in an aggravated case like this one, it will be at least three dollars apiece, and I don't know but more."

"Well, den, we'll take the money, Mars Tom, blame de 'pology. Hain't dat yo' notion, too? En hain't it yourn, Huck?"

We talked it over a little and allowed that that was as good a way as any, so we agreed to take the money. It was a new business to me, and I asked Tom if countries always apologized when they had done wrong, and he says:

"Yes; the little ones does."

We was sailing around examining the pyra-mids, you know, and now we soared up and roosted on the flat top of the biggest one, and found it was just like what the man said in the Sunday-school. It was like four pairs of stairs that start broad at the bottom and slants up and comes together in a point at the top, only these stair-steps couldn't be clumb the way you climb other stairs; no, for each step was as high as your chin, and you have to be boosted up from behind. The two other pyramids warn't far away, and the people moving about on the sand between looked like bugs crawling, we was so high above them.

Tom he couldn't hold himself he was so worked up with gladness and astonishment to be in such a celebrated place, and he just dripped history from every pore, seemed to me. He said he couldn't scarcely believe he was standing on the very identical spot the prince flew from on the Bronze Horse. It was in the *Arabian Nights* times, he said. Somebody give the prince the bronze horse with a peg in its shoulder, and he could git on him and fly through the air like a bird, and go all over the world, and steer it by turning the peg, and fly high or low and land wherever he wanted to.

When he got done telling it there was one of them uncomfortable silences that comes, you know, when a person has been telling a whopper and you feel sorry for him and wish you could think of some way to change the subject and let him down easy, but git stuck and don't see no way, and before you can pull your mind together and *do* something, that silence has got in and spared itself and done the business. I was embarrassed, Jim he was embarrassed, and neither of us couldn't say a word. Well, Tom he glowed at me a minute, and says:

"Come, out with it. What do you think?"

I says:

"Tom Sawyer, *you* don't believe that yourself."

"What's the reason I don't? What's to hender me?"

"There's one thing to hender you: it can't happen, that's all."

"What's the reason it couldn't happen?"

"You tell me the reason it *could* happen."

"This balloon is a good enough reason it could happen, I should reckon."

"*Why* is it?"

"*Why* is it? I never saw such an idiot. Ain't this balloon and the bronze horse the same thing under different names?"

"No, they're not. One is a balloon and the other's a horse. It's very different. Next you'll be saying a house and a cow is the same thing."

"By Jackson, Huck's got him ag'in! Dey ain't no wigglin' outer dat!"

"Shut your head, Jim; you don't know what you're talking about. And Huck don't. Look here, Huck, I'll make it plain to you, so you can understand. You see, it ain't the mere *form* that's got anything to do with their being similar or unsimilar, it's the *principle* involved; and the principle is the same in both. Don't you see, now?"

I turned it over in my mind, and says:

"Tom, it ain't no use. Principles is all very well but they don't git around that one big fact, that the thing that a balloon can do ain't no sort of proof of what a horse can do."

"Shucks, Huck, you don't get the idea at all. Now look here a minute—it's perfectly plain. Don't we fly through the air?"

"Yes."

"Very well. Don't we fly high or low, just as

we please?"

"Yes."

"Don't we steer whichever way we want to?"

"Yes."

"And don't we land when and where we please?"

"Yes."

"How do we move the balloon and steer it?"

"By touching the buttons."

"*Now* I reckon the thing is clear to you at last. In the other case the moving and steering was done by turning a peg. We touch a button, the prince turned a peg. There ain't an atom of difference, you see. I knowed I could git it through your head if I stuck to it long enough."

He felt so happy he began to whistle. But me and Jim was silent, so he broke off surprised, and says:

"Looky here, Huck Finn, don't you see it *yet*?"

I says:

"Tom Sawyer, I want to ask you some questions."

"Go ahead," he says, and I see Jim chirk up to listen.

"As I understand it, the whole thing is in the buttons and the peg—the rest ain't of no consequence. A button is one shape, a peg is another shape, but that ain't any matter?"

"No, that ain't any matter, as long as they've both got the same power."

"All right, then. What is the power that's in a candle and in a match?"

"It's the fire."

"It's the same in both, then?"

"Yes, just the same in both."

"All right. Suppose I set fire to a carpenter shop with a match. What will happen to that carpenter shop?"

"She'll burn up."

"And suppose I set fire to this pyramid with a candle—will she burn up?"

"Of course she won't."

"All right. Now the fire's the same, both times. *Why* does the shop burn, and the pyramid don't?"

"Because the pyramid *can't* burn."

"Ah! and *a horse can't fly!*"

"My lan', ef Huck ain't got him ag'in! Huck's landed him high en dry dis time, *I* tell you! Hit's de smartes' trap I ever see a body walk inter—en ef I—"

But Jim was so full of laugh he got to strangling and couldn't go on, and Tom was that mad to see how neat I had floored him, and turned his own agrument ag'in him and knocked him all to rags and flinders with it, that all he could manage to say was that whenever he heard me and Jim try to argue it made him ashamed of the human race. I never said nothing; I was feeling pretty well satisfied. When I have got the best of a person that way, it ain't my way to go around crowing about it the way some people does, for I consider that if I was in his place I wouldn't wish him to crow over me. It's better to be generous, that's what I think.

Chapter 13
Going for Tom's Pipe

By and by we left Jim to float around in the
neighborhood of the pyramids, and we clumb
down to the hole where you go into the tunnel,
and went in with some Arabs and candles, and
away in there in the middle of the pyramid we
found a room and a big stone box in it where
they used to keep that king, just as the man in
the Sunday-school said; but he was gone, now;
somebody had got him. But I didn't take no interest in the place, because there could be ghosts
there; of course, not fresh ones, but I don't like
no kind.

So then we come out and got some little donkeys and rode a piece, and then went in a boat
another piece, and then more donkeys, and got
to Cairo; and all the way the road was as smooth
and beautiful a road as ever I see, and had tall
date-pa'ms on both sides, and naked children
everywhere, and the men was as red as copper,

and fine and strong and handsome. And the city was a curiosity. Such narrow streets—why, they were just lanes, and crowded with people with turbans, and women with veils, and everybody rigged out in blazing bright clothes and all sorts of colors, and you wondered how the camels and the people got by each other in such narrow little cracks, but they done it—a perfect jam, you see, and everybody noisy. The stores warn't big enough to turn around in, but you don't have to go in; the storekeeper sat tailor fashion on his counter, smoking his snaky long pipe, and had his things where he could reach them to sell, and he was just as good as in the street, for the camel-loads rushed him as they went by.

Now and then a grand person flew by in a carriage with fancy dressed men running and yelling in front of it and whacking anybody with a long rod that didn't get out of the way. And by and by along comes the Sultan riding horseback at the head of a procession, and fairly took your breath away, his clothes was so splendid; and everybody fell flat and laid on his stomach while he went by. I forgot, but a feller helped me to remember. He was one that had a rod and run in front.

There was churches, but they don't know enough to keep Sunday; they keep Friday and break the Sabbath. You have to take off your shoes when you go in. There was crowds of men and boys in the church, setting in groups on the stone floor and making no end of noise— getting their lessons by heart, Tom said, out of the Koran, which they think is a Bible, and people that knows better knows enough to not let on. I never see such a big church in my life before, and most awful high, it was; it made you dizzy to look up; our village church at home ain't a circumstance to it; if you was to put it in there, people would think it was a dry-goods box.

What I wanted to see was a dervish, because I was interested in dervishes on account of the one that played the trick on the camel-driver. So we found a lot in a kind of church, and they called themselves Whirling Dervishes; and they did whirl, too. I never see anything like it. They had tall sugar-loaf hats on, and linen petticoats; and they spun and spun, round and round like tops, and the petticoats stood out on a slant, and it was the prettiest thing I ever see, and made me drunk to look at it. They was all Moslems, Tom said, and when I asked him what a Moslem was, he said it was a person that wasn't Presbyterian. So there is plenty of them in Missouri, though I didn't know it before.

We didn't see half there was to see in Cairo, because Tom was in such a sweat to hunt out places that was celebrated in history. We had a most tiresome time to find the granary where Joseph stored up the grain before the famine, and when he found it it warn't worth much to look at, being such an old tumbledown wreck; but Tom was satisfied, and made more fuss over it than I would make if I struck a nail in my foot. How he ever found that place was too many for me. We passed as much as forty just like it before we came to it, and any of them would 'a' done for me, but none but just the right one would suit him; I never see anybody so particular as Tom Sawyer. The minute he stuck the right one he reconnized it as easy as I would reconnize my other shirt if I had one, but how he done it he couldn't any more tell than he could fly; he said so himself.

Then we hunted a long time for the house where the boy lived that learned the cadi how to try the case of the old olives and the new ones, and said it was out of the *Arabian Nights,* and he would tell me and Jim about it when he got time. Well, we hunted and hunted till I was ready to drop, and I wanted Tom to give it up and come next day and git somebody that knowed the town and could talk Missourian and could go straight to the place; but no, he wanted to find it himself, and nothing else would answer. So on we went. Then at last the remarkablest thing happened I ever see. The house was gone—gone hundreds of years ago—every last rag of it gone but just one mud brick. Now a person wouldn't ever believe that a backwoods Missouri boy that hadn't ever been in that town before could go and hunt that place over and find that brick, but Tom Sawyer done it. I know he done it, because I seen him do it. I was right by his very side at the time, and see him see the brick and see him reconnize it. Well, I says to myself, how *does* he do it? Is it knowledge, or is it instink?

Now there's the facts, just as they happened: let everybody explain it in their own way. I've ciphered over it a good deal, and it's my opinion that some of it is knowledge but the main bulk of it is instink. The reason is this: Tom put the brick in his pocket to give to a museum with his name on it and the facts when he went home, and I slipped it out and put another brick considerable like it in its place, and he didn't know the difference—but there was a difference, you see. I think that settles it—it's mostly instink, not knowledge. Instink tells him where the exact *place* is for the brick to be in, and so he reconnizes it by the place it's in, not by the look of the brick. If it was knowledge, not instink, he would know the brick again by the look of it the next time he seen it—which he didn't. So it shows that for all the brag you hear about knowledge being such a wonderful thing, instink is worth forty of the real unerringness. Jim says the same.

When we got back Jim dropped down and took us in, and there was a young man there with a red skullcap and tassel on and a beautiful silk jacket and baggy trousers with a shawl around his waist and pistols in it that could talk English and wanted to hire to us as guide and take us to Mecca and Medina and Central Africa and everywheres for a half a dollar a day and his keep, and we hired him and left, and piled on the power, and by the time we was through dinner we was over the place where the Israelites crossed the Red Sea when Pharoah tried to overtake them and was caught by the waters. We stopped then, and had a good look at the place, and it done Jim good to see it. He said he could see the Israelites walking along between the walls of water, and the Egyptians coming, from away off yonder, hurrying all they could, and see them start in as the Israelites went out, and then when they was all in, see the walls tumble together and drown the last man of them. Then we piled on the power again and rushed away and huvvered over Mount Sinai, and saw the place where Moses broke the tables of stone, and where the children of Israel camped in the plain and worshiped the golden calf, and it was all just as interesting as could be, and the guide knowed every place as well as I knowed the village at home.

But we had an accident, now, and it fetched all the plans to a standstill. Tom's old orney corncob pipe had got so old and swelled and warped that she couldn't hold together any longer, notwithstanding the strings and bandages, but caved in and went to pieces. Tom he didn't know *what* to do. The professor's pipe wouldn't answer; it warn't anything but a mershum, and a person that's got used to a cob pipe knows it lays a long ways over all the pipes in this world, and you can't git him to smoke any other. He wouldn't take mine, I couldn't persuade him. So there he was.

He thought it over, and said we must scour around and see if we could roust out one in Egypt or Arabia or around in some of these countries, but the guide said no, warn't no use, they didn't have them. So Tom was pretty glum for a little while, then he chirked up and said he'd got the idea and knowed what to do. He says:

"I've got another corncob pipe, and it's a prime one, too, and nearly new. It's laying on the rafter that's right over the kitchen stove at home in the village. Jim, you and the guide go and get it, and me and Huck will camp here on Mount Sinai till you come back."

"But, Mars Tom, we couldn't ever find de village. I could find de pipe, 'case I knows de kitchen, but my lan', *we* can't ever find de village, nur Sent Louis, nur none o' dem places. We don't know de way, Mars Tom."

That was a fact, and it stumped Tom for a minute. Then he said:

"Looky here, it can be done, sure; and I'll tell you how. You set your compass and sail west as straight as a dart, till you find the United States. It ain't any trouble, because it's the first land you'll strike the other side of the Atlantic. If it's daytime when you strike it, bulge right on, straight west from the upper part of the Florida coast, and in an hour and three-quarters you'll hit the mouth of the Mississippi —at the speed that I'm going to send you. You'll be so high up in the air that the earth will be curved considerable—sorter like a washbowl turned upside down—and you'll see a raft of rivers crawling around every which way, long before you get there, and you can pick out the Mississippi without any trouble. Then you can follow the river north nearly an hour and three-quarters, till you see the Ohio come in; then you want to look sharp, because you're getting near. Away up to your left you'll see another thread coming in—that's the Missouri and is a little above St. Louis. You'll pass about twenty-five towns in the next fifteen minutes, and you'll recognize ours when you see it—and if you don't I reckon you can yell down and ask."

"Ef it's dat easy, Mars Tom, I reckon we kin do it—yassir, I knows we kin."

The guide was sure of it, too, and thought that he could learn to stand his watch in a little while.

"Jim can learn you the whole thing in half an hour," Tom said. "This balloon's as easy to manage as a canoe."

Tom got out the chart and marked out the course and measured it, and says:

"To go back west is the shortest way, you see. It's only about seven thousand miles. If you went east, and so on around, it's over twice as far." Then says to the guide, "I want you both to watch the telltale all through the watches, and whenever it don't mark three hundred miles an hour, you go higher or drop lower till you find a storm-current that's going your way. There's a hundred miles an hour in this old thing without any wind to help. There's two-hundred-mile gales to be found, any time you want to hunt for them."

"We'll hunt for them, sir."

"See that you do. Sometimes you may have to go up a couple of miles, and it'll be p'ison cold, but most of the time you'll find your storm a good deal lower. If you can only strike a cyclone—that's the ticket for you! You'll see by the professor's books that they travel west in these latitudes; and they travel low, too."

Then he ciphered on the time, and says:

"Seven thousand miles, three hundred miles an hour—you can make the trip in a day—twenty-four hours. This is Thursday; you'll be back here Saturday afternoon. Come, now, hustle out some blankets and food and books and things for me and Huck, and you can start right along. There ain't no occasion to fool around—I want a smoke, and the quicker you fetch that pipe the better."

All hands jumped for the things, and in eight minutes our things was out and the balloon was ready for America. So we shook hands goodbye, and Tom gave his last orders:

"It's ten minutes to 2 P.M. now, Mount Sinai time. In twenty-four hours you'll be home, and it'll be six tomorrow morning, village time. When you strike the village, land out of sight; then you rush down, Jim, and shove these letters in the post-office, and if you see anybody stirring, pull your slouch down over your face so they won't know you. Then you go and slip in the back way to the kitchen and git the pipe, and lay this piece of paper on the kitchen table, and put something on it to hold it, and then slide out and git away, and don't let Aunt Polly catch a sight of you, nor nobody else. Then you jump for the balloon and shove for Mount Sinai three hundred miles an hour. You won't have lost more than an hour. You'll start back at 7 or 8 A.M., village time, and be here in twenty-four hours, arriving at 2 or 3 P.M., Mount Sinai time."

Tom read the piece of paper to us. He had wrote it:

"THURSDAY AFTERNOON. *Tom Saw-yer the Erronort sends his love to Aunt Polly from Mount Sinai where the Ark was,*[1] *and so does Huck Finn, and she will get it tomorrow morning half-past six.*

"TOM SAWYER THE ERRONORT."

"That'll make her eyes bulge out and the tears come," he says. Then he says:

"Stand by! One—two—three—away you go!"

And away she *did* go! Why, she seemed to whiz out of sight in a second.

Then we found a most comfortable cave that looked out over the whole big plain, and there we camped to wait for the pipe.

The balloon came back alright, and brung the pipe; but Aunt Polly had catched Jim when he was getting it, and anybody can guess what happened: she sent for Tom. So Jim he says:

"Mars Tom, she's out on de porch wid her eye sot on de sky a-layin' for you, en she say she ain't gwyne to budge from dah tell she gits hold of you. Dey's gwyne to be trouble, Mars Tom, 'deed dey is."

So then we shoved for home, and not feeling very gay, neither.

[1]This misplacing of the Ark is probably Huck's error, not Tom's.—M.T.

NEW TESTAMENT

AUTHORIZED KING JAMES VERSION

Translated out of the original Greek:
and with the former translations
diligently compared and revised,
by His Majesty's special command

Transforming lives through God's Word

Call us today or visit us online to receive a free catalog featuring hundreds of
biblical resources priced for ministry.

Website: Biblica.com
E-mail: BiblicaDirectService@Biblica.com

Phone: 800-524-1588
Mail: 1820 Jet Stream Drive
Colorado Springs, CO 80921-3696

Biblica provides God's Word to people through Bible translation, Bible
publishing and Bible engagement in Africa, Asia Pacific, Europe, Latin
America, Middle East, North America, and South Asia. Through its
worldwide reach, Biblica engages people with God's Word so that their
lives are transformed through a relationship with Jesus Christ.

Eng. NT KJV 320101/320102/280853/BB503
20000/20000/20000/15000
320101: ISBN 978-1-56320-793-8
320102: ISBN 978-1-56320-794-5
280853: ISBN 978-1-56320-790-7

9/12
Printed in U.S.A.

THE **DRAMA** OF THE **BIBLE** IN SIX ACTS

The Bible is a collection of letters, poems, stories, visions, prophetic oracles, wisdom and other kinds of writing. The first step to good Bible reading and understanding is to engage these collected works as the different kinds of writing that they are, and to read them as whole books. We encourage you to read big, to not merely take in little fragments of the Bible. The introductions at the start of each book will help you to do this.

But it is also important not to view the Bible as a gathering of unrelated writings. Overall, the Bible is a narrative. These books come together to tell God's true story and his plan to set the world right again. This story of the Bible falls naturally into six key major acts, which are briefly summarized below.

> "I had always felt life first as a story: and if there is a story, there is a story-teller."
>
> G. K. Chesterton

But even more precisely, we can say the story of the Bible is a drama. The key to a drama is that it has to be acted out, performed, lived. It can't remain as only words on a page. A drama is an activated story. The Bible was written so we could enter into its story. It is meant to be lived.

All of us, without exception, live our lives as a drama. We are on stage every single day. What will we say? What will we do? According to which story will we live? If we are not answering these questions with the biblical script, we will follow another. We can't avoid living by someone's stage instructions, even if merely our own.

This is why another key to engaging the Bible well is to recognize that its story has not ended. God's saving action continues. We are all invited to take up our own roles in this ongoing story of redemption and new creation. So, welcome to the drama of the Bible. Welcome to the story of how God intends to renew your life, and the life of the world. God himself is calling you to engage with his word.

Act 1: GOD'S INTENTION

The drama begins (in the first pages of the book of Genesis) with God already on the stage creating a world. He makes a man and a woman, Adam and Eve, and places them in the Garden of Eden to work it and take care of it. The earth is created to be their home. God's intention is for humanity to be in close, trusting relationship with him and in harmony with the rest of creation that surrounds them.

In a startling passage, the Bible tells us that human beings are God's image-bearers, created to share in the task of bringing God's wise and beneficial rule to the rest of the world. Male and female together, we are significant, decision-making, world-shaping beings. This is our vocation, our purpose as defined in the biblical story.

An equally remarkable part of Act 1 is the description of God as coming into the garden to be with the first human beings. Not only is the earth the God-intended place for humanity, God himself comes to make the beautiful new creation his home as well. He takes up residence in it as his temple.

God then gives his own assessment of the whole creation: *God saw every thing he had made, and, behold, it was very good.* Act 1 reveals God's original desire for the world. It shows us that life itself is a gift from the Creator. It tells us what we were made for and provides the setting for all the action that follows.

Act 2: EXILE

Tension and conflict are introduced to the story when Adam and Eve decide to go their own way and seek their own wisdom. They listen to the deceptive voice of God's enemy, Satan, and doubt God's trustworthiness. They decide to live apart from the word that God himself has given them. They decide to be a law to themselves.

The disobedience of Adam and Eve—the introduction of sin into our world—is presented in the Bible as having devastating consequences. Humans were created for healthy, life-giving relationship: with God, with each other, and with the rest of creation. But now humanity must live with the fracturing of all these relations and with the resulting shame, brokenness, pain, loneliness—and death.

Heaven and earth—God's realm and our realm—were intended to be united. God's desire from the beginning was clearly to live with us in the world he made. But now God is hidden. Now it is possible to be in our world and not know him, not experience his presence, not follow his ways, not live in gratitude.

As a result of this rebellion, the first exile in the story takes place. The humans are driven away from God's presence. Their offspring throughout history will seek to find their way back to the source of life. They will devise any number of philosophies and religions, trying to make sense of a fallen, yet haunting world. But death now stalks them, and they will find that they cannot escape it. Having attempted to live apart from God and his good word, humans will find they have neither God nor life.

New questions arise in the drama: Can the curse on creation be overcome and the relationship between God and humanity restored? Can heaven and earth be reunited? Or did God's enemy effectively end the plan and subvert the story?

Act 3: CALLING ISRAEL TO A MISSION

 We see the direction of God's redemptive plan when he calls Abraham, promising to make him into a great nation. God narrows his focus and concentrates on one group of people. But the ultimate goal remains the same: to bless all the peoples on earth and remove the curse from creation.

When Abraham's descendants are enslaved in Egypt, a central pattern in the story is set: God hears their cries for help and comes to set them free. God makes a covenant with this new nation of Israel at Mt. Sinai. Israel is called by God to be a light to the nations, showing the world what it means to follow God's ways for living. If they will do this, he will bless them in their new land and will come to live with them.

However, God also warns them that if they are not faithful to the covenant, he will send them away, just as he did with Adam and Eve. In spite of God's repeated warnings through his prophets, Israel seems determined to break the covenant. So God abandons the holy temple—the sign of his presence with his people—and it is smashed by pagan invaders. Israel's capital city Jerusalem is sacked and burned.

Abraham's descendants, chosen to reverse the failure of Adam, have now apparently also failed. The problem this poses in the biblical story is profound. Israel, sent as the divine answer to Adam's fall, cannot escape Adam's sin. God, however, remains committed to his people and his plan, so he sows the seed of a different outcome. He promises to send a new king, a descendant of Israel's great King David, who will lead the nation back to its destiny. The very prophets who warned Israel of the dire consequences of its wrongdoing also pledge that the good news of God's victory will be heard in Israel once again.

Act 3 ends tragically, with God apparently absent and the pagan nations ruling over Israel. But the hope of a promise remains. There is one true God. He has chosen Israel. He will return to his people to live with them again. He will bring justice, peace and healing to Israel, and then to the world. He will do this in a final and climactic way. God will send his anointed one—the Messiah. He has given his word on this.

Act 4: THE SURPRISING VICTORY OF JESUS

 "He is the god made manifest . . . the universal savior of human life." These words, referring to Caesar Augustus (found in a Roman inscription from 4 BC in Ephesus), proclaim the gospel of the Roman Empire. This version of the good news announces that Caesar is the lord who brings peace and prosperity to the world.

Into this empire a son of David is born, and he announces the gospel of God's kingdom. Jesus of Nazareth brings the good news of the coming of God's reign. He begins to show what God's new creation looks like. He announces the end of Israel's exile and the forgiveness of sins. He heals the sick and raises the dead. He overcomes the dark spiritual powers. He welcomes sinners and those considered unclean. Jesus renews the nation, rebuilding the twelve tribes of Israel around himself in a symbolic way.

But the established religious leaders are threatened by Jesus and his kingdom, so they have him brought before the Roman governor. During the very week that the Jews were remembering and celebrating Passover—God's ancient rescue of his people from slavery in Egypt—the Romans nail Jesus to a cross and kill him as a false king.

But the Bible claims that this defeat is actually God's greatest victory. How? Jesus willingly gives up his life as a sacrifice on behalf of the nation, on behalf of the world. Jesus takes onto himself the full force of evil and empties it of its power. In this surprising way, Jesus fights and wins Israel's ultimate battle. The real enemy was never Rome, but the spiritual powers that lie behind Rome and every other kingdom whose weapon is death. Through his blood Jesus pays the price and reconciles everything in heaven and on earth to God.

God then publicly declares this victory by reversing Jesus' death sentence and raising him back to life. The resurrection of Israel's king shows that the great enemies of God's creation—sin and death—really have been defeated. The resurrection is the great sign that the new creation has begun.

Jesus is the fulfillment of Israel's story and a new start for the entire human race. Death came through the first man, Adam. The resurrection of the dead comes through the new man, Jesus. God's original intention is being reclaimed.

Act 5: THE RENEWED PEOPLE OF GOD

If the key victory has already been secured, why is there an Act 5? The answer is that God wants the victory of Jesus to spread to all the nations of the world. The risen Jesus says to his disciples, *Peace be unto you: as my Father hath sent me, even so send I you.* So this new act in the drama tells the story of how the earliest followers of Jesus began to spread the good news of God's reign.

According to the New Testament, all those who belong to Israel's Messiah are children of Abraham, heirs of both the ancient promises and the ancient mission. The task of bringing blessing to the peoples of the world has been given again to Abraham's family. Their mission is to live out the liberating message of the good news of God's kingdom.

God is gathering people from all around the world and forming them into assemblies of Jesus-followers—his church. Together they are God's new temple, the place where his Spirit lives. They are the community of those who have pledged their allegiance to Jesus as the true Lord of the world. They have crossed from death into new life, through the power of God's Spirit. They demonstrate God's love across the usual boundaries of race, class, tribe and nation.

Forgiveness of sins and reconciliation with God can now be announced to all. Following in the steps of Jesus, his followers proclaim this gospel in both word and deed. The power of this new, God-given life breaking into the world is meant to be shown by the real-world actions of the Christian community. But the message also has a warning. When the Messiah returns, he will come as the rightful judge of the world.

The Bible is the story of the central struggle weaving its way through the history of the world. And now the story arrives at our own time, enveloping us in its drama.

So the challenge of a decision confronts us. What will we do? How will we fit into this story? What role will we play? God is inviting us to be a part of his mission of re-creation—of bringing restoration, justice and forgiveness. We are to join in the task of making things new, to be a living sign of what is to come when the drama is complete.

Act 6: GOD COMES HOME

 God's future has come into our world through the work of Jesus the Messiah. But for now, the present evil age also continues. Brokenness, wrongdoing, sickness and even death remain. We live in the time of the overlap of the ages, the time of in-between. The final Act is coming, but it has not yet arrived.

We live in the time of invitation, when the call of the gospel goes out to every creature. Of course, many still live as though God doesn't exist. They do not acknowledge the rule of the Messiah. But the day is coming when Jesus will return to earth and the reign of God will become an uncontested reality throughout the world.

God's presence will be fully and openly with us once again, as it was at the beginning of the drama. God's plan of redemption will reach its goal. The creation will experience its own Exodus, finding freedom from its bondage to decay. Pain and tears, regret and shame, suffering and death will be no more.

When the day of resurrection arrives God's people will find that their hope has been realized. The dynamic force of an indestructible life will course through their bodies. Empowered by the Spirit, and unhindered by sin and death, we will pursue our original vocation as a renewed humanity. We will be culture makers, under God but over the world. Having been remade in the image of Christ, we will share in bringing his wise, caring rule to the earth.

At the center of it all will be God himself. He will return and make his home with us, this time in a new heavens and a new earth. We, along with the rest of creation, will worship him perfectly and fulfill our true calling. God will be all in all, and the whole world will be full of his glory.

WHAT NOW?

The preceding overview of the drama of the Bible is meant to give you a framework so you can begin to read the books that make up the story. The summary we've provided is merely an invitation for you to engage the sacred books themselves.

Many people today follow the practice of reading only small, fragmentary snippets of the Bible—verses—and often in isolation from the books of which they are a part. This does not lead to good Bible understanding. We encourage you instead to take in whole books, the way their authors wrote them. This is really the only way to gain deep insight to the Scriptures.

Go deep and read big.

The more you immerse yourself in the script of this drama, the better you will be able to find your own place in the story. The following page, called *Living the Script*, will help you with practical next steps for taking up your role in the Bible's drama of renewal.

LIVING
THE SCRIPT

From the beginning God made it clear that he intends for us to be significant players in his drama. No doubt, it is first and foremost God's story. But we can't passively sit back and just watch what happens. At every stage he invites humans to participate with him.

Here are three key steps to finding your place in the drama:

1. IMMERSE YOURSELF IN THE BIBLE

If we are unfamiliar with the text of the drama itself, there's no chance of living our parts well. Only when we read both deeply and widely in the Bible, marinating in it and letting it soak into our lives, will we be prepared to effectively take up our roles. The more we read the Bible, the better readers we will become. Rather than skimming the surface, we will become skilled at interpreting and practicing what we read.

2. COMMIT TO FOLLOW JESUS

We've all taken part in the brokenness and wrongdoing that came into the story in Act 2. The victory of Jesus in Act 4 now offers us the opportunity to have our lives turned around. Our sins can be forgiven. We can become part of God's story of new creation.

Turn away from your wrongdoing. God has acted through the death and resurrection of the Messiah to deal decisively with evil—in your life and in the life of the world. His death was a sacrifice, and his resurrection a new beginning. Acknowledge that Jesus is the rightful ruler of the world, and commit to follow him and join with God's people.

3. LIVE YOUR PART

Followers of Jesus are gospel players in local communities living out the biblical drama together. But we do not have an exact script for our lines and actions in the drama today. Our history has not yet been written. And we can't just repeat lines from earlier acts in the drama. So what do we do?

We read the Bible to understand what God has already done, especially through Jesus the Messiah, and to know how we carry this story forward. *The Bible helps us answer the key question about everything we say and do: Is this an appropriate and fitting way to live out the story of Jesus today?* This is how we put the Scriptures into action. Life's choices can be messy, but God has given us his word and promised us his Spirit to guide us on the way. You are God's artwork, created to do good works. May your life be a gift of beauty back to him.

For more help in understanding the Bible and finding your place in its story, go to Biblica.com/LivingTheScript.

Contents

THE NEW TESTAMENT

The Gospel According to
ST. MATTHEW

1 The book of the generation of Jesus Christ, the son of David, the son of Abraham.

2 Abraham begat Isaac; and Isaac begat Jacob; and Jacob begat Judas and his brethren; 3 And Judas begat Phares and Zara of Thamar; and Phares begat Esrom; and Esrom begat Aram; 4 And Aram begat Aminadab; and Aminadab begat Naasson; and Naasson begat Salmon; 5 And Salmon begat Booz of Rachab; and Booz begat Obed of Ruth; and Obed begat Jesse; 6 And Jesse begat David the king;

and David the king begat Solomon of her *that had been the wife* of Urias; 7 And Solomon begat Roboam; and Roboam begat Abia; and Abia begat Asa; 8 And Asa begat Josaphat; and Josaphat begat Joram; and Joram begat Ozias; 9 And Ozias begat Joatham; and Joatham begat Achaz; and Achaz begat Ezekias; 10 And Ezekias begat Manasses; and Manasses begat Amon; and Amon begat Josias; 11 And Josias begat Jechonias and his brethren, about the time they were carried away to Babylon:

12 And after they were brought to Babylon, Jechonias begat Salathiel; and Salathiel begat Zorobabel; 13 And Zorobabel begat Abiud; and Abiud begat Eliakim; and Eliakim begat Azor; 14 And Azor begat Sadoc; and Sadoc begat Achim; and Achim begat Eliud; 15 And Eliud begat Eleazar; and Eleazar begat Matthan; and Matthan begat Jacob; 16 And Jacob begat Joseph the husband of Mary, of whom was born Jesus, who is called Christ.

17 So all the generations from Abraham to David *are* fourteen generations; and from David until the carrying away into Babylon *are* fourteen generations; and from the carrying away into Babylon unto Christ *are* fourteen generations.

18 Now the birth of Jesus Christ was on this wise: When as his mother Mary was espoused to Joseph, before they came together, she was found with child of the Holy Ghost. 19 Then Joseph her husband, being a just *man*, and not willing to make her a publick example, was minded to put her away privily. 20 But while he thought on these things, behold, the angel of the Lord appeared unto him in a dream, saying, Joseph, thou son of David, fear not to take unto thee Mary thy wife: for that which is conceived in her is of the Holy Ghost. 21 And she shall bring forth a son, and thou shalt call his name JESUS: for he shall save his people from their sins. 22 Now all this was done, that it might be fulfilled which was spoken of the Lord by the prophet, saying, 23 Behold, a virgin shall be with child, and shall bring forth a son, and they shall call his name Emmanuel, which being interpreted is, God with us. 24 Then Joseph being raised from sleep did as the angel of the Lord had bidden him, and took unto him his wife: 25 And knew her not till she had brought forth her firstborn son: and he called his name JESUS.

2 Now when Jesus was born in Bethlehem of Judaea in the days of Herod the king, behold, there came wise men from the east to Jerusalem, 2 Saying, Where is he that is born King of the Jews? for we have seen his star in the east, and are come to worship him. 3 When Herod the king had heard *these things,* he was troubled, and all Jerusalem with him. 4 And when he had gathered all the chief priests and scribes of the people together, he demanded of them where Christ should be born. 5 And they said unto him, In Bethlehem of Judaea: for thus it is written by the prophet,

6 And thou Bethlehem, in the land of Juda, art not the least among the princes of Juda: for out of thee shall come a Governor, that shall rule my people Israel.

7 Then Herod, when he had privily called the wise men, enquired of them diligently what time the star appeared. 8 And he sent them to Bethlehem, and said, Go and search diligently for the young child; and when ye have found *him,* bring me word again, that I may come and worship him also. 9 When they had heard the king, they departed; and, lo, the star, which they saw

in the east, went before them, till it came and stood over where the young child was. [10]When they saw the star, they rejoiced with exceeding great joy.

[11]And when they were come into the house, they saw the young child with Mary his mother, and fell down, and worshipped him: and when they had opened their treasures, they presented unto him gifts; gold, and frankincense, and myrrh. [12]And being warned of God in a dream that they should not return to Herod, they departed into their own country another way. [13]And when they were departed, behold, the angel of the Lord appeareth to Joseph in a dream, saying, Arise, and take the young child and his mother, and flee into Egypt, and be thou there until I bring thee word: for Herod will seek the young child to destroy him. [14]When he arose, he took the young child and his mother by night, and departed into Egypt: [15]And was there until the death of Herod: that it might be fulfilled which was spoken of the Lord by the prophet, saying, Out of Egypt have I called my son.

[16]Then Herod, when he saw that he was mocked of the wise men, was exceeding wroth, and sent forth, and slew all the children that were in Bethlehem, and in all the coasts thereof, from two years old and under, according to the time which he had diligently enquired of the wise men. [17]Then was fulfilled that which was spoken by Jeremy the prophet, saying,

[18]In Rama was there a voice heard, lamentation, and weeping, and great mourning, Rachel weeping *for* her children, and would not be comforted, because they are not.

[19]But when Herod was dead, behold, an angel of the Lord appeareth in a dream to Joseph in Egypt, [20]Saying, Arise, and take the young child and his mother, and go into the land of Israel: for they are dead which sought the young child's life. [21]And he arose, and took the young child and his mother, and came into the land of Israel. [22]But when he heard that Archelaus did reign in Judaea in the room of his father Herod, he was afraid to go thither: notwithstanding, being warned of God in a dream, he turned aside into the parts of Galilee:

[23]And he came and dwelt in a city called Nazareth: that it might be fulfilled which was spoken by the prophets, He shall be called a Nazarene.

3 In those days came John the Baptist, preaching in the wilderness of Judaea, [2]And saying, Repent ye: for the kingdom of heaven is at hand. [3]For this is he that was spoken of by the prophet Esaias, saying,

The voice of one crying in the wilderness, Prepare ye the way of the Lord, make his paths straight.

[4]And the same John had his raiment of camel's hair, and a leathern girdle about his loins; and his meat was locusts and wild honey. [5]Then went out to him Jerusalem, and all Judaea, and all the region round about Jordan, [6]And were baptized of him in Jordan, confessing their sins.

[7]But when he saw many of the Pharisees and Sadducees come to his baptism, he said unto them, O generation of vipers, who hath warned you to flee from the wrath to come? [8]Bring forth therefore fruits meet for repentance: [9]And think not to say within yourselves, We have Abraham to *our* father: for I say unto you, that God is able of these stones to raise up children unto Abraham. [10]And now also the axe is laid unto the root of the trees: therefore every tree which bringeth not forth good fruit is hewn down, and cast into the fire. [11]I indeed baptize you with water unto repentance: but he that cometh after me is mightier than I, whose shoes I am not worthy to bear: he shall baptize you with the Holy Ghost, and *with* fire: [12]Whose fan *is* in his hand, and he will throughly purge his floor, and gather his wheat into the garner; but he will burn up the chaff with unquenchable fire.

[13]Then cometh Jesus from Galilee to Jordan unto John, to be baptized of him. [14]But John forbad him, saying, I have need to be baptized of thee, and comest thou to me? [15]And Jesus answering said unto him, Suffer *it to be so* now: for thus it becometh us to fulfil all righteousness. Then he suffered him. [16]And Jesus, when he was baptized, went up straightway out of the water: and, lo, the heavens were opened unto him, and he saw the Spirit of God descending like

a dove, and lighting upon him: ¹⁷And lo a voice from heaven, saying, This is my beloved Son, in whom I am well pleased.

4 Then was Jesus led up of the spirit into the wilderness to be tempted of the devil. ²And when he had fasted forty days and forty nights, he was afterward an hungred. ³And when the tempter came to him, he said, If thou be the Son of God, command that these stones be made bread. ⁴But he answered and said, It is written, Man shall not live by bread alone, but by every word that proceedeth out of the mouth of God. ⁵Then the devil taketh him up into the holy city, and setteth him on a pinnacle of the temple, ⁶And saith unto him, If thou be the Son of God, cast thyself down: for it is written,

He shall give his angels charge concerning thee: and in *their* hands they shall bear thee up, lest at any time thou dash thy foot against a stone.

⁷Jesus said unto him, It is written again, Thou shalt not tempt the Lord thy God. ⁸Again, the devil taketh him up into an exceeding high mountain, and sheweth him all the kingdoms of the world, and the glory of them; ⁹And saith unto him, All these things will I give thee, if thou wilt fall down and worship me. ¹⁰Then saith Jesus unto him, Get thee hence, Satan: for it is written, Thou shalt worship the Lord thy God, and him only shalt thou serve. ¹¹Then the devil leaveth him, and, behold, angels came and ministered unto him.

¹²Now when Jesus had heard that John was cast into prison, he departed into Galilee; ¹³And leaving Nazareth, he came and dwelt in Capernaum, which is upon the sea coast, in the borders of Zabulon and Nephthalim: ¹⁴That it might be fulfilled which was spoken by Esaias the prophet, saying,

¹⁵The land of Zabulon, and the land of Nephthalim, *by* the way of the sea, beyond Jordan, Galilee of the Gentiles; ¹⁶The people which sat in darkness saw great light; and to them which sat in the region and shadow of death light is sprung up.

¹⁷From that time Jesus began to preach, and to say, Repent: for the kingdom of heaven is at hand.

¹⁸And Jesus, walking by the sea of Galilee, saw two brethren, Simon called Peter, and Andrew his brother, casting a net into the sea: for they were fishers. ¹⁹And he saith unto them, Follow me, and I will make you fishers of men. ²⁰And they straightway left *their* nets, and followed him. ²¹And going on from thence, he saw other two brethren, James *the son* of Zebedee, and John his brother, in a ship with Zebedee their father, mending their nets; and he called them. ²²And they immediately left the ship and their father, and followed him.

²³And Jesus went about all Galilee, teaching in their synagogues, and preaching the gospel of the kingdom, and healing all manner of sickness and all manner of disease among the people. ²⁴And his fame went throughout all Syria: and they brought unto him all sick people that were taken with divers diseases and torments, and those which were possessed with devils, and those which were lunatick, and those that had the palsy; and he healed them. ²⁵And there followed him great multitudes of people from Galilee, and *from* Decapolis, and *from* Jerusalem, and *from* Judaea, and *from* beyond Jordan.

5 And seeing the multitudes, he went up into a mountain: and when he was set, his disciples came unto him: ²And he opened his mouth, and taught them, saying,

³Blessed *are* the poor in spirit: for theirs is the kingdom of heaven. ⁴Blessed *are* they that mourn: for they shall be comforted. ⁵Blessed *are* the meek: for they shall inherit the earth. ⁶Blessed *are* they which do hunger and thirst after righteousness: for they shall be filled. ⁷Blessed *are* the merciful: for they shall obtain mercy. ⁸Blessed *are* the pure in heart: for they shall see God. ⁹Blessed *are* the peacemakers: for they shall be called the children of God. ¹⁰Blessed *are* they which are persecuted for righteousness sake: for theirs is the kingdom of heaven.

¹¹Blessed are ye, when *men* shall revile you, and persecute *you,* and shall say all manner of evil against you falsely, for my sake. ¹²Rejoice, and be exceeding glad: for great *is* your reward in heaven: for so

persecuted they the prophets which were before you.

[13]Ye are the salt of the earth: but if the salt have lost his savour, wherewith shall it be salted? it is thenceforth good for nothing, but to be cast out, and to be trodden under foot of men. [14]Ye are the light of the world. A city that is set on an hill cannot be hid. [15]Neither do men light a candle, and put it under a bushel, but on a candlestick; and it giveth light unto all that are in the house. [16]Let your light so shine before men, that they may see your good works, and glorify your Father which is in heaven.

[17]Think not that I am come to destroy the law, or the prophets: I am not come to destroy, but to fulfil. [18]For verily I say unto you, Till heaven and earth pass, one jot or one tittle shall in no wise pass from the law, till all be fulfilled. [19]Whosoever therefore shall break one of these least commandments, and shall teach men so, he shall be called the least in the kingdom of heaven: but whosoever shall do and teach *them,* the same shall be called great in the kingdom of heaven. [20]For I say unto you, That except your righteousness shall exceed *the righteousness* of the scribes and Pharisees, ye shall in no case enter into the kingdom of heaven.

[21]Ye have heard that it was said by them of old time, Thou shalt not kill; and whosoever shall kill shall be in danger of the judgment: [22]But I say unto you, That whosoever is angry with his brother without a cause shall be in danger of the judgment: and whosoever shall say to his brother, Raca, shall be in danger of the council: but whosoever shall say, Thou fool, shall be in danger of hell fire. [23]Therefore if thou bring thy gift to the altar, and there rememberest that thy brother hath ought against thee; [24]Leave there thy gift before the altar, and go thy way; first be reconciled to thy brother, and then come and offer thy gift. [25]Agree with thine adversary quickly, whiles thou art in the way with him; lest at any time the adversary deliver thee to the judge, and the judge deliver thee to the officer, and thou be cast into prison. [26]Verily I say unto thee, Thou shalt by no means come out thence, till thou hast paid the uttermost farthing.

[27]Ye have heard that it was said by them of old time, Thou shalt not commit adultery: [28]But I say unto you, That whosoever looketh on a woman to lust after her hath committed adultery with her already in his heart. [29]And if thy right eye offend thee, pluck it out, and cast *it* from thee: for it is profitable for thee that one of thy members should perish, and not *that* thy whole body should be cast into hell. [30]And if thy right hand offend thee, cut if off, and cast it from thee: for it is profitable for thee that one of thy members should perish, and not *that* thy whole body should be cast into hell. [31]It hath been said, Whosoever shall put away his wife, let him give her a writing of divorcement: [32]But I say unto you, That whosoever shall put away his wife, saving for the cause of fornication, causeth her to commit adultery: and whosoever shall marry her that is divorced committeth adultery.

[33]Again, ye have heard that it hath been said by them of old time, Thou shalt not forswear thyself, but shalt perform unto the Lord thine oaths: [34]But I say unto you, Swear not at all; neither by heaven; for it is God's throne: [35]Nor by the earth; for it is his footstool: neither by Jerusalem; for it is the city of the great King. [36]Neither shalt thou swear by thy head, because thou canst not make one hair white or black. [37]But let your communication be, Yea, yea; Nay, nay: for whatsoever is more than these cometh of evil.

[38]Ye have heard that it hath been said, An eye for an eye, and a tooth for a tooth: [39]But I say unto you, That ye resist not evil: but whosoever shall smite thee on thy right cheek, turn to him the other also. [40]And if any man will sue thee at the law, and take away thy coat, let him have *thy* cloke also. [41]And whosoever shall compel thee to go a mile, go with him twain. [42]Give to him that asketh thee, and from him that would borrow of thee turn not thou away.

[43]Ye have heard that it hath been said, Thou shalt love thy neighbour, and hate thine enemy. [44]But I say unto you, Love your enemies, bless them that curse you, do good to them that hate you, and pray for them which despitefully use you, and persecute you; [45]That ye may be the children of your Father which is in heaven: for he

maketh his sun to rise on the evil and on the good, and sendeth rain on the just and on the unjust. ⁴⁶For if ye love them which love you, what reward have ye? do not even the publicans the same? ⁴⁷And if ye salute your brethren only, what do ye more *than others?* do not even the publicans so? ⁴⁸Be ye therefore perfect, even as your Father which is in heaven is perfect.

6 Take heed that ye do not your alms before men, to be seen of them: otherwise ye have no reward of your Father which is in heaven. ²Therefore when thou doest *thine* alms, do not sound a trumpet before thee, as the hypocrites do in the synagogues and in the streets, that they may have glory of men. Verily I say unto you, They have their reward. ³But when thou doest alms, let not thy left hand know what thy right hand doeth: ⁴That thine alms may be in secret: and thy Father which seeth in secret himself shall reward thee openly.

⁵And when thou prayest, thou shalt not be as the hypocrites *are:* for they love to pray standing in the synagogues and in the corners of the streets, that they may be seen of men. Verily I say unto you, They have their reward. ⁶But thou, when thou prayest, enter into thy closet, and when thou hast shut thy door, pray to thy Father which is in secret; and thy Father which seeth in secret shall reward thee openly. ⁷But when ye pray, use not vain repetitions, as the heathen *do:* for they think that they shall be heard for their much speaking. ⁸Be not ye therefore like unto them: for your Father knoweth what things ye have need of, before ye ask him. ⁹After this manner therefore pray ye:

Our Father which art in heaven, Hallowed be thy name. ¹⁰Thy kingdom come. Thy will be done in earth, as *it is* in heaven. ¹¹Give us this day our daily bread. ¹²And forgive us our debts, as we forgive our debtors. ¹³And lead us not into temptation, but deliver us from evil: For thine is the kingdom, and the power, and the glory, for ever. Amen.

¹⁴For if ye forgive men their trespasses, your heavenly Father will also forgive you: ¹⁵But if ye forgive not men their trespasses, neither will your Father forgive your trespasses.

¹⁶Moreover when ye fast, be not, as the hypocrites, of a sad countenance: for they disfigure their faces, that they may appear unto men to fast. Verily I say unto you, They have their reward. ¹⁷But thou, when thou fastest, anoint thine head, and wash thy face; ¹⁸That thou appear not unto men to fast, but unto thy Father which is in secret: and thy Father, which seeth in secret, shall reward thee openly.

¹⁹Lay not up for yourselves treasures upon earth, where moth and rust doth corrupt, and where thieves break through and steal: ²⁰But lay up for yourselves treasures in heaven, where neither moth nor rust doth corrupt, and where thieves do not break through nor steal: ²¹For where your treasure is, there will your heart be also. ²²The light of the body is the eye: if therefore thine eye be single, thy whole body shall be full of light. ²³But if thine eye be evil, thy whole body shall be full of darkness. If therefore the light that is in thee be darkness, how great *is* that darkness!

²⁴No man can serve two masters: for either he will hate the one, and love the other; or else he will hold to the one, and despise the other. Ye cannot serve God and mammon. ²⁵Therefore I say unto you, Take no thought for your life, what ye shall eat, or what ye shall drink; nor yet for your body, what ye shall put on. Is not the life more than meat, and the body than raiment? ²⁶Behold the fowls of the air: for they sow not, neither do they reap, nor gather into barns; yet your heavenly Father feedeth them. Are ye not much better than they? ²⁷Which of you by taking thought can add one cubit unto his stature? ²⁸And why take ye thought for raiment? Consider the lilies of the field, how they grow; they toil not, neither do they spin: ²⁹And yet I say unto you, That even Solomon in all his glory was not arrayed like one of these. ³⁰Wherefore, if God so clothe the grass of the field, which to day is, and to morrow is cast into the oven, *shall he* not much more *clothe* you, O ye of little faith? ³¹Therefore take no thought, saying, What shall we eat? or, What shall we drink? or, Wherewithal shall we be clothed? ³²(For after all these things do the Gentiles seek:) for your heavenly Father knoweth that ye have need of

all these things. ³³But seek ye first the kingdom of God, and his righteousness; and all these things shall be added unto you. ³⁴Take therefore no thought for the morrow: for the morrow shall take thought for the things of itself. Sufficient unto the day *is* the evil thereof.

7 Judge not, that ye be not judged. ²For with what judgment ye judge, ye shall be judged: and with what measure ye mete, it shall be measured to you again. ³And why beholdest thou the mote that is in thy brother's eye, but considerest not the beam that is in thine own eye? ⁴Or how wilt thou say to thy brother, Let me pull out the mote out of thine eye; and, behold, a beam *is* in thine own eye? ⁵Thou hypocrite, first cast out the beam out of thine own eye; and then shalt thou see clearly to cast out the mote out of thy brother's eye.

⁶Give not that which is holy unto the dogs, neither cast ye your pearls before swine, lest they trample them under their feet, and turn again and rend you.

⁷Ask, and it shall be given you; seek, and ye shall find; knock, and it shall be opened unto you: ⁸For every one that asketh receiveth; and he that seeketh findeth; and to him that knocketh it shall be opened. ⁹Or what man is there of you, whom if his son ask bread, will he give him a stone? ¹⁰Or if he ask a fish, will he give him a serpent? ¹¹If ye then, being evil, know how to give good gifts unto your children, how much more shall your Father which is in heaven give good things to them that ask him? ¹²Therefore all things whatsoever ye would that men should do to you, do ye even so to them: for this is the law and the prophets.

¹³Enter ye in at the strait gate: for wide *is* the gate, and broad *is* the way, that leadeth to destruction, and many there be which go in thereat: ¹⁴Because strait *is* the gate, and narrow *is* the way, which leadeth unto life, and few there be that find it.

¹⁵Beware of false prophets, which come to you in sheep's clothing, but inwardly they are ravening wolves. ¹⁶Ye shall know them by their fruits. Do men gather grapes of thorns, or figs of thistles? ¹⁷Even so every good tree bringeth forth good fruit; but a corrupt tree bringeth forth evil fruit. ¹⁸A good tree cannot bring forth evil fruit, neither *can* a corrupt tree bring forth good fruit. ¹⁹Every tree that bringeth not forth good fruit is hewn down, and cast into the fire. ²⁰Wherefore by their fruits ye shall know them.

²¹Not every one that saith unto me, Lord, Lord, shall enter into the kingdom of heaven; but he that doeth the will of my Father which is in heaven. ²²Many will say to me in that day, Lord, Lord, have we not prophesied in thy name? and in thy name have cast out devils? and in thy name done many wonderful works? ²³And then will I profess unto them, I never knew you: depart from me, ye that work iniquity.

²⁴Therefore whosoever heareth these sayings of mine, and doeth them, I will liken him unto a wise man, which built his house upon a rock: ²⁵And the rain descended, and the floods came, and the winds blew, and beat upon that house; and it fell not: for it was founded upon a rock. ²⁶And every one that heareth these sayings of mine, and doeth them not, shall be likened unto a foolish man, which built his house upon the sand: ²⁷And the rain descended, and the floods came, and the winds blew, and beat upon that house; and it fell: and great was the fall of it.

²⁸And it came to pass, when Jesus had ended these sayings, the people were astonished at his doctrine: ²⁹For he taught them as *one* having authority, and not as the scribes.

8 When he was come down from the mountain, great multitudes followed him. ²And, behold, there came a leper and worshipped him, saying, Lord, if thou wilt, thou canst make me clean. ³And Jesus put forth *his* hand, and touched him, saying, I will; be thou clean. And immediately his leprosy was cleansed. ⁴And Jesus saith unto him, See thou tell no man; but go thy way, shew thyself to the priest, and offer the gift that Moses commanded, for a testimony unto them.

⁵And when Jesus was entered into Capernaum, there came unto him a centurion, beseeching him, ⁶And saying, Lord, my servant lieth at home sick of the palsy, grievously tormented. ⁷And Jesus saith unto him, I will come and heal him. ⁸The

centurion answered and said, Lord, I am not worthy that thou shouldest come under my roof: but speak the word only, and my servant shall be healed. [9]For I am a man under authority, having soldiers under me: and I say to this *man*, Go, and he goeth; and to another, Come, and he cometh; and to my servant, Do this, and he doeth *it*. [10]When Jesus heard *it*, he marvelled, and said to them that followed, Verily I say unto you, I have not found so great faith, no, not in Israel. [11]And I say unto you, That many shall come from the east and west, and shall sit down with Abraham, and Isaac, and Jacob, in the kingdom of heaven. [12]But the children of the kingdom shall be cast out into outer darkness: there shall be weeping and gnashing of teeth. [13]And Jesus said unto the centurion, Go thy way; and as thou hast believed, so be it done unto thee. And his servant was healed in the selfsame hour.

[14]And when Jesus was come into Peter's house, he saw his wife's mother laid, and sick of a fever. [15]And he touched her hand, and the fever left her: and she arose, and ministered unto them.

[16]When the even was come, they brought unto him many that were possessed with devils: and he cast out the spirits with *his* word, and healed all that were sick: [17]That it might be fulfilled which was spoken by Esaias the prophet, saying,

Himself took our infirmities, and bare *our* sicknesses.

[18]Now when Jesus saw great multitudes about him, he gave commandment to depart unto the other side. [19]And a certain scribe came, and said unto him, Master, I will follow thee whithersoever thou goest. [20]And Jesus saith unto him, The foxes have holes, and the birds of the air *have* nests; but the Son of man hath not where to lay *his* head. [21]And another of his disciples said unto him, Lord, suffer me first to go and bury my father. [22]But Jesus said unto him, Follow me; and let the dead bury their dead.

[23]And when he was entered into a ship, his disciples followed him. [24]And, behold, there arose a great tempest in the sea, insomuch that the ship was covered with the waves: but he was asleep. [25]And his disciples came to *him*, and awoke him, saying, Lord, save us: we perish. [26]And he saith unto them, Why are ye fearful, O ye of little faith? Then he arose, and rebuked the winds and the sea; and there was a great calm. [27]But the men marvelled, saying, What manner of man is this, that even the winds and the sea obey him!

[28]And when he was come to the other side into the country of the Gergesenes, there met him two possessed with devils, coming out of the tombs, exceeding fierce, so that no man might pass by that way. [29]And, behold, they cried out, saying, What have we to do with thee, Jesus, thou Son of God? art thou come hither to torment us before the time? [30]And there was a good way off from them an herd of many swine feeding. [31]So the devils besought him, saying, If thou cast us out, suffer us to go away into the herd of swine. [32]And he said unto them, Go. And when they were come out, they went into the herd of swine: and, behold, the whole herd of swine ran violently down a steep place into the sea, and perished in the waters. [33]And they that kept them fled, and went their ways into the city, and told every thing, and what was befallen to the possessed of the devils. [34]And, behold, the whole city came out to meet Jesus: and when they saw him, they besought *him* that he would depart out of their coasts.

9 And he entered into a ship, and passed over, and came into his own city. [2]And, behold, they brought to him a man sick of the palsy, lying on a bed: and Jesus seeing their faith said unto the sick of the palsy; Son, be of good cheer; thy sins be forgiven thee. [3]And, behold, certain of the scribes said within themselves, This *man* blasphemeth. [4]And Jesus knowing their thoughts said, Wherefore think ye evil in your hearts? [5]For whether is easier, to say, *Thy* sins be forgiven thee; or to say, Arise, and walk? [6]But that ye may know that the Son of man hath power on earth to forgive sins, (then saith he to the sick of the palsy,) Arise, take up thy bed, and go unto thine house. [7]And he arose, and departed to his house. [8]But when the multitudes saw *it*, they

marvelled, and glorified God, which had given such power unto men.

⁹And as Jesus passed forth from thence, he saw a man, named Matthew, sitting at the receipt of custom: and he saith unto him, Follow me. And he arose, and followed him.

¹⁰And it came to pass, as Jesus sat at meat in the house, behold, many publicans and sinners came and sat down with him and his disciples. ¹¹And when the Pharisees saw *it,* they said unto his disciples, Why eateth your Master with publicans and sinners? ¹²But when Jesus heard *that,* he said unto them, They that be whole need not a physician, but they that are sick. ¹³But go ye and learn what *that* meaneth, I will have mercy, and not sacrifice: for I am not come to call the righteous, but sinners to repentance.

¹⁴Then came to him the disciples of John, saying, Why do we and the Pharisees fast oft, but thy disciples fast not? ¹⁵And Jesus said unto them, Can the children of the bridechamber mourn, as long as the bridegroom is with them? but the days will come, when the bridegroom shall be taken from them, and then shall they fast. ¹⁶No man putteth a piece of new cloth unto an old garment, for that which is put in to fill it up taketh from the garment, and the rent is made worse. ¹⁷Neither do men put new wine into old bottles: else the bottles break, and the wine runneth out, and the bottles perish: but they put new wine into new bottles, and both are preserved.

¹⁸While he spake these things unto them, behold, there came a certain ruler, and worshipped him, saying, My daughter is even now dead: but come and lay thy hand upon her, and she shall live. ¹⁹And Jesus arose, and followed him, and *so did* his disciples.

²⁰And, behold, a woman, which was diseased with an issue of blood twelve years, came behind *him,* and touched the hem of his garment: ²¹For she said within herself, If I may but touch his garment, I shall be whole. ²²But Jesus turned him about, and when he saw her, he said, Daughter, be of good comfort; thy faith hath made thee whole. And the woman was made whole from that hour. ²³And when Jesus came

into the ruler's house, and saw the minstrels and the people making a noise, ²⁴He said unto them, Give place: for the maid is not dead, but sleepeth. And they laughed him to scorn. ²⁵But when the people were put forth, he went in, and took her by the hand, and the maid arose. ²⁶And the fame hereof went abroad into all that land.

²⁷And when Jesus departed thence, two blind men followed him, crying, and saying, *Thou* Son of David, have mercy on us. ²⁸And when he was come into the house, the blind men came to him: and Jesus saith unto them, Believe ye that I am able to do this? They said unto him, Yea, Lord. ²⁹Then touched he their eyes, saying, According to your faith be it unto you. ³⁰And their eyes were opened; and Jesus straitly charged them, saying, See *that* no man know *it.* ³¹But they, when they were departed, spread abroad his fame in all that country.

³²As they went out, behold, they brought to him a dumb man possessed with a devil. ³³And when the devil was cast out, the dumb spake: and the multitudes marvelled, saying, It was never so seen in Israel. ³⁴But the Pharisees said, He casteth out devils through the prince of the devils. ³⁵And Jesus went about all the cities and villages, teaching in their synagogues, and preaching the gospel of the kingdom, and healing every sickness and every disease among the people.

³⁶But when he saw the multitudes, he was moved with compassion on them, because they fainted, and were scattered abroad, as sheep having no shepherd. ³⁷Then saith he unto his disciples, The harvest truly *is* plenteous, but the labourers *are* few; ³⁸Pray ye therefore the Lord of the harvest, that he will send forth labourers into his harvest.

10 And when he had called unto *him* his twelve disciples, he gave them power *against* unclean spirits, to cast them out, and to heal all manner of sickness and all manner of disease. ²Now the names of the twelve apostles are these; The first, Simon, who is called Peter, and Andrew his brother; James *the son* of Zebedee, and John his brother; ³Philip, and Bar-tholomew; Thomas, and Matthew the publican; James *the son* of Alphaeus, and Lebbaeus, whose surname was Thaddaeus; [4]Simon the Canaanite, and Judas Iscariot, who also betrayed him. [5]These twelve Jesus sent forth, and commanded them, saying, Go not into the way of the Gentiles, and into *any* city of the Samaritans enter ye not: [6]But go rather to the lost sheep of the house of Israel. [7]And as ye go, preach, saying, The kingdom of heaven is at hand. [8]Heal the sick, cleanse the lepers, raise the dead, cast out devils: freely ye have received, freely give. [9]Provide neither gold, nor silver, nor brass in your purses, [10]Nor scrip for *your* journey, neither two coats, neither shoes, nor yet staves: for the workman is worthy of his meat. [11]And into whatsoever city or town ye shall enter, enquire who in it is worthy; and there abide till ye go thence. [12]And when ye come into an house, salute it. [13]And if the house be worthy, let your peace come upon it: but if it be not worthy, let your peace return to you. [14]And whosoever shall not receive you, nor hear your words, when ye depart out of that house or city, shake off the dust of your feet. [15]Verily I say unto you, It shall be more tolerable for the land of Sodom and Gomorrha in the day of judgment, than for that city.

[16]Behold, I send you forth as sheep in the midst of wolves: be ye therefore wise as serpents, and harmless as doves. [17]But beware of men: for they will deliver you up to the councils, and they will scourge you in their synagogues; [18]And ye shall be brought before governors and kings for my sake, for a testimony against them and the Gentiles. [19]But when they deliver you up, take no thought how or what ye shall speak: for it shall be given you in that same hour what ye shall speak. [20]For it is not ye that speak, but the Spirit of your Father which speaketh in you. [21]And the brother shall deliver up the brother to death, and the father the child: and the children shall rise up against *their* parents, and cause them to be put to death. [22]And ye shall be hated of all *men* for my name's sake: but he that endureth to the end shall be saved. [23]But when they persecute you in this city, flee ye into another: for verily I say unto you, Ye shall not have gone over the cities of Israel, till the Son of man be come. [24]The disciple is not above *his* master, nor the servant above his lord. [25]It is enough for the disciple that he be as his master, and the servant as his lord. If they have called the master of the house Beelzebub, how much more *shall they call* them of his household? [26]Fear them not therefore: for there is nothing covered, that shall not be revealed; and hid, that shall not be known. [27]What I tell you in darkness, *that* speak ye in light: and what ye hear in the ear, *that* preach ye upon the housetops. [28]And fear not them which kill the body, but are not able to kill the soul: but rather fear him which is able to destroy both soul and body in hell. [29]Are not two sparrows sold for a farthing? and one of them shall not fall on the ground without your Father. [30]But the very hairs of your head are all numbered. [31]Fear ye not therefore, ye are of more value than many sparrows. [32]Whosoever therefore shall confess me before men, him will I confess also before my Father which is in heaven. [33]But whosoever shall deny me before men, him will I also deny before my Father which is in heaven. [34]Think not that I am come to send peace on earth: I came not to send peace, but a sword. [35]For I am come to set

a man at variance against his father, and the daughter against her mother, and the daughter in law against her mother in law. [36]And a man's foes *shall be* they of his own household.

[37]He that loveth father or mother more than me is not worthy of me: and he that loveth son or daughter more than me is not worthy of me. [38]And he that taketh not his cross, and followeth after me, is not worthy of me. [39]He that findeth his life shall lose it: and he that loseth his life for my sake shall find it.

[40]He that receiveth you receiveth me, and he that receiveth me receiveth him that sent me. [41]He that receiveth a prophet in the name of a prophet shall receive a prophet's reward; and he that receiveth a righteous man in the name of a righteous man shall receive a righteous man's reward. [42]And whosoever shall give to drink unto one of these little ones a cup of cold *water* only in the name of a disciple, verily I say unto you, he shall in no wise lose his reward.

11 And it came to pass, when Jesus had made an end of commanding his twelve disciples, he departed thence to teach and to preach in their cities. ²Now when John had heard in the prison the works of Christ, he sent two of his disciples, ³And said unto him, Art thou he that should come, or do we look for another? ⁴Jesus answered and said unto them, Go and shew John again those things which ye do hear and see: ⁵The blind receive their sight, and the lame walk, the lepers are cleansed, and the deaf hear, the dead are raised up, and the poor have the gospel preached to them. ⁶And blessed is *he,* whosoever shall not be offended in me.

⁷And as they departed, Jesus began to say unto the multitudes concerning John, What went ye out into the wilderness to see? A reed shaken with the wind? ⁸But what went ye out for to see? A man clothed in soft raiment? behold, they that wear soft *clothing* are in kings' houses. ⁹But what went ye out for to see? A prophet? yea, I say unto you, and more than a prophet. ¹⁰For this is *he,* of whom it is written,

Behold, I send my messenger before thy face, which shall prepare thy way before thee.

¹¹Verily I say unto you, Among them that are born of women there hath not risen a greater than John the Baptist: notwithstanding he that is least in the kingdom of heaven is greater than he. ¹²And from the days of John the Baptist until now the kingdom of heaven suffereth violence, and the violent take it by force. ¹³For all the prophets and the law prophesied until John. ¹⁴And if ye will receive *it,* this is Elias, which was for to come. ¹⁵He that hath ears to hear, let him hear.

¹⁶But whereunto shall I liken this generation? It is like unto children sitting in the markets, and calling unto their fellows,

¹⁷And saying, We have piped unto you, and ye have not danced; we have mourned unto you, and ye have not lamented.

¹⁸For John came neither eating nor drinking, and they say, He hath a devil. ¹⁹The Son of man came eating and drinking, and they say, Behold a man gluttonous, and a winebibber, a friend of publicans and sinners. But wisdom is justified of her children.

²⁰Then began he to upbraid the cities wherein most of his mighty works were done, because they repented not: ²¹Woe unto thee, Chorazin! woe unto thee, Bethsaida! for if the mighty works, which were done in you, had been done in Tyre and Sidon, they would have repented long ago in sackcloth and ashes. ²²But I say unto you, It shall be more tolerable for Tyre and Sidon at the day of judgment, than for you. ²³And thou, Capernaum, which art exalted unto heaven, shalt be brought down to hell: for if the mighty works, which have been done in thee, had been done in Sodom, it would have remained until this day. ²⁴But I say unto you, That it shall be more tolerable for the land of Sodom in the day of judgment, than for thee.

²⁵At that time Jesus answered and said, I thank thee, O Father, Lord of heaven and earth, because thou hast hid these things from the wise and prudent, and hast revealed them unto babes. ²⁶Even so, Father: for so it seemed good in thy sight. ²⁷All things are delivered unto me of my Father: and no man knoweth the Son, but the Father; neither knoweth any man the Father, save the Son, and *he* to whomsoever the Son will reveal *him.*

²⁸Come unto me, all *ye* that labour and are heavy laden, and I will give you rest. ²⁹Take my yoke upon you, and learn of me; for I am meek and lowly in heart: and ye shall find rest unto your souls. ³⁰For my yoke *is* easy, and my burden is light.

12 At that time Jesus went on the sabbath day through the corn; and his disciples were an hungred, and began to pluck the ears of corn, and to eat. ²But when the Pharisees saw *it,* they said unto him, Behold, thy disciples do that which is not lawful to do upon the sabbath day. ³But he said unto them, Have ye not read what David did, when he was an hungred, and they that were with him; ⁴How he entered into the house of God, and did eat the shewbread, which was not lawful for him to eat, neither for them which were with him, but only for the priests? ⁵Or have ye not read in the law, how that on the sabbath days the priests in the temple profane the sabbath, and are blameless? ⁶But I say unto you, That in this place is *one* greater than the temple. ⁷But if ye had known what *this* meaneth, I will have mercy, and not sacrifice, ye would not have condemned the guiltless. ⁸For the Son of man is Lord even of the sabbath day.

⁹And when he was departed thence, he went into their synagogue: ¹⁰And, behold, there was a man which had *his* hand withered. And they asked him, saying, Is it lawful to heal on the sabbath days? that they might accuse him. ¹¹And he said unto them, What man shall there be among you, that shall have one sheep, and if it fall into a pit on the sabbath day, will he not lay hold on it, and lift *it* out? ¹²How much then is a man better than a sheep? Wherefore it is lawful to do well on the sabbath days. ¹³Then saith he to the man, Stretch forth thine hand. And he stretched *it* forth; and it was restored whole, like as the other.

¹⁴Then the Pharisees went out, and held a council against him, how they might destroy him. ¹⁵But when Jesus knew *it,* he withdrew himself from thence: and great multitudes followed him, and he healed them all; ¹⁶And charged them that they should not make him known: ¹⁷That it might be fulfilled which was spoken by Esaias the prophet, saying,

¹⁸Behold my servant, whom I have chosen; my beloved, in whom my soul is well pleased: I will put my spirit upon him, and he shall shew judgment to the Gentiles. ¹⁹He shall not strive, nor cry; neither shall any man hear his voice in the streets. ²⁰A bruised reed shall he not break, and smoking flax shall he not quench, till he send forth judgment unto victory. ²¹And in his name shall the Gentiles trust.

²²Then was brought unto him one possessed with a devil, blind, and dumb: and he healed him, insomuch that the blind and dumb both spake and saw. ²³And all the people were amazed, and said, Is not this the son of David? ²⁴But when the Pharisees heard *it,* they said, This *fellow* doth not cast out devils, but by Beelzebub the prince of the devils. ²⁵And Jesus knew their thoughts, and said unto them, Every kingdom divid-

ed against itself is brought to desolation; and every city or house divided against itself shall not stand: ²⁶And if Satan cast out Satan, he is divided against himself; how shall then his kingdom stand? ²⁷And if I by Beelzebub cast out devils, by whom do your children cast *them* out? therefore they shall be your judges. ²⁸But if I cast out devils by the Spirit of God, then the kingdom of God is come unto you. ²⁹Or else how can one enter into a strong man's house, and spoil his goods, except he first bind the strong man? and then he will spoil his house. ³⁰He that is not with me is against me; and he that gathereth not with me scattereth abroad.

³¹Wherefore I say unto you, All manner of sin and blasphemy shall be forgiven unto men: but the blasphemy *against* the *Holy* Ghost shall not be forgiven unto men. ³²And whosoever speaketh a word against the Son of man, it shall be forgiven him: but whosoever speaketh against the Holy Ghost, it shall not be forgiven him, neither in this world, neither in the *world* to come. ³³Either make the tree good, and his fruit good; or else make the tree corrupt, and his fruit corrupt: for the tree is known by *his* fruit. ³⁴O generation of vipers, how can ye, being evil, speak good things? for out of the abundance of the heart the mouth speaketh. ³⁵A good man out of the good treasure of the heart bringeth forth good things: and an evil man out of the evil treasure bringeth forth evil things. ³⁶But I say unto you, That every idle word that men shall speak, they shall give account thereof in the day of judgment. ³⁷For by thy words thou shalt be justified, and by thy words thou shalt be condemned.

³⁸Then certain of the scribes and of the Pharisees answered, saying, Master, we would see a sign from thee. ³⁹But he answered and said unto them, An evil and adulterous generation seeketh after a sign; and there shall no sign be given to it, but the sign of the prophet Jonas: ⁴⁰For as Jonas was three days and three nights in the whale's belly; so shall the Son of man be three days and three nights in the heart of the earth. ⁴¹The men of Nineveh shall rise in judgment with this generation, and shall condemn it: because they repented at the preaching of Jonas; and, behold, a greater

than Jonas *is* here. ⁴²The queen of the south shall rise up in the judgment with this generation, and shall condemn it: for she came from the uttermost parts of the earth to hear the wisdom of Solomon; and, behold, a greater than Solomon *is* here. ⁴³When the unclean spirit is gone out of a man, he walketh through dry places, seeking rest, and findeth none. ⁴⁴Then he saith, I will return into my house from whence I came out; and when he is come, he findeth *it* empty, swept, and garnished. ⁴⁵Then goeth he, and taketh with himself seven other spirits more wicked than himself, and they enter in and dwell there: and the last *state* of that man is worse than the first. Even so shall it be also unto this wicked generation.

⁴⁶While he yet talked to the people, behold, *his* mother and his brethren stood without, desiring to speak with him. ⁴⁷Then one said unto him, Behold, thy mother and thy brethren stand without, desiring to speak with thee. ⁴⁸But he answered and said unto him that told him, Who is my mother? and who are my brethren? ⁴⁹And he stretched forth his hand toward his disciples, and said, Behold my mother and my brethren! ⁵⁰For whosoever shall do the will of my Father which is in heaven, the same is my brother, and sister, and mother.

13 The same day went Jesus out of the house, and sat by the sea side. ²And great multitudes were gathered together unto him, so that he went into a ship, and sat; and the whole multitude stood on the shore. ³And he spake many things unto them in parables, saying, Behold, a sower went forth to sow; ⁴And when he sowed, some *seeds* fell by the way side, and the fowls came and devoured them up: ⁵Some fell upon stony places, where they had not much earth: and forthwith they sprung up, because they had no deepness of earth: ⁶And when the sun was up, they were scorched; and because they had no root, they withered away. ⁷And some fell among thorns; and the thorns sprung up, and choked them: ⁸But other fell into good ground, and brought forth fruit, some an hundredfold, some sixtyfold, some thirtyfold. ⁹Who hath ears to hear, let him hear. ¹⁰And the disciples came, and said unto him, Why speakest thou unto them in par-

ables? ¹¹He answered and said unto them, Because it is given unto you to know the mysteries of the kingdom of heaven, but to them it is not given. ¹²For whosoever hath, to him shall be given, and he shall have more abundance: but whosoever hath not, from him shall be taken away even that he hath. ¹³Therefore speak I to them in parables:

because they seeing see not; and hearing they hear not, neither do they understand.

¹⁴And in them is fulfilled the prophecy of Esaias, which saith,

By hearing ye shall hear, and shall not understand; and seeing ye shall see, and shall not perceive: ¹⁵For this people's heart is waxed gross, and *their* ears are dull of hearing, and their eyes they have closed; lest at any time they should see with *their* eyes, and hear with *their* ears, and should understand with *their* heart, and should be converted, and I should heal them.

¹⁶But blessed *are* your eyes, for they see: and your ears, for they hear. ¹⁷For verily I say unto you, That many prophets and righteous *men* have desired to see *those things* which ye see, and have not seen *them;* and to hear *those things* which ye hear, and have not heard *them.*

¹⁸Hear ye therefore the parable of the sower. ¹⁹When any one heareth the word of the kingdom, and understandeth *it* not, then cometh the wicked *one,* and catcheth away that which was sown in his heart. This is he which received seed by the way side. ²⁰But he that received the seed into stony places, the same is he that heareth the word, and anon with joy receiveth it; ²¹Yet hath he not root in himself, but dureth for a while: for when tribulation or persecution ariseth because of the word, by and by he is offended. ²²He also that received seed among the thorns is he that heareth the word; and the care of this world, and the deceitfulness of riches, choke the word, and he becometh unfruitful. ²³But he that received seed into the good ground is he that heareth the word, and understandeth *it;* which also beareth fruit, and bringeth forth, some an hundredfold, some sixty, some thirty.

²⁴Another parable put he forth unto them, saying, The kingdom of heaven is likened unto a man which sowed good seed in his field: ²⁵But while men slept, his enemy came and sowed tares among the wheat, and went his way. ²⁶But when the blade was sprung up, and brought forth fruit, then appeared the tares also. ²⁷So the servants of the householder came and said unto him, Sir, didst not thou sow good seed in thy field? from whence then hath it tares? ²⁸He said unto them, An enemy hath done this. The servants said unto him, Wilt thou then that we go and gather them up? ²⁹But he said, Nay; lest while ye gather up the tares, ye root up also the wheat with them. ³⁰Let both grow together until the harvest: and in the time of harvest I will say to the reapers, Gather ye together first the tares, and bind them in bundles to burn them: but gather the wheat into my barn.

³¹Another parable put he forth unto them, saying, The kingdom of heaven is like to a grain of mustard seed, which a man took, and sowed in his field: ³²Which indeed is the least of all seeds: but when it is grown, it is the greatest among herbs, and becometh a tree, so that the birds of the air come and lodge in the branches thereof.

³³Another parable spake he unto them; The kingdom of heaven is like unto leaven, which a woman took, and hid in three measures of meal, till the whole was leavened. ³⁴All these things spake Jesus unto the multitude in parables; and without a parable spake he not unto them: ³⁵That it might be fulfilled which was spoken by the prophet, saying,

I will open my mouth in parables; I will utter things which have been kept secret from the foundation of the world.

³⁶Then Jesus sent the multitude away, and went into the house: and his disciples came unto him, saying, Declare unto us the parable of the tares of the field. ³⁷He answered and said unto them, He that soweth the good seed is the Son of man; ³⁸The field is the world; the good seed are the children of the kingdom; but the tares are the children of the wicked *one;* ³⁹The enemy that sowed them is the devil; the harvest is the end of the world; and the reapers are the angels. ⁴⁰As therefore the tares are gathered and burned in the fire; so shall it be in the end of this world. ⁴¹The Son of man shall send forth his angels, and they shall gather out of his kingdom all things that offend, and them which do iniquity; ⁴²And shall cast them into a furnace of fire: there shall be wailing and gnashing of teeth. ⁴³Then shall the righteous shine forth as the sun in the kingdom of their Father. Who hath ears to hear, let him hear.

⁴⁴Again, the kingdom of heaven is like unto treasure hid in a field; the which when a man hath found, he hideth, and for joy thereof goeth and selleth all that he hath, and buyeth that field.

⁴⁵Again, the kingdom of heaven is like unto a merchant man, seeking goodly pearls: ⁴⁶Who, when he had found one pearl of great price, went and sold all that he had, and bought it.

⁴⁷Again, the kingdom of heaven is like unto a net, that was cast into the sea, and gathered of every kind: ⁴⁸Which, when it was full, they drew to shore, and sat down, and gathered the good into vessels, but cast the bad away. ⁴⁹So shall it be at the end of the world: the angels shall come forth, and sever the wicked from among the just, ⁵⁰And shall cast them into the furnace of fire: there shall be wailing and gnashing of teeth. ⁵¹Jesus saith unto them, Have ye understood all these things? They say unto him, Yea, Lord. ⁵²Then said he unto them, Therefore every scribe *which is* instructed unto the kingdom of heaven is like unto a man *that is* an householder, which bringeth forth out of his treasure *things* new and old.

⁵³And it came to pass, *that* when Jesus had finished these parables, he departed thence. ⁵⁴And when he was come into his own country, he taught them in their synagogue, insomuch that they were astonished, and said, Whence hath this *man* this wisdom, and *these* mighty works? ⁵⁵Is not this the carpenter's son? is not his mother called Mary? and his brethren, James, and Joses, and Simon, and Judas? ⁵⁶And his sisters, are they not all with us? Whence then hath this *man* all these things? ⁵⁷And they were offended in him. But Jesus said unto them, A prophet is not without honour, save

in his own country, and in his own house. [58]And he did not many mighty works there because of their unbelief.

14 At that time Herod the tetrarch heard of the fame of Jesus, [2]And said unto his servants, This is John the Baptist; he is risen from the dead; and therefore mighty works do shew forth themselves in him.

[3]For Herod had laid hold on John, and bound him, and put *him* in prison for Herodias' sake, his brother Philip's wife. [4]For John said unto him, It is not lawful for thee to have her. [5]And when he would have put him to death, he feared the multitude, because they counted him as a prophet. [6]But when Herod's birthday was kept, the daughter of Herodias danced before them, and pleased Herod. [7]Whereupon he promised with an oath to give her whatsoever she would ask. [8]And she, being before instructed of her mother, said, Give me here John Baptist's head in a charger. [9]And the king was sorry: nevertheless for the oath's sake, and them which sat with him at meat, he commanded *it* to be given *her*. [10]And he sent, and beheaded John in the prison. [11]And his head was brought in a charger, and given to the damsel: and she brought *it* to her mother. [12]And his disciples came, and took up the body, and buried it, and went and told Jesus.

[13]When Jesus heard *of it*, he departed thence by ship into a desert place apart: and when the people had heard *thereof*, they followed him on foot out of the cities. [14]And Jesus went forth, and saw a great multitude, and was moved with compassion toward them, and he healed their sick.

[15]And when it was evening, his disciples came to him, saying, This is a desert place, and the time is now past; send the multitude away, that they may go into the villages, and buy themselves victuals. [16]But Jesus said unto them, They need not depart; give ye them to eat. [17]And they say unto him, We have here but five loaves, and two fishes. [18]He said, Bring them hither to me. [19]And he commanded the multitude to sit down on the grass, and took the five loaves, and the two fishes, and looking up to heaven, he blessed, and brake, and gave the loaves to *his* disciples, and the disciples to the multi-

tude. [20]And they did all eat, and were filled: and they took up of the fragments that remained twelve baskets full. [21]And they that had eaten were about five thousand men, beside women and children.

[22]And straightway Jesus constrained his disciples to get into a ship, and to go before him unto the other side, while he sent the multitudes away. [23]And when he had sent the multitudes away, he went up into a mountain apart to pray: and when the evening was come, he was there alone. [24]But the ship was now in the midst of the sea, tossed with waves: for the wind was contrary. [25]And in the fourth watch of the night Jesus went unto them, walking on the sea. [26]And when the disciples saw him walking on the sea, they were troubled, saying, It is a spirit; and they cried out for fear. [27]But straightway Jesus spake unto them, saying, Be of good cheer; it is I; be not afraid. [28]And Peter answered him and said, Lord, if it be thou, bid me come unto thee on the water. [29]And he said, Come. And when Peter was come down out of the ship, he walked on the water, to go to Jesus. [30]But when he saw the wind boisterous, he was afraid; and beginning to sink, he cried, saying, Lord, save me. [31]And immediately Jesus stretched forth *his* hand, and caught him, and said unto him, O thou of little faith, wherefore didst thou doubt? [32]And when they were come into the ship, the wind ceased. [33]Then they that were in the ship came and worshipped him, saying, Of a truth thou art the Son of God.

[34]And when they were gone over, they came into the land of Gennesaret. [35]And when the men of that place had knowledge of him, they sent out into all that country round about, and brought unto him all that were diseased; [36]And besought him that they might only touch the hem of his garment: and as many as touched were made perfectly whole.

15 Then came to Jesus scribes and Pharisees, which were of Jerusalem, saying, [2]Why do thy disciples transgress the tradition of the elders? for they wash not their hands when they eat bread. [3]But he answered and said unto them, Why do ye also transgress the commandment of God by your tradition? [4]For God commanded, saying, Honour thy father and mother: and, He that curseth father or mother, let him die the death. [5]But ye say, Whosoever shall say to *his* father or *his* mother, *It is* a gift, by whatsoever thou mightest be profited by me; [6]And honour not his father or his mother, *he shall be free.* Thus have ye made the commandment of God of none effect by your tradition. [7]Ye hypocrites, well did Esaias prophesy of you, saying,

[8]This people draweth nigh unto me with their mouth, and honoureth me with *their* lips; but their heart is far from me. [9]But in vain they do worship me, teaching *for* doctrines the commandments of men.

[10]And he called the multitude, and said unto them, Hear, and understand: [11]Not that which goeth into the mouth defileth a man; but that which cometh out of the mouth, this defileth a man. [12]Then came his disciples, and said unto him, Knowest thou that the Pharisees were offended, after they heard this saying? [13]But he answered and said, Every plant, which my heavenly Father hath not planted, shall be rooted up. [14]Let them alone: they be blind leaders of the blind. And if the blind lead the blind, both shall fall into the ditch. [15]Then answered Peter and said unto him, Declare unto us this parable. [16]And Jesus said, Are ye also yet without understanding? [17]Do not ye yet understand, that whatsoever entereth in at the mouth goeth into the belly, and is cast out into the draught? [18]But those things which proceed out of the mouth come forth from the heart; and they defile the man. [19]For out of the heart proceed evil thoughts, murders, adulteries, fornications, thefts, false witness, blasphemies: [20]These are *the things* which defile a man: but to eat with unwashen hands defileth not a man.

[21]Then Jesus went thence, and departed into the coasts of Tyre and Sidon. [22]And, behold, a woman of Canaan came out of the same coasts, and cried unto him, saying, Have mercy on me, O Lord, *thou* Son of David; my daughter is grievously vexed with a devil. [23]But he answered her not a word. And his disciples came and besought him, saying, Send her away; for she crieth after us. [24]But he answered and said, I am not sent but unto the lost sheep of the house of Israel. [25]Then came she and worshipped him, saying, Lord, help me. [26]But he answered and said, It is not meet to take the children's bread, and to cast *it* to dogs. [27]And she said, Truth, Lord: yet the dogs eat of the crumbs which fall from their masters' table. [28]Then Jesus answered and said unto her, O woman, great *is* thy faith: be it unto thee even as thou wilt. And her daughter was made whole from that very hour. [29]And Jesus departed from thence, and came nigh unto the sea of Galilee; and went up into a mountain, and sat down there. [30]And great multitudes came unto him, having with them *those that were* lame, blind, dumb, maimed, and many others, and cast them down at Jesus' feet; and he healed them: [31]Insomuch that the multitude wondered, when they saw the dumb to speak, the maimed to be whole, the lame to walk, and the blind to see: and they glorified the God of Israel.

[32]Then Jesus called his disciples *unto him,* and said, I have compassion on the multitude, because they continue with me now three days, and have nothing to eat: and I will not send them away fasting, lest they faint in the way. [33]And his disciples say unto him, Whence should we have so much bread in the wilderness, as to fill so great a multitude? [34]And Jesus saith unto them, How many loaves have ye? And they said, Seven, and a few little fishes. [35]And he commanded the multitude to sit down on the ground. [36]And he took the seven loaves and the fishes, and gave thanks, and brake *them,* and gave to his disciples, and the disciples to the multitude. [37]And they did all eat, and were filled: and they took up of the broken *meat* that was left seven baskets full. [38]And they that did eat were four thousand men, beside women and children. [39]And he sent away the multitude, and took ship, and came into the coasts of Magdala,

16 The Pharisees also with the Sadducees came, and tempting desired him that he would shew them a sign from heaven. [2]He answered and said unto them, When it is evening, ye say, *It will be* fair weather: for the sky is red. [3]And in the morning, *It will be* foul weather to day: for the sky is red and lowring. O *ye* hypocrites, ye can discern the face of the sky; but can ye not *discern* the signs of the times? ⁴A wicked and adulterous generation seeketh after a sign; and there shall no sign be given unto it, but the sign of the prophet Jonas. And he left them, and departed. ⁵And when his disciples were come to the other side, they had forgotten to take bread.

⁶Then Jesus said unto them, Take heed and beware of the leaven of the Pharisees and of the Sadducees. ⁷And they reasoned among themselves, saying, *It is* because we have taken no bread. ⁸*Which* when Jesus perceived, he said unto them, O ye of little faith, why reason ye among yourselves, because ye have brought no bread? ⁹Do ye not yet understand, neither remember the five loaves of the five thousand, and how many baskets ye took up? ¹⁰Neither the seven loaves of the four thousand, and how many baskets ye took up? ¹¹How is it that ye do not understand that I spake *it* not to you concerning bread, that ye should beware of the leaven of the Pharisees and of the Sadducees? ¹²Then understood they how that he bade *them* not beware of the leaven of bread, but of the doctrine of the Pharisees and of the Sadducees.

¹³When Jesus came into the coasts of Caesarea Philippi, he asked his disciples, saying, Whom do men say that I the Son of man am? ¹⁴And they said, Some *say that thou art* John the Baptist: some, Elias; and others, Jeremias, or one of the prophets. ¹⁵He saith unto them, But whom say ye that I am? ¹⁶And Simon Peter answered and said, Thou art the Christ, the Son of the living God. ¹⁷And Jesus answered and said unto him, Blessed art thou, Simon Barjona: for flesh and blood hath not revealed *it* unto thee, but my Father which is in heaven. ¹⁸And I say also unto thee, That thou art Peter, and upon this rock I will build my church; and the gates of hell shall not prevail against it. ¹⁹And I will give unto thee the keys of the kingdom of heaven: and whatsoever thou shalt bind on earth shall be bound in heaven: and whatsoever thou shalt loose on earth shall be loosed in heaven. ²⁰Then charged he his disciples that they should tell no man that he was Jesus the Christ.

²¹From that time forth began Jesus to shew unto his disciples, how that he must go unto Jerusalem, and suffer many things of the elders and chief priests and scribes, and be killed, and be raised again the third day. ²²Then Peter took him, and began to rebuke him, saying, Be it far from thee, Lord: this shall not be unto thee. ²³But he turned, and said unto Peter, Get thee behind me, Satan: thou art an offence unto me: for thou savourest not the things that be of God, but those that be of men.

²⁴Then said Jesus unto his disciples, If any *man* will come after me, let him deny himself, and take up his cross, and follow me. ²⁵For whosoever will save his life shall lose it: and whosoever will lose his life for my sake shall find it. ²⁶For what is a man profited, if he shall gain the whole world, and lose his own soul? or what shall a man give in exchange for his soul? ²⁷For the Son of man shall come in the glory of his Father with his angels; and then he shall reward every man according to his works. ²⁸Verily I say unto you, There be some standing here, which shall not taste of death, till they see the Son of man coming in his kingdom.

17 And after six days Jesus taketh Peter, James, and John his brother, and bringeth them up into an high mountain apart, ²And was transfigured before them: and his face did shine as the sun, and his raiment was white as the light. ³And, behold, there appeared unto them Moses and Elias talking with him. ⁴Then answered Peter, and said unto Jesus, Lord, it is good for us to be here: if thou wilt, let us make here three tabernacles; one for thee, and one for Moses, and one for Elias. ⁵While he yet spake, behold, a bright cloud overshadowed them: and behold a voice out of the cloud, which said, This is my beloved Son, in whom I am well pleased; hear ye him. ⁶And when the disciples heard *it*, they fell on their face, and were sore afraid. ⁷And Jesus came and touched them, and said, Arise, and be not afraid. ⁸And when they had lifted up their eyes, they saw no man, save Jesus only. ⁹And as they came down from the mountain, Jesus charged them, saying, Tell the vision to no man, until the Son of man be risen again from the dead. ¹⁰And his disciples asked him, saying, Why then say the scribes that Elias must first come? ¹¹And Jesus answered and said unto them, Elias truly shall first come, and restore all things. ¹²But I say unto you, That Elias is come already, and they knew him not, but have done unto him whatsoever they listed. Likewise shall also the Son of man suffer of them. ¹³Then the disciples understood that he spake unto them of John the Baptist.

¹⁴And when they were come to the multitude, there came to him a *certain* man, kneeling down to him, and saying, ¹⁵Lord, have mercy on my son: for he is lunatick, and sore vexed: for ofttimes he falleth into the fire, and oft into the water. ¹⁶And I brought him to thy disciples, and they could not cure him. ¹⁷Then Jesus answered and said, O faithless and perverse generation, how long shall I be with you? how long shall I suffer you? bring him hither to me. ¹⁸And Jesus rebuked the devil; and he departed out of him: and the child was cured from that very hour. ¹⁹Then came the disciples to Jesus apart, and said, Why could not we cast him out? ²⁰And Jesus said unto them, Because of your unbelief: for verily I say unto you, If ye have faith as a grain of mustard seed, ye shall say unto this mountain, Remove hence to yonder place; and it shall remove; and nothing shall be impossible unto you. ²¹Howbeit this kind goeth not out but by prayer and fasting.

²²And while they abode in Galilee, Jesus said unto them, The Son of man shall be betrayed into the hands of men: ²³And they shall kill him, and the third day he shall be raised again. And they were exceeding sorry.

²⁴And when they were come to Capernaum, they that received tribute *money* came to Peter, and said, Doth not your master pay tribute? ²⁵He saith, Yes. And when he was come into the house, Jesus prevented him, saying, What thinkest thou, Simon? of whom do the kings of the earth take custom or tribute? of their own children, or of strangers? ²⁶Peter saith unto him, Of strangers. Jesus saith unto him, Then are the children free. ²⁷Notwithstanding, lest we should offend them, go thou to the sea, and cast an hook, and take up the fish that first cometh up; and when thou hast opened his mouth, thou shalt find a piece of money: that take, and give unto them for me and thee.

18 At the same time came the disciples unto Jesus, saying, Who is the greatest in the kingdom of heaven? ²And Jesus called a little child unto him, and set him in the midst of them, ³And said, Verily I say unto you, Except ye be converted, and become as little children, ye shall not enter into the kingdom of heaven. ⁴Whosoever therefore shall humble himself as this little child, the same is greatest in the kingdom of heaven. ⁵And whoso shall receive one such little child in my name receiveth me. ⁶But whoso shall offend one of these little ones which believe in me, it were better for him that a millstone were hanged about his neck, and *that* he were drowned in the depth of the sea.

⁷Woe unto the world because of offences! for it must needs be that offences come; but woe to that man by whom the offence cometh! ⁸Wherefore if thy hand or thy foot offend thee, cut them off, and cast *them* from thee: it is better for thee to enter into life halt or maimed, rather than having two hands or two feet to be cast into everlasting fire. ⁹And if thine eye offend thee, pluck it out, and cast *it* from thee: it is better for thee to enter into life with one eye, rather than having two eyes to be cast into hell fire. ¹⁰Take heed that ye despise not one of these little ones; for I say unto you, That in heaven their angels do always behold the face of my Father which is in heaven. ¹¹For the Son of man is come to save that which was lost. ¹²How think ye? if a man have an hundred sheep, and one of them be gone astray, doth he not leave the ninety and nine, and goeth into the mountains, and seeketh that which is gone astray? ¹³And if so be that he find it, verily I say unto you, he rejoiceth more of that *sheep,* than of the ninety and nine which went not astray. ¹⁴Even so it is not the will of your Father which is in heaven, that one of these little ones should perish.

¹⁵Moreover if thy brother shall trespass against thee, go and tell him his fault between thee and him alone: if he shall hear thee, thou hast gained thy brother. ¹⁶But if he will not hear *thee, then* take with thee one or two more, that in the mouth of two or three witnesses every word may

be established. ¹⁷And if he shall neglect to hear them, tell *it* unto the church: but if he neglect to hear the church, let him be unto thee as an heathen man and a publican. ¹⁸Verily I say unto you, Whatsoever ye shall bind on earth shall be bound in heaven: and whatsoever ye shall loose on earth shall be loosed in heaven. ¹⁹Again I say unto you, That if two of you shall agree on earth as touching any thing that they shall ask, it shall be done for them of my Father which is in heaven. ²⁰For where two or three are gathered together in my name, there am I in the midst of them.

²¹Then came Peter to him, and said, Lord, how oft shall my brother sin against me, and I forgive him? till seven times? ²²Jesus saith unto him, I say not unto thee, Until seven times: but, Until seventy times seven.

²³Therefore is the kingdom of heaven likened unto a certain king, which would take account of his servants. ²⁴And when he had begun to reckon, one was brought unto him, which owed him ten thousand talents. ²⁵But forasmuch as he had not to pay, his lord commanded him to be sold, and his wife, and children, and all that he had, and payment to be made. ²⁶The servant therefore fell down, and worshipped him, saying, Lord, have patience with me, and I will pay thee all. ²⁷Then the lord of that servant was moved with compassion, and loosed him, and forgave him the debt. ²⁸But the same servant went out, and found one of his fellowservants, which owed him an hundred pence: and he laid hands on him, and took *him* by the throat, saying, Pay me that thou owest. ²⁹And his fellowservant fell down at his feet, and besought him, saying, Have patience with me, and I will pay thee all. ³⁰And he would not: but went and cast him into prison, till he should pay the debt. ³¹So when his fellowservants saw what was done, they were very sorry, and came and told unto their lord all that was done. ³²Then his lord, after that he had called him, said unto him, O thou wicked servant, I forgave thee all that debt, because thou desiredst me: ³³Shouldest not thou also have had compassion on thy fellowservant, even as I had pity on thee? ³⁴And his lord was wroth, and delivered him to the tormentors, till he should pay all that was due unto him. ³⁵So likewise shall my heavenly Father do also unto you, if ye from your hearts forgive not every one his brother their trespasses.

19 And it came to pass, *that* when Jesus had finished these sayings, he departed from Galilee, and came into the coasts of Judaea beyond Jordan; ²And great multitudes followed him; and he healed them there.

³The Pharisees also came unto him, tempting him, and saying unto him, Is it lawful for a man to put away his wife for every cause? ⁴And he answered and said unto them, Have ye not read, that he which made *them* at the beginning made them male and female, ⁵And said, For this cause shall a man leave father and mother, and shall cleave to his wife: and they twain shall be one flesh? ⁶Wherefore they are no more twain, but one flesh. What therefore God hath joined together, let not man put asunder. ⁷They say unto him, Why did Moses then command to give a writing of divorcement, and to put her away? ⁸He saith unto them, Moses because of the hardness of your hearts suffered you to put away your wives: but from the beginning it was not so. ⁹And I say unto you, Whosoever shall put away his wife, except *it be* for fornication, and shall marry another, committeth adultery: and whoso marrieth her which is put away doth commit adultery.

¹⁰His disciples say unto him, If the case of the man be so with *his* wife, it is not good to marry. ¹¹But he said unto them, All *men* cannot receive this saying, save *they* to whom it is given. ¹²For there are some eunuchs, which were so born from *their* mother's womb: and there are some eunuchs, which were made eunuchs of men: and there be eunuchs, which have made themselves eunuchs for the kingdom of heaven's sake. He that is able to receive *it*, let him receive *it.*

¹³Then were there brought unto him little children, that he should put *his* hands on them, and pray: and the disciples rebuked them. ¹⁴But Jesus said, Suffer little children, and forbid them not, to come unto me: for of such is the kingdom of heaven. ¹⁵And

he laid *his* hands on them, and departed thence.

¹⁶And, behold, one came and said unto him, Good Master, what good thing shall I do, that I may have eternal life? ¹⁷And he said unto him, Why callest thou me good? *there is* none good but one, *that is,* God: but if thou wilt enter into life, keep the commandments. ¹⁸He saith unto him, Which? Jesus said, Thou shalt do no murder, Thou shalt not commit adultery, Thou shalt not steal, Thou shalt not bear false witness, ¹⁹Honour thy father and *thy* mother: and, Thou shalt love thy neighbour as thyself. ²⁰The young man saith unto him, All these things have I kept from my youth up: what lack I yet? ²¹Jesus said unto him, If thou wilt be perfect, go *and* sell that thou hast, and give to the poor, and thou shalt have treasure in heaven: and come *and* follow me. ²²But when the young man heard that saying, he went away sorrowful: for he had great possessions.

²³Then said Jesus unto his disciples, Verily I say unto you, That a rich man shall hardly enter into the kingdom of heaven. ²⁴And again I say unto you, It is easier for a camel to go through the eye of a needle, than for a rich man to enter into the kingdom of God. ²⁵When his disciples heard *it,* they were exceedingly amazed, saying, Who then can be saved? ²⁶But Jesus beheld *them,* and said unto them, With men this is impossible; but with God all things are possible.

²⁷Then answered Peter and said unto him, Behold, we have forsaken all, and followed thee; what shall we have therefore? ²⁸And Jesus said unto them, Verily I say unto you, That ye which have followed me, in the regeneration when the Son of man shall sit in the throne of his glory, ye also shall sit upon twelve thrones, judging the twelve tribes of Israel. ²⁹And every one that hath forsaken houses, or brethren, or sisters, or father, or mother, or wife, or children, or lands, for my name's sake, shall receive an hundredfold, and shall inherit everlasting life. ³⁰But many *that are* first shall be last; and the last *shall be* first.

20 For the kingdom of heaven is like unto a man *that is* an householder, which went out early in the morning to hire labourers into his vineyard. ²And when he had agreed with the labourers for a penny a day, he sent them into his vineyard. ³And he went out about the third hour, and saw others standing idle in the marketplace, ⁴And said unto them; Go ye also into the vineyard, and whatsoever is right I will give you. And they went their way. ⁵Again he went out about the sixth and ninth hour, and did likewise. ⁶And about the eleventh hour he went out, and found others standing idle, and saith unto them, Why stand ye here all the day idle? ⁷They say unto him, Because no man hath hired us. He saith unto them, Go ye also into the vineyard; and whatsoever is right, *that* shall ye receive. ⁸So when even was come, the lord of the vineyard saith unto his steward, Call the labourers, and give them *their* hire, beginning from the last unto the first. ⁹And when they came that *were hired* about the eleventh hour, they received every man a penny. ¹⁰But when the first came, they supposed that they should have received more; and they likewise received every man a penny. ¹¹And when they had received it, they murmured against the goodman of the house, ¹²Saying, These last have wrought *but* one hour, and thou hast made them equal unto us, which have borne the burden and heat of the day. ¹³But he answered one of them, and said, Friend, I do thee no wrong: didst not thou agree with me for a penny? ¹⁴Take *that* thine *is,* and go thy way: I will give unto this last, even as unto thee. ¹⁵Is it not lawful for me to do what I will with mine own? Is thine eye evil, because I am good? ¹⁶So the last shall be first, and the first last: for many be called, but few chosen.

¹⁷And Jesus going up to Jerusalem took the twelve disciples apart in the way, and said unto them, ¹⁸Behold, we go up to Jerusalem; and the Son of man shall be betrayed unto the chief priests and unto the scribes, and they shall condemn him to death, ¹⁹And shall deliver him to the Gentiles to mock, and to scourge, and to crucify *him:* and the third day he shall rise again.

²⁰Then came to him the mother of Zebedee's children with her sons, worshipping *him,* and desiring a certain thing of him. ²¹And he said unto her, What wilt thou? She saith unto him, Grant that these my

two sons may sit, the one on thy right hand, and the other on the left, in thy kingdom. ²²But Jesus answered and said, Ye know not what ye ask. Are ye able to drink of the cup that I shall drink of, and to be baptized with the baptism that I am baptized with? They say unto him, We are able. ²³And he saith unto them, Ye shall drink indeed of my cup, and be baptized with the baptism that I am baptized with: but to sit on my right hand, and on my left, is not mine to give, but *it shall be given to them* for whom it is prepared of my Father. ²⁴And when the ten heard *it,* they were moved with indignation against the two brethren. ²⁵But Jesus called them *unto him,* and said, Ye know that the princes of the Gentiles exercise dominion over them, and they that are great exercise authority upon them. ²⁶But it shall not be so among you: but whosoever will be great among you, let him be your minister; ²⁷And whosoever will be chief among you, let him be your servant: ²⁸Even as the Son of man came not to be ministered unto, but to minister, and to give his life a ransom for many.

²⁹And as they departed from Jericho, a great multitude followed him. ³⁰And, behold, two blind men sitting by the way side, when they heard that Jesus passed by, cried out, saying, Have mercy on us, O Lord, *thou* Son of David. ³¹And the multitude rebuked them, because they should hold their peace: but they cried the more, saying, Have mercy on us, O Lord, *thou* Son of David. ³²And Jesus stood still, and called them, and said, What will ye that I shall do unto you? ³³They say unto him, Lord, that our eyes may be opened. ³⁴So Jesus had compassion *on them,* and touched their eyes: and immediately their eyes received sight, and they followed him.

21 And when they drew nigh unto Jerusalem, and were come to Bethphage, unto the mount of Olives, then sent Jesus two disciples, ²Saying unto them, Go into the village over against you, and straightway ye shall find an ass tied, and a colt with her: loose *them,* and bring *them* unto me. ³And if any *man* say ought unto you, ye shall say, The Lord hath need of them; and straightway he will send them. ⁴All this was done, that it might be fulfilled which was spoken by the prophet, saying,

⁵Tell ye the daughter of Sion, Behold, thy King cometh unto thee, meek, and sitting upon an ass, and a colt the foal of an ass.

⁶And the disciples went, and did as Jesus commanded them, ⁷And brought the ass, and the colt, and put on them their clothes, and they set *him* thereon. ⁸And a very great multitude spread their garments in the way; others cut down branches from the trees, and strawed *them* in the way. ⁹And the multitudes that went before, and that followed, cried, saying,

Hosanna to the Son of David:

Blessed *is* he that cometh in the name of the Lord;

Hosanna in the highest.

¹⁰And when he was come into Jerusalem, all the city was moved, saying, Who is this? ¹¹And the multitude said, This is Jesus the prophet of Nazareth of Galilee.

¹²And Jesus went into the temple of God, and cast out all them that sold and bought in the temple, and overthrew the tables of the moneychangers, and the seats of them that sold doves, ¹³And said unto them, It is written, My house shall be called the house of prayer; but ye have made it a den of thieves. ¹⁴And the blind and the lame came to him in the temple; and he healed them. ¹⁵And when the chief priests and scribes saw the wonderful things that he did, and the children crying in the temple, and saying, Hosanna to the Son of David; they were sore displeased, ¹⁶And said unto him, Hearest thou what these say? And Jesus saith unto them, Yea; have ye never read,

Out of the mouth of babes and sucklings thou hast perfected praise?

¹⁷And he left them, and went out of the city into Bethany; and he lodged there. ¹⁸Now in the morning as he returned into the city, he hungered. ¹⁹And when he saw a fig tree in the way, he came to it, and found nothing thereon, but leaves only, and said unto it, Let no fruit grow on thee henceforward for ever. And presently the fig tree withered away. ²⁰And when the disciples saw *it,* they marvelled, saying, How soon is the fig tree withered away! ²¹Jesus

answered and said unto them, Verily I say unto you, If ye have faith, and doubt not, ye shall not only do this *which is done* to the fig tree, but also if ye shall say unto this mountain, Be thou removed, and be thou cast into the sea; it shall be done. ²²And all things, whatsoever ye shall ask in prayer, believing, ye shall receive.

²³And when he was come into the temple, the chief priests and the elders of the people came unto him as he was teaching, and said, By what authority doest thou these things? and who gave thee this authority? ²⁴And Jesus answered and said unto them, I also will ask you one thing, which if ye tell me, I in like wise will tell you by what authority I do these things. ²⁵The baptism of John, whence was it? from heaven, or of men? And they reasoned with themselves, saying, If we shall say, From heaven; he will say unto us, Why did ye not then believe him? ²⁶But if we shall say, Of men; we fear the people; for all hold John as a prophet. ²⁷And they answered Jesus, and said, We cannot tell. And he said unto them, Neither tell I you by what authority I do these things.

²⁸But what think ye? A *certain* man had two sons; and he came to the first, and said, Son, go work to day in my vineyard. ²⁹He answered and said, I will not: but afterward he repented, and went. ³⁰And he came to the second, and said likewise. And he answered and said, I *go,* sir: and went not. ³¹Whether of them twain did the will of *his* father? They say unto him, The first. Jesus saith unto them, Verily I say unto you, That the publicans and the harlots go into the kingdom of God before you. ³²For John came unto you in the way of righteousness, and ye believed him not: but the publicans and the harlots believed him: and ye, when ye had seen *it,* repented not afterward, that ye might believe him.

³³Hear another parable: There was a certain householder, which planted a vineyard, and hedged it round about, and digged a winepress in it, and built a tower, and let it out to husbandmen, and went into a far country: ³⁴And when the time of the fruit drew near, he sent his servants to the husbandmen, that they might receive the fruits of it. ³⁵And the husbandmen took

his servants, and beat one, and killed another, and stoned another. ³⁶Again, he sent other servants more than the first: and they did unto them likewise. ³⁷But last of all he sent unto them his son, saying, They will reverence my son. ³⁸But when the husbandmen saw the son, they said among themselves, This is the heir; come, let us kill him, and let us seize on his inheritance. ³⁹And they caught him, and cast *him* out of the vineyard, and slew *him.* ⁴⁰When the lord therefore of the vineyard cometh, what will he do unto those husbandmen? ⁴¹They say unto him, He will miserably destroy those wicked men, and will let out *his* vineyard unto other husbandmen, which shall render him the fruits in their seasons. ⁴²Jesus saith unto them, Did ye never read in the scriptures,

The stone which the builders rejected, the same is become the head of the corner: this is the Lord's doing, and it is marvellous in our eyes?

⁴³Therefore say I unto you, The kingdom of God shall be taken from you, and given to a nation bringing forth the fruits thereof. ⁴⁴And whosoever shall fall on this stone shall be broken: but on whomsoever it shall fall, it will grind him to powder. ⁴⁵And when the chief priests and Pharisees had heard his parables, they perceived that he spake of them. ⁴⁶But when they sought to lay hands on him, they feared the multitude, because they took him for a prophet.

22 And Jesus answered and spake unto them again by parables, and said, ²The kingdom of heaven is like unto a certain king, which made a marriage for his son, ³And sent forth his servants to call them that were bidden to the wedding: and they would not come. ⁴Again, he sent forth other servants, saying, Tell them which are bidden, Behold, I have prepared my dinner: my oxen and *my* fatlings *are* killed, and all things *are* ready: come unto the marriage. ⁵But they made light of *it,* and went their ways, one to his farm, another to his merchandise: ⁶And the remnant took his servants, and entreated *them* spitefully, and slew *them.* ⁷But when the king heard *thereof,* he was wroth: and he sent forth his armies, and destroyed those murderers,

and burned up their city. ⁸Then saith he to his servants, The wedding is ready, but they which were bidden were not worthy. ⁹Go ye therefore into the highways, and as many as ye shall find, bid to the marriage. ¹⁰So those servants went out into the highways, and gathered together all as many as they found, both bad and good: and the wedding was furnished with guests.

¹¹And when the king came in to see the guests, he saw there a man which had not on a wedding garment: ¹²And he saith unto him, Friend, how camest thou in hither not having a wedding garment? And he was speechless. ¹³Then said the king to the servants, Bind him hand and foot, and take him away, and cast *him* into outer darkness; there shall be weeping and gnashing of teeth. ¹⁴For many are called, but few *are* chosen.

¹⁵Then went the Pharisees, and took counsel how they might entangle him in *his* talk. ¹⁶And they sent out unto him their disciples with the Herodians, saying, Master, we know that thou art true, and teachest the way of God in truth, neither carest thou for any *man:* for thou regardest not the person of men. ¹⁷Tell us therefore, What thinkest thou? Is it lawful to give tribute unto Caesar, or not? ¹⁸But Jesus perceived their wickedness, and said, Why tempt ye me, *ye* hypocrites? ¹⁹Shew me the tribute money. And they brought unto him a penny. ²⁰And he saith unto them, Whose *is* this image and superscription? ²¹They say unto him, Caesar's. Then saith he unto them, Render therefore unto Caesar the things which are Caesar's; and unto God the things that are God's. ²²When they had heard *these words,* they marvelled, and left him, and went their way.

²³The same day came to him the Sadducees, which say that there is no resurrection, and asked him, ²⁴Saying, Master, Moses said, If a man die, having no children, his brother shall marry his wife, and raise up seed unto his brother. ²⁵Now there were with us seven brethren: and the first, when he had married a wife, deceased, and, having no issue, left his wife unto his brother: ²⁶Likewise the second also, and the third, unto the seventh. ²⁷And last of all the woman died also. ²⁸Therefore in the resurrection whose wife shall she be of the seven? for they all had her. ²⁹Jesus answered and said unto them, Ye do err, not knowing the scriptures, nor the power of God. ³⁰For in the resurrection they neither marry, nor are given in marriage, but are as the angels of God in heaven. ³¹But as touching the resurrection of the dead, have ye not read that which was spoken unto you by God, saying, ³²I am the God of Abraham, and the God of Isaac, and the God of Jacob? God is not the God of the dead, but of the living. ³³And when the multitude heard *this,* they were astonished at his doctrine.

³⁴But when the Pharisees had heard that he had put the Sadducees to silence, they were gathered together. ³⁵Then one of them, *which was* a lawyer, asked *him a question,* tempting him, and saying, ³⁶Master, which *is* the great commandment in the law? ³⁷Jesus said unto him, Thou shalt love the Lord thy God with all thy heart, and with all thy soul, and with all thy mind. ³⁸This is the first and great commandment. ³⁹And the second *is* like unto it, Thou shalt love thy neighbour as thyself. ⁴⁰On these two commandments hang all the law and the prophets.

⁴¹While the Pharisees were gathered together, Jesus asked them, ⁴²Saying, What think ye of Christ? whose son is he? They say unto him, *The Son* of David. ⁴³He saith unto them, How then doth David in spirit call him Lord, saying,

⁴⁴The Lord said unto my Lord, Sit thou on my right hand, till I make thine enemies thy footstool?

⁴⁵If David then call him Lord, how is he his son? ⁴⁶And no man was able to answer him a word, neither durst any *man* from that day forth ask him any more *questions.*

23 Then spake Jesus to the multitude, and to his disciples, ²Saying, The scribes and the Pharisees sit in Moses' seat: ³All therefore whatsoever they bid you observe, *that* observe and do; but do not ye after their works: for they say, and do not. ⁴For they bind heavy burdens and grievous to be borne, and lay *them* on men's shoulders; but they *themselves* will not move them with one of their fingers. ⁵But all their works they do for to be seen of men: they make broad their phylacteries, and enlarge the borders of their garments, ⁶And love the uppermost rooms at feasts, and the chief seats in the synagogues, ⁷And greetings in the markets, and to be called of men, Rabbi, Rabbi. ⁸But be not ye called Rabbi: for one is your Master, *even* Christ; and all ye are brethren. ⁹And call no *man* your father upon the earth: for one is your Father, which is in heaven. ¹⁰Neither be ye called masters: for one is your Master, *even* Christ. ¹¹But he that is greatest among you shall be your servant. ¹²And whosoever shall exalt himself shall be abased; and he that shall humble himself shall be exalted.

¹³But woe unto you, scribes and Pharisees, hypocrites! for ye shut up the kingdom of heaven against men: for ye neither go in *yourselves,* neither suffer ye them that are entering to go in. ¹⁴Woe unto you, scribes and Pharisees, hypocrites! for ye devour widows' houses, and for a pretence make long prayer: therefore ye shall receive the greater damnation. ¹⁵Woe unto you, scribes and Pharisees, hypocrites! for ye compass sea and land to make one proselyte, and when he is made, ye make him twofold more the child of hell than yourselves. ¹⁶Woe unto you, *ye* blind guides, which say, Whosoever shall swear by the temple, it is nothing; but whosoever shall swear by the gold of the temple, he is a debtor! ¹⁷*Ye* fools and blind: for whether is greater, the gold, or the temple that sanctifieth the gold? ¹⁸And, Whosoever shall swear by the altar, it is nothing; but whosoever sweareth by the gift that is upon it, he is guilty. ¹⁹*Ye* fools and blind: for whether *is* greater, the gift, or the altar that sanctifieth the gift? ²⁰Whoso therefore shall swear by the altar, sweareth by it, and by all things thereon. ²¹And whoso shall swear by the temple, sweareth by it, and by him that dwelleth therein. ²²And he that shall swear by heaven, sweareth by the throne of God, and by him that sitteth thereon. ²³Woe unto you, scribes and Pharisees, hypocrites! for ye pay tithe of mint and anise and cummin, and have omitted the weightier *matters* of the law, judgment, mercy, and faith: these ought ye to have done, and not to leave the other undone. ²⁴*Ye* blind guides, which strain at a gnat, and swallow a camel.

²⁵Woe unto you, scribes and Pharisees, hypocrites! for ye make clean the outside of the cup and of the platter, but within they are full of extortion and excess. ²⁶*Thou* blind Pharisee, cleanse first that *which is* within the cup and platter, that the outside of them may be clean also. ²⁷Woe unto you, scribes and Pharisees, hypocrites! for ye are like unto whited sepulchres, which indeed appear beautiful outward, but are within full of dead *men's* bones, and of all uncleanness. ²⁸Even so ye also outwardly appear righteous unto men, but within ye are full of hypocrisy and iniquity. ²⁹Woe unto you, scribes and Pharisees, hypocrites! because ye build the tombs of the prophets, and garnish the sepulchres of the righteous, ³⁰And say, If we had been in the days of our fathers, we would not have been partakers with them in the blood of the prophets. ³¹Wherefore ye be witnesses unto yourselves, that ye are the children of them which killed the prophets. ³²Fill ye up then the measure of your fathers. ³³*Ye* serpents, *ye* generation of vipers, how can ye escape the damnation of hell?

³⁴Wherefore, behold, I send unto you prophets, and wise men, and scribes: and *some* of them ye shall kill and crucify; and *some* of them shall ye scourge in your synagogues, and persecute *them* from city to city: ³⁵That upon you may come all the righteous blood shed upon the earth, from the blood of righteous Abel unto the blood of Zacharias son of Barachias, whom ye slew between the temple and the altar. ³⁶Verily I say unto you, All these things shall come upon this generation. ³⁷O Jerusalem, Jerusalem, *thou* that killest the prophets, and stonest them which are sent unto thee, how often would I have gathered thy children together, even as a hen gathereth her chickens under *her* wings, and ye would not! ³⁸Behold, your house is left unto you desolate. ³⁹For I say unto you, Ye shall not see me henceforth, till ye shall say, Blessed *is* he that cometh in the name of the Lord.

24 And Jesus went out, and departed from the temple: and his disciples came to *him* for to shew him the buildings of the temple. ²And Jesus said unto them, See ye not all these things? verily I say unto you, There shall not be left here one stone

upon another, that shall not be thrown down.

³And as he sat upon the mount of Olives, the disciples came unto him privately, saying, Tell us, when shall these things be? and what *shall be* the sign of thy coming, and of the end of the world? ⁴And Jesus answered and said unto them, Take heed that no man deceive you. ⁵For many shall come in my name, saying, I am Christ; and shall deceive many. ⁶And ye shall hear of wars and rumours of wars: see that ye be not troubled: for all *these things* must come to pass, but the end is not yet. ⁷For nation shall rise against nation, and kingdom against kingdom: and there shall be famines, and pestilences, and earthquakes, in divers places. ⁸All these *are* the beginning of sorrows. ⁹Then shall they deliver you up to be afflicted, and shall kill you: and ye shall be hated of all nations for my name's sake. ¹⁰And then shall many be offended, and shall betray one another, and shall hate one another. ¹¹And many false prophets shall rise, and shall deceive many. ¹²And because iniquity shall abound, the love of many shall wax cold. ¹³But he that shall endure unto the end, the same shall be saved. ¹⁴And this gospel of the kingdom shall be preached in all the world for a witness unto all nations; and then shall the end come. ¹⁵When ye therefore shall see the abomination of desolation, spoken of by Daniel the prophet, stand in the holy place, (whoso readeth, let him understand:) ¹⁶Then let them which be in Judaea flee into the mountains: ¹⁷Let him which is on the housetop not come down to take any thing out of his house: ¹⁸Neither let him which is in the field return back to take his clothes. ¹⁹And woe unto them that are with child, and to them that give suck in those days! ²⁰But pray ye that your flight be not in the winter, neither on the sabbath day: ²¹For then shall be great tribulation, such as was not since the beginning of the world to this time, no, nor ever shall be. ²²And except those days should be shortened, there should no flesh be saved: but for the elect's sake those days shall be shortened. ²³Then if any man shall say unto you, Lo, here *is* Christ, or there; believe *it* not. ²⁴For there shall arise false Christs, and false prophets,

and shall shew great signs and wonders; insomuch that, if *it were* possible, they shall deceive the very elect. ²⁵Behold, I have told you before. ²⁶Wherefore if they shall say unto you, Behold, *he is* in the desert; go not forth: behold, he is in the secret chambers; believe *it* not. ²⁷For as the lightning cometh out of the east, and shineth even unto the west; so shall also the coming of the Son of man be. ²⁸For wheresoever the carcase is, there will the eagles be gathered together.

²⁹Immediately after the tribulation of those days

shall the sun be darkened, and the moon shall not give her light, and the stars shall fall from heaven, and the powers of the heavens shall be shaken:

³⁰And then shall appear the sign of the Son of man in heaven: and then shall all the tribes of the earth mourn, and they shall see the Son of man coming in the clouds of heaven with power and great glory. ³¹And he shall send his angels with a great sound of a trumpet, and they shall gather together his elect from the four winds, from one end of heaven to the other. ³²Now learn a parable of the fig tree; When his branch is yet tender, and putteth forth leaves, ye know that summer is nigh: ³³So likewise ye, when ye shall see all these things, know that it is near, *even* at the doors. ³⁴Verily I say unto you, This generation shall not pass, till all these things be fulfilled. ³⁵Heaven and earth shall pass away, but my words shall not pass away.

³⁶But of that day and hour knoweth no *man*, no, not the angels of heaven, but my Father only. ³⁷But as the days of Noe *were*, so shall also the coming of the Son of man be. ³⁸For as in the days that were before the flood they were eating and drinking, marrying and giving in marriage, until the day that Noe entered into the ark, ³⁹And knew not until the flood came, and took them all away; so shall also the coming of the Son of man be. ⁴⁰Then shall two be in the field; the one shall be taken, and the other left. ⁴¹Two *women shall be* grinding at the mill; the one shall be taken, and the other left.

⁴²Watch therefore: for ye know not what hour your Lord doth come. ⁴³But know this, that if the goodman of the

house had known in what watch the thief would come, he would have watched, and would not have suffered his house to be broken up. [44]Therefore be ye also ready: for in such an hour as ye think not the Son of man cometh. [45]Who then is a faithful and wise servant, whom his lord hath made ruler over his household, to give them meat in due season? [46]Blessed *is* that servant, whom his lord when he cometh shall find so doing. [47]Verily I say unto you, That he shall make him ruler over all his goods. [48]But and if that evil servant shall say in his heart, My lord delayeth his coming; [49]And shall begin to smite *his* fellowservants, and to eat and drink with the drunken; [50]The lord of that servant shall come in a day when he looketh not for *him,* and in an hour that he is not aware of, [51]And shall cut him asunder, and appoint *him* his portion with the hypocrites: there shall be weeping and gnashing of teeth.

25 Then shall the kingdom of heaven be likened unto ten virgins, which took their lamps, and went forth to meet the bridegroom. [2]And five of them were wise, and five *were* foolish. [3]They that *were* foolish took their lamps, and took no oil with them: [4]But the wise took oil in their vessels with their lamps. [5]While the bridegroom tarried, they all slumbered and slept. [6]And at midnight there was a cry made, Behold, the bridegroom cometh; go ye out to meet him. [7]Then all those virgins arose, and trimmed their lamps. [8]And the foolish said unto the wise, Give us of your oil; for our lamps are gone out. [9]But the wise answered, saying, *Not so;* lest there be not enough for us and you: but go ye rather to them that sell, and buy for yourselves. [10]And while they went to buy, the bridegroom came; and they that were ready went in with him to the marriage: and the door was shut. [11]Afterward came also the other virgins, saying, Lord, Lord, open to us. [12]But he answered and said, Verily I say unto you, I know you not. [13]Watch therefore, for ye know neither the day nor the hour wherein the Son of man cometh.

[14]For *the kingdom of heaven is* as a man travelling into a far country, *who* called his own servants, and delivered unto them his goods. [15]And unto one he gave five tal-

ents, to another two, and to another one; to every man according to his several ability; and straightway took his journey. [16]Then he that had received the five talents went and traded with the same, and made *them* other five talents. [17]And likewise he that *had received* two, he also gained other two. [18]But he that had received one went and digged in the earth, and hid his lord's money. [19]After a long time the lord of those servants cometh, and reckoneth with them. [20]And so he that had received five talents came and brought other five talents, saying, Lord, thou deliveredst unto me five talents: behold, I have gained beside them five talents more. [21]His lord said unto him, Well done, *thou* good and faithful servant: thou hast been faithful over a few things, I will make thee ruler over many things: enter thou into the joy of thy lord. [22]He also that had received two talents came and said, Lord, thou deliveredst unto me two talents: behold, I have gained two other talents beside them. [23]His lord said unto him, Well done, good and faithful servant; thou hast been faithful over a few things, I will make thee ruler over many things: enter thou into the joy of thy lord. [24]Then he which had received the one talent came and said, Lord, I knew thee that thou art an hard man, reaping where thou hast not sown, and gathering where thou hast not strawed: [25]And I was afraid, and went and hid thy talent in the earth: lo, *there* thou hast *that is* thine. [26]His lord answered and said unto him, *Thou* wicked and slothful servant, thou knewest that I reap where I sowed not, and gather where I have not strawed: [27]Thou oughtest therefore to have put my money to the exchangers, and *then* at my coming I should have received mine own with usury. [28]Take therefore the talent from him, and give *it* unto him which hath ten talents. [29]For unto every one that hath shall be given, and he shall have abundance: but from him that hath not shall be taken away even that which he hath. [30]And cast ye the unprofitable servant into outer darkness: there shall be weeping and gnashing of teeth.

[31]When the Son of man shall come in his glory, and all the holy angels with him, then shall he sit upon the throne of his

glory: ³²And before him shall be gathered all nations: and he shall separate them one from another, as a shepherd divideth *his* sheep from the goats: ³³And he shall set the sheep on his right hand, but the goats on the left. ³⁴Then shall the King say unto them on his right hand, Come, ye blessed of my Father, inherit the kingdom prepared for you from the foundation of the world: ³⁵For I was an hungred, and ye gave me meat: I was thirsty, and ye gave me drink: I was a stranger, and ye took me in: ³⁶Naked, and ye clothed me: I was sick, and ye visited me: I was in prison, and ye came unto me. ³⁷Then shall the righteous answer him, saying, Lord, when saw we thee an hungred, and fed *thee?* or thirsty, and gave *thee* drink? ³⁸When saw we thee a stranger, and took *thee* in? or naked, and clothed *thee?* ³⁹Or when saw we thee sick, or in prison, and came unto thee? ⁴⁰And the King shall answer and say unto them, Verily I say unto you, Inasmuch as ye have done *it* unto one of the least of these my brethren, ye have done *it* unto me. ⁴¹Then shall he say also unto them on the left hand, Depart from me, ye cursed, into everlasting fire, prepared for the devil and his angels: ⁴²For I was an hungred, and ye gave me no meat: I was thirsty, and ye gave me no drink: ⁴³I was a stranger, and ye took me not in: naked, and ye clothed me not: sick, and in prison, and ye visited me not. ⁴⁴Then shall they also answer him, saying, Lord, when saw we thee an hungred, or athirst, or a stranger, or naked, or sick, or in prison, and did not minister unto thee? ⁴⁵Then shall he answer them, saying, Verily I say unto you, Inasmuch as ye did *it* not to one of the least of these, ye did *it* not to me. ⁴⁶And these shall go away into everlasting punishment: but the righteous into life eternal.

26 And it came to pass, when Jesus had finished all these sayings, he said unto his disciples, ²Ye know that after two days is *the feast of* the passover, and the Son of man is betrayed to be crucified. ³Then assembled together the chief priests, and the scribes, and the elders of the people, unto the palace of the high priest, who was called Caiaphas, ⁴And consulted that they might take Jesus by subtilty, and kill

him. ⁵But they said, Not on the feast *day,* lest there be an uproar among the people.

⁶Now when Jesus was in Bethany, in the house of Simon the leper, ⁷There came unto him a woman having an alabaster box of very precious ointment, and poured it on his head, as he sat *at meat.* ⁸But when his disciples saw *it,* they had indignation, saying, To what purpose *is* this waste? ⁹For this ointment might have been sold for much, and given to the poor. ¹⁰When Jesus understood *it,* he said unto them, Why trouble ye the woman? for she hath wrought a good work upon me. ¹¹For ye have the poor always with you; but me ye have not always. ¹²For in that she hath poured this ointment on my body, she did *it* for my burial. ¹³Verily I say unto you, Wheresoever this gospel shall be preached in the whole world, *there* shall also this, that this woman hath done, be told for a memorial of her.

¹⁴Then one of the twelve, called Judas Iscariot, went unto the chief priests, ¹⁵And said *unto them,* What will ye give me, and I will deliver him unto you? And they covenanted with him for thirty pieces of silver. ¹⁶And from that time he sought opportunity to betray him.

¹⁷Now the first *day* of the *feast of* unleavened bread the disciples came to Jesus, saying unto him, Where wilt thou that we prepare for thee to eat the passover? ¹⁸And he said, Go into the city to such a man, and say unto him, The Master saith, My time is at hand; I will keep the passover at thy house with my disciples. ¹⁹And the disciples did as Jesus had appointed them; and they made ready the passover. ²⁰Now when the even was come, he sat down with the twelve. ²¹And as they did eat, he said, Verily I say unto you, that one of you shall betray me. ²²And they were exceeding sorrowful, and began every one of them to say unto him, Lord, is it I? ²³And he answered and said, He that dippeth *his* hand with me in the dish, the same shall betray me. ²⁴The Son of man goeth as it is written of him: but woe unto that man by whom the Son of man is betrayed! it had been good for that man if he had not been born. ²⁵Then Judas, which betrayed him, answered and said, Master, is it I? He said unto him, Thou hast said.

²⁶And as they were eating, Jesus took bread, and blessed *it*, and brake *it*, and gave *it* to the disciples, and said, Take, eat; this is my body. ²⁷And he took the cup, and gave thanks, and gave *it* to them, saying, Drink ye all of it; ²⁸For this is my blood of the new testament, which is shed for many for the remission of sins. ²⁹But I say unto you, I will not drink henceforth of this fruit of the vine, until that day when I drink it new with you in my Father's kingdom. ³⁰And when they had sung an hymn, they went out into the mount of Olives. ³¹Then saith Jesus unto them, All ye shall be offended because of me this night: for it is written,

I will smite the shepherd, and the sheep of the flock shall be scattered abroad.

³²But after I am risen again, I will go before you into Galilee. ³³Peter answered and said unto him, Though all *men* shall be offended because of thee, *yet* will I never be offended. ³⁴Jesus said unto him, Verily I say unto thee, That this night, before the cock crow, thou shalt deny me thrice. ³⁵Peter said unto him, Though I should die with thee, yet will I not deny thee. Likewise also said all the disciples.

³⁶Then cometh Jesus with them unto a place called Gethsemane, and saith unto the disciples, Sit ye here, while I go and pray yonder. ³⁷And he took with him Peter and the two sons of Zebedee, and began to be sorrowful and very heavy. ³⁸Then saith he unto them, My soul is exceeding sorrowful, even unto death: tarry ye here, and watch with me. ³⁹And he went a little farther, and fell on his face, and prayed, saying, O my Father, if it be possible, let this cup pass from me: nevertheless not as I will, but as thou *wilt*. ⁴⁰And he cometh unto the disciples, and findeth them asleep, and saith unto Peter, What, could ye not watch with me one hour? ⁴¹Watch and pray, that ye enter not into temptation: the spirit indeed *is* willing, but the flesh *is* weak. ⁴²He went away again the second time, and prayed, saying, O my Father, if this cup may not pass away from me, except I drink it, thy will be done. ⁴³And he came and found them asleep again: for their eyes were heavy. ⁴⁴And he left them, and went away again, and prayed the third time, saying the same words. ⁴⁵Then cometh he to his disciples, and saith unto them, Sleep on now, and take *your* rest: behold, the hour is at hand, and the Son of man is betrayed into the hands of sinners. ⁴⁶Rise, let us be going: behold, he is at hand that doth betray me.

⁴⁷And while he yet spake, lo, Judas, one of the twelve, came, and with him a great multitude with swords and staves, from the chief priests and elders of the people. ⁴⁸Now he that betrayed him gave them a sign, saying, Whomsoever I shall kiss, that same is he: hold him fast. ⁴⁹And forthwith he came to Jesus, and said, Hail, master; and kissed him. ⁵⁰And Jesus said unto him, Friend, wherefore art thou come? Then came they, and laid hands on Jesus, and took him. ⁵¹And, behold, one of them which were with Jesus stretched out *his* hand, and drew his sword, and struck a servant of the high priest's, and smote off his ear. ⁵²Then said Jesus unto him, Put up again thy sword into his place: for all they that take the sword shall perish with the sword. ⁵³Thinkest thou that I cannot now pray to my Father, and he shall presently give me more than twelve legions of angels? ⁵⁴But how then shall the scriptures be fulfilled, that thus it must be? ⁵⁵In that same hour said Jesus to the multitudes, Are ye come out as against a thief with swords and staves for to take me? I sat daily with you teaching in the temple, and ye laid no hold on me. ⁵⁶But all this was done, that the scriptures of the prophets might be fulfilled. Then all the disciples forsook him, and fled.

⁵⁷And they that had laid hold on Jesus led *him* away to Caiaphas the high priest, where the scribes and the elders were assembled. ⁵⁸But Peter followed him afar off unto the high priest's palace, and went in, and sat with the servants, to see the end. ⁵⁹Now the chief priests, and elders, and all the council, sought false witness against Jesus, to put him to death; ⁶⁰But found none: yea, though many false witnesses came, *yet* found they none. At the last came two false witnesses, ⁶¹And said, This *fellow* said, I am able to destroy the temple of God, and to build it in three days. ⁶²And the high priest arose, and said unto him, Answerest thou nothing? what *is it which* these witness against thee? ⁶³But Jesus held his

peace. And the high priest answered and said unto him, I adjure thee by the living God, that thou tell us whether thou be the Christ, the Son of God. ⁶⁴Jesus saith unto him, Thou hast said: nevertheless I say unto you, Hereafter shall ye see the Son of man sitting on the right hand of power, and coming in the clouds of heaven. ⁶⁵Then the high priest rent his clothes, saying, He hath spoken blasphemy; what further need have we of witnesses? behold, now ye have heard his blasphemy. ⁶⁶What think ye? They answered and said, He is guilty of death. ⁶⁷Then did they spit in his face, and buffeted him; and others smote *him* with the palms of their hands, ⁶⁸Saying, Prophesy unto us, thou Christ, Who is he that smote thee?

⁶⁹Now Peter sat without in the palace: and a damsel came unto him, saying, Thou also wast with Jesus of Galilee. ⁷⁰But he denied before *them* all, saying, I know not what thou sayest. ⁷¹And when he was gone out into the porch, another *maid* saw him, and said unto them that were there, This *fellow* was also with Jesus of Nazareth. ⁷²And again he denied with an oath, I do not know the man. ⁷³And after a while came unto *him* they that stood by, and said to Peter, Surely thou also art *one* of them; for thy speech bewrayeth thee. ⁷⁴Then began he to curse and to swear, *saying*, I know not the man. And immediately the cock crew. ⁷⁵And Peter remembered the word of Jesus, which said unto him, Before the cock crow, thou shalt deny me thrice. And he went out, and wept bitterly.

27 When the morning was come, all the chief priests and elders of the people took counsel against Jesus to put him to death: ²And when they had bound him, they led *him* away, and delivered him to Pontius Pilate the governor.

³Then Judas, which had betrayeth him, when he saw that he was condemned, repented himself, and brought again the thirty pieces of silver to the chief priests and elders, ⁴Saying, I have sinned in that I have betrayed the innocent blood. And they said, What *is that* to us? see thou *to that.* ⁵And he cast down the pieces of silver in the temple, and departed, and went and hanged himself. ⁶And the chief priests took the silver pieces, and said, It is not lawful for to put them into the treasury, because it is the price of blood. ⁷And they took counsel, and bought with them the potter's field, to bury strangers in. ⁸Wherefore that field was called, The field of blood, unto this day. ⁹Then was fulfilled that which was spoken by Jeremy the prophet, saying, And they took the thirty pieces of silver, the price of him that was valued, whom they of the children of Israel did value; ¹⁰And gave them for the potter's field, as the Lord appointed me. ¹¹And Jesus stood before the governor: and the governor asked him, saying, Art thou the King of the Jews? And Jesus said unto him, Thou sayest. ¹²And when he was accused of the chief priests and elders, he answered nothing. ¹³Then said Pilate unto him, Hearest thou not how many things they witness against thee? ¹⁴And he answered him to never a word; insomuch that the governor marvelled greatly. ¹⁵Now at *that* feast the governor was wont to release unto the people a prisoner, whom they would. ¹⁶And they had then a notable prisoner, called Barabbas. ¹⁷Therefore when they were gathered together, Pilate said unto them, Whom will ye that I release unto you? Barabbas, or Jesus which is called Christ? ¹⁸For he knew that for envy they had delivered him.

¹⁹When he was set down on the judgment seat, his wife sent unto him, saying, Have thou nothing to do with that just man: for I have suffered many things this day in a dream because of him. ²⁰But the chief priests and elders persuaded the multitude that they should ask Barabbas, and destroy Jesus. ²¹The governor answered and said unto them, Whether of the twain will ye that I release unto you? They said, Barabbas. ²²Pilate saith unto them, What shall I do then with Jesus which is called Christ? *They* all say unto him, Let him be crucified. ²³And the governor said, Why, what evil hath he done? But they cried out the more, saying, Let him be crucified.

²⁴When Pilate saw that he could prevail nothing, but *that* rather a tumult was made, he took water, and washed *his* hands before the multitude, saying, I am innocent of the blood of this just person: see ye *to it.*

²⁵Then answered all the people, and said, His blood *be* on us, and on our children.

²⁶Then released he Barabbas unto them: and when he had scourged Jesus, he delivered *him* to be crucified. ²⁷Then the soldiers of the governor took Jesus into the common hall, and gathered unto him the whole band *of soldiers.* ²⁸And they stripped him, and put on him a scarlet robe.

²⁹And when they had platted a crown of thorns, they put *it* upon his head, and a reed in his right hand: and they bowed the knee before him, and mocked him, saying, Hail, King of the Jews! ³⁰And they spit upon him, and took the reed, and smote him on the head. ³¹And after that they had mocked him, they took the robe off from him, and put his own raiment on him, and led him away to crucify *him.* ³²And as they came out, they found a man of Cyrene, Simon by name: him they compelled to bear his cross. ³³And when they were come unto a place called Golgotha, that is to say, a place of a skull, ³⁴They gave him vinegar to drink mingled with gall: and when he had tasted *thereof,* he would not drink. ³⁵And they crucified him, and parted his garments, casting lots: that it might be fulfilled which was spoken by the prophet, They parted my garments among them, and upon my vesture did they cast lots. ³⁶And sitting down they watched him there; ³⁷And set up over his head his accusation written, THIS IS JESUS THE KING OF THE JEWS. ³⁸Then were there two thieves crucified with him, one on the right hand, and another on the left.

³⁹And they that passed by reviled him, wagging their heads, ⁴⁰And saying, Thou that destroyest the temple, and buildest *it* in three days, save thyself. If thou be the Son of God, come down from the cross. ⁴¹Likewise also the chief priests mocking *him,* with the scribes and elders, said, ⁴²He saved others; himself he cannot save. If he be the King of Israel, let him now come down from the cross, and we will believe him. ⁴³He trusted in God; let him deliver him now, if he will have him: for he said, I am the Son of God. ⁴⁴The thieves also, which were crucified with him, cast the same in his teeth. ⁴⁵Now from the sixth hour there was darkness over all the land unto the ninth hour. ⁴⁶And about the ninth hour Jesus cried with a loud voice, saying, Eli, Eli, lama sabachthani? that is to say, My God, my God, why hast thou forsaken me? ⁴⁷Some of them that stood there, when they heard *that,* said, This *man* calleth for Elias. ⁴⁸And straightway one of them ran, and took a spunge, and filled *it* with vinegar, and put *it* on a reed, and gave him to drink. ⁴⁹The rest said, Let be, let us see whether Elias will come to save him.

⁵⁰Jesus, when he had cried again with a loud voice, yielded up the ghost. ⁵¹And, behold, the veil of the temple was rent in twain from the top to the bottom; and the earth did quake, and the rocks rent; ⁵²And the graves were opened; and many bodies of the saints which slept arose, ⁵³And came out of the graves after his resurrection, and went into the holy city, and appeared unto many. ⁵⁴Now when the centurion, and they that were with him, watching Jesus, saw the earthquake, and those things that were done, they feared greatly, saying, Truly this was the Son of God. ⁵⁵And many women were there beholding afar off, which followed Jesus from Galilee, ministering unto him: ⁵⁶Among which was Mary Magdalene, and Mary the mother of James and Joses, and the mother of Zebedee's children. ⁵⁷When the even was come, there came a rich man of Arimathaea, named Joseph, who also himself was Jesus' disciple: ⁵⁸He went to Pilate, and begged the body of Jesus. Then Pilate commanded the body to be delivered. ⁵⁹And when Joseph had taken the body, he wrapped it in a clean linen cloth, ⁶⁰And laid it in his own new tomb, which he had hewn out in the rock: and he rolled a great stone to the door of the sepulchre, and departed. ⁶¹And there was Mary Magdalene, and the other Mary, sitting over against the sepulchre.

⁶²Now the next day, that followed the day of the preparation, the chief priests and Pharisees came together unto Pilate, ⁶³Saying, Sir, we remember that that deceiver said, while he was yet alive, After three days I will rise again. ⁶⁴Command therefore that the sepulchre be made sure until the third day, lest his disciples come by night, and steal him away, and say unto the people,

He is risen from the dead: so the last error shall be worse than the first. ⁶⁵Pilate said unto them, Ye have a watch: go your way, make *it* as sure as ye can. ⁶⁶So they went, and made the sepulchre sure, sealing the stone, and setting a watch.

28 In the end of the sabbath, as it began to dawn toward the first *day* of the week, came Mary Magdalene and the other Mary to see the sepulchre. ²And, behold, there was a great earthquake: for the angel of the Lord descended from heaven, and came and rolled back the stone from the door, and sat upon it. ³His countenance was like lightning, and his raiment white as snow: ⁴And for fear of him the keepers did shake, and became as dead *men*. ⁵And the angel answered and said unto the women, Fear not ye: for I know that ye seek Jesus, which was crucified. ⁶He is not here: for he is risen, as he said. Come, see the place where the Lord lay. ⁷And go quickly, and tell his disciples that he is risen from the dead; and, behold, he goeth before you into Galilee; there shall ye see him: lo, I have told you. ⁸And they departed quickly from the sepulchre with fear and great joy; and did run to bring his disciples word.

⁹And as they went to tell his disciples, behold, Jesus met them, saying, All hail. And they came and held him by the feet, and worshipped him. ¹⁰Then said Jesus unto them, Be not afraid: go tell my brethren that they go into Galilee, and there shall they see me.

¹¹Now when they were going, behold, some of the watch came into the city, and shewed unto the chief priests all the things that were done. ¹²And when they were assembled with the elders, and had taken counsel, they gave large money unto the soldiers, ¹³Saying, Say ye, His disciples came by night, and stole him *away* while we slept. ¹⁴And if this come to the governor's ears, we will persuade him, and secure you. ¹⁵So they took the money, and did as they were taught: and this saying is commonly reported among the Jews until this day.

¹⁶Then the eleven disciples went away into Galilee, into a mountain where Jesus had appointed them. ¹⁷And when they saw him, they worshipped him: but some doubted. ¹⁸And Jesus came and spake unto them, saying, All power is given unto me in heaven and in earth.

¹⁹Go ye therefore, and teach all nations, baptizing them in the name of the Father, and of the Son, and of the Holy Ghost: ²⁰Teaching them to observe all things whatsoever I have commanded you: and, lo, I am with you alway, *even* unto the end of the world. Amen.

The Gospel According to
ST. MARK

1 The beginning of the gospel of Jesus Christ, the Son of God; [2]As it is written in the prophets,

Behold, I send my messenger before thy face, which shall prepare thy way before thee. [3]The voice of one crying in the wilderness, Prepare ye the way of the Lord, make his paths straight.

[4]John did baptize in the wilderness, and preach the baptism of repentance for the remission of sins. [5]And there went out unto him all the land of Judaea, and they of Jerusalem, and were all baptized of him in the river of Jordan, confessing their sins. [6]And John was clothed with camel's hair, and with a girdle of a skin about his loins; and he did eat locusts and wild honey; [7]And preached, saying, There cometh one mightier than I after me, the latchet of whose shoes I am not worthy to stoop down and unloose. [8]I indeed have baptized you with water: but he shall baptize you with the Holy Ghost.

[9]And it came to pass in those days, that Jesus came from Nazareth of Galilee, and was baptized of John in Jordan. [10]And straightway coming up out of the water, he saw the heavens opened, and the Spirit like a dove descending upon him: [11]And there came a voice from heaven, *saying*, Thou art my beloved Son, in whom I am well pleased.

[12]And immediately the Spirit driveth him into the wilderness. [13]And he was there in the wilderness forty days, tempted of Satan; and was with the wild beasts; and the angels ministered unto him.

[14]Now after that John was put in prison, Jesus came into Galilee, preaching the gospel of the kingdom of God, [15]And saying, The time is fulfilled, and the kingdom of God is at hand: repent ye, and believe the gospel.

[16]Now as he walked by the sea of Galilee, he saw Simon and Andrew his brother casting a net into the sea: for they were fishers. [17]And Jesus said unto them, Come ye after me, and I will make you to become fishers of men. [18]And straightway they forsook their nets, and followed him. [19]And when he had gone a little farther thence, he saw James the *son* of Zebedee, and John his brother, who also were in the ship mending their nets. [20]And straightway he called them: and they left their father Zebedee in the ship with the hired servants, and went after him.

[21]And they went into Capernaum; and straightway on the sabbath day he entered into the synagogue, and taught. [22]And they were astonished at his doctrine: for he taught them as one that had authority, and not as the scribes. [23]And there was in their synagogue a man with an unclean spirit; and he cried out, [24]Saying, Let *us* alone; what have we to do with thee, thou Jesus of Nazareth? art thou come to destroy us? I know thee who thou art, the Holy One of God. [25]And Jesus rebuked him, saying, Hold thy peace, and come out of him. [26]And when the unclean spirit had torn him, and cried with a loud voice, he came out of him. [27]And they were all amazed, insomuch that they questioned among themselves, saying, What thing is this? what new doctrine *is* this? for with authority commandeth he even the unclean spirits, and they do obey him. [28]And immediately his fame spread abroad throughout all the region round about Galilee.

[29]And forthwith, when they were come out of the synagogue, they entered into the house of Simon and Andrew, with James and John. [30]But Simon's wife's mother lay sick of a fever, and anon they tell him of her. [31]And he came and took her by the hand, and lifted her up; and immediately the fever left her, and she ministered unto them.

[32]And at even, when the sun did set, they brought unto him all that were diseased, and them that were possessed with devils. [33]And all the city was gathered together at the door. [34]And he healed many that were sick of divers diseases, and cast out many devils; and suffered not the devils to speak, because they knew him.

[35]And in the morning, rising up a great while before day, he went out, and departed into a solitary place, and there prayed. [36]And Simon and they that were with him

followed after him. [37] And when they had found him, they said unto him, All *men* seek for thee. [38] And he said unto them, Let us go into the next towns, that I may preach there also: for therefore came I forth. [39] And he preached in their synagogues throughout all Galilee, and cast out devils.

[40] And there came a leper to him, beseeching him, and kneeling down to him, and saying unto him, If thou wilt, thou canst make me clean. [41] And Jesus, moved with compassion, put forth *his* hand, and touched him, and saith unto him, I will; be thou clean. [42] And as soon as he had spoken, immediately the leprosy departed from him, and he was cleansed. [43] And he straitly charged him, and forthwith sent him away; [44] And saith unto him, See thou say nothing to any man: but go thy way, shew thyself to the priest, and offer for thy cleansing those things which Moses commanded, for a testimony unto them. [45] But he went out, and began to publish *it* much, and to blaze abroad the matter, insomuch that Jesus could no more openly enter into the city, but was without in desert places: and they came to him from every quarter.

2 And again he entered into Capernaum, after *some* days; and it was noised that he was in the house. [2] And straightway many were gathered together, insomuch that there was no room to receive *them,* no, not so much as about the door: and he preached the word unto them. [3] And they come unto him, bringing one sick of the palsy, which was borne of four. [4] And when they could not come nigh unto him for the press, they uncovered the roof where he was: and when they had broken *it* up, they let down the bed wherein the sick of the palsy lay. [5] When Jesus saw their faith, he said unto the sick of the palsy, Son, thy sins be forgiven thee. [6] But there were certain of the scribes sitting there, and reasoning in their hearts, [7] Why doth this *man* thus speak blasphemies? who can forgive sins but God only? [8] And immediately when Jesus perceived in his spirit that they so reasoned within themselves, he said unto them, Why reason ye these things in your hearts? [9] Whether is it easier to say to the sick of the palsy, *Thy* sins be forgiven thee; or to say, Arise, and take up thy bed, and

walk? [10] But that ye may know that the Son of man hath power on earth to forgive sins, (he saith to the sick of the palsy,) [11] I say unto thee, Arise, and take up thy bed, and go thy way into thine house. [12] And immediately he arose, took up the bed, and went forth before them all; insomuch that they were all amazed, and glorified God, saying, We never saw it on this fashion.

[13] And he went forth again by the sea side; and all the multitude resorted unto him, and he taught them. [14] And as he passed by, he saw Levi the *son* of Alphaeus sitting at the receipt of custom, and said unto him, Follow me. And he arose and followed him.

[15] And it came to pass, that, as Jesus sat at meat in his house, many publicans and sinners sat also together with Jesus and his disciples: for there were many, and they followed him. [16] And when the scribes and Pharisees saw him eat with publicans and sinners, they said unto his disciples, How is it that he eateth and drinketh with publicans and sinners? [17] When Jesus heard *it,* he saith unto them, They that are whole have no need of the physician, but they that are sick: I came not to call the righteous, but sinners to repentance.

[18] And the disciples of John and of the Pharisees used to fast: and they come and say unto him, Why do the disciples of John and of the Pharisees fast, but thy disciples fast not? [19] And Jesus said unto them, Can the children of the bridechamber fast, while the bridegroom is with them? as long as they have the bridegroom with them, they cannot fast. [20] But the days will come, when the bridegroom shall be taken away from them, and then shall they fast in those days.

[21] No man also seweth a piece of new cloth on an old garment: else the new piece that filled it up taketh away from the old, and the rent is made worse. [22] And no man putteth new wine into old bottles: else the new wine doth burst the bottles, and the wine is spilled, and the bottles will be marred: but new wine must be put into new bottles.

[23] And it came to pass, that he went through the corn fields on the sabbath day; and his disciples began, as they went, to pluck the ears of corn. [24] And the Pharisees

said unto him, Behold, why do they on the sabbath day that which is not lawful? ²⁵And he said unto them, Have ye never read what David did, when he had need, and was an hungred, he, and they that were with him? ²⁶How he went into the house of God in the days of Abiathar the high priest, and did eat the shewbread, which is not lawful to eat but for the priests, and gave also to them which were with him? ²⁷And he said unto them, The sabbath was made for man, and not man for the sabbath: ²⁸Therefore the Son of man is Lord also of the sabbath.

3 And he entered again into the synagogue; and there was a man there which had a withered hand. ²And they watched him, whether he would heal him on the sabbath day; that they might accuse him. ³And he saith unto the man which had the withered hand, Stand forth. ⁴And he saith unto them, Is it lawful to do good on the sabbath days, or to do evil? to save life, or to kill? But they held their peace. ⁵And when he had looked round about on them with anger, being grieved for the hardness of their hearts, he saith unto the man, Stretch forth thine hand. And he stretched it out: and his hand was restored whole as the other.

⁶And the Pharisees went forth, and straightway took counsel with the Herodians against him, how they might destroy him. ⁷But Jesus withdrew himself with his disciples to the sea: and a great multitude from Galilee followed him, and from Judaea, ⁸And from Jerusalem, and from Idumaea, and from beyond Jordan; and they about Tyre and Sidon, a great multitude, when they had heard what great things he did, came unto him. ⁹And he spake to his disciples, that a small ship should wait on him because of the multitude, lest they should throng him. ¹⁰For he had healed many; insomuch that they pressed upon him for to touch him, as many as had plagues. ¹¹And unclean spirits, when they saw him, fell down before him, and cried, saying, Thou art the Son of God. ¹²And he straitly charged them that they should not make him known.

¹³And he goeth up into a mountain, and calleth unto him whom he would: and they came unto him. ¹⁴And he ordained twelve, that they should be with him, and that he might send them forth to preach, ¹⁵And to have power to heal sicknesses, and to cast out devils: ¹⁶And Simon he surnamed Peter; ¹⁷And James the son of Zebedee, and John the brother of James; and he surnamed them Boanerges, which is, The sons of thunder: ¹⁸And Andrew, and Philip, and Bartholomew, and Matthew, and Thomas, and James the son of Alphaeus, and Thaddaeus, and Simon the Canaanite, ¹⁹And Judas Iscariot, which also betrayed him: and they went into an house. ²⁰And the multitude cometh together again, so that they could not so much as eat bread. ²¹And when his friends heard of it, they went out to lay hold on him: for they said, He is beside himself.

²²And the scribes which came down from Jerusalem said, He hath Beelzebub, and by the prince of the devils casteth he out devils. ²³And he called them unto him, and said unto them in parables, How can Satan cast out Satan? ²⁴And if a kingdom be divided against itself, that kingdom cannot stand. ²⁵And if a house be divided against itself, that house cannot stand. ²⁶And if Satan rise up against himself, and be divided, he cannot stand, but hath an end. ²⁷No man can enter into a strong man's house, and spoil his goods, except he will first bind the strong man; and then he will spoil his house. ²⁸Verily I say unto you, All sins shall be forgiven unto the sons of men, and blasphemies wherewith soever they shall blaspheme: ²⁹But he that shall blaspheme against the Holy Ghost hath never forgiveness, but is in danger of eternal damnation: ³⁰Because they said, He hath an unclean spirit.

³¹There came then his brethren and his mother, and, standing without, sent unto him, calling him. ³²And the multitude sat about him, and they said unto him, Behold, thy mother and thy brethren without seek for thee. ³³And he answered them, saying, Who is my mother, or my brethren? ³⁴And he looked round about on them which sat about him, and said, Behold my mother and my brethren! ³⁵For whosoever shall do the will of God, the same is my brother, and my sister, and mother.

4 And he began again to teach by the sea side: and there was gathered unto him a great multitude, so that he entered into a ship, and sat in the sea; and the whole multitude was by the sea on the land. ²And he taught them many things by parables, and said unto them in his doctrine, ³Hearken; Behold, there went out a sower to sow: ⁴And it came to pass, as he sowed, some fell by the way side, and the fowls of the air came and devoured it up. ⁵And some fell on stony ground, where it had not much earth; and immediately it sprang up, because it had no depth of earth: ⁶But when the sun was up, it was scorched; and because it had no root, it withered away. ⁷And some fell among thorns, and the thorns grew up, and choked it, and it yielded no fruit. ⁸And other fell on good ground, and did yield fruit that sprang up and increased; and brought forth, some thirty, and some sixty, and some an hundred. ⁹And he said unto them, He that hath ears to hear, let him hear. ¹⁰And when he was alone, they that were about him with the twelve asked of him the parable. ¹¹And he said unto them, Unto you it is given to know the mystery of the kingdom of God: but unto them that are without, all these *things* are done in parables: ¹²That

seeing they may see, and not perceive; and hearing they may hear, and not understand; lest at any time they should be converted, and *their* sins should be forgiven them.

¹³And he said unto them, Know ye not this parable? and how then will ye know all parables?

¹⁴The sower soweth the word. ¹⁵And these are they by the way side, where the word is sown; but when they have heard, Satan cometh immediately, and taketh away the word that was sown in their hearts. ¹⁶And these are they likewise which are sown on stony ground; who, when they have heard the word, immediately receive it with gladness; ¹⁷And have no root in themselves, and so endure but for a time: afterward, when affliction or persecution ariseth for the word's sake, immediately they are offended. ¹⁸And these are they which are sown among thorns; such

as hear the word, ¹⁹And the cares of this world, and the deceitfulness of riches, and the lusts of other things entering in, choke the word, and it becometh unfruitful. ²⁰And these are they which are sown on good ground; such as hear the word, and receive *it,* and bring forth fruit, some thirtyfold, some sixty, and some an hundred.

²¹And he said unto them, Is a candle brought to be put under a bushel, or under a bed? and not to be set on a candlestick? ²²For there is nothing hid, which shall not be manifested; neither was any thing kept secret, but that it should come abroad. ²³If any man have ears to hear, let him hear. ²⁴And he said unto them, Take heed what ye hear: with what measure ye mete, it shall be measured to you: and unto you that hear shall more be given. ²⁵For he that hath, to him shall be given: and he that hath not, from him shall be taken even that which he hath.

²⁶And he said, So is the kingdom of God, as if a man should cast seed into the ground; ²⁷And should sleep, and rise night and day, and the seed should spring and grow up, he knoweth not how. ²⁸For the earth bringeth forth fruit of herself; first the blade, then the ear, after that the full corn in the ear. ²⁹But when the fruit is brought forth, immediately he putteth in the sickle, because the harvest is come.

³⁰And he said, Whereunto shall we liken the kingdom of God? or with what comparison shall we compare it? ³¹*It is* like a grain of mustard seed, which, when it is sown in the earth, is less than all the seeds that be in the earth: ³²But when it is sown, it groweth up, and becometh greater than all herbs, and shooteth out great branches; so that the fowls of the air may lodge under the shadow of it. ³³And with many such parables spake he the word unto them, as they were able to hear *it.* ³⁴But without a parable spake he not unto them: and when they were alone, he expounded all things to his disciples.

³⁵And the same day, when the even was come, he saith unto them, Let us pass over unto the other side. ³⁶And when they had sent away the multitude, they took him even as he was in the ship. And there were also with him other little ships. ³⁷And

there arose a great storm of wind, and the waves beat into the ship, so that it was now full. ³⁸And he was in the hinder part of the ship, asleep on a pillow: and they awake him, and say unto him, Master, carest thou not that we perish? ³⁹And he arose, and rebuked the wind, and said unto the sea, Peace, be still. And the wind ceased, and there was a great calm. ⁴⁰And he said unto them, Why are ye so fearful? how is it that ye have no faith? ⁴¹And they feared exceedingly, and said one to another, What manner of man is this, that even the wind and the sea obey him?

5 And they came over unto the other side of the sea, into the country of the Gadarenes. ²And when he was come out of the ship, immediately there met him out of the tombs a man with an unclean spirit, ³Who had *his* dwelling among the tombs; and no man could bind him, no, not with chains: ⁴Because that he had been often bound with fetters and chains, and the chains had been plucked asunder by him, and the fetters broken in pieces: neither could any *man* tame him. ⁵And always, night and day, he was in the mountains, and in the tombs, crying, and cutting himself with stones. ⁶But when he saw Jesus afar off, he ran and worshipped him, ⁷And cried with a loud voice, and said, What have I to do with thee, Jesus, *thou* Son of the most high God? I adjure thee by God, that thou torment me not. ⁸For he said unto him, Come out of the man, *thou* unclean spirit. ⁹And he asked him, What *is* thy name? And he answered, saying, My name *is* Legion: for we are many. ¹⁰And he besought him much that he would not send them away out of the country. ¹¹Now there was there nigh unto the mountains a great herd of swine feeding. ¹²And all the devils besought him, saying, Send us into the swine, that we may enter into them. ¹³And forthwith Jesus gave them leave. And the unclean spirits went out, and entered into the swine: and the herd ran violently down a steep place into the sea, (they were about two thousand;) and were choked in the sea. ¹⁴And they that fed the swine fled, and told *it* in the city, and in the country. And they went out to see what it was that was done. ¹⁵And they come to Jesus, and see him that

was possessed with the devil, and had the legion, sitting, and clothed, and in his right mind: and they were afraid. ¹⁶And they that saw *it* told them how it befell to him that was possessed with the devil, and *also* concerning the swine. ¹⁷And they began to pray him to depart out of their coasts. ¹⁸And when he was come into the ship, he that had been possessed with the devil prayed him that he might be with him. ¹⁹Howbeit Jesus suffered him not, but saith unto him, Go home to thy friends, and tell them how great things the Lord hath done for thee, and hath had compassion on thee. ²⁰And he departed, and began to publish in Decapolis how great things Jesus had done for him: and all *men* did marvel.

²¹And when Jesus was passed over again by ship unto the other side, much people gathered unto him: and he was nigh unto the sea. ²²And, behold, there cometh one of the rulers of the synagogue, Jairus by name; and when he saw him, he fell at his feet, ²³And besought him greatly, saying, My little daughter lieth at the point of death: *I pray thee,* come and lay thy hands on her, that she may be healed; and she shall live. ²⁴And *Jesus* went with him; and much people followed him, and thronged him. ²⁵And a certain woman, which had an issue of blood twelve years, ²⁶And had suffered many things of many physicians, and had spent all that she had, and was nothing bettered, but rather grew worse, ²⁷When she had heard of Jesus, came in the press behind, and touched his garment. ²⁸For she said, If I may touch but his clothes, I shall be whole. ²⁹And straightway the fountain of her blood was dried up; and she felt in *her* body that she was healed of that plague. ³⁰And Jesus, immediately knowing in himself that virtue had gone out of him, turned him about in the press, and said, Who touched my clothes? ³¹And his disciples said unto him, Thou seest the multitude thronging thee, and sayest thou, Who touched me? ³²And he looked round about to see her that had done this thing. ³³But the woman fearing and trembling, knowing what was done in her, came and fell down before him, and told him all the truth. ³⁴And he said unto her, Daughter, thy

faith hath made thee whole; go in peace, and be whole of thy plague.

³⁵While he yet spake, there came from the ruler of the synagogue's *house certain* which said, Thy daughter is dead: why troublest thou the Master any further? ³⁶As soon as Jesus heard the word that was spoken, he saith unto the ruler of the synagogue, Be not afraid, only believe. ³⁷And he suffered no man to follow him, save Peter, and James, and John the brother of James. ³⁸And he cometh to the house of the ruler of the synagogue, and seeth the tumult, and them that wept and wailed greatly. ³⁹And when he was come in, he saith unto them, Why make ye this ado, and weep? the damsel is not dead, but sleepeth. ⁴⁰And they laughed him to scorn. But when he had put them all out, he taketh the father and the mother of the damsel, and them that were with him, and entereth in where the damsel was lying. ⁴¹And he took the damsel by the hand, and said unto her, Talitha cumi; which is, being interpreted, Damsel, I say unto thee, arise. ⁴²And straightway the damsel arose, and walked; for she was *of the age* of twelve years. And they were astonished with a great astonishment. ⁴³And he charged them straitly that no man should know it; and commanded that something should be given her to eat.

6 And he went out from thence, and came into his own country; and his disciples follow him. ²And when the sabbath day was come, he began to teach in the synagogue: and many hearing *him* were astonished, saying, From whence hath this *man* these things? and what wisdom *is* this which is given unto him, that even such mighty works are wrought by his hands? ³Is not this the carpenter, the son of Mary, the brother of James, and Joses, and of Juda, and Simon? and are not his sisters here with us? And they were offended at him. ⁴But Jesus said unto them, A prophet is not without honour, but in his own country, and among his own kin, and in his own house. ⁵And he could there do no mighty work, save that he laid his hands upon a few sick folk, and healed *them*. ⁶And he marvelled because of their unbelief. And he went round about the villages, teaching.

⁷And he called *unto him* the twelve, and began to send them forth by two and two; and gave them power over unclean spirits; ⁸And commanded them that they should take nothing for *their* journey, save a staff only; no scrip, no bread, no money in *their* purse: ⁹But *be* shod with sandals; and not put on two coats. ¹⁰And he said unto them, In what place soever ye enter into an house, there abide till ye depart from that place. ¹¹And whosoever shall not receive you, nor hear you, when ye depart thence, shake off the dust under your feet for a testimony against them. Verily I say unto you, It shall be more tolerable for Sodom and Gomorrha in the day of judgment, than for that city. ¹²And they went out, and preached that men should repent. ¹³And they cast out many devils, and anointed with oil many that were sick, and healed *them*.

¹⁴And king Herod heard *of him;* (for his name was spread abroad:) and he said, That John the Baptist was risen from the dead, and therefore mighty works do shew forth themselves in him. ¹⁵Others said, That it is Elias. And others said, That it is a prophet, or as one of the prophets. ¹⁶But when Herod heard *thereof,* he said, It is John, whom I beheaded: he is risen from the dead. ¹⁷For Herod himself had sent forth and laid hold upon John, and bound him in prison for Herodias' sake, his brother Philip's wife: for he had married her. ¹⁸For John had said unto Herod, It is not lawful for thee to have thy brother's wife. ¹⁹Therefore Herodias had a quarrel against him, and would have killed him; but she could not: ²⁰For Herod feared John, knowing that he was a just man and an holy, and observed him; and when he heard him, he did many things, and heard him gladly. ²¹And when a convenient day was come, that Herod on his birthday made a supper to his lords, high captains, and chief *estates* of Galilee; ²²And when the daughter of the said Herodias came in, and danced, and pleased Herod and them that sat with him, the king said unto the damsel, Ask of me whatsoever thou wilt, and I will give *it* thee. ²³And he sware unto her, Whatsoever thou shalt ask of me, I will give *it* thee, unto the half of my kingdom. ²⁴And she went forth, and said unto her mother, What shall I ask? And she

said, The head of John the Baptist. [25]And she came in straightway with haste unto the king, and asked, saying, I will that thou give me by and by in a charger the head of John the Baptist. [26]And the king was exceeding sorry; *yet* for his oath's sake, and for their sakes which sat with him, he would not reject her. [27]And immediately the king sent an executioner, and commanded his head to be brought: and he went and beheaded him in the prison, [28]And brought his head in a charger, and gave it to the damsel: and the damsel gave it to her mother. [29]And when his disciples heard *of it,* they came and took up his corpse, and laid it in a tomb.

[30]And the apostles gathered themselves together unto Jesus, and told him all things, both what they had done, and what they had taught. [31]And he said unto them, Come ye yourselves apart into a desert place, and rest a while: for there were many coming and going, and they had no leisure so much as to eat. [32]And they departed into a desert place by ship privately. [33]And the people saw them departing, and many knew him, and ran afoot thither out of all cities, and outwent them, and came together unto him. [34]And Jesus, when he came out, saw much people, and was moved with compassion toward them, because they were as sheep not having a shepherd: and he began to teach them many things. [35]And when the day was now far spent, his disciples came unto him, and said, This is a desert place, and now the time *is* far passed: [36]Send them away, that they may go into the country round about, and into the villages, and buy themselves bread: for they have nothing to eat. [37]He answered and said unto them, Give ye them to eat. And they say unto him, Shall we go and buy two hundred pennyworth of bread, and give them to eat? [38]He saith unto them, How many loaves have ye? go and see. And when they knew, they say, Five, and two fishes. [39]And he commanded them to make all sit down by companies upon the green grass. [40]And they sat down in ranks, by hundreds, and by fifties. [41]And when he had taken the five loaves and the two fishes, he looked up to heaven, and blessed, and brake the loaves, and gave *them* to his disciples to set before them; and the two fishes divided he among

them all. [42]And they did all eat, and were filled. [43]And they took up twelve baskets full of the fragments, and of the fishes. [44]And they that did eat of the loaves were about five thousand men. [45]And straightway he constrained his disciples to get into the ship, and to go to the other side before unto Bethsaida, while he sent away the people. [46]And when he had sent them away, he departed into a mountain to pray. [47]And when even was come, the ship was in the midst of the sea, and he alone on the land. [48]And he saw them toiling in rowing; for the wind was contrary unto them: and about the fourth watch of the night he cometh unto them, walking upon the sea, and would have passed by them. [49]But when they saw him walking upon the sea, they supposed it had been a spirit, and cried out: [50]For they all saw him, and were troubled. And immediately he talked with them, and saith unto them, Be of good cheer: it is I; be not afraid. [51]And he went up unto them into the ship; and the wind ceased: and they were sore amazed in themselves beyond measure, and wondered. [52]For they considered not *the miracle* of the loaves: for their heart was hardened.

[53]And when they had passed over, they came into the land of Gennesaret, and drew to the shore. [54]And when they were come out of the ship, straightway they knew him, [55]And ran through that whole region round about, and began to carry about in beds those that were sick, where they heard he was. [56]And whithersoever he entered, into villages, or cities, or country, they laid the sick in the streets, and besought him that they might touch if it were but the border of his garment: and as many as touched him were made whole.

7 Then came together unto him the Pharisees, and certain of the scribes, which came from Jerusalem. [2]And when they saw some of his disciples eat bread with defiled, that is to say, with unwashen, hands, they found fault. [3]For the Pharisees, and all the Jews, except they wash *their* hands oft, eat not, holding the tradition of the elders. [4]And *when they come* from the market, except they wash, they eat not. And many other things there be, which they have received to hold, *as* the washing of cups, and

pots, brasen vessels, and of tables. ⁵Then the Pharisees and scribes asked him, Why walk not thy disciples according to the tradition of the elders, but eat bread with unwashen hands? ⁶He answered and said unto them, Well hath Esaias prophesied of you hypocrites, as it is written,

This people honoureth me with *their* lips, but their heart is far from me. ⁷Howbeit in vain do they worship me, teaching *for* doctrines the commandments of men.

⁸For laying aside the commandment of God, ye hold the tradition of men, *as* the washing of pots and cups: and many other such like things ye do. ⁹And he said unto them, Full well ye reject the commandment of God, that ye may keep your own tradition. ¹⁰For Moses said, Honour thy father and thy mother; and, Whoso curseth father or mother, let him die the death: ¹¹But ye say, If a man shall say to his father or mother, *It is* Corban, that is to say, a gift, by whatsoever thou mightest be profited by me; *he shall be free.* ¹²And ye suffer him no more to do ought for his father or his mother; ¹³Making the word of God of none effect through your tradition, which ye have delivered: and many such like things do ye.

¹⁴And when he had called all the people *unto him,* he said unto them, Hearken unto me every one *of you,* and understand: ¹⁵There is nothing from without a man, that entering into him can defile him: but the things which come out of him, those are they that defile the man. ¹⁶If any man have ears to hear, let him hear. ¹⁷And when he was entered into the house from the people, his disciples asked him concerning the parable. ¹⁸And he saith unto them, Are ye so without understanding also? Do ye not perceive, that whatsoever thing from without entereth into the man, *it* cannot defile him; ¹⁹Because it entereth not into his heart, but into the belly, and goeth out into the draught, purging all meats? ²⁰And he said, That which cometh out of the man, that defileth the man. ²¹For from within, out of the heart of men, proceed evil thoughts, adulteries, fornications, murders, ²²Thefts, covetousness, wickedness, deceit, lasciviousness, an evil eye, blasphemy, pride, foolishness: ²³All these evil things come from within, and defile the man.

²⁴And from thence he arose, and went into the borders of Tyre and Sidon, and entered into an house, and would have no man know *it:* but he could not be hid. ²⁵For a *certain* woman, whose young daughter had an unclean spirit, heard of him, and came and fell at his feet: ²⁶The woman was a Greek, a Syrophenician by nation; and she besought him that he would cast forth the devil out of her daughter. ²⁷But Jesus said unto her, Let the children first be filled: for it is not meet to take the children's bread, and to cast *it* unto the dogs. ²⁸And she answered and said unto him, Yes, Lord: yet the dogs under the table eat of the children's crumbs. ²⁹And he said unto her, For this saying go thy way; the devil is gone out of thy daughter. ³⁰And when she was come to her house, she found the devil gone out, and her daughter laid upon the bed.

³¹And again, departing from the coasts of Tyre and Sidon, he came unto the sea of Galilee, through the midst of the coasts of Decapolis. ³²And they bring unto him one that was deaf, and had an impediment in his speech; and they beseech him to put his hand upon him. ³³And he took him aside from the multitude, and put his fingers into his ears, and he spit, and touched his tongue; ³⁴And looking up to heaven, he sighed, and saith unto him, Ephphatha, that is, Be opened. ³⁵And straightway his ears were opened, and the string of his tongue was loosed, and he spake plain. ³⁶And he charged them that they should tell no man: but the more he charged them, so much the more a great deal they published *it;* ³⁷And were beyond measure astonished, saying, He hath done all things well: he maketh both the deaf to hear, and the dumb to speak.

8 In those days the multitude being very great, and having nothing to eat, Jesus called his disciples *unto him,* and saith unto them, ²I have compassion on the multitude, because they have now been with me three days, and have nothing to eat: ³And if I send them away fasting to their own houses, they will faint by the way: for divers of them came from far. ⁴And his disciples answered him, From whence can a man satisfy these *men* with bread here in the wilderness? [5]And he asked them, How many loaves have ye? And they said, Seven. [6]And he commanded the people to sit down on the ground: and he took the seven loaves, and gave thanks, and brake, and gave to his disciples to set before *them;* and they did set *them* before the people. [7]And they had a few small fishes: and he blessed, and commanded to set them also before *them.* [8]So they did eat, and were filled: and they took up of the broken *meat* that was left seven baskets. [9]And they that had eaten were about four thousand: and he sent them away.

[10]And straightway he entered into a ship with his disciples, and came into the parts of Dalmanutha. [11]And the Pharisees came forth, and began to question with him, seeking of him a sign from heaven, tempting him. [12]And he sighed deeply in his spirit, and saith, Why doth this generation seek after a sign? verily I say unto you, There shall no sign be given unto this generation. [13]And he left them, and entering into the ship again departed to the other side.

[14]Now *the disciples* had forgotten to take bread, neither had they in the ship with them more than one loaf. [15]And he charged them, saying, Take heed, beware of the leaven of the Pharisees, and *of* the leaven of Herod. [16]And they reasoned among themselves, saying, *It is* because we have no bread. [17]And when Jesus knew *it,* he saith unto them, Why reason ye, because ye have no bread? perceive ye not yet, neither understand? have ye your heart yet hardened? [18]Having eyes, see ye not? and having ears, hear ye not? and do ye not remember? [19]When I brake the five loaves among five thousand, how many baskets full of fragments took ye up? They say unto him, Twelve. [20]And when the seven among four thousand, how many baskets full of fragments took ye up? And they said, Seven. [21]And he said unto them, How is it that ye do not understand?

[22]And he cometh to Bethsaida; and they bring a blind man unto him, and besought him to touch him. [23]And he took the blind man by the hand, and led him out of the town; and when he had spit on his eyes, and put his hands upon him, he asked him if he saw ought. [24]And he looked up, and said, I see men as trees, walking. [25]After that he put *his* hands again upon his eyes, and made him look up: and he was restored, and saw every man clearly. [26]And he sent him away to his house, saying, Neither go into the town, nor tell *it* to any in the town.

[27]And Jesus went out, and his disciples, into the towns of Caesarea Philippi: and by the way he asked his disciples, saying unto them, Whom do men say that I am? [28]And they answered, John the Baptist: but some *say,* Elias; and others, One of the prophets. [29]And he saith unto them, But whom say ye that I am? And Peter answereth and saith unto him, Thou art the Christ. [30]And he charged them that they should tell no man of him.

[31]And he began to teach them, that the Son of man must suffer many things, and be rejected of the elders, and *of* the chief priests, and scribes, and be killed, and after three days rise again. [32]And he spake that saying openly. And Peter took him, and began to rebuke him. [33]But when he had turned about and looked on his disciples, he rebuked Peter, saying, Get thee behind me, Satan: for thou savourest not the things that be of God, but the things that be of men.

[34]And when he had called the people *unto him* with his disciples also, he said unto them, Whosoever will come after me, let him deny himself, and take up his cross, and follow me. [35]For whosoever will save his life shall lose it; but whosoever shall lose his life for my sake and the gospel's, the same shall save it. [36]For what shall it profit a man, if he shall gain the whole world, and lose his own soul? [37]Or what shall a man give in exchange for his soul? [38]Whosoever therefore shall be ashamed of me and of my words in this adulterous and sinful generation; of him also shall the Son of man be ashamed, when he cometh in the glory of his Father with the holy angels.

9 And he said unto them, Verily I say unto you, That there be some of them that stand here, which shall not taste of death, till they have seen the kingdom of God come with power.

²And after six days Jesus taketh *with him* Peter, and James, and John, and leadeth them up into an high mountain apart by themselves: and he was transfigured before them. ³And his raiment became shining, exceeding white as snow; so as no fuller on earth can white them. ⁴And there appeared unto them Elias with Moses: and they were talking with Jesus. ⁵And Peter answered and said to Jesus, Master, it is good for us to be here: and let us make three tabernacles; one for thee, and one for Moses, and one for Elias. ⁶For he wist not what to say; for they were sore afraid. ⁷And there was a cloud that overshadowed them: and a voice came out of the cloud, saying, This is my beloved Son: hear him. ⁸And suddenly, when they had looked round about, they saw no man any more, save Jesus only with themselves.

⁹And as they came down from the mountain, he charged them that they should tell no man what things they had seen, till the Son of man were risen from the dead. ¹⁰And they kept that saying with themselves, questioning one with another what the rising from the dead should mean.

¹¹And they asked him, saying, Why say the scribes that Elias must first come? ¹²And he answered and told them, Elias verily cometh first, and restoreth all things; and how it is written of the Son of man, that he must suffer many things, and be set at nought. ¹³But I say unto you, That Elias is indeed come, and they have done unto him whatsoever they listed, as it is written of him.

¹⁴And when he came to *his* disciples, he saw a great multitude about them, and the scribes questioning with them. ¹⁵And straightway all the people, when they beheld him, were greatly amazed, and running to *him* saluted him. ¹⁶And he asked the scribes, What question ye with them? ¹⁷And one of the multitude answered and said, Master, I have brought unto thee my son, which hath a dumb spirit; ¹⁸And wheresoever he taketh him, he teareth him: and he foameth, and gnasheth with his teeth, and pineth away: and I spake to thy disciples that they should cast him out; and they could not. ¹⁹He answereth him, and saith, O faithless generation, how

long shall I be with you? how long shall I suffer you? bring him unto me. ²⁰And they brought him unto him: and when he saw him, straightway the spirit tare him; and he fell on the ground, and wallowed foaming. ²¹And he asked his father, How long is it ago since this came unto him? And he said, Of a child. ²²And ofttimes it hath cast him into the fire, and into the waters, to destroy him: but if thou canst do any thing, have compassion on us, and help us. ²³Jesus said unto him, If thou canst believe, all things *are* possible to him that believeth. ²⁴And straightway the father of the child cried out, and said with tears, Lord, I believe; help thou mine unbelief. ²⁵When Jesus saw that the people came running together, he rebuked the foul spirit, saying unto him, *Thou* dumb and deaf spirit, I charge thee, come out of him, and enter no more into him. ²⁶And *the spirit* cried, and rent him sore, and came out of him: and he was as one dead; insomuch that many said, He is dead. ²⁷But Jesus took him by the hand, and lifted him up; and he arose. ²⁸And when he was come into the house, his disciples asked him privately, Why could not we cast him out? ²⁹And he said unto them, This kind can come forth by nothing, but by prayer and fasting.

³⁰And they departed thence, and passed through Galilee; and he would not that any man should know *it.* ³¹For he taught his disciples, and said unto them, The Son of man is delivered into the hands of men, and they shall kill him; and after that he is killed, he shall rise the third day. ³²But they understood not that saying, and were afraid to ask him.

³³And he came to Capernaum: and being in the house he asked them, What was it that ye disputed among yourselves by the way? ³⁴But they held their peace: for by the way they had disputed among themselves, who *should be* the greatest. ³⁵And he sat down, and called the twelve, and saith unto them, If any man desire to be first, *the same* shall be last of all, and servant of all. ³⁶And he took a child, and set him in the midst of them: and when he had taken him in his arms, he said unto them, ³⁷Whosoever shall receive one of such children in my name, receiveth me: and whosoever shall

receive me, receiveth not me, but him that sent me.

[38] And John answered him, saying, Master, we saw one casting out devils in thy name, and he followeth not us: and we forbad him, because he followeth not us. [39] But Jesus said, Forbid him not: for there is no man which shall do a miracle in my name, that can lightly speak evil of me. [40] For he that is not against us is on our part. [41] For whosoever shall give you a cup of water to drink in my name, because ye belong to Christ, verily I say unto you, he shall not lose his reward. [42] And whosoever shall offend one of *these* little ones that believe in me, it is better for him that a millstone were hanged about his neck, and he were cast into the sea. [43] And if thy hand offend thee, cut it off: it is better for thee to enter into life maimed, than having two hands to go into hell, into the fire that never shall be quenched: [44] Where their worm dieth not, and the fire is not quenched. [45] And if thy foot offend thee, cut it off: it is better for thee to enter halt into life, than having two feet to be cast into hell, into the fire that never shall be quenched: [46] Where their worm dieth not, and the fire is not quenched. [47] And if thine eye offend thee, pluck it out: it is better for thee to enter into the kingdom of God with one eye, than having two eyes to be cast into hell fire: [48] Where

their worm dieth not, and the fire is not quenched.

[49] For every one shall be salted with fire, and every sacrifice shall be salted with salt. [50] Salt *is* good: but if the salt have lost his saltness, wherewith will ye season it? Have salt in yourselves, and have peace one with another.

10 And he arose from thence, and cometh into the coasts of Judaea by the farther side of Jordan: and the people resort unto him again; and, as he was wont, he taught them again.

[2] And the Pharisees came to him, and asked him, Is it lawful for a man to put away *his* wife? tempting him. [3] And he answered and said unto them, What did Moses command you? [4] And they said, Moses suffered to write a bill of divorcement, and to put *her* away. [5] And Jesus answered and said unto them, For the hardness of your heart he wrote you this precept. [6] But from the beginning of the creation God made them male and female. [7] For this cause shall a man leave his father and mother, and cleave to his wife; [8] And they twain shall be one flesh: so then they are no more twain, but one flesh. [9] What therefore God hath joined together, let not man put asunder. [10] And in the house his disciples asked him again of the same *matter.* [11] And he saith unto them, Whosoever shall put away his wife, and marry another, committeth adultery against her. [12] And if a woman shall put away her husband, and be married to another, she committeth adultery.

[13] And they brought young children to him, that he should touch them: and *his* disciples rebuked those that brought *them.* [14] But when Jesus saw *it,* he was much displeased, and said unto them, Suffer the little children to come unto me, and forbid them not: for of such is the kingdom of God. [15] Verily I say unto you, Whosoever shall not receive the kingdom of God as a little child, he shall not enter therein. [16] And he took them up in his arms, put *his* hands upon them, and blessed them.

[17] And when he was gone forth into the way, there came one running, and kneeled to him, and asked him, Good Master, what shall I do that I may inherit eternal life? [18] And Jesus said unto him, Why callest thou me good? *there is* none good but one, *that is,* God. [19] Thou knowest the commandments, Do not commit adultery, Do not kill, Do not steal, Do not bear false witness, Defraud not, Honour thy father and mother. [20] And he answered and said unto him, Master, all these have I observed from my youth. [21] Then Jesus beholding him loved him, and said unto him, One thing thou lackest: go thy way, sell whatsoever thou hast, and give to the poor, and thou shalt have treasure in heaven: and come, take up the cross, and follow me. [22] And he was sad at that saying, and went away grieved: for he had great possessions.

[23] And Jesus looked round about, and saith unto his disciples, How hardly shall they that have riches enter into the kingdom of God! [24] And the disciples were astonished at his words. But Jesus answereth

again, and saith unto them, Children, how hard is it for them that trust in riches to enter into the kingdom of God! ²⁵It is easier for a camel to go through the eye of a needle, than for a rich man to enter into the kingdom of God. ²⁶And they were astonished out of measure, saying among themselves, Who then can be saved? ²⁷And Jesus looking upon them saith, With men *it is* impossible, but not with God: for with God all things are possible.

²⁸Then Peter began to say unto him, Lo, we have left all, and have followed thee. ²⁹And Jesus answered and said, Verily I say unto you, There is no man that hath left house, or brethren, or sisters, or father, or mother, or wife, or children, or lands, for my sake, and the gospel's, ³⁰But he shall receive an hundredfold now in this time, houses, and brethren, and sisters, and mothers, and children, and lands, with persecutions; and in the world to come eternal life. ³¹But many *that are* first shall be last; and the last first.

³²And they were in the way going up to Jerusalem; and Jesus went before them: and they were amazed; and as they followed, they were afraid. And he took again the twelve, and began to tell them what things should happen unto him, ³³*Saying,* Behold, we go up to Jerusalem; and the Son of man shall be delivered unto the chief priests, and unto the scribes; and they shall condemn him to death, and shall deliver him to the Gentiles: ³⁴And they shall mock him, and shall scourge him, and shall spit upon him, and shall kill him: and the third day he shall rise again.

³⁵And James and John, the sons of Zebedee, come unto him, saying, Master, we would that thou shouldest do for us whatsoever we shall desire. ³⁶And he said unto them, What would ye that I should do for you? ³⁷They said unto him, Grant unto us that we may sit, one on thy right hand, and the other on thy left hand, in thy glory. ³⁸But Jesus said unto them, Ye know not what ye ask: can ye drink of the cup that I drink of? and be baptized with the baptism that I am baptized with? ³⁹And they said unto him, We can. And Jesus said unto them, Ye shall indeed drink of the cup that I drink of; and with the baptism that I am baptized withal

shall ye be baptized: ⁴⁰But to sit on my right hand and on my left hand is not mine to give; but *it shall be given to them* for whom it is prepared. ⁴¹And when the ten heard *it,* they began to be much displeased with James and John. ⁴²But Jesus called them *to him,* and saith unto them, Ye know that they which are accounted to rule over the Gentiles exercise lordship over them; and their great ones exercise authority upon them. ⁴³But so shall it not be among you: but whosoever will be great among you, shall be your minister: ⁴⁴And whosoever of you will be the chiefest, shall be servant of all. ⁴⁵For even the Son of man came not to be ministered unto, but to minister, and to give his life a ransom for many.

⁴⁶And they came to Jericho: and as he went out of Jericho with his disciples and a great number of people, blind Bartimaeus, the son of Timaeus, sat by the highway side begging. ⁴⁷And when he heard that it was Jesus of Nazareth, he began to cry out, and say, Jesus, *thou* Son of David, have mercy on me. ⁴⁸And many charged him that he should hold his peace: but he cried the more a great deal, *Thou* Son of David, have mercy on me. ⁴⁹And Jesus stood still, and commanded him to be called. And they call the blind man, saying unto him, Be of good comfort, rise; he calleth thee. ⁵⁰And he, casting away his garment, rose, and came to Jesus. ⁵¹And Jesus answered and said unto him, What wilt thou that I should do unto thee? The blind man said unto him, Lord, that I might receive my sight. ⁵²And Jesus said unto him, Go thy way; thy faith hath made thee whole. And immediately he received his sight, and followed Jesus in the way.

11 And when they came nigh to Jerusalem, unto Bethphage and Bethany, at the mount of Olives, he sendeth forth two of his disciples, ²And saith unto them, Go your way into the village over against you: and as soon as ye be entered into it, ye shall find a colt tied, whereon never man sat; loose him, and bring *him.* ³And if any man say unto you, Why do ye this? say ye that the Lord hath need of him; and straightway he will send him hither. ⁴And they went their way, and found the colt tied by the door without in a place where two ways met; and

they loose him. [5]And certain of them that stood there said unto them, What do ye, loosing the colt? [6]And they said unto them even as Jesus had commanded: and they let them go. [7]And they brought the colt to Jesus, and cast their garments on him; and he sat upon him. [8]And many spread their garments in the way: and others cut down branches off the trees, and strawed *them* in the way. [9]And they that went before, and they that followed, cried, saying,

Hosanna;

Blessed *is* he that cometh in the name of the Lord:

[10]Blessed *be* the kingdom of our father David, that cometh in the name of the Lord:

Hosanna in the highest.

[11]And Jesus entered into Jerusalem, and into the temple: and when he had looked round about upon all things, and now the eventide was come, he went out unto Bethany with the twelve. [12]And on the morrow, when they were come from Bethany, he was hungry: [13]And seeing a fig tree afar off having leaves, he came, if haply he might find any thing thereon: and when he came to it, he found nothing but leaves; for the time of figs was not *yet.* [14]And Jesus answered and said unto it, No man eat fruit of thee hereafter for ever. And his disciples heard *it.*

[15]And they come to Jerusalem: and Jesus went into the temple, and began to cast out them that sold and bought in the temple, and overthrew the tables of the moneychangers, and the seats of them that sold doves; [16]And would not suffer that any man should carry *any* vessel through the temple. [17]And he taught, saying unto them, Is it not written, My house shall be called of all nations the house of prayer? but ye have made it a den of thieves. [18]And the scribes and chief priests heard *it,* and sought how they might destroy him: for they feared him, because all the people was astonished at his doctrine. [19]And when even was come, he went out of the city.

[20]And in the morning, as they passed by, they saw the fig tree dried up from the roots. [21]And Peter calling to remembrance saith unto him, Master, behold, the fig tree which thou cursedst is withered away. [22]And Jesus answering saith unto them, Have faith in God. [23]For verily I say unto you, That whosoever shall say unto this mountain, Be thou removed, and be thou cast into the sea; and shall not doubt in his heart, but shall believe that those things which he saith shall come to pass; he shall have whatsoever he saith. [24]Therefore I say unto you, What things soever ye desire, when ye pray, believe that ye receive *them,* and ye shall have *them.* [25]And when ye stand praying, forgive, if ye have ought against any: that your Father also which is in heaven may forgive you your trespasses. [26]But if ye do not forgive, neither will your Father which is in heaven forgive your trespasses.

[27]And they come again to Jerusalem: and as he was walking in the temple, there come to him the chief priests, and the scribes, and the elders, [28]And say unto him, By what authority doest thou these things? and who gave thee this authority to do these things? [29]And Jesus answered and said unto them, I will also ask of you one question, and answer me, and I will tell you by what authority I do these things. [30]The baptism of John, was *it* from heaven, or of men? answer me. [31]And they reasoned with themselves, saying, If we shall say, From heaven; he will say, Why then did ye not believe him? [32]But if we shall say, Of men; they feared the people: for all *men* counted John, that he was a prophet indeed. [33]And they answered and said unto Jesus, We cannot tell. And Jesus answering saith unto them, Neither do I tell you by what authority I do these things.

12 And he began to speak unto them by parables. A *certain* man planted a vineyard, and set an hedge about *it,* and digged *a place for* the winefat, and built a tower, and let it out to husbandmen, and went into a far country. [2]And at the season he sent to the husbandmen a servant, that he might receive from the husbandmen of the fruit of the vineyard. [3]And they caught *him,* and beat him, and sent *him* away empty. [4]And again he sent unto them another servant; and at him they cast stones, and wounded *him* in the head, and sent *him* away shamefully handled. [5]And

again he sent another; and him they killed, and many others; beating some, and killing some. ⁶Having yet therefore one son, his wellbeloved, he sent him also last unto them, saying, They will reverence my son. ⁷But those husbandmen said among themselves, This is the heir; come, let us kill him, and the inheritance shall be ours. ⁸And they took him, and killed *him*, and cast *him* out of the vineyard. ⁹What shall therefore the lord of the vineyard do? he will come and destroy the husbandmen, and will give the vineyard unto others. ¹⁰And have ye not read this scripture;

The stone which the builders rejected is become the head of the corner: ¹¹This was the Lord's doing, and it is marvellous in our eyes?

¹²And they sought to lay hold on him, but feared the people: for they knew that he had spoken the parable against them: and they left him, and went their way.

¹³And they send unto him certain of the Pharisees and of the Herodians, to catch him in *his* words. ¹⁴And when they were come, they say unto him, Master, we know that thou art true, and carest for no man: for thou regardest not the person of men, but teachest the way of God in truth: Is it lawful to give tribute to Caesar, or not? ¹⁵Shall we give, or shall we not give? But he, knowing their hypocrisy, said unto them, Why tempt ye me? bring me a penny, that I may see *it.* ¹⁶And they brought *it.* And he saith unto them, Whose *is* this image and superscription? And they said unto him, Caesar's. ¹⁷And Jesus answering said unto them, Render to Caesar the things that are Caesar's, and to God the things that are God's. And they marvelled at him.

¹⁸Then come unto him the Sadducees, which say there is no resurrection; and they asked him, saying, ¹⁹Master, Moses wrote unto us, If a man's brother die, and leave *his* wife *behind him,* and leave no children, that his brother should take his wife, and raise up seed unto his brother. ²⁰Now there were seven brethren: and the first took a wife, and dying left no seed. ²¹And the second took her, and died, neither left he any seed: and the third likewise. ²²And the seven had her, and left no seed: last of all

the woman died also. ²³In the resurrection therefore, when they shall rise, whose wife shall she be of them? for the seven had her to wife. ²⁴And Jesus answering said unto them, Do ye not therefore err, because ye know not the scriptures, neither the power of God? ²⁵For when they shall rise from the dead, they neither marry, nor are given in marriage; but are as the angels which are in heaven. ²⁶And as touching the dead, that they rise: have ye not read in the book of Moses, how in the bush God spake unto him, saying, I *am* the God of Abraham, and the God of Isaac, and the God of Jacob? ²⁷He is not the God of the dead, but the God of the living: ye therefore do greatly err.

²⁸And one of the scribes came, and having heard them reasoning together, and perceiving that he had answered them well, asked him, Which is the first commandment of all? ²⁹And Jesus answered him, The first of all the commandments *is,* Hear, O Israel; The Lord our God is one Lord: ³⁰And thou shalt love the Lord thy God with all thy heart, and with all thy soul, and with all thy mind, and with all thy strength: this is the first commandment. ³¹And the second *is* like, *namely* this, Thou shalt love thy neighbour as thyself. There is none other commandment greater than these. ³²And the scribe said unto him, Well, Master, thou hast said the truth: for there is one God; and there is none other but he: ³³And to love him with all the heart, and with all the understanding, and with all the soul, and with all the strength, and to love *his* neighbour as himself, is more than all whole burnt offerings and sacrifices. ³⁴And when Jesus saw that he answered discreetly, he said unto him, Thou art not far from the kingdom of God. And no man after that durst ask him *any question.*

³⁵And Jesus answered and said, while he taught in the temple, How say the scribes that Christ is the Son of David? ³⁶For David himself said by the Holy Ghost,

The LORD said to my Lord, Sit thou on my right hand, till I make thine enemies thy footstool.

³⁷David therefore himself calleth him Lord; and whence is he *then* his son? And the common people heard him gladly.

[38] And he said unto them in his doctrine, Beware of the scribes, which love to go in long clothing, and *love* salutations in the marketplaces, [39] And the chief seats in the synagogues, and the uppermost rooms at feasts: [40] Which devour widows' houses, and for a pretence make long prayers: these shall receive greater damnation.

[41] And Jesus sat over against the treasury, and beheld how the people cast money into the treasury: and many that were rich cast in much. [42] And there came a certain poor widow, and she threw in two mites, which make a farthing. [43] And he called *unto him* his disciples, and saith unto them, Verily I say unto you, That this poor widow hath cast more in, than all they which have cast into the treasury: [44] For all *they* did cast in of their abundance; but she of her want did cast in all that she had, *even* all her living.

13 And as he went out of the temple, one of his disciples saith unto him, Master, see what manner of stones and what buildings *are here!* [2] And Jesus answering said unto him, Seest thou these great buildings? there shall not be left one stone upon another, that shall not be thrown down. [3] And as he sat upon the mount of Olives over against the temple, Peter and James and John and Andrew asked him privately, [4] Tell us, when shall these things be? and what *shall be* the sign when all these things shall be fulfilled? [5] And Jesus answering them began to say, Take heed lest any *man* deceive you: [6] For many shall come in my name, saying, I am *Christ;* and shall deceive many. [7] And when ye shall hear of wars and rumours of wars, be ye not troubled: for *such things* must needs be; but the end *shall* not *be* yet. [8] For nation shall rise against nation, and kingdom against kingdom: and there shall be earthquakes in divers places, and there shall be famines and troubles: these *are* the beginnings of sorrows.

[9] But take heed to yourselves: for they shall deliver you up to councils; and in the synagogues ye shall be beaten: and ye shall be brought before rulers and kings for my sake, for a testimony against them. [10] And the gospel must first be published among all nations. [11] But when they shall lead *you,* and deliver you up, take no thought beforehand what ye shall speak, neither do ye premeditate: but whatsoever shall be given you in that hour, that speak ye: for it is not ye that speak, but the Holy Ghost. [12] Now the brother shall betray the brother to death, and the father the son; and children shall rise up against *their* parents, and shall cause them to be put to death. [13] And ye shall be hated of all *men* for my name's sake: but he that shall endure unto the end, the same shall be saved.

[14] But when ye shall see the abomination of desolation, spoken of by Daniel the prophet, standing where it ought not, (let him that readeth understand,) then let them that be in Judaea flee to the mountains: [15] And let him that is on the housetop not go down into the house, neither enter *therein,* to take any thing out of his house: [16] And let him that is in the field not turn back again for to take up his garment. [17] But woe to them that are with child, and to them that give suck in those days! [18] And pray ye that your flight be not in the winter. [19] For *in* those days shall be affliction, such as was not from the beginning of the creation which God created unto this time, neither shall be. [20] And except that the Lord had shortened those days, no flesh should be saved: but for the elect's sake, whom he hath chosen, he hath shortened the days. [21] And then if any man shall say to you, Lo, here *is* Christ; or, lo, *he is* there; believe *him* not: [22] For false Christs and false prophets shall rise, and shall shew signs and wonders, to seduce, if *it were* possible, even the elect. [23] But take ye heed: behold, I have foretold you all things.

[24] But in those days, after that tribulation,

the sun shall be darkened, and the moon shall not give her light, [25] And the stars of heaven shall fall, and the powers that are in heaven shall be shaken.

[26] And then shall they see the Son of man coming in the clouds with great power and glory. [27] And then shall he send his angels, and shall gather together his elect from the four winds, from the uttermost part of the earth to the uttermost part of heaven. [28] Now learn a parable of the fig

tree; When her branch is yet tender, and putteth forth leaves, ye know that summer is near: ²⁹So ye in like manner, when ye shall see these things come to pass, know that it is nigh, *even* at the doors. ³⁰Verily I say unto you, that this generation shall not pass, till all these things be done. ³¹Heaven and earth shall pass away: but my words shall not pass away.

³²But of that day and *that* hour knoweth no man, no, not the angels which are in heaven, neither the Son, but the Father. ³³Take ye heed, watch and pray: for ye know not when the time is. ³⁴*For the Son of man is* as a man taking a far journey, who left his house, and gave authority to his servants, and to every man his work, and commanded the porter to watch. ³⁵Watch ye therefore: for ye know not when the master of the house cometh, at even, or at midnight, or at the cockcrowing, or in the morning: ³⁶Lest coming suddenly he find you sleeping. ³⁷And what I say unto you I say unto all, Watch.

14 After two days was *the feast of* the passover, and of unleavened bread: and the chief priests and the scribes sought how they might take him by craft, and put *him* to death. ²But they said, Not on the feast *day,* lest there be an uproar of the people.

³And being in Bethany in the house of Simon the leper, as he sat at meat, there came a woman having an alabaster box of ointment of spikenard very precious; and she brake the box, and poured *it* on his head. ⁴And there were some that had indignation within themselves, and said, Why was this waste of the ointment made? ⁵For it might have been sold for more than three hundred pence, and have been given to the poor. And they murmured against her. ⁶And Jesus said, Let her alone; why trouble ye her? she hath wrought a good work on me. ⁷For ye have the poor with you always, and whensoever ye will ye may do them good: but me ye have not always. ⁸She hath done what she could: she is come aforehand to anoint my body to the burying. ⁹Verily I say unto you, Wheresoever this gospel shall be preached throughout the whole world, *this* also that she hath done shall be spoken of for a memorial of her.

¹⁰And Judas Iscariot, one of the twelve, went unto the chief priests, to betray him unto them. ¹¹And when they heard *it,* they were glad, and promised to give him money. And he sought how he might conveniently betray him.

¹²And the first day of unleavened bread, when they killed the passover, his disciples said unto him, Where wilt thou that we go and prepare that thou mayest eat the passover? ¹³And he sendeth forth two of his disciples, and saith unto them, Go ye into the city, and there shall meet you a man bearing a pitcher of water: follow him. ¹⁴And wheresoever he shall go in, say ye to the goodman of the house, The Master saith, Where is the guestchamber, where I shall eat the passover with my disciples? ¹⁵And he will shew you a large upper room furnished *and* prepared: there make ready for us. ¹⁶And his disciples went forth, and came into the city, and found as he had said unto them: and they made ready the passover.

¹⁷And in the evening he cometh with the twelve. ¹⁸And as they sat and did eat, Jesus said, Verily I say unto you, One of you which eateth with me shall betray me. ¹⁹And they began to be sorrowful, and to say unto him one by one, *Is* it I? and another *said, Is* it I? ²⁰And he answered and said unto them, *It is* one of the twelve, that dippeth with me in the dish. ²¹The Son of man indeed goeth, as it is written of him: but woe to that man by whom the Son of man is betrayed! good were it for that man if he had never been born.

²²And as they did eat, Jesus took bread, and blessed, and brake *it,* and gave to them, and said, Take, eat: this is my body. ²³And he took the cup, and when he had given thanks, he gave *it* to them: and they all drank of it. ²⁴And he said unto them, This is my blood of the new testament, which is shed for many. ²⁵Verily I say unto you, I will drink no more of the fruit of the vine, until that day that I drink it new in the kingdom of God.

²⁶And when they had sung an hymn, they went out into the mount of Olives. ²⁷And Jesus saith unto them, All ye shall be offended because of me this night: for it is written,

I will smite the shepherd, and the sheep shall be scattered.

²⁸But after that I am risen, I will go before you into Galilee. ²⁹But Peter said unto him, Although all shall be offended, yet *will* not I. ³⁰And Jesus saith unto him, Verily I say unto thee, That this day, *even* in this night, before the cock crow twice, thou shalt deny me thrice. ³¹But he spake the more vehemently, If I should die with thee, I will not deny thee in any wise. Likewise also said they all. ³²And they came to a place which was named Gethsemane: and he saith to his disciples, Sit ye here, while I shall pray. ³³And he taketh with him Peter and James and John, and began to be sore amazed, and to be very heavy; ³⁴And saith unto them, My soul is exceeding sorrowful unto death: tarry ye here, and watch. ³⁵And he went forward a little, and fell on the ground, and prayed that, if it were possible, the hour might pass from him. ³⁶And he said, Abba, Father, all things *are* possible unto thee; take away this cup from me: nevertheless not what I will, but what thou wilt. ³⁷And he cometh, and findeth them sleeping, and saith unto Peter, Simon, sleepest thou? couldest not thou watch one hour? ³⁸Watch ye and pray, lest ye enter into temptation. The spirit truly is ready, but the flesh *is* weak. ³⁹And again he went away, and prayed, and spake the same words. ⁴⁰And when he returned, he found them asleep again, (for their eyes were heavy,) neither wist they what to answer him. ⁴¹And he cometh the third time, and saith unto them, Sleep on now, and take *your* rest: it is enough, the hour is come; behold, the Son of man is betrayed into the hands of sinners. ⁴²Rise up, let us go; lo, he that betrayeth me is at hand.

⁴³And immediately, while he yet spake, cometh Judas, one of the twelve, and with him a great multitude with swords and staves, from the chief priest and the scribes and the elders. ⁴⁴And he that betrayed him had given them a token, saying, Whomsoever I shall kiss, that same is he; take him, and lead *him* away safely. ⁴⁵And as soon as he was come, he goeth straightway to him, and saith, Master, master; and kissed him. ⁴⁶And they laid their hands on him, and took him. ⁴⁷And one of them that stood by drew a sword, and smote a servant of the high priest, and cut off his ear. ⁴⁸And Jesus answered and said unto them, Are ye come out, as against a thief, with swords and *with* staves to take me? ⁴⁹I was daily with you in the temple teaching, and ye took me not: but the scriptures must be fulfilled. ⁵⁰And they all forsook him, and fled. ⁵¹And there followed him a certain young man, having a linen cloth cast about *his* naked *body*; and the young men laid hold on him: ⁵²And he left the linen cloth, and fled from them naked.

⁵³And they led Jesus away to the high priest: and with him were assembled all the chief priests and the elders and the scribes. ⁵⁴And Peter followed him afar off, even into the palace of the high priest: and he sat with the servants, and warmed himself at the fire. ⁵⁵And the chief priests and all the council sought for witness against Jesus to put him to death; and found none. ⁵⁶For many bare false witness against him, but their witness agreed not together. ⁵⁷And there arose certain, and bare false witness against him, saying, ⁵⁸We heard him say, I will destroy this temple that is made with hands, and within three days I will build another made without hands. ⁵⁹But neither so did their witness agree together. ⁶⁰And the high priest stood up in the midst, and asked Jesus, saying, Answerest thou nothing? what *is it which* these witness against thee? ⁶¹But he held his peace, and answered nothing. Again the high priest asked him, and said unto him, Art thou the Christ, the Son of the Blessed? ⁶²And Jesus said, I am: and ye shall see the Son of man sitting on the right hand of power, and coming in the clouds of heaven. ⁶³Then the high priest rent his clothes, and saith, What need we any further witnesses? ⁶⁴Ye have heard the blasphemy: what think ye? And they all condemned him to be guilty of death. ⁶⁵And some began to spit on him, and to cover his face, and to buffet him, and to say unto him, Prophesy: and the servants did strike him with the palms of their hands.

⁶⁶And as Peter was beneath in the palace, there cometh one of the maids of the high priest: ⁶⁷And when she saw Peter warming himself, she looked upon him,

and said, And thou also wast with Jesus of Nazareth. ⁶⁸But he denied, saying, I know not, neither understand I what thou sayest. And he went out into the porch; and the cock crew. ⁶⁹And a maid saw him again, and began to say to them that stood by, This is *one* of them. ⁷⁰And he denied it again. And a little after, they that stood by said again to Peter, Surely thou art *one* of them: for thou art a Galilaean, and thy speech agreeth *thereto.* ⁷¹But he began to curse and to swear, *saying,* I know not this man of whom ye speak. ⁷²And the second time the cock crew. And Peter called to mind the word that Jesus said unto him, Before the cock crow twice, thou shalt deny me thrice. And when he thought thereon, he wept.

15 And straightway in the morning the chief priests held a consultation with the elders and scribes and the whole council, and bound Jesus, and carried *him* away, and delivered *him* to Pilate. ²And Pilate asked him, Art thou the King of the Jews? And he answering said unto him, Thou sayest *it.* ³And the chief priests accused him of many things: but he answered nothing. ⁴And Pilate asked him again, saying, Answerest thou nothing? behold how many things they witness against thee. ⁵But Jesus yet answered nothing; so that Pilate marvelled.

⁶Now at *that* feast he released unto them one prisoner, whomsoever they desired. ⁷And there was *one* named Barabbas, *which lay* bound with them that had made insurrection with him, who had committed murder in the insurrection. ⁸And the multitude crying aloud began to desire *him to do* as he had ever done unto them. ⁹But Pilate answered them, saying, Will ye that I release unto you the King of the Jews? ¹⁰For he knew that the chief priests had delivered him for envy. ¹¹But the chief priests moved the people, that he should rather release Barabbas unto them. ¹²And Pilate answered and said again unto them, What will ye then that I shall do *unto him* whom ye call the King of the Jews? ¹³And they cried out again, Crucify him. ¹⁴Then Pilate said unto them, Why, what evil hath he done? And they cried out the more exceedingly, Crucify him.

¹⁵And *so* Pilate, willing to content the people, released Barabbas unto them, and delivered Jesus, when he had scourged *him,* to be crucified. ¹⁶And the soldiers led him away into the hall, called Praetorium; and they call together the whole band. ¹⁷And they clothed him with purple, and platted a crown of thorns, and put it about his *head,* ¹⁸And began to salute him, Hail, King of the Jews! ¹⁹And they smote him on the head with a reed, and did spit upon him, and bowing *their* knees worshipped him. ²⁰And when they had mocked him, they took off the purple from him, and put his own clothes on him, and led him out to crucify him. ²¹And they compel one Simon a Cyrenian, who passed by, coming out of the country, the father of Alexander and Rufus, to bear his cross. ²²And they bring him unto the place Golgotha, which is, being interpreted, The place of a skull. ²³And they gave him to drink wine mingled with myrrh: but he received *it* not. ²⁴And when they had crucified him, they parted his garments, casting lots upon them, what every man should take. ²⁵And it was the third hour, and they crucified him. ²⁶And the superscription of his accusation was written over, THE KING OF THE JEWS. ²⁷And with him they crucify two thieves; the one on his right hand, and the other on his left. ²⁸And the scripture was fulfilled, which saith, And he was numbered with the transgressors. ²⁹And they that passed by railed on him, wagging their heads, and saying, Ah, thou that destroyest the temple, and buildest *it* in three days, ³⁰Save thyself, and come down from the cross. ³¹Likewise also the chief priests mocking said among themselves with the scribes, He saved others; himself he cannot save. ³²Let Christ the King of Israel descend now from the cross, that we may see and believe. And they that were crucified with him reviled him. ³³And when the sixth hour was come, there was darkness over the whole land until the ninth hour. ³⁴And at the ninth hour Jesus cried with a loud voice, saying, Eloi, Eloi, lama sabachthani? which is, being interpreted, My God, my God, why hast thou forsaken me? ³⁵And some of them that stood by, when they heard *it,* said, Behold, he calleth Elias. ³⁶And one ran and filled a spunge full of vinegar, and put *it* on a reed,

and gave him to drink, saying, Let alone; let us see whether Elias will come to take him down. ³⁷And Jesus cried with a loud voice, and gave up the ghost. ³⁸And the veil of the temple was rent in twain from the top to the bottom.

³⁹And when the centurion, which stood over against him, saw that he so cried out, and gave up the ghost, he said, Truly this man was the Son of God. ⁴⁰There were also women looking on afar off: among whom was Mary Magdalene, and Mary the mother of James the less and of Joses, and Salome; ⁴¹(Who also, when he was in Galilee, followed him, and ministered unto him;) and many other women which came up with him unto Jerusalem.

⁴²And now when the even was come, because it was the preparation, that is, the day before the sabbath, ⁴³Joseph of Arimathaea, an honourable counsellor, which also waited for the kingdom of God, came, and went in boldly unto Pilate, and craved the body of Jesus. ⁴⁴And Pilate marvelled if he were already dead: and calling *unto him* the centurion, he asked him whether he had been any while dead. ⁴⁵And when he knew *it* of the centurion, he gave the body to Joseph. ⁴⁶And he bought fine linen, and took him down, and wrapped him in the linen, and laid him in a sepulchre which was hewn out of a rock, and rolled a stone unto the door of the sepulchre. ⁴⁷And Mary Magdalene and Mary *the mother* of Joses beheld where he was laid.

16 And when the sabbath was past, Mary Magdalene, and Mary the *mother* of James, and Salome, had bought sweet spices, that they might come and anoint him. ²And very early in the morning the first *day* of the week, they came unto the sepulchre at the rising of the sun. ³And they said among themselves, Who shall roll us away the stone from the door of the sepulchre? ⁴And when they looked, they saw that the stone was rolled away: for it was very great. ⁵And entering into the sepulchre, they saw a young man sitting

on the right side, clothed in a long white garment; and they were affrighted. ⁶And he saith unto them, Be not affrighted: Ye seek Jesus of Nazareth, which was crucified: he is risen; he is not here: behold the place where they laid him. ⁷But go your way, tell his disciples and Peter that he goeth before you into Galilee: there shall ye see him, as he said unto you. ⁸And they went out quickly, and fled from the sepulchre; for they trembled and were amazed: neither said they any thing to any *man;* for they were afraid.

⁹Now when *Jesus* was risen early the first *day* of the week, he appeared first to Mary Magdalene, out of whom he had cast seven devils. ¹⁰*And* she went and told them that had been with him, as they mourned and wept. ¹¹And they, when they had heard that he was alive, and had been seen of her, believed not.

¹²After that he appeared in another form unto two of them, as they walked, and went into the country. ¹³And they went and told *it* unto the residue: neither believed they them.

¹⁴Afterward he appeared unto the eleven as they sat at meat, and upbraided them with their unbelief and hardness of heart, because they believed not them which had seen him after he was risen. ¹⁵And he said unto them, Go ye into all the world, and preach the gospel to every creature. ¹⁶He that believeth and is baptized shall be saved; but he that believeth not shall be damned. ¹⁷And these signs shall follow them that believe; In my name shall they cast out devils; they shall speak with new tongues; ¹⁸They shall take up serpents; and if they drink any deadly thing, it shall not hurt them; they shall lay hands on the sick, and they shall recover.

¹⁹So then after the Lord had spoken unto them, he was received up into heaven, and sat on the right hand of God. ²⁰And they went forth, and preached every where, the Lord working with *them,* and confirming the word with signs following. Amen.

ST. LUKE

1 Forasmuch as many have taken in hand to set forth in order a declaration of those things which are most surely believed among us, ²Even as they delivered them unto us, which from the beginning were eyewitnesses, and ministers of the word; ³It seemed good to me also, having had perfect understanding of all things from the very first, to write unto thee in order, most excellent Theophilus, ⁴That thou mightest know the certainty of those things, wherein thou hast been instructed.

⁵There was in the days of Herod, the king of Judaea, a certain priest named Zacharias, of the course of Abia: and his wife *was* of the daughters of Aaron, and her name *was* Elisabeth. ⁶And they were both righteous before God, walking in all the commandments and ordinances of the Lord blameless. ⁷And they had no child, because that Elisabeth was barren, and they both were *now* well stricken in years. ⁸And it came to pass, that while he executed the priest's office before God in the order of his course, ⁹According to the custom of the priest's office, his lot was to burn incense when he went into the temple of the Lord. ¹⁰And the whole multitude of the people were praying without at the time of incense. ¹¹And there appeared unto him an angel of the Lord standing on the right side of the altar of incense. ¹²And when Zacharias saw *him,* he was troubled, and fear fell upon him. ¹³But the angel said unto him, Fear not, Zacharias: for thy prayer is heard; and thy wife Elisabeth shall bear thee a son, and thou shalt call his name John. ¹⁴And thou shalt have joy and gladness; and many shall rejoice at his birth. ¹⁵For he shall be great in the sight of the Lord, and shall drink neither wine nor strong drink; and he shall be filled with the Holy Ghost, even from his mother's womb. ¹⁶And many of the children of Israel shall he turn to the Lord their God. ¹⁷And he shall go before him in the spirit and power of Elias, to turn the hearts of the fathers to the children, and the disobedient to the wisdom of the just; to make ready a people prepared for the Lord. ¹⁸And Zacharias said unto the angel, Whereby shall I know this? for I am an old man, and my wife well stricken in years. ¹⁹And the angel answering said unto him, I am Gabriel, that stand in the presence of God; and am sent to speak unto thee, and to shew thee these glad tidings. ²⁰And, behold, thou shalt be dumb, and not able to speak, until the day that these things shall be performed, because thou believest not my words, which shall be fulfilled in their season. ²¹And the people waited for Zacharias, and marvelled that he tarried so long in the temple. ²²And when he came out, he could not speak unto them: and they perceived that he had seen a vision in the temple: for he beckoned unto them, and remained speechless. ²³And it came to pass, that, as soon as the days of his ministration were accomplished, he departed to his own house. ²⁴And after those days his wife Elisabeth conceived, and hid herself five months, saying, ²⁵Thus hath the Lord dealt with me in the days wherein he looked on *me,* to take away my reproach among men.

²⁶And in the sixth month the angel Gabriel was sent from God unto a city of Galilee, named Nazareth, ²⁷To a virgin espoused to a man whose name was Joseph, of the house of David; and the virgin's name *was* Mary. ²⁸And the angel came in unto her, and said, Hail, *thou that art* highly favoured, the Lord *is* with thee: blessed *art* thou among women. ²⁹And when she saw *him,* she was troubled at his saying, and cast in her mind what manner of salutation this should be. ³⁰And the angel said unto her, Fear not, Mary: for thou hast found favour with God. ³¹And, behold, thou shalt conceive in thy womb, and bring forth a son, and shalt call his name JESUS. ³²He shall be great, and shall be called the Son of the Highest: and the Lord God shall give unto him the throne of his father David: ³³And he shall reign over the house of Jacob for ever; and of his kingdom there shall be no end. ³⁴Then said Mary unto the angel, How shall this be, seeing I know not a man? ³⁵And the angel answered and said unto her, The Holy Ghost shall come upon

thee, and the power of the Highest shall overshadow thee: therefore also that holy thing which shall be.born of thee shall be called the Son of God. ³⁶And, behold, thy cousin Elisabeth, she hath also conceived a son in her old age: and this is the sixth month with her, who was called barren. ³⁷For with God nothing shall be impossible. ³⁸And Mary said, Behold the handmaid of the Lord; be it unto me according to thy word. And the angel departed from her. ³⁹And Mary arose in those days, and went into the hill country with haste, into a city of Juda; ⁴⁰And entered into the house of Zacharias, and saluted Elisabeth. ⁴¹And it came to pass, that, when Elisabeth heard the salutation of Mary, the babe leaped in her womb; and Elisabeth was filled with the Holy Ghost: ⁴²And she spake out with a loud voice, and said, Blessed *art* thou among women, and blessed *is* the fruit of thy womb. ⁴³And whence *is* this to me, that the mother of my Lord should come to me? ⁴⁴For, lo, as soon as the voice of thy salutation sounded in mine ears, the babe leaped in my womb for joy. ⁴⁵And blessed *is* she that believed: for there shall be a performance of those things which were told her from the Lord. ⁴⁶And Mary said,

My soul doth magnify the Lord, ⁴⁷And my spirit hath rejoiced in God my Saviour. ⁴⁸For he hath regarded the low estate of his handmaiden: for, behold, from henceforth all generations shall call me blessed. ⁴⁹For he that is mighty hath done to me great things; and holy *is* his name. ⁵⁰And his mercy *is* on them that fear him from generation to generation. ⁵¹He hath shewed strength with his arm; he hath scattered the proud in the imagination of their hearts. ⁵²He hath put down the mighty from *their* seats, and exalted them of low degree. ⁵³He hath filled the hungry with good things; and the rich he hath sent empty away. ⁵⁴He hath holpen his servant Israel, in remembrance of *his* mercy; ⁵⁵As he spake to our fathers, to Abraham, and to his seed for ever.

⁵⁶And Mary abode with her about three months, and returned to her own house.

⁵⁷Now Elisabeth's full time came that she should be delivered; and she brought forth a son. ⁵⁸And her neighbours and her cousins heard how the Lord had shewed great mercy upon her; and they rejoiced with her. ⁵⁹And it came to pass, that on the eighth day they came to circumcise the child; and they called him Zacharias, after the name of his father. ⁶⁰And his mother answered and said, Not *so;* but he shall be called John. ⁶¹And they said unto her, There is none of thy kindred that is called by this name. ⁶²And they made signs to his father, how he would have him called. ⁶³And he asked for a writing table, and wrote, saying, His name is John. And they marvelled all. ⁶⁴And his mouth was opened immediately, and his tongue *loosed,* and he spake, and praised God. ⁶⁵And fear came on all that dwelt round about them: and all these sayings were noised abroad throughout all the hill country of Judaea. ⁶⁶And all they that heard *them* laid *them* up in their hearts, saying, What manner of child shall this be! And the hand of the Lord was with him.

⁶⁷And his father Zacharias was filled with the Holy Ghost, and prophesied, saying,

⁶⁸Blessed *be* the Lord God of Israel; for he hath visited and redeemed his people, ⁶⁹And hath raised up an horn of salvation for us in the house of his servant David; ⁷⁰As he spake by the mouth of his holy prophets, which have been since the world began: ⁷¹That we should be saved from our enemies, and from the hand of all that hate us; ⁷²To perform the mercy *promised* to our fathers, and to remember his holy covenant; ⁷³The oath which he sware to our father Abraham, ⁷⁴That he would grant unto us, that we being delivered out of the hand of our enemies might serve him without fear, ⁷⁵In holiness and righteousness before him, all the days of our life.

⁷⁶And thou, child, shalt be called the prophet of the Highest: for thou shalt go before the face of the Lord to prepare his ways; ⁷⁷To give knowledge of salvation unto his people by the remission of their sins, ⁷⁸Through the tender mercy of our God; whereby the dayspring from on high hath visited us, ⁷⁹To give light to them that sit in darkness and *in* the shadow of death, to guide our feet into the way of peace.

⁸⁰And the child grew, and waxed strong in spirit, and was in the deserts till the day of his shewing unto Israel.

2 And it came to pass in those days, that there went out a decree from Caesar Augustus, that all the world should be taxed. ²(*And* this taxing was first made when Cyrenius was governor of Syria.) ³And all went to be taxed, every one into his own city. ⁴And Joseph also went up from Galilee, out of the city of Nazareth, into Judaea, unto the city of David, which is called Bethlehem; (because he was of the house and lineage of David:) ⁵To be taxed with Mary his espoused wife, being great with child. ⁶And so it was, that, while they were there, the days were accomplished that she should be delivered. ⁷And she brought forth her firstborn son, and wrapped him in swaddling clothes, and laid him in a manger; because there was no room for them in the inn.

⁸And there were in the same country shepherds abiding in the field, keeping watch over their flock by night. ⁹And, lo, the angel of the Lord came upon them, and the glory of the Lord shone round about them: and they were sore afraid. ¹⁰And the angel said unto them, Fear not: for, behold, I bring you good tidings of great joy, which shall be to all people. ¹¹For unto you is born this day in the city of David a Saviour, which is Christ the Lord. ¹²And this *shall be* a sign unto you; Ye shall find the babe wrapped in swaddling clothes, lying in a manger. ¹³And suddenly there was with the angel a multitude of the heavenly host praising God, and saying,

¹⁴Glory to God in the highest, and on earth peace, good will toward men.

¹⁵And it came to pass, as the angels were gone away from them into heaven, the shepherds said one to another, Let us now go even unto Bethlehem, and see this thing which is come to pass, which the Lord hath made known unto us. ¹⁶And they came with haste, and found Mary, and Joseph, and the babe lying in a manger. ¹⁷And when they had seen *it*, they made known abroad the saying which was told them concerning this child. ¹⁸And all they that heard *it* wondered at those things which were told them by the shepherds. ¹⁹But Mary kept all these things, and pondered *them* in her heart. ²⁰And the shepherds returned, glorifying and praising God for all the things that they had heard and seen, as it was told unto them.

²¹And when eight days were accomplished for the circumcising of the child, his name was called JESUS, which was so named of the angel before he was conceived in the womb. ²²And when the days of her purification according to the law of Moses were accomplished, they brought him to Jerusalem, to present *him* to the Lord; ²³(As it is written in the law of the Lord, Every male that openeth the womb shall be called holy to the Lord;) ²⁴And to offer a sacrifice according to that which is said in the law of the Lord, A pair of turtledoves, or two young pigeons.

²⁵And, behold, there was a man in Jerusalem, whose name *was* Simeon; and the same man *was* just and devout, waiting for the consolation of Israel: and the Holy Ghost was upon him. ²⁶And it was revealed unto him by the Holy Ghost, that he should not see death, before he had seen the Lord's Christ. ²⁷And he came by the Spirit into the temple: and when the parents brought in the child Jesus, to do for him after the custom of the law, ²⁸Then took he him up in his arms, and blessed God, and said,

²⁹Lord, now lettest thou thy servant depart in peace, according to thy word: ³⁰For mine eyes have seen thy salvation, ³¹Which thou hast prepared before the face of all people; ³²A light to lighten the Gentiles, and the glory of thy people Israel.

³³And Joseph and his mother marvelled at those things which were spoken of him. ³⁴And Simeon blessed them, and said unto Mary his mother, Behold, this *child* is set for the fall and rising again of many in Israel; and for a sign which shall be spoken against; ³⁵(Yea, a sword shall pierce through thy own soul also,) that the thoughts of many hearts may be revealed.

³⁶And there was one Anna, a prophetess, the daughter of Phanuel, of the tribe of Aser: she was of a great age, and had lived with an husband seven years from her

virginity; [37]And she *was* a widow of about fourscore and four years, which departed not from the temple, but served *God* with fastings and prayers night and day. [38]And she coming in that instant gave thanks likewise unto the Lord, and spake of him to all them that looked for redemption in Jerusalem.

[39]And when they had performed all things according to the law of the Lord, they returned into Galilee, to their own city Nazareth. [40]And the child grew, and waxed strong in spirit, filled with wisdom: and the grace of God was upon him.

[41]Now his parents went to Jerusalem every year at the feast of the passover. [42]And when he was twelve years old, they went up to Jerusalem after the custom of the feast. [43]And when they had fulfilled the days, as they returned, the child Jesus tarried behind in Jerusalem; and Joseph and his mother knew not *of it.* [44]But they, supposing him to have been in the company, went a day's journey; and they sought him among *their* kinsfolk and acquaintance. [45]And when they found him not, they turned back again to Jerusalem, seeking him. [46]And it came to pass, that after three days they found him in the temple, sitting in the midst of the doctors, both hearing them, and asking them questions. [47]And all that heard him were astonished at his understanding and answers. [48]And when they saw him, they were amazed: and his mother said unto him, Son, why hast thou thus dealt with us? behold, thy father and I have sought thee sorrowing. [49]And he said unto them, How is it that ye sought me? wist ye not that I must be about my Father's business? [50]And they understood not the saying which he spake unto them. [51]And he went down with them, and came to Nazareth, and was subject unto them: but his mother kept all these sayings in her heart. [52]And Jesus increased in wisdom and stature, and in favour with God and man.

3 Now in the fifteenth year of the reign of Tiberius Caesar, Pontius Pilate being governor of Judaea, and Herod being tetrarch of Galilee, and his brother Philip tetrarch of Ituraea and of the region of Trachonitis, and Lysanias the tetrarch of Abilene, [2]Annas and Caiaphas being the high priests, the word of God came unto John the son of Zacharias in the wilderness. [3]And he came into all the country about Jordan, preaching the baptism of repentance for the remission of sins; [4]As it is written in the book of the words of Esaias the prophet, saying,

The voice of one crying in the wilderness, Prepare ye the way of the Lord, make his paths straight. [5]Every valley shall be filled, and every mountain and hill shall be brought low; and the crooked shall be made straight, and the rough ways *shall be* made smooth; [6]And all flesh shall see the salvation of God.

[7]Then said he to the multitude that came forth to be baptized of him, O generation of vipers, who hath warned you to flee from the wrath to come? [8]Bring forth therefore fruits worthy of repentance, and begin not to say within yourselves, We have Abraham to *our* father: for I say unto you, That God is able of these stones to raise up children unto Abraham. [9]And now also the axe is laid unto the root of the trees: every tree therefore which bringeth not forth good fruit is hewn down, and cast into the fire. [10]And the people asked him, saying, What shall we do then? [11]He answereth and saith unto them, He that hath two coats, let him impart to him that hath none; and he that hath meat, let him do likewise. [12]Then came also publicans to be baptized, and said unto him, Master, what shall we do? [13]And he said unto them, Exact no more than that which is appointed you. [14]And the soldiers likewise demanded of him, saying, And what shall we do? And he said unto them, Do violence to no man, neither accuse *any* falsely; and be content with your wages. [15]And as the people were in expectation, and all men mused in their hearts of John, whether he were the Christ, or not; [16]John answered, saying unto *them* all, I indeed baptize you with water; but one mightier than I cometh, the latchet of whose shoes I am not worthy to unloose: he shall baptize you with the Holy Ghost and with fire: [17]Whose fan *is* in his hand, and he will throughly purge his floor, and will gather the wheat into his garner; but the chaff he will burn with fire unquenchable.

[18]And many other things in his exhortation preached he unto the people. [19]But Herod the tetrarch, being reproved by him for Herodias his brother Philip's wife, and for all the evils which Herod had done, [20]Added yet this above all, that he shut up John in prison.

[21]Now when all the people were baptized, it came to pass, that Jesus also being baptized, and praying, the heaven was opened, [22]And the Holy Ghost descended in a bodily shape like a dove upon him, and a voice came from heaven, which said, Thou art my beloved Son; in thee I am well pleased.

[23]And Jesus himself began to be about thirty years of age, being (as was supposed) the son of Joseph,

which was *the son* of Heli, [24]Which was *the son* of Matthat, which was *the son* of Levi, which was *the son* of Melchi, which was *the son* of Janna, which was *the son* of Joseph, [25]Which was *the son* of Mattathias, which was *the son* of Amos, which was *the son* of Naum, which was *the son* of Esli, which was *the son* of Nagge, [26]Which was *the son* of Maath, which was *the son* of Mattathias, which was *the son* of Semei, which was *the son* of Joseph, which was *the son* of Juda, [27]Which was *the son* of Joanna, which was *the son* of Rhesa, which was *the son* of Zorobabel, which was *the son* of Salathiel, which was *the son* of Neri, [28]Which was *the son* of Melchi, which was *the son* of Addi, which was *the son* of Cosam, which was *the son* of Elmodam, which was *the son* of Er, [29]Which was *the son* of Jose, which was *the son* of Eliezer, which was *the son* of Jorim, which was *the son* of Matthat, which was *the son* of Levi, [30]Which was *the son* of Simeon, which was *the son* of Juda, which was *the son* of Joseph, which was *the son* of Jonan, which was *the son* of Eliakim, [31]Which was *the son* of Melea, which was *the son* of Menan, which was *the son* of Mattatha, which was *the son* of Nathan, which was *the son* of David, [32]Which was *the son* of Jesse, which was *the son* of Obed, which was *the son* of Booz, which was *the son* of Salmon, which was *the son* of Naasson, [33]Which was *the son* of Aminadab, which was *the son* of Aram, which was *the*

son of Esrom, which was *the son* of Phares, which was *the son* of Juda, [34]Which was *the son* of Jacob, which was *the son* of Isaac, which was *the son* of Abraham, which was *the son* of Thara, which was *the son* of Nachor, [35]Which was *the son* of Saruch, which was *the son* of Ragau, which was *the son* of Phalec, which was *the son* of Heber, which was *the son* of Sala, [36]Which was *the son* of Cainan, which was *the son* of Arphaxad, which was *the son* of Sem, which was *the son* of Noe, which was *the son* of Lamech, [37]Which was *the son* of Mathusala, which was *the son* of Enoch, which was *the son* of Jared, which was *the son* of Maleleel, which was *the son* of Cainan, [38]Which was *the son* of Enos, which was *the son* of Seth, which was *the son* of Adam, which was *the son* of God.

4 And Jesus being full of the Holy Ghost returned from Jordan, and was led by the Spirit into the wilderness, [2]Being forty days tempted of the devil. And in those days he did eat nothing: and when they were ended, he afterward hungered. [3]And the devil said unto him, If thou be the Son of God, command this stone that it be made bread. [4]And Jesus answered him, saying, It is written, That man shall not live by bread alone, but by every word of God. [5]And the devil, taking him up into an high mountain, shewed unto him all the kingdoms of the world in a moment of time. [6]And the devil said unto him, All this power will I give thee, and the glory of them: for that is delivered unto me; and to whomsoever I will I give it. [7]If thou therefore wilt worship me, all shall be thine. [8]And Jesus answered and said unto him, Get thee behind me, Satan: for it is written, Thou shalt worship the Lord thy God, and him only shalt thou serve. [9]And he brought him to Jerusalem, and set him on a pinnacle of the temple, and said unto him, If thou be the Son of God, cast thyself down from hence: [10]For it is written,

He shall give his angels charge over thee, to keep thee: [11]And in *their* hands they shall bear thee up, lest at any time thou dash thy foot against a stone.

[12]And Jesus answering said unto him, It is said, Thou shalt not tempt the Lord thy

God. [13]And when the devil had ended all the temptation, he departed from him for a season.

[14]And Jesus returned in the power of the Spirit into Galilee: and there went out a fame of him through all the region round about. [15]And he taught in their synagogues, being glorified of all.

[16]And he came to Nazareth, where he had been brought up: and, as his custom was, he went into the synagogue on the sabbath day, and stood up for to read. [17]And there was delivered unto him the book of the prophet Esaias. And when he had opened the book, he found the place where it was written,

[18]The Spirit of the Lord is upon me, because he hath anointed me to preach the gospel to the poor; he hath sent me to heal the brokenhearted, to preach deliverance to the captives, and recovering of sight to the blind, to set at liberty them that are bruised, [19]To preach the acceptable year of the Lord.

[20]And he closed the book, and he gave it again to the minister, and sat down. And the eyes of all them that were in the synagogue were fastened on him. [21]And he began to say unto them, This day is this scripture fulfilled in your ears. [22]And all bare him witness, and wondered at the gracious words which proceeded out of his mouth. And they said, Is not this Joseph's son? [23]And he said unto them, Ye will surely say unto me this proverb, Physician, heal thyself: whatsoever we have heard done in Capernaum, do also here in thy country. [24]And he said, Verily I say unto you, No prophet is accepted in his own country. [25]But I tell you of a truth, many widows were in Israel in the days of Elias, when the heaven was shut up three years and six months, when great famine was throughout all the land; [26]But unto none of them was Elias sent, save unto Sarepta, a city of Sidon, unto a woman that was a widow. [27]And many lepers were in Israel in the time of Eliseus the prophet; and none of them was cleansed, saving Naaman the Syrian. [28]And all they in the synagogue, when they heard these things, were filled with wrath, [29]And rose up, and thrust him out of the city, and led him unto the brow of the hill whereon their city was built, that they might cast him down headlong. [30]But he passing through the midst of them went his way, [31]And came down to Capernaum, a city of Galilee, and taught them on the sabbath days. [32]And they were astonished at his doctrine: for his word was with power.

[33]And in the synagogue there was a man, which had a spirit of an unclean devil, and cried out with a loud voice, [34]Saying, Let us alone; what have we to do with thee, thou Jesus of Nazareth? art thou come to destroy us? I know thee who thou art; the Holy One of God. [35]And Jesus rebuked him, saying, Hold thy peace, and come out of him. And when the devil had thrown him in the midst, he came out of him, and hurt him not. [36]And they were all amazed, and spake among themselves, saying, What a word is this! for with authority and power he commandeth the unclean spirits, and they come out. [37]And the fame of him went out into every place of the country round about.

[38]And he arose out of the synagogue, and entered into Simon's house. And Simon's wife's mother was taken with a great fever; and they besought him for her. [39]And he stood over her, and rebuked the fever; and it left her: and immediately she arose and ministered unto them.

[40]Now when the sun was setting, all they that had any sick with divers diseases brought them unto him; and he laid his hands on every one of them, and healed them. [41]And devils also came out of many, crying out, and saying, Thou art Christ the Son of God. And he rebuking them suffered them not to speak: for they knew that he was Christ. [42]And when it was day, he departed and went into a desert place: and the people sought him, and came unto him, and stayed him, that he should not depart from them. [43]And he said unto them, I must preach the kingdom of God to other cities also: for therefore am I sent. [44]And he preached in the synagogues of Galilee.

5 And it came to pass, that, as the people pressed upon him to hear the word of God, he stood by the lake of Gennesaret, [2]And saw two ships standing by the lake: but the fishermen were gone out of them,

and were washing *their* nets. ³And he entered into one of the ships, which was Simon's, and prayed him that he would thrust out a little from the land. And he sat down, and taught the people out of the ship. ⁴Now when he had left speaking, he said unto Simon, Launch out into the deep, and let down your nets for a draught. ⁵And Simon answering said unto him, Master, we have toiled all the night, and have taken nothing: nevertheless at thy word I will let down the net. ⁶And when they had this done, they inclosed a great multitude of fishes: and their net brake. ⁷And they beckoned unto *their* partners, which were in the other ship, that they should come and help them. And they came, and filled both the ships, so that they began to sink. ⁸When Simon Peter saw *it,* he fell down at Jesus' knees, saying, Depart from me; for I am a sinful man, O Lord. ⁹For he was astonished, and all that were with him, at the draught of the fishes which they had taken: ¹⁰And so *was* also James, and John, the sons of Zebedee, which were partners with Simon. And Jesus said unto Simon, Fear not; from henceforth thou shalt catch men. ¹¹And when they had brought their ships to land, they forsook all, and followed him.

¹²And it came to pass, when he was in a certain city, behold a man full of leprosy: who seeing Jesus fell on *his* face, and besought him, saying, Lord, if thou wilt, thou canst make me clean. ¹³And he put forth *his* hand, and touched him, saying, I will: be thou clean. And immediately the leprosy departed from him. ¹⁴And he charged him to tell no man: but go, and shew thyself to the priest, and offer for thy cleansing, according as Moses commanded, for a testimony unto them. ¹⁵But so much the more went there a fame abroad of him: and great multitudes came together to hear, and to be healed by him of their infirmities.

¹⁶And he withdrew himself into the wilderness, and prayed. ¹⁷And it came to pass on a certain day, as he was teaching, that there were Pharisees and doctors of the law sitting by, which were come out of every town of Galilee, and Judaea, and Jerusalem: and the power of the Lord was *present* to heal them. ¹⁸And, behold, men brought in a bed a man which was taken with a palsy: and they sought *means* to bring him in, and to lay *him* before him. ¹⁹And when they could not find by what *way* they might bring him in because of the multitude, they went upon the housetop, and let him down through the tiling with *his* couch into the midst before Jesus. ²⁰And when he saw their faith, he said unto him, Man, thy sins are forgiven thee. ²¹And the scribes and the Pharisees began to reason, saying, Who is this which speaketh blasphemies? Who can forgive sins, but God alone? ²²But when Jesus perceived their thoughts, he answering said unto them, What reason ye in your hearts? ²³Whether is easier, to say, Thy sins be forgiven thee; or to say, Rise up and walk? ²⁴But that ye may know that the Son of man hath power upon earth to forgive sins, (he said unto the sick of the palsy,) I say unto thee, Arise, and take up thy couch, and go into thine house. ²⁵And immediately he rose up before them, and took up that whereon he lay, and departed to his own house, glorifying God. ²⁶And they were all amazed, and they glorified God, and were filled with fear, saying, We have seen strange things to day.

²⁷And after these things he went forth, and saw a publican, named Levi, sitting at the receipt of custom: and he said unto him, Follow me. ²⁸And he left all, rose up, and followed him. ²⁹And Levi made him a great feast in his own house: and there was a great company of publicans and of others that sat down with them. ³⁰But their scribes and Pharisees murmured against his disciples, saying, Why do ye eat and drink with publicans and sinners? ³¹And Jesus answering said unto them, They that are whole need not a physician; but they that are sick. ³²I came not to call the righteous, but sinners to repentance.

³³And they said unto him, Why do the disciples of John fast often, and make prayers, and likewise *the disciples* of the Pharisees; but thine eat and drink? ³⁴And he said unto them, Can ye make the children of the bridechamber fast, while the bridegroom is with them? ³⁵But the days will come, when the bridegroom shall be taken away from them, and then shall they fast in those days.

³⁶And he spake also a parable unto them; No man putteth a piece of a new garment upon an old; if otherwise, then both the new maketh a rent, and the piece that was *taken* out of the new agreeth not with the old. ³⁷And no man putteth new wine into old bottles; else the new wine will burst the bottles, and be spilled, and the bottles shall perish. ³⁸But new wine must be put into new bottles; and both are preserved. ³⁹No man also having drunk old *wine* straightway desireth new: for he saith, The old is better.

6 And it came to pass on the second sabbath after the first, that he went through the corn fields; and his disciples plucked the ears of corn, and did eat, rubbing *them* in *their* hands. ²And certain of the Pharisees said unto them, Why do ye that which is not lawful to do on the sabbath days? ³And Jesus answering them said, Have ye not read so much as this, what David did, when himself was an hungred, and they which were with him; ⁴How he went into the house of God, and did take and eat the shewbread, and gave also to them that were with him; which it is not lawful to eat but for the priests alone? ⁵And he said unto them, That the Son of man is Lord also of the sabbath.

⁶And it came to pass also on another sabbath, that he entered into the synagogue and taught: and there was a man whose right hand was withered. ⁷And the scribes and Pharisees watched him, whether he would heal on the sabbath day; that they might find an accusation against him. ⁸But he knew their thoughts, and said to the man which had the withered hand, Rise up, and stand forth in the midst. And he arose and stood forth. ⁹Then said Jesus unto them, I will ask you one thing; Is it lawful on the sabbath days to do good, or to do evil? to save life, or to destroy *it?* ¹⁰And looking round about upon them all, he said unto the man, Stretch forth thy hand. And he did so: and his hand was restored whole as the other. ¹¹And they were filled with madness; and communed one with another what they might do to Jesus. ¹²And it came to pass in those days, that he went out into a mountain to pray, and continued all night in prayer to God.

¹³And when it was day, he called *unto him* his disciples: and of them he chose twelve, whom also he named apostles; ¹⁴Simon, (whom he also named Peter,) and Andrew his brother, James and John, Philip and Bartholomew, ¹⁵Matthew and Thomas, James the *son* of Alphaeus, and Simon called Zelotes, ¹⁶And Judas *the brother* of James, and Judas Iscariot, which also was the traitor.

¹⁷And he came down with them, and stood in the plain, and the company of his disciples, and a great multitude of people out of all Judaea and Jerusalem, and from the sea coast of Tyre and Sidon, which came to hear him, and to be healed of their diseases; ¹⁸And they that were vexed with unclean spirits: and they were healed. ¹⁹And the whole multitude sought to touch him: for there went virtue out of him, and healed *them* all.

²⁰And he lifted up his eyes on his disciples, and said,

Blessed *be ye* poor: for yours is the kingdom of God. ²¹Blessed *are ye* that hunger now: for ye shall be filled. Blessed *are ye* that weep now: for ye shall laugh. ²²Blessed are ye, when men shall hate you, and when they shall separate you *from their company,* and shall reproach *you,* and cast out your name as evil, for the Son of man's sake.

²³Rejoice ye in that day, and leap for joy: for, behold, your reward *is* great in heaven: for in the like manner did their fathers unto the prophets.

²⁴But woe unto you that are rich! for ye have received your consolation. ²⁵Woe unto you that are full! for ye shall hunger. Woe unto you that laugh now! for ye shall mourn and weep. ²⁶Woe unto you, when all men shall speak well of you! for so did their fathers to the false prophets.

²⁷But I say unto you which hear, Love your enemies, do good to them which hate you, ²⁸Bless them that curse you, and pray for them which despitefully use you. ²⁹And unto him that smiteth thee on the *one* cheek offer also the other; and him that taketh away thy cloke forbid not *to take thy* coat also. ³⁰Give to every man that asketh of thee; and of him that taketh

away thy goods ask *them* not again. ³¹And as ye would that men should do to you, do ye also to them likewise. ³²For if ye love them which love you, what thank have ye? for sinners also love those that love them. ³³And if ye do good to them which do good to you, what thank have ye? for sinners also do even the same. ³⁴And if ye lend *to them* of whom ye hope to receive, what thank have ye? for sinners also lend to sinners, to receive as much again. ³⁵But love ye your enemies, and do good, and lend, hoping for nothing again; and your reward shall be great, and ye shall be the children of the Highest: for he is kind unto the unthankful and *to* the evil. ³⁶Be ye therefore merciful, as your Father also is merciful. ³⁷Judge not, and ye shall not be judged: condemn not, and ye shall not be condemned: forgive, and ye shall be forgiven: ³⁸Give, and it shall be given unto you; good measure, pressed down, and shaken together, and running over, shall men give into your bosom. For with the same measure that ye mete withal it shall be measured to you again. ³⁹And he spake a parable unto them, Can the blind lead the blind? shall they not both fall into the ditch? ⁴⁰The disciple is not above his master: but every one that is perfect shall be as his master. ⁴¹And why beholdest thou the mote that is in thy brother's eye, but perceivest not the beam that is in thine own eye? ⁴²Either how canst thou say to thy brother, Brother, let me pull out the mote that is in thine eye, when thou thyself beholdest not the beam that is in thine own eye? Thou hypocrite, cast out first the beam out of thine own eye, and then shalt thou see clearly to pull out the mote that is in thy brother's eye. ⁴³For a good tree bringeth not forth corrupt fruit; neither doth a corrupt tree bring forth good fruit. ⁴⁴For every tree is known by his own fruit. For of thorns men do not gather figs, nor of a bramble bush gather they grapes. ⁴⁵A good man out of the good treasure of his heart bringeth forth that which is good; and an evil man out of the evil treasure of his heart bringeth forth that which is evil: for of the abundance of the heart his mouth speaketh.

⁴⁶And why call ye me, Lord, Lord, and do not the things which I say? ⁴⁷Whosoever cometh to me, and heareth my sayings, and doeth them, I will shew you to whom he is like: ⁴⁸He is like a man which built an house, and digged deep, and laid the foundation on a rock: and when the flood arose, the stream beat vehemently upon that house, and could not shake it: for it was founded upon a rock. ⁴⁹But he that heareth, and doeth not, is like a man that without a foundation built an house upon the earth; against which the stream did beat vehemently, and immediately it fell; and the ruin of that house was great.

7 Now when he had ended all his sayings in the audience of the people, he entered into Capernaum. ²And a certain centurion's servant, who was dear unto him, was sick, and ready to die. ³And when he heard of Jesus, he sent unto him the elders of the Jews, beseeching him that he would come and heal his servant. ⁴And when they came to Jesus, they besought him instantly, saying, That he was worthy for whom he should do this: ⁵For he loveth our nation, and he hath built us a synagogue. ⁶Then Jesus went with them. And when he was now not far from the house, the centurion sent friends to him, saying unto him, Lord, trouble not thyself: for I am not worthy that thou shouldest enter under my roof: ⁷Wherefore neither thought I myself worthy to come unto thee: but say in a word, and my servant shall be healed. ⁸For I also am a man set under authority, having under me soldiers, and I say unto one, Go, and he goeth; and to another, Come, and he cometh; and to my servant, Do this, and he doeth *it*. ⁹When Jesus heard these things, he marvelled at him, and turned him about, and said unto the people that followed him, I say unto you, I have not found so great faith, no, not in Israel. ¹⁰And they that were sent, returning to the house, found the servant whole that had been sick.

¹¹And it came to pass the day after, that he went into a city called Nain; and many of his disciples went with him, and much people. ¹²Now when he came nigh to the gate of the city, behold, there was a dead man carried out, the only son of his mother, and she was a widow: and much people of the city was with her. ¹³And when the Lord saw her, he had compassion on her, and said unto her, Weep not. ¹⁴And he came and touched

the bier: and they that bare *him* stood still. And he said, Young man, I say unto thee, Arise. [15]And he that was dead sat up, and began to speak. And he delivered him to his mother. [16]And there came a fear on all: and they glorified God, saying, That a great prophet is risen up among us; and, That God hath visited his people. [17]And this rumour of him went forth throughout all Judaea, and throughout all the region round about. [18]And the disciples of John shewed him of all these things.

[19]And John calling *unto him* two of his disciples sent *them* to Jesus, saying, Art thou he that should come? or look we for another? [20]When the men were come unto him, they said, John Baptist hath sent us unto thee, saying, Art thou he that should come? or look we for another? [21]And in that same hour he cured many of *their* infirmities and plagues, and of evil spirits; and unto many *that were* blind he gave sight. [22]Then Jesus answering said unto them, Go your way, and tell John what things ye have seen and heard; how that the blind see, the lame walk, the lepers are cleansed, the deaf hear, the dead are raised, to the poor the gospel is preached. [23]And blessed is *he*, whosoever shall not be offended in me.

[24]And when the messengers of John were departed, he began to speak unto the people concerning John, What went ye out into the wilderness for to see? A reed shaken with the wind? [25]But what went ye out for to see? A man clothed in soft raiment? Behold, they which are gorgeously apparelled, and live delicately, are in kings courts. [26]But what went ye out for to see? A prophet? Yea, I say unto you, and much more than a prophet. [27]This is *he*, of whom it is written,

Behold, I send my messenger before thy face, which shall prepare thy way before thee.

[28]For I say unto you, Among those that are born of women there is not a greater prophet than John the Baptist: but he that is least in the kingdom of God is greater than he. [29]And all the people that heard *him*, and the publicans, justified God, being baptized with the baptism of John. [30]But the Pharisees and lawyers rejected the counsel of God against themselves, being not baptized of him.

[31]And the Lord said, Whereunto then shall I liken the men of this generation? and to what are they like? [32]They are like unto children sitting in the marketplace, and calling one to another, and saying,

We have piped unto you, and ye have not danced; we have mourned to you, and ye have not wept.

[33]For John the Baptist came neither eating bread nor drinking wine; and ye say, He hath a devil. [34]The Son of man is come eating and drinking; and ye say, Behold a gluttonous man, and a winebibber, a friend of publicans and sinners! [35]But wisdom is justified of all her children.

[36]And one of the Pharisees desired him that he would eat with him. And he went into the Pharisee's house, and sat down to meat. [37]And, behold, a woman in the city, which was a sinner, when she knew that *Jesus* sat at meat in the Pharisee's house, brought an alabaster box of ointment, [38]And stood at his feet behind *him* weeping, and began to wash his feet with tears, and did wipe *them* with the hairs of her head, and kissed his feet, and anointed *them* with the ointment. [39]Now when the Pharisee which had bidden him saw *it*, he spake within himself, saying, This man, if he were a prophet, would have known who and what manner of woman *this is* that toucheth him: for she is a sinner. [40]And Jesus answering said unto him, Simon, I have somewhat to say unto thee. And he saith, Master, say on. [41]There was a certain creditor which had two debtors: the one owed five hundred pence, and the other fifty. [42]And when they had nothing to pay, he frankly forgave them both. Tell me therefore, which of them will love him most? [43]Simon answered and said, I suppose that *he*, to whom he forgave most. And he said unto him, Thou hast rightly judged. [44]And he turned to the woman, and said unto Simon, Seest thou this woman? I entered into thine house, thou gavest me no water for my feet: but she hath washed my feet with tears, and wiped *them* with the hairs of her head. [45]Thou gavest me no kiss: but this woman since the time I came in hath not

ceased to kiss my feet. ⁴⁶My head with oil thou didst not anoint: but this woman hath anointed my feet with ointment. ⁴⁷Wherefore I say unto thee, Her sins, which are many, are forgiven; for she loved much: but to whom little is forgiven, *the same* loveth little. ⁴⁸And he said unto her, Thy sins are forgiven. ⁴⁹And they that sat at meat with him began to say within themselves, Who is this that forgiveth sins also? ⁵⁰And he said to the woman, Thy faith hath saved thee; go in peace.

8 And it came to pass afterward, that he went throughout every city and village, preaching and shewing the glad tidings of the kingdom of God: and the twelve *were* with him, ²And certain women, which had been healed of evil spirits and infirmities, Mary called Magdalene, out of whom went seven devils, ³And Joanna the wife of Chuza Herod's steward, and Susanna, and many others, which ministered unto him of their substance.

⁴And when much people were gathered together, and were come to him out of every city, he spake by a parable: ⁵A sower went out to sow his seed: and as he sowed, some fell by the way side; and it was trodden down, and the fowls of the air devoured it. ⁶And some fell upon a rock; and as soon as it was sprung up, it withered away, because it lacked moisture. ⁷And some fell among thorns; and the thorns sprang up with it, and choked it. ⁸And other fell on good ground, and sprang up, and bare fruit an hundredfold. And when he had said these things, he cried, He that hath ears to hear, let him hear. ⁹And his disciples asked him, saying, What might this parable be? ¹⁰And he said, Unto you it is given to know the mysteries of the kingdom of God: but to others in parables;

that seeing they might not see, and hearing they might not understand.

¹¹Now the parable is this: The seed is the word of God. ¹²Those by the way side are they that hear; then cometh the devil, and taketh away the word out of their hearts, lest they should believe and be saved. ¹³They on the rock *are they,* which, when they hear, receive the word with joy; and these have no root, which for a while

believe, and in time of temptation fall away. ¹⁴And that which fell among thorns are they, which, when they have heard, go forth, and are choked with cares and riches and pleasures of *this* life, and bring no fruit to perfection. ¹⁵But that on the good ground are they, which in an honest and good heart, having heard the word, keep *it,* and bring forth fruit with patience.

¹⁶No man, when he hath lighted a candle, covereth it with a vessel, or putteth *it* under a bed; but setteth *it* on a candlestick, that they which enter in may see the light. ¹⁷For nothing is secret, that shall not be made manifest; neither *any thing* hid, that shall not be known and come abroad. ¹⁸Take heed therefore how ye hear: for whosoever hath, to him shall be given; and whosoever hath not, from him shall be taken even that which he seemeth to have.

¹⁹Then came to him *his* mother and his brethren, and could not come at him for the press. ²⁰And it was told him *by certain* which said, Thy mother and thy brethren stand without, desiring to see thee. ²¹And he answered and said unto them, My mother and my brethren are these which hear the word of God, and do it.

²²Now it came to pass on a certain day, that he went into a ship with his disciples: and he said unto them, Let us go over unto the other side of the lake. And they launched forth. ²³But as they sailed he fell asleep: and there came down a storm of wind on the lake; and they were filled *with water,* and were in jeopardy. ²⁴And they came to him, and awoke him, saying, Master, master, we perish. Then he arose, and rebuked the wind and the raging of the water: and they ceased, and there was a calm. ²⁵And he said unto them, Where is your faith? And they being afraid wondered, saying one to another, What manner of man is this! for he commandeth even the winds and water, and they obey him.

²⁶And they arrived at the country of the Gadarenes, which is over against Galilee. ²⁷And when he went forth to land, there met him out of the city a certain man, which had devils long time, and ware no clothes, neither abode in *any* house, but in the tombs. ²⁸When he saw Jesus, he cried out, and fell down before him, and with

a loud voice said, What have I to do with thee, Jesus, *thou* Son of God most high? I beseech thee, torment me not. [29](For he had commanded the unclean spirit to come out of the man. For oftentimes it had caught him: and he was kept bound with chains and in fetters; and he brake the bands, and was driven of the devil into the wilderness.) [30]And Jesus asked him, saying, What is thy name? And he said, Legion: because many devils were entered into him. [31]And they besought him that he would not command them to go out into the deep. [32]And there was there an herd of many swine feeding on the mountain: and they besought him that he would suffer them to enter into them. And he suffered them. [33]Then went the devils out of the man, and entered into the swine: and the herd ran violently down a steep place into the lake, and were choked. [34]When they that fed *them* saw what was done, they fled, and went and told *it* in the city and in the country. [35]Then they went out to see what was done; and came to Jesus, and found the man, out of whom the devils were departed, sitting at the feet of Jesus, clothed, and in his right mind: and they were afraid. [36]They also which saw *it* told them by what means he that was possessed of the devils was healed.

[37]Then the whole multitude of the country of the Gadarenes round about besought him to depart from them; for they were taken with great fear: and he went up into the ship, and returned back again. [38]Now the man out of whom the devils were departed besought him that he might be with him: but Jesus sent him away, saying, [39]Return to thine own house, and shew how great things God hath done unto thee. And he went his way, and published throughout the whole city how great things Jesus had done unto him. [40]And it came to pass, that, when Jesus was returned, the people *gladly* received him: for they were all waiting for him. [41]And, behold, there came a man named Jairus, and he was a ruler of the synagogue: and he fell down at Jesus' feet, and besought him that he would come into his house: [42]For he had one only daughter, about twelve years of age, and she lay a dying. But as he went the people thronged him.

[43]And a woman having an issue of blood twelve years, which had spent all her living upon physicians, neither could be healed of any, [44]Came behind *him,* and touched the border of his garment: and immediately her issue of blood stanched. [45]And Jesus said, Who touched me? When all denied, Peter and they that were with him said, Master, the multitude throng thee and press *thee,* and sayest thou, Who touched me? [46]And Jesus said, Somebody hath touched me: for I perceive that virtue is gone out of me. [47]And when the woman saw that she was not hid, she came trembling, and falling down before him, she declared unto him before all the people for what cause she had touched him and how she was healed immediately. [48]And he said unto her, Daughter, be of good comfort: thy faith hath made thee whole; go in peace.

[49]While he yet spake, there cometh one from the ruler of the synagogue's *house,* saying to him, Thy daughter is dead; trouble not the Master. [50]But when Jesus heard *it,* he answered him, saying, Fear not: believe only, and she shall be made whole. [51]And when he came into the house, he suffered no man to go in, save Peter, and James, and John, and the father and the mother of the maiden. [52]And all wept, and bewailed her: but he said, Weep not; she is not dead, but sleepeth. [53]And they laughed him to scorn, knowing that she was dead. [54]And he put them all out, and took her by the hand, and called, saying, Maid, arise. [55]And her spirit came again, and she arose straightway: and he commanded to give her meat. [56]And her parents were astonished: but he charged them that they should tell no man what was done.

9 Then he called his twelve disciples together, and gave them power and authority over all devils, and to cure diseases. [2]And he sent them to preach the kingdom of God, and to heal the sick. [3]And he said unto them, Take nothing for *your* journey, neither staves, nor scrip, neither bread, neither money; neither have two coats apiece. [4]And whatsoever house ye enter into, there abide, and thence depart. [5]And whosoever will not receive you, when ye go out of that city, shake off the very dust from your feet for a testimony against them. [6]And they

departed, and went through the towns, preaching the gospel, and healing every where.

⁷Now Herod the tetrarch heard of all that was done by him: and he was perplexed, because that it was said of some, that John was risen from the dead; ⁸And of some, that Elias had appeared; and of others, that one of the old prophets was risen again. ⁹And Herod said, John have I beheaded: but who is this, of whom I hear such things? And he desired to see him.

¹⁰And the apostles, when they were returned, told him all that they had done. And he took them, and went aside privately into a desert place belonging to the city called Bethsaida. ¹¹And the people, when they knew *it*, followed him: and he received them, and spake unto them of the kingdom of God, and healed them that had need of healing. ¹²And when the day began to wear away, then came the twelve, and said unto him, Send the multitude away, that they may go into the towns and country round about, and lodge, and get victuals: for we are here in a desert place. ¹³But he said unto them, Give ye them to eat. And they said, We have no more but five loaves and two fishes; except we should go and buy meat for all this people. ¹⁴For they were about five thousand men. And he said to his disciples, Make them sit down by fifties in a company. ¹⁵And they did so, and made them all sit down. ¹⁶Then he took the five loaves and the two fishes, and looking up to heaven, he blessed them, and brake, and gave to the disciples to set before the multitude. ¹⁷And they did eat, and were all filled: and there was taken up of fragments that remained to them twelve baskets.

¹⁸And it came to pass, as he was alone praying, his disciples were with him: and he asked them, saying, Whom say the people that I am? ¹⁹They answering said, John the Baptist; but some *say*, Elias; and others *say*, that one of the old prophets is risen again. ²⁰He said unto them, But whom say ye that I am? Peter answering said, The Christ of God. ²¹And he straitly charged them, and commanded *them* to tell no man that thing; ²²Saying, The Son of man must suffer many things, and be rejected of the elders and chief priests and scribes, and be slain, and be raised the third day.

²³And he said to *them* all, If any *man* will come after me, let him deny himself, and take up his cross daily, and follow me. ²⁴For whosoever will save his life shall lose it: but whosoever will lose his life for my sake, the same shall save it. ²⁵For what is a man advantaged, if he gain the whole world, and lose himself, or be cast away? ²⁶For whosoever shall be ashamed of me and of my words, of him shall the Son of man be ashamed, when he shall come in his own glory, and *in his* Father's, and of the holy angels. ²⁷But I tell you of a truth, there be some standing here, which shall not taste of death, till they see the kingdom of God.

²⁸And it came to pass about an eight days after these sayings, he took Peter and John and James, and went up into a mountain to pray. ²⁹And as he prayed, the fashion of his countenance was altered, and his raiment *was* white *and* glistering. ³⁰And, behold, there talked with him two men, which were Moses and Elias: ³¹Who appeared in glory, and spake of his decease which he should accomplish at Jerusalem. ³²But Peter and they that were with him were heavy with sleep: and when they were awake, they saw his glory, and the two men that stood with him. ³³And it came to pass, as they departed from him, Peter said unto Jesus, Master, it is good for us to be here: and let us make three tabernacles; one for thee, and one for Moses, and one for Elias: not knowing what he said. ³⁴While he thus spake, there came a cloud, and overshadowed them: and they feared as they entered into the cloud. ³⁵And there came a voice out of the cloud, saying, This is my beloved Son: hear him. ³⁶And when the voice was past, Jesus was found alone. And they kept *it* close, and told no man in those days any of those things which they had seen.

³⁷And it came to pass, that on the next day, when they were come down from the hill, much people met him. ³⁸And, behold, a man of the company cried out, saying, Master, I beseech thee, look upon my son: for he is mine only child. ³⁹And, lo, a spirit taketh him, and he suddenly crieth out; and it teareth him that he foameth again, and bruising him hardly departeth from

him. [40]And I besought thy disciples to cast him out; and they could not. [41]And Jesus answering said, O faithless and perverse generation, how long shall I be with you, and suffer you? Bring thy son hither. [42]And as he was yet a coming, the devil threw him down, and tare *him*. And Jesus rebuked the unclean spirit, and healed the child, and delivered him again to his father.

[43]And they were all amazed at the mighty power of God. But while they wondered every one at all things which Jesus did, he said unto his disciples, [44]Let these sayings sink down into your ears: for the Son of man shall be delivered into the hands of men. [45]But they understood not this saying, and it was hid from them, that they perceived it not: and they feared to ask him of that saying.

[46]Then there arose a reasoning among them, which of them should be greatest. [47]And Jesus, perceiving the thought of their heart, took a child, and set him by him, [48]And said unto them, Whosoever shall receive this child in my name receiveth me: and whosoever shall receive me receiveth him that sent me: for he that is least among you all, the same shall be great.

[49]And John answered and said, Master, we saw one casting out devils in thy name; and we forbad him, because he followeth not with us. [50]And Jesus said unto him, Forbid *him* not: for he that is not against us is for us.

[51]And it came to pass, when the time was come that he should be received up, he stedfastly set his face to go to Jerusalem, [52]And sent messengers before his face: and they went, and entered into a village of the Samaritans, to make ready for him. [53]And they did not receive him, because his face was as though he would go to Jerusalem. [54]And when his disciples James and John saw *this,* they said, Lord, wilt thou that we command fire to come down from heaven, and consume them, even as Elias did? [55]But he turned, and rebuked them, and said, Ye know not what manner of spirit ye are of. [56]For the Son of man is not come to destroy men's lives, but to save *them*. And they went to another village.

[57]And it came to pass, that, as they went in the way, a certain *man* said unto him, Lord, I will follow thee whithersoever thou goest. [58]And Jesus said unto him, Foxes have holes, and birds of the air *have* nests; but the Son of man hath not where to lay *his* head. [59]And he said unto another, Follow me. But he said, Lord, suffer me first to go and bury my father. [60]Jesus said unto him, Let the dead bury their dead: but go thou and preach the kingdom of God. [61]And another also said, Lord, I will follow thee; but let me first go bid them farewell, which are at home at my house. [62]And Jesus said unto him, No man, having put his hand to the plough, and looking back, is fit for the kingdom of God.

10 After these things the Lord appointed other seventy also, and sent them two and two before his face into every city and place, whither he himself would come. [2]Therefore said he unto them, The harvest truly *is* great, but the labourers *are* few: pray ye therefore the Lord of the harvest, that he would send forth labourers into his harvest. [3]Go your ways: behold, I send you forth as lambs among wolves. [4]Carry neither purse, nor scrip, nor shoes: and salute no man by the way. [5]And into whatsoever house ye enter, first say, Peace *be* to this house. [6]And if the son of peace be there, your peace shall rest upon it: if not, it shall turn to you again. [7]And in the same house remain, eating and drinking such things as they give: for the labourer is worthy of his hire. Go not from house to house. [8]And into whatsoever city ye enter, and they receive you, eat such things as are set before you: [9]And heal the sick that are therein, and say unto them, The kingdom of God is come nigh unto you. [10]But into whatsoever city ye enter, and they receive you not, go your ways out into the streets of the same, and say, [11]Even the very dust of your city, which cleaveth on us, we do wipe off against you: notwithstanding be ye sure of this, that the kingdom of God is come nigh unto you. [12]But I say unto you, that it shall be more tolerable in that day for Sodom, than for that city. [13]Woe unto thee, Chorazin! woe unto thee, Bethsaida! for if the mighty works had been done in Tyre and Sidon, which have been done in you, they had a great while ago repented, sitting in sackcloth and ashes. [14]But it shall be more tolerable for Tyre and Sidon at the judgment, than for you. [15]And thou, Capernaum, which art exalted to heaven, shalt be thrust down to hell. [16]He that heareth you heareth me; and he that despiseth you despiseth me; and he that despiseth me despiseth him that sent me.

[17]And the seventy returned again with joy, saying, Lord, even the devils are subject unto us through thy name. [18]And he said unto them, I beheld Satan as lightning fall from heaven. [19]Behold, I give unto you power to tread on serpents and scorpions, and over all the power of the enemy: and nothing shall by any means hurt you. [20]Notwithstanding in this rejoice not, that the spirits are subject unto you; but rather rejoice, because your names are written in heaven.

[21]In that hour Jesus rejoiced in spirit, and said, I thank thee, O Father, Lord of heaven and earth, that thou hast hid these things from the wise and prudent, and hast revealed them unto babes: even so, Father; for so it seemed good in thy sight. [22]All things are delivered to me of my Father: and no man knoweth who the Son is, but the Father; and who the Father is, but the Son, and *he* to whom the Son will reveal *him*.

[23]And he turned him unto *his* disciples, and said privately, Blessed *are* the eyes which see the things that ye see: [24]For I tell you, that many prophets and kings have desired to see those things which ye see, and have not seen *them;* and to hear those things which ye hear, and have not heard *them.*

[25]And, behold, a certain lawyer stood up, and tempted him, saying, Master, what shall I do to inherit eternal life? [26]He said unto him, What is written in the law? how readest thou? [27]And he answering said, Thou shalt love the Lord thy God with all thy heart, and with all thy soul, and with all thy strength, and with all thy mind; and thy neighbour as thyself. [28]And he said unto him, Thou hast answered right: this do, and thou shalt live. [29]But he, willing to justify himself, said unto Jesus, And who is my neighbour? [30]And Jesus answering said, A certain *man* went down from Je-

rusalem to Jericho, and fell among thieves, which stripped him of his raiment, and wounded *him,* and departed, leaving *him* half dead. [31]And by chance there came down a certain priest that way: and when he saw him, he passed by on the other side. [32]And likewise a Levite, when he was at the place, came and looked *on him,* and passed by on the other side. [33]But a certain Samaritan, as he journeyed, came where he was: and when he saw him, he had compassion *on him,* [34]And went to *him,* and bound up his wounds, pouring in oil and wine, and set him on his own beast, and brought him to an inn, and took care of him. [35]And on the morrow when he departed, he took out two pence, and gave *them* to the host, and said unto him, Take care of him; and whatsoever thou spendest more, when I come again, I will repay thee. [36]Which now of these three, thinkest thou, was neighbour unto him that fell among the thieves? [37]And he said, He that shewed mercy on him. Then said Jesus unto him, Go, and do thou likewise.

[38]Now it came to pass, as they went, that he entered into a certain village: and a certain woman named Martha received him into her house. [39]And she had a sister called Mary, which also sat at Jesus' feet, and heard his word. [40]But Martha was cumbered about much serving, and came to him, and said, Lord, dost thou not care that my sister hath left me to serve alone? bid her therefore that she help me. [41]And Jesus answered and said unto her, Martha, Martha, thou art careful and troubled about many things: [42]But one thing is needful: and Mary hath chosen that good part, which shall not be taken away from her.

11 And it came to pass, that, as he was praying in a certain place, when he ceased, one of his disciples said unto him, Lord, teach us to pray, as John also taught his disciples. [2]And he said unto them, When ye pray, say,

Our Father which art in heaven, Hallowed be thy name. Thy kingdom come. Thy will be done, as in heaven, so in earth. [3]Give us day by day our daily bread. [4]And forgive us our sins; for we also forgive every one that is indebted to us. And lead us not into temptation; but deliver us from evil.

⁵And he said unto them, Which of you shall have a friend, and shall go unto him at midnight, and say unto him, Friend, lend me three loaves; ⁶For a friend of mine in his journey is come to me, and I have nothing to set before him? ⁷And he from within shall answer and say, Trouble me not: the door is now shut, and my children are with me in bed; I cannot rise and give thee. ⁸I say unto you, Though he will not rise and give him, because he is his friend, yet because of his importunity he will rise and give him as many as he needeth. ⁹And I say unto you, Ask, and it shall be given you; seek, and ye shall find; knock, and it shall be opened unto you. ¹⁰For every one that asketh receiveth; and he that seeketh findeth; and to him that knocketh it shall be opened. ¹¹If a son shall ask bread of any of you that is a father, will he give him a stone? or if *he ask* a fish, will he for a fish give him a serpent? ¹²Or if he shall ask an egg, will he offer him a scorpion? ¹³If ye then, being evil, know how to give good gifts unto your children: how much more shall *your* heavenly Father give the Holy Spirit to them that ask him?

¹⁴And he was casting out a devil, and it was dumb. And it came to pass, when the devil was gone out, the dumb spake; and the people wondered. ¹⁵But some of them said, He casteth out devils through Beelzebub the chief of the devils. ¹⁶And others, tempting *him,* sought of him a sign from heaven. ¹⁷But he, knowing their thoughts, said unto them, Every kingdom divided against itself is brought to desolation; and a house *divided* against a house falleth. ¹⁸If Satan also be divided against himself, how shall his kingdom stand? because ye say that I cast out devils through Beelzebub. ¹⁹And if I by Beelzebub cast out devils, by whom do your sons cast *them* out? therefore shall they be your judges. ²⁰But if I with the finger of God cast out devils, no doubt the kingdom of God is come upon you. ²¹When a strong man armed keepeth his palace, his goods are in peace: ²²But when a stronger than he shall come upon him, and overcome him, he taketh from him all his armour wherein he trusted, and divid-

eth his spoils. ²³He that is not with me is against me: and he that gathereth not with me scattereth.

²⁴When the unclean spirit is gone out of a man, he walketh through dry places, seeking rest; and finding none, he saith, I will return unto my house whence I came out. ²⁵And when he cometh, he findeth *it* swept and garnished. ²⁶Then goeth he, and taketh *to him* seven other spirits more wicked than himself; and they enter in, and dwell there: and the last *state* of that man is worse than the first.

²⁷And it came to pass, as he spake these things, a certain woman of the company lifted up her voice, and said unto him, Blessed is the womb that bare thee, and the paps which thou hast sucked. ²⁸But he said, Yea rather, blessed *are* they that hear the word of God, and keep it.

²⁹And when the people were gathered thick together, he began to say, This is an evil generation: they seek a sign; and there shall no sign be given it, but the sign of Jonas the prophet. ³⁰For as Jonas was a sign unto the Ninevites, so shall also the Son of man be to this generation. ³¹The queen of the south shall rise up in the judgment with the men of this generation, and condemn them: for she came from the utmost parts of the earth to hear the wisdom of Solomon; and, behold, a greater than Solomon is here. ³²The men of Nineve shall rise up in the judgment with this generation, and shall condemn it: for they repented at the preaching of Jonas; and, behold, a greater than Jonas *is* here. ³³No man, when he hath lighted a candle, putteth *it* in a secret place, neither under a bushel, but on a candlestick, that they which come in may see the light. ³⁴The light of the body is the eye: therefore when thine eye is single, thy whole body also is full of light; but when *thine eye* is evil, thy body also *is* full of darkness. ³⁵Take heed therefore that the light which is in thee be not darkness. ³⁶If thy whole body therefore *be* full of light, having no part dark, the whole shall be full of light, as when the bright shining of a candle doth give thee light.

³⁷And as he spake, a certain Pharisee besought him to dine with him: and he went in, and sat down to meat. ³⁸And when

the Pharisee saw *it*, he marvelled that he had not first washed before dinner. ³⁹And the Lord said unto him, Now do ye Pharisees make clean the outside of the cup and the platter; but your inward part is full of ravening and wickedness. ⁴⁰*Ye* fools, did not he that made that which is without make that which is within also? ⁴¹But rather give alms of such things as ye have; and, behold, all things are clean unto you. ⁴²But woe unto you, Pharisees! for ye tithe mint and rue and all manner of herbs, and pass over judgment and the love of God: these ought ye to have done, and not to leave the other undone. ⁴³Woe unto you, Pharisees! for ye love the uppermost seats in the synagogues, and greetings in the markets. ⁴⁴Woe unto you, scribes and Pharisees, hypocrites! for ye are as graves which appear not, and the men that walk over *them* are not aware *of them*.

⁴⁵Then answered one of the lawyers, and said unto him, Master, thus saying thou reproachest us also. ⁴⁶And he said,

Woe unto you also, *ye* lawyers! for ye lade men with burdens grievous to be borne, and ye yourselves touch not the burdens with one of your fingers. ⁴⁷Woe unto you! for ye build the sepulchres of the prophets, and your fathers killed them. ⁴⁸Truly ye bear witness that ye allow the deeds of your fathers: for they indeed killed them, and ye build their sepulchres. ⁴⁹Therefore also said the wisdom of God, I will send them prophets and apostles, and *some* of them they shall slay and persecute: ⁵⁰That the blood of all the prophets, which was shed from the foundation of the world, may be required of this generation; ⁵¹From the blood of Abel unto the blood of Zacharias, which perished between the altar and the temple: verily I say unto you, It shall be required of this generation. ⁵²Woe unto you, lawyers! for ye have taken away the key of knowledge: ye entered not in yourselves, and them that were entering in ye hindered. ⁵³And as he said these things unto them, the scribes and the Pharisees began to urge *him* vehemently, and to provoke him to speak of many things: ⁵⁴Laying wait for him, and seeking to catch something out of his mouth, that they might accuse him.

12 In the mean time, when there were gathered together an innumerable multitude of people, insomuch that they trode one upon another, he began to say unto his disciples first of all, Beware ye of the leaven of the Pharisees, which is hypocrisy. ²For there is nothing covered, that shall not be revealed; neither hid, that shall not be known. ³Therefore whatsoever ye have spoken in darkness shall be heard in the light; and that which ye have spoken in the ear in closets shall be proclaimed upon the housetops. ⁴And I say unto you my friends, Be not afraid of them that kill the body, and after that have no more that they can do. ⁵But I will forewarn you whom ye shall fear: Fear him, which after he hath killed hath power to cast into hell; yea, I say unto you, Fear him. ⁶Are not five sparrows sold for two farthings, and not one of them is forgotten before God? ⁷But even the very hairs of your head are all numbered. Fear not therefore: ye are of more value than many sparrows. ⁸Also I say unto you, Whosoever shall confess me before men, him shall the Son of man also confess before the angels of God: ⁹But he that denieth me before men shall be denied before the angels of God. ¹⁰And whosoever shall speak a word against the Son of man, it shall be forgiven him: but unto him that blasphemeth against the Holy Ghost it shall not be forgiven. ¹¹And when they bring you unto the synagogues, and *unto* magistrates, and powers, take ye no thought how or what thing ye shall answer, or what ye shall say: ¹²For the Holy Ghost shall teach you in the same hour what ye ought to say.

¹³And one of the company said unto him, Master, speak to my brother, that he divide the inheritance with me. ¹⁴And he said unto him, Man, who made me a judge or a divider over you? ¹⁵And he said unto them, Take heed, and beware of covetousness: for a man's life consisteth not in the abundance of the things which he possesseth.

¹⁶And he spake a parable unto them, saying, The ground of a certain rich man brought forth plentifully: ¹⁷And he thought within himself, saying, What shall I do, because I have no room where to bestow my fruits? ¹⁸And he said, This will I do: I

will pull down my barns, and build greater; and there will I bestow all my fruits and my goods. [19]And I will say to my soul, Soul, thou hast much goods laid up for many years; take thine ease, eat, drink, *and* be merry. [20]But God said unto him, *Thou* fool, this night thy soul shall be required of thee: then whose shall those things be, which thou hast provided? [21]So *is* he that layeth up treasure for himself, and is not rich toward God.

[22]And he said unto his disciples, Therefore I say unto you, Take no thought for your life, what ye shall eat; neither for the body, what ye shall put on. [23]The life is more than meat, and the body *is more* than raiment. [24]Consider the ravens: for they neither sow nor reap; which neither have storehouse nor barn; and God feedeth them: how much more are ye better than the fowls? [25]And which of you with taking thought can add to his stature one cubit? [26]If ye then be not able to do that thing which is least, why take ye thought for the rest? [27]Consider the lilies how they grow: they toil not, they spin not; and yet I say unto you, that Solomon in all his glory was not arrayed like one of these. [28]If then God so clothe the grass, which is to day in the field, and to morrow is cast into the oven; how much more *will he clothe* you, O ye of little faith? [29]And seek not ye what ye shall eat, or what ye shall drink, neither be ye of doubtful mind. [30]For all these things do the nations of the world seek after: and your Father knoweth that ye have need of these things.

[31]But rather seek ye the kingdom of God; and all these things shall be added unto you. [32]Fear not, little flock; for it is your Father's good pleasure to give you the kingdom. [33]Sell that ye have, and give alms; provide yourselves bags which wax not old, a treasure in the heavens that faileth not, where no thief approacheth, neither moth corrupteth. [34]For where your treasure is, there will your heart be also. [35]Let your loins be girded about, and *your* lights burning; [36]And ye yourselves like unto men that wait for their lord, when he will return from the wedding; that when he cometh and knocketh, they may open unto him immediately. [37]Blessed *are* those servants,

whom the lord when he cometh shall find watching: verily I say unto you, that he shall gird himself, and make them to sit down to meat, and will come forth and serve them. [38]And if he shall come in the second watch, or come in the third watch, and find *them* so, blessed are those servants. [39]And this know, that if the goodman of the house had known what hour the thief would come, he would have watched, and not have suffered his house to be broken through. [40]Be ye therefore ready also: for the Son of man cometh at an hour when ye think not.

[41]Then Peter said unto him, Lord, speakest thou this parable unto us, or even to all? [42]And the Lord said, Who then is that faithful and wise steward, whom *his* lord shall make ruler over his household, to give *them their* portion of meat in due season? [43]Blessed *is* that servant, whom his lord when he cometh shall find so doing. [44]Of a truth I say unto you, that he will make him ruler over all that he hath. [45]But and if that servant say in his heart, My lord delayeth his coming; and shall begin to beat the menservants and maidens, and to eat and drink, and to be drunken; [46]The lord of that servant will come in a day when he looketh not for *him,* and at an hour when he is not aware, and will cut him in sunder, and will appoint him his portion with the unbelievers. [47]And that servant, which knew his lord's will, and prepared not *himself,* neither did according to his will, shall be beaten with many *stripes.* [48]But he that knew not, and did commit things worthy of stripes, shall be beaten with few *stripes.* For unto whomsoever much is given, of him shall be much required: and to whom men have committed much, of him they will ask the more.

[49]I am come to send fire on the earth; and what will I if it be already kindled? [50]But I have a baptism to be baptized with; and how am I straitened till it be accomplished! [51]Suppose ye that I am come to give peace on earth? I tell you, Nay; but rather division: [52]For from henceforth there shall be five in one house divided, three against two, and two against three. [53]The father shall be divided against the son, and the son against the father; the mother against the daughter, and the daughter against

the mother; the mother in law against her daughter in law, and the daughter in law against her mother in law.

⁵⁴And he said also to the people, When ye see a cloud rise out of the west, straightway ye say, There cometh a shower; and so it is. ⁵⁵And when *ye see* the south wind blow, ye say, There will be heat; and it cometh to pass. ⁵⁶*Ye* hypocrites, ye can discern the face of the sky and of the earth; but how is it that ye do not discern this time? ⁵⁷Yea, and why even of yourselves judge ye not what is right?

⁵⁸When thou goest with thine adversary to the magistrate, *as thou art* in the way, give diligence that thou mayest be delivered from him; lest he hale thee to the judge, and the judge deliver thee to the officer, and the officer cast thee into prison. ⁵⁹I tell thee, thou shalt not depart thence, till thou hast paid the very last mite.

13 There were present at that season some that told him of the Galilaeans, whose blood Pilate had mingled with their sacrifices. ²And Jesus answering said unto them, Suppose ye that these Galilaeans were sinners above all the Galilaeans, because they suffered such things? ³I tell you, Nay: but, except ye repent, ye shall all likewise perish. ⁴Or those eighteen, upon whom the tower in Siloam fell, and slew them, think ye that they were sinners above all men that dwelt in Jerusalem? ⁵I tell you, Nay: but, except ye repent, ye shall all likewise perish.

⁶He spake also this parable; A certain *man* had a fig tree planted in his vineyard; and he came and sought fruit thereon, and found none. ⁷Then said he unto the dresser of his vineyard, Behold, these three years I come seeking fruit on this fig tree, and find none: cut it down; why cumbereth it the ground? ⁸And he answering said unto him, Lord, let it alone this year also, till I shall dig about it, and dung *it:* ⁹And if it bear fruit, *well:* and if not, *then* after that thou shalt cut it down.

¹⁰And he was teaching in one of the synagogues on the sabbath. ¹¹And, behold, there was a woman which had a spirit of infirmity eighteen years, and was bowed together, and could in no wise lift up *herself.* ¹²And when Jesus saw her, he called *her*

to him, and said unto her, Woman, thou art loosed from thine infirmity. ¹³And he laid *his* hands on her: and immediately she was made straight, and glorified God. ¹⁴And the ruler of the synagogue answered with indignation, because that Jesus had healed on the sabbath day, and said unto the people, There are six days in which men ought to work: in them therefore come and be healed, and not on the sabbath day. ¹⁵The Lord then answered him, and said, *Thou* hypocrite, doth not each one of you on the sabbath loose his ox or *his* ass from the stall, and lead *him* away to watering? ¹⁶And ought not this woman, being a daughter of Abraham, whom Satan hath bound, lo, these eighteen years, be loosed from this bond on the sabbath day? ¹⁷And when he had said these things, all his adversaries were ashamed: and all the people rejoiced for all the glorious things that were done by him.

¹⁸Then said he, Unto what is the kingdom of God like? and whereunto shall I resemble it? ¹⁹It is like a grain of mustard seed, which a man took, and cast into his garden; and it grew, and waxed a great tree; and the fowls of the air lodged in the branches of it. ²⁰And again he said, Whereunto shall I liken the kingdom of God? ²¹It is like leaven, which a woman took and hid in three measures of meal, till the whole was leavened.

²²And he went through the cities and villages, teaching, and journeying toward Jerusalem. ²³Then said one unto him, Lord, are there few that be saved? And he said unto them,

²⁴Strive to enter in at the strait gate: for many, I say unto you, will seek to enter in, and shall not be able. ²⁵When once the master of the house is risen up, and hath shut to the door, and ye begin to stand without, and to knock at the door, saying, Lord, Lord, open unto us; and he shall answer and say unto you, I know you not whence ye are: ²⁶Then shall ye begin to say, We have eaten and drunk in thy presence, and thou hast taught in our streets. ²⁷But he shall say, I tell you, I know you not whence ye are; depart from me, all *ye* workers of iniquity. ²⁸There shall be weeping and gnashing of teeth, when ye shall see Abraham, and

Isaac, and Jacob, and all the prophets, in the kingdom of God, and you *yourselves* thrust out. ²⁹And they shall come from the east, and *from* the west, and from the north, and *from* the south, and shall sit down in the kingdom of God. ³⁰And, behold, there are last which shall be first, and there are first which shall be last.

³¹The same day there came certain of the Pharisees, saying unto him, Get thee out, and depart hence: for Herod will kill thee. ³²And he said unto them, Go ye, and tell that fox, Behold, I cast out devils, and I do cures to day and to morrow, and the third *day* I shall be perfected. ³³Nevertheless I must walk to day, and to morrow, and the *day* following: for it cannot be that a prophet perish out of Jerusalem. ³⁴O Jerusalem, Jerusalem, which killest the prophets, and stonest them that are sent unto thee; how often would I have gathered thy children together, as a hen *doth gather* her brood under *her* wings, and ye would not! ³⁵Behold, your house is left unto you desolate: and verily I say unto you, Ye shall not see me, until *the time* come when ye shall say, Blessed *is* he that cometh in the name of the Lord.

14 And it came to pass, as he went into the house of one of the chief Pharisees to eat bread on the sabbath day, that they watched him. ²And, behold, there was a certain man before him which had the dropsy. ³And Jesus answering spake unto the lawyers and Pharisees, saying, Is it lawful to heal on the sabbath day? ⁴And they held their peace. And he took *him*, and healed him, and let him go; ⁵And answered them, saying, Which of you shall have an ass or an ox fallen into a pit, and will not straightway pull him out on the sabbath day? ⁶And they could not answer him again to these things.

⁷And he put forth a parable to those which were bidden, when he marked how they chose out the chief rooms; saying unto them, ⁸When thou art bidden of any *man* to a wedding, sit not down in the highest room; lest a more honourable man than thou be bidden of him; ⁹And he that bade thee and him come and say to thee, Give this man place; and thou begin with shame to take the lowest room. ¹⁰But when thou art bidden, go and sit down in the lowest room; that when he that bade thee cometh, he may say unto thee, Friend, go up higher: then shalt thou have worship in the presence of them that sit at meat with thee. ¹¹For whosoever exalteth himself shall be abased; and he that humbleth himself shall be exalted.

¹²Then said he also to him that bade him, When thou makest a dinner or a supper, call not thy friends, nor thy brethren, neither thy kinsmen, nor *thy* rich neighbours; lest they also bid thee again, and a recompence be made thee. ¹³But when thou makest a feast, call the poor, the maimed, the lame, the blind: ¹⁴And thou shalt be blessed; for they cannot recompense thee: for thou shalt be recompensed at the resurrection of the just.

¹⁵And when one of them that sat at meat with him heard these things, he said unto him, Blessed *is* he that shall eat bread in the kingdom of God. ¹⁶Then said he unto him, A certain man made a great supper, and bade many: ¹⁷And sent his servant at supper time to say to them that were bidden, Come; for all things are now ready. ¹⁸And they all with one *consent* began to make excuse. The first said unto him, I have bought a piece of ground, and I must needs go and see it: I pray thee have me excused. ¹⁹And another said, I have bought five yoke of oxen, and I go to prove them: I pray thee have me excused. ²⁰And another said, I have married a wife, and therefore I cannot come. ²¹So that servant came, and shewed his lord these things. Then the master of the house being angry said to his servant, Go out quickly into the streets and lanes of the city, and bring in hither the poor, and the maimed, and the halt, and the blind. ²²And the servant said, Lord, it is done as thou hast commanded, and yet there is room. ²³And the lord said unto the servant, Go out into the highways and hedges, and compel *them* to come in, that my house may be filled. ²⁴For I say unto you, That none of those men which were bidden shall taste of my supper.

²⁵And there went great multitudes with him: and he turned, and said unto them, ²⁶If any *man* come to me, and hate not his father, and mother, and wife, and children,

and brethren, and sisters, yea, and his own life also, he cannot be my disciple. [27]And whosoever doth not bear his cross, and come after me, cannot be my disciple. [28]For which of you, intending to build a tower, sitteth not down first, and counteth the cost, whether he have *sufficient* to finish *it?* [29]Lest haply, after he hath laid the foundation, and is not able to finish *it,* all that behold *it* begin to mock him, [30]Saying, This man began to build, and was not able to finish. [31]Or what king, going to make war against another king, sitteth not down first, and consulteth whether he be able with ten thousand to meet him that cometh against him with twenty thousand? [32]Or else, while the other is yet a great way off, he sendeth an ambassage, and desireth conditions of peace. [33]So likewise, whosoever he be of you that forsaketh not all that he hath, he cannot be my disciple.

[34]Salt *is* good: but if the salt have lost his savour, wherewith shall it be seasoned? [35]It is neither fit for the land, nor yet for the dunghill; *but* men cast it out. He that hath ears to hear, let him hear.

15 Then drew near unto him all the publicans and sinners for to hear him. [2]And the Pharisees and scribes murmured, saying, This man receiveth sinners, and eateth with them.

[3]And he spake this parable unto them, saying, [4]What man of you, having an hundred sheep, if he lose one of them, doth not leave the ninety and nine in the wilderness, and go after that which is lost, until he find it? [5]And when he hath found *it,* he layeth *it* on his shoulders, rejoicing. [6]And when he cometh home, he calleth together *his* friends and neighbours, saying unto them, Rejoice with me; for I have found my sheep which was lost. [7]I say unto you, that likewise joy shall be in heaven over one sinner that repenteth, more than over ninety and nine just persons, which need no repentance.

[8]Either what woman having ten pieces of silver, if she lose one piece, doth not light a candle, and sweep the house, and seek diligently till she find *it?* [9]And when she hath found *it,* she calleth *her* friends and *her* neighbours together, saying, Rejoice with me; for I have found the piece which I had lost. [10]Likewise, I say unto you, there is joy in the presence of the angels of God over one sinner that repenteth.

[11]And he said, A certain man had two sons: [12]And the younger of them said to *his* father, Father, give me the portion of goods that falleth *to me.* And he divided unto them *his* living. [13]And not many days after the younger son gathered all together, and took his journey into a far country, and there wasted his substance with riotous living. [14]And when he had spent all, there arose a mighty famine in that land; and he began to be in want. [15]And he went and joined himself to a citizen of that country; and he sent him into his fields to feed swine. [16]And he would fain have filled his belly with the husks that the swine did eat: and no man gave unto him. [17]And when he came to himself, he said, How many hired servants of my father's have bread enough and to spare, and I perish with hunger! [18]I will arise and go to my father, and will say unto him, Father, I have sinned against heaven, and before thee, [19]And am no more worthy to be called thy son: make me as one of thy hired servants. [20]And he arose, and came to his father. But when he was yet a great way off, his father saw him, and had compassion, and ran, and fell on his neck, and kissed him. [21]And the son said unto him, Father, I have sinned against heaven, and in thy sight, and am no more worthy to be called thy son. [22]But the father said to his servants, Bring forth the best robe, and put *it* on him; and put a ring on his hand, and shoes on *his* feet: [23]And bring hither the fatted calf, and kill *it;* and let us eat, and be merry: [24]For this my son was dead, and is alive again; he was lost, and is found. And they began to be merry. [25]Now his elder son was in the field: and as he came and drew nigh to the house, he heard musick and dancing. [26]And he called one of the servants, and asked what these things meant. [27]And he said unto him, Thy brother is come; and thy father hath killed the fatted calf, because he hath received him safe and sound. [28]And he was angry, and would not go in: therefore came his father out, and intreated him. [29]And he answering said to *his* father, Lo, these many years do I serve thee, neither transgressed I at any time thy

commandment: and yet thou never gavest me a kid, that I might make merry with my friends: ³⁰But as soon as this thy son was come, which hath devoured thy living with harlots, thou hast killed for him the fatted calf. ³¹And he said unto him, Son, thou art ever with me, and all that I have is thine. ³²It was meet that we should make merry, and be glad: for this thy brother was dead, and is alive again; and was lost, and is found.

16 And he said also unto his disciples, There was a certain rich man, which had a steward; and the same was accused unto him that he had wasted his goods. ²And he called him, and said unto him, How is it that I hear this of thee? give an account of thy stewardship; for thou mayest be no longer steward. ³Then the steward said within himself, What shall I do? for my lord taketh away from me the stewardship: I cannot dig; to beg I am ashamed. ⁴I am resolved what to do, that, when I am put out of the stewardship, they may receive me into their houses. ⁵So he called every one of his lord's debtors *unto him*, and said unto the first, How much owest thou unto my lord? ⁶And he said, An hundred measures of oil. And he said unto him, Take thy bill, and sit down quickly, and write fifty. ⁷Then said he to another, And how much owest thou? And he said, An hundred measures of wheat. And he said unto him, Take thy bill, and write fourscore. ⁸And the lord commended the unjust steward, because he had done wisely: for the children of this world are in their generation wiser than the children of light. ⁹And I say unto you, Make to yourselves friends of the mammon of unrighteousness; that, when ye fail, they may receive you into everlasting habitations. ¹⁰He that is faithful in that which is least is faithful also in much: and he that is unjust in the least is unjust also in much. ¹¹If therefore ye have not been faithful in the unrighteous mammon, who will commit to your trust the true *riches?* ¹²And if ye have not been faithful in that which is another man's, who shall give you that which is your own? ¹³No servant can serve two masters: for either he will hate the one, and love the other; or else he will hold to the one, and despise the other. Ye cannot serve God and mammon.

¹⁴And the Pharisees also, who were covetous, heard all these things: and they derided him. ¹⁵And he said unto them, Ye are they which justify yourselves before men; but God knoweth your hearts: for that which is highly esteemed among men is abomination in the sight of God. ¹⁶The law and the prophets *were* until John: since that time the kingdom of God is preached, and every man presseth into it. ¹⁷And it is easier for heaven and earth to pass, than one tittle of the law to fail.

¹⁸Whosoever putteth away his wife, and marrieth another, committeth adultery: and whosoever marrieth her that is put away from *her* husband committeth adultery.

¹⁹There was a certain rich man, which was clothed in purple and fine linen, and fared sumptuously every day: ²⁰And there was a certain beggar named Lazarus, which was laid at his gate, full of sores, ²¹And desiring to be fed with the crumbs which fell from the rich man's table: moreover the dogs came and licked his sores. ²²And it came to pass, that the beggar died, and was carried by the angels into Abraham's bosom: the rich man also died, and was buried; ²³And in hell he lift up his eyes, being in torments, and seeth Abraham afar off, and Lazarus in his bosom. ²⁴And he cried and said, Father Abraham, have mercy on me, and send Lazarus, that he may dip the tip of his finger in water, and cool my tongue; for I am tormented in this flame. ²⁵But Abraham said, Son, remember that thou in thy lifetime receivedst thy good things, and likewise Lazarus evil things: but now he is comforted, and thou art tormented. ²⁶And beside all this, between us and you there is a great gulf fixed: so that they which would pass from hence to you cannot; neither can they pass to us, that *would come* from thence. ²⁷Then he said, I pray thee therefore, father, that thou wouldest send him to my father's house: ²⁸For I have five brethren; that he may testify unto them, lest they also come into this place of torment. ²⁹Abraham saith unto him, They have Moses and the prophets; let them hear them. ³⁰And he said, Nay, father Abraham: but if one went unto them from the dead, they will repent. ³¹And he said unto him,

If they hear not Moses and the prophets, neither will they be persuaded, though one rose from the dead.

17 Then said he unto the disciples, It is impossible but that offences will come: but woe *unto him,* through whom they come! ²It were better for him that a millstone were hanged about his neck, and he cast into the sea, than that he should offend one of these little ones.

³Take heed to yourselves: If thy brother trespass against thee, rebuke him; and if he repent, forgive him. ⁴And if he trespass against thee seven times in a day, and seven times in a day turn again to thee, saying, I repent; thou shalt forgive him. ⁵And the apostles said unto the Lord, Increase our faith. ⁶And the Lord said, If ye had faith as a grain of mustard seed, ye might say unto this sycamine tree, Be thou plucked up by the root, and be thou planted in the sea; and it should obey you.

⁷But which of you, having a servant plowing or feeding cattle, will say unto him by and by, when he is come from the field, Go and sit down to meat? ⁸And will not rather say unto him, Make ready wherewith I may sup, and gird thyself, and serve me, till I have eaten and drunken; and afterward thou shalt eat and drink? ⁹Doth he thank that servant because he did the things that were commanded him? I trow not. ¹⁰So likewise ye, when ye shall have done all those things which are commanded you, say, We are unprofitable servants: we have done that which was our duty to do.

¹¹And it came to pass, as he went to Jerusalem, that he passed through the midst of Samaria and Galilee. ¹²And as he entered into a certain village, there met him ten men that were lepers, which stood afar off: ¹³And they lifted up *their* voices, and said, Jesus, Master, have mercy on us. ¹⁴And when he saw *them,* he said unto them, Go shew yourselves unto the priests. And it came to pass, that, as they went, they were cleansed. ¹⁵And one of them, when he saw that he was healed, turned back, and with a loud voice glorified God, ¹⁶And fell down on *his* face at his feet, giving him thanks: and he was a Samaritan. ¹⁷And Jesus answering said, Were there not ten cleansed? but

where *are* the nine? ¹⁸There are not found that returned to give glory to God, save this stranger. ¹⁹And he said unto him, Arise, go thy way: thy faith hath made thee whole.

²⁰And when he was demanded of the Pharisees, when the kingdom of God should come, he answered them and said, The kingdom of God cometh not with observation: ²¹Neither shall they say, Lo here! or, lo there! for, behold, the kingdom of God is within you.

²²And he said unto the disciples, The days will come, when ye shall desire to see one of the days of the Son of man, and ye shall not see *it.* ²³And they shall say to you, See here; or, see there: go not after *them,* nor follow *them.* ²⁴For as the lightning, that lighteneth out of the one *part* under heaven, shineth unto the other *part* under heaven; so shall also the Son of man be in his day. ²⁵But first must he suffer many things, and be rejected of this generation. ²⁶And as it was in the days of Noe, so shall it be also in the days of the Son of man. ²⁷They did eat, they drank, they married wives, they were given in marriage, until the day that Noe entered into the ark, and the flood came, and destroyed them all. ²⁸Likewise also as it was in the days of Lot; they did eat, they drank, they bought, they sold, they planted, they builded; ²⁹But the same day that Lot went out of Sodom it rained fire and brimstone from heaven, and destroyed *them* all. ³⁰Even thus shall it be in the day when the Son of man is revealed. ³¹In that day, he which shall be upon the housetop, and his stuff in the house, let him not come down to take it away: and he that is in the field, let him likewise not return back. ³²Remember Lot's wife. ³³Whosoever shall seek to save his life shall lose it; and whosoever shall lose his life shall preserve it. ³⁴I tell you, in that night there shall be two *men* in one bed; the one shall be taken, and the other shall be left. ³⁵Two *women* shall be grinding together; the one shall be taken, and the other left. ³⁶Two *men* shall be in the field; the one shall be taken, and the other left. ³⁷And they answered and said unto him, Where, Lord? And he said unto them, Wheresoever the body is, thither will the eagles be gathered together.

18 And he spake a parable unto them *to this end,* that men ought always to pray, and not to faint; ²Saying, There was in a city a judge, which feared not God, neither regarded man: ³And there was a widow in that city; and she came unto him, saying, Avenge me of mine adversary. ⁴And he would not for a while: but afterward he said within himself, Though I fear not God, nor regard man; ⁵Yet because this widow troubleth me, I will avenge her, lest by her continual coming she weary me. ⁶And the Lord said, Hear what the unjust judge saith. ⁷And shall not God avenge his own elect, which cry day and night unto him, though he bear long with them? ⁸I tell you that he will avenge them speedily. Nevertheless when the Son of man cometh, shall he find faith on the earth?

⁹And he spake this parable unto certain which trusted in themselves that they were righteous, and despised others: ¹⁰Two men went up into the temple to pray; the one a Pharisee, and the other a publican. ¹¹The Pharisee stood and prayed thus with himself, God, I thank thee, that I am not as other men *are,* extortioners, unjust, adulterers, or even as this publican. ¹²I fast twice in the week, I give tithes of all that I possess. ¹³And the publican, standing afar off, would not lift up so much as *his* eyes unto heaven, but smote upon his breast, saying, God be merciful to me a sinner. ¹⁴I tell you, this man went down to his house justified *rather* than the other: for every one that exalteth himself shall be abased; and he that humbleth himself shall be exalted.

¹⁵And they brought unto him also infants, that he would touch them: but when *his* disciples saw *it,* they rebuked them. ¹⁶But Jesus called them *unto him,* and said, Suffer little children to come unto me, and forbid them not: for of such is the kingdom of God. ¹⁷Verily I say unto you, Whosoever shall not receive the kingdom of God as a little child shall in no wise enter therein.

¹⁸And a certain ruler asked him, saying, Good Master, what shall I do to inherit eternal life? ¹⁹And Jesus said unto him, Why callest thou me good? none *is* good, save one, *that is,* God. ²⁰Thou knowest the commandments, Do not commit adultery, Do not kill, Do not steal, Do not bear false witness, Honour thy father and thy mother. ²¹And he said, All these have I kept from my youth up. ²²Now when Jesus heard these things, he said unto him, Yet lackest thou one thing: sell all that thou hast, and distribute unto the poor, and thou shalt have treasure in heaven: and come, follow me. ²³And when he heard this, he was very sorrowful: for he was very rich. ²⁴And when Jesus saw that he was very sorrowful, he said, How hardly shall they that have riches enter into the kingdom of God! ²⁵For it is easier for a camel to go through a needle's eye, than for a rich man to enter into the kingdom of God. ²⁶And they that heard *it* said, Who then can be saved? ²⁷And he said, The things which are impossible with men are possible with God. ²⁸Then Peter said, Lo, we have left all, and followed thee. ²⁹And he said unto them, Verily I say unto you, There is no man that hath left house, or parents, or brethren, or wife, or children, for the kingdom of God's sake, ³⁰Who shall not receive manifold more in this present time, and in the world to come life everlasting.

³¹Then he took *unto him* the twelve, and said unto them, Behold, we go up to Jerusalem, and all things that are written by the prophets concerning the Son of man shall be accomplished. ³²For he shall be delivered unto the Gentiles, and shall be mocked, and spitefully entreated, and spitted on: ³³And they shall scourge *him,* and put him to death: and the third day he shall rise again. ³⁴And they understood none of these things: and this saying was hid from them, neither knew they the things which were spoken.

³⁵And it came to pass, that as he was come nigh unto Jericho, a certain blind man sat by the way side begging: ³⁶And hearing the multitude pass by, he asked what it meant. ³⁷And they told him, that Jesus of Nazareth passeth by. ³⁸And he cried, saying, Jesus, *thou* Son of David, have mercy on me. ³⁹And they which went before rebuked him, that he should hold his peace: but he cried so much the more, *Thou* Son of David, have mercy on me. ⁴⁰And Jesus stood, and commanded him to be brought unto him: and when he was come near, he asked him, ⁴¹Saying, What wilt thou that I

shall do unto thee? And he said, Lord, that I may receive my sight. ⁴²And Jesus said unto him, Receive thy sight: thy faith hath saved thee. ⁴³And immediately he received his sight, and followed him, glorifying God: and all the people, when they saw *it*, gave praise unto God.

19 And *Jesus* entered and passed through Jericho. ²And, behold, *there was* a man named Zacchaeus, which was the chief among the publicans, and he was rich. ³And he sought to see Jesus who he was; and could not for the press, because he was little of stature. ⁴And he ran before, and climbed up into a sycomore tree to see him: for he was to pass that *way*. ⁵And when Jesus came to the place, he looked up, and saw him, and said unto him, Zacchaeus, make haste, and come down; for to day I must abide at thy house. ⁶And he made haste, and came down, and received him joyfully. ⁷And when they saw *it,* they all murmured, saying, That he was gone to be guest with a man that is a sinner. ⁸And Zacchaeus stood, and said unto the Lord; Behold, Lord, the half of my goods I give to the poor; and if I have taken any thing from any man by false accusation, I restore *him* fourfold. ⁹And Jesus said unto him, This day is salvation come to this house, forsomuch as he also is a son of Abraham. ¹⁰For the Son of man is come to seek and to save that which was lost.

¹¹And as they heard these things, he added and spake a parable, because he was nigh to Jerusalem, and because they thought that the kingdom of God should immediately appear. ¹²He said therefore, A certain nobleman went into a far country to receive for himself a kingdom, and to return. ¹³And he called his ten servants, and delivered them ten pounds, and said unto them, Occupy till I come. ¹⁴But his citizens hated him, and sent a message after him, saying, We will not have this *man* to reign over us. ¹⁵And it came to pass, that when he was returned, having received the kingdom, then he commanded these servants to be called unto him, to whom he had given the money, that he might know how much every man had gained by trading. ¹⁶Then came the first, saying, Lord, thy pound hath gained ten pounds. ¹⁷And he

said unto him, Well, thou good servant: because thou hast been faithful in a very little, have thou authority over ten cities. ¹⁸And the second came, saying, Lord, thy pound hath gained five pounds. ¹⁹And he said likewise to him, Be thou also over five cities. ²⁰And another came, saying, Lord, behold, *here is* thy pound, which I have kept laid up in a napkin: ²¹For I feared thee, because thou art an austere man: thou takest up that thou layedst not down, and reapest that thou didst not sow. ²²And he saith unto him, Out of thine own mouth will I judge thee, *thou* wicked servant. Thou knewest that I was an austere man, taking up that I laid not down, and reaping that I did not sow: ²³Wherefore then gavest not thou my money into the bank, that at my coming I might have required mine own with usury? ²⁴And he said unto them that stood by, Take from him the pound, and give *it* to him that hath ten pounds. ²⁵(And they said unto him, Lord, he hath ten pounds.) ²⁶For I say unto you, That unto every one which hath shall be given; and from him that hath not, even that he hath shall be taken away from him. ²⁷But those mine enemies, which would not that I should reign over them, bring hither, and slay *them* before me.

²⁸And when he had thus spoken, he went before, ascending up to Jerusalem. ²⁹And it came to pass, when he was come nigh to Bethphage and Bethany, at the mount called *the mount* of Olives, he sent two of his disciples, ³⁰Saying, Go ye into the village over against *you;* in the which at your entering ye shall find a colt tied, whereon yet never man sat: loose him, and bring *him hither.* ³¹And if any man ask you, Why do ye loose *him?* thus shall ye say unto him, Because the Lord hath need of him. ³²And they that were sent went their way, and found even as he had said unto them. ³³And as they were loosing the colt, the owners thereof said unto them, Why loose ye the colt? ³⁴And they said, The Lord hath need of him. ³⁵And they brought him to Jesus: and they cast their garments upon the colt, and they set Jesus thereon. ³⁶And as he went, they spread their clothes in the way. ³⁷And when he was come nigh, even now at the descent of the mount of Olives,

the whole multitude of the disciples began to rejoice and praise God with a loud voice for all the mighty works that they had seen;

[38]Saying, Blessed *be* the King that cometh in the name of the Lord:

peace in heaven, and glory in the highest.

[39]And some of the Pharisees from among the multitude said unto him, Master, rebuke thy disciples. [40]And he answered and said unto them, I tell you that, if these should hold their peace, the stones would immediately cry out.

[41]And when he was come near, he beheld the city, and wept over it, [42]Saying, If thou hadst known, even thou, at least in this thy day, the things *which belong* unto thy peace! but now they are hid from thine eyes. [43]For the days shall come upon thee, that thine enemies shall cast a trench about thee, and compass thee round, and keep thee in on every side, [44]And shall lay thee even with the ground, and thy children within thee; and they shall not leave in thee one stone upon another; because thou knewest not the time of thy visitation.

[45]And he went into the temple, and began to cast out them that sold therein, and them that bought; [46]Saying unto them, It is written, My house is the house of prayer: but ye have made it a den of thieves. [47]And he taught daily in the temple. But the chief priests and the scribes and the chief of the people sought to destroy him, [48]And could not find what they might do: for all the people were very attentive to hear him.

20 And it came to pass, *that* on one of those days, as he taught the people in the temple, and preached the gospel, the chief priests and the scribes came upon *him* with the elders, [2]And spake unto him, saying, Tell us, by what authority doest thou these things? or who is he that gave thee this authority? [3]And he answered and said unto them, I will also ask you one thing; and answer me: [4]The baptism of John, was it from heaven, or of men? [5]And they reasoned with themselves, saying, If we shall say, From heaven; he will say, Why then believed ye him not? [6]But and if we say, Of men; all the people will stone us: for they be persuaded

that John was a prophet. [7]And they answered, that they could not tell whence *it* was. [8]And Jesus said unto them, Neither tell I you by what authority I do these things.

[9]Then began he to speak to the people this parable; A certain man planted a vineyard, and let it forth to husbandmen, and went into a far country for a long time. [10]And at the season he sent a servant to the husbandmen, that they should give him of the fruit of the vineyard: but the husbandmen beat him, and sent *him* away empty. [11]And again he sent another servant: and they beat him also, and entreated *him* shamefully, and sent *him* away empty. [12]And again he sent a third: and they wounded him also, and cast *him* out. [13]Then said the lord of the vineyard, What shall I do? I will send my beloved son: it may be they will reverence *him* when they see him. [14]But when the husbandmen saw him, they reasoned among themselves, saying, This is the heir: come, let us kill him, that the inheritance may be ours. [15]So they cast him out of the vineyard, and killed *him*. What therefore shall the lord of the vineyard do unto them? [16]He shall come and destroy these husbandmen, and shall give the vineyard to others. And when they heard *it,* they said, God forbid. [17]And he beheld them, and said, What is this then that is written,

The stone which the builders rejected, the same is become the head of the corner?

[18]Whosoever shall fall upon that stone shall be broken; but on whomsoever it shall fall, it will grind him to powder.

[19]And the chief priests and the scribes the same hour sought to lay hands on him; and they feared the people: for they perceived that he had spoken this parable against them. [20]And they watched *him,* and sent forth spies, which should feign themselves just men, that they might take hold of his words, that so they might deliver him unto the power and authority of the governor. [21]And they asked him, saying, Master, we know that thou sayest and teachest rightly, neither acceptest thou the person *of any,* but teachest the way of God truly: [22]Is it lawful for us to give tribute unto Caesar, or no? [23]But he perceived their craftiness, and said unto them, Why tempt ye me? [24]Shew

me a penny. Whose image and superscription hath it? They answered and said, Caesar's. 25 And he said unto them, Render therefore unto Caesar the things which be Caesar's, and unto God the things which be God's. 26 And they could not take hold of his words before the people: and they marvelled at his answer, and held their peace.

27 Then came to *him* certain of the Sadducees, which deny that there is any resurrection; and they asked him, 28 Saying, Master, Moses wrote unto us, If any man's brother die, having a wife, and he die without children, that his brother should take his wife, and raise up seed unto his brother. 29 There were therefore seven brethren: and the first took a wife, and died without children. 30 And the second took her to wife, and he died childless. 31 And the third took her; and in like manner the seven also: and they left no children, and died. 32 Last of all the woman died also. 33 Therefore in the resurrection whose wife of them is she? for seven had her to wife. 34 And Jesus answering said unto them, The children of this world marry, and are given in marriage: 35 But they which shall be accounted worthy to obtain that world, and the resurrection from the dead, neither marry, nor are given in marriage: 36 Neither can they die any more: for they are equal unto the angels; and are the children of God, being the children of the resurrection. 37 Now that the dead are raised, even Moses shewed at the bush, when he calleth the Lord the God of Abraham, and the God of Isaac, and the God of Jacob. 38 For he is not a God of the dead, but of the living: for all live unto him.

39 Then certain of the scribes answering said, Master, thou hast well said. 40 And after that they durst not ask him any *question at all.* 41 And he said unto them, How say they that Christ is David's son? 42 And David himself saith in the book of Psalms,

The LORD said unto my Lord, Sit thou on my right hand, 43 Till I make thine enemies thy footstool.

44 David therefore calleth him Lord, how is he then his son?

45 Then in the audience of all the people he said unto his disciples, 46 Beware of the scribes, which desire to walk in long robes, and love greetings in the markets, and the highest seats in the synagogues, and the chief rooms at feasts; 47 Which devour widows' houses, and for a shew make long prayers: the same shall receive greater damnation.

21 And he looked up, and saw the rich men casting their gifts into the treasury. 2 And he saw also a certain poor widow casting in thither two mites. 3 And he said, Of a truth I say unto you, that this poor widow hath cast in more than they all: 4 For all these have of their abundance cast in unto the offerings of God: but she of her penury hath cast in all the living that she had.

5 And as some spake of the temple, how it was adorned with goodly stones and gifts, he said, 6 *As for* these things which ye behold, the days will come, in the which there shall not be left one stone upon another, that shall not be thrown down. 7 And they asked him, saying, Master, but when shall these things be? and what sign *will there be* when these things shall come to pass? 8 And he said, Take heed that ye be not deceived: for many shall come in my name, saying, I am *Christ;* and the time draweth near: go ye not therefore after them. 9 But when ye shall hear of wars and commotions, be not terrified: for these things must first come to pass; but the end *is* not by and by. 10 Then said he unto them, Nation shall rise against nation, and kingdom against kingdom: 11 And great earthquakes shall be in divers places, and famines, and pestilences; and fearful sights and great signs shall there be from heaven. 12 But before all these, they shall lay their hands on you, and persecute *you,* delivering *you* up to the synagogues, and into prisons, being brought before kings and rulers for my name's sake. 13 And it shall turn to you for a testimony. 14 Settle *it* therefore in your hearts, not to meditate before what ye shall answer: 15 For I will give you a mouth and wisdom, which all your adversaries shall not be able to gainsay nor resist. 16 And ye shall be betrayed both by parents, and brethren, and kinsfolks, and friends; and *some* of you shall they cause to be put to death. 17 And ye shall be hated of all *men* for my name's sake. 18 But there

shall not an hair of your head perish. [19]In your patience possess ye your souls. [20]And when ye shall see Jerusalem compassed with armies, then know that the desolation thereof is nigh. [21]Then let them which are in Judaea flee to the mountains; and let them which are in the midst of it depart out; and let not them that are in the countries enter thereinto. [22]For these be the days of vengeance, that all things which are written may be fulfilled. [23]But woe unto them that are with child, and to them that give suck, in those days! for there shall be great distress in the land, and wrath upon this people. [24]And they shall fall by the edge of the sword, and shall be led away captive into all nations: and Jerusalem shall be trodden down of the Gentiles, until the times of the Gentiles be fulfilled.

[25]And there shall be signs in the sun, and in the moon, and in the stars; and upon the earth distress of nations, with perplexity; the sea and the waves roaring; [26]Men's hearts failing them for fear, and for looking after those things which are coming on the earth: for the powers of heaven shall be shaken. [27]And then shall they see the Son of man coming in a cloud with power and great glory. [28]And when these things begin to come to pass, then look up, and lift up your heads; for your redemption draweth nigh.

[29]And he spake to them a parable; Behold the fig tree, and all the trees; [30]When they now shoot forth, ye see and know of your own selves that summer is now nigh at hand. [31]So likewise ye, when ye see these things come to pass, know ye that the kingdom of God is nigh at hand. [32]Verily I say unto you, This generation shall not pass away, till all be fulfilled. [33]Heaven and earth shall pass away: but my words shall not pass away.

[34]And take heed to yourselves, lest at any time your hearts be overcharged with surfeiting, and drunkenness, and cares of this life, and so that day come upon you unawares. [35]For as a snare shall it come on all them that dwell on the face of the whole earth. [36]Watch ye therefore, and pray always, that ye may be accounted worthy to escape all these things that shall come to pass, and to stand before the Son of man.

[37]And in the day time he was teaching in the temple; and at night he went out, and abode in the mount that is called *the mount* of Olives. [38]And all the people came early in the morning to him in the temple, for to hear him.

22 Now the feast of unleavened bread drew nigh, which is called the Passover. [2]And the chief priests and scribes sought how they might kill him; for they feared the people.

[3]Then entered Satan into Judas surnamed Iscariot, being of the number of the twelve. [4]And he went his way, and communed with the chief priests and captains, how he might betray him unto them. [5]And they were glad, and covenanted to give him money. [6]And he promised, and sought opportunity to betray him unto them in the absence of the multitude.

[7]Then came the day of unleavened bread, when the passover must be killed. [8]And he sent Peter and John, saying, Go and prepare us the passover, that we may eat. [9]And they said unto him, Where wilt thou that we prepare? [10]And he said unto them, Behold, when ye are entered into the city, there shall a man meet you, bearing a pitcher of water; follow him into the house where he entereth in. [11]And ye shall say unto the goodman of the house, The Master saith unto thee, Where is the guest-chamber, where I shall eat the passover with my disciples? [12]And he shall shew you a large upper room furnished: there make ready. [13]And they went, and found as he had said unto them: and they made ready the passover.

[14]And when the hour was come, he sat down, and the twelve apostles with him. [15]And he said unto them, With desire I have desired to eat this passover with you before I suffer: [16]For I say unto you, I will not any more eat thereof, until it be fulfilled in the kingdom of God. [17]And he took the cup, and gave thanks, and said, Take this, and divide *it* among yourselves: [18]For I say unto you, I will not drink of the fruit of the vine, until the kingdom of God shall come.

[19]And he took bread, and gave thanks, and brake *it*, and gave unto them, saying, This is my body which is given for you: this

do in remembrance of me. ²⁰Likewise also the cup after supper, saying, This cup *is* the new testament in my blood, which is shed for you.

²¹But, behold, the hand of him that betrayeth me *is* with me on the table. ²²And truly the Son of man goeth, as it was determined: but woe unto that man by whom he is betrayed! ²³And they began to enquire among themselves, which of them it was that should do this thing.

²⁴And there was also a strife among them, which of them should be accounted the greatest. ²⁵And he said unto them, The kings of the Gentiles exercise lordship over them; and they that exercise authority upon them are called benefactors. ²⁶But ye *shall* not *be* so: but he that is greatest among you, let him be as the younger; and he that is chief, as he that doth serve. ²⁷For whether *is* greater, he that sitteth at meat, or he that serveth? *is* not he that sitteth at meat? but I am among you as he that serveth. ²⁸Ye are they which have continued with me in my temptations. ²⁹And I appoint unto you a kingdom, as my Father hath appointed unto me; ³⁰That ye may eat and drink at my table in my kingdom, and sit on thrones judging the twelve tribes of Israel.

³¹And the Lord said, Simon, Simon, behold, Satan hath desired *to have* you, that he may sift *you* as wheat: ³²But I have prayed for thee, that thy faith fail not: and when thou art converted, strengthen thy brethren. ³³And he said unto him, Lord, I am ready to go with thee, both into prison, and to death. ³⁴And he said, I tell thee, Peter, the cock shall not crow this day, before that thou shalt thrice deny that thou knowest me.

³⁵And he said unto them, When I sent you without purse, and scrip, and shoes, lacked ye any thing? And they said, Nothing. ³⁶Then said he unto them, But now, he that hath a purse, let him take *it*, and likewise *his* scrip: and he that hath no sword, let him sell his garment, and buy one. ³⁷For I say unto you, that this that is written must yet be accomplished in me, And he was reckoned among the transgressors: for the things concerning me have an end. ³⁸And they said, Lord, behold, here *are* two swords. And he said unto them, It is enough.

³⁹And he came out, and went, as he was wont, to the mount of Olives; and his disciples also followed him. ⁴⁰And when he was at the place, he said unto them, Pray that ye enter not into temptation. ⁴¹And he was withdrawn from them about a stone's cast, and kneeled down, and prayed, ⁴²Saying, Father, if thou be willing, remove this cup from me: nevertheless not my will, but thine, be done. ⁴³And there appeared an angel unto him from heaven, strengthening him. ⁴⁴And being in an agony he prayed more earnestly: and his sweat was as it were great drops of blood falling down to the ground. ⁴⁵And when he rose up from prayer, and was come to his disciples, he found them sleeping for sorrow, ⁴⁶And said unto them, Why sleep ye? rise and pray, lest ye enter into temptation.

⁴⁷And while he yet spake, behold a multitude, and he that was called Judas, one of the twelve, went before them, and drew near unto Jesus to kiss him. ⁴⁸But Jesus said unto him, Judas, betrayest thou the Son of man with a kiss? ⁴⁹When they which were about him saw what would follow, they said unto him, Lord, shall we smite with the sword?

⁵⁰And one of them smote the servant of the high priest, and cut off his right ear. ⁵¹And Jesus answered and said, Suffer ye thus far. And he touched his ear, and healed him. ⁵²Then Jesus said unto the chief priests, and captains of the temple, and the elders, which were come to him, Be ye come out, as against a thief, with swords and staves? ⁵³When I was daily with you in the temple, ye stretched forth no hands against me: but this is your hour, and the power of darkness.

⁵⁴Then took they him, and led *him*, and brought him into the high priest's house. And Peter followed afar off. ⁵⁵And when they had kindled a fire in the midst of the hall, and were set down together, Peter sat down among them. ⁵⁶But a certain maid beheld him as he sat by the fire, and earnestly looked upon him, and said, This man was also with him. ⁵⁷And he denied him, saying, Woman, I know him not. ⁵⁸And after a little while another saw him,

and said, Thou art also of them. And Peter said, Man, I am not. ⁵⁹And about the space of one hour after another confidently affirmed, saying, Of a truth this *fellow* also was with him: for he is a Galilaean. ⁶⁰And Peter said, Man, I know not what thou sayest. And immediately, while he yet spake, the cock crew. ⁶¹And the Lord turned, and looked upon Peter. And Peter remembered the word of the Lord, how he had said unto him, Before the cock crow, thou shalt deny me thrice. ⁶²And Peter went out, and wept bitterly.

⁶³And the men that held Jesus mocked him, and smote *him*. ⁶⁴And when they had blindfolded him, they struck him on the face, and asked him, saying, Prophesy, who is it that smote thee? ⁶⁵And many other things blasphemously spake they against him.

⁶⁶And as soon as it was day, the elders of the people and the chief priests and the scribes came together, and led him into their council, saying, ⁶⁷Art thou the Christ? tell us. And he said unto them, If I tell you, ye will not believe: ⁶⁸And if I also ask *you*, ye will not answer me, nor let *me* go. ⁶⁹Hereafter shall the Son of man sit on the right hand of the power of God. ⁷⁰Then said they all, Art thou then the Son of God? And he said unto them, Ye say that I am. ⁷¹And they said, What need we any further witness? for we ourselves have heard of his own mouth.

23 And the whole multitude of them arose, and led him unto Pilate. ²And they began to accuse him, saying, We found this *fellow* perverting the nation, and forbidding to give tribute to Caesar, saying that he himself is Christ a King. ³And Pilate asked him, saying, Art thou the King of the Jews? And he answered him and said, Thou sayest *it*. ⁴Then said Pilate to the chief priests and *to* the people, I find no fault in this man. ⁵And they were the more fierce, saying, He stirreth up the people, teaching throughout all Jewry, beginning from Galilee to this place.

⁶When Pilate heard of Galilee, he asked whether the man were a Galilaean. ⁷And as soon as he knew that he belonged unto Herod's jurisdiction, he sent him to Herod,

who himself also was at Jerusalem at that time.

⁸And when Herod saw Jesus, he was exceeding glad: for he was desirous to see him of a long *season*, because he had heard many things of him; and he hoped to have seen some miracle done by him. ⁹Then he questioned with him in many words; but he answered him nothing. ¹⁰And the chief priests and scribes stood and vehemently accused him. ¹¹And Herod with his men of war set him at nought, and mocked *him*, and arrayed him in a gorgeous robe, and sent him again to Pilate.

¹²And the same day Pilate and Herod were made friends together: for before they were at enmity between themselves.

¹³And Pilate, when he had called together the chief priests and the rulers and the people, ¹⁴Said unto them, Ye have brought this man unto me, as one that perverteth the people: and, behold, I, having examined *him* before you, have found no fault in this man touching those things whereof ye accuse him: ¹⁵No, nor yet Herod: for I sent you to him; and, lo, nothing worthy of death is done unto him. ¹⁶I will therefore chastise him, and release *him*. ¹⁷(For of necessity he must release one unto them at the feast.) ¹⁸And they cried out all at once, saying, Away with this *man*, and release unto us Barabbas: ¹⁹(Who for a certain sedition made in the city, and for murder, was cast into prison.) ²⁰Pilate therefore, willing to release Jesus, spake again to them. ²¹But they cried, saying, Crucify *him*, crucify him. ²²And he said unto them the third time, Why, what evil hath he done? I have found no cause of death in him: I will therefore chastise him, and let *him* go. ²³And they were instant with loud voices, requiring that he might be crucified. And the voices of them and of the chief priests prevailed. ²⁴And Pilate gave sentence that it should be as they required. ²⁵And he released unto them him that for sedition and murder was cast into prison, whom they had desired; but he delivered Jesus to their will.

²⁶And as they led him away, they laid hold upon one Simon, a Cyrenian, coming out of the country, and on him they laid the cross, that he might bear *it* after Jesus.

²⁷And there followed him a great company of people, and of women, which also bewailed and lamented him. ²⁸But Jesus turning unto them said, Daughters of Jerusalem, weep not for me, but weep for yourselves, and for your children. ²⁹For, behold, the days are coming, in the which they shall say, Blessed *are* the barren, and the wombs that never bare, and the paps which never gave suck. ³⁰Then

shall they begin to say to the mountains, Fall on us; and to the hills, Cover us.

³¹For if they do these things in a green tree, what shall be done in the dry? ³²And there were also two others, malefactors, led with him to be put to death. ³³And when they were come to the place, which is called Calvary, there they crucified him, and the malefactors, one on the right hand, and the other on the left.

³⁴Then said Jesus, Father, forgive them; for they know not what they do. And they parted his raiment, and cast lots. ³⁵And the people stood beholding. And the rulers also with them derided *him,* saying, He saved others; let him save himself, if he be Christ, the chosen of God. ³⁶And the soldiers also mocked him, coming to him, and offering him vinegar, ³⁷And saying, If thou be the king of the Jews, save thyself. ³⁸And a superscription also was written over him in letters of Greek, and Latin, and Hebrew, THIS IS THE KING OF THE JEWS.

³⁹And one of the malefactors which were hanged railed on him, saying, If thou be Christ, save thyself and us. ⁴⁰But the other answering rebuked him, saying, Dost not thou fear God, seeing thou art in the same condemnation? ⁴¹And we indeed justly; for we receive the due reward of our deeds: but this man hath done nothing amiss. ⁴²And he said unto Jesus, Lord, remember me when thou comest into thy kingdom. ⁴³And Jesus said unto him, Verily I say unto thee, To day shalt thou be with me in paradise.

⁴⁴And it was about the sixth hour, and there was a darkness over all the earth until the ninth hour. ⁴⁵And the sun was darkened, and the veil of the temple was rent in the midst.

⁴⁶And when Jesus had cried with a loud voice, he said, Father, into thy hands I commend my spirit: and having said thus, he gave up the ghost. ⁴⁷Now when the centurion saw what was done, he glorified God, saying, Certainly this was a righteous man. ⁴⁸And all the people that came together to that sight, beholding the things which were done, smote their breasts, and returned. ⁴⁹And all his acquaintance, and the women that followed him from Galilee, stood afar off, beholding these things.

⁵⁰And, behold, *there was* a man named Joseph, a counsellor; *and he was* a good man, and a just: ⁵¹(The same had not consented to the counsel and deed of them;) *he was* of Arimathaea, a city of the Jews: who also himself waited for the kingdom of God. ⁵²This *man* went unto Pilate, and begged the body of Jesus. ⁵³And he took it down, and wrapped it in linen, and laid it in a sepulchre that was hewn in stone, wherein never man before was laid. ⁵⁴And that day was the preparation, and the sabbath drew on. ⁵⁵And the women also, which came with him from Galilee, followed after, and beheld the sepulchre, and how his body was laid. ⁵⁶And they returned, and prepared spices and ointments; and rested the sabbath day according to the commandment.

24 Now upon the first *day* of the week, very early in the morning, they came unto the sepulchre, bringing the spices which they had prepared, and certain *others* with them. ²And they found the stone rolled away from the sepulchre. ³And they entered in, and found not the body of the Lord Jesus. ⁴And it came to pass, as they were much perplexed thereabout, behold, two men stood by them in shining garments: ⁵And as they were afraid, and bowed down *their* faces to the earth, they said unto them, Why seek ye the living among the dead? ⁶He is not here, but is risen: remember how he spake unto you when he was yet in Galilee, ⁷Saying, The Son of man must be delivered into the hands of sinful men, and be crucified, and the third day rise again. ⁸And they remembered his words, ⁹And returned from the sepulchre, and told all these things unto the eleven, and to all the rest. ¹⁰It was Mary Magdalene, and Joanna, and Mary *the mother* of

James, and other *women that were* with them, which told these things unto the apostles. [11]And their words seemed to them as idle tales, and they believed them not. [12]Then arose Peter, and ran unto the sepulchre; and stooping down, he beheld the linen clothes laid by themselves, and departed, wondering in himself at that which was come to pass.

[13]And, behold, two of them went that same day to a village called Emmaus, which was from Jerusalem *about* threescore furlongs. [14]And they talked together of all these things which had happened. [15]And it came to pass, that, while they communed *together* and reasoned, Jesus himself drew near, and went with them. [16]But their eyes were holden that they should not know him. [17]And he said unto them, What manner of communications *are* these that ye have one to another, as ye walk, and are sad? [18]And the one of them, whose name was Cleopas, answering said unto him, Art thou only a stranger in Jerusalem, and hast not known the things which are come to pass there in these days? [19]And he said unto them, What things? And they said unto him, Concerning Jesus of Nazareth, which was a prophet mighty in deed and word before God and all the people: [20]And how the chief priests and our rulers delivered him to be condemned to death, and have crucified him. [21]But we trusted that it had been he which should have redeemed Israel: and beside all this, to day is the third day since these things were done. [22]Yea, and certain women also of our company made us astonished, which were early at the sepulchre; [23]And when they found not his body, they came, saying, that they had also seen a vision of angels, which said that he was alive. [24]And certain of them which were with us went to the sepulchre, and found *it* even so as the women had said: but him they saw not. [25]Then he said unto them, O fools, and slow of heart to believe all that the prophets have spoken: [26]Ought not Christ to have suffered these things, and to enter into his glory? [27]And beginning at Moses and all the prophets, he expounded unto them in all the scriptures the things concerning himself. [28]And they drew nigh unto the village, whither they went: and he made as

though he would have gone further. [29]But they constrained him, saying, Abide with us: for it is toward evening, and the day is far spent. And he went in to tarry with them. [30]And it came to pass, as he sat at meat with them, he took bread, and blessed *it,* and brake, and gave to them. [31]And their eyes were opened, and they knew him; and he vanished out of their sight. [32]And they said one to another, Did not our heart burn within us, while he talked with us by the way, and while he opened to us the scriptures? [33]And they rose up the same hour, and returned to Jerusalem, and found the eleven gathered together, and them that were with them, [34]Saying, The Lord is risen indeed, and hath appeared to Simon. [35]And they told what things *were done* in the way, and how he was known of them in breaking of bread.

[36]And as they thus spake, Jesus himself stood in the midst of them, and saith unto them, Peace *be* unto you. [37]But they were terrified and affrighted, and supposed that they had seen a spirit. [38]And he said unto them, Why are ye troubled? and why do thoughts arise in your hearts? [39]Behold my hands and my feet, that it is I myself: handle me, and see; for a spirit hath not flesh and bones, as ye see me have. [40]And when he had thus spoken, he shewed them *his* hands and *his* feet. [41]And while they yet believed not for joy, and wondered, he said unto them, Have ye here any meat? [42]And they gave him a piece of a broiled fish, and of an honeycomb. [43]And he took *it,* and did eat before them.

[44]And he said unto them, These *are* the words which I spake unto you, while I was yet with you, that all things must be fulfilled, which were written in the law of Moses, and *in* the prophets, and *in* the psalms, concerning me. [45]Then opened he their understanding, that they might understand the scriptures, [46]And said unto them, Thus it is written, and thus it behoved Christ to suffer, and to rise from the dead the third day: [47]And that repentance and remission of sins should be preached in his name among all nations, beginning at Jerusalem. [48]And ye are witnesses of these things.

[49]And, behold, I send the promise of my

Father upon you: but tarry ye in the city of Jerusalem, until ye be endued with power from on high.

⁵⁰And he led them out as far as to Bethany, and he lifted up his hands, and blessed them. ⁵¹And it came to pass, while he blessed them, he was parted from them, and carried up into heaven. ⁵²And they worshipped him, and returned to Jerusalem with great joy: ⁵³And were continually in the temple, praising and blessing God. Amen.

The Gospel According to
ST. JOHN

1 In the beginning was the Word, and the Word was with God, and the Word was God. ²The same was in the beginning with God. ³All things were made by him; and without him was not any thing made that was made. ⁴In him was life; and the life was the light of men. ⁵And the light shineth in darkness; and the darkness comprehended it not.

⁶There was a man sent from God, whose name *was* John. ⁷The same came for a witness, to bear witness of the Light, that all *men* through him might believe. ⁸He was not that Light, but *was sent* to bear witness of that Light. ⁹*That* was the true Light, which lighteth every man that cometh into the world. ¹⁰He was in the world, and the world was made by him, and the world knew him not. ¹¹He came unto his own, and his own received him not. ¹²But as many as received him, to them gave he power to become the sons of God, *even* to them that believe on his name: ¹³Which were born, not of blood, nor of the will of the flesh, nor of the will of man, but of God. ¹⁴And the Word was made flesh, and dwelt among us, (and we beheld his glory, the glory as of the only begotten of the Father,) full of grace and truth.

¹⁵John bare witness of him, and cried, saying, This was he of whom I spake, He that cometh after me is preferred before me: for he was before me. ¹⁶And of his fulness have all we received, and grace for grace. ¹⁷For the law was given by Moses, *but* grace and truth came by Jesus Christ. ¹⁸No man hath seen God at any time; the only begotten Son, which is in the bosom of the Father, he hath declared *him.*

¹⁹And this is the record of John, when the Jews sent priests and Levites from Jerusalem to ask him, Who art thou? ²⁰And he confessed, and denied not; but confessed, I am not the Christ. ²¹And they asked him, What then? Art thou Elias? And he saith, I am not. Art thou that prophet? And he answered, No. ²²Then said they unto him, Who art thou? that we may give an answer to them that sent us. What sayest thou of thyself? ²³He said, I *am* the voice of one crying in the wilderness, Make straight the way of the Lord, as said the prophet Esaias. ²⁴And they which were sent were of the Pharisees. ²⁵And they asked him, and said unto him, Why baptizest thou then, if thou be not that Christ, nor Elias, neither that prophet? ²⁶John answered them, saying, I baptize with water: but there standeth one among you, whom ye know not; ²⁷He it is, who coming after me is preferred before me, whose shoe's latchet I am not worthy to unloose. ²⁸These things were done in Bethabara beyond Jordan, where John was baptizing.

²⁹The next day John seeth Jesus coming unto him, and saith, Behold the Lamb of God, which taketh away the sin of the world. ³⁰This is he of whom I said, After me cometh a man which is preferred before me: for he was before me. ³¹And I knew him not: but that he should be made manifest to Israel, therefore am I come baptizing with water. ³²And John bare record, saying, I saw the Spirit descending from heaven like a dove, and it abode upon him. ³³And I knew him not: but he that sent me to baptize with water, the same said unto me, Upon whom thou shalt see the Spirit descending, and remaining on him, the same is he which baptizeth with the Holy Ghost. ³⁴And I saw, and bare record that this is the Son of God.

³⁵Again the next day after John stood, and two of his disciples; ³⁶And looking upon Jesus as he walked, he saith, Behold the Lamb of God! ³⁷And the two disciples heard him speak, and they followed Jesus. ³⁸Then Jesus turned, and saw them following, and saith unto them, What seek ye? They said unto him, Rabbi, (which is to say, being interpreted, Master,) where dwellest thou? ³⁹He saith unto them, Come and see. They came and saw where he dwelt, and abode with him that day: for it was about the tenth hour. ⁴⁰One of the two which heard John *speak,* and followed him, was Andrew, Simon Peter's brother. ⁴¹He first findeth his own brother Simon, and saith unto him, We have found the Messias,

which is, being interpreted, the Christ. [42]And he brought him to Jesus. And when Jesus beheld him, he said, Thou art Simon the son of Jona: thou shalt be called Cephas, which is by interpretation, A stone. [43]The day following Jesus would go forth into Galilee, and findeth Philip, and saith unto him, Follow me. [44]Now Philip was of Bethsaida, the city of Andrew and Peter. [45]Philip findeth Nathanael, and saith unto him, We have found him, of whom Moses in the law, and the prophets, did write, Jesus of Nazareth, the son of Joseph. [46]And Nathanael said unto him, Can there any good thing come out of Nazareth? Philip saith unto him, Come and see. [47]Jesus saw Nathanael coming to him, and saith of him, Behold an Israelite indeed, in whom is no guile! [48]Nathanael saith unto him, Whence knowest thou me? Jesus answered and said unto him, Before that Philip called thee, when thou wast under the fig tree, I saw thee. [49]Nathanael answered and saith unto him, Rabbi, thou art the Son of God; thou art the King of Israel. [50]Jesus answered and said unto him, Because I said unto thee, I saw thee under the fig tree, believest thou? thou shalt see greater things than these. [51]And he saith unto him, Verily, verily, I say unto you, Hereafter ye shall see heaven open, and the angels of God ascending and descending upon the Son of man.

2 And the third day there was a marriage in Cana of Galilee; and the mother of Jesus was there: [2]And both Jesus was called, and his disciples, to the marriage. [3]And when they wanted wine, the mother of Jesus saith unto him, They have no wine. [4]Jesus saith unto her, Woman, what have I to do with thee? mine hour is not yet come. [5]His mother saith unto the servants, Whatsoever he saith unto you, do it. [6]And there were set there six waterpots of stone, after the manner of the purifying of the Jews, containing two or three firkins apiece. [7]Jesus saith unto them, Fill the waterpots with water. And they filled them up to the brim. [8]And he saith unto them, Draw out now, and bear unto the governor of the feast. And they bare it. [9]When the ruler of the feast had tasted the water that was made wine, and knew not whence it was:

(but the servants which drew the water knew;) the governor of the feast called the bridegroom, [10]And saith unto him, Every man at the beginning doth set forth good wine; and when men have well drunk, then that which is worse: but thou hast kept the good wine until now. [11]This beginning of miracles did Jesus in Cana of Galilee, and manifested forth his glory; and his disciples believed on him.

[12]After this he went down to Capernaum, he, and his mother, and his brethren, and his disciples: and they continued there not many days.

[13]And the Jews' passover was at hand, and Jesus went up to Jerusalem, [14]And found in the temple those that sold oxen and sheep and doves, and the changers of money sitting: [15]And when he had made a scourge of small cords, he drove them all out of the temple, and the sheep, and the oxen; and poured out the changers' money, and overthrew the tables; [16]And said unto them that sold doves, Take these things hence; make not my Father's house an house of merchandise. [17]And his disciples remembered that it was written, The zeal of thine house hath eaten me up.

[18]Then answered the Jews and said unto him, What sign shewest thou unto us, seeing that thou doest these things? [19]Jesus answered and said unto them, Destroy this temple, and in three days I will raise it up. [20]Then said the Jews, Forty and six years was this temple in building, and wilt thou rear it up in three days? [21]But he spake of the temple of his body. [22]When therefore he was risen from the dead, his disciples remembered that he had said this unto them; and they believed the scripture, and the word which Jesus had said.

[23]Now when he was in Jerusalem at the passover, in the feast day, many believed in his name, when they saw the miracles which he did. [24]But Jesus did not commit himself unto them, because he knew all men, [25]And needed not that any should testify of man: for he knew what was in man.

3 There was a man of the Pharisees, named Nicodemus, a ruler of the Jews: [2]The same came to Jesus by night, and said unto him, Rabbi, we know that thou art a

teacher come from God: for no man can do these miracles that thou doest, except God be with him. ³Jesus answered and said unto him, Verily, verily, I say unto thee, Except a man be born again, he cannot see the kingdom of God. ⁴Nicodemus saith unto him, How can a man be born when he is old? can he enter the second time into his mother's womb, and be born? ⁵Jesus answered, Verily, verily, I say unto thee, Except a man be born of water and *of* the Spirit, he cannot enter into the kingdom of God. ⁶That which is born of the flesh is flesh; and that which is born of the Spirit is spirit. ⁷Marvel not that I said unto thee, Ye must be born again. ⁸The wind bloweth where it listeth, and thou hearest the sound thereof, but canst not tell whence it cometh, and whither it goeth: so is every one that is born of the Spirit. ⁹Nicodemus answered and said unto him, How can these things be? ¹⁰Jesus answered and said unto him, Art thou a master of Israel, and knowest not these things? ¹¹Verily, verily, I say unto thee, We speak that we do know, and testify that we have seen; and ye receive not our witness. ¹²If I have told you earthly things, and ye believe not, how shall ye believe, if I tell you *of* heavenly things? ¹³And no man hath ascended up to heaven, but he that came down from heaven, *even* the Son of man which is in heaven.

¹⁴And as Moses lifted up the serpent in the wilderness, even so must the Son of man be lifted up: ¹⁵That whosoever believeth in him should not perish, but have eternal life.

¹⁶For God so loved the world, that he gave his only begotten Son, that whosoever believeth in him should not perish, but have everlasting life. ¹⁷For God sent not his Son into the world to condemn the world; but that the world through him might be saved.

¹⁸He that believeth on him is not condemned: but he that believeth not is condemned already, because he hath not believed in the name of the only begotten Son of God. ¹⁹And this is the condemnation, that light is come into the world, and men loved darkness rather than light, because their deeds were evil. ²⁰For every one that doeth evil hateth the light, neither cometh to the light, lest his deeds should be reproved. ²¹But he that doeth truth cometh to the light, that his deeds may be made manifest, that they are wrought in God.

²²After these things came Jesus and his disciples into the land of Judaea; and there he tarried with them, and baptized.

²³And John also was baptizing in Aenon near to Salim, because there was much water there: and they came, and were baptized. ²⁴For John was not yet cast into prison.

²⁵Then there arose a question between *some* of John's disciples and the Jews about purifying. ²⁶And they came unto John, and said unto him, Rabbi, he that was with thee beyond Jordan, to whom thou barest witness, behold, the same baptizeth, and all *men* come to him. ²⁷John answered and said, A man can receive nothing, except it be given him from heaven. ²⁸Ye yourselves bear me witness, that I said, I am not the Christ, but that I am sent before him. ²⁹He that hath the bride is the bridegroom: but the friend of the bridegroom, which standeth and heareth him, rejoiceth greatly because of the bridegroom's voice: this my joy therefore is fulfilled. ³⁰He must increase, but I *must* decrease. ³¹He that cometh from above is above all: he that is of the earth is earthly, and speaketh of the earth: he that cometh from heaven is above all. ³²And what he hath seen and heard, that he testifieth; and no man receiveth his testimony. ³³He that hath received his testimony hath set to his seal that God is true. ³⁴For he whom God hath sent speaketh the words of God: for God giveth not the Spirit by measure *unto him.* ³⁵The Father loveth the Son, and hath given all things into his hand. ³⁶He that believeth on the Son hath everlasting life: and he that believeth not the Son shall not see life; but the wrath of God abideth on him.

4 When therefore the Lord knew how the Pharisees had heard that Jesus made and baptized more disciples than John, ²(Though Jesus himself baptized not, but his disciples,) ³He left Judaea, and departed again into Galilee. ⁴And he must needs go through Samaria. ⁵Then cometh he to a city of Samaria, which is called Sychar, near to the parcel of ground

that Jacob gave to his son Joseph. ⁶Now Jacob's well was there. Jesus therefore, being wearied with *his* journey, sat thus on the well: *and* it was about the sixth hour. ⁷There cometh a woman of Samaria to draw water: Jesus saith unto her, Give me to drink. ⁸(For his disciples were gone away unto the city to buy meat.) ⁹Then saith the woman of Samaria unto him, How is it that thou, being a Jew, askest drink of me, which am a woman of Samaria? for the Jews have no dealings with the Samaritans. ¹⁰Jesus answered and said unto her, If thou knewest the gift of God, and who it is that saith to thee, Give me to drink; thou wouldest have asked of him, and he would have given thee living water. ¹¹The woman saith unto him, Sir, thou hast nothing to draw with, and the well is deep: from whence then hast thou that living water? ¹²Art thou greater than our father Jacob, which gave us the well, and drank thereof himself, and his children, and his cattle? ¹³Jesus answered and said unto her, Whosoever drinketh of this water shall thirst again: ¹⁴But whosoever drinketh of the water that I shall give him shall never thirst; but the water that I shall give him shall be in him a well of water springing up into everlasting life. ¹⁵The woman saith unto him, Sir, give me this water, that I thirst not, neither come hither to draw. ¹⁶Jesus saith unto her, Go, call thy husband, and come hither. ¹⁷The woman answered and said, I have no husband. Jesus said unto her, Thou hast well said, I have no husband: ¹⁸For thou hast had five husbands; and he whom thou now hast is not thy husband: in that saidst thou truly. ¹⁹The woman saith unto him, Sir, I perceive that thou art a prophet. ²⁰Our fathers worshipped in this mountain; and ye say, that in Jerusalem is the place where men ought to worship. ²¹Jesus saith unto her, Woman, believe me, the hour cometh, when ye shall neither in this mountain, nor yet at Jerusalem, worship the Father. ²²Ye worship ye know not what: we know what we worship: for salvation is of the Jews. ²³But the hour cometh, and now is, when the true worshippers shall worship the Father in spirit and in truth: for the Father seeketh such to worship him. ²⁴God *is* a Spirit: and

they that worship him must worship *him* in spirit and in truth. ²⁵The woman saith unto him, I know that Messias cometh, which is called Christ: when he is come, he will tell us all things. ²⁶Jesus saith unto her, I that speak unto thee am *he*.

²⁷And upon this came his disciples, and marvelled that he talked with the woman: yet no man said, What seekest thou? or, Why talkest thou with her? ²⁸The woman then left her waterpot, and went her way into the city, and saith to the men, ²⁹Come, see a man, which told me all things that ever I did: is not this the Christ? ³⁰Then they went out of the city, and came unto him.

³¹In the mean while his disciples prayed him, saying, Master, eat. ³²But he said unto them, I have meat to eat that ye know not of. ³³Therefore said the disciples one to another, Hath any man brought him *ought* to eat? ³⁴Jesus saith unto them, My meat is to do the will of him that sent me, and to finish his work. ³⁵Say not ye, There are yet four months, and *then* cometh harvest? behold, I say unto you, Lift up your eyes, and look on the fields; for they are white already to harvest. ³⁶And he that reapeth receiveth wages, and gathereth fruit unto life eternal: that both he that soweth and he that reapeth may rejoice together. ³⁷And herein is that saying true, One soweth, and another reapeth. ³⁸I sent you to reap that whereon ye bestowed no labour: other men laboured, and ye are entered into their labours.

³⁹And many of the Samaritans of that city believed on him for the saying of the woman, which testified, He told me all that ever I did. ⁴⁰So when the Samaritans were come unto him, they besought him that he would tarry with them: and he abode there two days. ⁴¹And many more believed because of his own word; ⁴²And said unto the woman, Now we believe, not because of thy saying: for we have heard *him* ourselves, and know that this is indeed the Christ, the Saviour of the world.

⁴³Now after two days he departed thence, and went into Galilee. ⁴⁴For Jesus himself testified, that a prophet hath no honour in his own country. ⁴⁵Then when he was come into Galilee, the Galilaeans

received him, having seen all the things that he did at Jerusalem at the feast: for they also went unto the feast. ⁴⁶So Jesus came again into Cana of Galilee, where he made the water wine. And there was a certain nobleman, whose son was sick at Capernaum. ⁴⁷When he heard that Jesus was come out of Judaea into Galilee, he went unto him, and besought him that he would come down, and heal his son: for he was at the point of death. ⁴⁸Then said Jesus unto him, Except ye see signs and wonders, ye will not believe. ⁴⁹The nobleman saith unto him, Sir, come down ere my child die. ⁵⁰Jesus saith unto him, Go thy way; thy son liveth. And the man believed the word that Jesus had spoken unto him, and he went his way. ⁵¹And as he was now going down, his servants met him, and told *him*, saying, Thy son liveth. ⁵²Then enquired he of them the hour when he began to amend. And they said unto him, Yesterday at the seventh hour the fever left him. ⁵³So the father knew that *it was* at the same hour, in the which Jesus said unto him, Thy son liveth: and himself believed, and his whole house. ⁵⁴This *is* again the second miracle *that* Jesus did, when he was come out of Judaea into Galilee.

5 After this there was a feast of the Jews; and Jesus went up to Jerusalem. ²Now there is at Jerusalem by the sheep *market* a pool, which is called in the Hebrew tongue Bethesda, having five porches. ³In these lay a great multitude of impotent folk, of blind, halt, withered, waiting for the moving of the water. ⁴For an angel went down at a certain season into the pool, and troubled the water: whosoever then first after the troubling of the water stepped in was made whole of whatsoever disease he had. ⁵And a certain man was there, which had an infirmity thirty and eight years. ⁶When Jesus saw him lie, and knew that he had been now a long time *in that case*, he saith unto him, Wilt thou be made whole? ⁷The impotent man answered him, Sir, I have no man, when the water is troubled, to put me into the pool: but while I am coming, another steppeth down before me. ⁸Jesus saith unto him, Rise, take up thy bed, and walk. ⁹And immediately the man was made whole,

and took up his bed, and walked: and on the same day was the sabbath.

¹⁰The Jews therefore said unto him that was cured, It is the sabbath day: it is not lawful for thee to carry *thy* bed. ¹¹He answered them, He that made me whole, the same said unto me, Take up thy bed, and walk. ¹²Then asked they him, What man is that which said unto thee, Take up thy bed, and walk? ¹³And he that was healed wist not who it was: for Jesus had conveyed himself away, a multitude being in *that* place. ¹⁴Afterward Jesus findeth him in the temple, and said unto him, Behold, thou art made whole: sin no more, lest a worse thing come unto thee. ¹⁵The man departed, and told the Jews that it was Jesus, which had made him whole. ¹⁶And therefore did the Jews persecute Jesus, and sought to slay him, because he had done these things on the sabbath day.

¹⁷But Jesus answered them, My Father worketh hitherto, and I work. ¹⁸Therefore the Jews sought the more to kill him, because he not only had broken the sabbath, but said also that God was his Father, making himself equal with God. ¹⁹Then answered Jesus and said unto them, Verily, verily, I say unto you, The Son can do nothing of himself, but what he seeth the Father do: for what things soever he doeth, these also doeth the Son likewise. ²⁰For the Father loveth the Son, and sheweth him all things that himself doeth: and he will shew him greater works than these, that ye may marvel. ²¹For as the Father raiseth up the dead, and quickeneth *them;* even so the Son quickeneth whom he will. ²²For the Father judgeth no man, but hath committed all judgment unto the Son: ²³That all *men* should honour the Son, even as they honour the Father. He that honoureth not the Son honoureth not the Father which hath sent him. ²⁴Verily, verily, I say unto you, He that heareth my word, and believeth on him that sent me, hath everlasting life, and shall not come into condemnation; but is passed from death unto life. ²⁵Verily, verily, I say unto you, The hour is coming, and now is, when the dead shall hear the voice of the Son of God: and they that hear shall live. ²⁶For as the Father hath life in himself; so hath he given to the Son to have life in

himself; [27]And hath given him authority to execute judgment also, because he is the Son of man. [28]Marvel not at this: for the hour is coming, in the which all that are in the graves shall hear his voice, [29]And shall come forth; they that have done good, unto the resurrection of life; and they that have done evil, unto the resurrection of damnation. [30]I can of mine own self do nothing: as I hear, I judge: and my judgment is just; because I seek not mine own will, but the will of the Father which hath sent me. [31]If I bear witness of myself, my witness is not true.

[32]There is another that beareth witness of me; and I know that the witness which he witnesseth of me is true. [33]Ye sent unto John, and he bare witness unto the truth. [34]But I receive not testimony from man: but these things I say, that ye might be saved. [35]He was a burning and a shining light: and ye were willing for a season to rejoice in his light.

[36]But I have greater witness than *that* of John: for the works which the Father hath given me to finish, the same works that I do, bear witness of me, that the Father hath sent me. [37]And the Father himself, which hath sent me, hath borne witness of me. Ye have neither heard his voice at any time, nor seen his shape. [38]And ye have not his word abiding in you: for whom he hath sent, him ye believe not.

[39]Search the scriptures; for in them ye think ye have eternal life: and they are they which testify of me. [40]And ye will not come to me, that ye might have life. [41]I receive not honour from men. [42]But I know you, that ye have not the love of God in you. [43]I am come in my Father's name, and ye receive me not: if another shall come in his own name, him ye will receive. [44]How can ye believe, which receive honour one of another, and seek not the honour that *cometh* from God only? [45]Do not think that I will accuse you to the Father: there is *one* that accuseth you, *even* Moses, in whom ye trust. [46]For had ye believed Moses, ye would have believed me: for he wrote of me. [47]But if ye believe not his writings, how shall ye believe my words?

6 After these things Jesus went over the sea of Galilee, which is *the sea* of Tiberias. [2]And a great multitude followed him, because they saw his miracles which he did on them that were diseased. [3]And Jesus went up into a mountain, and there he sat with his disciples. [4]And the passover, a feast of the Jews, was nigh.

[5]When Jesus then lifted up *his* eyes, and saw a great company come unto him, he saith unto Philip, Whence shall we buy bread, that these may eat? [6]And this he said to prove him: for he himself knew what he would do. [7]Philip answered him, Two hundred pennyworth of bread is not sufficient for them, that every one of them may take a little. [8]One of his disciples, Andrew, Simon Peter's brother, saith unto him, [9]There is a lad here, which hath five barley loaves, and two small fishes: but what are they among so many? [10]And Jesus said, Make the men sit down. Now there was much grass in the place. So the men sat down, in number about five thousand. [11]And Jesus took the loaves; and when he had given thanks, he distributed to the disciples, and the disciples to them that were set down; and likewise of the fishes as much as they would. [12]When they were filled, he said unto his disciples, Gather up the fragments that remain, that nothing be lost. [13]Therefore they gathered *them* together, and filled twelve baskets with the fragments of the five barley loaves, which remained over and above unto them that had eaten. [14]Then those men, when they had seen the miracle that Jesus did, said, This is of a truth that prophet that should come into the world.

[15]When Jesus therefore perceived that they would come and take him by force, to make him a king, he departed again into a mountain himself alone. [16]And when even was *now* come, his disciples went down unto the sea, [17]And entered into a ship, and went over the sea toward Capernaum. And it was now dark, and Jesus was not come to them. [18]And the sea arose by reason of a great wind that blew. [19]So when they had rowed about five and twenty or thirty furlongs, they see Jesus walking on the sea, and drawing nigh unto the ship: and they were afraid. [20]But he saith unto them, It is I; be not afraid. [21]Then they willingly received him into the ship: and immediately the ship was at the land whither they went.

²²The day following, when the people which stood on the other side of the sea saw that there was none other boat there, save that one whereinto his disciples were entered, and that Jesus went not with his disciples into the boat, but *that* his disciples were gone away alone; ²³(Howbeit there came other boats from Tiberias nigh unto the place where they did eat bread, after that the Lord had given thanks:) ²⁴When the people therefore saw that Jesus was not there, neither his disciples, they also took shipping, and came to Capernaum, seeking for Jesus. ²⁵And when they had found him on the other side of the sea, they said unto him, Rabbi, when camest thou hither? ²⁶Jesus answered them and said, Verily, verily, I say unto you, Ye seek me, not because ye saw the miracles, but because ye did eat of the loaves, and were filled. ²⁷Labour not for the meat which perisheth, but for that meat which endureth unto everlasting life, which the Son of man shall give unto you: for him hath God the Father sealed. ²⁸Then said they unto him, What shall we do, that we might work the works of God? ²⁹Jesus answered and said unto them, This is the work of God, that ye believe on him whom he hath sent. ³⁰They said therefore unto him, What sign shewest thou then, that we may see, and believe thee? what dost thou work? ³¹Our fathers did eat manna in the desert; as it is written, He gave them bread from heaven to eat. ³²Then Jesus said unto them, Verily, verily, I say unto you, Moses gave you not that bread from heaven; but my Father giveth you the true bread from heaven. ³³For the bread of God is he which cometh down from heaven, and giveth life unto the world. ³⁴Then said they unto him, Lord, evermore give us this bread. ³⁵And Jesus said unto them, I am the bread of life: he that cometh to me shall never hunger; and he that believeth on me shall never thirst. ³⁶But I said unto you, That ye also have seen me, and believe not. ³⁷All that the Father giveth me shall come to me; and him that cometh to me I will in no wise cast out. ³⁸For I came down from heaven, not to do mine own will, but the will of him that sent me. ³⁹And this is the Father's will which hath sent me, that of all which he hath

given me I should lose nothing, but should raise it up again at the last day. ⁴⁰And this is the will of him that sent me, that every one which seeth the Son, and believeth on him, may have everlasting life: and I will raise him up at the last day. ⁴¹The Jews then murmured at him, because he said, I am the bread which came down from heaven. ⁴²And they said, Is not this Jesus, the son of Joseph, whose father and mother we know? how is it then that he saith, I came down from heaven? ⁴³Jesus therefore answered and said unto them, Murmur not among yourselves. ⁴⁴No man can come to me, except the Father which hath sent me draw him: and I will raise him up at the last day. ⁴⁵It is written in the prophets, And they shall be all taught of God. Every man therefore that hath heard, and hath learned of the Father, cometh unto me. ⁴⁶Not that any man hath seen the Father, save he which is of God, he hath seen the Father. ⁴⁷Verily, verily, I say unto you, He that believeth on me hath everlasting life. ⁴⁸I am that bread of life. ⁴⁹Your fathers did eat manna in the wilderness, and are dead. ⁵⁰This is the bread which cometh down from heaven, that a man may eat thereof, and not die. ⁵¹I am the living bread which came down from heaven: if any man eat of this bread, he shall live for ever: and the bread that I will give is my flesh, which I will give for the life of the world. ⁵²The Jews therefore strove among themselves, saying, How can this man give us *his* flesh to eat? ⁵³Then Jesus said unto them, Verily, verily, I say unto you, Except ye eat the flesh of the Son of man, and drink his blood, ye have no life in you. ⁵⁴Whoso eateth my flesh, and drinketh my blood, hath eternal life; and I will raise him up at the last day. ⁵⁵For my flesh is meat indeed, and my blood is drink indeed. ⁵⁶He that eateth my flesh, and drinketh my blood, dwelleth in me, and I in him. ⁵⁷As the living Father hath sent me, and I live by the Father: so he that eateth me, even he shall live by me. ⁵⁸This is that bread which came down from heaven: not as your fathers did eat manna, and are dead: he that eateth of this bread shall live for ever. ⁵⁹These things said he in the synagogue, as he taught in Capernaum. ⁶⁰Many therefore of his disciples, when they had heard *this*, said, This is an hard saying; who can hear it? ⁶¹When Jesus knew in himself that his disciples murmured at it, he said unto them, Doth this offend you? ⁶²*What* and if ye shall see the Son of man ascend up where he was before? ⁶³It is the spirit that quickeneth; the flesh profiteth nothing: the words that I speak unto you, *they* are spirit, and *they* are life. ⁶⁴But there are some of you that believe not. For Jesus knew from the beginning who they were that believed not, and who should betray him. ⁶⁵And he said, Therefore said I unto you, that no man can come unto me, except it were given unto him of my Father.

⁶⁶From that *time* many of his disciples went back, and walked no more with him. ⁶⁷Then said Jesus unto the twelve, Will ye also go away? ⁶⁸Then Simon Peter answered him, Lord, to whom shall we go? thou hast the words of eternal life. ⁶⁹And we believe and are sure that thou art that Christ, the Son of the living God. ⁷⁰Jesus answered them, Have not I chosen you twelve, and one of you is a devil? ⁷¹He spake of Judas Iscariot *the son* of Simon: for he it was that should betray him, being one of the twelve.

7 After these things Jesus walked in Galilee: for he would not walk in Jewry, because the Jews sought to kill him. ²Now the Jews' feast of tabernacles was at hand. ³His brethren therefore said unto him, Depart hence, and go into Judaea, that thy disciples also may see the works that thou doest. ⁴For *there is* no man *that* doeth any thing in secret, and he himself seeketh to be known openly. If thou do these things, shew thyself to the world. ⁵For neither did his brethren believe in him. ⁶Then Jesus said unto them, My time is not yet come: but your time is alway ready. ⁷The world cannot hate you; but me it hateth, because I testify of it, that the works thereof are evil. ⁸Go ye up unto this feast: I go not up yet unto this feast; for my time is not yet full come. ⁹When he had said these words unto them, he abode *still* in Galilee.

¹⁰But when his brethren were gone up, then went he also up unto the feast, not openly, but as it were in secret. ¹¹Then the Jews sought him at the feast, and said, Where is he? ¹²And there was much murmuring among the people concerning him: for some said, He is a good man: others said, Nay; but he deceiveth the people. ¹³Howbeit no man spake openly of him for fear of the Jews.

¹⁴Now about the midst of the feast Jesus went up into the temple, and taught. ¹⁵And the Jews marvelled, saying, How knoweth this man letters, having never learned? ¹⁶Jesus answered them, and said, My doctrine is not mine, but his that sent me. ¹⁷If any man will do his will, he shall know of the doctrine, whether it be of God, or *whether* I speak of myself. ¹⁸He that speaketh of himself seeketh his own glory: but he that seeketh his glory that sent him, the same is true, and no unrighteousness is in him. ¹⁹Did not Moses give you the law, and *yet* none of you keepeth the law? Why go ye about to kill me? ²⁰The people answered and said, Thou hast a devil: who goeth about to kill thee? ²¹Jesus answered and said unto them, I have done one work, and ye all marvel. ²²Moses therefore gave unto you circumcision; (not because it is of Moses, but of the fathers;) and ye on the sabbath day circumcise a man. ²³If a man on the sabbath day receive circumcision, that the law of Moses should not be broken; are ye angry at me, because I have made a man every whit whole on the sabbath day? ²⁴Judge not according to the appearance, but judge righteous judgment. ²⁵Then said some of them of Jerusalem, Is not this he, whom they seek to kill? ²⁶But, lo, he speaketh boldly, and they say nothing unto him. Do the rulers know indeed that this is the very Christ? ²⁷Howbeit we know this man whence he is: but when Christ cometh, no man knoweth whence he is. ²⁸Then cried Jesus in the temple as he taught, saying, Ye both know me, and ye know whence I am: and I am not come of myself, but he that sent me is true, whom ye know not. ²⁹But I know him: for I am from him, and he hath sent me. ³⁰Then they sought to take him: but no man laid hands on him, because his hour was not yet come. ³¹And many of the people believed on him, and said, When Christ cometh, will he do more miracles than these which this *man* hath done? ³²The Pharisees heard that the people

murmured such things concerning him; and the Pharisees and the chief priests sent officers to take him. ³³Then said Jesus unto them, Yet a little while am I with you, and *then* I go unto him that sent me. ³⁴Ye shall seek me, and shall not find *me:* and where I am, *thither* ye cannot come. ³⁵Then said the Jews among themselves, Whither will he go, that we shall not find him? will he go unto the dispersed among the Gentiles, and teach the Gentiles? ³⁶What *manner of* saying is this that he said, Ye shall seek me, and shall not find *me:* and where I am, *thither* ye cannot come? ³⁷In the last day, that great *day* of the feast, Jesus stood and cried, saying, If any man thirst, let him come unto me, and drink. ³⁸He that believeth on me, as the scripture hath said, out of his belly shall flow rivers of living water. ³⁹(But this spake he of the Spirit, which they that believe on him should receive: for the Holy Ghost was not yet *given;* because that Jesus was not yet glorified.)

⁴⁰Many of the people therefore, when they heard this saying, said, Of a truth this is the Prophet. ⁴¹Others said, This is the Christ. But some said, Shall Christ come out of Galilee? ⁴²Hath not the scripture said, That Christ cometh of the seed of David, and out of the town of Bethlehem, where David was? ⁴³So there was a division among the people because of him. ⁴⁴And some of them would have taken him; but no man laid hands on him.

⁴⁵Then came the officers to the chief priests and Pharisees; and they said unto them, Why have ye not brought him? ⁴⁶The officers answered, Never man spake like this man. ⁴⁷Then answered them the Pharisees, Are ye also deceived? ⁴⁸Have any of the rulers or of the Pharisees believed on him? ⁴⁹But this people who knoweth not the law are cursed. ⁵⁰Nicodemus saith unto them, (he that came to Jesus by night, being one of them,) ⁵¹Doth our law judge *any* man, before it hear him, and know what he doeth? ⁵²They answered and said unto him, Art thou also of Galilee? Search, and look: for out of Galilee ariseth no prophet. ⁵³And every man went unto his own house.

8 Jesus went unto the mount of Olives. ²And early in the morning he came again into the temple, and all the people came unto him; and he sat down, and taught them. ³And the scribes and Pharisees brought unto him a woman taken in adultery; and when they had set her in the midst, ⁴They say unto him, Master, this woman was taken in adultery, in the very act. ⁵Now Moses in the law commanded us, that such should be stoned: but what sayest thou? ⁶This they said, tempting him, that they might have to accuse him. But Jesus stooped down, and with *his* finger wrote on the ground, *as though he heard them not.* ⁷So when they continued asking him, he lifted up himself, and said unto them, He that is without sin among you, let him first cast a stone at her. ⁸And again he stooped down, and wrote on the ground. ⁹And they which heard *it,* being convicted by *their own* conscience, went out one by one, beginning at the eldest, *even* unto the last: and Jesus was left alone, and the woman standing in the midst. ¹⁰When Jesus had lifted up himself, and saw none but the woman, he said unto her, Woman, where are those thine accusers? hath no man condemned thee? ¹¹She said, No man, Lord. And Jesus said unto her, Neither do I condemn thee: go, and sin no more.

¹²Then spake Jesus again unto them, saying, I am the light of the world: he that followeth me shall not walk in darkness, but shall have the light of life. ¹³The Pharisees therefore said unto him, Thou bearest record of thyself; thy record is not true. ¹⁴Jesus answered and said unto them, Though I bear record of myself, *yet* my record is true: for I know whence I came, and whither I go; but ye cannot tell whence I come, and whither I go. ¹⁵Ye judge after the flesh; I judge no man. ¹⁶And yet if I judge, my judgment is true: for I am not alone, but I and the Father that sent me. ¹⁷It is also written in your law, that the testimony of two men is true. ¹⁸I am one that bear witness of myself, and the Father that sent me beareth witness of me. ¹⁹Then said they unto him, Where is thy Father? Jesus answered, Ye neither know me, nor my Father: if ye had known me, ye should have known my Father also. ²⁰These words spake Jesus in the treasury, as he taught in the temple: and no man laid hands on him; for his hour was not yet come. ²¹Then said

Jesus again unto them, I go my way, and ye shall seek me, and shall die in your sins: whither I go, ye cannot come. [22] Then said the Jews, Will he kill himself? because he saith, Whither I go, ye cannot come. [23] And he said unto them, Ye are from beneath; I am from above: ye are of this world; I am not of this world. [24] I said therefore unto you, that ye shall die in your sins: for if ye believe not that I am *he,* ye shall die in your sins. [25] Then said they unto him, Who art thou? And Jesus saith unto them, Even *the same* that I said unto you from the beginning. [26] I have many things to say and to judge of you: but he that sent me is true; and I speak to the world those things which I have heard of him. [27] They understood not that he spake to them of the Father. [28] Then said Jesus unto them, When ye have lifted up the Son of man, then shall ye know that I am *he,* and *that* I do nothing of myself; but as my Father hath taught me, I speak these things. [29] And he that sent me is with me: the Father hath not left me alone; for I do always those things that please him. [30] As he spake these words, many believed on him. [31] Then said Jesus to those Jews which believed on him, If ye continue in my word, *then* are ye my disciples indeed; [32] And ye shall know the truth, and the truth shall make you free.

[33] They answered him, We be Abraham's seed, and were never in bondage to any man: how sayest thou, Ye shall be made free? [34] Jesus answered them, Verily, verily, I say unto you, Whosoever committeth sin is the servant of sin. [35] And the servant abideth not in the house for ever: *but* the Son abideth ever. [36] If the Son therefore shall make you free, ye shall be free indeed. [37] I know that ye are Abraham's seed; but ye seek to kill me, because my word hath no place in you. [38] I speak that which I have seen with my Father: and ye do that which ye have seen with your father. [39] They answered and said unto him, Abraham is our father. Jesus saith unto them, If ye were Abraham's children, ye would do the works of Abraham. [40] But now ye seek to kill me, a man that hath told you the truth, which I have heard of God: this did not Abraham. [41] Ye do the deeds of your father. Then said they to him, We be not born of fornication;

we have one Father, *even* God. [42] Jesus said unto them, If God were your Father, ye would love me: for I proceeded forth and came from God; neither came I of myself, but he sent me. [43] Why do ye not understand my speech? *even* because ye cannot hear my word. [44] Ye are of your father the devil, and the lusts of *your* father ye will do. He was a murderer from the beginning, and abode not in the truth, because there is no truth in him. When he speaketh a lie, he speaketh of his own: for he is a liar, and the father of it. [45] And because I tell *you* the truth, ye believe me not. [46] Which of you convinceth me of sin? And if I say the truth, why do ye not believe me? [47] He that is of God heareth God's words: ye therefore hear *them* not, because ye are not of God. [48] Then answered the Jews, and said unto him, Say we not well that thou art a Samaritan, and hast a devil? [49] Jesus answered, I have not a devil; but I honour my Father, and ye do dishonour me. [50] And I seek not mine own glory: there is one that seeketh and judgeth. [51] Verily, verily, I say unto you, If a man keep my saying, he shall never see death. [52] Then said the Jews unto him, Now we know that thou hast a devil. Abraham is dead, and the prophets; and thou sayest, If a man keep my saying, he shall never taste of death. [53] Art thou greater than our father Abraham, which is dead? and the prophets are dead: whom makest thou thyself? [54] Jesus answered, If I honour myself, my honour is nothing: it is my Father that honoureth me; of whom ye say, that he is your God: [55] Yet ye have not known him; but I know him: and if I should say, I know him not, I shall be a liar like unto you: but I know him, and keep his saying. [56] Your father Abraham rejoiced to see my day: and he saw *it,* and was glad. [57] Then said the Jews unto him, Thou art not yet fifty years old, and hast thou seen Abraham? [58] Jesus said unto them, Verily, verily, I say unto you, Before Abraham was, I am. [59] Then took they up stones to cast at him: but Jesus hid himself, and went out of the temple, going through the midst of them, and so passed by.

9 And as *Jesus* passed by, he saw a man which was blind from *his* birth. [2] And his disciples asked him, saying, Master, who did sin, this man, or his parents, that he was born blind? ³Jesus answered, Neither hath this man sinned, nor his parents: but that the works of God should be made manifest in him. ⁴I must work the works of him that sent me, while it is day: the night cometh, when no man can work. ⁵As long as I am in the world, I am the light of the world. ⁶When he had thus spoken, he spat on the ground, and made clay of the spittle, and he anointed the eyes of the blind man with the clay, ⁷And said unto him, Go, wash in the pool of Siloam, (which is by interpretation, Sent.) He went his way therefore, and washed, and came seeing.

⁸The neighbours therefore, and they which before had seen him that he was blind, said, Is not this he that sat and begged? ⁹Some said, This is he: others *said,* He is like him: *but* he said, I am *he.* ¹⁰Therefore said they unto him, How were thine eyes opened? ¹¹He answered and said, A man that is called Jesus made clay, and anointed mine eyes, and said unto me, Go to the pool of Siloam, and wash: and I went and washed, and I received sight. ¹²Then said they unto him, Where is he? He said, I know not.

¹³They brought to the Pharisees him that aforetime was blind. ¹⁴And it was the sabbath day when Jesus made the clay, and opened his eyes. ¹⁵Then again the Pharisees also asked him how he had received his sight. He said unto them, He put clay upon mine eyes, and I washed, and do see. ¹⁶Therefore said some of the Pharisees, This man is not of God, because he keepeth not the sabbath day. Others said, How can a man that is a sinner do such miracles? And there was a division among them. ¹⁷They say unto the blind man again, What sayest thou of him, that he hath opened thine eyes? He said, He is a prophet. ¹⁸But the Jews did not believe concerning him, that he had been blind, and received his sight, until they called the parents of him that had received his sight. ¹⁹And they asked them, saying, Is this your son, who ye say was born blind? how then doth he now see? ²⁰His parents answered them and said, We know that this is our son, and that he was born blind: ²¹But by what means he now seeth, we know not; or who hath opened his eyes, we know not: he is of age;

ask him: he shall speak for himself. ²²These *words* spake his parents, because they feared the Jews: for the Jews had agreed already, that if any man did confess that he was Christ, he should be put out of the synagogue. ²³Therefore said his parents, He is of age; ask him. ²⁴Then again called they the man that was blind, and said unto him, Give God the praise: we know that this man is a sinner. ²⁵He answered and said, Whether he be a sinner *or no,* I know not: one thing I know, that, whereas I was blind, now I see. ²⁶Then said they to him again, What did he to thee? how opened he thine eyes? ²⁷He answered them, I have told you already, and ye did not hear: wherefore would ye hear *it* again? will ye also be his disciples? ²⁸Then they reviled him, and said, Thou art his disciple; but we are Moses' disciples. ²⁹We know that God spake unto Moses: *as for* this *fellow,* we know not from whence he is. ³⁰The man answered and said unto them, Why herein is a marvellous thing, that ye know not from whence he is, and *yet* he hath opened mine eyes. ³¹Now we know that God heareth not sinners: but if any man be a worshipper of God, and doeth his will, him he heareth. ³²Since the world began was it not heard that any man opened the eyes of one that was born blind. ³³If this man were not of God, he could do nothing. ³⁴They answered and said unto him, Thou wast altogether born in sins, and dost thou teach us? And they cast him out. ³⁵Jesus heard that they had cast him out; and when he had found him, he said unto him, Dost thou believe on the Son of God? ³⁶He answered and said, Who is he, Lord, that I might believe on him? ³⁷And Jesus said unto him, Thou hast both seen him, and it is he that talketh with thee. ³⁸And he said, Lord, I believe. And he worshipped him.

³⁹And Jesus said, For judgment I am come into this world, that they which see not might see; and that they which see might be made blind. ⁴⁰And *some* of the Pharisees which were with him heard these words, and said unto him, Are we blind also? ⁴¹Jesus said unto them, If ye were blind, ye should have no sin: but now ye say, We see; therefore your sin remaineth.

10 Verily, verily, I say unto you, He that entereth not by the door into the sheepfold, but climbeth up some other way, the same is a thief and a robber. [2]But he that entereth in by the door is the shepherd of the sheep. [3]To him the porter openeth; and the sheep hear his voice: and he calleth his own sheep by name, and leadeth them out. [4]And when he putteth forth his own sheep, he goeth before them, and the sheep follow him: for they know his voice. [5]And a stranger will they not follow, but will flee from him: for they know not the voice of strangers. [6]This parable spake Jesus unto them: but they understood not what things they were which he spake unto them. [7]Then said Jesus unto them again, Verily, verily, I say unto you, I am the door of the sheep. [8]All that ever came before me are thieves and robbers: but the sheep did not hear them. [9]I am the door: by me if any man enter in, he shall be saved, and shall go in and out, and find pasture. [10]The thief cometh not, but for to steal, and to kill, and to destroy: I am come that they might have life, and that they might have it more abundantly. [11]I am the good shepherd: the good shepherd giveth his life for the sheep. [12]But he that is an hireling, and not the shepherd, whose own the sheep are not, seeth the wolf coming, and leaveth the sheep, and fleeth: and the wolf catcheth them, and scattereth the sheep. [13]The hireling fleeth, because he is an hireling, and careth not for the sheep. [14]I am the good shepherd, and know my *sheep,* and am known of mine. [15]As the Father knoweth me, even so know I the Father: and I lay down my life for the sheep. [16]And other sheep I have, which are not of this fold: them also I must bring, and they shall hear my voice; and there shall be one fold, *and* one shepherd. [17]Therefore doth my Father love me, because I lay down my life, that I might take it again. [18]No man taketh it from me, but I lay it down of myself. I have power to lay it down, and I have power to take it again. This commandment have I received of my Father.

[19]There was a division therefore again among the Jews for these sayings. [20]And many of them said, He hath a devil, and is mad; why hear ye him? [21]Others said, These are not the words of him that hath a devil. Can a devil open the eyes of the blind?

[22]And it was at Jerusalem the feast of the dedication, and it was winter. [23]And Jesus walked in the temple in Solomon's porch. [24]Then came the Jews round about him, and said unto him, How long dost thou make us to doubt? If thou be the Christ, tell us plainly. [25]Jesus answered them, I told you, and ye believed not: the works that I do in my Father's name, they bear witness of me. [26]But ye believe not, because ye are not of my sheep, as I said unto you. [27]My sheep hear my voice, and I know them, and they follow me: [28]And I give unto them eternal life; and they shall never perish, neither shall any *man* pluck them out of my hand. [29]My Father, which gave *them* me, is greater than all; and no *man* is able to pluck *them* out of my Father's hand. [30]I and *my* Father are one. [31]Then the Jews took up stones again to stone him. [32]Jesus answered them, Many good works have I shewed you from my Father; for which of those works do ye stone me? [33]The Jews answered him, saying, For a good work we stone thee not; but for blasphemy; and because that thou, being a man, makest thyself God. [34]Jesus answered them, Is it not written in your law, I said, Ye are gods? [35]If he called them gods, unto whom the word of God came, and the scripture cannot be broken; [36]Say ye of him, whom the Father hath sanctified, and sent into the world, Thou blasphemest; because I said, I am the Son of God? [37]If I do not the works of my Father, believe me not. [38]But if I do, though ye believe not me, believe the works: that ye may know, and believe, that the Father is in me, and I in him. [39]Therefore they sought again to take him: but he escaped out of their hand, [40]And went away again beyond Jordan into the place where John at first baptized; and there he abode. [41]And many resorted unto him, and said, John did no miracle: but all things that John spake of this man were true. [42]And many believed on him there.

11 Now a certain *man* was sick, *named* Lazarus, of Bethany, the town of Mary and her sister Martha. [2](It was *that* Mary which anointed the Lord with ointment, and wiped his feet with her hair, whose brother Lazarus was sick.) [3]Therefore his sisters sent unto him, saying, Lord, behold, he whom thou lovest is sick. [4]When Jesus heard *that,* he said, This sickness is not unto death, but for the glory of God, that the Son of God might be glorified thereby. [5]Now Jesus loved Martha, and her sister, and Lazarus. [6]When he had heard therefore that he was sick, he abode two days still in the same place where he was. [7]Then after that saith he to *his* disciples, Let us go into Judaea again. [8]*His* disciples say unto him, Master, the Jews of late sought to stone thee; and goest thou thither again? [9]Jesus answered, Are there not twelve hours in the day? If any man walk in the day, he stumbleth not, because he seeth the light of this world. [10]But if a man walk in the night, he stumbleth, because there is no light in him. [11]These things said he: and after that he saith unto them, Our friend Lazarus sleepeth; but I go, that I may awake him out of sleep. [12]Then said his disciples, Lord, if he sleep, he shall do well. [13]Howbeit Jesus spake of his death: but they thought that he had spoken of taking of rest in sleep. [14]Then said Jesus unto them plainly, Lazarus is dead. [15]And I am glad for your sakes that I was not there, to the intent ye may believe; nevertheless let us go unto him. [16]Then said Thomas, which is called Didymus, unto his fellowdisciples, Let us also go, that we may die with him. [17]Then when Jesus came, he found that he had *lain* in the grave four days already. [18]Now Bethany was nigh unto Jerusalem, about fifteen furlongs off: [19]And many of the Jews came to Martha and Mary, to comfort them concerning their brother. [20]Then Martha, as soon as she heard that Jesus was coming, went and met him: but Mary sat *still* in the house. [21]Then said Martha unto Jesus, Lord, if thou hadst been here, my brother had not died. [22]But I know, that even now, whatsoever thou wilt ask of God, God will give *it* thee. [23]Jesus saith unto her, Thy brother shall rise again. [24]Martha saith unto him, I know that he shall rise again in the resurrection at the last day. [25]Jesus said unto her, I am the resurrection, and the life: he that believeth in me, though he were dead, yet shall he live: [26]And whosoever liveth and

believeth in me shall never die. Believest thou this? [27]She saith unto him, Yea, Lord: I believe that thou art the Christ, the Son of God, which should come into the world. [28]And when she had so said, she went her way, and called Mary her sister secretly, saying, The Master is come, and calleth for thee. [29]As soon as she heard *that,* she arose quickly, and came unto him. [30]Now Jesus was not yet come into the town, but was in that place where Martha met him. [31]The Jews then which were with her in the house, and comforted her, when they saw Mary, that she rose up hastily and went out, followed her, saying, She goeth unto the grave to weep there. [32]Then when Mary was come where Jesus was, and saw him, she fell down at his feet, saying unto him, Lord, if thou hadst been here, my brother had not died. [33]When Jesus therefore saw her weeping, and the Jews also weeping which came with her, he groaned in the spirit, and was troubled, [34]And said, Where have ye laid him? They said unto him, Lord, come and see. [35]Jesus wept. [36]Then said the Jews, Behold how he loved him! [37]And some of them said, Could not this man, which opened the eyes of the blind, have caused that even this man should not have died? [38]Jesus therefore again groaning in himself cometh to the grave. It was a cave, and a stone lay upon it. [39]Jesus said, Take ye away the stone. Martha, the sister of him that was dead, saith unto him, Lord, by this time he stinketh: for he hath been *dead* four days. [40]Jesus saith unto her, Said I not unto thee, that, if thou wouldest believe, thou shouldest see the glory of God? [41]Then they took away the stone *from the place* where the dead was laid. And Jesus lifted up *his* eyes, and said, Father, I thank thee that thou hast heard me. [42]And I knew that thou hearest me always: but because of the people which stand by I said *it,* that they may believe that thou hast sent me. [43]And when he thus had spoken, he cried with a loud voice, Lazarus, come forth. [44]And he that was dead came forth, bound hand and foot with graveclothes: and his face was bound about with a napkin. Jesus saith unto them, Loose him, and let him go. [45]Then many of the Jews which came to Mary, and had seen the things which Jesus did, believed on him. ⁴⁶But some of them went their ways to the Pharisees, and told them what things Jesus had done.

⁴⁷Then gathered the chief priests and the Pharisees a council, and said, What do we? for this man doeth many miracles. ⁴⁸If we let him thus alone, all *men* will believe on him: and the Romans shall come and take away both our place and nation. ⁴⁹And one of them, *named* Caiaphas, being the high priest that same year, said unto them, Ye know nothing at all, ⁵⁰Nor consider that it is expedient for us, that one man should die for the people, and that the whole nation perish not. ⁵¹And this spake he not of himself: but being high priest that year, he prophesied that Jesus should die for that nation; ⁵²And not for that nation only, but that also he should gather together in one the children of God that were scattered abroad. ⁵³Then from that day forth they took counsel together for to put him to death. ⁵⁴Jesus therefore walked no more openly among the Jews; but went thence unto a country near to the wilderness, into a city called Ephraim, and there continued with his disciples.

⁵⁵And the Jews' passover was nigh at hand: and many went out of the country up to Jerusalem before the passover, to purify themselves. ⁵⁶Then sought they for Jesus, and spake among themselves, as they stood in the temple, What think ye, that he will not come to the feast? ⁵⁷Now both the chief priests and the Pharisees had given a commandment, that, if any man knew where he were, he should shew *it*, that they might take him.

12 Then Jesus six days before the passover came to Bethany, where Lazarus was which had been dead, whom he raised from the dead. ²There they made him a supper; and Martha served: but Lazarus was one of them that sat at the table with him. ³Then took Mary a pound of ointment of spikenard, very costly, and anointed the feet of Jesus, and wiped his feet with her hair: and the house was filled with the odour of the ointment. ⁴Then saith one of his disciples, Judas Iscariot, Simon's *son*, which should betray him, ⁵Why was not this ointment sold for three hundred pence, and given to the poor? ⁶This he said,

not that he cared for the poor; but because he was a thief, and had the bag, and bare what was put therein. ⁷Then said Jesus, Let her alone: against the day of my burying hath she kept this. ⁸For the poor always ye have with you; but me ye have not always. ⁹Much people of the Jews therefore knew that he was there: and they came not for Jesus' sake only, but that they might see Lazarus also, whom he had raised from the dead.

¹⁰But the chief priests consulted that they might put Lazarus also to death; ¹¹Because that by reason of him many of the Jews went away, and believed on Jesus.

¹²On the next day much people that were come to the feast, when they heard that Jesus was coming to Jerusalem, ¹³Took branches of palm trees, and went forth to meet him, and cried,

Hosanna:

Blessed *is* the King of Israel that cometh in the name of the Lord.

¹⁴And Jesus, when he had found a young ass, sat thereon; as it is written,

¹⁵Fear not, daughter of Sion: behold, thy King cometh, sitting on an ass's colt.

¹⁶These things understood not his disciples at the first: but when Jesus was glorified, then remembered they that these things were written of him, and *that* they had done these things unto him. ¹⁷The people therefore that was with him when he called Lazarus out of his grave, and raised him from the dead, bare record. ¹⁸For this cause the people also met him, for that they heard that he had done this miracle. ¹⁹The Pharisees therefore said among themselves, Perceive ye how ye prevail nothing? behold, the world is gone after him.

²⁰And there were certain Greeks among them that came up to worship at the feast: ²¹The same came therefore to Philip, which was of Bethsaida of Galilee, and desired him, saying, Sir, we would see Jesus. ²²Philip cometh and telleth Andrew: and again Andrew and Philip tell Jesus.

²³And Jesus answered them, saying, The hour is come, that the Son of man should be glorified. ²⁴Verily, verily, I say

unto you, Except a corn of wheat fall into the ground and die, it abideth alone: but if it die, it bringeth forth much fruit. ²⁵He that loveth his life shall lose it; and he that hateth his life in this world shall keep it unto life eternal. ²⁶If any man serve me, let him follow me; and where I am, there shall also my servant be: if any man serve me, him will *my* Father honour. ²⁷Now is my soul troubled; and what shall I say? Father, save me from this hour: but for this cause came I unto this hour. ²⁸Father, glorify thy name. Then came there a voice from heaven, *saying,* I have both glorified *it,* and will glorify *it* again. ²⁹The people therefore, that stood by, and heard *it,* said that it thundered: others said, An angel spake to him. ³⁰Jesus answered and said, This voice came not because of me, but for your sakes. ³¹Now is the judgment of this world: now shall the prince of this world be cast out. ³²And I, if I be lifted up from the earth, will draw all *men* unto me. ³³This he said, signifying what death he should die. ³⁴The people answered him, We have heard out of the law that Christ abideth for ever: and how sayest thou, The Son of man must be lifted up? who is this Son of man? ³⁵Then Jesus said unto them, Yet a little while is the light with you. Walk while ye have the light, lest darkness come upon you: for he that walketh in darkness knoweth not whither he goeth. ³⁶While ye have light, believe in the light, that ye may be the children of light. These things spake Jesus, and departed, and did hide himself from them.

³⁷But though he had done so many miracles before them, yet they believed not on him: ³⁸That the saying of Esaias the prophet might be fulfilled, which he spake,

. Lord, who hath believed our report? and to whom hath the arm of the Lord been revealed?

³⁹Therefore they could not believe, because that Esaias said again,

⁴⁰He hath blinded their eyes, and hardened their heart; that they should not see with *their* eyes, nor understand with *their* heart, and be converted, and I should heal them.

⁴¹These things said Esaias, when he saw his glory, and spake of him.

⁴²Nevertheless among the chief rulers also many believed on him; but because of the Pharisees they did not confess *him,* lest they should be put out of the synagogue: ⁴³For they loved the praise of men more than the praise of God.

⁴⁴Jesus cried and said, He that believeth on me, believeth not on me, but on him that sent me. ⁴⁵And he that seeth me seeth him that sent me. ⁴⁶I am come a light into the world, that whosoever believeth on me should not abide in darkness. ⁴⁷And if any man hear my words, and believe not, I judge him not: for I came not to judge the world, but to save the world. ⁴⁸He that rejecteth me, and receiveth not my words, hath one that judgeth him: the word that I have spoken, the same shall judge him in the last day. ⁴⁹For I have not spoken of myself; but the Father which sent me, he gave me a commandment, what I should say, and what I should speak. ⁵⁰And I know that his commandment is life everlasting: whatsoever I speak therefore, even as the Father said unto me, so I speak.

13 Now before the feast of the passover, when Jesus knew that his hour was come that he should depart out of this world unto the Father, having loved his own which were in the world, he loved them unto the end. ²And supper being ended, the devil having now put into the heart of Judas Iscariot, Simon's *son,* to betray him; ³Jesus knowing that the Father had given all things into his hands, and that he was come from God, and went to God; ⁴He riseth from supper, and laid aside his garments; and took a towel, and girded himself. ⁵After that he poureth water into a bason, and began to wash the disciples' feet, and to wipe *them* with the towel wherewith he was girded. ⁶Then cometh he to Simon Peter: and Peter saith unto him, Lord, dost thou wash my feet? ⁷Jesus answered and said unto him, What I do thou knowest not now; but thou shalt know hereafter. ⁸Peter saith unto him, Thou shalt never wash my feet. Jesus answered him, If I wash thee not, thou hast no part with me. ⁹Simon Peter saith unto him, Lord, not my feet only, but also *my* hands and *my* head. [10]Jesus saith to him, He that is washed needeth not save to wash *his* feet, but is clean every whit: and ye are clean, but not all. [11]For he knew who should betray him; therefore said he, Ye are not all clean. [12]So after he had washed their feet, and had taken his garments, and was set down again, he said unto them, Know ye what I have done to you? [13]Ye call me Master and Lord: and ye say well; for so I am. [14]If I then, *your* Lord and Master, have washed your feet; ye also ought to wash one another's feet. [15]For I have given you an example, that ye should do as I have done to you. [16]Verily, verily, I say unto you, The servant is not greater than his lord; neither he that is sent greater than he that sent him. [17]If ye know these things, happy are ye if ye do them.

[18]I speak not of you all: I know whom I have chosen: but that the scripture may be fulfilled, He that eateth bread with me hath lifted up his heel against me. [19]Now I tell you before it come, that, when it is come to pass, ye may believe that I am *he.* [20]Verily, verily, I say unto you, He that receiveth whomsoever I send receiveth me; and he that receiveth me receiveth him that sent me. [21]When Jesus had thus said, he was troubled in spirit, and testified, and said, Verily, verily, I say unto you, that one of you shall betray me. [22]Then the disciples looked one on another, doubting of whom he spake. [23]Now there was leaning on Jesus' bosom one of his disciples, whom Jesus loved. [24]Simon Peter therefore beckoned to him, that he should ask who it should be of whom he spake. [25]He then lying on Jesus' breast saith unto him, Lord, who is it? [26]Jesus answered, He it is, to whom I shall give a sop, when I have dipped *it.* And when he had dipped the sop, he gave *it* to Judas Iscariot, *the son* of Simon. [27]And after the sop Satan entered into him. Then said Jesus unto him, That thou doest, do quickly. [28]Now no man at the table knew for what intent he spake this unto him. [29]For some *of them* thought, because Judas had the bag, that Jesus had said unto him, Buy *those things* that we have need of against the feast; or, that he should give something to the poor. [30]He then having received the sop went immediately out: and it was night.

[31]Therefore, when he was gone out, Jesus said, Now is the Son of man glorified, and God is glorified in him. [32]If God be glorified in him, God shall also glorify him in himself, and shall straightway glorify him. [33]Little children, yet a little while I am with you. Ye shall seek me: and as I said unto the Jews, Whither I go, ye cannot come; so now I say to you. [34]A new commandment I give unto you, That ye love one another; as I have loved you, that ye also love one another. [35]By this shall all *men* know that ye are my disciples, if ye have love one to another.

[36]Simon Peter said unto him, Lord, whither goest thou? Jesus answered him, Whither I go, thou canst not follow me now; but thou shalt follow me afterwards. [37]Peter said unto him, Lord, why cannot I follow thee now? I will lay down my life for thy sake. [38]Jesus answered him, Wilt thou lay down thy life for my sake? Verily, verily, I say unto thee, The cock shall not crow, till thou hast denied me thrice.

14 Let not your heart be troubled: ye believe in God, believe also in me. [2]In my Father's house are many mansions: if *it were* not so, I would have told you. I go to prepare a place for you. [3]And if I go and prepare a place for you, I will come again, and receive you unto myself; that where I am, *there* ye may be also. [4]And whither I go ye know, and the way ye know. [5]Thomas saith unto him, Lord, we know not whither thou goest; and how can we know the way? [6]Jesus saith unto him, I am the way, the truth, and the life: no man cometh unto the Father, but by me. [7]If ye had known me, ye should have known my Father also: and from henceforth ye know him, and have seen him. [8]Philip saith unto him, Lord, shew us the Father, and it sufficeth us. [9]Jesus saith unto him, Have I been so long time with you, and yet hast thou not known me, Philip? he that hath seen me hath seen the Father; and how sayest thou *then,* Shew us the Father? [10]Believest thou not that I am in the Father, and the Father in me? the words that I speak unto you I speak not of myself: but the Father that dwelleth in me, he doeth the works. [11]Believe me that I *am* in the Father, and the Father in me: or else believe me for the very works' sake. [12]Verily, verily, I say unto you, He that believeth on me, the works that I do shall he do also; and greater *works* than these shall he do; because I go unto my Father. [13]And whatsoever ye shall ask in my name, that will I do, that the Father may be glorified in the Son. [14]If ye shall ask any thing in my name, I will do *it*.

[15]If ye love me, keep my commandments. [16]And I will pray the Father, and he shall give you another Comforter, that he may abide with you for ever; [17]*Even* the Spirit of truth; whom the world cannot receive, because it seeth him not, neither knoweth him: but ye know him; for he dwelleth with you, and shall be in you. [18]I will not leave you comfortless: I will come to you. [19]Yet a little while, and the world seeth me no more; but ye see me: because I live, ye shall live also. [20]At that day ye shall know that I *am* in my Father, and ye in me, and I in you. [21]He that hath my commandments, and keepeth them, he it is that loveth me: and he that loveth me shall be loved of my Father, and I will love him, and will manifest myself to him. [22]Judas saith unto him, not Iscariot, Lord, how is it that thou wilt manifest thyself unto us, and not unto the world? [23]Jesus answered and said unto him, If a man love me, he will keep my words: and my Father will love him, and we will come unto him, and make our abode with him. [24]He that loveth me not keepeth not my sayings: and the word which ye hear is not mine, but the Father's which sent me. [25]These things have I spoken unto you, being *yet* present with you. [26]But the Comforter, *which is* the Holy Ghost, whom the Father will send in my name, he shall teach you all things, and bring all things to your remembrance, whatsoever I have said unto you. [27]Peace I leave with you, my peace I give unto you: not as the world giveth, give I unto you. Let not your heart be troubled, neither let it be afraid. [28]Ye have heard how I said unto you, I go away, and come *again* unto you. If ye loved me, ye would rejoice, because I said, I go unto the Father: for my Father is greater than I. [29]And now I have told you before it come to pass, that, when it is come to pass, ye might believe. [30]Hereafter I will not talk much with you: for the prince of this world cometh, and hath noth-

ing in me. [31]But that the world may know that I love the Father; and as the Father gave me commandment, even so I do. Arise, let us go hence.

15 I am the true vine, and my Father is the husbandman. [2]Every branch in me that beareth not fruit he taketh away: and every *branch* that beareth fruit, he purgeth it, that it may bring forth more fruit. [3]Now ye are clean through the word which I have spoken unto you. [4]Abide in me, and I in you. As the branch cannot bear fruit of itself, except it abide in the vine; no more can ye, except ye abide in me. [5]I am the vine, ye *are* the branches: He that abideth in me, and I in him, the same bringeth forth much fruit: for without me ye can do nothing. [6]If a man abide not in me, he is cast forth as a branch, and is withered; and men gather them, and cast *them* into the fire, and they are burned. [7]If ye abide in me, and my words abide in you, ye shall ask what ye will, and it shall be done unto you. [8]Herein is my Father glorified, that ye bear much fruit; so shall ye be my disciples. [9]As the Father hath loved me, so have I loved you: continue ye in my love. [10]If ye keep my commandments, ye shall abide in my love; even as I have kept my Father's commandments, and abide in his love. [11]These things have I spoken unto you, that my joy might remain in you, and *that* your joy might be full. [12]This is my commandment, That ye love one another, as I have loved you. [13]Greater love hath no man than this, that a man lay down his life for his friends. [14]Ye are my friends, if ye do whatsoever I command you. [15]Henceforth I call you not servants; for the servant knoweth not what his lord doeth: but I have called you friends; for all things that I have heard of my Father I have made known unto you. [16]Ye have not chosen me, but I have chosen you, and ordained you, that ye should go and bring forth fruit, and *that* your fruit should remain: that whatsoever ye shall ask of the Father in my name, he may give it you. [17]These things I command you, that ye love one another. [18]If the world hate you, ye know that *it hated* me before it hated you. [19]If ye were of the world, the world would love his own: but because ye are not of the world, but I have chosen you

out of the world, therefore the world hateth you. ²⁰Remember the word that I said unto you, The servant is not greater than his lord. If they have persecuted me, they will also persecute you; if they have kept my saying, they will keep yours also. ²¹But all these things will they do unto you for my name's sake, because they know not him that sent me. ²²If I had not come and spoken unto them, they had not had sin: but now they have no cloke for their sin. ²³He that hateth me hateth my Father also. ²⁴If I had not done among them the works which none other man did, they had not had sin: but now have they both seen and hated both me and my Father. ²⁵But *this cometh to pass,* that the word might be fulfilled that is written in their law, They hated me without a cause. ²⁶But when the Comforter is come, whom I will send unto you from the Father, *even* the Spirit of truth, which proceedeth from the Father, he shall testify of me: ²⁷And ye also shall bear witness, because ye have been with me from the beginning.

16 These things have I spoken unto you, that ye should not be offended. ²They shall put you out of the synagogues: yea, the time cometh, that whosoever killeth you will think that he doeth God service. ³And these things will they do unto you, because they have not known the Father, nor me. ⁴But these things have I told you, that when the time shall come, ye may remember that I told you of them. And these things I said not unto you at the beginning, because I was with you. ⁵But now I go my way to him that sent me; and none of you asketh me, Whither goest thou? ⁶But because I have said these things unto you, sorrow hath filled your heart. ⁷Nevertheless I tell you the truth; It is expedient for you that I go away: for if I go not away, the Comforter will not come unto you; but if I depart, I will send him unto you. ⁸And when he is come, he will reprove the world of sin, and of righteousness, and of judgment: ⁹Of sin, because they believe not on me; ¹⁰Of righteousness, because I go to my Father, and ye see me no more; ¹¹Of judgment, because the prince of this world is judged. ¹²I have yet many things to say unto you, but ye cannot bear them now. ¹³Howbeit when he, the Spirit of truth, is come, he

will guide you into all truth: for he shall not speak of himself; but whatsoever he shall hear, *that* shall he speak: and he will shew you things to come. ¹⁴He shall glorify me: for he shall receive of mine, and shall shew *it* unto you. ¹⁵All things that the Father hath are mine: therefore said I, that he shall take of mine, and shall shew *it* unto you. ¹⁶A little while, and ye shall not see me: and again, a little while, and ye shall see me, because I go to the Father. ¹⁷Then said *some* of his disciples among themselves, What is this that he saith unto us, A little while, and ye shall not see me: and again, a little while, and ye shall see me: and, Because I go to the Father? ¹⁸They said therefore, What is this that he saith, A little while? we cannot tell what he saith. ¹⁹Now Jesus knew that they were desirous to ask him, and said unto them, Do ye enquire among yourselves of that I said, A little while, and ye shall not see me: and again, a little while, and ye shall see me? ²⁰Verily, verily, I say unto you, That ye shall weep and lament, but the world shall rejoice: and ye shall be sorrowful, but your sorrow shall be turned into joy. ²¹A woman when she is in travail hath sorrow, because her hour is come: but as soon as she is delivered of the child, she remembereth no more the anguish, for joy that a man is born into the world. ²²And ye now therefore have sorrow: but I will see you again, and your heart shall rejoice, and your joy no man taketh from you. ²³And in that day ye shall ask me nothing. Verily, verily, I say unto you, Whatsoever ye shall ask the Father in my name, he will give *it* you. ²⁴Hitherto have ye asked nothing in my name: ask, and ye shall receive, that your joy may be full. ²⁵These things have I spoken unto you in proverbs: but the time cometh, when I shall no more speak unto you in proverbs, but I shall shew you plainly of the Father. ²⁶At that day ye shall ask in my name: and I say not unto you, that I will pray the Father for you: ²⁷For the Father himself loveth you, because ye have loved me, and have believed that I came out from God. ²⁸I came forth from the Father, and am come into the world: again, I leave the world, and go to the Father. ²⁹His disciples said unto him, Lo, now speakest thou plainly, and speakest no proverb. ³⁰Now are we sure that thou knowest all things, and needest not that any man should ask thee: by this we believe that thou camest forth from God. [31]Jesus answered them, Do ye now believe? [32]Behold, the hour cometh, yea, is now come, that ye shall be scattered, every man to his own, and shall leave me alone: and yet I am not alone, because the Father is with me. [33]These things I have spoken unto you, that in me ye might have peace. In the world ye shall have tribulation: but be of good cheer; I have overcome the world.

17 These words spake Jesus, and lifted up his eyes to heaven, and said,

Father, the hour is come; glorify thy Son, that thy Son also may glorify thee: [2]As thou hast given him power over all flesh, that he should give eternal life to as many as thou hast given him. [3]And this is life eternal, that they might know thee the only true God, and Jesus Christ, whom thou hast sent. [4]I have glorified thee on the earth: I have finished the work which thou gavest me to do. [5]And now, O Father, glorify thou me with thine own self with the glory which I had with thee before the world was. [6]I have manifested thy name unto the men which thou gavest me out of the world: thine they were, and thou gavest them me; and they have kept thy word. [7]Now they have known that all things whatsoever thou hast given me are of thee. [8]For I have given unto them the words which thou gavest me; and they have received *them*, and have known surely that I came out from thee, and they have believed that thou didst send me. [9]I pray for them: I pray not for the world, but for them which thou hast given me; for they are thine. [10]And all mine are thine, and thine are mine; and I am glorified in them. [11]And now I am no more in the world, but these are in the world, and I come to thee. Holy Father, keep through thine own name those whom thou hast given me, that they may be one, as we *are*. [12]While I was with them in the world, I kept them in thy name: those that thou gavest me I have kept, and none of them is lost, but the son of perdition; that the scripture might be fulfilled. [13]And now come I to thee; and these things I speak in the world, that they might have my joy fulfilled in themselves. [14]I have given them thy word; and the world hath hated them, because they are not of the world, even as I am not of the world. [15]I pray not that thou shouldest take them out of the world, but that thou shouldest keep them from the evil. [16]They are not of the world, even as I am not of the world. [17]Sanctify them through thy truth: thy word is truth. [18]As thou hast sent me into the world, even so have I also sent them into the world. [19]And for their sakes I sanctify myself, that they also might be sanctified through the truth. [20]Neither pray I for these alone, but for them also which shall believe on me through their word; [21]That they all may be one; as thou, Father, *art* in me, and I in thee, that they also may be one in us: that the world may believe that thou hast sent me. [22]And the glory which thou gavest me I have given them; that they may be one, even as we are one: [23]I in them, and thou in me, that they may be made perfect in one; and that the world may know that thou hast sent me, and hast loved them, as thou hast loved me. [24]Father, I will that they also, whom thou hast given me, be with me where I am; that they may behold my glory, which thou hast given me: for thou lovedst me before the foundation of the world. [25]O righteous Father, the world hath not known thee: but I have known thee, and these have known that thou hast sent me. [26]And I have declared unto them thy name, and will declare *it*: that the love wherewith thou hast loved me may be in them, and I in them.

18 When Jesus had spoken these words, he went forth with his disciples over the brook Cedron, where was a garden, into the which he entered, and his disciples. [2]And Judas also, which betrayed him, knew the place: for Jesus ofttimes resorted thither with his disciples. [3]Judas then, having received a band *of men* and officers from the chief priests and Pharisees, cometh thither with lanterns and torches and weapons. [4]Jesus therefore, knowing all things that should come upon him, went forth, and said unto them, Whom seek ye? [5]They answered him, Jesus of Nazareth. Jesus saith unto them, I am *he*. And Judas also, which betrayed him, stood with them. ⁶As soon then as he had said unto them, I am *he*, they went backward, and fell to the ground. ⁷Then asked he them again, Whom seek ye? And they said, Jesus of Nazareth. ⁸Jesus answered, I have told you that I am *he*: if therefore ye seek me, let these go their way: ⁹That the saying might be fulfilled, which he spake, Of them which thou gavest me have I lost none. ¹⁰Then Simon Peter having a sword drew it, and smote the high priest's servant, and cut off his right ear. The servant's name was Malchus. ¹¹Then said Jesus unto Peter, Put up thy sword into the sheath: the cup which my Father hath given me, shall I not drink it? ¹²Then the band and the captain and officers of the Jews took Jesus, and bound him, ¹³And led him away to Annas first; for he was father in law to Caiaphas, which was the high priest that same year. ¹⁴Now Caiaphas was he, which gave counsel to the Jews, that it was expedient that one man should die for the people.

¹⁵And Simon Peter followed Jesus, and *so did* another disciple: that disciple was known unto the high priest, and went in with Jesus into the palace of the high priest. ¹⁶But Peter stood at the door without. Then went out that other disciple, which was known unto the high priest, and spake unto her that kept the door, and brought in Peter. ¹⁷Then saith the damsel that kept the door unto Peter, Art not thou also *one* of this man's disciples? He saith, I am not. ¹⁸And the servants and officers stood there, who had made a fire of coals; for it was cold: and they warmed themselves: and Peter stood with them, and warmed himself.

¹⁹The high priest then asked Jesus of his disciples, and of his doctrine. ²⁰Jesus answered him, I spake openly to the world; I ever taught in the synagogue, and in the temple, whither the Jews always resort; and in secret have I said nothing. ²¹Why askest thou me? ask them which heard me, what I have said unto them: behold, they know what I said. ²²And when he had thus spoken, one of the officers which stood by struck Jesus with the palm of his hand, saying, Answerest thou the high priest so? ²³Jesus answered him, If I have spoken evil, bear witness of the evil: but if well, why smitest thou me? ²⁴Now Annas had sent him bound unto Caiaphas the high priest. ²⁵And Simon Peter stood and warmed himself. They said therefore unto him, Art not thou also *one* of his disciples? He denied *it*, and said, I am not. ²⁶One of the servants of the high priest, being *his* kinsman whose ear Peter cut off, saith, Did not I see thee in the garden with him? ²⁷Peter then denied again: and immediately the cock crew.

²⁸Then led they Jesus from Caiaphas unto the hall of judgment: and it was early; and they themselves went not into the judgment hall, lest they should be defiled; but that they might eat the passover. ²⁹Pilate then went out unto them, and said, What accusation bring ye against this man? ³⁰They answered and said unto him, If he were not a malefactor, we would not have delivered him up unto thee. ³¹Then said Pilate unto them, Take ye him, and judge him according to your law. The Jews therefore said unto him, It is not lawful for us to put any man to death: ³²That the saying of Jesus might be fulfilled, which he spake, signifying what death he should die. ³³Then Pilate entered into the judgment hall again, and called Jesus, and said unto him, Art thou the King of the Jews? ³⁴Jesus answered him, Sayest thou this thing of thyself, or did others tell it thee of me? ³⁵Pilate answered, Am I a Jew? Thine own nation and the chief priests have delivered thee unto me: what hast thou done? ³⁶Jesus answered, My kingdom is not of this world: if my kingdom were of this world, then would my servants fight, that I should not be delivered to the Jews: but now is my kingdom not from hence. ³⁷Pilate therefore said unto him, Art thou a king then? Jesus answered, Thou sayest that I am a king. To this end was I born, and for this cause came I into the world, that I should bear witness unto the truth. Every one that is of the truth heareth my voice. ³⁸Pilate saith unto him, What is truth? And when he had said this, he went out again unto the Jews, and saith unto them, I find in him no fault *at all*. ³⁹But ye have a custom, that I should release unto you one at the passover: will ye therefore

that I release unto you the King of the Jews? ⁴⁰Then cried they all again, saying, Not this man, but Barabbas. Now Barabbas was a robber.

19 Then Pilate therefore took Jesus, and scourged *him*. ²And the soldiers platted a crown of thorns, and put *it* on his head, and they put on him a purple robe, ³And said, Hail, King of the Jews! and they smote him with their hands. ⁴Pilate therefore went forth again, and saith unto them, Behold, I bring him forth to you, that ye may know that I find no fault in him. ⁵Then came Jesus forth, wearing the crown of thorns, and the purple robe. And *Pilate* saith unto them, Behold the man! ⁶When the chief priests therefore and officers saw him, they cried out, saying, Crucify *him*, crucify *him*. Pilate saith unto them, Take ye him, and crucify *him:* for I find no fault in him. ⁷The Jews answered him, We have a law, and by our law he ought to die, because he made himself the Son of God.

⁸When Pilate therefore heard that saying, he was the more afraid; ⁹And went again into the judgment hall, and saith unto Jesus, Whence art thou? But Jesus gave him no answer. ¹⁰Then saith Pilate unto him, Speakest thou not unto me? knowest thou not that I have power to crucify thee, and have power to release thee? ¹¹Jesus answered, Thou couldest have no power *at all* against me, except it were given thee from above: therefore he that delivered me unto thee hath the greater sin. ¹²And from thenceforth Pilate sought to release him: but the Jews cried out, saying, If thou let this man go, thou art not Caesar's friend: whosoever maketh himself a king speaketh against Caesar.

¹³When Pilate therefore heard that saying, he brought Jesus forth, and sat down in the judgment seat in a place that is called the Pavement, but in the Hebrew, Gabbatha. ¹⁴And it was the preparation of the passover, and about the sixth hour: and he saith unto the Jews, Behold your King! ¹⁵But they cried out, Away with *him*, away with *him*, crucify him. Pilate saith unto them, Shall I crucify your King? The chief priests answered, We have no king but Caesar. ¹⁶Then delivered he him therefore unto them to be crucified. And they took Jesus, and led *him* away. ¹⁷And he bearing his cross went forth into a place called *the place* of a skull, which is called in the Hebrew Golgotha: ¹⁸Where they crucified him, and two others with him, on either side one, and Jesus in the midst.

¹⁹And Pilate wrote a title, and put *it* on the cross. And the writing was, JESUS OF NAZARETH THE KING OF THE JEWS. ²⁰This title then read many of the Jews: for the place where Jesus was crucified was nigh to the city: and it was written in Hebrew, *and* Greek, *and* Latin. ²¹Then said the chief priests of the Jews to Pilate, Write not, The King of the Jews; but that he said, I am King of the Jews. ²²Pilate answered, What I have written I have written.

²³Then the soldiers, when they had crucified Jesus, took his garments, and made four parts, to every soldier a part; and also *his* coat: now the coat was without seam, woven from the top throughout. ²⁴They said therefore among themselves, Let us not rend it, but cast lots for it, whose it shall be: that the scripture might be fulfilled, which saith,

They parted my raiment among them, and for my vesture they did cast lots.

These things therefore the soldiers did.

²⁵Now there stood by the cross of Jesus his mother, and his mother's sister, Mary the *wife* of Cleophas, and Mary Magdalene. ²⁶When Jesus therefore saw his mother, and the disciple standing by, whom he loved, he saith unto his mother, Woman, behold thy son! ²⁷Then saith he to the disciple, Behold thy mother! And from that hour that disciple took her unto his own *home*.

²⁸After this, Jesus knowing that all things were now accomplished, that the scripture might be fulfilled, saith, I thirst. ²⁹Now there was set a vessel full of vinegar: and they filled a spunge with vinegar, and put *it* upon hyssop, and put *it* to his mouth. ³⁰When Jesus therefore had received the vinegar, he said, It is finished: and he bowed his head, and gave up the ghost. ³¹The Jews therefore, because it was the preparation, that the bodies should not remain upon the cross on the sabbath day, (for that sabbath day was an high day,) besought Pilate

that their legs might be broken, and *that* they might be taken away. ³²Then came the soldiers, and brake the legs of the first, and of the other which was crucified with him. ³³But when they came to Jesus, and saw that he was dead already, they brake not his legs: ³⁴But one of the soldiers with a spear pierced his side, and forthwith came there out blood and water. ³⁵And he that saw *it* bare record, and his record is true: and he knoweth that he saith true, that ye might believe. ³⁶For these things were done, that the scripture should be fulfilled, A bone of him shall not be broken. ³⁷And again another scripture saith, They shall look on him whom they pierced.

³⁸And after this Joseph of Arimathaea, being a disciple of Jesus, but secretly for fear of the Jews, besought Pilate that he might take away the body of Jesus: and Pilate gave *him* leave. He came therefore, and took the body of Jesus. ³⁹And there came also Nicodemus, which at the first came to Jesus by night, and brought a mixture of myrrh and aloes, about an hundred pound *weight.* ⁴⁰Then took they the body of Jesus, and wound it in linen clothes with the spices, as the manner of the Jews is to bury. ⁴¹Now in the place where he was crucified there was a garden; and in the garden a new sepulchre, wherein was never man yet laid. ⁴²There laid they Jesus therefore because of the Jews' preparation *day;* for the sepulchre was nigh at hand.

20 The first *day* of the week cometh Mary Magdalene early, when it was yet dark, unto the sepulchre, and seeth the stone taken away from the sepulchre. ²Then she runneth, and cometh to Simon Peter, and to the other disciple, whom Jesus loved, and saith unto them, They have taken away the Lord out of the sepulchre, and we know not where they have laid him. ³Peter therefore went forth, and that other disciple, and came to the sepulchre. ⁴So they ran both together: and the other disciple did outrun Peter, and came first to the sepulchre. ⁵And he stooping down, *and looking in,* saw the linen clothes lying; yet went he not in. ⁶Then cometh Simon Peter following him, and went into the sepulchre, and seeth the linen clothes lie, ⁷And the napkin, that was about his head, not

lying with the linen clothes, but wrapped together in a place by itself. ⁸Then went in also that other disciple, which came first to the sepulchre, and he saw, and believed. ⁹For as yet they knew not the scripture, that he must rise again from the dead. ¹⁰Then the disciples went away again unto their own home.

¹¹But Mary stood without at the sepulchre weeping: and as she wept, she stooped down, *and looked* into the sepulchre, ¹²And seeth two angels in white sitting, the one at the head, and the other at the feet, where the body of Jesus had lain. ¹³And they say unto her, Woman, why weepest thou? She saith unto them, Because they have taken away my Lord, and I know not where they have laid him. ¹⁴And when she had thus said, she turned herself back, and saw Jesus standing, and knew not that it was Jesus. ¹⁵Jesus saith unto her, Woman, why weepest thou? whom seekest thou? She, supposing him to be the gardener, saith unto him, Sir, if thou have borne him hence, tell me where thou hast laid him, and I will take him away. ¹⁶Jesus saith unto her, Mary. She turned herself, and saith unto him, Rabboni; which is to say, Master. ¹⁷Jesus saith unto her, Touch me not; for I am not yet ascended to my Father: but go to my brethren, and say unto them, I ascend unto my Father, and your Father; and *to* my God, and your God. ¹⁸Mary Magdalene came and told the disciples that she had seen the Lord, and *that* he had spoken these things unto her.

¹⁹Then the same day at evening, being the first *day* of the week, when the doors were shut where the disciples were assembled for fear of the Jews, came Jesus and stood in the midst, and saith unto them, Peace *be* unto you. ²⁰And when he had so said, he shewed unto them *his* hands and his side. Then were the disciples glad, when they saw the Lord. ²¹Then said Jesus to them again, Peace *be* unto you: as *my* Father hath sent me, even so send I you. ²²And when he had said this, he breathed on *them,* and saith unto them, Receive ye the Holy Ghost: ²³Whose soever sins ye remit, they are remitted unto them; *and* whose soever *sins* ye retain, they are retained.

²⁴But Thomas, one of the twelve, called

Didymus, was not with them when Jesus came. ²⁵The other disciples therefore said unto him, We have seen the Lord. But he said unto them, Except I shall see in his hands the print of the nails, and put my finger into the print of the nails, and thrust my hand into his side, I will not believe.

²⁶And after eight days again his disciples were within, and Thomas with them: *then* came Jesus, the doors being shut, and stood in the midst, and said, Peace *be* unto you. ²⁷Then saith he to Thomas, reach hither thy finger, and behold my hands; and reach hither thy hand, and thrust *it* into my side: and be not faithless, but believing. ²⁸And Thomas answered and said unto him, My Lord and my God. ²⁹Jesus saith unto him, Thomas, because thou hast seen me, thou hast believed: blessed *are* they that have not seen, and *yet* have believed.

³⁰And many other signs truly did Jesus in the presence of his disciples, which are not written in this book: ³¹But these are written, that ye might believe that Jesus is the Christ, the Son of God; and that believing ye might have life through his name.

21 After these things Jesus shewed himself again to the disciples at the sea of Tiberias; and on this wise shewed he *himself.* ²There were together Simon Peter, and Thomas called Didymus, and Nathanael of Cana in Galilee, and the *sons* of Zebedee, and two other of his disciples. ³Simon Peter saith unto them, I go a fishing. They say unto him, We also go with thee. They went forth, and entered into a ship immediately; and that night they caught nothing. ⁴But when the morning was now come, Jesus stood on the shore: but the disciples knew not that it was Jesus. ⁵Then Jesus saith unto them, Children, have ye any meat? They answered him, No. ⁶And he said unto them, Cast the net on the right side of the ship, and ye shall find. They cast therefore, and now they were not able to draw it for the multitude of fishes. ⁷Therefore that disciple whom Jesus loved saith unto Peter, It is the Lord. Now when Simon Peter heard that it was the Lord, he girt *his* fisher's coat *unto him,* (for he was naked,) and did cast himself into the sea. ⁸And the other disciples came in a little ship; (for

they were not far from land, but as it were two hundred cubits,) dragging the net with fishes. ⁹As soon then as they were come to land, they saw a fire of coals there, and fish laid thereon, and bread. ¹⁰Jesus saith unto them, Bring of the fish which ye have now caught. ¹¹Simon Peter went up, and drew the net to land full of great fishes, and hundred and fifty and three: and for all there were so many, yet was not the net broken. ¹²Jesus saith unto them, Come *and* dine. And none of the disciples durst ask him, Who art thou? knowing that it was the Lord. ¹³Jesus then cometh, and taketh bread, and giveth them, and fish likewise. ¹⁴This is now the third time that Jesus shewed himself to his disciples, after that he was risen from the dead.

¹⁵So when they had dined, Jesus saith to Simon Peter, Simon, *son* of Jonas, lovest thou me more than these? He saith unto him, Yea, Lord; thou knowest that I love thee. He saith unto him, Feed my lambs. ¹⁶He saith to him again the second time, Simon, *son* of Jonas, lovest thou me? He saith unto him, Yea, Lord; thou knowest that I love thee. He saith unto him, Feed my sheep. ¹⁷He saith unto him the third time, Simon, *son* of Jonas, lovest thou me? Peter was grieved because he said unto him the third time, Lovest thou me? And he said unto him, Lord, thou knowest all things; thou knowest that I love thee. Jesus saith unto him, Feed my sheep. ¹⁸Verily, verily, I say unto thee, When thou wast young, thou girdedst thyself, and walkedst whither thou wouldest: but when thou shalt be old, thou shalt stretch forth thy hands, and another shall gird thee, and carry *thee* whither thou wouldest not. ¹⁹This spake he, signifying by what death he should glorify God. And when he had spoken this, he saith unto him, Follow me. ²⁰Then Peter, turning about, seeth the disciple whom Jesus loved following; which also leaned on his breast at supper, and said, Lord, which is he that betrayeth thee? ²¹Peter seeing him saith to Jesus, Lord, and what *shall* this man *do?* ²²Jesus saith unto him, If I will that he tarry till I come, what *is that* to thee? follow thou me. ²³Then went this saying abroad among the brethren, that that disciple should not die: yet Jesus

said not unto him, He shall not die; but, If I will that he tarry till I come, what *is that* to thee? [24] This is the disciple which testifieth of these things, and wrote these things: and we know that his testimony is true.

[25] And there are also many other things which Jesus did, the which, if they should be written every one, I suppose that even the world itself could not contain the books that should be written. Amen.

THE ACTS
of the Apostles

1 The former treatise have I made, O Theophilus, of all that Jesus began both to do and teach, [2]Until the day in which he was taken up, after that he through the Holy Ghost had given commandments unto the apostles whom he had chosen: [3]To whom also he shewed himself alive after his passion by many infallible proofs, being seen of them forty days, and speaking of the things pertaining to the kingdom of God: [4]And, being assembled together with *them,* commanded them that they should not depart from Jerusalem, but wait for the promise of the Father, which, *saith he,* ye have heard of me. [5]For John truly baptized with water; but ye shall be baptized with the Holy Ghost not many days hence. [6]When they therefore were come together, they asked of him, saying, Lord, wilt thou at this time restore again the kingdom to Israel? [7]And he said unto them, It is not for you to know the times or the seasons, which the Father hath put in his own power. [8]But ye shall receive power, after that the Holy Ghost is come upon you: and ye shall be witnesses unto me both in Jerusalem, and in all Judaea, and in Samaria, and unto the uttermost part of the earth. [9]And when he had spoken these things, while they beheld, he was taken up; and a cloud received him out of their sight. [10]And while they looked stedfastly toward heaven as he went up, behold, two men stood by them in white apparel; [11]Which also said, Ye men of Galilee, why stand ye gazing up into heaven? this same Jesus, which is taken up from you into heaven, shall so come in like manner as ye have seen him go into heaven. [12]Then returned they unto Jerusalem from the mount called Olivet, which is from Jerusalem a sabbath day's journey. [13]And when they were come in, they went up into an upper room, where abode both Peter, and James, and John, and Andrew, Philip, and Thomas, Bartholomew, and Matthew, James *the son* of Alphaeus, and Simon Zelotes, and Judas *the brother* of James. [14]These all continued with one accord in prayer and supplication, with the women, and Mary the mother of Jesus, and with his brethren.

[15]And in those days Peter stood up in the midst of the disciples, and said, (the number of names together were about an hundred and twenty,) [16]Men *and* brethren, this scripture must needs have been fulfilled, which the Holy Ghost by the mouth of David spake before concerning Judas, which was guide to them that took Jesus. [17]For he was numbered with us, and had obtained part of this ministry. [18]Now this man purchased a field with the reward of iniquity; and falling headlong, he burst asunder in the midst, and all his bowels gushed out. [19]And it was known unto all the dwellers at Jerusalem; insomuch as that field is called in their proper tongue, Aceldama, that is to say, The field of blood. [20]For it is written in the book of Psalms,

Let his habitation be desolate, and let no man dwell therein:

and

his bishoprick let another take.

[21]Wherefore of these men which have companied with us all the time that the Lord Jesus went in and out among us, [22]Beginning from the baptism of John, unto that same day that he was taken up from us, must one be ordained to be a witness with us of his resurrection. [23]And they appointed two, Joseph called Barsabas, who was surnamed Justus, and Matthias. [24]And they prayed, and said, Thou, Lord, which knowest the hearts of all *men,* shew whether of these two thou hast chosen, [25]That he may take part of this ministry and apostleship, from which Judas by transgression fell, that he might go to his own place. [26]And they gave forth their lots; and the lot fell upon Matthias; and he was numbered with the eleven apostles.

2 And when the day of Pentecost was fully come, they were all with one accord in one place. [2]And suddenly there came a sound from heaven as of a rushing mighty wind, and it filled all the house where they were sitting. [3]And there appeared unto

them cloven tongues like as of fire, and it sat upon each of them. ⁴And they were all filled with the Holy Ghost, and began to speak with other tongues, as the Spirit gave them utterance. ⁵And there were dwelling at Jerusalem Jews, devout men, out of every nation under heaven. ⁶Now when this was noised abroad, the multitude came together, and were confounded, because that every man heard them speak in his own language. ⁷And they were all amazed and marvelled, saying one to another, Behold, are not all these which speak Galilaeans? ⁸And how hear we every man in our own tongue, wherein we were born? ⁹Parthians, and Medes, and Elamites, and the dwellers in Mesopotamia, and in Judaea, and Cappadocia, in Pontus, and Asia, ¹⁰Phrygia, and Pamphylia, in Egypt, and in the parts of Libya about Cyrene, and strangers of Rome, Jews and proselytes, ¹¹Cretes and Arabians, we do hear them speak in our tongues the wonderful works of God. ¹²And they were all amazed, and were in doubt, saying one to another, What meaneth this? ¹³Others mocking said, These men are full of new wine.

¹⁴But Peter, standing up with the eleven, lifted up his voice, and said unto them, Ye men of Judaea, and all *ye* that dwell at Jerusalem, be this known unto you, and hearken to my words: ¹⁵For these are not drunken, as ye suppose, seeing it is *but* the third hour of the day. ¹⁶But this is that which was spoken by the prophet Joel;

¹⁷And it shall come to pass in the last days, saith God,I will pour out of my Spirit upon all flesh: and your sons and your daughters shall prophesy, and your young men shall see visions, and your old men shall dream dreams: ¹⁸And on my servants and on my handmaidens I will pour out in those days of my Spirit; and they shall prophesy: ¹⁹And I will shew wonders in heaven above, and signs in the earth beneath; blood, and fire, and vapour of smoke: ²⁰The sun shall be turned into darkness, and the moon into blood, before that great and notable day of the Lord come: ²¹And it shall come to pass, *that* whosoever shall call on the name of the Lord shall be saved.

²²Ye men of Israel, hear these words; Jesus of Nazareth, a man approved of God among you by miracles and wonders and signs, which God did by him in the midst of you, as ye yourselves also know: ²³Him, being delivered by the determinate counsel and foreknowledge of God, ye have taken, and by wicked hands have crucified and slain: ²⁴Whom God hath raised up, having loosed the pains of death: because it was not possible that he should be holden of it. ²⁵For David speaketh concerning him,

I foresaw the Lord always before my face, for he is on my right hand, that I should not be moved: ²⁶Therefore did my heart rejoice, and my tongue was glad; moreover also my flesh shall rest in hope: ²⁷Because thou wilt not leave my soul in hell, neither wilt thou suffer thine Holy One to see corruption. ²⁸Thou hast made known to me the ways of life; thou shalt make me full of joy with thy countenance.

²⁹Men *and* brethren, let me freely speak unto you of the patriarch David, that he is both dead and buried, and his sepulchre is with us unto this day. ³⁰Therefore being a prophet, and knowing that God had sworn with an oath to him, that of the fruit of his loins, according to the flesh, he would raise up Christ to sit on his throne; ³¹He seeing this before spake of the resurrection of Christ, that his soul was not left in hell, neither his flesh did see corruption. ³²This Jesus hath God raised up, whereof we all are witnesses. ³³Therefore being by the right hand of God exalted, and having received of the Father the promise of the Holy Ghost, he hath shed forth this, which ye now see and hear. ³⁴For David is not ascended into the heavens: but he saith himself,

The Lord said unto my Lord, Sit thou on my right hand, ³⁵Until I make thy foes thy footstool.

³⁶Therefore let all the house of Israel know assuredly, that God hath made that same Jesus, whom ye have crucified, both Lord and Christ.

³⁷Now when they heard *this*, they were pricked in their heart, and said unto Peter and to the rest of the apostles, Men *and*

brethren, what shall we do? [38]Then Peter said unto them, Repent, and be baptized every one of you in the name of Jesus Christ for the remission of sins, and ye shall receive the gift of the Holy Ghost. [39]For the promise is unto you, and to your children, and to all that are afar off, *even* as many as the Lord our God shall call. [40]And with many other words did he testify and exhort, saying, Save yourselves from this untoward generation.

[41]Then they that gladly received his word were baptized: and the same day there were added *unto them* about three thousand souls. [42]And they continued stedfastly in the apostles' doctrine and fellowship, and in breaking of bread, and in prayers. [43]And fear came upon every soul: and many wonders and signs were done by the apostles. [44]And all that believed were together, and had all things common; [45]And sold their possessions and goods, and parted them to all *men,* as every man had need. [46]And they, continuing daily with one accord in the temple, and breaking bread from house to house, did eat their meat with gladness and singleness of heart, [47]Praising God, and having favour with all the people. And the Lord added to the church daily such as should be saved.

3 Now Peter and John went up together into the temple at the hour of prayer, *being* the ninth *hour.* [2]And a certain man lame from his mother's womb was carried, whom they laid daily at the gate of the temple which is called Beautiful, to ask alms of them that entered into the temple; [3]Who seeing Peter and John about to go into the temple asked an alms. [4]And Peter, fastening his eyes upon him with John, said, Look on us. [5]And he gave heed unto them, expecting to receive something of them. [6]Then Peter said, Silver and gold have I none; but such as I have give I thee: In the name of Jesus Christ of Nazareth rise up and walk. [7]And he took him by the right hand, and lifted *him* up: and immediately his feet and ancle bones received strength. [8]And he leaping up stood, and walked, and entered with them into the temple, walking, and leaping, and praising God. [9]And all the people saw him walking and praising God: [10]And they knew that it was he which sat for alms at the Beautiful gate of the temple: and they were filled with wonder and amazement at that which had happened unto him. [11]And as the lame man which was healed held Peter and John, all the people ran together unto them in the porch that is called Solomon's, greatly wondering.

[12]And when Peter saw *it,* he answered unto the people, Ye men of Israel, why marvel ye at this? or why look ye so earnestly on us, as though by our own power or holiness we had made this man to walk? [13]The God of Abraham, and of Isaac, and of Jacob, the God of our fathers, hath glorified his Son Jesus; whom ye delivered up, and denied him in the presence of Pilate, when he was determined to let *him* go. [14]But ye denied the Holy One and the Just, and desired a murderer to be granted unto you; [15]And killed the Prince of life, whom God hath raised from the dead; whereof we are witnesses. [16]And his name through faith in his name hath made this man strong, whom ye see and know: yea, the faith which is by him hath given him this perfect soundness in the presence of you all. [17]And now, brethren, I wot that through ignorance ye did *it,* as *did* also your rulers. [18]But those things, which God before had shewed by the mouth of all his prophets, that Christ should suffer, he hath so fulfilled.

[19]Repent ye therefore, and be converted, that your sins may be blotted out, when the times of refreshing shall come from the presence of the Lord; [20]And he shall send Jesus Christ, which before was preached unto you: [21]Whom the heaven must receive until the times of restitution of all things, which God hath spoken by the mouth of all his holy prophets since the world began. [22]For Moses truly said unto the fathers, A prophet shall the Lord your God raise up unto you of your brethren, like unto me; him shall ye hear in all things whatsoever he shall say unto you. [23]And it shall come to pass, *that* every soul, which will not hear that prophet, shall be destroyed from among the people. [24]Yea, and all the prophets from Samuel and those that follow after, as many as have spoken, have likewise foretold of these days. [25]Ye are the children of the prophets, and of the covenant which

God made with our fathers, saying unto Abraham, And in thy seed shall all the kindreds of the earth be blessed. [26]Unto you first God, having raised up his Son Jesus, sent him to bless you, in turning away every one of you from his iniquities.

4 And as they spake unto the people, the priests, and the captain of the temple, and the Sadducees, came upon them, [2]Being grieved that they taught the people, and preached through Jesus the resurrection from the dead. [3]And they laid hands on them, and put *them* in hold unto the next day: for it was now eventide. [4]Howbeit many of them which heard the word believed; and the number of the men was about five thousand.

[5]And it came to pass on the morrow, that their rulers, and elders, and scribes, [6]And Annas the high priest, and Caiaphas, and John, and Alexander, and as many as were of the kindred of the high priest, were gathered together at Jerusalem. [7]And when they had set them in the midst, they asked, By what power, or by what name, have ye done this? [8]Then Peter, filled with the Holy Ghost, said unto them, Ye rulers of the people, and elders of Israel, [9]If we this day be examined of the good deed done to the impotent man, by what means he is made whole; [10]Be it known unto you all, and to all the people of Israel, that by the name of Jesus Christ of Nazareth, whom ye crucified, whom God raised from the dead, *even* by him doth this man stand here before you whole.

[11]This is the stone which was set at nought of you builders, which is become the head of the corner.

[12]Neither is there salvation in any other: for there is none other name under heaven given among men, whereby we must be saved.

[13]Now when they saw the boldness of Peter and John, and perceived that they were unlearned and ignorant men, they marvelled; and they took knowledge of them, that they had been with Jesus. [14]And beholding the man which was healed standing with them, they could say nothing against it. [15]But when they had commanded them to go aside out of the council, they conferred among themselves, [16]Saying, What shall we do to these men? for that indeed a notable miracle hath been done by them *is* manifest to all them that dwell in Jerusalem; and we cannot deny *it.* [17]But that it spread no further among the people, let us straitly threaten them, that they speak henceforth to no man in this name. [18]And they called them, and commanded them not to speak at all nor teach in the name of Jesus. [19]But Peter and John answered and said unto them, Whether it be right in the sight of God to hearken unto you more than unto God, judge ye. [20]For we cannot but speak the things which we have seen and heard. [21]So when they had further threatened them, they let them go, finding nothing how they might punish them, because of the people: for all *men* glorified God for that which was done. [22]For the man was above forty years old, on whom this miracle of healing was shewed.

[23]And being let go, they went to their own company, and reported all that the chief priests and elders had said unto them. [24]And when they heard that, they lifted up their voice to God with one accord, and said, Lord, thou *art* God, which hast made heaven, and earth, and the sea, and all that in them is; [25]Who by the mouth of thy servant David hast said,

Why did the heathen rage, and the people imagine vain things? [26]The kings of the earth stood up, and the rulers were gathered together against the Lord, and against his Christ.

[27]For of a truth against thy holy child Jesus, whom thou hast anointed, both Herod, and Pontius Pilate, with the Gentiles, and the people of Israel, were gathered together, [28]For to do whatsoever thy hand and thy counsel determined before to be done. [29]And now, Lord, behold their threatenings: and grant unto thy servants, that with all boldness they may speak thy word, [30]By stretching forth thine hand to heal; and that signs and wonders may be done by the name of thy holy child Jesus.

[31]And when they had prayed, the place was shaken where they were assembled together; and they were all filled with the

Holy Ghost, and they spake the word of God with boldness.

³²And the multitude of them that believed were of one heart and of one soul: neither said any *of them* that ought of the things which he possessed was his own; but they had all things common. ³³And with great power gave the apostles witness of the resurrection of the Lord Jesus: and great grace was upon them all. ³⁴Neither was there any among them that lacked: for as many as were possessors of lands or houses sold them, and brought the prices of the things that were sold, ³⁵And laid *them* down at the apostles' feet: and distribution was made unto every man according as he had need. ³⁶And Joses, who by the apostles was surnamed Barnabas, (which is, being interpreted, The son of consolation,) a Levite, *and* of the country of Cyprus, ³⁷Having land, sold *it,* and brought the money, and laid *it* at the apostles' feet.

5 But a certain man named Ananias, with Sapphira his wife, sold a possession, ²And kept back *part* of the price, his wife also being privy *to it,* and brought a certain part, and laid *it* at the apostles' feet. ³But Peter said, Ananias, why hath Satan filled thine heart to lie to the Holy Ghost, and to keep back *part* of the price of the land? ⁴Whiles it remained, was it not thine own? and after it was sold, was it not in thine own power? why hast thou conceived this thing in thine heart? thou hast not lied unto men, but unto God. ⁵And Ananias hearing these words fell down, and gave up the ghost: and great fear came on all them that heard these things. ⁶And the young men arose, wound him up, and carried *him* out, and buried *him.* ⁷And it was about the space of three hours after, when his wife, not knowing what was done, came in. ⁸And Peter answered unto her, Tell me whether ye sold the land for so much? And she said, Yea, for so much. ⁹Then Peter said unto her, How is it that ye have agreed together to tempt the Spirit of the Lord? behold, the feet of them which have buried thy husband *are* at the door, and shall carry thee out. ¹⁰Then fell she down straightway at his feet, and yielded up the ghost: and the young men came in, and found her dead, and, carrying *her* forth, buried *her* by her husband. ¹¹And great fear came upon all the church, and upon as many as heard these things.

¹²And by the hands of the apostles were many signs and wonders wrought among the people; (and they were all with one accord in Solomon's porch. ¹³And of the rest durst no man join himself to them: but the people magnified them. ¹⁴And believers were the more added to the Lord, multitudes both of men and women.) ¹⁵Insomuch that they brought forth the sick into the streets, and laid *them* on beds and couches, that at the least the shadow of Peter passing by might overshadow some of them. ¹⁶There came also a multitude *out* of the cities round about unto Jerusalem, bringing sick folks, and them which were vexed with unclean spirits: and they were healed every one.

¹⁷Then the high priest rose up, and all they that were with him, (which is the sect of the Sadducees,) and were filled with indignation, ¹⁸And laid their hands on the apostles, and put them in the common prison. ¹⁹But the angel of the Lord by night opened the prison doors, and brought them forth, and said, ²⁰Go, stand and speak in the temple to the people all the words of this life. ²¹And when they heard *that,* they entered into the temple early in the morning, and taught. But the high priest came, and they that were with him, and called the council together, and all the senate of the children of Israel and sent to the prison to have them brought. ²²But when the officers came, and found them not in the prison, they returned, and told, ²³Saying, The prison truly found we shut with all safety, and the keepers standing without before the doors: but when we had opened, we found no man within. ²⁴Now when the high priest and the captain of the temple and the chief priests heard these things, they doubted of them whereunto this would grow. ²⁵Then came one and told them, saying, Behold, the men whom ye put in prison are standing in the temple, and teaching the people. ²⁶Then went the captain with the officers, and brought them without violence: for they feared the people, lest they should have been stoned. ²⁷And when they had brought them, they set *them* before the

council: and the high priest asked them, [28]Saying, Did not we straitly command you that ye should not teach in this name? and, behold, ye have filled Jerusalem with your doctrine, and intend to bring this man's blood upon us.

[29]Then Peter and the *other* apostles answered and said, We ought to obey God rather than men. [30]The God of our fathers raised up Jesus, whom ye slew and hanged on a tree. [31]Him hath God exalted with his right hand *to be* a Prince and a Saviour, for to give repentance to Israel, and forgiveness of sins. [32]And we are his witnesses of these things; and *so is* also the Holy Ghost, whom God hath given to them that obey him.

[33]When they heard *that,* they were cut *to the heart,* and took counsel to slay them. [34]Then stood there up one in the council, a Pharisee, named Gamaliel, a doctor of the law, had in reputation among all the people, and commanded to put the apostles forth a little space; [35]And said unto them, Ye men of Israel, take heed to yourselves what ye intend to do as touching these men. [36]For before these days rose up Theudas, boasting himself to be somebody; to whom a number of men, about four hundred, joined themselves: who was slain; and all, as many as obeyed him, were scattered, and brought to nought. [37]After this man rose up Judas of Galilee in the days of the taxing, and drew away much people after him: he also perished; and all, *even* as many as obeyed him, were dispersed. [38]And now I say unto you, Refrain from these men, and let them alone: for if this counsel or this work be of men, it will come to nought: [39]But if it be of God, ye cannot overthrow it; lest haply ye be found even to fight against God. [40]And to him they agreed: and when they had called the apostles, and beaten *them,* they commanded that they should not speak in the name of Jesus, and let them go.

[41]And they departed from the presence of the council, rejoicing that they were counted worthy to suffer shame for his name. [42]And daily in the temple, and in every house, they ceased not to teach and preach Jesus Christ.

6 And in those days, when the number of the disciples was multiplied, there arose a murmuring of the Grecians against the Hebrews, because their widows were neglected in the daily ministration. [2]Then the twelve called the multitude of the disciples *unto them,* and said, It is not reason that we should leave the word of God, and serve tables. [3]Wherefore, brethren, look ye out among you seven men of honest report, full of the Holy Ghost and wisdom, whom we may appoint over this business. [4]But we will give ourselves continually to prayer, and to the ministry of the word.

[5]And the saying pleased the whole multitude: and they chose Stephen, a man full of faith and of the Holy Ghost, and Philip, and Prochorus, and Nicanor, and Timon, and Parmenas, and Nicolas a proselyte of Antioch: [6]Whom they set before the apostles: and when they had prayed, they laid *their* hands on them. [7]And the word of God increased; and the number of the disciples multiplied in Jerusalem greatly; and a great company of the priests were obedient to the faith.

[8]And Stephen, full of faith and power, did great wonders and miracles among the people.

[9]Then there arose certain of *the synagogue,* which is called the synagogue of the Libertines, and Cyrenians, and Alexandrians, and of them of Cilicia and of Asia, disputing with Stephen. [10]And they were not able to resist the wisdom and the spirit by which he spake. [11]Then they suborned men, which said, We have heard him speak blasphemous words against Moses, and *against* God. [12]And they stirred up the people, and the elders, and the scribes, and came upon *him,* and caught him, and brought *him* to the council, [13]And set up false witnesses, which said, This man ceaseth not to speak blasphemous words against this holy place, and the law: [14]For we have heard him say, that this Jesus of Nazareth shall destroy this place, and shall change the customs which Moses delivered us. [15]And all that sat in the council, looking stedfastly on him, saw his face as it had been the face of an angel.

7 Then said the high priest, Are these things so? [2]And he said, Men, brethren, and fathers, hearken; The God of glory appeared unto our father Abraham, when

he was in Mesopotamia, before he dwelt in Charran, ³And said unto him, Get thee out of thy country, and from thy kindred, and come into the land which I shall shew thee. ⁴Then came he out of the land of the Chaldaeans, and dwelt in Charran: and from thence, when his father was dead, he removed him into this land, wherein ye now dwell. ⁵And he gave him none inheritance in it, no, not *so much as* to set his foot on: yet he promised that he would give it to him for a possession, and to his seed after him, when *as yet* he had no child. ⁶And God spake on this wise, That his seed should sojourn in a strange land; and that they should bring them into bondage, and entreat *them* evil four hundred years. ⁷And the nation to whom they shall be in bondage will I judge, said God: and after that shall they come forth, and serve me in this place. ⁸And he gave him the covenant of circumcision: and so *Abraham* begat Isaac, and circumcised him the eighth day; and Isaac *begat* Jacob; and Jacob *begat* the twelve patriarchs. ⁹And the patriarchs, moved with envy, sold Joseph into Egypt: but God was with him, ¹⁰And delivered him out of all his afflictions, and gave him favour and wisdom in the sight of Pharaoh king of Egypt; and he made him governor over Egypt and all his house. ¹¹Now there came a dearth over all the land of Egypt and Chanaan, and great affliction: and our fathers found no sustenance. ¹²But when Jacob heard that there was corn in Egypt, he sent out our fathers first. ¹³And at the second *time* Joseph was made known to his brethren; and Joseph's kindred was made known unto Pharaoh. ¹⁴Then sent Joseph, and called his father Jacob to *him*, and all his kindred, threescore and fifteen souls. ¹⁵So Jacob went down into Egypt, and died, he, and our fathers, ¹⁶And were carried over into Sychem, and laid in the sepulchre that Abraham bought for a sum of money of the sons of Emmor *the father* of Sychem. ¹⁷But when the time of the promise drew nigh, which God had sworn to Abraham, the people grew and multiplied in Egypt, ¹⁸Till another king arose, which knew not Joseph. ¹⁹The same dealt subtilly with our kindred, and evil entreated our fathers, so that they cast out their young children,

to the end they might not live. ²⁰In which time Moses was born, and was exceeding fair, and nourished up in his father's house three months: ²¹And when he was cast out, Pharaoh's daughter took him up, and nourished him for her own son. ²²And Moses was learned in all the wisdom of the Egyptians, and was mighty in words and in deeds. ²³And when he was full forty years old, it came into his heart to visit his brethren the children of Israel. ²⁴And seeing one *of them* suffer wrong, he defended *him*, and avenged him that was oppressed, and smote the Egyptian: ²⁵For he supposed his brethren would have understood how that God by his hand would deliver them: but they understood not. ²⁶And the next day he shewed himself unto them as they strove, and would have set them at one again, saying, Sirs, ye are brethren; why do ye wrong one to another? ²⁷But he that did his neighbour wrong thrust him away, saying, Who made thee a ruler and a judge over us? ²⁸Wilt thou kill me, as thou diddest the Egyptian yesterday? ²⁹Then fled Moses at this saying, and was a stranger in the land of Madian, where he begat two sons. ³⁰And when forty years were expired, there appeared to him in the wilderness of mount Sina an angel of the Lord in a flame of fire in a bush. ³¹When Moses saw *it*, he wondered at the sight: and as he drew near to behold *it*, the voice of the Lord came unto him, ³²*Saying*, I *am* the God of thy fathers, the God of Abraham, and the God of Isaac, and the God of Jacob. Then Moses trembled, and durst not behold. ³³Then said the Lord to him, Put off thy shoes from thy feet: for the place where thou standest is holy ground. ³⁴I have seen, I have seen the affliction of my people which is in Egypt, and I have heard their groaning, and am come down to deliver them. And now come, I will send thee into Egypt. ³⁵This Moses whom they refused, saying, Who made thee a ruler and a judge? the same did God send *to be* a ruler and a deliverer by the hand of the angel which appeared to him in the bush. ³⁶He brought them out, after that he had shewed wonders and signs in the land of Egypt, and in the Red sea, and in the wilderness forty years. ³⁷This is that Moses, which said unto the children of Israel, A prophet shall the Lord your God raise up unto you of your brethren, like unto me; him shall ye hear. ³⁸This is he, that was in the church in the wilderness with the angel which spake to him in the mount Sina, and *with* our fathers: who received the lively oracles to give unto us: ³⁹To whom our fathers would not obey, but thrust *him* from them, and in their hearts turned back again into Egypt, ⁴⁰Saying unto Aaron, Make us gods to go before us: for *as for* this Moses, which brought us out of the land of Egypt, we wot not what is become of him. ⁴¹And they made a calf in those days, and offered sacrifice unto the idol, and rejoiced in the works of their own hands. ⁴²Then God turned, and gave them up to worship the host of heaven; as it is written in the book of the prophets,

O ye house of Israel, have ye offered to me slain beasts and sacrifices *by the space of* forty years in the wilderness? ⁴³Yea, ye took up the tabernacle of Moloch, and the star of your god Remphan, figures which ye made to worship them: and I will carry you away beyond Babylon.

⁴⁴Our fathers had the tabernacle of witness in the wilderness, as he had appointed, speaking unto Moses, that he should make it according to the fashion that he had seen. ⁴⁵Which also our fathers that came after brought in with Jesus into the possession of the Gentiles, whom God drave out before the face of our fathers, unto the days of David; ⁴⁶Who found favour before God, and desired to find a tabernacle for the God of Jacob. ⁴⁷But Solomon built him an house. ⁴⁸Howbeit the most High dwelleth not in temples made with hands; as saith the prophet,

⁴⁹Heaven *is* my throne, and earth *is* my footstool: what house will ye build me? saith the Lord: or what *is* the place of my rest? ⁵⁰Hath not my hand made all these things?

⁵¹Ye stiffnecked and uncircumcised in heart and ears, ye do always resist the Holy Ghost: as your fathers *did,* so *do* ye. ⁵²Which of the prophets have not your fathers persecuted? and they have slain them which shewed before of the coming of the Just One; of whom ye have been now the betrayers and murderers: ⁵³Who have received the law by the disposition of angels, and have not kept *it.*

⁵⁴When they heard these things, they were cut to the heart, and they gnashed on him with *their* teeth. ⁵⁵But he, being full of the Holy Ghost, looked up stedfastly into heaven, and saw the glory of God, and Jesus standing on the right hand of God, ⁵⁶And said, Behold, I see the heavens opened, and the Son of man standing on the right hand of God. ⁵⁷Then they cried out with a loud voice, and stopped their ears, and ran upon him with one accord, ⁵⁸And cast *him* out of the city, and stoned *him:* and the witnesses laid down their clothes at a young man's feet, whose name was Saul. ⁵⁹And they stoned Stephen, calling upon *God,* and saying, Lord Jesus, receive my spirit. ⁶⁰And he kneeled down, and cried with a loud voice, Lord, lay not this sin to their charge. And when he had said this, he fell asleep.

8 And Saul was consenting unto his death. And at that time there was a great persecution against the church which was at Jerusalem; and they were all scattered abroad throughout the regions of Judaea and Samaria, except the apostles. ²And devout men carried Stephen *to his burial,* and made great lamentation over him. ³As for Saul, he made havock of the church, entering into every house, and haling men and women committed *them* to prison. ⁴Therefore they that were scattered abroad went every where preaching the word. ⁵Then Philip went down to the city of Samaria, and preached Christ unto them. ⁶And the people with one accord gave heed unto those things which Philip spake, hearing and seeing the miracles which he did. ⁷For unclean spirits, crying with loud voice, came out of many that were possessed *with them:* and many taken with palsies, and that were lame, were healed. ⁸And there was great joy in that city. ⁹But there was a certain man, called Simon, which beforetime in the same city used sorcery, and bewitched the people of Samaria, giving out that himself was some great one: ¹⁰To whom they all gave heed, from the least to the greatest, saying, This man is the great power of God.

¹¹And to him they had regard, because that of long time he had bewitched them with sorceries. ¹²But when they believed Philip preaching the things concerning the kingdom of God, and the name of Jesus Christ, they were baptized, both men and women. ¹³Then Simon himself believed also: and when he was baptized, he continued with Philip, and wondered, beholding the miracles and signs which were done. ¹⁴Now when the apostles which were at Jerusalem heard that Samaria had received the word of God, they sent unto them Peter and John: ¹⁵Who, when they were come down, prayed for them, that they might receive the Holy Ghost: ¹⁶(For as yet he was fallen upon none of them: only they were baptized in the name of the Lord Jesus.) ¹⁷Then laid they *their* hands on them, and they received the Holy Ghost. ¹⁸And when Simon saw that through laying on of the apostles' hands the Holy Ghost was given, he offered them money, ¹⁹Saying, Give me also this power, that on whomsoever I lay hands, he may receive the Holy Ghost. ²⁰But Peter said unto him, Thy money perish with thee, because thou hast thought that the gift of God may be purchased with money. ²¹Thou hast neither part nor lot in this matter: for thy heart is not right in the sight of God. ²²Repent therefore of this thy wickedness, and pray God, if perhaps the thought of thine heart may be forgiven thee. ²³For I perceive that thou art in the gall of bitterness, and *in* the bond of iniquity. ²⁴Then answered Simon, and said, Pray ye to the Lord for me, that none of these things which ye have spoken come upon me. ²⁵And they, when they had testified and preached the word of the Lord, returned to Jerusalem, and preached the gospel in many villages of the Samaritans. ²⁶And the angel of the Lord spake unto Philip, saying, Arise, and go toward the south unto the way that goeth down from Jerusalem unto Gaza, which is desert. ²⁷And he arose and went: and, behold, a man of Ethiopia, an eunuch of great authority under Candace queen of the Ethiopians, who had the charge of all her treasure, and had come to Jerusalem for to worship, ²⁸Was returning, and sitting in his chariot read Esaias the prophet.

²⁹Then the Spirit said unto Philip, Go near, and join thyself to this chariot. ³⁰And Philip ran thither to *him*, and heard him read the prophet Esaias, and said, Understandest thou what thou readest? ³¹And he said, How can I, except some man should guide me? And he desired Philip that he would come up and sit with him. ³²The place of the scripture which he read was this,

He was led as a sheep to the slaughter; and like a lamb dumb before his shearer, so opened he not his mouth: ³³In his humiliation his judgment was taken away: and who shall declare his generation? for his life is taken from the earth.

³⁴And the eunuch answered Philip, and said, I pray thee, of whom speaketh the prophet this? of himself, or of some other man? ³⁵Then Philip opened his mouth, and began at the same scripture, and preached unto him Jesus. ³⁶And as they went on *their* way, they came unto a certain water: and the eunuch said, See, *here is* water; what doth hinder me to be baptized? ³⁷And Philip said, If thou believest with all thine heart, thou mayest. And he answered and said, I believe that Jesus Christ is the Son of God. ³⁸And he commanded the chariot to stand still: and they went down both into the water, both Philip and the eunuch; and he baptized him. ³⁹And when they were come up out of the water, the Spirit of the Lord caught away Philip, that the eunuch saw him no more: and he went on his way rejoicing. ⁴⁰But Philip was found at Azotus: and passing through he preached in all the cities, till he came to Caesarea.

9 And Saul, yet breathing out threatenings and slaughter against the disciples of the Lord, went unto the high priest, ²And desired of him letters to Damascus to the synagogues, that if he found any of this way, whether they were men or women, he might bring them bound unto Jerusalem. ³And as he journeyed, he came near Damascus: and suddenly there shined round about him a light from heaven: ⁴And he fell to the earth, and heard a voice saying unto him, Saul, Saul, why persecutest thou me? ⁵And he said, Who art thou, Lord? And the Lord said, I am Jesus whom thou persecutest: *it is* hard for thee to kick against the pricks. [6]And he trembling and astonished said, Lord, what wilt thou have me to do? And the Lord *said* unto him, Arise, and go into the city, and it shall be told thee what thou must do. [7]And the men which journeyed with him stood speechless, hearing a voice, but seeing no man. [8]And Saul arose from the earth; and when his eyes were opened, he saw no man: but they led him by the hand, and brought *him* into Damascus. [9]And he was three days without sight, and neither did eat nor drink.

[10]And there was a certain disciple at Damascus, named Ananias; and to him said the Lord in a vision, Ananias. And he said, Behold, I *am here,* Lord. [11]And the Lord *said* unto him, Arise, and go into the street which is called Straight, and enquire in the house of Judas for *one* called Saul, of Tarsus: for, behold, he prayeth, [12]And hath seen in a vision a man named Ananias coming in, and putting *his* hand on him, that he might receive his sight. [13]Then Ananias answered, Lord, I have heard by many of this man, how much evil he hath done to thy saints at Jerusalem: [14]And here he hath authority from the chief priests to bind all that call on thy name. [15]But the Lord said unto him, Go thy way: for he is a chosen vessel unto me, to bear my name before the Gentiles, and kings, and the children of Israel: [16]For I will shew him how great things he must suffer for my name's sake. [17]And Ananias went his way, and entered into the house; and putting his hands on him said, Brother Saul, the Lord, *even* Jesus, that appeared unto thee in the way as thou camest, hath sent me, that thou mightest receive thy sight, and be filled with the Holy Ghost. [18]And immediately there fell from his eyes as it had been scales: and he received sight forthwith, and arose, and was baptized. [19]And when he had received meat, he was strengthened. Then was Saul certain days with the disciples which were at Damascus. [20]And straightway he preached Christ in the synagogues, that he is the Son of God. [21]But all that heard *him* were amazed, and said; Is not this he that destroyed them which called on this name in Jerusalem, and came hither for that intent, that he might bring them bound unto the chief priests? [22]But Saul increased the more in strength, and confounded the Jews which dwelt at Damascus, proving that this is very Christ.

[23]And after that many days were fulfilled, the Jews took counsel to kill him: [24]But their laying await was known of Saul. And they watched the gates day and night to kill him. [25]Then the disciples took him by night, and let *him* down by the wall in a basket. [26]And when Saul was come to Jerusalem, he assayed to join himself to the disciples: but they were all afraid of him, and believed not that he was a disciple. [27]But Barnabas took him, and brought *him* to the apostles, and declared unto them how he had seen the Lord in the way, and that he had spoken to him, and how he had preached boldly at Damascus in the name of Jesus. [28]And he was with them coming in and going out at Jerusalem. [29]And he spake boldly in the name of the Lord Jesus, and disputed against the Grecians: but they went about to slay him. [30]*Which* when the brethren knew, they brought him down to Caesarea, and sent him forth to Tarsus. [31]Then had the churches rest throughout all Judaea and Galilee and Samaria, and were edified; and walking in the fear of the Lord, and in the comfort of the Holy Ghost, were multiplied.

[32]And it came to pass, as Peter passed throughout all *quarters,* he came down also to the saints which dwelt at Lydda. [33]And there he found a certain man named Aeneas, which had kept his bed eight years, and was sick of the palsy. [34]And Peter said unto him, Aeneas, Jesus Christ maketh thee whole: arise, and make thy bed. And he arose immediately. [35]And all that dwelt at Lydda and Saron saw him, and turned to the Lord.

[36]Now there was at Joppa a certain disciple named Tabitha, which by interpretation is called Dorcas: this woman was full of good works and almsdeeds which she did. [37]And it came to pass in those days, that she was sick, and died: whom when they had washed, they laid *her* in an upper chamber. [38]And forasmuch as Lydda was nigh to Joppa, and the disciples had heard that Peter was there, they sent unto him two men, desiring *him* that he would not delay

to come to them. ³⁹Then Peter arose and went with them. When he was come, they brought him into the upper chamber: and all the widows stood by him weeping, and shewing the coats and garments which Dorcas made, while she was with them. ⁴⁰But Peter put them all forth, and kneeled down, and prayed; and turning *him* to the body said, Tabitha, arise. And she opened her eyes: and when she saw Peter, she sat up. ⁴¹And he gave her *his* hand, and lifted her up, and when he had called the saints and widows, presented her alive. ⁴²And it was known throughout all Joppa; and many believed in the Lord. ⁴³And it came to pass, that he tarried many days in Joppa with one Simon a tanner.

10 There was a certain man in Caesarea called Cornelius, a centurion of the band called the Italian *band,* ²A devout *man,* and one that feared God with all his house, which gave much alms to the people, and prayed to God alway. ³He saw in a vision evidently about the ninth hour of the day an angel of God coming in to him, and saying unto him, Cornelius. ⁴And when he looked on him, he was afraid, and said, What is it, Lord? And he said unto him, Thy prayers and thine alms are come up for a memorial before God. ⁵And now send men to Joppa, and call for *one* Simon, whose surname is Peter: ⁶He lodgeth with one Simon a tanner, whose house is by the sea side: he shall tell thee what thou oughtest to do. ⁷And when the angel which spake unto Cornelius was departed, he called two of his household servants, and a devout soldier of them that waited on him continually; ⁸And when he had declared all *these* things unto them, he sent them to Joppa.

⁹On the morrow, as they went on their journey, and drew nigh unto the city, Peter went up upon the housetop to pray about the sixth hour: ¹⁰And he became very hungry, and would have eaten: but while they made ready, he fell into a trance, ¹¹And saw heaven opened, and a certain vessel descending unto him, as it had been a great sheet knit at the four corners, and let down to the earth: ¹²Wherein were all manner of fourfooted beasts of the earth, and wild beasts, and creeping things, and fowls of the air. ¹³And there came a voice to him,

Rise, Peter; kill, and eat. ¹⁴But Peter said, Not so, Lord; for I have never eaten any thing that is common or unclean. ¹⁵And the voice *spake* unto him again the second time, What God hath cleansed, *that* call not thou common. ¹⁶This was done thrice: and the vessel was received up again into heaven. ¹⁷Now while Peter doubted in himself what this vision which he had seen should mean, behold, the men which were sent from Cornelius had made enquiry for Simon's house, and stood before the gate, ¹⁸And called, and asked whether Simon, which was surnamed Peter, were lodged there.

¹⁹While Peter thought on the vision, the Spirit said unto him, Behold, three men seek thee. ²⁰Arise therefore, and get thee down, and go with them, doubting nothing: for I have sent them. ²¹Then Peter went down to the men which were sent unto him from Cornelius; and said, Behold, I am he whom ye seek: what *is* the cause wherefore ye are come? ²²And they said, Cornelius the centurion, a just man, and one that feareth God, and of good report among all the nation of the Jews, was warned from God by an holy angel to send for thee into his house, and to hear words of thee. ²³Then called he them in, and lodged *them.* And on the morrow Peter went away with them, and certain brethren from Joppa accompanied him. ²⁴And the morrow after they entered into Caesarea. And Cornelius waited for them, and had called together his kinsmen and near friends. ²⁵And as Peter was coming in, Cornelius met him, and fell down at his feet, and worshipped *him.* ²⁶But Peter took him up, saying, Stand up; I myself also am a man. ²⁷And as he talked with him, he went in, and found many that were come together. ²⁸And he said unto them, Ye know how that it is an unlawful thing for a man that is a Jew to keep company, or come unto one of another nation; but God hath shewed me that I should not call any man common or unclean. ²⁹Therefore came I *unto you* without gainsaying, as soon as I was sent for: I ask therefore for what intent ye have sent for me? ³⁰And Cornelius said, Four days ago I was fasting until this hour; and at the ninth hour I prayed in my house, and, behold, a man stood before me

in bright clothing, ³¹And said, Cornelius, thy prayer is heard, and thine alms are had in remembrance in the sight of God. ³²Send therefore to Joppa, and call hither Simon, whose surname is Peter; he is lodged in the house of *one* Simon a tanner by the sea side: who, when he cometh, shall speak unto thee. ³³Immediately therefore I sent to thee; and thou hast well done that thou art come. Now therefore are we all here present before God, to hear all things that are commanded thee of God.

³⁴Then Peter opened *his* mouth, and said, Of a truth I perceive that God is no respecter of persons: ³⁵But in every nation he that feareth him, and worketh righteousness, is accepted with him. ³⁶The word which *God* sent unto the children of Israel, preaching peace by Jesus Christ: (he is Lord of all:) ³⁷That word, *I say,* ye know, which was published throughout all Judaea, and began from Galilee, after the baptism which John preached; ³⁸How God anointed Jesus of Nazareth with the Holy Ghost and with power: who went about doing good, and healing all that were oppressed of the devil; for God was with him. ³⁹And we are witnesses of all things which he did both in the land of the Jews, and in Jerusalem; whom they slew and hanged on a tree: ⁴⁰Him God raised up the third day, and shewed him openly; ⁴¹Not to all the people, but unto witnesses chosen before of God, *even* to us, who did eat and drink with him after he rose from the dead. ⁴²And he commanded us to preach unto the people, and to testify that it is he which was ordained of God *to be* the Judge of quick and dead. ⁴³To him give all the prophets witness, that through his name whosoever believeth in him shall receive remission of sins.

⁴⁴While Peter yet spake these words, the Holy Ghost fell on all them which heard the word. ⁴⁵And they of the circumcision which believed were astonished, as many as came with Peter, because that on the Gentiles also was poured out the gift of the Holy Ghost. ⁴⁶For they heard them speak with tongues, and magnify God. Then answered Peter, ⁴⁷Can any man forbid water, that these should not be baptized, which have received the Holy Ghost as well as we? ⁴⁸And he commanded them to be baptized

in the name of the Lord. Then prayed they him to tarry certain days.

11 And the apostles and brethren that were in Judaea heard that the Gentiles had also received the word of God. ²And when Peter was come up to Jerusalem, they that were of the circumcision contended with him, ³Saying, Thou wentest in to men uncircumcised, and didst eat with them. ⁴But Peter rehearsed *the matter* from the beginning, and expounded *it* by order unto them, saying, ⁵I was in the city of Joppa praying: and in a trance I saw a vision, A certain vessel descend, as it had been a great sheet, let down from heaven by four corners; and it came even to me: ⁶Upon the which when I had fastened mine eyes, I considered, and saw fourfooted beasts of the earth, and wild beasts, and creeping things, and fowls of the air. ⁷And I heard a voice saying unto me, Arise, Peter; slay and eat. ⁸But I said, Not so, Lord: for nothing common or unclean hath at any time entered into my mouth. ⁹But the voice answered me again from heaven, What God hath cleansed, *that* call not thou common. ¹⁰And this was done three times: and all were drawn up again into heaven. ¹¹And, behold, immediately there were three men already come unto the house where I was, sent from Caesarea unto me. ¹²And the spirit bade me go with them, nothing doubting. Moreover these six brethren accompanied me, and we entered into the man's house: ¹³And he shewed us how he had seen an angel in his house, which stood and said unto him, Send men to Joppa, and call for Simon, whose surname is Peter; ¹⁴Who shall tell thee words, whereby thou and all thy house shall be saved. ¹⁵And as I began to speak, the Holy Ghost fell on them, as on us at the beginning. ¹⁶Then remembered I the word of the Lord, how that he said, John indeed baptized with water; but ye shall be baptized with the Holy Ghost. ¹⁷Forasmuch then as God gave them the like gift as *he did* unto us, who believed on the Lord Jesus Christ; what was I, that I could withstand God? ¹⁸When they heard these things, they held their peace, and glorified God, saying, Then hath God also to the Gentiles granted repentance unto life.

¹⁹Now they which were scattered abroad upon the persecution that arose about Stephen travelled as far as Phenice, and Cyprus, and Antioch, preaching the word to none but unto the Jews only. ²⁰And some of them were men of Cyprus and Cyrene, which, when they were come to Antioch, spake unto the Grecians, preaching the Lord Jesus. ²¹And the hand of the Lord was with them: and a great number believed, and turned unto the Lord.

²²Then tidings of these things came unto the ears of the church which was in Jerusalem: and they sent forth Barnabas, that he should go as far as Antioch. ²³Who, when he came, and had seen the grace of God, was glad, and exhorted them all, that with purpose of heart they would cleave unto the Lord. ²⁴For he was a good man, and full of the Holy Ghost and of faith: and much people was added unto the Lord. ²⁵Then departed Barnabas to Tarsus, for to seek Saul: ²⁶And when he had found him, he brought him unto Antioch. And it came to pass, that a whole year they assembled themselves with the church, and taught much people. And the disciples were called Christians first in Antioch.

²⁷And in these days came prophets from Jerusalem unto Antioch. ²⁸And there stood up one of them named Agabus, and signified by the spirit that there should be great dearth throughout all the world: which came to pass in the days of Claudius Caesar. ²⁹Then the disciples, every man according to his ability, determined to send relief unto the brethren which dwelt in Judaea: ³⁰Which also they did, and sent it to the elders by the hands of Barnabas and Saul.

12 Now about that time Herod the king stretched forth *his* hands to vex certain of the church. ²And he killed James the brother of John with the sword. ³And because he saw it pleased the Jews, he proceeded further to take Peter also. (Then were the days of unleavened bread.) ⁴And when he had apprehended him, he put *him* in prison, and delivered *him* to four quaternions of soldiers to keep him; intending after Easter to bring him forth to the people. ⁵Peter therefore was kept in prison: but prayer was made without ceasing of the church unto God for him. ⁶And when Herod would have brought him forth, the same night Peter was sleeping between two soldiers, bound with two chains: and the keepers before the door kept the prison. ⁷And, behold, the angel of the Lord came upon *him*, and a light shined in the prison: and he smote Peter on the side, and raised him up, saying, Arise up quickly. And his chains fell off from *his* hands. ⁸And the angel said unto him, Gird thyself, and bind on thy sandals. And so he did. And he saith unto him, Cast thy garment about thee, and follow me. ⁹And he went out, and followed him; and wist not that it was true which was done by the angel; but thought he saw a vision. ¹⁰When they were past the first and the second ward, they came unto the iron gate that leadeth unto the city; which opened to them of his own accord: and they went out, and passed on through one street; and forthwith the angel departed from him. ¹¹And when Peter was come to himself, he said, Now I know of a surety, that the Lord hath sent his angel, and hath delivered me out of the hand of Herod, and *from* all the expectation of the people of the Jews. ¹²And when he had considered *the thing*, he came to the house of Mary the mother of John, whose surname was Mark; where many were gathered together praying. ¹³And as Peter knocked at the door of the gate, a damsel came to hearken, named Rhoda. ¹⁴And when she knew Peter's voice, she opened not the gate for gladness, but ran in, and told how Peter stood before the gate. ¹⁵And they said unto her, Thou art mad. But she constantly affirmed that it was even so. Then said they, It is his angel. ¹⁶But Peter continued knocking: and when they had opened *the door*, and saw him, they were astonished. ¹⁷But he, beckoning unto them with the hand to hold their peace, declared unto them how the Lord had brought him out of the prison. And he said, Go shew these things unto James, and to the brethren. And he departed, and went into another place. ¹⁸Now as soon as it was day, there was no small stir among the soldiers, what was become of Peter. ¹⁹And when Herod had sought for him, and found him not, he examined the keepers, and commanded that *they* should be put to death. And he went down from Judaea to Caesarea, and *there* abode.

²⁰And Herod was highly displeased with them of Tyre and Sidon: but they came with one accord to him, and, having made Blastus the king's chamberlain their friend, desired peace; because their country was nourished by the king's *country.* ²¹And upon a set day Herod, arrayed in royal apparel, sat upon his throne, and made an oration unto them. ²²And the people gave a shout, *saying, It is* the voice of a god, and not of a man. ²³And immediately the angel of the Lord smote him, because he gave not God the glory: and he was eaten of worms, and gave up the ghost.

²⁴But the word of God grew and multiplied.

²⁵And Barnabas and Saul returned from Jerusalem, when they had fulfilled *their* ministry, and took with them John, whose surname was Mark.

13 Now there were in the church that was at Antioch certain prophets and teachers; as Barnabas, and Simeon that was called Niger, and Lucius of Cyrene, and Manaen, which had been brought up with Herod the tetrarch, and Saul. ²As they ministered to the Lord, and fasted, the Holy Ghost said, Separate me Barnabas and Saul for the work whereunto I have called them. ³And when they had fasted and prayed, and laid *their* hands on them, they sent *them* away.

⁴So they, being sent forth by the Holy Ghost, departed unto Seleucia; and from thence they sailed to Cyprus. ⁵And when they were at Salamis, they preached the word of God in the synagogues of the Jews: and they had also John to *their* minister. ⁶And when they had gone through the isle unto Paphos, they found a certain sorcerer, a false prophet, a Jew, whose name *was* Bar-jesus: ⁷Which was with the deputy of the country, Sergius Paulus, a prudent man; who called for Barnabas and Saul, and desired to hear the word of God. ⁸But Elymas the sorcerer (for so is his name by interpretation) withstood them, seeking to turn away the deputy from the faith. ⁹Then Saul, (who also *is called* Paul,) filled with the Holy Ghost, set his eyes on him, ¹⁰And said,

O full of all subtilty and all mischief, *thou* child of the devil, *thou* enemy of all righteousness, wilt thou not cease to pervert the right ways of the Lord? ¹¹And now, behold, the hand of the Lord *is* upon thee, and thou shalt be blind, not seeing the sun for a season. And immediately there fell on him a mist and a darkness; and he went about seeking some to lead him by the hand. ¹²Then the deputy, when he saw what was done, believed, being astonished at the doctrine of the Lord. ¹³Now when Paul and his company loosed from Paphos, they came to Perga in Pamphylia: and John departing from them returned to Jerusalem.

¹⁴But when they departed from Perga, they came to Antioch in Pisidia, and went into the synagogue on the sabbath day, and sat down. ¹⁵And after the reading of the law and the prophets the rulers of the synagogue sent unto them, saying, Ye men *and* brethren, if ye have any word of exhortation for the people, say on. ¹⁶Then Paul stood up, and beckoning with *his* hand said,

Men of Israel, and ye that fear God, give audience. ¹⁷The God of this people of Israel chose our fathers, and exalted the people when they dwelt as strangers in the land of Egypt, and with an high arm brought he them out of it. ¹⁸And about the time of forty years suffered he their manners in the wilderness. ¹⁹And when he had destroyed seven nations in the land of Chanaan, he divided their land to them by lot. ²⁰And after that he gave *unto them* judges about the space of four hundred and fifty years, until Samuel the prophet. ²¹And afterward they desired a king: and God gave unto them Saul the son of Cis, a man of the tribe of Benjamin, by the space of forty years. ²²And when he had removed him, he raised up unto them David to be their king; to whom also he gave testimony, and said, I have found David the *son* of Jesse, a man after mine own heart, which shall fulfil all my will. ²³Of this man's seed hath God according to *his* promise raised unto Israel a Saviour, Jesus: ²⁴When John had first preached before his coming the baptism of repentance to all the people of Israel. ²⁵And as John fulfilled his course, he said, Whom think ye that I am? I am not *he.* But, behold, there cometh one after me, whose shoes of *his* feet I am not worthy to loose. ²⁶Men *and* brethren, children of the stock of Abraham, and whosoever among you feareth God, to you is the word of this salvation sent. ²⁷For they that dwell at Jerusalem, and their rulers, because they knew him not, nor yet the voices of the prophets which are read every sabbath day, they have fulfilled *them* in condemning *him*. ²⁸And though they found no cause of death *in him*, yet desired they Pilate that he should be slain. ²⁹And when they had fulfilled all that was written of him, they took *him* down from the tree, and laid *him* in a sepulchre. ³⁰But God raised him from the dead: ³¹And he was seen many days of them which came up with him from Galilee to Jerusalem, who are his witnesses unto the people. ³²And we declare unto you glad tidings, how that the promise which was made unto the fathers, ³³God hath fulfilled the same unto us their children, in that he hath raised up Jesus again; as it is also written in the second psalm,

Thou art my Son, this day have I begotten thee.

³⁴And as concerning that he raised him up from the dead, *now* no more to return to corruption, he said on this wise,

I will give you the sure mercies of David.

³⁵Wherefore he saith also in another *psalm,*

Thou shalt not suffer thine Holy One to see corruption.

³⁶For David, after he had served his own generation by the will of God, fell on sleep, and was laid unto his fathers, and saw corruption: ³⁷But he, whom God raised again, saw no corruption. ³⁸Be it known unto you therefore, men *and* brethren, that through this man is preached unto you the forgiveness of sins: ³⁹And by him all that believe are justified from all things, from which ye could not be justified by the law of Moses. ⁴⁰Beware therefore, lest that come upon you, which is spoken of in the prophets;

⁴¹Behold, ye despisers, and wonder, and perish: for I work a work in your days,

a work which ye shall in no wise believe, though a man declare it unto you.

⁴²And when the Jews were gone out of the synagogue, the Gentiles besought that these words might be preached to them the next sabbath. ⁴³Now when the congregation was broken up, many of the Jews and religious proselytes followed Paul and Barnabas: who, speaking to them, persuaded them to continue in the grace of God.

⁴⁴And the next sabbath day came almost the whole city together to hear the word of God. ⁴⁵But when the Jews saw the multitudes, they were filled with envy, and spake against those things which were spoken by Paul, contradicting and blaspheming. ⁴⁶Then Paul and Barnabas waxed bold, and said, It was necessary that the word of God should first have been spoken to you: but seeing ye put it from you, and judge yourselves unworthy of everlasting life, lo, we turn to the Gentiles. ⁴⁷For so hath the Lord commanded us, *saying,*

I have set thee to be a light of the Gentiles, that thou shouldest be for salvation unto the ends of the earth.

⁴⁸And when the Gentiles heard this, they were glad, and glorified the word of the Lord: and as many as were ordained to eternal life believed. ⁴⁹And the word of the Lord was published throughout all the region. ⁵⁰But the Jews stirred up the devout and honourable women, and the chief men of the city, and raised persecution against Paul and Barnabas, and expelled them out of their coasts. ⁵¹But they shook off the dust of their feet against them, and came unto Iconium. ⁵²And the disciples were filled with joy, and with the Holy Ghost.

14 And it came to pass in Iconium, that they went both together into the synagogue of the Jews, and so spake, that a great multitude both of the Jews and also of the Greeks believed. ²But the unbelieving Jews stirred up the Gentiles, and made their minds evil affected against the brethren. ³Long time therefore abode they speaking boldly in the Lord, which gave testimony unto the word of his grace, and granted signs and wonders to be done by their hands. ⁴But the multitude of the city was divided: and part held with the Jews, and part with the apostles. ⁵And when there was an assault made both of the Gentiles, and also of the Jews with their rulers, to use *them* despitefully, and to stone them, ⁶They were ware of *it*, and fled unto Lystra and Derbe, cities of Lycaonia, and unto the region that lieth round about: ⁷And there they preached the gospel.

⁸And there sat a certain man at Lystra, impotent in his feet, being a cripple from his mother's womb, who never had walked: ⁹The same heard Paul speak: who stedfastly beholding him, and perceiving that he had faith to be healed, ¹⁰Said with a loud voice, Stand upright on thy feet. And he leaped and walked. ¹¹And when the people saw what Paul had done, they lifted up their voices, saying in the speech of Lycaonia, The gods are come down to us in the likeness of men. ¹²And they called Barnabas, Jupiter; and Paul, Mercurius, because he was the chief speaker. ¹³Then the priest of Jupiter, which was before their city, brought oxen and garlands unto the gates, and would have done sacrifice with the people. ¹⁴*Which* when the apostles, Barnabas and Paul, heard *of*, they rent their clothes, and ran in among the people, crying out, ¹⁵And saying, Sirs, why do ye these things? We also are men of like passions with you, and preach unto you that ye should turn from these vanities unto the living God, which made heaven, and earth, and the sea, and all things that are therein: ¹⁶Who in times past suffered all nations to walk in their own ways. ¹⁷Nevertheless he left not himself without witness, in that he did good, and gave us rain from heaven, and fruitful seasons, filling our hearts with food and gladness. ¹⁸And with these sayings scarce restrained they the people, that they had not done sacrifice unto them.

¹⁹And there came thither *certain* Jews from Antioch and Iconium, who persuaded the people, and, having stoned Paul, drew *him* out of the city, supposing he had been dead. ²⁰Howbeit, as the disciples stood round about him, he rose up, and came into the city: and the next day he departed with Barnabas to Derbe. ²¹And when they had preached the gospel to that city, and had

taught many, they returned again to Lystra, and *to* Iconium, and Antioch, ²²Confirming the souls of the disciples, *and* exhorting them to continue in the faith, and that we must through much tribulation enter into the kingdom of God. ²³And when they had ordained them elders in every church, and had prayed with fasting, they commended them to the Lord, on whom they believed. ²⁴And after they had passed throughout Pisidia, they came to Pamphylia. ²⁵And when they had preached the word in Perga, they went down into Attalia: ²⁶And thence sailed to Antioch, from whence they had been recommended to the grace of God for the work which they fulfilled. ²⁷And when they were come, and had gathered the church together, they rehearsed all that God had done with them, and how he had opened the door of faith unto the Gentiles. ²⁸And there they abode long time with the disciples.

15 And certain men which came down from Judaea taught the brethren, *and said,* Except ye be circumcised after the manner of Moses, ye cannot be saved. ²When therefore Paul and Barnabas had no small dissension and disputation with them, they determined that Paul and Barnabas, and certain other of them, should go up to Jerusalem unto the apostles and elders about this question. ³And being brought on their way by the church, they passed through Phenice and Samaria, declaring the conversion of the Gentiles: and they caused great joy unto all the brethren. ⁴And when they were come to Jerusalem, they were received of the church, and *of* the apostles and elders, and they declared all things that God had done with them. ⁵But there rose up certain of the sect of the Pharisees which believed, saying, That it was needful to circumcise them, and to command *them* to keep the law of Moses.

⁶And the apostles and elders came together for to consider of this matter. ⁷And when there had been much disputing, Peter rose up, and said unto them, Men *and* brethren, ye know how that a good while ago God made choice among us, that the Gentiles by my mouth should hear the word of the gospel, and believe. ⁸And God, which knoweth the hearts, bare them wit-

ness, giving them the Holy Ghost, even as *he did* unto us; [9]And put no difference between us and them, purifying their hearts by faith. [10]Now therefore why tempt ye God, to put a yoke upon the neck of the disciples, which neither our fathers nor we were able to bear? [11]But we believe that through the grace of the Lord Jesus Christ we shall be saved, even as they.

[12]Then all the multitude kept silence, and gave audience to Barnabas and Paul, declaring what miracles and wonders God had wrought among the Gentiles by them.

[13]And after they had held their peace, James answered, saying, Men *and* brethren, hearken unto me: [14]Simeon hath declared how God at the first did visit the Gentiles, to take out of them a people for his name. [15]And to this agree the words of the prophets; as it is written,

[16]After this I will return, and will build again the tabernacle of David, which is fallen down; and I will build again the ruins thereof, and I will set it up: [17]That the residue of men might seek after the Lord, and all the Gentiles, upon whom my name is called, saith the Lord, who doeth all these things. [18]Known unto God are all his works from the beginning of the world.

[19]Wherefore my sentence is, that we trouble not them, which from among the Gentiles are turned to God: [20]But that we write unto them, that they abstain from pollutions of idols, and *from* fornication, and *from* things strangled, and *from* blood. [21]For Moses of old time hath in every city them that preach him, being read in the synagogues every sabbath day. [22]Then pleased it the apostles and elders, with the whole church, to send chosen men of their own company to Antioch with Paul and Barnabas; *namely,* Judas surnamed Barsabas, and Silas, chief men among the brethren: [23]And they wrote *letters* by them after this manner;

The apostles and elders and brethren *send*

greeting

unto the brethren which are of the Gentiles in Antioch and Syria and Cilicia:

[24]Forasmuch as we have heard, that certain which went out from us have troubled you with words, subverting your souls, saying, *Ye must* be circumcised, and keep the law: to whom we gave no *such* commandment: [25]It seemed good unto us, being assembled with one accord, to send chosen men unto you with our beloved Barnabas and Paul, [26]Men that have hazarded their lives for the name of our Lord Jesus Christ. [27]We have sent therefore Judas and Silas, who shall also tell *you* the same things by mouth. [28]For it seemed good to the Holy Ghost, and to us, to lay upon you no greater burden than these necessary things; [29]That ye abstain from meats offered to idols, and from blood, and from things strangled, and from fornication: from which if ye keep yourselves, ye shall do well.

Fare ye well.

[30]So when they were dismissed, they came to Antioch: and when they had gathered the multitude together, they delivered the epistle: [31]*Which* when they had read, they rejoiced for the consolation. [32]And Judas and Silas, being prophets also themselves, exhorted the brethren with many words, and confirmed *them.* [33]And after they had tarried *there* a space, they were let go in peace from the brethren unto the apostles. [34]Notwithstanding it pleased Silas to abide there still. [35]Paul also and Barnabas continued in Antioch, teaching and preaching the word of the Lord, with many others also.

[36]And some days after Paul said unto Barnabas, Let us go again and visit our brethren in every city where we have preached the word of the Lord, *and see* how they do. [37]And Barnabas determined to take with them John, whose surname was Mark. [38]But Paul thought not good to take him with them, who departed from them from Pamphylia, and went not with them to the work. [39]And the contention was so sharp between them, that they departed asunder one from the other: and so Barnabas took Mark, and sailed unto Cyprus; [40]And Paul chose Silas, and departed, being recommended by the brethren unto the

grace of God. [41]And he went through Syria and Cilicia, confirming the churches.

16 Then came he to Derbe and Lystra: and, behold, a certain disciple was there, named Timotheus, the son of a certain woman, which was a Jewess, and believed; but his father *was* a Greek: [2]Which was well reported of by the brethren that were at Lystra and Iconium. [3]Him would Paul have to go forth with him; and took and circumcised him because of the Jews which were in those quarters: for they knew all that his father was a Greek. [4]And as they went through the cities, they delivered them the decrees for to keep, that were ordained of the apostles and elders which were at Jerusalem. [5]And so were the churches established in the faith, and increased in number daily.

[6]Now when they had gone throughout Phrygia and the region of Galatia, and were forbidden of the Holy Ghost to preach the word in Asia, [7]After they were come to Mysia, they assayed to go into Bithynia: but the Spirit suffered them not. [8]And they passing by Mysia came down to Troas. [9]And a vision appeared to Paul in the night; There stood a man of Macedonia, and prayed him, saying, Come over into Macedonia, and help us. [10]And after he had seen the vision, immediately we endeavoured to go into Macedonia, assuredly gathering that the Lord had called us for to preach the gospel unto them. [11]Therefore loosing from Troas, we came with a straight course to Samothracia, and the next day to Neapolis; [12]And from thence to Philippi, which is the chief city of that part of Macedonia, *and* a colony: and we were in that city abiding certain days. [13]And on the sabbath we went out of the city by a river side, where prayer was wont to be made; and we sat down, and spake unto the women which resorted *thither.*

[14]And a certain woman named Lydia, a seller of purple, of the city of Thyatira, which worshipped God, heard *us:* whose heart the Lord opened, that she attended unto the things which were spoken of Paul. [15]And when she was baptized, and her household, she besought *us,* saying, If ye have judged me to be faithful to the Lord,

come into my house, and abide *there.* And she constrained us.

[16]And it came to pass, as we went to prayer, a certain damsel possessed with a spirit of divination met us, which brought her masters much gain by soothsaying: [17]The same followed Paul and us, and cried, saying, These men are the servants of the most high God, which shew unto us the way of salvation. [18]And this did she many days. But Paul, being grieved, turned and said to the spirit, I command thee in the name of Jesus Christ to come out of her. And he came out the same hour.

[19]And when her masters saw that the hope of their gains was gone, they caught Paul and Silas, and drew *them* into the marketplace unto the rulers, [20]And brought them to the magistrates, saying, These men, being Jews, do exceedingly trouble our city, [21]And teach customs, which are not lawful for us to receive, neither to observe, being Romans. [22]And the multitude rose up together against them: and the magistrates rent off their clothes, and commanded to beat *them.* [23]And when they had laid many stripes upon them, they cast *them* into prison, charging the jailer to keep them safely: [24]Who, having received such a charge, thrust them into the inner prison, and made their feet fast in the stocks.

[25]And at midnight Paul and Silas prayed, and sang praises unto God: and the prisoners heard them. [26]And suddenly there was a great earthquake, so that the foundations of the prison were shaken: and immediately all the doors were opened, and every one's bands were loosed. [27]And the keeper of the prison awaking out of his sleep, and seeing the prison doors open, he drew out his sword, and would have killed himself, supposing that the prisoners had been fled. [28]But Paul cried with a loud voice, saying, Do thyself no harm: for we are all here. [29]Then he called for a light, and sprang in, and came trembling, and fell down before Paul and Silas, [30]And brought them out, and said, Sirs, what must I do to be saved? [31]And they said, Believe on the Lord Jesus Christ, and thou shalt be saved, and thy house. [32]And they spake unto him the word of the Lord, and to all that were in his house. [33]And he took them the same hour

of the night, and washed *their* stripes; and was baptized, he and all his, straightway. ³⁴And when he had brought them into his house, he set meat before them, and rejoiced, believing in God with all his house. ³⁵And when it was day, the magistrates sent the serjeants, saying, Let those men go. ³⁶And the keeper of the prison told this saying to Paul, The magistrates have sent to let you go: now therefore depart, and go in peace. ³⁷But Paul said unto them, They have beaten us openly uncondemned, being Romans, and have cast *us* into prison; and now do they thrust us out privily? nay verily; but let them come themselves and fetch us out. ³⁸And the serjeants told these words unto the magistrates: and they feared, when they heard that they were Romans. ³⁹And they came and besought them, and brought *them* out, and desired *them* to depart out of the city. ⁴⁰And they went out of the prison, and entered into *the house of* Lydia and when they had seen the brethren, they comforted them, and departed.

17 Now when they had passed through Amphipolis and Apollonia, they came to Thessalonica, where was a synagogue of the Jews: ²And Paul, as his manner was, went in unto them, and three sabbath days reasoned with them out of the scriptures, ³Opening and alleging, that Christ must needs have suffered, and risen again from the dead; and that this Jesus, whom I preach unto you, is Christ. ⁴And some of them believed, and consorted with Paul and Silas; and of the devout Greeks a great multitude, and of the chief women not a few.

⁵But the Jews which believed not, moved with envy, took unto them certain lewd fellows of the baser sort, and gathered a company, and set all the city on an uproar, and assaulted the house of Jason, and sought to bring them out to the people. ⁶And when they found them not, they drew Jason and certain brethren unto the rulers of the city, crying, These that have turned the world upside down are come hither also; ⁷Whom Jason hath received: and these all do contrary to the decrees of Caesar, saying that there is another king, *one* Jesus. ⁸And they troubled the people and the rulers of the

city, when they heard these things. ⁹And when they had taken security of Jason, and of the other, they let them go.

¹⁰And the brethren immediately sent away Paul and Silas by night unto Berea: who coming *thither* went into the synagogue of the Jews. ¹¹These were more noble than those in Thessalonica, in that they received the word with all readiness of mind, and searched the scriptures daily, whether those things were so. ¹²Therefore many of them believed; also of honourable women which were Greeks, and of men, not a few. ¹³But when the Jews of Thessalonica had knowledge that the word of God was preached of Paul at Berea, they came thither also, and stirred up the people. ¹⁴And then immediately the brethren sent away Paul to go as it were to the sea: but Silas and Timotheus abode there still. ¹⁵And they that conducted Paul brought him unto Athens: and receiving a commandment unto Silas and Timotheus for to come to him with all speed, they departed.

¹⁶Now while Paul waited for them at Athens, his spirit was stirred in him, when he saw the city wholly given to idolatry. ¹⁷Therefore disputed he in the synagogue with the Jews, and with the devout persons, and in the market daily with them that met with him. ¹⁸Then certain philosophers of the Epicureans, and of the Stoicks, encountered him. And some said, What will this babbler say? other some, He seemeth to be a setter forth of strange gods: because he preached unto them Jesus, and the resurrection. ¹⁹And they took him, and brought him unto Areopagus, saying, May we know what this new doctrine, whereof thou speakest, *is?* ²⁰For thou bringest certain strange things to our ears: we would know therefore what these things mean. ²¹(For all the Athenians and strangers which were there spent their time in nothing else, but either to tell, or to hear some new thing.)

²²Then Paul stood in the midst of Mars' hill, and said, *Ye* men of Athens, I perceive that in all things ye are too superstitious. ²³For as I passed by, and beheld your devotions, I found an altar with this inscription, TO THE UNKNOWN GOD. Whom therefore ye ignorantly worship, him declare I unto you. ²⁴God that made the world and

all things therein, seeing that he is Lord of heaven and earth, dwelleth not in temples made with hands; [25]Neither is worshipped with men's hands, as though he needed any thing, seeing he giveth to all life, and breath, and all things; [26]And hath made of one blood all nations of men for to dwell on all the face of the earth, and hath determined the times before appointed, and the bounds of their habitation; [27]That they should seek the Lord, if haply they might feel after him, and find him, though he be not far from every one of us: [28]For in him we live, and move, and have our being; as certain also of your own poets have said, For we are also his offspring. [29]Forasmuch then as we are the offspring of God, we ought not to think that the Godhead is like unto gold, or silver, or stone, graven by art and man's device. [30]And the times of this ignorance God winked at; but now commandeth all men every where to repent: [31]Because he hath appointed a day, in the which he will judge the world in righteousness by *that* man whom he hath ordained; *whereof* he hath given assurance unto all *men,* in that he hath raised him from the dead.

[32]And when they heard of the resurrection of the dead, some mocked: and others said, We will hear thee again of this *matter.* [33]So Paul departed from among them. [34]Howbeit certain men clave unto him, and believed: among the which *was* Dionysius the Areopagite, and a woman named Damaris, and others with them.

18 After these things Paul departed from Athens, and came to Corinth; [2]And found a certain Jew named Aquila, born in Pontus, lately come from Italy, with his wife Priscilla; (because that Claudius had commanded all Jews to depart from Rome:) and came unto them. [3]And because he was of the same craft, he abode with them, and wrought: for by their occupation they were tentmakers. [4]And he reasoned in the synagogue every sabbath, and persuaded the Jews and the Greeks. [5]And when Silas and Timotheus were come from Macedonia, Paul was pressed in the spirit, and testified to the Jews *that* Jesus *was* Christ. [6]And when they opposed themselves, and blasphemed, he shook *his*

raiment, and said unto them, Your blood *be* upon your own heads; I *am* clean: from henceforth I will go unto the Gentiles.

[7]And he departed thence, and entered into a certain *man's* house, named Justus, *one* that worshipped God, whose house joined hard to the synagogue. [8]And Crispus, the chief ruler of the synagogue, believed on the Lord with all his house; and many of the Corinthians hearing believed, and were baptized. [9]Then spake the Lord to Paul in the night by a vision, Be not afraid, but speak, and hold not thy peace: [10]For I am with thee, and no man shall set on thee to hurt thee: for I have much people in this city. [11]And he continued *there* a year and six months, teaching the word of God among them.

[12]And when Gallio was the deputy of Achaia, the Jews made insurrection with one accord against Paul, and brought him to the judgment seat, [13]Saying, This *fellow* persuadeth men to worship God contrary to the law. [14]And when Paul was now about to open *his* mouth, Gallio said unto the Jews, If it were a matter of wrong or wicked lewdness, O *ye* Jews, reason would that I should bear with you: [15]But if it be a question of words and names, and *of* your law, look ye *to it;* for I will be no judge of such *matters.* [16]And he drave them from the judgment seat. [17]Then all the Greeks took Sosthenes, the chief ruler of the synagogue, and beat *him* before the judgment seat. And Gallio cared for none of those things.

[18]And Paul *after this* tarried *there* yet a good while, and then took his leave of the brethren, and sailed thence into Syria, and with him Priscilla and Aquila; having shorn *his* head in Cenchrea: for he had a vow. [19]And he came to Ephesus, and left them there: but he himself entered into the synagogue, and reasoned with the Jews. [20]When they desired *him* to tarry longer time with them, he consented not; [21]But bade them farewell, saying, I must by all means keep this feast that cometh in Jerusalem: but I will return again unto you, if God will. And he sailed from Ephesus. [22]And when he had landed at Caesarea, and gone up, and saluted the church, he went down to Antioch.

[23]And after he had spent some time

there, he departed, and went over *all* the country of Galatia and Phrygia in order, strengthening all the disciples. ²⁴And a certain Jew named Apollos, born at Alexandria, an eloquent man, *and* mighty in the scriptures, came to Ephesus. ²⁵This man was instructed in the way of the Lord; and being fervent in the spirit, he spake and taught diligently the things of the Lord, knowing only the baptism of John. ²⁶And he began to speak boldly in the synagogue: whom when Aquila and Priscilla had heard, they took him unto *them,* and expounded unto him the way of God more perfectly. ²⁷And when he was disposed to pass into Achaia, the brethren wrote, exhorting the disciples to receive him: who, when he was come, helped them much which had believed through grace: ²⁸For he mightily convinced the Jews, *and that* publickly, shewing by the scriptures that Jesus was Christ.

19 And it came to pass, that, while Apollos was at Corinth, Paul having passed through the upper coasts came to Ephesus: and finding certain disciples, ²He said unto them, Have ye received the Holy Ghost since ye believed? And they said unto him, We have not so much as heard whether there be any Holy Ghost. ³And he said unto them, Unto what then were ye baptized? And they said, Unto John's baptism. ⁴Then said Paul, John verily baptized with the baptism of repentance, saying unto the people, that they should believe on him which should come after him, that is, on Christ Jesus. ⁵When they heard *this,* they were baptized in the name of the Lord Jesus. ⁶And when Paul had laid *his* hands upon them, the Holy Ghost came on them; and they spake with tongues, and prophesied. ⁷And all the men were about twelve. ⁸And he went into the synagogue, and spake boldly for the space of three months, disputing and persuading the things concerning the kingdom of God. ⁹But when divers were hardened, and believed not, but spake evil of that way before the multitude, he departed from them, and separated the disciples, disputing daily in the school of one Tyrannus. ¹⁰And this continued by the space of two years; so that all they which dwelt in Asia heard the word of the Lord

Jesus, both Jews and Greeks. ¹¹And God wrought special miracles by the hands of Paul: ¹²So that from his body were brought unto the sick handkerchiefs or aprons, and the diseases departed from them, and the evil spirits went out of them.

¹³Then certain of the vagabond Jews, exorcists, took upon them to call over them which had evil spirits the name of the Lord Jesus, saying, We adjure you by Jesus whom Paul preacheth. ¹⁴And there were seven sons of *one* Sceva, a Jew, *and* chief of the priests, which did so. ¹⁵And the evil spirit answered and said, Jesus I know, and Paul I know; but who are ye? ¹⁶And the man in whom the evil spirit was leaped on them, and overcame them, and prevailed against them, so that they fled out of that house naked and wounded. ¹⁷And this was known to all the Jews and Greeks also dwelling at Ephesus; and fear fell on them all, and the name of the Lord Jesus was magnified. ¹⁸And many that believed came, and confessed, and shewed their deeds. ¹⁹Many of them also which used curious arts brought their books together, and burned them before all *men:* and they counted the price of them, and found it fifty thousand *pieces* of silver. ²⁰So mightily grew the word of God and prevailed.

²¹After these things were ended, Paul purposed in the spirit, when he had passed through Macedonia and Achaia, to go to Jerusalem, saying, After I have been there, I must also see Rome. ²²So he sent into Macedonia two of them that ministered unto him, Timotheus and Erastus; but he himself stayed in Asia for a season. ²³And the same time there arose no small stir about that way. ²⁴For a certain *man* named Demetrius, a silversmith, which made silver shrines for Diana, brought no small gain unto the craftsmen; ²⁵Whom he called together with the workmen of like occupation, and said, Sirs, ye know that by this craft we have our wealth. ²⁶Moreover ye see and hear, that not alone at Ephesus, but almost throughout all Asia, this Paul hath persuaded and turned away much people, saying that they be no gods, which are made with hands: ²⁷So that not only this our craft is in danger to be set at nought;

but also that the temple of the great goddess Diana should be despised, and her magnificence should be destroyed, whom all Asia and the world worshippeth. ²⁸And when they heard *these sayings,* they were full of wrath, and cried out, saying, Great *is* Diana of the Ephesians. ²⁹And the whole city was filled with confusion: and having caught Gaius and Aristarchus, men of Macedonia, Paul's companions in travel, they rushed with one accord into the theatre. ³⁰And when Paul would have entered in unto the people, the disciples suffered him not. ³¹And certain of the chief of Asia, which were his friends, sent unto him, desiring *him* that he would not adventure himself into the theatre. ³²Some therefore cried one thing, and some another: for the assembly was confused; and the more part knew not wherefore they were come together. ³³And they drew Alexander out of the multitude, the Jews putting him forward. And Alexander beckoned with the hand, and would have made his defence unto the people. ³⁴But when they knew that he was a Jew, all with one voice about the space of two hours cried out, Great *is* Diana of the Ephesians. ³⁵And when the townclerk had appeased the people, he said, *Ye* men of Ephesus, what man is there that knoweth not how that the city of the Ephesians is a worshipper of the great goddess Diana, and of the *image* which fell down from Jupiter? ³⁶Seeing then that these things cannot be spoken against, ye ought to be quiet, and to do nothing rashly. ³⁷For ye have brought hither these men, which are neither robbers of churches, nor yet blasphemers of your goddess. ³⁸Wherefore if Demetrius, and the craftsmen which are with him, have a matter against any man, the law is open, and there are deputies: let them implead one another. ³⁹But if ye enquire any thing concerning other matters, it shall be determined in a lawful assembly. ⁴⁰For we are in danger to be called in question for this day's uproar, there being no cause whereby we may give an account of this concourse. ⁴¹And when he had thus spoken, he dismissed the assembly.

20 And after the uproar was ceased, Paul called unto *him* the disciples, and embraced *them,* and departed for to go into Macedonia. ²And when he had gone over those parts, and had given them much exhortation, he came into Greece, ³And *there* abode three months. And when the Jews laid wait for him, as he was about to sail into Syria, he purposed to return through Macedonia. ⁴And there accompanied him into Asia Sopater of Berea; and of the Thessalonians, Aristarchus and Secundus; and Gaius of Derbe, and Timotheus; and of Asia, Tychicus and Trophimus. ⁵These going before tarried for us at Troas.

⁶And we sailed away from Philippi after the days of unleavened bread, and came unto them to Troas in five days; where we abode seven days. ⁷And upon the first *day* of the week, when the disciples came together to break bread, Paul preached unto them, ready to depart on the morrow; and continued his speech until midnight. ⁸And there were many lights in the upper chamber, where they were gathered together. ⁹And there sat in a window a certain young man named Eutychus, being fallen into a deep sleep: and as Paul was long preaching, he sunk down with sleep, and fell down from the third loft, and was taken up dead. ¹⁰And Paul went down, and fell on him, and embracing *him* said, Trouble not yourselves; for his life is in him. ¹¹When he therefore was come up again, and had broken bread, and eaten, and talked a long while, even till break of day, so he departed. ¹²And they brought the young man alive, and were not a little comforted.

¹³And we went before to ship, and sailed unto Assos, there intending to take in Paul: for so had he appointed, minding himself to go afoot. ¹⁴And when he met with us at Assos, we took him in, and came to Mitylene. ¹⁵And we sailed thence, and came the next *day* over against Chios; and the next *day* we arrived at Samos, and tarried at Trogyllium; and the next *day* we came to Miletus. ¹⁶For Paul had determined to sail by Ephesus, because he would not spend the time in Asia: for he hasted, if it were possible for him, to be at Jerusalem the day of Pentecost.

¹⁷And from Miletus he sent to Ephesus, and called the elders of the church. ¹⁸And when they were come to him, he said unto

them, Ye know, from the first day that I came into Asia, after what manner I have been with you at all seasons, [19]Serving the Lord with all humility of mind, and with many tears, and temptations, which befell me by the lying in wait of the Jews: [20]*And* how I kept back nothing that was profitable *unto you,* but have shewed you, and have taught you publickly, and from house to house, [21]Testifying both to the Jews, and also to the Greeks, repentance toward God, and faith toward our Lord Jesus Christ. [22]And now, behold, I go bound in the spirit unto Jerusalem, not knowing the things that shall befall me there: [23]Save that the Holy Ghost witnesseth in every city, saying that bonds and afflictions abide me. [24]But none of these things move me, neither count I my life dear unto myself, so that I might finish my course with joy, and the ministry, which I have received of the Lord Jesus, to testify the gospel of the grace of God. [25]And now, behold, I know that ye all, among whom I have gone preaching the kingdom of God, shall see my face no more. [26]Wherefore I take you to record this day, that I *am* pure from the blood of all *men.* [27]For I have not shunned to declare unto you all the counsel of God.

[28]Take heed therefore unto yourselves, and to all the flock, over the which the Holy Ghost hath made you overseers, to feed the church of God, which he hath purchased with his own blood. [29]For I know this, that after my departing shall grievous wolves enter in among you, not sparing the flock. [30]Also of your own selves shall men arise, speaking perverse things, to draw away disciples after them. [31]Therefore watch, and remember, that by the space of three years I ceased not to warn every one night and day with tears. [32]And now, brethren, I commend you to God, and to the word of his grace, which is able to build you up, and to give you an inheritance among all them which are sanctified. [33]I have coveted no man's silver, or gold, or apparel. [34]Yea, ye yourselves know, that these hands have ministered unto my necessities, and to them that were with me. [35]I have shewed you all things, how that so labouring ye ought to support the weak, and to remember the words of the Lord Jesus, how he said, It is more blessed to give than to receive.

[36]And when he had thus spoken, he kneeled down, and prayed with them all. [37]And they all wept sore, and fell on Paul's neck, and kissed him, [38]Sorrowing most of all for the words which he spake, that they should see his face no more. And they accompanied him unto the ship.

21 And it came to pass, that after we were gotten from them, and had launched, we came with a straight course unto Coos, and the *day* following unto Rhodes, and from thence unto Patara: [2]And finding a ship sailing over unto Phenicia, we went aboard, and set forth. [3]Now when we had discovered Cyprus, we left it on the left hand, and sailed into Syria, and landed at Tyre: for there the ship was to unlade her burden. [4]And finding disciples, we tarried there seven days: who said to Paul through the Spirit, that he should not go up to Jerusalem. [5]And when we had accomplished those days, we departed and went our way; and they all brought us on our way, with wives and children, till *we were* out of the city: and we kneeled down on the shore, and prayed. [6]And when we had taken our leave one of another, we took ship; and they returned home again. [7]And when we had finished *our* course from Tyre, we came to Ptolemais, and saluted the brethren, and abode with them one day. [8]And the next *day* we that were of Paul's company departed, and came unto Caesarea: and we entered into the house of Philip the evangelist, which was *one* of the seven; and abode with him. [9]And the same man had four daughters, virgins, which did prophesy. [10]And as we tarried *there* many days, there came down from Judaea a certain prophet, named Agabus. [11]And when he was come unto us, he took Paul's girdle, and bound his own hands and feet, and said, Thus saith the Holy Ghost, So shall the Jews at Jerusalem bind the man that owneth this girdle, and shall deliver *him* into the hands of the Gentiles. [12]And when we heard these things, both we, and they of that place, besought him not to go up to Jerusalem. [13]Then Paul answered, What mean ye to weep and to break mine heart? for I am ready not to be bound only,

but also to die at Jerusalem for the name of the Lord Jesus. ¹⁴And when he would not be persuaded, we ceased, saying, The will of the Lord be done.

¹⁵And after those days we took up our carriages, and went up to Jerúsalem. ¹⁶There went with us also *certain* of the disciples of Caesarea, and brought with them one Mnason of Cyprus, an old disciple, with whom we should lodge. ¹⁷And when we were come to Jerusalem, the brethren received us gladly. ¹⁸And the *day* following Paul went in with us unto James; and all the elders were present. ¹⁹And when he had saluted them, he declared particularly what things God had wrought among the Gentiles by his ministry. ²⁰And when they heard *it,* they glorified the Lord, and said unto him, Thou seest, brother, how many thousands of Jews there are which believe; and they are all zealous of the law: ²¹And they are informed of thee, that thou teachest all the Jews which are among the Gentiles to forsake Moses, saying that they ought not to circumcise *their* children, neither to walk after the customs. ²²What is it therefore? the multitude must needs come together: for they will hear that thou art come. ²³Do therefore this that we say to thee: We have four men which have a vow on them; ²⁴Them take, and purify thyself with them, and be at charges with them, that they may shave *their* heads: and all may know that those things, whereof they were informed concerning thee, are nothing; but *that* thou thyself also walkest orderly, and keepest the law. ²⁵As touching the Gentiles which believe, we have written *and* concluded that they observe no such thing, save only that they keep themselves from *things* offered to idols, and from blood, and from strangled, and from fornication. ²⁶Then Paul took the men, and the next day purifying himself with them entered into the temple, to signify the accomplishment of the days of purification, until that an offering should be offered for every one of them.

²⁷And when the seven days were almost ended, the Jews which were of Asia, when they saw him in the temple, stirred up all the people, and laid hands on him, ²⁸Crying out, Men of Israel, help: This is the man,

that teacheth all *men* every where against the people, and the law, and this place: and further brought Greeks also into the temple, and hath polluted this holy place. ²⁹(For they had seen before with him in the city Trophimus an Ephesian, whom they supposed that Paul had brought into the temple.) ³⁰And all the city was moved, and the people ran together: and they took Paul, and drew him out of the temple: and forthwith the doors were shut. ³¹And as they went about to kill him, tidings came unto the chief captain of the band, that all Jerusalem was in an uproar. ³²Who immediately took soldiers and centurions, and ran down unto them: and when they saw the chief captain and the soldiers, they left beating of Paul. ³³Then the chief captain came near, and took him, and commanded *him* to be bound with two chains; and demanded who he was, and what he had done. ³⁴And some cried one thing, some another, among the multitude: and when he could not know the certainty for the tumult, he commanded him to be carried into the castle. ³⁵And when he came upon the stairs, so it was, that he was borne of the soldiers for the violence of the people. ³⁶For the multitude of the people followed after, crying, Away with him. ³⁷And as Paul was to be led into the castle, he said unto the chief captain, May I speak unto thee? Who said, Canst thou speak Greek? ³⁸Art not thou that Egyptian, which before these days madest an uproar, and leddest out into the wilderness four thousand men that were murderers? ³⁹But Paul said, I am a man *which am* a Jew of Tarsus, *a city* in Cilicia, a citizen of no mean city: and, I beseech thee, suffer me to speak unto the people. ⁴⁰And when he had given him licence, Paul stood on the stairs, and beckoned with the hand unto the people. And when there was made a great silence, he spake unto *them* in the Hebrew tongue, saying,

22 Men, brethren, and fathers, hear ye my defence *which I make* now unto you. ²(And when they heard that he spake in the Hebrew tongue to them, they kept the more silence: and he saith,) ³I am verily a man *which am* a Jew, born in Tarsus, a city in Cilicia, yet brought up in this city at the feet of Gamaliel, *and* taught according to the perfect manner of the law of the fathers, and was zealous toward God, as ye all are this day. ⁴And I persecuted this way unto the death, binding and delivering into prisons both men and women. ⁵As also the high priest doth bear me witness, and all the estate of the elders: from whom also I received letters unto the brethren, and went to Damascus, to bring them which were there bound unto Jerusalem, for to be punished. ⁶And it came to pass, that, as I made my journey, and was come nigh unto Damascus about noon, suddenly there shone from heaven a great light round about me. ⁷And I fell unto the ground, and heard a voice saying unto me, Saul, Saul, why persecutest thou me? ⁸And I answered, Who art thou, Lord? And he said unto me, I am Jesus of Nazareth, whom thou persecutest. ⁹And they that were with me saw indeed the light, and were afraid; but they heard not the voice of him that spake to me. ¹⁰And I said, What shall I do, Lord? And the Lord said unto me, Arise, and go into Damascus; and there it shall be told thee of all things which are appointed for thee to do. ¹¹And when I could not see for the glory of that light, being led by the hand of them that were with me, I came into Damascus. ¹²And one Ananias, a devout man according to the law, having a good report of all the Jews which dwelt *there*, ¹³Came unto me, and stood, and said unto me, Brother Saul, receive thy sight. And the same hour I looked up upon him. ¹⁴And he said, The God of our fathers hath chosen thee, that thou shouldest know his will, and see that Just One, and shouldest hear the voice of his mouth. ¹⁵For thou shalt be his witness unto all men of what thou hast seen and heard. ¹⁶And now why tarriest thou? arise, and be baptized, and wash away thy sins, calling on the name of the Lord. ¹⁷And it came to pass, that, when I was come again to Jerusalem, even while I prayed in the temple, I was in a trance; ¹⁸And saw him saying unto me, Make haste, and get thee quickly out of Jerusalem: for they will not receive thy testimony concerning me. ¹⁹And I said, Lord, they know that I imprisoned and beat in every synagogue them that believed on thee: ²⁰And when the blood of thy martyr Stephen was shed,

I also was standing by, and consenting unto his death, and kept the raiment of them that slew him. ²¹And he said unto me, Depart: for I will send thee far hence unto the Gentiles. ²²And they gave him audience unto this word, and *then* lifted up their voices, and said, Away with such a *fellow* from the earth: for it is not fit that he should live. ²³And as they cried out, and cast off *their* clothes, and threw dust into the air, ²⁴The chief captain commanded him to be brought into the castle, and bade that he should be examined by scourging; that he might know wherefore they cried so against him. ²⁵And as they bound him with thongs, Paul said unto the centurion that stood by, Is it lawful for you to scourge a man that is a Roman, and uncondemned? ²⁶When the centurion heard *that,* he went and told the chief captain, saying, Take heed what thou doest: for this man is a Roman. ²⁷Then the chief captain came, and said unto him, Tell me, art thou a Roman? He said, Yea. ²⁸And the chief captain answered, With a great sum obtained I this freedom. And Paul said, But I was *free* born. ²⁹Then straightway they departed from him which should have examined him: and the chief captain also was afraid, after he knew that he was a Roman, and because he had bound him. ³⁰On the morrow, because he would have known the certainty wherefore he was accused of the Jews, he loosed him from *his* bands, and commanded the chief priests and all their council to appear, and brought Paul down, and set him before them.

23 And Paul, earnestly beholding the council, said, Men *and* brethren, I have lived in all good conscience before God until this day. ²And the high priest Ananias commanded them that stood by him to smite him on the mouth. ³Then said Paul unto him, God shall smite thee, *thou* whited wall: for sittest thou to judge me after the law, and commandest me to be smitten contrary to the law? ⁴And they that stood by said, Revilest thou God's high priest? ⁵Then said Paul, I wist not, brethren, that he was the high priest: for it is written, Thou shalt not speak evil of the ruler of thy people. ⁶But when Paul perceived that the one part were Sadducees, and the other

Pharisees, he cried out in the council, Men *and* brethren, I am a Pharisee, the son of a Pharisee: of the hope and resurrection of the dead I am called in question. [7]And when he had so said, there arose a dissension between the Pharisees and the Sadducees: and the multitude was divided. [8]For the Sadducees say that there is no resurrection, neither angel, nor spirit: but the Pharisees confess both. [9]And there arose a great cry: and the scribes *that were* of the Pharisees' part arose, and strove, saying, We find no evil in this man: but if a spirit or an angel hath spoken to him, let us not fight against God. [10]And when there arose a great dissension, the chief captain, fearing lest Paul should have been pulled in pieces of them, commanded the soldiers to go down, and to take him by force from among them, and to bring *him* into the castle. [11]And the night following the Lord stood by him, and said, Be of good cheer, Paul: for as thou hast testified of me in Jerusalem, so must thou bear witness also at Rome. [12]And when it was day, certain of the Jews banded together, and bound themselves under a curse, saying that they would neither eat nor drink till they had killed Paul. [13]And they were more than forty which had made this conspiracy. [14]And they came to the chief priests and elders, and said, We have bound ourselves under a great curse, that we will eat nothing until we have slain Paul. [15]Now therefore ye with the council signify to the chief captain that he bring him down unto you to morrow, as though ye would enquire something more perfectly concerning him: and we, or ever he come near, are ready to kill him. [16]And when Paul's sister's son heard of their lying in wait, he went and entered into the castle, and told Paul. [17]Then Paul called one of the centurions unto *him,* and said, Bring this young man unto the chief captain: for he hath a certain thing to tell him. [18]So he took him, and brought *him* to the chief captain, and said, Paul the prisoner called me unto *him,* and prayed me to bring this young man unto thee, who hath something to say unto thee. [19]Then the chief captain took him by the hand, and went *with him* aside privately, and asked *him,* What is that thou hast to tell me? [20]And he said,

The Jews have agreed to desire thee that thou wouldest bring down Paul to morrow into the council, as though they would enquire somewhat of him more perfectly. [21]But do not thou yield unto them: for there lie in wait for him of them more than forty men, which have bound themselves with an oath, that they will neither eat nor drink till they have killed him: and now are they ready, looking for a promise from thee. [22]So the chief captain *then* let the young man depart, and charged *him, See thou* tell no man that thou hast shewed these things to me. [23]And he called unto *him* two centurions, saying, Make ready two hundred soldiers to go to Caesarea, and horsemen threescore and ten, and spearmen two hundred, at the third hour of the night; [24]And provide *them* beasts, that they may set Paul on, and bring *him* safe unto Felix the governor. [25]And he wrote a letter after this manner:

[26]Claudius Lysias

unto the most excellent governor Felix *sendeth*

greeting.

[27]This man was taken of the Jews, and should have been killed of them: then came I with an army, and rescued him, having understood that he was a Roman. [28]And when I would have known the cause wherefore they accused him, I brought him forth into their council: [29]Whom I perceived to be accused of questions of their law, but to have nothing laid to his charge worthy of death or of bonds. [30]And when it was told me how that the Jews laid wait for the man, I sent straightway to thee, and gave commandment to his accusers also to say before thee what *they had* against him. Farewell.

[31]Then the soldiers, as it was commanded them, took Paul, and brought *him* by night to Antipatris. [32]On the morrow they left the horsemen to go with him, and returned to the castle: [33]Who, when they came to Caesarea, and delivered the epistle to the governor, presented Paul also before him. [34]And when the governor had

read *the letter,* he asked of what province he was. And when he understood that *he was* of Cilicia; ³⁵I will hear thee, said he, when thine accusers are also come. And he commanded him to be kept in Herod's judgment hall.

24 And after five days Ananias the high priest descended with the elders, and *with* a certain orator *named* Tertullus, who informed the governor against Paul. ²And when he was called forth, Tertullus began to accuse *him,* saying,

Seeing that by thee we enjoy great quietness, and that very worthy deeds are done unto this nation by thy providence, ³We accept *it* always, and in all places, most noble Felix, with all thankfulness. ⁴Notwithstanding, that I be not further tedious unto thee, I pray thee that thou wouldest hear us of thy clemency a few words. ⁵For we have found this man *a* pestilent *fellow,* and a mover of sedition among all the Jews throughout the world, and a ringleader of the sect of the Nazarenes: ⁶Who also hath gone about to profane the temple: whom we took, and would have judged according to our law. ⁷But the chief captain Lysias came *upon us,* and with great violence took *him* away out of our hands, ⁸Commanding his accusers to come unto thee: by examining of whom thyself mayest take knowledge of all these things, whereof we accuse him. ⁹And the Jews also assented, saying that these things were so. ¹⁰Then Paul, after that the governor had beckoned unto him to speak, answered, Forasmuch as I know that thou hast been of many years a judge unto this nation, I do the more cheerfully answer for myself: ¹¹Because that thou mayest understand, that there are yet but twelve days since I went up to Jerusalem for to worship. ¹²And they neither found me in the temple disputing with any man, neither raising up the people, neither in the synagogues, nor in the city: ¹³Neither can they prove the things whereof they now accuse me. ¹⁴But this I confess unto thee, that after the way which they call heresy, so worship I the God of my fathers, believing all things which are written in the law and in the prophets: ¹⁵And have hope toward God, which they themselves also allow, that there shall be a resurrection of the dead, both of the just and unjust. ¹⁶And herein do I exercise myself, to have always a conscience void of offence toward God, and *toward* men. ¹⁷Now after many years I came to bring alms to my nation, and offerings. ¹⁸Whereupon certain Jews from Asia found me purified in the temple, neither with multitude, nor with tumult. ¹⁹Who ought to have been here before thee, and object, if they had ought against me. ²⁰Or else let these same *here* say, if they have found any evil doing in me, while I stood before the council, ²¹Except it be for this one voice, that I cried standing among them, Touching the resurrection of the dead I am called in question by you this day.

²²And when Felix heard these things, having more perfect knowledge of *that* way, he deferred them, and said, When Lysias the chief captain shall come down, I will know the uttermost of your matter. ²³And he commanded a centurion to keep Paul, and to let *him* have liberty, and that he should forbid none of his acquaintance to minister or come unto him.

²⁴And after certain days, when Felix came with his wife Drusilla, which was a Jewess, he sent for Paul, and heard him concerning the faith in Christ. ²⁵And as he reasoned of righteousness, temperance, and judgment to come Felix trembled, and answered, Go thy way for this time; when I have a convenient season, I will call for thee. ²⁶He hoped also that money should have been given him of Paul, that he might loose him: wherefore he sent for him the oftener, and communed with him. ²⁷But after two years Porcius Festus came into Felix' room: and Felix, willing to shew the Jews a pleasure, left Paul bound.

25 Now when Festus was come into the province, after three days he ascended from Caesarea to Jerusalem. ²Then the high priest and the chief of the Jews informed him against Paul, and besought him, ³And desired favour against him, that he would send for him to Jerusalem, laying wait in the way to kill him. ⁴But Festus answered, that Paul should be kept at Caesarea, and that he himself would depart shortly *thither.* ⁵Let them therefore, said he, which among you are able, go down with *me*, and accuse this man, if there be any wickedness in him. [6]And when he had tarried among them more than ten days, he went down unto Caesarea; and the next day sitting on the judgment seat commanded Paul to be brought. [7]And when he was come, the Jews which came down from Jerusalem stood round about, and laid many and grievous complaints against Paul, which they could not prove. [8]While he answered for himself, Neither against the law of the Jews, neither against the temple, nor yet against Caesar, have I offended any thing at all. [9]But Festus, willing to do the Jews a pleasure, answered Paul, and said, Wilt thou go up to Jerusalem, and there be judged of these things before me? [10]Then said Paul, I stand at Caesar's judgment seat, where I ought to be judged: to the Jews have I done no wrong, as thou very well knowest. [11]For if I be an offender, or have committed any thing worthy of death, I refuse not to die: but if there be none of these things whereof these accuse me, no man may deliver me unto them. I appeal unto Caesar. [12]Then Festus, when he had conferred with the council, answered, Hast thou appealed unto Caesar? unto Caesar shalt thou go.

[13]And after certain days king Agrippa and Bernice came unto Caesarea to salute Festus. [14]And when they had been there many days, Festus declared Paul's cause unto the king, saying, There is a certain man left in bonds by Felix: [15]About whom, when I was at Jerusalem, the chief priests and the elders of the Jews informed *me*, desiring *to have* judgment against him. [16]To whom I answered, It is not the manner of the Romans to deliver any man to die, before that he which is accused have the accusers face to face, and have licence to answer for himself concerning the crime laid against him. [17]Therefore, when they were come hither, without any delay on the morrow I sat on the judgment seat, and commanded the man to be brought forth. [18]Against whom when the accusers stood up, they brought none accusation of such things as I supposed: [19]But had certain questions against him of their own superstition, and of one Jesus, which was dead, whom Paul affirmed to be alive. [20]And be-

cause I doubted of such manner of questions, I asked *him* whether he would go to Jerusalem, and there be judged of these matters. [21]But when Paul had appealed to be reserved unto the hearing of Augustus, I commanded him to be kept till I might send him to Caesar. [22]Then Agrippa said unto Festus, I would also hear the man myself. To morrow, said he, thou shalt hear him.

[23]And on the morrow, when Agrippa was come, and Bernice, with great pomp, and was entered into the place of hearing, with the chief captains, and principal men of the city, at Festus' commandment Paul was brought forth. [24]And Festus said, King Agrippa, and all men which are here present with us, ye see this man, about whom all the multitude of the Jews have dealt with me, both at Jerusalem, and *also* here, crying that he ought not to live any longer. [25]But when I found that he had committed nothing worthy of death, and that he himself hath appealed to Augustus, I have determined to send him. [26]Of whom I have no certain thing to write unto my lord. Wherefore I have brought him forth before you, and specially before thee, O king Agrippa, that, after examination had, I might have somewhat to write. [27]For it seemeth to me unreasonable to send a prisoner, and not withal to signify the crimes *laid* against him.

26 Then Agrippa said unto Paul, Thou art permitted to speak for thyself. Then Paul stretched forth the hand, and answered for himself: [2]I think myself happy, king Agrippa, because I shall answer for myself this day before thee touching all the things whereof I am accused of the Jews: [3]Especially *because I know* thee to be expert in all customs and questions which are among the Jews: wherefore I beseech thee to hear me patiently. [4]My manner of life from my youth, which was at the first among mine own nation at Jerusalem, know all the Jews; [5]Which knew me from the beginning, if they would testify, that after the most straitest sect of our religion I lived a Pharisee. [6]And now I stand and am judged for the hope of the promise made of God unto our fathers: [7]Unto which *promise* our twelve tribes, instantly serving *God*

day and night, hope to come. For which hope's sake, king Agrippa, I am accused of the Jews. [8] Why should it be thought a thing incredible with you, that God should raise the dead? [9] I verily thought with myself, that I ought to do many things contrary to the name of Jesus of Nazareth. [10] Which thing I also did in Jerusalem: and many of the saints did I shut up in prison, having received authority from the chief priests; and when they were put to death, I gave my voice against *them*. [11] And I punished them oft in every synagogue, and compelled *them* to blaspheme; and being exceedingly mad against them, I persecuted *them* even unto strange cities. [12] Whereupon as I went to Damascus with authority and commission from the chief priests, [13] At midday, O king, I saw in the way a light from heaven, above the brightness of the sun, shining round about me and them which journeyed with me. [14] And when we were all fallen to the earth, I heard a voice speaking unto me, and saying in the Hebrew tongue, Saul, Saul, why persecutest thou me? *it is* hard for thee to kick against the pricks. [15] And I said, Who art thou, Lord? And he said, I am Jesus whom thou persecutest. [16] But rise, and stand upon thy feet: for I have appeared unto thee for this purpose, to make thee a minister and a witness both of these things which thou hast seen, and of those things in the which I will appear unto thee; [17] Delivering thee from the people, and *from* the Gentiles, unto whom now I send thee, [18] To open their eyes, *and* to turn *them* from darkness to light, and *from* the power of Satan unto God, that they may receive forgiveness of sins, and inheritance among them which are sanctified by faith that is in me. [19] Whereupon, O king Agrippa, I was not disobedient unto the heavenly vision: [20] But shewed first unto them of Damascus, and at Jerusalem, and throughout all the coasts of Judaea, and *then* to the Gentiles, that they should repent and turn to God, and do works meet for repentance. [21] For these causes the Jews caught me in the temple, and went about to kill *me*. [22] Having therefore obtained help of God, I continue unto this day, witnessing both to small and great, saying none other things than those which the prophets and Moses did say should come: [23] That Christ should suffer, *and* that he should be the first that should rise from the dead, and should shew light unto the people, and to the Gentiles.

[24] And as he thus spake for himself, Festus said with a loud voice, Paul, thou art beside thyself; much learning doth make thee mad. [25] But he said, I am not mad, most noble Festus; but speak forth the words of truth and soberness. [26] For the king knoweth of these things, before whom also I speak freely: for I am persuaded that none of these things are hidden from him; for this thing was not done in a corner. [27] King Agrippa, believest thou the prophets? I know that thou believest. [28] Then Agrippa said unto Paul, Almost thou persuadest me to be a Christian. [29] And Paul said, I would to God, that not only thou, but also all that hear me this day, were both almost, and altogether such as I am, except these bonds. [30] And when he had thus spoken, the king rose up, and the governor, and Bernice, and they that sat with them: [31] And when they were gone aside, they talked between themselves, saying, This man doeth nothing worthy of death or of bonds. [32] Then said Agrippa unto Festus, This man might have been set at liberty, if he had not appealed unto Caesar.

27 And when it was determined that we should sail into Italy, they delivered Paul and certain other prisoners unto *one* named Julius, a centurion of Augustus' band. [2] And entering into a ship of Adramyttium, we launched, meaning to sail by the coasts of Asia; *one* Aristarchus, a Macedonian of Thessalonica, being with us. [3] And the next *day* we touched at Sidon. And Julius courteously entreated Paul, and gave *him* liberty to go unto his friends to refresh himself. [4] And when we had launched from thence, we sailed under Cyprus, because the winds were contrary. [5] And when we had sailed over the sea of Cilicia and Pamphylia, we came to Myra, *a city* of Lycia. [6] And there the centurion found a ship of Alexandria sailing into Italy; and he put us therein. [7] And when we had sailed slowly many days, and scarce were come over against Cnidus, the wind not suffering us, we sailed under Crete,

over against Salmone; [8]And, hardly passing it, came unto a place which is called The fair havens; nigh whereunto was the city *of* Lasea.

[9]Now when much time was spent, and when sailing was now dangerous, because the fast was now already past, Paul admonished *them*, [10]And said unto them, Sirs, I perceive that this voyage will be with hurt and much damage, not only of the lading and ship, but also of our lives. [11]Nevertheless the centurion believed the master and the owner of the ship, more than those things which were spoken by Paul. [12]And because the haven was not commodious to winter in, the more part advised to depart thence also, if by any means they might attain to Phenice, *and there* to winter; *which is* an haven of Crete, and lieth toward the south west and north west. [13]And when the south wind blew softly, supposing that they had obtained *their* purpose, loosing *thence*, they sailed close by Crete. [14]But not long after there arose against it a tempestuous wind, called Euroclydon. [15]And when the ship was caught, and could not bear up into the wind, we let *her* drive. [16]And running under a certain island which is called Clauda, we had much work to come by the boat: [17]Which when they had taken up, they used helps, undergirding the ship; and, fearing lest they should fall into the quicksands, strake sail, and so were driven. [18]And we being exceedingly tossed with a tempest, the next *day* they lightened the ship; [19]And the third *day* we cast out with our own hands the tackling of the ship. [20]And when neither sun nor stars in many days appeared, and no small tempest lay on *us*, all hope that we should be saved was then taken away. [21]But after long abstinence Paul stood forth in the midst of them, and said, Sirs, ye should have hearkened unto me, and not have loosed from Crete, and to have gained this harm and loss. [22]And now I exhort you to be of good cheer: for there shall be no loss of *any man's* life among you, but of the ship. [23]For there stood by me this night the angel of God, whose I am, and whom I serve, [24]Saying, Fear not, Paul; thou must be brought before Caesar: and, lo, God hath given thee all them that sail with thee. [25]Wherefore,

sirs, be of good cheer: for I believe God, that it shall be even as it was told me. [26]Howbeit we must be cast upon a certain island. [27]But when the fourteenth night was come, as we were driven up and down in Adria, about midnight the shipmen deemed that they drew near to some country; [28]And sounded, and found *it* twenty fathoms: and when they had gone a little further, they sounded again, and found *it* fifteen fathoms. [29]Then fearing lest we should have fallen upon rocks, they cast four anchors out of the stern, and wished for the day. [30]And as the shipmen were about to flee out of the ship, when they had let down the boat into the sea, under colour as though they would have cast anchors out of the foreship, [31]Paul said to the centurion and to the soldiers, Except these abide in the ship, ye cannot be saved. [32]Then the soldiers cut off the ropes of the boat, and let her fall off. [33]And while the day was coming on, Paul besought *them* all to take meat, saying, This day is the fourteenth day that ye have tarried and continued fasting, having taken nothing. [34]Wherefore I pray you to take *some* meat: for this is for your health: for there shall not an hair fall from the head of any of you. [35]And when he had thus spoken, he took bread, and gave thanks to God in presence of them all: and when he had broken *it*, he began to eat. [36]Then were they all of good cheer, and they also took *some* meat. [37]And we were in all in the ship two hundred threescore and sixteen souls. [38]And when they had eaten enough, they lightened the ship, and cast out the wheat into the sea. [39]And when it was day, they knew not the land: but they discovered a certain creek with a shore, into the which they were minded, if it were possible, to thrust in the ship. [40]And when they had taken up the anchors, they committed *themselves* unto the sea, and loosed the rudder bands, and hoised up the mainsail to the wind, and made toward shore. [41]And falling into a place where two seas met, they ran the ship aground; and the forepart stuck fast, and remained unmoveable, but the hinder part was broken with the violence of the waves. [42]And the soldiers' counsel was to kill the prisoners, lest any of them should swim out, and escape. [43]But the centurion, willing to save Paul, kept them from *their* purpose; and commanded that they which could swim should cast *themselves* first *into the sea*, and get to land: [44]And the rest, some on boards, and some on *broken pieces* of the ship. And so it came to pass, that they escaped all safe to land.

28 And when they were escaped, then they knew that the island was called Melita. [2]And the barbarous people shewed us no little kindness: for they kindled a fire, and received us every one, because of the present rain, and because of the cold. [3]And when Paul had gathered a bundle of sticks, and laid *them* on the fire, there came a viper out of the heat, and fastened on his hand. [4]And when the barbarians saw the *venomous* beast hang on his hand, they said among themselves, No doubt this man is a murderer, whom, though he hath escaped the sea, yet vengeance suffereth not to live. [5]And he shook off the beast into the fire, and felt no harm. [6]Howbeit they looked when he should have swollen, or fallen down dead suddenly: but after they had looked a great while, and saw no harm come to him, they changed their minds, and said that he was a god.

[7]In the same quarters were possessions of the chief man of the island, whose name was Publius; who received us, and lodged us three days courteously. [8]And it came to pass, that the father of Publius lay sick of a fever and of a bloody flux: to whom Paul entered in, and prayed, and laid his hands on him, and healed him. [9]So when this was done, others also, which had diseases in the island, came, and were healed: [10]Who also honoured us with many honours; and when we departed, they laded *us* with such things as were necessary.

[11]And after three months we departed in a ship of Alexandria, which had wintered in the isle, whose sign was Castor and Pollux. [12]And landing at Syracuse, we tarried *there* three days. [13]And from thence we fetched a compass, and came to Rhegium: and after one day the south wind blew, and we came the next day to Puteoli: [14]Where we found brethren, and were desired to tarry with them seven days: and so we went toward Rome. [15]And from thence, when the brethren heard of us, they came to meet us as far as Appii Forum, and The three taverns: whom when Paul saw, he thanked God, and took courage. [16]And when we came to Rome, the centurion delivered the prisoners to the captain of the guard: but Paul was suffered to dwell by himself with a soldier that kept him.

[17]And it came to pass, that after three days Paul called the chief of the Jews together: and when they were come together, he said unto them, Men *and* brethren, though I have committed nothing against the people, or customs of our fathers, yet was I delivered prisoner from Jerusalem into the hands of the Romans. [18]Who, when they had examined me, would have let *me* go, because there was no cause of death in me. [19]But when the Jews spake against *it*, I was constrained to appeal unto Caesar; not that I had ought to accuse my nation of. [20]For this cause therefore have I called for you, to see *you*, and to speak with *you*: because that for the hope of Israel I am bound with this chain. [21]And they said unto him, We neither received letters out of Judaea concerning thee, neither any of the brethren that came shewed or spake any harm of thee. [22]But we desire to hear of thee what thou thinkest: for as concerning this sect, we know that every where it is spoken against. [23]And when they had appointed him a day, there came many to him into *his* lodging; to whom he expounded and testified the kingdom of God, persuading them concerning Jesus, both out of the law of Moses, and *out of* the prophets, from morning till evening. [24]And some believed the things which were spoken, and some believed not. [25]And when they agreed not among themselves, they departed, after that Paul had spoken one word, Well spake the Holy Ghost by Esaias the prophet unto our fathers, [26]Saying,

Go unto this people, and say, Hearing ye shall hear, and shall not understand; and seeing ye shall see, and not perceive: [27]For the heart of this people is waxed gross, and their ears are dull of hearing, and their eyes have they closed; lest they should see with *their* eyes, and hear with *their* ears, and understand with *their* heart, and should be converted, and I should heal them.

²⁸Be it known therefore unto you, that the salvation of God is sent unto the Gentiles, and *that* they will hear it. ²⁹And when he had said these words, the Jews departed,

and had great reasoning among themselves.

³⁰And Paul dwelt two whole years in his own hired house, and received all that came in unto him, ³¹Preaching the kingdom of God, and teaching those things which concern the Lord Jesus Christ, with all confidence, no man forbidding him.

ROMANS

1 Paul, a servant of Jesus Christ, called *to be* an apostle, separated unto the gospel of God, [2](Which he had promised afore by his prophets in the holy scriptures,) [3]Concerning his Son Jesus Christ our Lord, which was made of the seed of David according to the flesh; [4]And declared *to be* the Son of God with power, according to the spirit of holiness, by the resurrection from the dead: [5]By whom we have received grace and apostleship, for obedience to the faith among all nations, for his name: [6]Among whom are ye also the called of Jesus Christ:

[7]To all that be in Rome, beloved of God, called *to be* saints:

Grace to you and peace from God our Father, and the Lord Jesus Christ.

[8]First, I thank my God through Jesus Christ for you all, that your faith is spoken of throughout the whole world. [9]For God is my witness, whom I serve with my spirit in the gospel of his Son, that without ceasing I make mention of you always in my prayers; [10]Making request, if by any means now at length I might have a prosperous journey by the will of God to come unto you. [11]For I long to see you, that I may impart unto you some spiritual gift, to the end ye may be established; [12]That is, that I may be comforted together with you by the mutual faith both of you and me. [13]Now I would not have you ignorant, brethren, that oftentimes I purposed to come unto you, (but was let hitherto,) that I might have some fruit among you also, even as among other Gentiles. [14]I am debtor both to the Greeks, and to the Barbarians; both to the wise, and to the unwise. [15]So, as much as in me is, I am ready to preach the gospel to you that are at Rome also. [16]For I am not ashamed of the gospel of Christ: for it is the power of God unto salvation to every one that believeth; to the Jew first, and also to the Greek. [17]For therein is the righteousness of God revealed from faith to faith: as it is written, The just shall live by faith.

[18]For the wrath of God is revealed from heaven against all ungodliness and unrighteousness of men, who hold the truth in unrighteousness; [19]Because that which may be known of God is manifest in them; for God hath shewed *it* unto them. [20]For the invisible things of him from the creation of the world are clearly seen, being understood by the things that are made, *even* his eternal power and Godhead; so that they are without excuse: [21]Because that, when they knew God, they glorified *him* not as God, neither were thankful; but became vain in their imaginations, and their foolish heart was darkened. [22]Professing themselves to be wise, they became fools, [23]And changed the glory of the uncorruptible God into an image made like to corruptible man, and to birds, and fourfooted beasts, and creeping things.

[24]Wherefore God also gave them up to uncleanness through the lusts of their own hearts, to dishonour their own bodies between themselves: [25]Who changed the truth of God into a lie, and worshipped and served the creature more than the Creator, who is blessed for ever. Amen. [26]For this cause God gave them up unto vile affections: for even their women did change the natural use into that which is against nature: [27]And likewise also the men, leaving the natural use of the woman, burned in their lust one toward another; men with men working that which is unseemly, and receiving in themselves that recompence of their error which was meet. [28]And even as they did not like to retain God in *their* knowledge, God gave them over to a reprobate mind, to do those things which are not convenient; [29]Being filled with all unrighteousness, fornication, wickedness, covetousness, maliciousness; full of envy, murder, debate, deceit, malignity; whisperers, [30]Backbiters, haters of God, despiteful, proud, boasters, inventors of evil things, disobedient to parents, [31]Without understanding, covenantbreakers, without natural affection, implacable, unmerciful: [32]Who knowing the judgment of God, that they which commit such things are worthy of death, not only do the same, but have pleasure in them that do them.

2 Therefore thou art inexcusable, O man, whosoever thou art that judgest: for wherein thou judgest another, thou condemnest thyself; for thou that judgest doest the same things. ²But we are sure that the judgment of God is according to truth against them which commit such things. ³And thinkest thou this, O man, that judgest them which do such things, and doest the same, that thou shalt escape the judgment of God? ⁴Or despisest thou the riches of his goodness and forbearance and longsuffering; not knowing that the goodness of God leadeth thee to repentance? ⁵But after thy hardness and impenitent heart treasurest up unto thyself wrath against the day of wrath and revelation of the righteous judgment of God; ⁶Who will render to every man according to his deeds: ⁷To them who by patient continuance in well doing seek for glory and honour and immortality, eternal life: ⁸But unto them that are contentious, and do not obey the truth, but obey unrighteousness, indignation and wrath, ⁹Tribulation and anguish, upon every soul of man that doeth evil, of the Jew first, and also of the Gentile; ¹⁰But glory, honour, and peace, to every man that worketh good, to the Jew first, and also to the Gentile: ¹¹For there is no respect of persons with God. ¹²For as many as have sinned without law shall also perish without law: and as many as have sinned in the law shall be judged by the law; ¹³(For not the hearers of the law *are* just before God, but the doers of the law shall be justified. ¹⁴For when the Gentiles, which have not the law, do by nature the things contained in the law, these, having not the law, are a law unto themselves: ¹⁵Which shew the work of the law written in their hearts, their conscience also bearing witness, and *their* thoughts the mean while accusing or else excusing one another;) ¹⁶In the day when God shall judge the secrets of men by Jesus Christ according to my gospel.

¹⁷Behold, thou art called a Jew, and restest in the law, and makest thy boast of God, ¹⁸And knowest *his* will, and approvest the things that are more excellent, being instructed out of the law; ¹⁹And art confident that thou thyself art a guide of the blind, a light of them which are in darkness, ²⁰An instructor of the foolish, a teacher of babes, which hast the form of knowledge and of the truth in the law. ²¹Thou therefore which teachest another, teachest thou not thyself? thou that preachest a man should not steal, dost thou steal? ²²Thou that sayest a man should not commit adultery, dost thou commit adultery? thou that abhorrest idols, dost thou commit sacrilege? ²³Thou that makest thy boast of the law, through breaking the law dishonourest thou God? ²⁴For the name of God is blasphemed among the Gentiles through you, as it is written. ²⁵For circumcision verily profiteth, if thou keep the law: but if thou be a breaker of the law, thy circumcision is made uncircumcision. ²⁶Therefore if the uncircumcision keep the righteousness of the law, shall not his uncircumcision be counted for circumcision? ²⁷And shall not uncircumcision which is by nature, if it fulfil the law, judge thee, who by the letter and circumcision dost transgress the law? ²⁸For he is not a Jew, which is one outwardly; neither *is that* circumcision, which is outward in the flesh: ²⁹But he *is* a Jew, which is one inwardly; and circumcision *is that* of the heart, in the spirit, *and* not in the letter; whose praise *is* not of men, but of God.

3 What advantage then hath the Jew? or what profit *is there* of circumcision? ²Much every way: chiefly, because that unto them were committed the oracles of God. ³For what if some did not believe? shall their unbelief make the faith of God without effect? ⁴God forbid: yea, let God be true, but every man a liar; as it is written,

That thou mightest be justified in thy sayings, and mightest overcome when thou art judged.

⁵But if our unrighteousness commend the righteousness of God, what shall we say? *Is* God unrighteous who taketh vengeance? (I speak as a man) ⁶God forbid: for then how shall God judge the world? ⁷For if the truth of God hath more abounded through my lie unto his glory; why yet am I also judged as a sinner? ⁸And not *rather,* (as we be slanderously reported, and as some affirm that we say,) Let us do evil, that good may come? whose damnation is just.

⁹What then? are we better *than they?* No,

in no wise: for we have before proved both Jews and Gentiles, that they are all under sin; [10]As it is written,

There is none righteous, no, not one: [11]There is none that understandeth, there is none that seeketh after God. [12]They are all gone out of the way, they are together become unprofitable; there is none that doeth good, no, not one. [13]Their throat *is* an open sepulchre; with their tongues they have used deceit; the poison of asps *is* under their lips: [14]Whose mouth *is* full of cursing and bitterness: [15]Their feet *are* swift to shed blood: [16]Destruction and misery *are* in their ways: [17]And the way of peace have they not known: [18]There is no fear of God before their eyes.

[19]Now we know that what things soever the law saith, it saith to them who are under the law: that every mouth may be stopped, and all the world may become guilty before God. [20]Therefore by the deeds of the law there shall no flesh be justified in his sight: for by the law *is* the knowledge of sin. [21]But now the righteousness of God without the law is manifested, being witnessed by the law and the prophets; [22]Even the righteousness of God *which is* by faith of Jesus Christ unto all and upon all them that believe: for there is no difference: [23]For all have sinned, and come short of the glory of God; [24]Being justified freely by his grace through the redemption that is in Christ Jesus: [25]Whom God hath set forth *to be* a propitiation through faith in his blood, to declare his righteousness for the remission of sins that are past, through the forbearance of God; [26]To declare, *I say,* at this time his righteousness: that he might be just, and the justifier of him which believeth in Jesus. [27]Where *is* boasting then? It is excluded. By what law? of works? Nay: but by the law of faith. [28]Therefore we conclude that a man is justified by faith without the deeds of the law. [29]*Is he* the God of the Jews only? *is he* not also of the Gentiles? Yes, of the Gentiles also: [30]Seeing *it is* one God, which shall justify the circumcision by faith, and uncircumcision through faith. [31]Do we then make void the law through faith? God forbid: yea, we establish the law.

4 What shall we say then that Abraham our father, as pertaining to the flesh, hath found? [2]For if Abraham were justified by works, he hath *whereof* to glory; but not before God. [3]For what saith the scripture? Abraham believed God, and it was counted unto him for righteousness. [4]Now to him that worketh is the reward not reckoned of grace, but of debt. [5]But to him that worketh not, but believeth on him that justifieth the ungodly, his faith is counted for righteousness. [6]Even as David also describeth the blessedness of the man, unto whom God imputeth righteousness without works, [7]Saying,

Blessed *are* they whose iniquities are forgiven, and whose sins are covered. [8]Blessed *is* the man to whom the Lord will not impute sin.

[9]*Cometh* this blessedness then upon the circumcision *only,* or upon the uncircumcision also? for we say that faith was reckoned to Abraham for righteousness. [10]How was it then reckoned? when he was in circumcision, or in uncircumcision? Not in circumcision, but in uncircumcision. [11]And he received the sign of circumcision, a seal of the righteousness of the faith which *he had yet* being uncircumcised: that he might be the father of all them that believe, though they be not circumcised; that righteousness might be imputed unto them also: [12]And the father of circumcision to them who are not of the circumcision only, but who also walk in the steps of that faith of our father Abraham, which *he had* being *yet* uncircumcised. [13]For the promise, that he should be the heir of the world, *was* not to Abraham, or to his seed, through the law, but through the righteousness of faith. [14]For if they which are of the law *be* heirs, faith is made void, and the promise made of none effect: [15]Because the law worketh wrath: for where no law is, *there is* no transgression. [16]Therefore *it is of* faith, that *it might be* by grace; to the end the promise might be sure to all the seed; not to that only which is of the law, but to that also which is of the faith of Abraham; who is the father of us all, [17](As it is written, I have made thee a father of many nations,) before him whom he believed,

even God, who quickeneth the dead, and calleth those things which be not as though they were. [18] Who against hope believed in hope, that he might become the father of many nations; according to that which was spoken, So shall thy seed be. [19] And being not weak in faith, he considered not his own body now dead, when he was about an hundred years old, neither yet the deadness of Sarah's womb: [20] He staggered not at the promise of God through unbelief; but was strong in faith, giving glory to God; [21] And being fully persuaded that, what he had promised, he was able also to perform. [22] And therefore it was imputed to him for righteousness. [23] Now it was not written for his sake alone, that it was imputed to him; [24] But for us also, to whom it shall be imputed, if we believe on him that raised up Jesus our Lord from the dead; [25] Who was delivered for our offences, and was raised again for our justification.

5 Therefore being justified by faith, we have peace with God through our Lord Jesus Christ: [2] By whom also we have access by faith into this grace wherein we stand, and rejoice in hope of the glory of God. [3] And not only *so,* but we glory in tribulations also: knowing that tribulation worketh patience; [4] And patience, experience; and experience, hope: [5] And hope maketh not ashamed; because the love of God is shed abroad in our hearts by the Holy Ghost which is given unto us. [6] For when we were yet without strength, in due time Christ died for the ungodly. [7] For scarcely for a righteous man will one die: yet peradventure for a good man some would even dare to die. [8] But God commendeth his love toward us, in that, while we were yet sinners, Christ died for us. [9] Much more then, being now justified by his blood, we shall be saved from wrath through him. [10] For if, when we were enemies, we were reconciled to God by the death of his Son, much more, being reconciled, we shall be saved by his life. [11] And not only *so,* but we also joy in God through our Lord Jesus Christ, by whom we have now received the atonement.

[12] Wherefore, as by one man sin entered into the world, and death by sin; and so death passed upon all men, for that all have sinned: [13] (For until the law sin was in the world: but sin is not imputed when there is no law. [14] Nevertheless death reigned from Adam to Moses, even over them that had not sinned after the similitude of Adam's transgression, who is the figure of him that was to come. [15] But not as the offence, so also *is* the free gift. For if through the offence of one many be dead, much more the grace of God, and the gift by grace, *which is* by one man, Jesus Christ, hath abounded unto many. [16] And not as *it was* by one that sinned, *so is* the gift: for the judgment *was* by one to condemnation, but the free gift *is* of many offences unto justification. [17] For if by one man's offence death reigned by one; much more they which receive abundance of grace and of the gift of righteousness shall reign in life by one, Jesus Christ.) [18] Therefore as by the offence of one *judgment came* upon all men to condemnation; even so by the righteousness of one *the free gift came* upon all men unto justification of life. [19] For as by one man's disobedience many were made sinners, so by the obedience of one shall many be made righteous. [20] Moreover the law entered, that the offence might abound. But where sin abounded, grace did much more abound: [21] That as sin hath reigned unto death, even so might grace reign through righteousness unto eternal life by Jesus Christ our Lord.

6 What shall we say then? Shall we continue in sin, that grace may abound? [2] God forbid. How shall we, that are dead to sin, live any longer therein? [3] Know ye not, that so many of us as were baptized into Jesus Christ were baptized into his death? [4] Therefore we are buried with him by baptism into death: that like as Christ was raised up from the dead by the glory of the Father, even so we also should walk in newness of life. [5] For if we have been planted together in the likeness of his death, we shall be also *in the likeness of his* resurrection: [6] Knowing this, that our old man is crucified with *him,* that the body of sin might be destroyed, that henceforth we should not serve sin. [7] For he that is dead is freed from sin. [8] Now if we be dead with Christ, we believe that we shall also live with him: [9] Knowing that Christ being raised from the dead dieth no more; death hath

no more dominion over him. ¹⁰For in that he died, he died unto sin once: but in that he liveth, he liveth unto God. ¹¹Likewise reckon ye also yourselves to be dead indeed unto sin, but alive unto God through Jesus Christ our Lord. ¹²Let not sin therefore reign in your mortal body, that ye should obey it in the lusts thereof. ¹³Neither yield ye your members *as* instruments of un-righteousness unto sin: but yield yourselves unto God, as those that are alive from the dead, and your members *as* instruments of righteousness unto God. ¹⁴For sin shall not have dominion over you: for ye are not un-der the law, but under grace. ¹⁵What then? shall we sin, because we are not under the law, but under grace? God forbid. ¹⁶Know ye not, that to whom ye yield yourselves servants to obey, his servants ye are to whom ye obey; whether of sin unto death, or of obedience unto righteousness? ¹⁷But God be thanked, that ye were the servants of sin, but ye have obeyed from the heart that form of doctrine which was delivered you. ¹⁸Being then made free from sin, ye became the servants of righteousness. ¹⁹I speak after the manner of men because of the infirmity of your flesh: for as ye have yielded your members servants to unclean-ness and to iniquity unto iniquity; even so now yield your members servants to righ-teousness unto holiness. ²⁰For when ye were the servants of sin, ye were free from righteousness. ²¹What fruit had ye then in those things whereof ye are now ashamed? for the end of those things *is* death. ²²But now being made free from sin, and become servants to God, ye have your fruit unto ho-liness, and the end everlasting life. ²³For the wages of sin *is* death; but the gift of God *is* eternal life through Jesus Christ our Lord.

7 Know ye not, brethren, (for I speak to them that know the law,) how that the law hath dominion over a man as long as he liveth? ²For the woman which hath an hus-band is bound by the law to *her* husband so long as he liveth; but if the husband be dead, she is loosed from the law of *her* hus-band. ³So then if, while *her* husband liveth, she be married to another man, she shall be called an adulteress: but if her husband be dead, she is free from that law; so that she is no adulteress, though she be married

to another man. ⁴Wherefore, my brethren, ye also are become dead to the law by the body of Christ; that ye should be married to another, *even* to him who is raised from the dead, that we should bring forth fruit unto God. ⁵For when we were in the flesh, the motions of sins, which were by the law, did work in our members to bring forth fruit unto death. ⁶But now we are delivered from the law, that being dead wherein we were held; that we should serve in newness of spirit, and not *in* the oldness of the letter.

⁷What shall we say then? *Is* the law sin? God forbid. Nay, I had not known sin, but by the law: for I had not known lust, except the law had said, Thou shalt not covet. ⁸But sin, taking occasion by the com-mandment, wrought in me all manner of concupiscence. For without the law sin *was* dead. ⁹For I was alive without the law once: but when the commandment came, sin revived, and I died. ¹⁰And the command-ment, which *was ordained* to life, I found *to be* unto death. ¹¹For sin, taking occasion by the commandment, deceived me, and by it slew *me.* ¹²Wherefore the law *is* holy, and the commandment holy, and just, and good. ¹³Was then that which is good made death unto me? God forbid. But sin, that it might appear sin, working death in me by that which is good; that sin by the com-mandment might become exceeding sinful. ¹⁴For we know that the law is spiritual: but I am carnal, sold under sin. ¹⁵For that which I do I allow not: for what I would, that do I not; but what I hate, that do I. ¹⁶If then I do that which I would not, I consent unto the law that *it is* good. ¹⁷Now then it is no more I that do it, but sin that dwelleth in me. ¹⁸For I know that in me (that is, in my flesh,) dwell-eth no good thing: for to will is present with me; but *how* to perform that which is good I find not. ¹⁹For the good that I would I do not: but the evil which I would not, that I do. ²⁰Now if I do that I would not, it is no more I that do it, but sin that dwelleth in me. ²¹I find then a law, that, when I would do good, evil is present with me. ²²For I delight in the law of God after the inward man: ²³But I see another law in my members, warring against the law of my mind, and bringing me into captivity to the law of sin which is in my members. ²⁴O wretched man that I

am! who shall deliver me from the body of this death? [25]I thank God through Jesus Christ our Lord. So then with the mind I myself serve the law of God; but with the flesh the law of sin.

8 *There is* therefore now no condemnation to them which are in Christ Jesus, who walk not after the flesh, but after the Spirit. [2]For the law of the Spirit of life in Christ Jesus hath made me free from the law of sin and death. [3]For what the law could not do, in that it was weak through the flesh, God sending his own Son in the likeness of sinful flesh, and for sin, condemned sin in the flesh: [4]That the righteousness of the law might be fulfilled in us, who walk not after the flesh, but after the Spirit. [5]For they that are after the flesh do mind the things of the flesh; but they that are after the Spirit the things of the Spirit. [6]For to be carnally minded *is* death; but to be spiritually minded *is* life and peace. [7]Because the carnal mind *is* enmity against God: for it is not subject to the law of God, neither indeed can be. [8]So then they that are in the flesh cannot please God. [9]But ye are not in the flesh, but in the Spirit, if so be that the Spirit of God dwell in you. Now if any man have not the Spirit of Christ, he is none of his. [10]And if Christ *be* in you, the body *is* dead because of sin; but the Spirit *is* life because of righteousness. [11]But if the Spirit of him that raised up Jesus from the dead dwell in you, he that raised up Christ from the dead shall also quicken your mortal bodies by his Spirit that dwelleth in you.

[12]Therefore, brethren, we are debtors, not to the flesh, to live after the flesh. [13]For if ye live after the flesh, ye shall die: but if ye through the Spirit do mortify the deeds of the body, ye shall live. [14]For as many as are led by the Spirit of God, they are the sons of God. [15]For ye have not received the spirit of bondage again to fear; but ye have received the Spirit of adoption, whereby we cry, Abba, Father. [16]The Spirit itself beareth witness with our spirit, that we are the children of God: [17]And if children, then heirs; heirs of God, and joint-heirs with Christ; if so be that we suffer with *him*, that we may be also glorified together.

[18]For I reckon that the sufferings of this present time *are* not worthy *to be compared* with the glory which shall be revealed in us. [19]For the earnest expectation of the creature waiteth for the manifestation of the sons of God. [20]For the creature was made subject to vanity, not willingly, but by reason of him who hath subjected *the same* in hope, [21]Because the creature itself also shall be delivered from the bondage of corruption into the glorious liberty of the children of God. [22]For we know that the whole creation groaneth and travaileth in pain together until now. [23]And not only *they*, but ourselves also, which have the firstfruits of the Spirit, even we ourselves groan within ourselves, waiting for the adoption, *to wit*, the redemption of our body. [24]For we are saved by hope: but hope that is seen is not hope: for what a man seeth, why doth he yet hope for? [25]But if we hope for that we see not, *then* do we with patience wait for *it*. [26]Likewise the Spirit also helpeth our infirmities: for we know not what we should pray for as we ought: but the Spirit itself maketh intercession for us with groanings which cannot be uttered. [27]And he that searcheth the hearts knoweth what *is* the mind of the Spirit, because he maketh intercession for the saints according to *the will of* God. [28]And we know that all things work together for good to them that love God, to them who are the called according to *his* purpose. [29]For whom he did foreknow, he also did predestinate *to be* conformed to the image of his Son, that he might be the firstborn among many brethren. [30]Moreover whom he did predestinate, them he also called: and whom he called, them he also justified: and whom he justified, them he also glorified. [31]What shall we then say to these things? If God *be* for us, who *can be* against us? [32]He that spared not his own Son, but delivered him up for us all, how shall he not with him also freely give us all things? [33]Who shall lay any thing to the charge of God's elect? *It is* God that justifieth. [34]Who *is* he that condemneth? *It is* Christ that died, yea rather, that is risen again, who is even at the right hand of God, who also maketh intercession for us. [35]Who shall separate us from the love of Christ? *shall* tribulation, or distress, or persecution, or famine, or nakedness, or peril, or sword? [36]As it is written,

For thy sake we are killed all the day long; we are accounted as sheep for the slaughter.

³⁷Nay, in all these things we are more than conquerors through him that loved us. ³⁸For I am persuaded, that neither death, nor life, nor angels, nor principalities, nor powers, nor things present, nor things to come, ³⁹Nor height, nor depth, nor any other creature, shall be able to separate us from the love of God, which is in Christ Jesus our Lord.

9 I say the truth in Christ, I lie not, my conscience also bearing me witness in the Holy Ghost, ²That I have great heaviness and continual sorrow in my heart. ³For I could wish that myself were accursed from Christ for my brethren, my kinsmen according to the flesh: ⁴Who are Israelites; to whom *pertaineth* the adoption, and the glory, and the covenants, and the giving of the law, and the service *of God,* and the promises; ⁵Whose *are* the fathers, and of whom as concerning the flesh Christ *came,* who is over all, God blessed for ever. Amen.

⁶Not as though the word of God hath taken none effect. For they *are* not all Israel, which are of Israel: ⁷Neither, because they are the seed of Abraham, *are they* all children: but, In Isaac shall thy seed be called. ⁸That is, They which are the children of the flesh, these *are* not the children of God: but the children of the promise are counted for the seed. ⁹For this *is* the word of promise, At this time will I come, and Sarah shall have a son. ¹⁰And not only *this;* but when Rebecca also had conceived by one, *even* by our father Isaac; ¹¹(For *the children* being not yet born, neither having done any good or evil, that the purpose of God according to election might stand, not of works, but of him that calleth;) ¹²It was said unto her, The elder shall serve the younger. ¹³As it is written, Jacob have I loved, but Esau have I hated.

¹⁴What shall we say then? *Is there* unrighteousness with God? God forbid. ¹⁵For he saith to Moses,

I will have mercy on whom I will have mercy, and I will have compassion on whom I will have compassion.

¹⁶So then *it is* not of him that willeth, nor of him that runneth, but of God that sheweth mercy. ¹⁷For the scripture saith unto Pharaoh, Even for this same purpose have I raised thee up, that I might shew my power in thee, and that my name might be declared throughout all the earth. ¹⁸Therefore hath he mercy on whom he will *have mercy,* and whom he will he hardeneth. ¹⁹Thou wilt say then unto me, Why doth he yet find fault? For who hath resisted his will? ²⁰Nay but, O man, who art thou that repliest against God? Shall the thing formed say to him that formed *it,* Why hast thou made me thus? ²¹Hath not the potter power over the clay, of the same lump to make one vessel unto honour, and another unto dishonour? ²²*What* if God, willing to shew *his* wrath, and to make his power known, endured with much longsuffering the vessels of wrath fitted to destruction: ²³And that he might make known the riches of his glory on the vessels of mercy, which he had afore prepared unto glory, ²⁴Even us, whom he hath called, not of the Jews only, but also of the Gentiles? ²⁵As he saith also in Osee,

I will call them my people, which were not my people; and her beloved, which was not beloved.

²⁶And it shall come to pass, *that* in the place where it was said unto them, Ye *are* not my people; there shall they be called the children of the living God.

²⁷Esaias also crieth concerning Israel,

Though the number of the children of Israel be as the sand of the sea, a remnant shall be saved: ²⁸For he will finish the work, and cut *it* short in righteousness: because a short work will the Lord make upon the earth.

²⁹And as Esaias said before,

Except the Lord of Sabaoth had left us a seed, we had been as Sodoma, and been made like unto Gomorrha.

³⁰What shall we say then? That the Gentiles, which followed not after righteousness, have attained to righteousness, even the righteousness which is of faith. ³¹But Israel, which followed after the law of

righteousness, hath not attained to the law of righteousness. [32] Wherefore? Because *they sought it* not by faith, but as it were by the works of the law. For they stumbled at that stumblingstone; [33] As it is written,

Behold, I lay in Sion a stumblingstone and rock of offence: and whosoever believeth on him shall not be ashamed.

10 Brethren, my heart's desire and prayer to God for Israel is, that they might be saved. [2] For I bear them record that they have a zeal of God, but not according to knowledge. [3] For they being ignorant of God's righteousness, and going about to establish their own righteousness, have not submitted themselves unto the righteousness of God. [4] For Christ *is* the end of the law for righteousness to every one that believeth. [5] For Moses describeth the righteousness which is of the law, That the man which doeth those things shall live by them. [6] But the righteousness which is of faith speaketh on this wise, Say not in thine heart, Who shall ascend into heaven? (that is, to bring Christ down *from above*:) [7] Or, Who shall descend into the deep? (that is, to bring up Christ again from the dead.) [8] But what saith it? The word is nigh thee, *even* in thy mouth, and in thy heart: that is, the word of faith, which we preach; [9] That if thou shalt confess with thy mouth the Lord Jesus, and shalt believe in thine heart that God hath raised him from the dead, thou shalt be saved. [10] For with the heart man believeth unto righteousness; and with the mouth confession is made unto salvation. [11] For the scripture saith, Whosoever believeth on him shall not be ashamed. [12] For there is no difference between the Jew and the Greek: for the same Lord over all is rich unto all that call upon him. [13] For whosoever shall call upon the name of the Lord shall be saved. [14] How then shall they call on him in whom they have not believed? and how shall they believe in him of whom they have not heard? and how shall they hear without a preacher? [15] And how shall they preach, except they be sent? as it is written, How beautiful are the feet of them that preach the gospel of peace, and bring glad tidings of good things! [16] But they have not all obeyed the gospel. For Esaias saith, Lord, who hath believed our report? [17] So then faith *cometh* by hearing, and hearing by the word of God. [18] But I say, Have they not heard? Yes verily,

their sound went into all the earth, and their words unto the ends of the world.

[19] But I say, Did not Israel know? First Moses saith,

I will provoke you to jealousy by *them that are* no people, *and* by a foolish nation I will anger you.

[20] But Esaias is very bold, and saith,

I was found of them that sought me not; I was made manifest unto them that asked not after me.

[21] But to Israel he saith,

All day long I have stretched forth my hands unto a disobedient and gainsaying people.

11 I say then, Hath God cast away his people? God forbid. For I also am an Israelite, of the seed of Abraham, *of* the tribe of Benjamin. [2] God hath not cast away his people which he foreknew. Wot ye not what the scripture saith of Elias? how he maketh intercession to God against Israel, saying, [3] Lord, they have killed thy prophets, and digged down thine altars; and I am left alone, and they seek my life. [4] But what saith the answer of God unto him? I have reserved to myself seven thousand men, who have not bowed the knee to *the image of* Baal. [5] Even so then at this present time also there is a remnant according to the election of grace. [6] And if by grace, then *is it* no more of works: otherwise grace is no more grace. But if *it be* of works, then is it no more grace: otherwise work is no more work.

[7] What then? Israel hath not obtained that which he seeketh for; but the election hath obtained it, and the rest were blinded [8] (According as it is written,

God hath given them the spirit of slumber, eyes that they should not see, and ears that they should not hear;) unto this day.

[9] And David saith,

Let their table be made a snare, and a trap, and a stumblingblock, and a recompence unto them: [10]Let their eyes be darkened, that they may not see, and bow down their back alway.

[11]I say then, Have they stumbled that they should fall? God forbid: but *rather* through their fall salvation *is come* unto the Gentiles, for to provoke them to jealousy. [12]Now if the fall of them *be* the riches of the world, and the diminishing of them the riches of the Gentiles; how much more their fulness?

[13]For I speak to you Gentiles, inasmuch as I am the apostle of the Gentiles, I magnify mine office: [14]If by any means I may provoke to emulation *them which are* my flesh, and might save some of them. [15]For if the casting away of them *be* the reconciling of the world, what *shall* the receiving *of them be,* but life from the dead? [16]For if the firstfruit *be* holy, the lump *is* also *holy:* and if the root *be* holy, so *are* the branches. [17]And if some of the branches be broken off, and thou, being a wild olive tree, wert graffed in among them, and with them partakest of the root and fatness of the olive tree; [18]Boast not against the branches. But if thou boast, thou bearest not the root, but the root thee. [19]Thou wilt say then, The branches were broken off, that I might be graffed in. [20]Well; because of unbelief they were broken off, and thou standest by faith. Be not highminded, but fear: [21]For if God spared not the natural branches, *take heed* lest he also spare not thee. [22]Behold therefore the goodness and severity of God: on them which fell, severity; but toward thee, goodness, if thou continue in *his* goodness: otherwise thou also shalt be cut off. [23]And they also, if they abide not still in unbelief, shall be graffed in: for God is able to graff them in again. [24]For if thou wert cut out of the olive tree which is wild by nature, and wert graffed contrary to nature into a good olive tree: how much more shall these, which be the natural *branches,* be graffed into their own olive tree?

[25]For I would not, brethren, that ye should be ignorant of this mystery, lest ye should be wise in your own conceits; that blindness in part is happened to Israel, until the fulness of the Gentiles be come in. [26]And so all Israel shall be saved: as it is written,

There shall come out of Sion the Deliverer, and shall turn away ungodliness from Jacob: [27]For this *is* my covenant unto them, when I shall take away their sins.

[28]As concerning the gospel, *they are* enemies for your sakes: but as touching the election, *they are* beloved for the fathers' sakes. [29]For the gifts and calling of God *are* without repentance. [30]For as ye in times past have not believed God, yet have now obtained mercy through their unbelief: [31]Even so have these also now not believed, that through your mercy they also may obtain mercy. [32]For God hath concluded them all in unbelief, that he might have mercy upon all.

[33]O the depth of the riches both of the wisdom and knowledge of God! how unsearchable *are* his judgments, and his ways past finding out! [34]For who hath known the mind of the Lord? or who hath been his counsellor? [35]Or who hath first given to him, and it shall be recompensed unto him again? [36]For of him, and through him, and to him, *are* all things: to whom *be* glory for ever. Amen.

12 I beseech you therefore, brethren, by the mercies of God, that ye present your bodies a living sacrifice, holy, acceptable unto God, *which is* your reasonable service. [2]And be not conformed to this world: but be ye transformed by the renewing of your mind, that ye may prove what is that good, and acceptable, and perfect, will of God.

[3]For I say, through the grace given unto me, to every man that is among you, not to think *of himself* more highly than he ought to think; but to think soberly, according as God hath dealt to every man the measure of faith. [4]For as we have many members in one body, and all members have not the same office: [5]So we, *being* many, are one body in Christ, and every one members one of another. [6]Having then gifts differing according to the grace that is given to us, whether prophecy, *let us prophesy*

according to the proportion of faith; ⁷Or ministry, *let us wait* on *our* ministering: or he that teacheth, on teaching; ⁸Or he that exhorteth, on exhortation: he that giveth, *let him do it* with simplicity; he that ruleth, with diligence; he that sheweth mercy, with cheerfulness.

⁹*Let* love be without dissimulation. Abhor that which is evil; cleave to that which is good. ¹⁰*Be* kindly affectioned one to another with brotherly love; in honour preferring one another; ¹¹Not slothful in business; fervent in spirit; serving the Lord; ¹²Rejoicing in hope; patient in tribulation; continuing instant in prayer; ¹³Distributing to the necessity of saints; given to hospitality. ¹⁴Bless them which persecute you: bless, and curse not. ¹⁵Rejoice with them that do rejoice, and weep with them that weep. ¹⁶*Be* of the same mind one toward another. Mind not high things, but condescend to men of low estate. Be not wise in your own conceits. ¹⁷Recompense to no man evil for evil. Provide things honest in the sight of all men. ¹⁸If it be possible, as much as lieth in you, live peaceably with all men. ¹⁹Dearly beloved, avenge not yourselves, but *rather* give place unto wrath: for it is written, Vengeance *is* mine; I will repay, saith the Lord.

²⁰Therefore if thine enemy hunger, feed him; if he thirst, give him drink: for in so doing thou shalt heap coals of fire on his head.

²¹Be not overcome of evil, but overcome evil with good.

13 Let every soul be subject unto the higher powers. For there is no power but of God: the powers that be are ordained of God. ²Whosoever therefore resisteth the power, resisteth the ordinance of God: and they that resist shall receive to themselves damnation. ³For rulers are not a terror to good works, but to the evil. Wilt thou then not be afraid of the power? do that which is good, and thou shalt have praise of the same: ⁴For he is the minister of God to thee for good. But if thou do that which is evil, be afraid; for he beareth not the sword in vain: for he is the minister of God, a revenger to *execute* wrath upon him that doeth evil. ⁵Wherefore *ye* must needs be subject, not only for wrath, but also for

conscience sake. ⁶For for this cause pay ye tribute also: for they are God's ministers, attending continually upon this very thing. ⁷Render therefore to all their dues: tribute to whom tribute *is due;* custom to whom custom; fear to whom fear; honour to whom honour. ⁸Owe no man any thing, but to love one another: for he that loveth another hath fulfilled the law. ⁹For this, Thou shalt not commit adultery, Thou shalt not kill, Thou shalt not steal, Thou shalt not bear false witness, Thou shalt not covet; and if *there be* any other commandment, it is briefly comprehended in this saying, namely, Thou shalt love thy neighbour as thyself. ¹⁰Love worketh no ill to his neighbour: therefore love *is* the fulfilling of the law. ¹¹And that, knowing the time, that now *it is* high time to awake out of sleep: for now *is* our salvation nearer than when we believed. ¹²The night is far spent, the day is at hand: let us therefore cast off the works of darkness, and let us put on the armour of light. ¹³Let us walk honestly, as in the day; not in rioting and drunkenness, not in chambering and wantonness, not in strife and envying. ¹⁴But put ye on the Lord Jesus Christ, and make not provision for the flesh, to *fulfil* the lusts *thereof.*

14 Him that is weak in the faith receive ye, *but* not to doubtful disputations. ²For one believeth that he may eat all things: another, who is weak, eateth herbs. ³Let not him that eateth despise him that eateth not; and let not him which eateth not judge him that eateth: for God hath received him. ⁴Who art thou that judgest another man's servant? to his own master he standeth or falleth. Yea, he shall be holden up: for God is able to make him stand. ⁵One man esteemeth one day above another: another esteemeth every day *alike.* Let every man be fully persuaded in his own mind. ⁶He that regardeth the day, regardeth *it* unto the Lord; and he that regardeth not the day, to the Lord he doth not regard *it.* He that eateth, eateth to the Lord, for he giveth God thanks; and he that eateth not, to the Lord he eateth not, and giveth God thanks. ⁷For none of us liveth to himself, and no man dieth to himself. ⁸For whether we live, we live unto the Lord; and whether we die, we die unto the Lord: whether we live therefore, or die, we are the Lord's. [9]For to this end Christ both died, and rose, and revived, that he might be Lord both of the dead and living. [10]But why dost thou judge thy brother? or why dost thou set at nought thy brother? for we shall all stand before the judgment seat of Christ. [11]For it is written,

As I live, saith the Lord, every knee shall bow to me, and every tongue shall confess to God.

[12]So then every one of us shall give account of himself to God. [13]Let us not therefore judge one another any more: but judge this rather, that no man put a stumbling-block or an occasion to fall in *his* brother's way. [14]I know, and am persuaded by the Lord Jesus, that *there is* nothing unclean of itself: but to him that esteemeth any thing to be unclean, to him *it is* unclean. [15]But if thy brother be grieved with *thy* meat, now walkest thou not charitably. Destroy not him with thy meat, for whom Christ died. [16]Let not then your good be evil spoken of: [17]For the kingdom of God is not meat and drink; but righteousness, and peace, and joy in the Holy Ghost. [18]For he that in these things serveth Christ *is* acceptable to God, and approved of men. [19]Let us therefore follow after the things which make for peace, and things wherewith one may edify another. [20]For meat destroy not the work of God. All things indeed *are* pure; but *it is* evil for that man who eateth with offence. [21]*It is* good neither to eat flesh, nor to drink wine, nor *any thing* whereby thy brother stumbleth, or is offended, or is made weak. [22]Hast thou faith? have *it* to thyself before God. Happy *is* he that condemneth not himself in that thing which he alloweth. [23]And he that doubteth is damned if he eat, because *he eateth* not of faith: for whatsoever *is* not of faith is sin.

15 We then that are strong ought to bear the infirmities of the weak, and not to please ourselves. [2]Let every one of us please *his* neighbour for *his* good to edification. [3]For even Christ pleased not himself; but, as it is written, The reproaches of them that reproached thee fell on me. [4]For whatsoever things were written aforetime were written for our learning, that we through patience and comfort of the

scriptures might have hope. [5]Now the God of patience and consolation grant you to be likeminded one toward another according to Christ Jesus: [6]That ye may with one mind *and* one mouth glorify God, even the Father of our Lord Jesus Christ.

[7]Wherefore receive ye one another, as Christ also received us to the glory of God. [8]Now I say that Jesus Christ was a minister of the circumcision for the truth of God, to confirm the promises *made* unto the fathers: [9]And that the Gentiles might glorify God for *his* mercy; as it is written,

For this cause I will confess to thee among the Gentiles, and sing unto thy name.

[10]And again he saith,

Rejoice, ye Gentiles, with his people.

[11]And again,

Praise the Lord, all ye Gentiles; and laud him, all ye people.

[12]And again, Esaias saith,

There shall be a root of Jesse, and he that shall rise to reign over the Gentiles; in him shall the Gentiles trust.

[13]Now the God of hope fill you with all joy and peace in believing, that ye may abound in hope, through the power of the Holy Ghost.

[14]And I myself also am persuaded of you, my brethren, that ye also are full of goodness, filled with all knowledge, able also to admonish one another. [15]Nevertheless, brethren, I have written the more boldly unto you in some sort, as putting you in mind, because of the grace that is given to me of God, [16]That I should be the minister of Jesus Christ to the Gentiles, ministering the gospel of God, that the offering up of the Gentiles might be acceptable, being sanctified by the Holy Ghost. [17]I have therefore whereof I may glory through Jesus Christ in those things which pertain to God. [18]For I will not dare to speak of any of those things which Christ hath not wrought by me, to make the Gentiles obedient, by word and deed, [19]Through mighty signs and wonders, by the power of the Spirit of God;

so that from Jerusalem, and round about unto Illyricum, I have fully preached the gospel of Christ. [20]Yea, so have I strived to preach the gospel, not where Christ was named, lest I should build upon another man's foundation: [21]But as it is written,

To whom he was not spoken of, they shall see: and they that have not heard shall understand.

[22]For which cause also I have been much hindered from coming to you. [23]But now having no more place in these parts, and having a great desire these many years to come unto you; [24]Whensoever I take my journey into Spain, I will come to you: for I trust to see you in my journey, and to be brought on my way thitherward by you, if first I be somewhat filled with your *company*. [25]But now I go unto Jerusalem to minister unto the saints. [26]For it hath pleased them of Macedonia and Achaia to make a certain contribution for the poor saints which are at Jerusalem. [27]It hath pleased them verily; and their debtors they are. For if the Gentiles have been made partakers of their spiritual things, their duty is also to minister unto them in carnal things. [28]When therefore I have performed this, and have sealed to them this fruit, I will come by you into Spain. [29]And I am sure that, when I come unto you, I shall come in the fulness of the blessing of the gospel of Christ. [30]Now I beseech you, brethren, for the Lord Jesus Christ's sake, and for the love of the Spirit, that ye strive together with me in *your* prayers to God for me; [31]That I may be delivered from them that do not believe in Judaea; and that my service which *I have* for Jerusalem may be accepted of the saints; [32]That I may come unto you with joy by the will of God, and may with you be refreshed. [33]Now the God of peace *be* with you all. Amen.

16 I commend unto you Phebe our sister, which is a servant of the church which is at Cenchrea: [2]That ye receive her in the Lord, as becometh saints, and that ye assist her in whatsoever business she hath need of you: for she hath been a succourer of many, and of myself also.

[3]Greet Priscilla and Aquila my helpers in Christ Jesus: [4]Who have for my life laid down their own necks: unto whom not only I give thanks, but also all the churches of the Gentiles. [5]Likewise *greet* the church that is in their house. Salute my wellbeloved Epaenetus, who is the firstfruits of Achaia unto Christ. [6]Greet Mary, who bestowed much labour on us. [7]Salute Andronicus and Junia, my kinsmen, and my fellowprisoners, who are of note among the apostles, who also were in Christ before me. [8]Greet Amplias my beloved in the Lord. [9]Salute Urbane, our helper in Christ, and Stachys my beloved. [10]Salute Apelles approved in Christ. Salute them which are of Aristobulus' *household*. [11]Salute Herodion my kinsman. Greet them that be of the *household* of Narcissus, which are in the Lord. [12]Salute Tryphena and Tryphosa, who labour in the Lord. Salute the beloved Persis, which laboured much in the Lord. [13]Salute Rufus chosen in the Lord, and his mother and mine. [14]Salute Asyncritus, Phlegon, Hermas, Patrobas, Hermes, and the brethren which are with them. [15]Salute Philologus, and Julia, Nereus, and his sister, and Olympas, and all the saints which are with them. [16]Salute one another with an holy kiss. The churches of Christ salute you.

[17]Now I beseech you, brethren, mark them which cause divisions and offences contrary to the doctrine which ye have learned; and avoid them. [18]For they that are such serve not our Lord Jesus Christ, but their own belly; and by good words and fair speeches deceive the hearts of the simple. [19]For your obedience is come abroad unto all *men*. I am glad therefore on your behalf: but yet I would have you wise unto that which is good, and simple concerning evil. [20]And the God of peace shall bruise Satan under your feet shortly. The grace of our Lord Jesus Christ *be* with you. Amen.

[21]Timotheus my workfellow, and Lucius, and Jason, and Sosipater, my kinsmen, salute you. [22]I Tertius, who wrote *this* epistle, salute you in the Lord. [23]Gaius mine host, and of the whole church, saluteth you. Erastus the chamberlain of the city saluteth you, and Quartus a brother. [24]The grace

of our Lord Jesus Christ *be* with you all. Amen.

²⁵Now to him that is of power to stablish you according to my gospel, and the preaching of Jesus Christ, according to the revelation of the mystery, which was kept secret since the world began, ²⁶But now is made manifest, and by the scriptures of the prophets, according to the commandment of the everlasting God, made known to all nations for the obedience of faith: ²⁷To God only wise, *be* glory through Jesus Christ for ever. Amen.

The First Epistle of Paul the Apostle to the
CORINTHIANS

1 Paul, called *to be* an apostle of Jesus Christ through the will of God, and Sosthenes *our* brother,

²Unto the church of God which is at Corinth, to them that are sanctified in Christ Jesus, called *to be* saints, with all that in every place call upon the name of Jesus Christ our Lord, both theirs and ours:

³Grace *be* unto you, and peace, from God our Father, and *from* the Lord Jesus Christ.

⁴I thank my God always on your behalf, for the grace of God which is given you by Jesus Christ; ⁵That in every thing ye are enriched by him, in all utterance, and *in* all knowledge; ⁶Even as the testimony of Christ was confirmed in you: ⁷So that ye come behind in no gift; waiting for the coming of our Lord Jesus Christ: ⁸Who shall also confirm you unto the end, *that ye may be* blameless in the day of our Lord Jesus Christ. ⁹God *is* faithful, by whom ye were called unto the fellowship of his Son Jesus Christ our Lord.

¹⁰Now I beseech you, brethren, by the name of our Lord Jesus Christ, that ye all speak the same thing, and *that* there be no divisions among you; but *that* ye be perfectly joined together in the same mind and in the same judgment. ¹¹For it hath been declared unto me of you, my brethren, by them *which are of the house* of Chloe, that there are contentions among you. ¹²Now this I say, that every one of you saith, I am of Paul; and I of Apollos; and I of Cephas; and I of Christ. ¹³Is Christ divided? was Paul crucified for you? or were ye baptized in the name of Paul? ¹⁴I thank God that I baptized none of you, but Crispus and Gaius; ¹⁵Lest any should say that I had baptized in mine own name. ¹⁶And I baptized also the household of Stephanas: besides, I know not whether I baptized any other. ¹⁷For Christ sent me not to baptize, but to preach the gospel: not with wisdom of words, lest the cross of Christ should be made of none effect.

¹⁸For the preaching of the cross is to them that perish foolishness; but unto us which are saved it is the power of God. ¹⁹For it is written,

I will destroy the wisdom of the wise, and will bring to nothing the understanding of the prudent.

²⁰Where *is* the wise? where *is* the scribe? where *is* the disputer of this world? hath not God made foolish the wisdom of this world? ²¹For after that in the wisdom of God the world by wisdom knew not God, it pleased God by the foolishness of preaching to save them that believe. ²²For the Jews require a sign, and the Greeks seek after wisdom: ²³But we preach Christ crucified, unto the Jews a stumblingblock, and unto the Greeks foolishness; ²⁴But unto them which are called, both Jews and Greeks, Christ the power of God, and the wisdom of God. ²⁵Because the foolishness of God is wiser than men; and the weakness of God is stronger than men. ²⁶For ye see your calling, brethren, how that not many wise men after the flesh, not many mighty, not many noble, *are called:* ²⁷But God hath chosen the foolish things of the world to confound the wise; and God hath chosen the weak things of the world to confound the things which are mighty; ²⁸And base things of the world, and things which are despised, hath God chosen, *yea,* and things which are not, to bring to nought things that are: ²⁹That no flesh should glory in his presence. ³⁰But of him are ye in Christ Jesus, who of God is made unto us wisdom, and righteousness, and sanctification, and redemption: ³¹That, according as it is written, He that glorieth, let him glory in the Lord.

2 And I, brethren, when I came to you, came not with excellency of speech or of wisdom, declaring unto you the testimony of God. ²For I determined not to know any thing among you, save Jesus Christ, and him crucified. ³And I was with you in weakness, and in fear, and in much trembling. ⁴And my speech and my preaching *was* not with enticing words of man's wisdom, but in demonstration of the Spirit and of power: [5]That your faith should not stand in the wisdom of men, but in the power of God. [6]Howbeit we speak wisdom among them that are perfect: yet not the wisdom of this world, nor of the princes of this world, that come to nought: [7]But we speak the wisdom of God in a mystery, *even* the hidden *wisdom,* which God ordained before the world unto our glory: [8]Which none of the princes of this world knew: for had they known *it,* they would not have crucified the Lord of glory. [9]But as it is written,

Eye hath not seen, nor ear heard, neither have entered into the heart of man, the things which God hath prepared for them that love him.

[10]But God hath revealed *them* unto us by his Spirit: for the Spirit searcheth all things, yea, the deep things of God. [11]For what man knoweth the things of a man, save the spirit of man which is in him? even so the things of God knoweth no man, but the Spirit of God. [12]Now we have received, not the spirit of the world, but the spirit which is of God; that we might know the things that are freely given to us of God. [13]Which things also we speak, not in the words which man's wisdom teacheth, but which the Holy Ghost teacheth; comparing spiritual things with spiritual. [14]But the natural man receiveth not the things of the Spirit of God: for they are foolishness unto him: neither can he know *them,* because they are spiritually discerned. [15]But he that is spiritual judgeth all things, yet he himself is judged of no man. [16]For

who hath known the mind of the Lord, that he may instruct him?

But we have the mind of Christ.

3 And I, brethren, could not speak unto you as unto spiritual, but as unto carnal, *even* as unto babes in Christ. [2]I have fed you with milk, and not with meat: for hitherto ye were not able *to bear it,* neither yet now are ye able.

[3]For ye are yet carnal: for whereas *there is* among you envying, and strife, and divisions, are ye not carnal, and walk as men? [4]For while one saith, I am of Paul; and another, I *am* of Apollos; are ye not carnal? [5]Who then is Paul, and who *is* Apollos,

but ministers by whom ye believed, even as the Lord gave to every man? [6]I have planted, Apollos watered; but God gave the increase. [7]So then neither is he that planteth any thing, neither he that watereth; but God that giveth the increase. [8]Now he that planteth and he that watereth are one: and every man shall receive his own reward according to his own labour. [9]For we are labourers together with God: ye are God's husbandry, *ye are* God's building. [10]According to the grace of God which is given unto me, as a wise masterbuilder, I have laid the foundation, and another buildeth thereon. But let every man take heed how he buildeth thereupon. [11]For other foundation can no man lay than that is laid, which is Jesus Christ. [12]Now if any man build upon this foundation gold, silver, precious stones, wood, hay, stubble; [13]Every man's work shall be made manifest: for the day shall declare it, because it shall be revealed by fire; and the fire shall try every man's work of what sort it is. [14]If any man's work abide which he hath built thereupon, he shall receive a reward. [15]If any man's work shall be burned, he shall suffer loss: but he himself shall be saved; yet so as by fire. [16]Know ye not that ye are the temple of God, and *that* the Spirit of God dwelleth in you? [17]If any man defile the temple of God, him shall God destroy; for the temple of God is holy, which *temple* ye are.

[18]Let no man deceive himself. If any man among you seemeth to be wise in this world, let him become a fool, that he may be wise. [19]For the wisdom of this world is foolishness with God. For it is written, He taketh the wise in their own craftiness. [20]And again, The Lord knoweth the thoughts of the wise, that they are vain. [21]Therefore let no man glory in men. For all things are yours; [22]Whether Paul, or Apollos, or Cephas, or the world, or life, or death, or things present, or things to come; all are yours; [23]And ye are Christ's; and Christ *is* God's.

4 Let a man so account of us, as of the ministers of Christ, and stewards of the mysteries of God. [2]Moreover it is required in stewards, that a man be found faithful. [3]But with me it is a very small thing that I should be judged of you, or of man's judgment: yea, I judge not mine own self. ⁴For I know nothing by myself; yet am I not hereby justified: but he that judgeth me is the Lord. ⁵Therefore judge nothing before the time, until the Lord come, who both will bring to light the hidden things of darkness, and will make manifest the counsels of the hearts: and then shall every man have praise of God. ⁶And these things, brethren, I have in a figure transferred to myself and *to* Apollos for your sakes; that ye might learn in us not to think *of men* above that which is written, that no one of you be puffed up for one against another. ⁷For who maketh thee to differ *from another?* and what hast thou that thou didst not receive? now if thou didst receive *it,* why dost thou glory, as if thou hadst not received *it?* ⁸Now ye are full, now ye are rich, ye have reigned as kings without us: and I would to God ye did reign, that we also might reign with you. ⁹For I think that God hath set forth us the apostles last, as it were appointed to death: for we are made a spectacle unto the world, and to angels, and to men. ¹⁰We *are* fools for Christ's sake, but ye *are* wise in Christ; we *are* weak, but ye *are* strong; ye *are* honourable, but we *are* despised. ¹¹Even unto this present hour we both hunger, and thirst, and are naked, and are buffeted, and have no certain dwellingplace; ¹²And labour, working with our own hands: being reviled, we bless; being persecuted, we suffer it: ¹³Being defamed, we intreat: we are made as the filth of the world, *and are* the offscouring of all things unto this day. ¹⁴I write not these things to shame you, but as my beloved sons I warn *you.* ¹⁵For though ye have ten thousand instructors in Christ, yet *have ye* not many fathers: for in Christ Jesus I have begotten you through the gospel. ¹⁶Wherefore I beseech you, be ye followers of me. ¹⁷For this cause have I sent unto you Timotheus, who is my beloved son, and faithful in the Lord, who shall bring you into remembrance of my ways which be in Christ, as I teach every where in every church. ¹⁸Now some are puffed up, as though I would not come to you. ¹⁹But I will come to you shortly, if the Lord will, and will know, not the speech of them which are puffed up, but the power. ²⁰For the kingdom of God *is* not in word, but in power. ²¹What will ye? shall I come unto you with a rod, or in love, and *in* the spirit of meekness?

5 It is reported commonly *that there is* fornication among you, and such fornication as is not so much as named among the Gentiles, that one should have his father's wife. ²And ye are puffed up, and have not rather mourned, that he that hath done this deed might be taken away from among you. ³For I verily, as absent in body, but present in spirit, have judged already, as though I were present, *concerning* him that hath so done this deed, ⁴In the name of our Lord Jesus Christ, when ye are gathered together, and my spirit, with the power of our Lord Jesus Christ, ⁵To deliver such an one unto Satan for the destruction of the flesh, that the spirit may be saved in the day of the Lord Jesus. ⁶Your glorying *is* not good. Know ye not that a little leaven leaveneth the whole lump? ⁷Purge out therefore the old leaven, that ye may be a new lump, as ye are unleavened. For even Christ our passover is sacrificed for us: ⁸Therefore let us keep the feast, not with old leaven, neither with the leaven of malice and wickedness; but with the unleavened *bread* of sincerity and truth. ⁹I wrote unto you in an epistle not to company with fornicators: ¹⁰Yet not altogether with the fornicators of this world, or with the covetous, or extortioners, or with idolaters; for then must ye needs go out of the world. ¹¹But now I have written unto you not to keep company, if any man that is called a brother be a fornicator, or covetous, or an idolater, or a railer, or a drunkard, or an extortioner; with such an one no not to eat. ¹²For what have I to do to judge them also that are without? do not ye judge them that are within? ¹³But them that are without God judgeth. Therefore put away from among yourselves that wicked person.

6 Dare any of you, having a matter against another, go to law before the unjust, and not before the saints? ²Do ye not know that the saints shall judge the world? and if the world shall be judged by you, are ye unworthy to judge the smallest matters? ³Know ye not that we shall judge angels? how much more things that pertain to this life? ⁴If then ye have judgments of things pertaining to this life, set them to judge who are least esteemed in the church. ⁵I speak to your shame. Is it so, that there is not a wise man among you? no, not one that shall be able to judge between his brethren? ⁶But brother goeth to law with brother, and that before the unbelievers. ⁷Now therefore there is utterly a fault among you, because ye go to law one with another. Why do ye not rather take wrong? why do ye not rather *suffer yourselves to* be defrauded? ⁸Nay, ye do wrong, and defraud, and that *your* brethren. ⁹Know ye not that the unrighteous shall not inherit the kingdom of God? Be not deceived: neither fornicators, nor idolaters, nor adulterers, nor effeminate, nor abusers of themselves with mankind, ¹⁰Nor thieves, nor covetous, nor drunkards, nor revilers, nor extortioners, shall inherit the kingdom of God. ¹¹And such were some of you: but ye are washed, but ye are sanctified, but ye are justified in the name of the Lord Jesus, and by the Spirit of our God.

¹²All things are lawful unto me, but all things are not expedient: all things are lawful for me, but I will not be brought under the power of any. ¹³Meats for the belly, and the belly for meats: but God shall destroy both it and them. Now the body *is* not for fornication, but for the Lord; and the Lord for the body. ¹⁴And God hath both raised up the Lord, and will also raise up us by his own power. ¹⁵Know ye not that your bodies are the members of Christ? shall I then take the members of Christ, and make *them* the members of an harlot? God forbid. ¹⁶What? know ye not that he which is joined to an harlot is one body? for two, saith he, shall be one flesh. ¹⁷But he that is joined unto the Lord is one spirit. ¹⁸Flee fornication. Every sin that a man doeth is without the body; but he that committeth fornication sinneth against his own body. ¹⁹What? know ye not that your body is the temple of the Holy Ghost *which is* in you, which ye have of God, and ye are not your own? ²⁰For ye are bought with a price: therefore glorify God in your body, and in your spirit, which are God's.

7 Now concerning the things whereof ye wrote unto me: *It is* good for a man not to touch a woman. ²Nevertheless, *to avoid* fornication, let every man have his own wife, and let every woman have her own husband. ³Let the husband render unto the wife due benevolence: and likewise also the wife unto the husband. ⁴The wife hath not power of her own body, but the husband: and likewise also the husband hath not power of his own body, but the wife. ⁵Defraud ye not one the other, except *it be* with consent for a time, that ye may give yourselves to fasting and prayer; and come together again, that Satan tempt you not for your incontinency. ⁶But I speak this by permission, *and* not of commandment. ⁷For I would that all men were even as I myself. But every man hath his proper gift of God, one after this manner, and another after that.

⁸I say therefore to the unmarried and widows, It is good for them if they abide even as I. ⁹But if they cannot contain, let them marry: for it is better to marry than to burn. ¹⁰And unto the married I command, *yet* not I, but the Lord, Let not the wife depart from *her* husband: ¹¹But and if she depart, let her remain unmarried, or be reconciled to *her* husband: and let not the husband put away *his* wife. ¹²But to the rest speak I, not the Lord: If any brother hath a wife that believeth not, and she be pleased to dwell with him, let him not put her away. ¹³And the woman which hath an husband that believeth not, and if he be pleased to dwell with her, let her not leave him. ¹⁴For the unbelieving husband is sanctified by the wife, and the unbelieving wife is sanctified by the husband: else were your children unclean; but now are they holy. ¹⁵But if the unbelieving depart, let him depart. A brother or a sister is not under bondage in such *cases:* but God hath called us to peace. ¹⁶For what knowest thou, O wife, whether thou shalt save *thy* husband? or how knowest thou, O man, whether thou shalt save *thy* wife? ¹⁷But as God hath distributed to every man, as the Lord hath called every one, so let him walk. And so ordain I in all churches. ¹⁸Is any man called being circumcised? let him not become uncircumcised. Is any called in uncircumcision? let

him not be circumcised. ¹⁹Circumcision is nothing, and uncircumcision is nothing, but the keeping of the commandments of God. ²⁰Let every man abide in the same calling wherein he was called. ²¹Art thou called *being* a servant? care not for it: but if thou mayest be made free, use *it* rather. ²²For he that is called in the Lord, *being* a servant, is the Lord's freeman: likewise also he that is called, *being* free, is Christ's servant. ²³Ye are bought with a price; be not ye the servants of men. ²⁴Brethren, let every man, wherein he is called, therein abide with God.

²⁵Now concerning virgins I have no commandment of the Lord: yet I give my judgment, as one that hath obtained mercy of the Lord to be faithful. ²⁶I suppose therefore that this is good for the present distress, *I say,* that *it is* good for a man so to be. ²⁷Art thou bound unto a wife? seek not to be loosed. Art thou loosed from a wife? seek not a wife. ²⁸But and if thou marry, thou hast not sinned; and if a virgin marry, she hath not sinned. Nevertheless such shall have trouble in the flesh: but I spare you. ²⁹But this I say, brethren, the time *is* short: it remaineth, that both they that have wives be as though they had none; ³⁰And they that weep, as though they wept not; and they that rejoice, as though they rejoiced not; and they that buy, as though they possessed not; ³¹And they that use this world, as not abusing *it:* for the fashion of this world passeth away. ³²But I would have you without carefulness. He that is unmarried careth for the things that belong to the Lord, how he may please the Lord: ³³But he that is married careth for the things that are of the world, how he may please *his* wife. ³⁴There is difference *also* between a wife and a virgin. The unmarried woman careth for the things of the Lord, that she may be holy both in body and in spirit: but she that is married careth for the things of the world, how she may please *her* husband. ³⁵And this I speak for your own profit; not that I may cast a snare upon you, but for that which is comely, and that ye may attend upon the Lord without distraction. ³⁶But if any man think that he behaveth himself uncomely toward his vir-

gin, if she pass the flower of *her* age, and need so require, let him do what he will, he sinneth not: let them marry. ³⁷Nevertheless he that standeth stedfast in his heart, having no necessity, but hath power over his own will, and hath so decreed in his heart that he will keep his virgin, doeth well. ³⁸So then he that giveth *her* in marriage doeth well; but he that giveth *her* not in marriage doeth better. ³⁹The wife is bound by the law as long as her husband liveth; but if her husband be dead, she is at liberty to be married to whom she will; only in the Lord. ⁴⁰But she is happier if she so abide, after my judgment: and I think also that I have the Spirit of God.

8 Now as touching things offered unto idols, we know that we all have knowledge. Knowledge puffeth up, but charity edifieth. ²And if any man think that he knoweth any thing, he knoweth nothing yet as he ought to know. ³But if any man love God, the same is known of him. ⁴As concerning therefore the eating of those things that are offered in sacrifice unto idols, we know that an idol *is* nothing in the world, and that *there is* none other God but one. ⁵For though there be that are called gods, whether in heaven or in earth, (as there be gods many, and lords many,) ⁶But to us *there is but* one God, the Father, of whom *are* all things, and we in him; and one Lord Jesus Christ, by whom *are* all things, and we by him. ⁷Howbeit *there is* not in every man that knowledge: for some with conscience of the idol unto this hour eat *it* as a thing offered unto an idol; and their conscience being weak is defiled. ⁸But meat commendeth us not to God: for neither, if we eat, are we the better; neither, if we eat not, are we the worse. ⁹But take heed lest by any means this liberty of yours become a stumblingblock to them that are weak. ¹⁰For if any man see thee which hast knowledge sit at meat in the idol's temple, shall not the conscience of him which is weak be emboldened to eat those things which are offered to idols; ¹¹And through thy knowledge shall the weak brother perish, for whom Christ died? ¹²But when ye sin so against the brethren, and wound their weak conscience, ye sin against Christ. ¹³Wherefore, if meat make my brother to offend, I will eat no flesh while the world standeth, lest I make my brother to offend.

9 Am I not an apostle? am I not free? have I not seen Jesus Christ our Lord? are not ye my work in the Lord? ²If I be not an apostle unto others, yet doubtless I am to you: for the seal of mine apostleship are ye in the Lord. ³Mine answer to them that do examine me is this, ⁴Have we not power to eat and to drink? ⁵Have we not power to lead about a sister, a wife, as well as other apostles, and *as* the brethren of the Lord, and Cephas? ⁶Or I only and Barnabas, have not we power to forbear working? ⁷Who goeth a warfare any time at his own charges? who planteth a vineyard, and eateth not of the fruit thereof? or who feedeth a flock, and eateth not of the milk of the flock? ⁸Say I these things as a man? or saith not the law the same also? ⁹For it is written in the law of Moses, Thou shalt not muzzle the mouth of the ox that treadeth out the corn. Doth God take care for oxen? ¹⁰Or saith he *it* altogether for our sakes? For our sakes, no doubt, *this* is written: that he that ploweth should plow in hope; and that he that thresheth in hope should be partaker of his hope. ¹¹If we have sown unto you spiritual things, *is it* a great thing if we shall reap your carnal things? ¹²If others be partakers of *this* power over you, *are* not we rather? Nevertheless we have not used this power; but suffer all things, lest we should hinder the gospel of Christ. ¹³Do ye not know that they which minister about holy things live *of the things* of the temple? and they which wait at the altar are partakers with the altar? ¹⁴Even so hath the Lord ordained that they which preach the gospel should live of the gospel. ¹⁵But I have used none of these things: neither have I written these things, that it should be so done unto me: for *it were* better for me to die, than that any man should make my glorying void. ¹⁶For though I preach the gospel, I have nothing to glory of: for necessity is laid upon me; yea, woe is unto me, if I preach not the gospel! ¹⁷For if I do this thing willingly, I have a reward: but if against my will, a dispensation *of the gospel* is committed unto me. ¹⁸What is my reward then? *Verily* that, when I preach the gospel, I may make the gospel of Christ without charge, that I abuse not my power in the gospel. ¹⁹For though I be free from all *men,* yet have I made myself servant unto all, that I might gain the more. ²⁰And unto the Jews I became as a Jew, that I might gain the Jews; to them that are under the law, as under the law, that I might gain them that are under the law; ²¹To them that are without law, as without law, (being not without law to God, but under the law to Christ,) that I might gain them that are without law. ²²To the weak became I as weak, that I might gain the weak: I am made all things to all *men,* that I might by all means save some. ²³And this I do for the gospel's sake, that I might be partaker thereof with *you.* ²⁴Know ye not that they which run in a race run all, but one receiveth the prize? So run, that ye may obtain. ²⁵And every man that striveth for the mastery is temperate in all things. Now they *do it* to obtain a corruptible crown; but we an incorruptible. ²⁶I therefore so run, not as uncertainly; so fight I, not as one that beateth the air: ²⁷But I keep under my body, and bring *it* into subjection: lest that by any means, when I have preached to others, I myself should be a castaway.

10 Moreover, brethren, I would not that ye should be ignorant, how that all our fathers were under the cloud, and all passed through the sea; ²And were all baptized unto Moses in the cloud and in the sea; ³And did all eat the same spiritual meat; ⁴And did all drink the same spiritual drink: for they drank of that spiritual Rock that followed them: and that Rock was Christ. ⁵But with many of them God was not well pleased: for they were overthrown in the wilderness. ⁶Now these things were our examples, to the intent we should not lust after evil things, as they also lusted. ⁷Neither be ye idolaters, as *were* some of them; as it is written, The people sat down to eat and drink, and rose up to play. ⁸Neither let us commit fornication, as some of them committed, and fell in one day three and twenty thousand. ⁹Neither let us tempt Christ, as some of them also tempted, and were destroyed of serpents. ¹⁰Neither murmur ye, as some of them also murmured, and were destroyed of the destroyer. ¹¹Now all these things happened unto them for ensamples: and they are written for our admonition, upon whom the ends of the world are come. [12]Wherefore let him that thinketh he standeth take heed lest he fall. [13]There hath no temptation taken you but such as is common to man: but God is faithful, who will not suffer you to be tempted above that ye are able; but will with the temptation also make a way to escape, that ye may be able to bear it.

[14]Wherefore, my dearly beloved, flee from idolatry. [15]I speak as to wise men; judge ye what I say. [16]The cup of blessing which we bless, is it not the communion of the blood of Christ? The bread which we break, is it not the communion of the body of Christ? [17]For we being many are one bread, and one body: for we are all partakers of that one bread. [18]Behold Israel after the flesh: are not they which eat of the sacrifices partakers of the altar? [19]What say I then? that the idol is any thing, or that which is offered in sacrifice to idols is any thing? [20]But I say, that the things which the Gentiles sacrifice, they sacrifice to devils, and not to God: and I would not that ye should have fellowship with devils. [21]Ye cannot drink the cup of the Lord, and the cup of devils: ye cannot be partakers of the Lord's table, and of the table of devils. [22]Do we provoke the Lord to jealousy? are we stronger than he? [23]All things are lawful for me, but all things are not expedient: all things are lawful for me, but all things edify not. [24]Let no man seek his own, but every man another's wealth. [25]Whatsoever is sold in the shambles, that eat, asking no question for conscience sake: [26]For the earth is the Lord's, and the fulness thereof. [27]If any of them that believe not bid you to a feast, and ye be disposed to go; whatsoever is set before you, eat, asking no question for conscience sake. [28]But if any man say unto you, This is offered in sacrifice unto idols, eat not for his sake that shewed it, and for conscience sake: for the earth is the Lord's, and the fulness thereof: [29]Conscience, I say, not thine own, but of the other: for why is my liberty judged of another man's conscience? [30]For if I by grace be a partaker, why am I evil spoken of for that for which I give thanks? [31]Whether therefore ye eat, or drink, or whatsoever ye do, do all to the glory of God. [32]Give none offence, neither to the Jews, nor to the Gentiles, nor to the church of God: [33]Even as I please all men in all things, not seeking mine own profit, but the profit of many, that they may be saved.

11 Be ye followers of me, even as I also am of Christ.

[2]Now I praise you, brethren, that ye remember me in all things, and keep the ordinances, as I delivered them to you. [3]But I would have you know, that the head of every man is Christ; and the head of the woman is the man; and the head of Christ is God. [4]Every man praying or prophesying, having his head covered, dishonoureth his head. [5]But every woman that prayeth or prophesieth with her head uncovered dishonoureth her head: for that is even all one as if she were shaven. [6]For if the woman be not covered, let her also be shorn: but if it be a shame for a woman to be shorn or shaven, let her be covered. [7]For a man indeed ought not to cover his head, forasmuch as he is the image and glory of God: but the woman is the glory of the man. [8]For the man is not of the woman; but the woman of the man. [9]Neither was the man created for the woman; but the woman for the man. [10]For this cause ought the woman to have power on her head because of the angels. [11]Nevertheless neither is the man without the woman, neither the woman without the man, in the Lord. [12]For as the woman is of the man, even so is the man also by the woman; but all things of God. [13]Judge in yourselves: is it comely that a woman pray unto God uncovered? [14]Doth not even nature itself teach you, that, if a man have long hair, it is a shame unto him? [15]But if a woman have long hair, it is a glory to her: for her hair is given her for a covering. [16]But if any man seem to be contentious, we have no such custom, neither the churches of God.

[17]Now in this that I declare unto you I praise you not, that ye come together not for the better, but for the worse. [18]For first of all, when ye come together in the church, I hear that there be divisions among you; and I partly believe it. [19]For there must be also heresies among you, that they which are approved may be made mani-

fest among you. ²⁰When ye come together therefore into one place, *this* is not to eat the Lord's supper. ²¹For in eating every one taketh before *other* his own supper: and one is hungry, and another is drunken. ²²What? have ye not houses to eat and to drink in? or despise ye the church of God, and shame them that have not? What shall I say to you? shall I praise you in this? I praise *you* not. ²³For I have received of the Lord that which also I delivered unto you, That the Lord Jesus the *same* night in which he was betrayed took bread: ²⁴And when he had given thanks, he brake *it,* and said, Take, eat: this is my body, which is broken for you: this do in remembrance of me. ²⁵After the same manner also *he took* the cup, when he had supped, saying, This cup is the new testament in my blood: this do ye, as oft as ye drink *it,* in remembrance of me. ²⁶For as often as ye eat this bread, and drink *this* cup, ye do shew the Lord's death till he come. ²⁷Wherefore whosoever shall eat this bread, and drink this cup of the Lord, unworthily, shall be guilty of the body and blood of the Lord. ²⁸But let a man examine himself, and so let him eat of *that* bread, and drink of *that* cup. ²⁹For he that eateth and drinketh unworthily, eateth and drinketh damnation to himself, not discerning the Lord's body. ³⁰For this cause many *are* weak and sickly among you, and many sleep. ³¹For if we would judge ourselves, we should not be judged. ³²But when we are judged, we are chastened of the Lord, that we should not be condemned with the world. ³³Wherefore, my brethren, when ye come together to eat, tarry one for another. ³⁴And if any man hunger, let him eat at home; that ye come not together unto condemnation. And the rest will I set in order when I come.

12 Now concerning spiritual *gifts,* brethren, I would not have you ignorant. ²Ye know that ye were Gentiles, carried away unto these dumb idols, even as ye were led. ³Wherefore I give you to understand, that no man speaking by the Spirit of God calleth Jesus accursed: and *that* no man can say that Jesus is the Lord, but by the Holy Ghost. ⁴Now there are diversities of gifts, but the same Spirit. ⁵And there are differences of administrations, but the same Lord. ⁶And there are diversities of operations, but it is the same God which worketh all in all. ⁷But the manifestation of the Spirit is given to every man to profit withal. ⁸For to one is given by the Spirit the word of wisdom; to another the word of knowledge by the same Spirit; ⁹To another faith by the same Spirit; to another the gifts of healing by the same Spirit; ¹⁰To another the working of miracles; to another prophecy; to another discerning of spirits; to another *divers* kinds of tongues; to another the interpretation of tongues: ¹¹But all these worketh that one and the selfsame Spirit, dividing to every man severally as he will. ¹²For as the body is one, and hath many members, and all the members of that one body, being many, are one body: so also *is* Christ. ¹³For by one Spirit are we all baptized into one body, whether *we be* Jews or Gentiles, whether *we be* bond or free; and have been all made to drink into one Spirit. ¹⁴For the body is not one member, but many. ¹⁵If the foot shall say, Because I am not the hand, I am not of the body; is it therefore not of the body? ¹⁶And if the ear shall say, Because I am not the eye, I am not of the body; is it therefore not of the body? ¹⁷If the whole body *were* an eye, where *were* the hearing? If the whole *were* hearing, where *were* the smelling? ¹⁸But now hath God set the members every one of them in the body, as it hath pleased him. ¹⁹And if they were all one member, where *were* the body? ²⁰But now *are they* many members, yet but one body. ²¹And the eye cannot say unto the hand, I have no need of thee: nor again the head to the feet, I have no need of you. ²²Nay, much more those members of the body, which seem to be more feeble, are necessary: ²³And those *members* of the body, which we think to be less honourable, upon these we bestow more abundant honour; and our uncomely *parts* have more abundant comeliness. ²⁴For our comely *parts* have no need: but God hath tempered the body together, having given more abundant honour to that *part* which lacked: ²⁵That there should be no schism in the body; but *that* the members should have the same care one for another. ²⁶And whether one member suffer, all the members suffer with it; or one member be honoured, all the members rejoice with it. 27Now ye are the body of Christ, and members in particular. 28And God hath set some in the church, first apostles, secondarily prophets, thirdly teachers, after that miracles, then gifts of healings, helps, governments, diversities of tongues. 29*Are* all apostles? *are* all prophets? *are* all teachers? *are* all workers of miracles? 30Have all the gifts of healing? do all speak with tongues? do all interpret? 31But covet earnestly the best gifts: and yet shew I unto you a more excellent way.

13 Though I speak with the tongues of men and of angels, and have not charity, I am become *as* sounding brass, or a tinkling cymbal. 2And though I have *the gift of* prophecy, and understand all mysteries, and all knowledge; and though I have all faith, so that I could remove mountains, and have not charity, I am nothing. 3And though I bestow all my goods to feed *the poor,* and though I give my body to be burned, and have not charity, it profiteth me nothing. 4Charity suffereth long, *and* is kind; charity envieth not; charity vaunteth not itself, is not puffed up, 5Doth not behave itself unseemly, seeketh not her own, is not easily provoked, thinketh no evil; 6Rejoiceth not in iniquity, but rejoiceth in the truth; 7Beareth all things, believeth all things, hopeth all things, endureth all things. 8Charity never faileth: but whether *there be* prophecies, they shall fail; whether *there be* tongues, they shall cease; whether *there be* knowledge, it shall vanish away. 9For we know in part, and we prophesy in part. 10But when that which is perfect is come, then that which is in part shall be done away. 11When I was a child, I spake as a child, I understood as a child, I thought as a child: but when I became a man, I put away childish things. 12For now we see through a glass, darkly; but then face to face: now I know in part; but then shall I know even as also I am known. 13And now abideth faith, hope, charity, these three; but the greatest of these *is* charity.

14 Follow after charity, and desire spiritual *gifts,* but rather that ye may prophesy. 2For he that speaketh in an *unknown* tongue speaketh not unto men, but unto God: for no man understandeth *him;*

howbeit in the spirit he speaketh mysteries. 3But he that prophesieth speaketh unto men *to* edification, and exhortation, and comfort. 4He that speaketh in an *unknown* tongue edifieth himself; but he that prophesieth edifieth the church. 5I would that ye all spake with tongues, but rather that ye prophesied: for greater *is* he that prophesieth than he that speaketh with tongues, except he interpret, that the church may receive edifying. 6Now, brethren, if I come unto you speaking with tongues, what shall I profit you, except I shall speak to you either by revelation, or by knowledge, or by prophesying, or by doctrine? 7And even things without life giving sound, whether pipe or harp, except they give a distinction in the sounds, how shall it be known what is piped or harped? 8For if the trumpet give an uncertain sound, who shall prepare himself to the battle? 9So likewise ye, except ye utter by the tongue words easy to be understood, how shall it be known what is spoken? for ye shall speak into the air. 10There are, it may be, so many kinds of voices in the world, and none of them *is* without signification. 11Therefore if I know not the meaning of the voice, I shall be unto him that speaketh a barbarian, and he that speaketh *shall be* a barbarian unto me. 12Even so ye, forasmuch as ye are zealous of spiritual *gifts,* seek that ye may excel to the edifying of the church. 13Wherefore let him that speaketh in an *unknown* tongue pray that he may interpret. 14For if I pray in an *unknown* tongue, my spirit prayeth, but my understanding is unfruitful. 15What is it then? I will pray with the spirit, and I will pray with the understanding also: I will sing with the spirit, and I will sing with the understanding also. 16Else when thou shalt bless with the spirit, how shall he that occupieth the room of the unlearned say Amen at thy giving of thanks, seeing he understandeth not what thou sayest? 17For thou verily givest thanks well, but the other is not edified. 18I thank my God, I speak with tongues more than ye all: 19Yet in the church I had rather speak five words with my understanding, that *by my voice* I might teach others also, than ten thousand words in an *unknown* tongue. 20Brethren, be not children in understanding: howbeit in malice be ye children, but in understanding be men. ²¹In the law it is written,

With *men of* other tongues and other lips will I speak unto this people; and yet for all that will they not hear me, saith the Lord.

²²Wherefore tongues are for a sign, not to them that believe, but to them that believe not: but prophesying *serveth* not for them that believe not, but for them which believe. ²³If therefore the whole church be come together into one place, and all speak with tongues, and there come in *those that are* unlearned, or unbelievers, will they not say that ye are mad? ²⁴But if all prophesy, and there come in one that believeth not, or *one* unlearned, he is convinced of all, he is judged of all: ²⁵And thus are the secrets of his heart made manifest; and so falling down on *his* face he will worship God, and report that God is in you of a truth. ²⁶How is it then, brethren? when ye come together, every one of you hath a psalm, hath a doctrine, hath a tongue, hath a revelation, hath an interpretation. Let all things be done unto edifying. ²⁷If any man speak in an *unknown* tongue, *let it be* by two, or at the most *by* three, and *that* by course; and let one interpret. ²⁸But if there be no interpreter, let him keep silence in the church; and let him speak to himself, and to God. ²⁹Let the prophets speak two or three, and let the other judge. ³⁰If *any thing* be revealed to another that sitteth by, let the first hold his peace. ³¹For ye may all prophesy one by one, that all may learn, and all may be comforted. ³²And the spirits of the prophets are subject to the prophets. ³³For God is not *the author* of confusion, but of peace, as in all churches of the saints. ³⁴Let your women keep silence in the churches: for it is not permitted unto them to speak; but *they are commanded* to be under obedience, as also saith the law. ³⁵And if they will learn any thing, let them ask their husbands at home: for it is a shame for women to speak in the church. ³⁶What? came the word of God out from you? or came it unto you only? ³⁷If any man think himself to be a prophet, or spiritual, let him acknowledge that the things that I write unto you are the commandments of the Lord. ³⁸But if any man

be ignorant, let him be ignorant. ³⁹Wherefore, brethren, covet to prophesy, and forbid not to speak with tongues. ⁴⁰Let all things be done decently and in order.

15 Moreover, brethren, I declare unto you the gospel which I preached unto you, which also ye have received, and wherein ye stand; ²By which also ye are saved, if ye keep in memory what I preached unto you, unless ye have believed in vain. ³For I delivered unto you first of all that which I also received, how that Christ died for our sins according to the scriptures; ⁴And that he was buried, and that he rose again the third day according to the scriptures: ⁵And that he was seen of Cephas, then of the twelve: ⁶After that, he was seen of above five hundred brethren at once; of whom the greater part remain unto this present, but some are fallen asleep. ⁷After that, he was seen of James; then of all the apostles. ⁸And last of all he was seen of me also, as of one born out of due time. ⁹For I am the least of the apostles, that am not meet to be called an apostle, because I persecuted the church of God. ¹⁰But by the grace of God I am what I am: and his grace *which was bestowed* upon me was not in vain; but I laboured more abundantly than they all: yet not I, but the grace of God which was with me. ¹¹Therefore whether *it were* I or they, so we preach, and so ye believed. ¹²Now if Christ be preached that he rose from the dead, how say some among you that there is no resurrection of the dead? ¹³But if there be no resurrection of the dead, then is Christ not risen: ¹⁴And if Christ be not risen, then *is* our preaching vain, and your faith *is* also vain. ¹⁵Yea, and we are found false witnesses of God; because we have testified of God that he raised up Christ: whom he raised not up, if so be that the dead rise not. ¹⁶For if the dead rise not, then is not Christ raised: ¹⁷And if Christ be not raised, your faith *is* vain; ye are yet in your sins. ¹⁸Then they also which are fallen asleep in Christ are perished. ¹⁹If in this life only we have hope in Christ, we are of all men most miserable. ²⁰But now is Christ risen from the dead, *and* become the firstfruits of them that slept. ²¹For since by man *came* death, by man *came* also the resurrection of the dead. [22]For as in Adam all die, even so in Christ shall all be made alive. [23]But every man in his own order: Christ the firstfruits; afterward they that are Christ's at his coming. [24]Then *cometh* the end, when he shall have delivered up the kingdom to God, even the Father; when he shall have put down all rule and all authority and power. [25]For he must reign, till he hath put all enemies under his feet. [26]The last enemy *that* shall be destroyed *is* death. [27]For he hath put all things under his feet. But when he saith, all things are put under *him, it is* manifest that he is excepted, which did put all things under him. [28]And when all things shall be subdued unto him, then shall the Son also himself be subject unto him that put all things under him, that God may be all in all. [29]Else what shall they do which are baptized for the dead, if the dead rise not at all? why are they then baptized for the dead? [30]And why stand we in jeopardy every hour? [31]I protest by your rejoicing which I have in Christ Jesus our Lord, I die daily. [32]If after the manner of men I have fought with beasts at Ephesus, what advantageth it me, if the dead rise not?

let us eat and drink; for to morrow we die.

[33]Be not deceived: evil communications corrupt good manners. [34]Awake to righteousness, and sin not; for some have not the knowledge of God: I speak *this* to your shame.

[35]But some *man* will say, How are the dead raised up? and with what body do they come? [36]*Thou fool,* that which thou sowest is not quickened, except it die: [37]And that which thou sowest, thou sowest not that body that shall be, but bare grain, it may chance of wheat, or of some other *grain:* [38]But God giveth it a body as it hath pleased him, and to every seed his own body. [39]All flesh *is* not the same flesh: but *there is* one *kind of* flesh of men, another flesh of beasts, another of fishes, *and* another of birds. [40]*There are* also celestial bodies, and bodies terrestrial: but the glory of the celestial *is* one, and the *glory* of the terrestrial *is* another. [41]*There is* one glory of the sun, and another glory of the moon, and another glory of the stars: for *one* star dif-

fereth from *another* star in glory. [42]So also *is* the resurrection of the dead. It is sown in corruption; it is raised in incorruption: [43]It is sown in dishonour; it is raised in glory: it is sown in weakness; it is raised in power: [44]It is sown a natural body; it is raised a spiritual body. There is a natural body, and there is a spiritual body. [45]And so it is written, The first man Adam was made a living soul; the last Adam *was made* a quickening spirit. [46]Howbeit that *was* not first which is spiritual, but that which is natural; and afterward that which is spiritual. [47]The first man *is* of the earth, earthy: the second man *is* the Lord from heaven. [48]As *is* the earthy, such *are* they also that are earthy: and as *is* the heavenly, such *are* they also that are heavenly. [49]And as we have borne the image of the earthy, we shall also bear the image of the heavenly. [50]Now this I say, brethren, that flesh and blood cannot inherit the kingdom of God; neither doth corruption inherit incorruption. [51]Behold, I shew you a mystery; We shall not all sleep, but we shall all be changed, [52]In a moment, in the twinkling of an eye, at the last trump: for the trumpet shall sound, and the dead shall be raised incorruptible, and we shall be changed. [53]For this corruptible must put on incorruption, and this mortal *must* put on immortality. [54]So when this corruptible shall have put on incorruption, and this mortal shall have put on immortality, then shall be brought to pass the saying that is written, Death is swallowed up in victory.

[55]O death, where *is* thy sting? O grave, where *is* thy victory?

[56]The sting of death *is* sin; and the strength of sin *is* the law. [57]But thanks *be* to God, which giveth us the victory through our Lord Jesus Christ. [58]Therefore, my beloved brethren, be ye stedfast, unmovable, always abounding in the work of the Lord, forasmuch as ye know that your labour is not in vain in the Lord.

16 Now concerning the collection for the saints, as I have given order to the churches of Galatia, even so do ye. [2]Upon the first *day* of the week let every one of you lay by him in store, as God hath prospered him, that there be no gatherings when I come. [3]And when I come, whomsoever ye shall approve by *your* letters, them will I send to bring your liberality unto Jerusalem. [4]And if it be meet that I go also, they shall go with me.

[5]Now I will come unto you, when I shall pass through Macedonia: for I do pass through Macedonia. [6]And it may be that I will abide, yea, and winter with you, that ye may bring me on my journey whithersoever I go. [7]For I will not see you now by the way; but I trust to tarry *a* while with you, if the Lord permit. [8]But I will tarry at Ephesus until Pentecost. [9]For a great door and effectual is opened unto me, and *there are* many adversaries. [10]Now if Timotheus come, see that he may be with you without fear: for he worketh the work of the Lord, as I also *do*. [11]Let no man therefore despise him: but conduct him forth in peace, that he may come unto me: for I look for him with the brethren. [12]As touching *our* brother Apollos, I greatly desired him to come unto you with the brethren: but his will was not at all to come at this time; but he will come when

he shall have convenient time. [13]Watch ye, stand fast in the faith, quit you like men, be strong. [14]Let all your things be done with charity. [15]I beseech you, brethren, (ye know the house of Stephanas, that it is the firstfruits of Achaia, and *that* they have addicted themselves to the ministry of the saints,) [16]That ye submit yourselves unto such, and to every one that helpeth with *us*, and laboureth. [17]I am glad of the coming of Stephanas and Fortunatus and Achaicus: for that which was lacking on your part they have supplied. [18]For they have refreshed my spirit and yours: therefore acknowledge ye them that are such.

[19]The churches of Asia salute you. Aquila and Priscilla salute you much in the Lord, with the church that is in their house. [20]All the brethren greet you. Greet ye one another with an holy kiss. [21]The salutation of *me* Paul with mine own hand. [22]If any man love not the Lord Jesus Christ, let him be Anathema Maranatha. [23]The grace of our Lord Jesus Christ *be* with you. [24]My love *be* with you all in Christ Jesus. Amen.

1 Paul, an apostle of Jesus Christ by the will of God, and Timothy *our* brother,

unto the church of God which is at Corinth, with all the saints which are in all Achaia:

[2] Grace be to you and peace from God our Father, and *from* the Lord Jesus Christ.

[3] Blessed *be* God, even the Father of our Lord Jesus Christ, the Father of mercies, and the God of all comfort; [4] Who comforteth us in all our tribulation, that we may be able to comfort them which are in any trouble, by the comfort wherewith we ourselves are comforted of God. [5] For as the sufferings of Christ abound in us, so our consolation also aboundeth by Christ. [6] And whether we be afflicted, *it is* for your consolation and salvation, which is effectual in the enduring of the same sufferings which we also suffer: or whether we be comforted, *it is* for your consolation and salvation. [7] And our hope of you *is* stedfast, knowing, that as ye are partakers of the sufferings, so *shall ye be* also of the consolation.

[8] For we would not, brethren, have you ignorant of our trouble which came to us in Asia, that we were pressed out of measure, above strength, insomuch that we despaired even of life: [9] But we had the sentence of death in ourselves, that we should not trust in ourselves, but in God which raiseth the dead: [10] Who delivered us from so great a death, and doth deliver: in whom we trust that he will yet deliver *us;* [11] Ye also helping together by prayer for us, that for the gift *bestowed* upon us by the means of many persons thanks may be given by many on our behalf.

[12] For our rejoicing is this, the testimony of our conscience, that in simplicity and godly sincerity, not with fleshly wisdom, but by the grace of God, we have had our conversation in the world, and more abundantly to you-ward. [13] For we write none other things unto you, than what ye read or acknowledge; and I trust ye shall acknowledge even to the end; [14] As also ye have acknowledged us in part, that we are your rejoicing, even as ye also *are* ours in the day of the Lord Jesus.

[15] And in this confidence I was minded to come unto you before, that ye might have a second benefit; [16] And to pass by you into Macedonia, and to come again out of Macedonia unto you, and of you to be brought on my way toward Judaea. [17] When I therefore was thus minded, did I use lightness? or the things that I purpose, do I purpose according to the flesh, that with me there should be yea yea, and nay nay? [18] But *as* God *is* true, our word toward you was not yea and nay. [19] For the Son of God, Jesus Christ, who was preached among you by us, *even* by me and Silvanus and Timotheus, was not yea and nay, but in him was yea. [20] For all the promises of God in him *are* yea, and in him Amen, unto the glory of God by us. [21] Now he which stablisheth us with you in Christ, and hath anointed us, *is* God; [22] Who hath also sealed us, and given the earnest of the Spirit in our hearts. [23] Moreover I call God for a record upon my soul, that to spare you I came not as yet unto Corinth. [24] Not for that we have dominion over your faith, but are helpers of your joy: for by faith ye stand.

2 But I determined this with myself, that I would not come again to you in heaviness. [2] For if I make you sorry, who is he then that maketh me glad, but the same which is made sorry by me? [3] And I wrote this same unto you, lest, when I came, I should have sorrow from them of whom I ought to rejoice; having confidence in you all, that my joy is *the joy* of you all. [4] For out of much affliction and anguish of heart I wrote unto you with many tears; not that ye should be grieved, but that ye might know the love which I have more abundantly unto you. [5] But if any have caused grief, he hath not grieved me, but in part: that I may not overcharge you all. [6] Sufficient to such a man is this punishment, which *was inflicted* of many. [7] So that contrariwise ye *ought* rather to forgive *him,* and comfort *him,* lest perhaps such a one should be swallowed up with overmuch sorrow. [8] Wherefore I beseech you that ye would confirm *your* love toward him. ⁹For to this end also did I write, that I might know the proof of you, whether ye be obedient in all things. ¹⁰To whom ye forgive any thing, I *forgive* also: for if I forgave any thing, to whom I forgave *it*, for your sakes *forgave I it* in the person of Christ; ¹¹Lest Satan should get an advantage of us: for we are not ignorant of his devices.

¹²Furthermore, when I came to Troas to *preach* Christ's gospel, and a door was opened unto me of the Lord, ¹³I had no rest in my spirit, because I found not Titus my brother: but taking my leave of them, I went from thence into Macedonia. ¹⁴Now thanks *be* unto God, which always causeth us to triumph in Christ, and maketh manifest the savour of his knowledge by us in every place. ¹⁵For we are unto God a sweet savour of Christ, in them that are saved, and in them that perish: ¹⁶To the one *we are* the savour of death unto death; and to the other the savour of life unto life. And who *is* sufficient for these things? ¹⁷For we are not as many, which corrupt the word of God: but as of sincerity, but as of God, in the sight of God speak we in Christ.

3 Do we begin again to commend ourselves? or need we, as some *others*, epistles of commendation to you, or *letters* of commendation from you? ²Ye are our epistle written in our hearts, known and read of all men: ³*Forasmuch as ye are* manifestly declared to be the epistle of Christ ministered by us, written not with ink, but with the Spirit of the living God; not in tables of stone, but in fleshy tables of the heart.

⁴And such trust have we through Christ to God-ward: ⁵Not that we are sufficient of ourselves to think any thing as of ourselves; but our sufficiency *is* of God; ⁶Who also hath made us able ministers of the new testament; not of the letter, but of the spirit: for the letter killeth, but the spirit giveth life. ⁷But if the ministration of death, written *and* engraven in stones, was glorious, so that the children of Israel could not stedfastly behold the face of Moses for the glory of his countenance; which *glory* was to be done away: ⁸How shall not the ministration of the spirit be rather glorious? ⁹For if the ministration of condemnation

be glory, much more doth the ministration of righteousness exceed in glory. ¹⁰For even that which was made glorious had no glory in this respect, by reason of the glory that excelleth. ¹¹For if that which is done away *was* glorious, much more that which remaineth *is* glorious. ¹²Seeing then that we have such hope, we use great plainness of speech: ¹³And not as Moses, *which* put a vail over his face, that the children of Israel could not stedfastly look to the end of that which is abolished: ¹⁴But their minds were blinded: for until this day remaineth the same vail untaken away in the reading of the old testament; which *vail* is done away in Christ. ¹⁵But even unto this day, when Moses is read, the vail is upon their heart. ¹⁶Nevertheless when it shall turn to the Lord, the vail shall be taken away. ¹⁷Now the Lord is that Spirit: and where the Spirit of the Lord *is*, there *is* liberty. ¹⁸But we all, with open face beholding as in a glass the glory of the Lord, are changed into the same image from glory to glory, *even* as by the Spirit of the Lord.

4 Therefore seeing we have this ministry, as we have received mercy, we faint not; ²But have renounced the hidden things of dishonesty, not walking in craftiness, nor handling the word of God deceitfully; but by manifestation of the truth commending ourselves to every man's conscience in the sight of God. ³But if our gospel be hid, it is hid to them that are lost: ⁴In whom the god of this world hath blinded the minds of them which believe not, lest the light of the glorious gospel of Christ, who is the image of God, should shine unto them. ⁵For we preach not ourselves, but Christ Jesus the Lord; and ourselves your servants for Jesus' sake. ⁶For God, who commanded the light to shine out of darkness, hath shined in our hearts, to *give* the light of the knowledge of the glory of God in the face of Jesus Christ.

⁷But we have this treasure in earthen vessels, that the excellency of the power may be of God, and not of us. ⁸*We are* troubled on every side, yet not distressed; *we are* perplexed, but not in despair; ⁹Persecuted, but not forsaken; cast down, but not destroyed; ¹⁰Always bearing about in the body the dying of the Lord Jesus, that the life also of Jesus might be made manifest in

our body. [11]For we which live are alway delivered unto death for Jesus' sake, that the life also of Jesus might be made manifest in our mortal flesh. [12]So then death worketh in us, but life in you. [13]We having the same spirit of faith, according as it is written, I believed, and therefore have I spoken; we also believe, and therefore speak; [14]Knowing that he which raised up the Lord Jesus shall raise up us also by Jesus, and shall present *us* with you. [15]For all things *are* for your sakes, that the abundant grace might through the thanksgiving of many redound to the glory of God. [16]For which cause we faint not; but though our outward man perish, yet the inward *man* is renewed day by day. [17]For our light affliction, which is but for a moment, worketh for us a far more exceeding *and* eternal weight of glory; [18]While we look not at the things which are seen, but at the things which are not seen: for the things which are seen *are* temporal; but the things which are not seen *are* eternal.

5 For we know that if our earthly house of *this* tabernacle were dissolved, we have a building of God, an house not made with hands, eternal in the heavens. [2]For in this we groan, earnestly desiring to be clothed upon with our house which is from heaven: [3]If so be that being clothed we shall not be found naked. [4]For we that are in *this* tabernacle do groan, being burdened: not for that we would be unclothed, but clothed upon, that mortality might be swallowed up of life. [5]Now he that hath wrought us for the selfsame thing *is* God, who also hath given unto us the earnest of the Spirit. [6]Therefore *we are* always confident, knowing that, whilst we are at home in the body, we are absent from the Lord: [7](For we walk by faith, not by sight:) [8]We are confident, *I say,* and willing rather to be absent from the body, and to be present with the Lord. [9]Wherefore we labour, that, whether present or absent, we may be accepted of him. [10]For we must all appear before the judgment seat of Christ; that every one may receive the things *done* in *his* body, according to that he hath done, whether *it be* good or bad.

[11]Knowing therefore the terror of the Lord, we persuade men; but we are made manifest unto God; and I trust also are made manifest in your consciences. [12]For we commend not ourselves again unto you, but give you occasion to glory on our behalf, that ye may have somewhat to *answer* them which glory in appearance, and not in heart. [13]For whether we be beside ourselves, *it is* to God: or whether we be sober, *it is* for your cause. [14]For the love of Christ constraineth us; because we thus judge, that if one died for all, then were all dead: [15]And *that* he died for all, that they which live should not henceforth live unto themselves, but unto him which died for them, and rose again. [16]Wherefore henceforth know we no man after the flesh: yea, though we have known Christ after the flesh, yet now henceforth know we *him* no more. [17]Therefore if any man *be* in Christ, *he is* a new creature: old things are passed away; behold, all things are become new. [18]And all things *are* of God, who hath reconciled us to himself by Jesus Christ, and hath given to us the ministry of reconciliation; [19]To wit, that God was in Christ, reconciling the world unto himself, not imputing their trespasses unto them; and hath committed unto us the word of reconciliation. [20]Now then we are ambassadors for Christ, as though God did beseech *you* by us: we pray *you* in Christ's stead, be ye reconciled to God. [21]For he hath made him *to be* sin for us, who knew no sin; that we might be made the righteousness of God in him.

6 We then, *as* workers together *with him,* beseech *you* also that ye receive not the grace of God in vain. [2](For he saith,

I have heard thee in a time accepted, and in the day of salvation have I succoured thee:

behold, now *is* the accepted time; behold, now *is* the day of salvation.) [3]Giving no offence in any thing, that the ministry be not blamed: [4]But in all *things* approving ourselves as the ministers of God, in much patience, in afflictions, in necessities, in distresses, [5]In stripes, in imprisonments, in tumults, in labours, in watchings, in fastings; [6]By pureness, by knowledge, by longsuffering, by kindness, by the Holy Ghost, by love unfeigned, [7]By the word of truth, by the power of God, by the armour of righteousness on the right hand and on the left, [8]By honour and dishonour, by evil report and good report: as deceivers, and *yet* true; [9]As unknown, and *yet* well known; as dying, and, behold, we live; as chastened, and not killed; [10]As sorrowful, yet alway rejoicing; as poor, yet making many rich; as having nothing, and *yet* possessing all things.

[11]O *ye* Corinthians, our mouth is open unto you, our heart is enlarged. [12]Ye are not straitened in us, but ye are straitened in your own bowels. [13]Now for a recompence in the same, (I speak as unto *my* children,) be ye also enlarged. [14]Be ye not unequally yoked together with unbelievers: for what fellowship hath righteousness with unrighteousness? and what communion hath light with darkness? [15]And what concord hath Christ with Belial? or what part hath he that believeth with an infidel? [16]And what agreement hath the temple of God with idols? for ye are the temple of the living God; as God hath said,

I will dwell in them, and walk in *them;* and I will be their God, and they shall be my people.

[17]Wherefore

come out from among them, and be ye separate, saith the Lord, and touch not the unclean *thing;* and I will receive you,

[18]And

will be a Father unto you, and ye shall be my sons and daughters, saith the Lord Almighty.

7 Having therefore these promises, dearly beloved, let us cleanse ourselves from all filthiness of the flesh and spirit, perfecting holiness in the fear of God. [2]Receive us; we have wronged no man, we have corrupted no man, we have defrauded no man. [3]I speak not *this* to condemn *you:* for I have said before, that ye are in our hearts to die and live with *you.* [4]Great *is* my boldness of speech toward you, great *is* my glorying of you: I am filled with comfort, I am exceeding joyful in all our tribulation.

[5]For, when we were come into Macedonia, our flesh had no rest, but we were troubled on every side; without *were* fightings, within *were* fears. [6]Nevertheless God, that comforteth those that are cast down, comforted us by the coming of Titus; [7]And not by his coming only, but by the consolation wherewith he was comforted in you, when he told us your earnest desire, your mourning, your fervent mind toward me; so that I rejoiced the more. [8]For though I made you sorry with a letter, I do not repent, though I did repent: for I perceive that the same epistle hath made you sorry, though *it were* but for a season. [9]Now I rejoice, not that ye were made sorry, but that ye sorrowed to repentance: for ye were made sorry after a godly manner, that ye might receive damage by us in nothing. [10]For godly sorrow worketh repentance to salvation not to be repented of: but the sorrow of the world worketh death. [11]For behold this selfsame thing, that ye sorrowed after a godly sort, what carefulness it wrought in you, yea, *what* clearing of yourselves, yea, *what* indignation, yea, *what* fear, yea, *what* vehement desire, yea, *what* zeal, yea, *what* revenge! In all *things* ye have approved yourselves to be clear in this matter. [12]Wherefore, though I wrote unto you, *I did it* not for his cause that had done the wrong, nor for his cause that suffered wrong, but that our care for you in the sight of God might appear unto you. [13]Therefore we were comforted in your comfort: yea, and exceedingly the more joyed we for the joy of Titus, because his spirit was refreshed by you all. [14]For if I have boasted any thing to him of you, I am not ashamed; but as we spake all things to you in truth, even so our boasting, which *I made* before Titus, is found a truth. [15]And his inward affection is more abundant toward you, whilst he remembereth the obedience of you all, how with fear and trembling ye received him. [16]I rejoice therefore that I have confidence in you in all *things.*

8 Moreover, brethren, we do you to wit of the grace of God bestowed on the churches of Macedonia; [2]How that in a great trial of affliction the abundance of their joy and their deep poverty abounded unto the riches of their liberality. [3]For to *their* power, I bear record, yea, and beyond *their* power *they were* willing of themselves;

[4]Praying us with much intreaty that we would receive the gift, and *take upon us* the fellowship of the ministering to the saints. [5]And *this they did,* not as we hoped, but first gave their own selves to the Lord, and unto us by the will of God. [6]Insomuch that we desired Titus, that as he had begun, so he would also finish in you the same grace also. [7]Therefore, as ye abound in every *thing, in* faith, and utterance, and knowledge, and *in* all diligence, and *in* your love to us, *see* that ye abound in this grace also. [8]I speak not by commandment, but by occasion of the forwardness of others, and to prove the sincerity of your love. [9]For ye know the grace of our Lord Jesus Christ, that, though he was rich, yet for your sakes he became poor, that ye through his poverty might be rich. [10]And herein I give *my* advice: for this is expedient for you, who have begun before, not only to do, but also to be forward a year ago. [11]Now therefore perform the doing *of it;* that as *there was* a readiness to will, so *there may be* a performance also out of that which ye have. [12]For if there be first a willing mind, *it is* accepted according to that a man hath, *and* not according to that he hath not. [13]For *I mean* not that other men be eased, and ye burdened: [14]But by an equality, *that* now at this time your abundance *may be a supply* for their want, that their abundance also may be *a supply* for your want: that there may be equality: [15]As it is written, He that *had gathered* much had nothing over; and he that *had gathered* little had no lack. [16]But thanks *be* to God, which put the same earnest care into the heart of Titus for you. [17]For indeed he accepted the exhortation; but being more forward, of his own accord he went unto you. [18]And we have sent with him the brother, whose praise is in the gospel throughout all the churches; [19]And not *that* only, but who was also chosen of the churches to travel with us with this grace, which is administered by us to the glory of the same Lord, and *declaration of* your ready mind: [20]Avoiding this, that no man should blame us in this abundance which is administered by us: [21]Providing for honest things, not only in the sight of the Lord, but also in the sight of men. [22]And we have sent with them our brother, whom we have oftentimes proved diligent in many things, but now much more diligent, upon the great confidence which I *have* in you. [23]Whether *any do* enquire of Titus, *he is* my partner and fellowhelper concerning you: or our brethren *be enquired of, they are* the messengers of the churches, *and* the glory of Christ. [24]Wherefore shew ye to them, and before the churches, the proof of your love, and of our boasting on your behalf.

9 For as touching the ministering to the saints, it is superfluous for me to write to you: [2]For I know the forwardness of your mind, for which I boast of you to them of Macedonia, that Achaia was ready a year ago; and your zeal hath provoked very many. [3]Yet have I sent the brethren, lest our boasting of you should be in vain in this behalf; that, as I said, ye may be ready: [4]Lest haply if they of Macedonia come with me, and find you unprepared, we (that we say not, ye) should be ashamed in this same confident boasting. [5]Therefore I thought it necessary to exhort the brethren, that they would go before unto you, and make up beforehand your bounty, whereof ye had notice before, that the same might be ready, as *a matter of* bounty, and not as *of* covetousness. [6]But this *I say,* He which soweth sparingly shall reap also sparingly; and he which soweth bountifully shall reap also bountifully. [7]Every man according as he purposeth in his heart, *so let him give;* not grudgingly, or of necessity: for God loveth a cheerful giver. [8]And God *is* able to make all grace abound toward you; that ye, always having all sufficiency in all *things,* may abound to every good work: [9](As it is written,

He hath dispersed abroad; he hath given to the poor: his righteousness remaineth for ever.

[10]Now he that ministereth seed to the sower both minister bread for *your* food, and multiply your seed sown, and increase the fruits of your righteousness;) [11]Being enriched in every thing to all bountifulness, which causeth through us thanksgiving to God. [12]For the administration of this service not only supplieth the want of the saints, but is abundant also by many thanksgivings unto God; [13]Whiles by the

experiment of this ministration they glorify God for your professed subjection into the gospel of Christ, and for *your* liberal distribution unto them, and unto all *men;* ¹⁴And by their prayer for you, which long after you for the exceeding grace of God in you. ¹⁵Thanks *be* unto God for his unspeakable gift.

10 Now I Paul myself beseech you by the meekness and gentleness of Christ, who in presence *am* base among you, but being absent am bold toward you: ²But I beseech *you,* that I may not be bold when I am present with that confidence, wherewith I think to be bold against some, which think of us as if we walked according to the flesh. ³For though we walk in the flesh, we do not war after the flesh: ⁴(For the weapons of our warfare *are* not carnal, but mighty through God to the pulling down of strong holds;) ⁵Casting down imaginations, and every high thing that exalteth itself against the knowledge of God, and bringing into captivity every thought to the obedience of Christ; ⁶And having in a readiness to revenge all disobedience, when your obedience is fulfilled. ⁷Do ye look on things after the outward appearance? If any man trust to himself that he is Christ's, let him of himself think this again, that, as he *is* Christ's, even so *are* we Christ's. ⁸For though I should boast somewhat more of our authority, which the Lord hath given us for edification, and not for your destruction, I should not be ashamed: ⁹That I may not seem as if I would terrify you by letters. ¹⁰For *his* letters, say they, *are* weighty and powerful; but *his* bodily presence *is* weak, and *his* speech contemptible. ¹¹Let such an one think this, that, such as we are in word by letters when we are absent, such *will we be* also in deed when we are present. ¹²For we dare not make ourselves of the number, or compare ourselves with some that commend themselves: but they measuring themselves by themselves, and comparing themselves among themselves, are not wise. ¹³But we will not boast of things without *our* measure, but according to the measure of the rule which God hath distributed to us, a measure to reach even unto you. ¹⁴For we stretch not ourselves beyond *our measure,* as though we reached not unto you: for we are come as far as to you also in *preaching* the gospel of Christ: ¹⁵Not boasting of things without *our* measure, *that is,* of other men's labours; but having hope, when your faith is increased, that we shall be enlarged by you according to our rule abundantly, ¹⁶To preach the gospel in the *regions* beyond you, *and* not to boast in another man's line of things made ready to our hand. ¹⁷But he that glorieth, let him glory in the Lord. ¹⁸For not he that commendeth himself is approved, but whom the Lord commendeth.

11 Would to God ye could bear with me a little in *my* folly: and indeed bear with me. ²For I am jealous over you with godly jealousy: for I have espoused you to one husband, that I may present *you* as a chaste virgin to Christ. ³But I fear, lest by any means, as the serpent beguiled Eve through his subtilty, so your minds should be corrupted from the simplicity that is in Christ. ⁴For if he that cometh preacheth another Jesus, whom we have not preached, or *if* ye receive another spirit, which ye have not received, or another gospel, which ye have not accepted, ye might well bear with *him.* ⁵For I suppose I was not a whit behind the very chiefest apostles. ⁶But though *I be* rude in speech, yet not in knowledge; but we have been throughly made manifest among you in all things. ⁷Have I committed an offence in abasing myself that ye might be exalted, because I have preached to you the gospel of God freely? ⁸I robbed other churches, taking wages *of them,* to do you service. ⁹And when I was present with you, and wanted, I was chargeable to no man: for that which was lacking to me the brethren which came from Macedonia supplied: and in all *things* I have kept myself from being burdensome unto you, and so will I keep *myself.* ¹⁰As the truth of Christ is in me, no man shall stop me of this boasting in the regions of Achaia. ¹¹Wherefore? because I love you not? God knoweth. ¹²But what I do, that I will do, that I may cut off occasion from them which desire occasion; that wherein they glory, they may be found even as we. ¹³For such *are* false apostles, deceitful workers, transforming themselves into the apostles of Christ. ¹⁴And no marvel; for Satan himself is transformed into an angel of light. ¹⁵Therefore *it is* no great thing if his ministers also be transformed as the ministers of righteousness; whose end shall be according to their works.

¹⁶I say again, Let no man think me a fool; if otherwise, yet as a fool receive me, that I may boast myself a little. ¹⁷That which I speak, I speak *it* not after the Lord, but as it were foolishly, in this confidence of boasting. ¹⁸Seeing that many glory after the flesh, I will glory also. ¹⁹For ye suffer fools gladly, seeing ye *yourselves* are wise. ²⁰For ye suffer, if a man bring you into bondage, if a man devour *you*, if a man take *of you*, if a man exalt himself, if a man smite you on the face. ²¹I speak as concerning reproach, as though we had been weak. Howbeit whereinsoever any is bold, (I speak foolishly,) I am bold also. ²²Are they Hebrews? so *am* I. Are they Israelites? so *am* I. Are they the seed of Abraham? so *am* I. ²³Are they ministers of Christ? (I speak as a fool) I *am* more; in labours more abundant, in stripes above measure, in prisons more frequent, in deaths oft. ²⁴Of the Jews five times received I forty *stripes* save one. ²⁵Thrice was I beaten with rods, once was I stoned, thrice I suffered shipwreck, a night and a day I have been in the deep; ²⁶*In* journeyings often, *in* perils of waters, *in* perils of robbers, *in* perils by *mine own* countrymen, *in* perils by the heathen, *in* perils in the city, *in* perils in the wilderness, *in* perils in the sea, *in* perils among false brethren; ²⁷In weariness and painfulness, in watchings often, in hunger and thirst, in fastings often, in cold and nakedness. ²⁸Beside those things that are without, that which cometh upon me daily, the care of all the churches. ²⁹Who is weak, and I am not weak? who is offended, and I burn not? ³⁰If I must needs glory, I will glory of the things which concern mine infirmities. ³¹The God and Father of our Lord Jesus Christ, which is blessed for evermore, knoweth that I lie not. ³²In Damascus the governor under Aretas the king kept the city of the Damascenes with a garrison, desirous to apprehend me: ³³And through a window in a basket was I let down by the wall, and escaped his hands.

12 It is not expedient for me doubtless to glory. I will come to visions and revelations of the Lord. ²I knew a man in Christ above fourteen years ago, (whether in the body, I cannot tell; or whether out of the body, I cannot tell: God knoweth;) such an one caught up to the third heaven. ³And I knew such a man, (whether in the body, or out of the body, I cannot tell: God knoweth;) ⁴How that he was caught up into paradise, and heard unspeakable words, which it is not lawful for a man to utter. ⁵Of such an one will I glory: yet of myself I will not glory, but in mine infirmities. ⁶For though I would desire to glory, I shall not be a fool; for I will say the truth: but *now* I forbear, lest any man should think of me above that which he seeth me *to be*, or *that* he heareth of me. ⁷And lest I should be exalted above measure through the abundance of the revelations, there was given to me a thorn in the flesh, the messenger of Satan to buffet me, lest I should be exalted above measure. ⁸For this thing I besought the Lord thrice, that it might depart from me. ⁹And he said unto me, My grace is sufficient for thee: for my strength is made perfect in weakness. Most gladly therefore will I rather glory in my infirmities, that the power of Christ may rest upon me. ¹⁰Therefore I take pleasure in infirmities, in reproaches, in necessities, in persecutions, in distresses for Christ's sake: for when I am weak, then am I strong.

¹¹I am become a fool in glorying; ye have compelled me: for I ought to have been commended of you: for in nothing am I behind the very chiefest apostles, though I be nothing. ¹²Truly the signs of an apostle were wrought among you in all patience, in signs, and wonders, and mighty deeds. ¹³For what is it wherein ye were inferior to other churches, except *it be* that I myself was not burdensome to you? forgive me this wrong. ¹⁴Behold, the third time I am ready to come to you; and I will not be burdensome to you: for I seek not yours, but you: for the children ought not to lay up for the parents, but the parents for the children. ¹⁵And I will very gladly spend and be spent for you; though the more abundantly I love you, the less I be loved. ¹⁶But be it so, I did not burden you:

nevertheless, being crafty, I caught you with guile. [17]Did I make a gain of you by any of them whom I sent unto you? [18]I desired Titus, and with *him* I sent a brother. Did Titus make a gain of you? walked we not in the same spirit? *walked we* not in the same steps? [19]Again, think ye that we excuse ourselves unto you? we speak before God in Christ: but *we do* all things, dearly beloved, for your edifying. [20]For I fear, lest, when I come, I shall not find you such as I would, and *that* I shall be found unto you such as ye would not: lest *there be* debates, envyings, wraths, strifes, backbitings, whisperings, swellings, tumults: [21]*And* lest, when I come again, my God will humble me among you, and *that* I shall bewail many which have sinned already, and have not repented of the uncleanness and fornication and lasciviousness which they have committed.

13 This *is* the third *time* I am coming to you. In the mouth of two or three witnesses shall every word be established. [2]I told you before, and foretell you, as if I were present, the second time; and being absent now I write to them which heretofore have sinned, and to all other, that, if I come again, I will not spare: [3]Since ye seek a proof of Christ speaking in me, which to you-ward is not weak, but is mighty in you. [4]For though he was crucified through weakness, yet he liveth by the power of God. For we also are weak in him, but we shall live with him by the power of God toward you. [5]Examine yourselves, whether ye be in the faith; prove your own selves. Know ye not your own selves, how that Jesus Christ is in you, except ye be reprobates? [6]But I trust that ye shall know that we are not reprobates. [7]Now I pray to God that ye do no evil; not that we should appear approved, but that ye should do that which is honest, though we be as reprobates. [8]For we can do nothing against the truth, but for the truth. [9]For we are glad, when we are weak, and ye are strong: and this also we wish, *even* your perfection. [10]Therefore I write these things being absent, lest being present I should use sharpness, according to the power which the Lord hath given me to edification, and not to destruction.

[11]Finally, brethren, farewell. Be perfect, be of good comfort, be of one mind, live in peace; and the God of love and peace shall be with you. [12]Greet one another with an holy kiss.

[13]All the saints salute you. [14]The grace of the Lord Jesus Christ, and the love of God, and the communion of the Holy Ghost, *be* with you all. Amen.

GALATIANS

1 Paul, an apostle, (not of men, neither by man, but by Jesus Christ, and God the Father, who raised him from the dead;) ²And all the brethren which are with me,

unto the churches of Galatia:

³Grace *be* to you and peace from God the Father, and *from* our Lord Jesus Christ, ⁴Who gave himself for our sins, that he might deliver us from this present evil world, according to the will of God and our Father: ⁵To whom *be* glory for ever and ever. Amen.

⁶I marvel that ye are so soon removed from him that called you into the grace of Christ unto another gospel: ⁷Which is not another; but there be some that trouble you, and would pervert the gospel of Christ. ⁸But though we, or an angel from heaven, preach any other gospel unto you than that which we have preached unto you, let him be accursed. ⁹As we said before, so say I now again, If any *man* preach any other gospel unto you than that ye have received, let him be accursed.

¹⁰For do I now persuade men, or God? or do I seek to please men? for if I yet pleased men, I should not be the servant of Christ. ¹¹But I certify you, brethren, that the gospel which was preached of me is not after man. ¹²For I neither received it of man, neither was I taught *it,* but by the revelation of Jesus Christ. ¹³For ye have heard of my conversation in time past in the Jews' religion, how that beyond measure I persecuted the church of God, and wasted it: ¹⁴And profited in the Jews' religion above many my equals in mine own nation, being more exceedingly zealous of the traditions of my fathers. ¹⁵But when it pleased God, who separated me from my mother's womb, and called *me* by his grace, ¹⁶To reveal his Son in me, that I might preach him among the heathen; immediately I conferred not with flesh and blood: ¹⁷Neither went I up to Jerusalem to them which were apostles before me; but I went into Arabia, and returned again unto Damascus. ¹⁸Then after three years I went up to Jerusalem to see Pe-

ter, and abode with him fifteen days. ¹⁹But other of the apostles saw I none, save James the Lord's brother. ²⁰Now the things which I write unto you, behold, before God, I lie not. ²¹Afterwards I came into the regions of Syria and Cilicia; ²²And was unknown by face unto the churches of Judaea which were in Christ: ²³But they had heard only, That he which persecuted us in times past now preacheth the faith which once he destroyed. ²⁴And they glorified God in me.

2 Then fourteen years after I went up again to Jerusalem with Barnabas, and took Titus with *me* also. ²And I went up by revelation, and communicated unto them that gospel which I preach among the Gentiles, but privately to them which were of reputation, lest by any means I should run, or had run, in vain. ³But neither Titus, who was with me, being a Greek, was compelled to be circumcised: ⁴And that because of false brethren unawares brought in, who came in privily to spy out our liberty which we have in Christ Jesus, that they might bring us into bondage: ⁵To whom we gave place by subjection, no, not for an hour; that the truth of the gospel might continue with you. ⁶But of these who seemed to be somewhat, (whatsoever they were, it maketh no matter to me: God accepteth no man's person:) for they who seemed *to be somewhat* in conference added nothing to me: ⁷But contrariwise, when they saw that the gospel of the uncircumcision was committed unto me, as *the gospel* of the circumcision *was* unto Peter; ⁸(For he that wrought effectually in Peter to the apostleship of the circumcision, the same was mighty in me toward the Gentiles:) ⁹And when James, Cephas, and John, who seemed to be pillars, perceived the grace that was given unto me, they gave to me and Barnabas the right hands of fellowship; that we *should go* unto the heathen, and they unto the circumcision. ¹⁰Only *they would* that we should remember the poor; the same which I also was forward to do. ¹¹But when Peter was come to Antioch, I withstood him to the face, because he was to be blamed. ¹²For before that certain came from James, he

did eat with the Gentiles: but when they were come, he withdrew and separated himself, fearing them which were of the circumcision. [13]And the other Jews dissembled likewise with him; insomuch that Barnabas also was carried away with their dissimulation. [14]But when I saw that they walked not uprightly according to the truth of the gospel, I said unto Peter before *them* all, If thou, being a Jew, livest after the manner of Gentiles, and not as do the Jews, why compellest thou the Gentiles to live as do the Jews? [15]We *who are* Jews by nature, and not sinners of the Gentiles, [16]Knowing that a man is not justified by the works of the law, but by the faith of Jesus Christ, even we have believed in Jesus Christ, that we might be justified by the faith of Christ, and not by the works of the law: for by the works of the law shall no flesh be justified. [17]But if, while we seek to be justified by Christ, we ourselves also are found sinners, *is* therefore Christ the minister of sin? God forbid. [18]For if I build again the things which I destroyed, I make myself a transgressor. [19]For I through the law am dead to the law, that I might live unto God. [20]I am crucified with Christ: nevertheless I live; yet not I, but Christ liveth in me: and the life which I now live in the flesh I live by the faith of the Son of God, who loved me, and gave himself for me. [21]I do not frustrate the grace of God: for if righteousness *come* by the law, then Christ is dead in vain.

3 O foolish Galatians, who hath bewitched you, that ye should not obey the truth, before whose eyes Jesus Christ hath been evidently set forth, crucified among you? [2]This only would I learn of you, Received ye the Spirit by the works of the law, or by the hearing of faith? [3]Are ye so foolish? having begun in the Spirit, are ye now made perfect by the flesh? [4]Have ye suffered so many things in vain? if *it be* yet in vain. [5]He therefore that ministereth to you the Spirit, and worketh miracles among you, *doeth he it* by the works of the law, or by the hearing of faith? [6]Even as Abraham believed God, and it was accounted to him for righteousness.

[7]Know ye therefore that they which are of faith, the same are the children of Abraham. [8]And the scripture, foreseeing that God would justify the heathen through faith, preached before the gospel unto Abraham, *saying,* In thee shall all nations be blessed. [9]So then they which be of faith are blessed with faithful Abraham. [10]For as many as are of the works of the law are under the curse: for it is written, Cursed *is* every one that continueth not in all things which are written in the book of the law to do them. [11]But that no man is justified by the law in the sight of God, *it is* evident: for, The just shall live by faith. [12]And the law is not of faith: but, The man that doeth them shall live in them. [13]Christ hath redeemed us from the curse of the law, being made a curse for us: for it is written, Cursed *is* every one that hangeth on a tree: [14]That the blessing of Abraham might come on the Gentiles through Jesus Christ; that we might receive the promise of the Spirit through faith. [15]Brethren, I speak after the manner of men; Though *it be* but a man's covenant, yet *if it be* confirmed, no man disannulleth, or addeth thereto. [16]Now to Abraham and his seed were the promises made. He saith not, And to seeds, as of many; but as of one, And to thy seed, which is Christ. [17]And this I say, *that* the covenant, that was confirmed before of God in Christ, the law, which was four hundred and thirty years after, cannot disannul, that it should make the promise of none effect. [18]For if the inheritance *be* of the law, *it is* no more of promise: but God gave *it* to Abraham by promise. [19]Wherefore then *serveth* the law? It was added because of transgressions, till the seed should come to whom the promise was made; *and it was* ordained by angels in the hand of a mediator. [20]Now a mediator is not *a mediator* of one, but God is one. [21]*Is* the law then against the promises of God? God forbid: for if there had been a law given which could have given life, verily righteousness should have been by the law. [22]But the scripture hath concluded all under sin, that the promise by faith of Jesus Christ might be given to them that believe.

[23]But before faith came, we were kept under the law, shut up unto the faith which should afterwards be revealed. [24]Wherefore the law was our schoolmaster *to bring us* unto Christ, that we might be justified by faith. [25]But after that faith is come, we

are no longer under a schoolmaster. ²⁶For ye are all the children of God by faith in Christ Jesus. ²⁷For as many of you as have been baptized into Christ have put on Christ. ²⁸There is neither Jew nor Greek, there is neither bond nor free, there is neither male nor female: for ye are all one in Christ Jesus. ²⁹And if ye *be* Christ's, then are ye Abraham's seed, and heirs according to the promise.

4 Now I say, *That* the heir, as long as he is a child, differeth nothing from a servant, though he be lord of all; ²But is under tutors and governors until the time appointed of the father. ³Even so we, when we were children, were in bondage under the elements of the world: ⁴But when the fulness of the time was come, God sent forth his Son, made of a woman, made under the law, ⁵To redeem them that were under the law, that we might receive the adoption of sons. ⁶And because ye are sons, God hath sent forth the Spirit of his Son into your hearts, crying, Abba, Father. ⁷Wherefore thou art no more a servant, but a son; and if a son, then an heir of God through Christ.

⁸Howbeit then, when ye knew not God, ye did service unto them which by nature are no gods. ⁹But now, after that ye have known God, or rather are known of God, how turn ye again to the weak and beggarly elements, whereunto ye desire again to be in bondage? ¹⁰Ye observe days, and months, and times, and years. ¹¹I am afraid of you, lest I have bestowed upon you labour in vain.

¹²Brethren, I beseech you, be as I *am;* for I *am* as ye *are:* ye have not injured me at all. ¹³Ye know how through infirmity of the flesh I preached the gospel unto you at the first. ¹⁴And my temptation which was in my flesh ye despised not, nor rejected; but received me as an angel of God, *even* as Christ Jesus. ¹⁵Where is then the blessedness ye spake of? for I bear you record, that, if *it had been* possible, ye would have plucked out your own eyes, and have given them to me. ¹⁶Am I therefore become your enemy, because I tell you the truth? ¹⁷They zealously affect you, *but* not well; yea, they would exclude you, that ye might affect them. ¹⁸But *it is* good to be zealously affected always in *a* good *thing,* and not only

when I am present with you. ¹⁹My little children, of whom I travail in birth again until Christ be formed in you, ²⁰I desire to be present with you now, and to change my voice; for I stand in doubt of you.

²¹Tell me, ye that desire to be under the law, do ye not hear the law? ²²For it is written, that Abraham had two sons, the one by a bondmaid, the other by a freewoman. ²³But he *who was* of the bondwoman was born after the flesh; but he of the freewoman *was* by promise. ²⁴Which things are an allegory: for these are the two covenants; the one from the mount Sinai, which gendereth to bondage, which is Agar. ²⁵For this Agar is mount Sinai in Arabia, and answereth to Jerusalem which now is, and is in bondage with her children. ²⁶But Jerusalem which is above is free, which is the mother of us all. ²⁷For it is written,

Rejoice, *thou* barren that bearest not; break forth and cry, thou that travailest not: for the desolate hath many more children than she which hath an husband.

²⁸Now we, brethren, as Isaac was, are the children of promise. ²⁹But as then he that was born after the flesh persecuted him *that was born* after the Spirit, even so *it is* now. ³⁰Nevertheless what saith the scripture? Cast out the bondwoman and her son: for the son of the bondwoman shall not be heir with the son of the free woman. ³¹So then, brethren, we are not children of the bondwoman, but of the free.

5 Stand fast therefore in the liberty wherewith Christ hath made us free, and be not entangled again with the yoke of bondage.

²Behold, I Paul say unto you, that if ye be circumcised, Christ shall profit you nothing. ³For I testify again to every man that is circumcised, that he is a debtor to do the whole law. ⁴Christ is become of no effect unto you, whosoever of you are justified by the law; ye are fallen from grace. ⁵For we through the Spirit wait for the hope of righteousness by faith. ⁶For in Jesus Christ neither circumcision availeth any thing, nor uncircumcision; but faith which worketh by love. ⁷Ye did run well; who did hinder you that ye should not obey the truth? ⁸This persuasion *cometh* not of him that

calleth you. ⁹A little leaven leaveneth the whole lump. ¹⁰I have confidence in you through the Lord, that ye will be none otherwise minded: but he that troubleth you shall bear his judgment, whosoever he be. ¹¹And I, brethren, if I yet preach circumcision, why do I yet suffer persecution? then is the offence of the cross ceased. ¹²I would they were even cut off which trouble you.

¹³For, brethren, ye have been called unto liberty; only *use* not liberty for an occasion to the flesh, but by love serve one another. ¹⁴For all the law is fulfilled in one word, *even* in this; Thou shalt love thy neighbour as thyself. ¹⁵But if ye bite and devour one another, take heed that ye be not consumed one of another. ¹⁶*This* I say then, Walk in the Spirit, and ye shall not fulfil the lust of the flesh. ¹⁷For the flesh lusteth against the Spirit, and the Spirit against the flesh: and these are contrary the one to the other: so that ye cannot do the things that ye would. ¹⁸But if ye be led of the Spirit, ye are not under the law. ¹⁹Now the works of the flesh are manifest, which are *these;* Adultery, fornication, uncleanness, lasciviousness, ²⁰Idolatry, witchcraft, hatred, variance, emulations, wrath, strife, seditions, heresies, ²¹Envyings, murders, drunkenness, revellings, and such like: of the which I tell you before, as I have also told *you* in time past, that they which do such things shall not inherit the kingdom of God. ²²But the fruit of the Spirit is love, joy, peace, longsuffering, gentleness, goodness, faith, ²³Meekness, temperance: against such there is no law. ²⁴And they that are Christ's have crucified the flesh with the affections and lusts. ²⁵If we live in the Spirit, let us also walk in the Spirit. ²⁶Let us not be desirous of vain glory, provoking one another, envying one another.

6 Brethren, if a man be overtaken in a fault, ye which are spiritual, restore such an one in the spirit of meekness; considering thyself, lest thou also be tempted. ²Bear ye one another's burdens, and so fulfil the law of Christ. ³For if a man think himself to be something, when he is nothing, he deceiveth himself. ⁴But let every man prove his own work, and then shall he have rejoicing in himself alone, and not in another. ⁵For every man shall bear his own burden. ⁶Let him that is taught in the word communicate unto him that teacheth in all good things. ⁷Be not deceived; God is not mocked: for whatsoever a man soweth, that shall he also reap. ⁸For he that soweth to his flesh shall of the flesh reap corruption; but he that soweth to the Spirit shall of the Spirit reap life everlasting. ⁹And let us not be weary in well doing: for in due season we shall reap, if we faint not. ¹⁰As we have therefore opportunity, let us do good unto all *men*, especially unto them who are of the household of faith.

¹¹Ye see how large a letter I have written unto you with mine own hand. ¹²As many as desire to make a fair shew in the flesh, they constrain you to be circumcised; only lest they should suffer persecution for the cross of Christ. ¹³For neither they themselves who are circumcised keep the law; but desire to have you circumcised, that they may glory in your flesh. ¹⁴But God forbid that I should glory, save in the cross of our Lord Jesus Christ, by whom the world is crucified unto me, and I unto the world. ¹⁵For in Christ Jesus neither circumcision availeth any thing, nor uncircumcision, but a new creature. ¹⁶And as many as walk according to this rule, peace *be* on them, and mercy, and upon the Israel of God.

¹⁷From henceforth let no man trouble me: for I bear in my body the marks of the Lord Jesus.

¹⁸Brethren, the grace of our Lord Jesus Christ *be* with your spirit. Amen.

The Epistle of Paul the Apostle to the
EPHESIANS

1 Paul, an apostle of Jesus Christ by the will of God,

to the saints which are at Ephesus, and to the faithful in Christ Jesus:

[2] Grace *be* to you, and peace, from God our Father, and *from* the Lord Jesus Christ.

[3] Blessed *be* the God and Father of our Lord Jesus Christ, who hath blessed us with all spiritual blessings in heavenly *places* in Christ: [4] According as he hath chosen us in him before the foundation of the world, that we should be holy and without blame before him in love: [5] Having predestinated us unto the adoption of children by Jesus Christ to himself, according to the good pleasure of his will, [6] To the praise of the glory of his grace, wherein he hath made us accepted in the beloved. [7] In whom we have redemption through his blood, the forgiveness of sins, according to the riches of his grace; [8] Wherein he hath abounded toward us in all wisdom and prudence; [9] Having made known unto us the mystery of his will, according to his good pleasure which he hath purposed in himself: [10] That in the dispensation of the fulness of times he might gather together in one all things in Christ, both which are in heaven, and which are on earth; *even* in him: [11] In whom also we have obtained an inheritance, being predestinated according to the purpose of him who worketh all things after the counsel of his own will: [12] That we should be to the praise of his glory, who first trusted in Christ. [13] In whom ye also *trusted,* after that ye heard the word of truth, the gospel of your salvation: in whom also after that ye believed, ye were sealed with that holy Spirit of promise, [14] Which is the earnest of our inheritance until the redemption of the purchased possession, unto the praise of his glory.

[15] Wherefore I also, after I heard of your faith in the Lord Jesus, and love unto all the saints, [16] Cease not to give thanks for you, making mention of you in my prayers; [17] That the God of our Lord Jesus Christ, the Father of glory, may give unto you the spirit of wisdom and revelation in the knowledge of him: [18] The eyes of your understanding being enlightened; that ye may know what is the hope of his calling, and what the riches of the glory of his inheritance in the saints, [19] And what *is* the exceeding greatness of his power to us-ward who believe, according to the working of his mighty power, [20] Which he wrought in Christ, when he raised him from the dead, and set *him* at his own right hand in the heavenly *places,* [21] Far above all principality, and power, and might, and dominion, and every name that is named, not only in this world, but also in that which is to come: [22] And hath put all *things* under his feet, and gave him *to be* the head over all *things* to the church, [23] Which is his body, the fulness of him that filleth all in all.

2 And you *hath he quickened,* who were dead in trespasses and sins; [2] Wherein in time past ye walked according to the course of this world, according to the prince of the power of the air, the spirit that now worketh in the children of disobedience: [3] Among whom also we all had our conversation in times past in the lusts of our flesh, fulfilling the desires of the flesh and of the mind; and were by nature the children of wrath, even as others. [4] But God, who is rich in mercy, for his great love wherewith he loved us, [5] Even when we were dead in sins, hath quickened us together with Christ, (by grace ye are saved;) [6] And hath raised *us* up together, and made *us* sit together in heavenly *places* in Christ Jesus: [7] That in the ages to come he might shew the exceeding riches of his grace in *his* kindness toward us through Christ Jesus. [8] For by grace are ye saved through faith; and that not of yourselves: *it is* the gift of God: [9] Not of works, lest any man should boast. [10] For we are his workmanship, created in Christ Jesus unto good works, which God hath before ordained that we should walk in them.

[11] Wherefore remember, that ye *being* in time past Gentiles in the flesh, who are called Uncircumcision by that which is called the Circumcision in the flesh made by hands; [12] That at that time ye were with-

out Christ, being aliens from the commonwealth of Israel, and strangers from the covenants of promise, having no hope, and without God in the world: ¹³But now in Christ Jesus ye who sometimes were far off are made nigh by the blood of Christ. ¹⁴For he is our peace, who hath made both one, and hath broken down the middle wall of partition *between us;* ¹⁵Having abolished in his flesh the enmity, *even* the law of commandments *contained* in ordinances; for to make in himself of twain one new man, *so* making peace; ¹⁶And that he might reconcile both unto God in one body by the cross, having slain the enmity thereby: ¹⁷And came and preached peace to you which were afar off, and to them that were nigh. ¹⁸For through him we both have access by one Spirit unto the Father. ¹⁹Now therefore ye are no more strangers and foreigners, but fellowcitizens with the saints, and of the household of God; ²⁰And are built upon the foundation of the apostles and prophets, Jesus Christ himself being the chief corner *stone;* ²¹In whom all the building fitly framed together groweth unto an holy temple in the Lord: ²²In whom ye also are builded together for an habitation of God through the Spirit.

3 For this cause I Paul, the prisoner of Jesus Christ for you Gentiles, ²If ye have heard of the dispensation of the grace of God which is given me to youward: ³How that by revelation he made known unto me the mystery; (as I wrote afore in few words, ⁴Whereby, when ye read, ye may understand my knowledge in the mystery of Christ) ⁵Which in other ages was not made known unto the sons of men, as it is now revealed unto his holy apostles and prophets by the Spirit; ⁶That the Gentiles should be fellowheirs, and of the same body, and partakers of his promise in Christ by the gospel: ⁷Whereof I was made a minister, according to the gift of the grace of God given unto me by the effectual working of his power. ⁸Unto me, who am less than the least of all saints, is this grace given, that I should preach among the Gentiles the unsearchable riches of Christ; ⁹And to make all *men* see what *is* the fellowship of the mystery, which from the beginning of the world hath been hid in God, who created all things by Jesus Christ: ¹⁰To the intent that now unto the principalities and powers in heavenly *places* might be known by the church the manifold wisdom of God, ¹¹According to the eternal purpose which he purposed in Christ Jesus our Lord: ¹²In whom we have boldness and access with confidence by the faith of him. ¹³Wherefore I desire that ye faint not at my tribulations for you, which is your glory. ¹⁴For this cause I bow my knees unto the Father of our Lord Jesus Christ, ¹⁵Of whom the whole family in heaven and earth is named, ¹⁶That he would grant you, according to the riches of his glory, to be strengthened with might by his Spirit in the inner man; ¹⁷That Christ may dwell in your hearts by faith; that ye, being rooted and grounded in love, ¹⁸May be able to comprehend with all saints what *is* the breadth, and length, and depth, and height; ¹⁹And to know the love of Christ, which passeth knowledge, that ye might be filled with all the fulness of God.

²⁰Now unto him that is able to do exceeding abundantly above all that we ask or think, according to the power that worketh in us, ²¹Unto him *be* glory in the church by Christ Jesus throughout all ages, world without end. Amen.

4 I therefore, the prisoner of the Lord, beseech you that ye walk worthy of the vocation wherewith ye are called, ²With all lowliness and meekness, with longsuffering, forbearing one another in love; ³Endeavouring to keep the unity of the Spirit in the bond of peace. ⁴*There is* one body, and one Spirit, even as ye are called in one hope of your calling; ⁵One Lord, one faith, one baptism, ⁶One God and Father of all, who *is* above all, and through all, and in you all. ⁷But unto every one of us is given grace according to the measure of the gift of Christ. ⁸Wherefore he saith,

When he ascended up on high, he led captivity captive, and gave gifts unto men.

⁹(Now that he ascended, what is it but that he also descended first into the lower parts of the earth? ¹⁰He that descended is the same also that ascended up far above all heavens, that he might fill all things.) ¹¹And he gave some, apostles; and some,

prophets; and some, evangelists; and some, pastors and teachers; [12]For the perfecting of the saints, for the work of the ministry, for the edifying of the body of Christ: [13]Till we all come in the unity of the faith, and of the knowledge of the Son of God, unto a perfect man, unto the measure of the stature of the fulness of Christ: [14]That we *henceforth* be no more children, tossed to and fro, and carried about with every wind of doctrine, by the sleight of men, *and* cunning craftiness, whereby they lie in wait to deceive; [15]But speaking the truth in love, may grow up into him in all things, which is the head, *even* Christ: [16]From whom the whole body fitly joined together and compacted by that which every joint supplieth, according to the effectual working in the measure of every part, maketh increase of the body unto the edifying of itself in love.

[17]This I say therefore, and testify in the Lord, that ye henceforth walk not as other Gentiles walk, in the vanity of their mind, [18]Having the understanding darkened, being alienated from the life of God through the ignorance that is in them, because of the blindness of their heart: [19]Who being past feeling have given themselves over unto lasciviousness, to work all uncleanness with greediness. [20]But ye have not so learned Christ; [21]If so be that ye have heard him, and have been taught by him, as the truth is in Jesus: [22]That ye put off concerning the former conversation the old man, which is corrupt according to the deceitful lusts; [23]And be renewed in the spirit of your mind; [24]And that ye put on the new man, which after God is created in righteousness and true holiness.

[25]Wherefore putting away lying, speak every man truth with his neighbour: for we are members one of another. [26]Be ye angry, and sin not: let not the sun go down upon your wrath: [27]Neither give place to the devil. [28]Let him that stole steal no more: but rather let him labour, working with *his* hands the thing which is good, that he may have to give to him that needeth. [29]Let no corrupt communication proceed out of your mouth, but that which is good to the use of edifying, that it may minister grace unto the hearers. [30]And grieve not the holy Spirit of God, whereby ye are sealed unto the day of redemption. [31]Let all bitterness, and wrath, and anger, and clamour, and evil speaking, be put away from you, with all malice: [32]And be ye kind one to another, tenderhearted, forgiving one another, even as God for Christ's sake hath forgiven you.

5 Be ye therefore followers of God, as dear children; [2]And walk in love, as Christ also hath loved us, and hath given himself for us an offering and a sacrifice to God for a sweetsmelling savour. [3]But fornication, and all uncleanness, or covetousness, let it not be once named among you, as becometh saints; [4]Neither filthiness, nor foolish talking, nor jesting, which are not convenient: but rather giving of thanks. [5]For this ye know, that no whoremonger, nor unclean person, nor covetous man, who is an idolater, hath any inheritance in the kingdom of Christ and of God. [6]Let no man deceive you with vain words: for because of these things cometh the wrath of God upon the children of disobedience. [7]Be not ye therefore partakers with them. [8]For ye were sometimes darkness, but now *are ye* light in the Lord: walk as children of light: [9](For the fruit of the Spirit is in all goodness and righteousness and truth;) [10]Proving what is acceptable unto the Lord. [11]And have no fellowship with the unfruitful works of darkness, but rather reprove *them.* [12]For it is a shame even to speak of those things which are done of them in secret. [13]But all things that are reproved are made manifest by the light: for whatsoever doth make manifest is light. [14]Wherefore he saith,

Awake thou that sleepest, and arise from the dead, and Christ shall give thee light.

[15]See then that ye walk circumspectly, not as fools, but as wise, [16]Redeeming the time, because the days are evil. [17]Wherefore be ye not unwise, but understanding what the will of the Lord *is.* [18]And be not drunk with wine, wherein is excess; but be filled with the Spirit; [19]Speaking to yourselves in psalms and hymns and spiritual songs, singing and making melody in your heart to the Lord; [20]Giving thanks always for all things unto God and the Father in the name of our Lord Jesus Christ; [21]Submit-

ting yourselves one to another in the fear of God. [22]Wives, submit yourselves unto your own husbands, as unto the Lord. [23]For the husband is the head of the wife, even as Christ is the head of the church: and he is the saviour of the body. [24]Therefore as the church is subject unto Christ, so *let* the wives *be* to their own husbands in every thing. [25]Husbands, love your wives, even as Christ also loved the church, and gave himself for it; [26]That he might sanctify and cleanse it with the washing of water by the word, [27]That he might present it to himself a glorious church, not having spot, or wrinkle, or any such thing; but that it should be holy and without blemish. [28]So ought men to love their wives as their own bodies. He that loveth his wife loveth himself. [29]For no man ever yet hated his own flesh; but nourisheth and cherisheth it, even as the Lord the church: [30]For we are members of his body, of his flesh, and of his bones. [31]For this cause shall a man leave his father and mother, and shall be joined unto his wife, and they two shall be one flesh. [32]This is a great mystery: but I speak concerning Christ and the church. [33]Nevertheless let every one of you in particular so love his wife even as himself; and the wife *see* that she reverence *her* husband.

6 Children, obey your parents in the Lord: for this is right. [2]Honour thy father and mother; (which is the first commandment with promise;) [3]That it may be well with thee, and thou mayest live long on the earth. [4]And, ye fathers, provoke not your children to wrath: but bring them up in the nurture and admonition of the Lord. [5]Servants, be obedient to them that are *your* masters according to the flesh, with fear and trembling, in singleness of your heart, as unto Christ; [6]Not with eyeservice, as menpleasers; but as the servants of Christ, doing the will of God from the heart; [7]With good will doing service, as to the Lord, and not to men: [8]Knowing that whatsoever good thing any man doeth, the same shall he receive of the Lord, whether

he be bond or free. [9]And, ye masters, do the same things unto them, forbearing threatening: knowing that your Master also is in heaven; neither is there respect of persons with him.

[10]Finally, my brethren, be strong in the Lord, and in the power of his might. [11]Put on the whole armour of God, that ye may be able to stand against the wiles of the devil. [12]For we wrestle not against flesh and blood, but against principalities, against powers, against the rulers of the darkness of this world, against spiritual wickedness in high *places*. [13]Wherefore take unto you the whole armour of God, that ye may be able to withstand in the evil day, and having done all, to stand. [14]Stand therefore, having your loins girt about with truth, and having on the breastplate of righteousness; [15]And your feet shod with the preparation of the gospel of peace; [16]Above all, taking the shield of faith, wherewith ye shall be able to quench all the fiery darts of the wicked. [17]And take the helmet of salvation, and the sword of the Spirit, which is the word of God: [18]Praying always with all prayer and supplication in the Spirit, and watching thereunto with all perseverance and supplication for all saints; [19]And for me, that utterance may be given unto me, that I may open my mouth boldly, to make known the mystery of the gospel, [20]For which I am an ambassador in bonds: that therein I may speak boldly, as I ought to speak.

[21]But that ye also may know my affairs, *and* how I do, Tychicus, a beloved brother and faithful minister in the Lord, shall make known to you all things: [22]Whom I have sent unto you for the same purpose, that ye might know our affairs, and *that* he might comfort your hearts.

[23]Peace *be* to the brethren, and love with faith, from God the Father and the Lord Jesus Christ. [24]Grace *be* with all them that love our Lord Jesus Christ in sincerity. Amen.

PHILIPPIANS

1 Paul and Timotheus, the servants of Jesus Christ,

to all the saints in Christ Jesus which are at Philippi, with the bishops and deacons:

[2]Grace *be* unto you, and peace, from God our Father, and *from* the Lord Jesus Christ.

[3]I thank my God upon every remembrance of you, [4]Always in every prayer of mine for you all making request with joy, [5]For your fellowship in the gospel from the first day until now; [6]Being confident of this very thing, that he which hath begun a good work in you will perform *it* until the day of Jesus Christ: [7]Even as it is meet for me to think this of you all, because I have you in my heart; inasmuch as both in my bonds, and in the defence and confirmation of the gospel, ye all are partakers of my grace. [8]For God is my record, how greatly I long after you all in the bowels of Jesus Christ. [9]And this I pray, that your love may abound yet more and more in knowledge and *in* all judgment; [10]That ye may approve things that are excellent; that ye may be sincere and without offence till the day of Christ; [11]Being filled with the fruits of righteousness, which are by Jesus Christ, unto the glory and praise of God.

[12]But I would ye should understand, brethren, that the things *which happened* unto me have fallen out rather unto the furtherance of the gospel; [13]So that my bonds in Christ are manifest in all the palace, and in all other *places;* [14]And many of the brethren in the Lord, waxing confident by my bonds, are much more bold to speak the word without fear. [15]Some indeed preach Christ even of envy and strife; and some also of good will: [16]The one preach Christ of contention, not sincerely, supposing to add affliction to my bonds: [17]But the other of love, knowing that I am set for the defence of the gospel. [18]What then? notwithstanding, every way, whether in pretence, or in truth, Christ is preached; and I therein do rejoice, yea, and will rejoice. [19]For I know that this shall turn to my salvation through your prayer, and the supply of the Spirit of Jesus Christ, [20]According to my earnest expectation and *my* hope, that in nothing I shall be ashamed, but *that* with all boldness, as always, *so* now also Christ shall be magnified in my body, whether *it be* by life, or by death. [21]For to me to live *is* Christ, and to die *is* gain. [22]But if I live in the flesh, this *is* the fruit of my labour: yet what I shall choose I wot not. [23]For I am in a strait betwixt two, having a desire to depart, and to be with Christ; which is far better: [24]Nevertheless to abide in the flesh *is* more needful for you. [25]And having this confidence, I know that I shall abide and continue with you all for your furtherance and joy of faith; [26]That your rejoicing may be more abundant in Jesus Christ for me by my coming to you again. [27]Only let your conversation be as it becometh the gospel of Christ: that whether I come and see you, or else be absent, I may hear of your affairs, that ye stand fast in one spirit, with one mind striving together for the faith of the gospel; [28]And in nothing terrified by your adversaries: which is to them an evident token of perdition, but to you of salvation, and that of God. [29]For unto you it is given in the behalf of Christ, not only to believe on him, but also to suffer for his sake; [30]Having the same conflict which ye saw in me, and now hear *to be* in me.

2 If *there be* therefore any consolation in Christ, if any comfort of love, if any fellowship of the Spirit, if any bowels and mercies, [2]Fulfil ye my joy, that ye be likeminded, having the same love, *being* of one accord, of one mind. [3]*Let* nothing *be done* through strife or vainglory; but in lowliness of mind let each esteem other better than themselves. [4]Look not every man on his own things, but every man also on the things of others. [5]Let this mind be in you, which was also in Christ Jesus:

[6]Who, being in the form of God, thought it not robbery to be equal with God: [7]But made himself of no reputation, and took upon him the form of a servant, and was made in the likeness of men: [8]And being

found in fashion as a man, he humbled himself, and became obedient unto death, even the death of the cross.

[9]Wherefore God also hath highly exalted him, and given him a name which is above every name: [10]That at the name of Jesus every knee should bow, of *things* in heaven, and *things* in earth, and *things* under the earth; [11]And *that* every tongue should confess that Jesus Christ *is* Lord, to the glory of God the Father.

[12]Wherefore, my beloved, as ye have always obeyed, not as in my presence only, but now much more in my absence, work out your own salvation with fear and trembling. [13]For it is God which worketh in you both to will and to do of *his* good pleasure. [14]Do all things without murmurings and disputings: [15]That ye may be blameless and harmless, the sons of God, without rebuke, in the midst of a crooked and perverse nation, among whom ye shine as lights in the world; [16]Holding forth the word of life; that I may rejoice in the day of Christ, that I have not run in vain, neither laboured in vain. [17]Yea, and if I be offered upon the sacrifice and service of your faith, I joy, and rejoice with you all. [18]For the same cause also do ye joy, and rejoice with me.

[19]But I trust in the Lord Jesus to send Timotheus shortly unto you, that I also may be of good comfort, when I know your state. [20]For I have no man likeminded, who will naturally care for your state. [21]For all seek their own, not the things which are Jesus Christ's. [22]But ye know the proof of him, that, as a son with the father, he hath served with me in the gospel. [23]Him therefore I hope to send presently, so soon as I shall see how it will go with me. [24]But I trust in the Lord that I also myself shall come shortly. [25]Yet I supposed it necessary to send to you Epaphroditus, my brother, and companion in labour, and fellow soldier, but your messenger, and he that ministered to my wants. [26]For he longed after you all, and was full of heaviness, because that ye had heard that he had been sick. [27]For indeed he was sick nigh unto death: but God had mercy on him; and not on him only, but on me also, lest I should have sorrow upon sorrow. [28]I sent him therefore the more carefully, that,

when ye see him again, ye may rejoice, and that I may be the less sorrowful. [29]Receive him therefore in the Lord with all gladness; and hold such in reputation: [30]Because for the work of Christ he was nigh unto death, not regarding his life, to supply your lack of service toward me.

3 Finally, my brethren, rejoice in the Lord. To write the same things to you, to me indeed *is* not grievous, but for you *it is* safe.

[2]Beware of dogs, beware of evil workers, beware of the concision. [3]For we are the circumcision, which worship God in the spirit, and rejoice in Christ Jesus, and have no confidence in the flesh. [4]Though I might also have confidence in the flesh. If any other man thinketh that he hath whereof he might trust in the flesh, I more: [5]Circumcised the eighth day, of the stock of Israel, *of* the tribe of Benjamin, an Hebrew of the Hebrews; as touching the law, a Pharisee; [6]Concerning zeal, persecuting the church; touching the righteousness which is in the law, blameless. [7]But what things were gain to me, those I counted loss for Christ. [8]Yea doubtless, and I count all things *but* loss for the excellency of the knowledge of Christ Jesus my Lord: for whom I have suffered the loss of all things, and do count them *but* dung, that I may win Christ, [9]And be found in him, not having mine own righteousness, which is of the law, but that which is through the faith of Christ, the righteousness which is of God by faith: [10]That I may know him, and the power of his resurrection, and the fellowship of his sufferings, being made conformable unto his death; [11]If by any means I might attain unto the resurrection of the dead. [12]Not as though I had already attained, either were already perfect: but I follow after, if that I may apprehend that for which also I am apprehended of Christ Jesus. [13]Brethren, I count not myself to have apprehended: but *this* one thing *I do,* forgetting those things which are behind, and reaching forth unto those things which are before, [14]I press toward the mark for the prize of the high calling of God in Christ Jesus. [15]Let us therefore, as many as be perfect, be thus minded: and if in any thing ye be otherwise minded, God shall reveal

even this unto you. [16]Nevertheless, whereto we have already attained, let us walk by the same rule, let us mind the same thing. [17]Brethren, be followers together of me, and mark them which walk so as ye have us for an ensample. [18](For many walk, of whom I have told you often, and now tell you even weeping, *that they are* the enemies of the cross of Christ: [19]Whose end *is* destruction, whose God *is their* belly, and *whose* glory *is* in their shame, who mind earthly things.) [20]For our conversation is in heaven; from whence also we look for the Saviour, the Lord Jesus Christ: [21]Who shall change our vile body, that it may be fashioned like unto his glorious body, according to the working whereby he is able even to subdue all things unto himself.

4 Therefore, my brethren dearly beloved and longed for, my joy and crown, so stand fast in the Lord, *my* dearly beloved. [2]I beseech Euodias, and beseech Syntyche, that they be of the same mind in the Lord. [3]And I intreat thee also, true yokefellow, help those women which laboured with me in the gospel, with Clement also, and *with* other my fellowlabourers, whose names *are* in the book of life. [4]Rejoice in the Lord alway: *and* again I say, Rejoice. [5]Let your moderation be known unto all men. The Lord *is* at hand. [6]Be careful for nothing; but in every thing by prayer and supplication with thanksgiving let your requests be made known unto God. [7]And the peace of God, which passeth all understanding, shall keep your hearts and minds through Christ Jesus. [8]Finally, brethren, whatsoever things are true, whatsoever things *are* honest, whatsoever things *are* just, whatsoever things *are* pure, whatsoever things *are* lovely, whatsoever things *are* of good report; if *there be* any virtue, and if *there be*

any praise, think on these things. [9]Those things, which ye have both learned, and received, and heard, and seen in me, do: and the God of peace shall be with you.

[10]But I rejoiced in the Lord greatly, that now at the last your care of me hath flourished again; wherein ye were also careful, but ye lacked opportunity. [11]Not that I speak in respect of want: for I have learned, in whatsoever state I am, *therewith* to be content. [12]I know both how to be abased, and I know how to abound: every where and in all things I am instructed both to be full and to be hungry, both to abound and to suffer need. [13]I can do all things through Christ which strengtheneth me. [14]Notwithstanding ye have well done, that ye did communicate with my affliction. [15]Now ye Philippians know also, that in the beginning of the gospel, when I departed from Macedonia, no church communicated with me as concerning giving and receiving, but ye only. [16]For even in Thessalonica ye sent once and again unto my necessity. [17]Not because I desire a gift: but I desire fruit that may abound to your account. [18]But I have all, and abound: I am full, having received of Epaphroditus the things *which were sent* from you, an odour of a sweet smell, a sacrifice acceptable, wellpleasing to God. [19]But my God shall supply all your need according to his riches in glory by Christ Jesus. [20]Now unto God and our Father *be* glory for ever and ever. Amen.

[21]Salute every saint in Christ Jesus. The brethren which are with me greet you. [22]All the saints salute you, chiefly they that are of Caesar's household.

[23]The grace of our Lord Jesus Christ *be* with you all. Amen.

The Epistle of Paul the Apostle to the
COLOSSIANS

1 Paul, an apostle of Jesus Christ by the will of God, and Timotheus *our* brother,

² To the saints and faithful brethren in Christ which are at Colosse:

Grace *be* unto you, and peace, from God our Father and the Lord Jesus Christ.

³ We give thanks to God and the Father of our Lord Jesus Christ, praying always for you, ⁴ Since we heard of your faith in Christ Jesus, and of the love *which ye have* to all the saints, ⁵ For the hope which is laid up for you in heaven, whereof ye heard before in the word of the truth of the gospel; ⁶ Which is come unto you, as *it is* in all the world; and bringeth forth fruit, as *it doth* also in you, since the day ye heard *of it,* and knew the grace of God in truth: ⁷ As ye also learned of Epaphras our dear fellowservant, who is for you a faithful minister of Christ; ⁸ Who also declared unto us your love in the Spirit. ⁹ For this cause we also, since the day we heard *it,* do not cease to pray for you, and to desire that ye might be filled with the knowledge of his will in all wisdom and spiritual understanding; ¹⁰ That ye might walk worthy of the Lord unto all pleasing, being fruitful in every good work, and increasing in the knowledge of God; ¹¹ Strengthened with all might, according to his glorious power, unto all patience and longsuffering with joyfulness; ¹² Giving thanks unto the Father, which hath made us meet to be partakers of the inheritance of the saints in light: ¹³ Who hath delivered us from the power of darkness, and hath translated *us* into the kingdom of his dear Son: ¹⁴ In whom we have redemption through his blood, *even* the forgiveness of sins: ¹⁵ Who is the image of the invisible God, the firstborn of every creature: ¹⁶ For by him were all things created, that are in heaven, and that are in earth, visible and invisible, whether *they be* thrones, or dominions, or principalities, or powers: all things were created by him, and for him: ¹⁷ And he is before all things, and by him all things consist. ¹⁸ And he is the head of the body, the church: who is the beginning, the firstborn from the dead; that in all *things* he might have the preeminence. ¹⁹ For it pleased *the Father* that in him should all fulness dwell; ²⁰ And, having made peace through the blood of his cross, by him to reconcile all things unto himself; by him, *I say,* whether *they be* things in earth, or things in heaven. ²¹ And you, that were sometime alienated and enemies in *your* mind by wicked works, yet now hath he reconciled ²² In the body of his flesh through death, to present you holy and unblameable and unreproveable in his sight: ²³ If ye continue in the faith grounded and settled, and *be* not moved away from the hope of the gospel, which ye have heard, *and* which was preached to every creature which is under heaven; whereof I Paul am made a minister; ²⁴ Who now rejoice in my sufferings for you, and fill up that which is behind of the afflictions of Christ in my flesh for his body's sake, which is the church: ²⁵ Whereof I am made a minister, according to the dispensation of God which is given to me for you, to fulfil the word of God; ²⁶ *Even* the mystery which hath been hid from ages and from generations, but now is made manifest to his saints: ²⁷ To whom God would make known what *is* the riches of the glory of this mystery among the Gentiles; which is Christ in you, the hope of glory: ²⁸ Whom we preach, warning every man, and teaching every man in all wisdom; that we may present every man perfect in Christ Jesus: ²⁹ Whereunto I also labour, striving according to his working, which worketh in me mightily.

2 For I would that ye knew what great conflict I have for you, and *for* them at Laodicea, and *for* as many as have not seen my face in the flesh; ² That their hearts might be comforted, being knit together in love, and unto all riches of the full assurance of understanding, to the acknowledgement of the mystery of God, and of the Father, and of Christ; ³ In whom are hid all the treasures of wisdom and knowledge. ⁴ And this I say, lest any man should beguile you with enticing words. ⁵ For though I be absent in the flesh, yet am I with you in the spirit, joying and beholding your order, and the stedfastness of your faith in Christ.

⁶As ye have therefore received Christ Jesus the Lord, *so* walk ye in him: ⁷Rooted and built up in him, and stablished in the faith, as ye have been taught, abounding therein with thanksgiving. ⁸Beware lest any man spoil you through philosophy and vain deceit, after the tradition of men, after the rudiments of the world, and not after Christ. ⁹For in him dwelleth all the fulness of the Godhead bodily. ¹⁰And ye are complete in him, which is the head of all principality and power: ¹¹In whom also ye are circumcised with the circumcision made without hands, in putting off the body of the sins of the flesh by the circumcision of Christ: ¹²Buried with him in baptism, wherein also ye are risen with *him* through the faith of the operation of God, who hath raised him from the dead. ¹³And you, being dead in your sins and the uncircumcision of your flesh, hath he quickened together with him, having forgiven you all trespasses; ¹⁴Blotting out the handwriting of ordinances that was against us, which was contrary to us, and took it out of the way, nailing it to his cross; ¹⁵*And* having spoiled principalities and powers, he made a shew of them openly, triumphing over them in it. ¹⁶Let no man therefore judge you in meat, or in drink, or in respect of an holyday, or of the new moon, or of the sabbath *days:* ¹⁷Which are a shadow of things to come; but the body *is* of Christ. ¹⁸Let no man beguile you of your reward in a voluntary humility and worshipping of angels, intruding into those things which he hath not seen, vainly puffed up by his fleshly mind, ¹⁹And not holding the Head, from which all the body by joints and bands having nourishment ministered, and knit together, increaseth with the increase of God.

²⁰Wherefore if ye be dead with Christ from the rudiments of the world, why, as though living in the world, are ye subject to ordinances, ²¹(Touch not; taste not; handle not; ²²Which all are to perish with the using;) after the commandments and doctrines of men? ²³Which things have indeed a shew of wisdom in will worship, and humility, and neglecting of the body; not in any honour to the satisfying of the flesh.

3 If ye then be risen with Christ, seek those things which are above, where Christ sitteth on the right hand of God. ²Set your affection on things above, not on things on the earth. ³For ye are dead, and your life is hid with Christ in God. ⁴When Christ, *who is* our life, shall appear, then shall ye also appear with him in glory.

⁵Mortify therefore your members which are upon the earth; fornication, uncleanness, inordinate affection, evil concupiscence, and covetousness, which is idolatry: ⁶For which things' sake the wrath of God cometh on the children of disobedience: ⁷In the which ye also walked some time, when ye lived in them. ⁸But now ye also put off all these; anger, wrath, malice, blasphemy, filthy communication out of your mouth. ⁹Lie not one to another, seeing that ye have put off the old man with his deeds; ¹⁰And have put on the new *man,* which is renewed in knowledge after the image of him that created him: ¹¹Where there is neither Greek nor Jew, circumcision nor uncircumcision, Barbarian, Scythian, bond *nor* free: but Christ *is* all, and in all. ¹²Put on therefore, as the elect of God, holy and beloved, bowels of mercies, kindness, humbleness of mind, meekness, longsuffering; ¹³Forbearing one another, and forgiving one another, if any man have a quarrel against any: even as Christ forgave you, so also *do* ye. ¹⁴And above all these things *put on* charity, which is the bond of perfectness. ¹⁵And let the peace of God rule in your hearts, to the which also ye are called in one body; and be ye thankful. ¹⁶Let the word of Christ dwell in you richly in all wisdom; teaching and admonishing one another in psalms and hymns and spiritual songs, singing with grace in your hearts to the Lord. ¹⁷And whatsoever ye do in word or deed, *do* all in the name of the Lord Jesus, giving thanks to God and the Father by him.

¹⁸Wives, submit yourselves unto your own husbands, as it is fit in the Lord. ¹⁹Husbands, love *your* wives, and be not bitter against them. ²⁰Children, obey *your* parents in all things: for this is well pleasing unto the Lord. ²¹Fathers, provoke not your children *to anger,* lest they be discouraged. ²²Servants, obey in all things *your* masters according to the flesh; not with eyeservice,

as menpleasers; but in singleness of heart, fearing God: [23]And whatsoever ye do, do *it* heartily, as to the Lord, and not unto men; [24]Knowing that of the Lord ye shall receive the reward of the inheritance: for ye serve the Lord Christ. [25]But he that doeth wrong shall receive for the wrong which he hath done: and there is no respect of persons.

4 Masters, give unto *your* servants that which is just and equal; knowing that ye also have a Master in heaven.

[2]Continue in prayer, and watch in the same with thanksgiving; [3]Withal praying also for us, that God would open unto us a door of utterance, to speak the mystery of Christ, for which I am also in bonds: [4]That I may make it manifest, as I ought to speak. [5]Walk in wisdom toward them that are without, redeeming the time. [6]Let your speech *be* alway with grace, seasoned with salt, that ye may know how ye ought to answer every man.

[7]All my state shall Tychicus declare unto you, *who is* a beloved brother, and a faithful minister and fellowservant in the Lord: [8]Whom I have sent unto you for the same purpose, that he might know your estate, and comfort your hearts; [9]With Onesimus, a faithful and beloved brother, who is one

of you. They shall make known unto you all things which *are done* here.

[10]Aristarchus my fellowprisoner saluteth you, and Marcus, sister's son to Barnabas, (touching whom ye received commandments: if he come unto you, receive him;) [11]And Jesus, which is called Justus, who are of the circumcision. These only *are my* fellow workers unto the kingdom of God, which have been a comfort unto me. [12]Epaphras, who is *one* of you, a servant of Christ, saluteth you, always labouring fervently for you in prayers, that ye may stand perfect and complete in all the will of God. [13]For I bear him record, that he hath a great zeal for you, and them *that are* in Laodicea, and them in Hierapolis. [14]Luke, the beloved physician, and Demas, greet you. [15]Salute the brethren which are in Laodicea, and Nymphas, and the church which is in his house. [16]And when this epistle is read among you, cause that it be read also in the church of the Laodiceans; and that ye likewise read the *epistle* from Laodicea. [17]And say to Archippus, Take heed to the ministry which thou hast received in the Lord, that thou fulfil it.

[18]The salutation by the hand of me Paul. Remember my bonds. Grace *be* with you. Amen.

The First Epistle of Paul the Apostle to the
THESSALONIANS

1 Paul, and Silvanus, and Timotheus,

unto the church of the Thessalonians *which is* in God the Father and *in* the Lord Jesus Christ:

Grace *be* unto you, and peace, from God our Father, and the Lord Jesus Christ.

[2] We give thanks to God always for you all, making mention of you in our prayers; [3] Remembering without ceasing your work of faith, and labour of love, and patience of hope in our Lord Jesus Christ, in the sight of God and our Father; [4] Knowing, brethren beloved, your election of God. [5] For our gospel came not unto you in word only, but also in power, and in the Holy Ghost, and in much assurance; as ye know what manner of men we were among you for your sake. [6] And ye became followers of us, and of the Lord, having received the word in much affliction, with joy of the Holy Ghost: [7] So that ye were ensamples to all that believe in Macedonia and Achaia. [8] For from you sounded out the word of the Lord not only in Macedonia and Achaia, but also in every place your faith to God-ward is spread abroad; so that we need not to speak any thing. [9] For they themselves shew of us what manner of entering in we had unto you, and how ye turned to God from idols to serve the living and true God; [10] And to wait for his Son from heaven, whom he raised from the dead, *even* Jesus, which delivered us from the wrath to come.

2 For yourselves, brethren, know our entrance in unto you, that it was not in vain: [2] But even after that we had suffered before, and were shamefully entreated, as ye know, at Philippi, we were bold in our God to speak unto you the gospel of God with much contention. [3] For our exhortation *was* not of deceit, nor of uncleanness, nor in guile: [4] But as we were allowed of God to be put in trust with the gospel, even so we speak; not as pleasing men, but God, which trieth our hearts. [5] For neither at any time used we flattering words, as ye know, nor a cloke of covetousness; God *is* witness:

[6] Nor of men sought we glory, neither of you, nor *yet* of others, when we might have been burdensome, as the apostles of Christ. [7] But we were gentle among you, even as a nurse cherisheth her children: [8] So being affectionately desirous of you, we were willing to have imparted unto you, not the gospel of God only, but also our own souls, because ye were dear unto us. [9] For ye remember, brethren, our labour and travail: for labouring night and day, because we would not be chargeable unto any of you, we preached unto you the gospel of God. [10] Ye *are* witnesses, and God *also,* how holily and justly and unblameably we behaved ourselves among you that believe: [11] As ye know how we exhorted and comforted and charged every one of you, as a father *doth* his children, [12] That ye would walk worthy of God, who hath called you unto his kingdom and glory.

[13] For this cause also thank we God without ceasing, because, when ye received the word of God which ye heard of us, ye received *it* not *as* the word of men, but as it is in truth, the word of God, which effectually worketh also in you that believe. [14] For ye, brethren, became followers of the churches of God which in Judaea are in Christ Jesus: for ye also have suffered like things of your own countrymen, even as they *have* of the Jews: [15] Who both killed the Lord Jesus, and their own prophets, and have persecuted us; and they please not God, and are contrary to all men: [16] Forbidding us to speak to the Gentiles that they might be saved, to fill up their sins alway: for the wrath is come upon them to the uttermost.

[17] But we, brethren, being taken from you for a short time in presence, not in heart, endeavoured the more abundantly to see your face with great desire. [18] Wherefore we would have come unto you, even I Paul, once and again; but Satan hindered us. [19] For what *is* our hope, or joy, or crown of rejoicing? *Are* not even ye in the presence of our Lord Jesus Christ at his coming? [20] For ye are our glory and joy.

3 Wherefore when we could no longer forbear, we thought it good to be left at Athens alone; ²And sent Timotheus, our brother, and minister of God, and our fellowlabourer in the gospel of Christ, to establish you, and to comfort you concerning your faith: ³That no man should be moved by these afflictions: for yourselves know that we are appointed thereunto. ⁴For verily, when we were with you, we told you before that we should suffer tribulation; even as it came to pass, and ye know. ⁵For this cause, when I could no longer forbear, I sent to know your faith, lest by some means the tempter have tempted you, and our labour be in vain. ⁶But now when Timotheus came from you unto us, and brought us good tidings of your faith and charity, and that ye have good remembrance of us always, desiring greatly to see us, as we also *to see* you: ⁷Therefore, brethren, we were comforted over you in all our affliction and distress by your faith: ⁸For now we live, if ye stand fast in the Lord. ⁹For what thanks can we render to God again for you, for all the joy wherewith we joy for your sakes before our God; ¹⁰Night and day praying exceedingly that we might see your face, and might perfect that which is lacking in your faith? ¹¹Now God himself and our Father, and our Lord Jesus Christ, direct our way unto you. ¹²And the Lord make you to increase and abound in love one toward another, and toward all *men,* even as we *do* toward you: ¹³To the end he may stablish your hearts unblameable in holiness before God, even our Father, at the coming of our Lord Jesus Christ with all his saints.

4 Furthermore then we beseech you, brethren, and exhort *you* by the Lord Jesus, that as ye have received of us how ye ought to walk and to please God, *so* ye would abound more and more. ²For ye know what commandments we gave you by the Lord Jesus. ³For this is the will of God, *even* your sanctification, that ye should abstain from fornication: ⁴That every one of you should know how to possess his vessel in sanctification and honour; ⁵Not in the lust of concupiscence, even as the Gentiles which know not God: ⁶That no *man* go beyond and defraud his brother in *any* matter: because that the Lord *is* the avenger of all such, as we also have forewarned you and testified. ⁷For God hath not called us

unto uncleanness, but unto holiness. ⁸He therefore that despiseth, despiseth not man, but God, who hath also given unto us his holy Spirit. ⁹But as touching brotherly love ye need not that I write unto you: for ye yourselves are taught of God to love one another. ¹⁰And indeed ye do it toward all the brethren which are in all Macedonia: but we beseech you, brethren, that ye increase more and more; ¹¹And that ye study to be quiet, and to do your own business, and to work with your own hands, as we commanded you; ¹²That ye may walk honestly toward them that are without, and *that* ye may have lack of nothing.

¹³But I would not have you to be ignorant, brethren, concerning them which are asleep, that ye sorrow not, even as others which have no hope. ¹⁴For if we believe that Jesus died and rose again, even so them also which sleep in Jesus will God bring with him. ¹⁵For this we say unto you by the word of the Lord, that we which are alive *and* remain unto the coming of the Lord shall not prevent them which are asleep. ¹⁶For the Lord himself shall descend from heaven with a shout, with the voice of the archangel, and with the trump of God: and the dead in Christ shall rise first: ¹⁷Then we which are alive *and* remain shall be caught up together with them in the clouds, to meet the Lord in the air: and so shall we ever be with the Lord. ¹⁸Wherefore comfort one another with these words.

5 But of the times and the seasons, brethren, ye have no need that I write unto you. ²For yourselves know perfectly that the day of the Lord so cometh as a thief in the night. ³For when they shall say, Peace and safety; then sudden destruction cometh upon them, as travail upon a woman with child; and they shall not escape. ⁴But ye, brethren, are not in darkness, that that day should overtake you as a thief. ⁵Ye are all the children of light, and the children of the day: we are not of the night, nor of darkness. ⁶Therefore let us not sleep, as *do* others; but let us watch and be sober. ⁷For they that sleep sleep in the night; and they that be drunken are drunken in the night. ⁸But let us, who are of the day, be sober, putting on the breastplate of faith and love; and for an helmet, the hope of salvation. ⁹For

God hath not appointed us to wrath, but to obtain salvation by our Lord Jesus Christ, [10]Who died for us, that, whether we wake or sleep, we should live together with him. [11]Wherefore comfort yourselves together, and edify one another, even as also ye do.

[12]And we beseech you, brethren, to know them which labour among you, and are over you in the Lord, and admonish you; [13]And to esteem them very highly in love for their work's sake. *And* be at peace among yourselves. [14]Now we exhort you, brethren, warn them that are unruly, comfort the feebleminded, support the weak, be patient toward all *men.* [15]See that none render evil for evil unto any *man;* but ever follow that which is good, both among yourselves, and to all *men.* [16]Rejoice evermore. [17]Pray without ceasing. [18]In every thing give thanks: for this is the will of God in Christ Jesus concerning you. [19]Quench not the Spirit. [20]Despise not prophesyings. [21]Prove all things; hold fast that which is good. [22]Abstain from all appearance of evil. [23]And the very God of peace sanctify you wholly; and *I pray God* your whole spirit and soul and body be preserved blameless unto the coming of our Lord Jesus Christ. [24]Faithful *is* he that calleth you, who also will do *it.*

[25]Brethren, pray for us.

[26]Greet all the brethren with an holy kiss. [27]I charge you by the Lord that this epistle be read unto all the holy brethren.

[28]The grace of our Lord Jesus Christ *be* with you. Amen.

1 Paul, and Silvanus, and Timotheus,

unto the church of the Thessalonians in God our Father and the Lord Jesus Christ:

²Grace unto you, and peace, from God our Father and the Lord Jesus Christ.

³We are bound to thank God always for you, brethren, as it is meet, because that your faith groweth exceedingly, and the charity of every one of you all toward each other aboundeth; ⁴So that we ourselves glory in you in the churches of God for your patience and faith in all your persecutions and tribulations that ye endure: ⁵*Which is* a manifest token of the righteous judgment of God, that ye may be counted worthy of the kingdom of God, for which ye also suffer: ⁶Seeing *it is* a righteous thing with God to recompense tribulation to them that trouble you; ⁷And to you who are troubled rest with us, when the Lord Jesus shall be revealed from heaven with his mighty angels, ⁸In flaming fire taking vengeance on them that know not God, and that obey not the gospel of our Lord Jesus Christ: ⁹Who shall be punished with everlasting destruction from the presence of the Lord, and from the glory of his power; ¹⁰When he shall come to be glorified in his saints, and to be admired in all them that believe (because our testimony among you was believed) in that day. ¹¹Wherefore also we pray always for you, that our God would count you worthy of *this* calling, and fulfil all the good pleasure of *his* goodness, and the work of faith with power: ¹²That the name of our Lord Jesus Christ may be glorified in you, and ye in him, according to the grace of our God and the Lord Jesus Christ.

2 Now we beseech you, brethren, by the coming of our Lord Jesus Christ, and *by* our gathering together unto him, ²That ye be not soon shaken in mind, or be troubled, neither by spirit, nor by word, nor by letter as from us, as that the day of Christ is at hand. ³Let no man deceive you by any means: for *that day shall not come,* except

there come a falling away first, and that man of sin be revealed, the son of perdition; ⁴Who opposeth and exalteth himself above all that is called God, or that is worshipped; so that he as God sitteth in the temple of God, shewing himself that he is God. ⁵Remember ye not, that, when I was yet with you, I told you these things? ⁶And now ye know what withholdeth that he might be revealed in his time. ⁷For the mystery of iniquity doth already work: only he who now letteth *will let,* until he be taken out of the way. ⁸And then shall that Wicked be revealed, whom the Lord shall consume with the spirit of his mouth, and shall destroy with the brightness of his coming: ⁹*Even him,* whose coming is after the working of Satan with all power and signs and lying wonders, ¹⁰And with all deceivableness of unrighteousness in them that perish; because they received not the love of the truth, that they might be saved. ¹¹And for this cause God shall send them strong delusion, that they should believe a lie: ¹²That they all might be damned who believed not the truth, but had pleasure in unrighteousness.

¹³But we are bound to give thanks alway to God for you, brethren beloved of the Lord, because God hath from the beginning chosen you to salvation through sanctification of the Spirit and belief of the truth: ¹⁴Whereunto he called you by our gospel, to the obtaining of the glory of our Lord Jesus Christ. ¹⁵Therefore, brethren, stand fast, and hold the traditions which ye have been taught, whether by word, or our epistle. ¹⁶Now our Lord Jesus Christ himself, and God, even our Father, which hath loved us, and hath given *us* everlasting consolation and good hope through grace, ¹⁷Comfort your hearts, and stablish you in every good word and work.

3 Finally, brethren, pray for us, that the word of the Lord may have *free* course, and be glorified, even as *it is* with you: ²And that we may be delivered from unreasonable and wicked men: for all *men* have not faith. ³But the Lord is faithful, who shall stablish you, and keep *you* from evil. ⁴And we have confidence in the Lord touching you, that ye both do and will do the things which we command you. ⁵And the Lord direct your hearts into the love of God, and into the patient waiting for Christ.

⁶Now we command you, brethren, in the name of our Lord Jesus Christ, that ye withdraw yourselves from every brother that walketh disorderly, and not after the tradition which he received of us. ⁷For yourselves know how ye ought to follow us: for we behaved not ourselves disorderly among you; ⁸Neither did we eat any man's bread for nought; but wrought with labour and travail night and day, that we might not be chargeable to any of you: ⁹Not because we have not power, but to make ourselves an ensample unto you to follow us. ¹⁰For even when we were with you, this we commanded you, that if any would not

work, neither should he eat. ¹¹For we hear that there are some which walk among you disorderly, working not at all, but are busybodies. ¹²Now them that are such we command and exhort by our Lord Jesus Christ, that with quietness they work, and eat their own bread. ¹³But ye, brethren, be not weary in well doing. ¹⁴And if any man obey not our word by this epistle, note that man, and have no company with him, that he may be ashamed. ¹⁵Yet count *him* not as an enemy, but admonish *him* as a brother.

¹⁶Now the Lord of peace himself give you peace always by all means. The Lord *be* with you all.

¹⁷The salutation of Paul with mine own hand, which is the token in every epistle: so I write. ¹⁸The grace of our Lord Jesus Christ *be* with you all. Amen.

1 Paul, an apostle of Jesus Christ by the commandment of God our Saviour, and Lord Jesus Christ, *which is* our hope;

²Unto Timothy, *my* own son in the faith:

Grace, mercy, *and* peace, from God our Father and Jesus Christ our Lord.

³As I besought thee to abide still at Ephesus, when I went into Macedonia, that thou mightest charge some that they teach no other doctrine, ⁴Neither give heed to fables and endless genealogies, which minister questions, rather than godly edifying which is in faith: *so do.* ⁵Now the end of the commandment is charity out of a pure heart, and *of* a good conscience, and *of* faith unfeigned: ⁶From which some having swerved have turned aside unto vain jangling; ⁷Desiring to be teachers of the law; understanding neither what they say, nor whereof they affirm. ⁸But we know that the law *is* good, if a man use it lawfully; ⁹Knowing this, that the law is not made for a righteous man, but for the lawless and disobedient, for the ungodly and for sinners, for unholy and profane, for murderers of fathers and murderers of mothers, for manslayers, ¹⁰For whoremongers, for them that defile themselves with mankind, for menstealers, for liars, for perjured persons, and if there be any other thing that is contrary to sound doctrine; ¹¹According to the glorious gospel of the blessed God, which was committed to my trust. ¹²And I thank Christ Jesus our Lord, who hath enabled me, for that he counted me faithful, putting me into the ministry; ¹³Who was before a blasphemer, and a persecutor, and injurious: but I obtained mercy, because I did *it* ignorantly in unbelief. ¹⁴And the grace of our Lord was exceeding abundant with faith and love which is in Christ Jesus. ¹⁵This *is* a faithful saying, and worthy of all acceptation, that Christ Jesus came into the world to save sinners; of whom I am chief. ¹⁶Howbeit for this cause I obtained mercy, that in me first Jesus Christ might shew forth all longsuffering, for a pattern to them which should hereafter believe on him to life everlasting. ¹⁷Now unto the King eternal, immortal, invisible, the only wise God, *be* honour and glory for ever and ever. Amen. ¹⁸This charge I commit unto thee, son Timothy, according to the prophecies which went before on thee, that thou by them mightest war a good warfare; ¹⁹Holding faith, and a good conscience; which some having put away concerning faith have made shipwreck: ²⁰Of whom is Hymenaeus and Alexander; whom I have delivered unto Satan, that they may learn not to blaspheme.

2 I exhort therefore, that, first of all, supplications, prayers, intercessions, *and* giving of thanks, be made for all men; ²For kings, and *for* all that are in authority; that we may lead a quiet and peaceable life in all godliness and honesty. ³For this *is* good and acceptable in the sight of God our Saviour; ⁴Who will have all men to be saved, and to come unto the knowledge of the truth. ⁵For *there is* one God, and one mediator between God and men, the man Christ Jesus; ⁶Who gave himself a ransom for all, to be testified in due time. ⁷Whereunto I am ordained a preacher, and an apostle, (I speak the truth in Christ, *and* lie not;) a teacher of the Gentiles in faith and verity. ⁸I will therefore that men pray every where, lifting up holy hands, without wrath and doubting. ⁹In like manner also, that women adorn themselves in modest apparel, with shamefacedness and sobriety; not with broided hair, or gold, or pearls, or costly array; ¹⁰But (which becometh women professing godliness) with good works. ¹¹Let the woman learn in silence with all subjection. ¹²But I suffer not a woman to teach, nor to usurp authority over the man, but to be in silence. ¹³For Adam was first formed, then Eve. ¹⁴And Adam was not deceived, but the woman being deceived was in the transgression. ¹⁵Notwithstanding she shall be saved in childbearing, if they continue in faith and charity and holiness with sobriety.

3 This *is* a true saying, If a man desire the office of a bishop, he desireth a good work. ²A bishop then must be blameless, the husband of one wife, vigilant, sober, of good behaviour, given to hospitality, apt to teach; ³Not given to wine, no striker, not greedy of filthy lucre; but patient, not a brawler, not covetous; ⁴One that ruleth well his own house, having his children in subjection with all gravity; ⁵(For if a man know not how to rule his own house, how shall he take care of the church of God?) ⁶Not a novice, lest being lifted up with pride he fall into the condemnation of the devil. ⁷Moreover he must have a good report of them which are without; lest he fall into reproach and the snare of the devil. ⁸Likewise *must* the deacons *be* grave, not doubletongued, not given to much wine, not greedy of filthy lucre; ⁹Holding the mystery of the faith in a pure conscience. ¹⁰And let these also first be proved; then let them use the office of a deacon, being *found* blameless. ¹¹Even so *must their* wives be grave, not slanderers, sober, faithful in all things. ¹²Let the deacons be the husbands of one wife, ruling their children and their own houses well. ¹³For they that have used the office of a deacon well purchase to themselves a good degree, and great boldness in the faith which is in Christ Jesus. ¹⁴These things write I unto thee, hoping to come unto thee shortly: ¹⁵But if I tarry long, that thou mayest know how thou oughtest to behave thyself in the house of God, which is the church of the living God, the pillar and ground of the truth. ¹⁶And without controversy great is the mystery of godliness:

God was manifest in the flesh, justified in the Spirit, seen of angels, preached unto the Gentiles, believed on in the world, received up into glory.

4 Now the Spirit speaketh expressly, that in the latter times some shall depart from the faith, giving heed to seducing spirits, and doctrines of devils; ²Speaking lies in hypocrisy; having their conscience seared with a hot iron; ³Forbidding to marry, *and commanding* to abstain from meats, which God hath created to be received with thanksgiving of them which believe and know the truth. ⁴For every

creature of God *is* good, and nothing to be refused, if it be received with thanksgiving: ⁵For it is sanctified by the word of God and prayer. ⁶If thou put the brethren in remembrance of these things, thou shalt be a good minister of Jesus Christ, nourished up in the words of faith and of good doctrine, whereunto thou hast attained. ⁷But refuse profane and old wives' fables, and exercise thyself *rather* unto godliness. ⁸For bodily exercise profiteth little: but godliness is profitable unto all things, having promise of the life that now is, and of that which is to come. ⁹This *is* a faithful saying and worthy of all acceptation. ¹⁰For therefore we both labour and suffer reproach, because we trust in the living God, who is the Saviour of all men, specially of those that believe.

¹¹These things command and teach. ¹²Let no man despise thy youth; but be thou an example of the believers, in word, in conversation, in charity, in spirit, in faith, in purity. ¹³Till I come, give attendance to reading, to exhortation, to doctrine. ¹⁴Neglect not the gift that is in thee, which was given thee by prophecy, with the laying on of the hands of the presbytery. ¹⁵Meditate upon these things; give thyself wholly to them; that thy profiting may appear to all. ¹⁶Take heed unto thyself, and unto the doctrine; continue in them: for in doing this thou shalt both save thyself, and them that hear thee.

5 Rebuke not an elder, but intreat *him* as a father; *and* the younger men as brethren; ²The elder women as mothers; the younger as sisters, with all purity. ³Honour widows that are widows indeed. ⁴But if any widow have children or nephews, let them learn first to shew piety at home, and to requite their parents: for that is good and acceptable before God. ⁵Now she that is a widow indeed, and desolate, trusteth in God, and continueth in supplications and prayers night and day. ⁶But she that liveth in pleasure is dead while she liveth. ⁷And these things give in charge, that they may be blameless. ⁸But if any provide not for his own, and specially for those of his own house, he hath denied the faith, and is worse than an infidel. ⁹Let not a widow be taken into

the number under threescore years old, having been the wife of one man, ¹⁰Well reported of for good works; if she have brought up children, if she have lodged strangers, if she have washed the saints' feet, if she have relieved the afflicted, if she have diligently followed every good work. ¹¹But the younger widows refuse: for when they have begun to wax wanton against Christ, they will marry; ¹²Having damnation, because they have cast off their first faith. ¹³And withal they learn *to be* idle, wandering about from house to house; and not only idle, but tattlers also and busybodies, speaking things which they ought not. ¹⁴I will therefore that the younger women marry, bear children, guide the house, give none occasion to the adversary to speak reproachfully. ¹⁵For some are already turned aside after Satan. ¹⁶If any man or woman that believeth have widows, let them relieve them, and let not the church be charged; that it may relieve them that are widows indeed. ¹⁷Let the elders that rule well be counted worthy of double honour, especially they who labour in the word and doctrine. ¹⁸For the scripture saith, Thou shalt not muzzle the ox that treadeth out the corn. And, The labourer *is* worthy of his reward. ¹⁹Against an elder receive not an accusation, but before two or three witnesses. ²⁰Them that sin rebuke before all, that others also may fear. ²¹I charge *thee* before God, and the Lord Jesus Christ, and the elect angels, that thou observe these things without preferring one before another, doing nothing by partiality. ²²Lay hands suddenly on no man, neither be partaker of other men's sins: keep thyself pure. ²³Drink no longer water, but use a little wine for thy stomach's sake and thine often infirmities. ²⁴Some men's sins are open beforehand, going before to judgment; and some *men* they follow after. ²⁵Likewise also the good works *of some* are manifest beforehand; and they that are otherwise cannot be hid.

6 Let as many servants as are under the yoke count their own masters worthy of all honour, that the name of God and *his* doctrine be not blasphemed. ²And they that have believing masters, let them not despise *them*, because they are brethren; but rather do *them* service, because they are faithful and beloved, partakers of the benefit. These things teach and exhort.

³If any man teach otherwise, and consent not to wholesome words, *even* the words of our Lord Jesus Christ, and to the doctrine which is according to godliness; ⁴He is proud, knowing nothing, but doting about questions and strifes of words, whereof cometh envy, strife, railings, evil surmisings, ⁵Perverse disputings of men of corrupt minds, and destitute of the truth, supposing that gain is godliness: from such withdraw thyself. ⁶But godliness with contentment is great gain. ⁷For we brought nothing into *this* world, *and it is* certain we can carry nothing out. ⁸And having food and raiment let us be therewith content. ⁹But they that will be rich fall into temptation and a snare, and *into* many foolish and hurtful lusts, which drown men in destruction and perdition. ¹⁰For the love of money is the root of all evil: which while some coveted after, they have erred from the faith, and pierced themselves through with many sorrows. ¹¹But thou, O man of God, flee these things; and follow after righteousness, godliness, faith, love, patience, meekness. ¹²Fight the good fight of faith, lay hold on eternal life, whereunto thou art also called, and hast professed a good profession before many witnesses. ¹³I give thee charge in the sight of God, who quickeneth all things, and *before* Christ Jesus, who before Pontius Pilate witnessed a good confession; ¹⁴That thou keep *this* commandment without spot, unrebukeable, until the appearing of our Lord Jesus Christ: ¹⁵Which in his times he shall shew, *who is* the blessed and only Potentate, the King of kings, and Lord of lords; ¹⁶Who only hath immortality, dwelling in the light which no man can approach unto; whom no man hath seen, nor can see: to whom *be* honour and power everlasting. Amen. ¹⁷Charge them that are rich in this world, that they be not highminded, nor trust in uncertain riches, but in the living God, who giveth us richly all things to enjoy; ¹⁸That they do good, that they be rich in good works,

ready to distribute, willing to communicate; [19]Laying up in store for themselves a good foundation against the time to come, that they may lay hold on eternal life. [20]O Timothy, keep that which is committed to thy trust, avoiding profane *and* vain babblings, and oppositions of science falsely so called: [21]Which some professing have erred concerning the faith. Grace *be* with thee. Amen.

The Second Epistle of Paul the Apostle to
TIMOTHY

1 Paul, an apostle of Jesus Christ by the will of God, according to the promise of life which is in Christ Jesus,

[2] To Timothy, *my* dearly beloved son:

Grace, mercy, *and* peace, from God the Father and Christ Jesus our Lord.

[3] I thank God, whom I serve from *my* forefathers with pure conscience, that without ceasing I have remembrance of thee in my prayers night and day; [4] Greatly desiring to see thee, being mindful of thy tears, that I may be filled with joy; [5] When I call to remembrance the unfeigned faith that is in thee, which dwelt first in thy grandmother Lois, and thy mother Eunice; and I am persuaded that in thee also. [6] Wherefore I put thee in remembrance that thou stir up the gift of God, which is in thee by the putting on of my hands. [7] For God hath not given us the spirit of fear; but of power, and of love, and of a sound mind. [8] Be not thou therefore ashamed of the testimony of our Lord, nor of me his prisoner: but be thou partaker of the afflictions of the gospel according to the power of God; [9] Who hath saved us, and called *us* with an holy calling, not according to our works, but according to his own purpose and grace, which was given us in Christ Jesus before the world began, [10] But is now made manifest by the appearing of our Saviour Jesus Christ, who hath abolished death, and hath brought life and immortality to light through the gospel: [11] Whereunto I am appointed a preacher, and an apostle, and a teacher of the Gentiles. [12] For the which cause I also suffer these things: nevertheless I am not ashamed: for I know whom I have believed, and am persuaded that he is able to keep that which I have committed unto him against that day. [13] Hold fast the form of sound words, which thou hast heard of me, in faith and love which is in Christ Jesus. [14] That good thing which was committed unto thee keep by the Holy Ghost which dwelleth in us. [15] This thou knowest, that all they which are in Asia be turned away from me; of whom are Phygellus and Hermogenes. [16] The Lord give mercy unto the house of Onesiphorus; for he oft refreshed me, and was not ashamed of my chain: [17] But, when he was in Rome, he sought me out very diligently, and found *me*. [18] The Lord grant unto him that he may find mercy of the Lord in that day: and in how many things he ministered unto me at Ephesus, thou knowest very well.

2 Thou therefore, my son, be strong in the grace that is in Christ Jesus. [2] And the things that thou hast heard of me among many witnesses, the same commit thou to faithful men, who shall be able to teach others also. [3] Thou therefore endure hardness, as a good soldier of Jesus Christ. [4] No man that warreth entangleth himself with the affairs of *this* life; that he may please him who hath chosen him to be a soldier. [5] And if a man also strive for masteries, *yet* is he not crowned, except he strive lawfully. [6] The husbandman that laboureth must be first partaker of the fruits. [7] Consider what I say; and the Lord give thee understanding in all things. [8] Remember that Jesus Christ of the seed of David was raised from the dead according to my gospel: [9] Wherein I suffer trouble, as an evil doer, *even* unto bonds; but the word of God is not bound. [10] Therefore I endure all things for the elect's sakes, that they may also obtain the salvation which is in Christ Jesus with eternal glory. [11] *It is* a faithful saying:

For if we be dead with *him,* we shall also live with *him:* [12] If we suffer, we shall also reign with *him:* if we deny *him,* he also will deny us: [13] If we believe not, *yet* he abideth faithful: he cannot deny himself.

[14] Of these things put *them* in remembrance, charging *them* before the Lord that they strive not about words to no profit, *but* to the subverting of the hearers. [15] Study to shew thyself approved unto God, a workman that needeth not to be ashamed, rightly dividing the word of truth. [16] But shun profane *and* vain babblings: for they will increase unto more ungodliness. [17] And their word will eat as doth a canker: of whom is Hymenaeus and Philetus; [18] Who

concerning the truth have erred, saying that the resurrection is past already; and overthrow the faith of some. [19]Nevertheless the foundation of God standeth sure, having this seal, The Lord knoweth them that are his. And, Let every one that nameth the name of Christ depart from iniquity. [20]But in a great house there are not only vessels of gold and of silver, but also of wood and of earth; and some to honour, and some to dishonour. [21]If a man therefore purge himself from these, he shall be a vessel unto honour, sanctified, and meet for the master's use, *and* prepared unto every good work. [22]Flee also youthful lusts: but follow righteousness, faith, charity, peace, with them that call on the Lord out of a pure heart. [23]But foolish and unlearned questions avoid, knowing that they do gender strifes. [24]And the servant of the Lord must not strive; but be gentle unto all *men,* apt to teach, patient, [25]In meekness instructing those that oppose themselves; if God peradventure will give them repentance to the acknowledging of the truth; [26]And *that* they may recover themselves out of the snare of the devil, who are taken captive by him at his will.

3 This know also, that in the last days perilous times shall come. [2]For men shall be lovers of their own selves, covetous, boasters, proud, blasphemers, disobedient to parents, unthankful, unholy, [3]Without natural affection, trucebreakers, false accusers, incontinent, fierce, despisers of those that are good, [4]Traitors, heady, highminded, lovers of pleasures more than lovers of God; [5]Having a form of godliness, but denying the power thereof: from such turn away. [6]For of this sort are they which creep into houses, and lead captive silly women laden with sins, led away with divers lusts, [7]Ever learning, and never able to come to the knowledge of the truth. [8]Now as Jannes and Jambres withstood Moses, so do these also resist the truth: men of corrupt minds, reprobate concerning the faith. [9]But they shall proceed no further: for their folly shall be manifest unto all *men,* as theirs also was. [10]But thou hast fully known my doctrine, manner of life, purpose, faith, longsuffering, charity, patience, [11]Persecutions, afflictions, which came unto me at Antioch, at Iconium, at Lystra; what persecutions I endured: but out of *them* all the Lord delivered me. [12]Yea, and all that will live godly in Christ Jesus shall suffer persecution. [13]But evil men and seducers shall wax worse and worse, deceiving, and being deceived. [14]But continue thou in the things which thou hast learned and hast been assured of, knowing of whom thou hast learned *them;* [15]And that from a child thou hast known the holy scriptures, which are able to make thee wise unto salvation through faith which is in Christ Jesus. [16]All scripture *is* given by inspiration of God, and *is* profitable for doctrine, for reproof, for correction, for instruction in righteousness: [17]That the man of God may be perfect, throughly furnished unto all good works.

4 I charge *thee* therefore before God, and the Lord Jesus Christ, who shall judge the quick and the dead at his appearing and his kingdom; [2]Preach the word; be instant in season, out of season; reprove, rebuke, exhort with all longsuffering and doctrine. [3]For the time will come when they will not endure sound doctrine; but after their own lusts shall they heap to themselves teachers, having itching ears; [4]And they shall turn away *their* ears from the truth, and shall be turned unto fables. [5]But watch thou in all things, endure afflictions, do the work of an evangelist, make full proof of thy ministry. [6]For I am now ready to be offered, and the time of my departure is at hand. [7]I have fought a good fight, I have finished *my* course, I have kept the faith: [8]Henceforth there is laid up for me a crown of righteousness, which the Lord, the righteous judge, shall give me at that day: and not to me only, but unto all them also that love his appearing.

[9]Do thy diligence to come shortly unto me: [10]For Demas hath forsaken me, having loved this present world, and is departed unto Thessalonica; Crescens to Galatia, Titus unto Dalmatia. [11]Only Luke is with me. Take Mark, and bring him with thee: for he is profitable to me for the ministry. [12]And Tychicus have I sent to Ephesus. [13]The cloke that I left at Troas with Carpus, when thou comest, bring *with thee,* and

the books, *but* especially the parchments. [14]Alexander the coppersmith did me much evil: the Lord reward him according to his works: [15]Of whom be thou ware also; for he hath greatly withstood our words. [16]At my first answer no man stood with me, but all *men* forsook me: *I pray God* that it may not be laid to their charge. [17]Notwithstanding the Lord stood with me, and strengthened me; that by me the preaching might be fully known, and *that* all the Gentiles might hear: and I was delivered out of the mouth of the lion. [18]And the Lord shall deliver me from every evil work, and will preserve *me* unto his heavenly kingdom: to whom *be* glory for ever and ever. Amen.

[19]Salute Prisca and Aquila, and the household of Onesiphorus. [20]Erastus abode at Corinth: but Trophimus have I left at Miletum sick. [21]Do thy diligence to come before winter. Eubulus greeteth thee, and Pudens, and Linus, and Claudia, and all the brethren.

[22]The Lord Jesus Christ *be* with thy spirit. Grace *be* with you. Amen.

TITUS

1 Paul, a servant of God, and an apostle of Jesus Christ, according to the faith of God's elect, and the acknowledging of the truth which is after godliness; ²In hope of eternal life, which God, that cannot lie, promised before the world began; ³But hath in due times manifested his word through preaching, which is committed unto me according to the commandment of God our Saviour;

⁴To Titus, *mine* own son after the common faith: ·

Grace, mercy, *and* peace, from God the Father and the Lord Jesus Christ our Saviour.

⁵For this cause left I thee in Crete, that thou shouldest set in order the things that are wanting, and ordain elders in every city, as I had appointed thee: ⁶If any be blameless, the husband of one wife, having faithful children not accused of riot or unruly. ⁷For a bishop must be blameless, as the steward of God; not selfwilled, not soon angry, not given to wine, no striker, not given to filthy lucre; ⁸But a lover of hospitality, a lover of good men, sober, just, holy, temperate; ⁹Holding fast the faithful word as he hath been taught, that he may be able by sound doctrine both to exhort and to convince the gainsayers. ¹⁰For there are many unruly and vain talkers and deceivers, specially they of the circumcision: ¹¹Whose mouths must be stopped, who subvert whole houses, teaching things which they ought not, for filthy lucre's sake. ¹²One of themselves, *even* a prophet of their own, said, The Cretians *are* alway liars, evil beasts, slow bellies. ¹³This witness is true. Wherefore rebuke them sharply, that they may be sound in the faith; ¹⁴Not giving heed to Jewish fables, and commandments of men, that turn from the truth. ¹⁵Unto the pure all things *are* pure: but unto them that are defiled and unbelieving *is* nothing pure; but even their mind and conscience is defiled. ¹⁶They profess that they know God; but in works they deny *him*, being abominable, and disobedient, and unto every good work reprobate.

2 But speak thou the things which become sound doctrine: ²That the aged men be sober, grave, temperate, sound in faith, in charity, in patience. ³The aged women likewise, that *they be* in behaviour as becometh holiness, not false accusers, not given to much wine, teachers of good things; ⁴That they may teach the young women to be sober, to love their husbands, to love their children, ⁵*To be* discreet, chaste, keepers at home, good, obedient to their own husbands, that the word of God be not blasphemed. ⁶Young men likewise exhort to be sober minded. ⁷In all things shewing thyself a pattern of good works: in doctrine *shewing* uncorruptness, gravity, sincerity, ⁸Sound speech, that cannot be condemned; that he that is of the contrary part may be ashamed, having no evil thing to say of you. ⁹*Exhort* servants to be obedient unto their own masters, *and* to please *them* well in all *things;* not answering again; ¹⁰Not purloining, but shewing all good fidelity; that they may adorn the doctrine of God our Saviour in all things. ¹¹For the grace of God that bringeth salvation hath appeared to all men, ¹²Teaching us that, denying ungodliness and worldly lusts, we should live soberly, righteously, and godly, in this present world; ¹³Looking for that blessed hope, and the glorious appearing of the great God and our Saviour Jesus Christ; ¹⁴Who gave himself for us, that he might redeem us from all iniquity, and purify unto himself a peculiar people, zealous of good works. ¹⁵These things speak, and exhort, and rebuke with all authority. Let no man despise thee.

3 Put them in mind to be subject to principalities and powers, to obey magistrates, to be ready to every good work, ²To speak evil of no man, to be no brawlers, *but* gentle, shewing all meekness unto all men. ³For we ourselves also were sometimes foolish, disobedient, deceived, serving divers lusts and pleasures, living in malice and envy, hateful, *and* hating one another. ⁴But after that the kindness and love of God our Saviour toward man appeared, ⁵Not by works of righteousness which we have done, but according to his mercy he saved us, by the washing of regeneration, and renewing of the Holy Ghost; ⁶Which he shed on us abundantly through Jesus Christ our Saviour; ⁷That being justified by his grace, we should be made heirs according to the hope of eternal life. ⁸*This is* a faithful saying, and these things I will that thou affirm constantly, that they which have believed in God might be careful to maintain good works. These things are good and profitable unto men. ⁹But avoid foolish questions, and genealogies, and contentions, and strivings about the law; for they are unprofitable and vain. ¹⁰A man that is an heretick after the first and second admonition reject; ¹¹Knowing that he that is such is subverted, and sinneth, being condemned of himself.

¹²When I shall send Artemas unto thee, or Tychicus, be diligent to come unto me to Nicopolis: for I have determined there to winter. ¹³Bring Zenas the lawyer and Apollos on their journey diligently, that nothing be wanting unto them. ¹⁴And let ours also learn to maintain good works for necessary uses, that they be not unfruitful.

¹⁵All that are with me salute thee. Greet them that love us in the faith. Grace *be* with you all. Amen.

The Epistle of Paul the Apostle to

PHILEMON

¹Paul, a prisoner of Jesus Christ, and Timothy our brother,

unto Philemon our dearly beloved, and fellowlabourer, ²And to *our* beloved Apphia, and Archippus our fellowsoldier, and to the church in thy house:

³Grace to you, and peace, from God our Father and the Lord Jesus Christ.

⁴I thank my God, making mention of thee always in my prayers, ⁵Hearing of thy love and faith, which thou hast toward the Lord Jesus, and toward all saints; ⁶That the communication of thy faith may become effectual by the acknowledging of every good thing which is in you in Christ Jesus. ⁷For we have great joy and consolation in thy love, because the bowels of the saints are refreshed by thee, brother. ⁸Wherefore, though I might be much bold in Christ to enjoin thee that which is convenient, ⁹Yet for love's sake I rather beseech *thee,* being such an one as Paul the aged, and now also a prisoner of Jesus Christ. ¹⁰I beseech thee for my son Onesimus, whom I have begotten in my bonds: ¹¹Which in time past was to thee unprofitable, but now profitable to thee and to me: ¹²Whom I have sent again: thou therefore receive him, that is, mine own bowels: ¹³Whom I would have retained with me, that in thy stead he might have ministered unto me in the bonds of the gospel: ¹⁴But without thy mind would I do nothing; that thy benefit should not be as it were of necessity, but willingly. ¹⁵For perhaps he therefore departed for a season, that thou shouldest receive him for ever; ¹⁶Not now as a servant, but above a servant, a brother beloved, specially to me, but how much more unto thee, both in the flesh, and in the Lord? ¹⁷If thou count me therefore a partner, receive him as myself. ¹⁸If he hath wronged thee, or oweth *thee* ought, put that on mine account; ¹⁹I Paul have written *it* with mine own hand, I will repay *it:* albeit I do not say to thee how thou owest unto me even thine own self besides. ²⁰Yea, brother, let me have joy of thee in the Lord: refresh my bowels in the Lord.

²¹Having confidence in thy obedience I wrote unto thee, knowing that thou wilt also do more than I say. ²²But withal prepare me also a lodging: for I trust that through your prayers I shall be given unto you.

²³There salute thee Epaphras, my fellowprisoner in Christ Jesus; ²⁴Marcus, Aristarchus, Demas, Lucas, my fellowlabourers.

²⁵The grace of our Lord Jesus Christ *be* with your spirit. Amen.

HEBREWS

1 God, who at sundry times and in divers manners spake in time past unto the fathers by the prophets, [2]Hath in these last days spoken unto us by *his* Son, whom he hath appointed heir of all things, by whom also he made the worlds; [3]Who being the brightness of *his* glory, and the express image of his person, and upholding all things by the word of his power, when he had by himself purged our sins, sat down on the right hand of the Majesty on high; [4]Being made so much better than the angels, as he hath by inheritance obtained a more excellent name than they. [5]For unto which of the angels said he at any time,

Thou art my Son, this day have I begotten thee?

And again,

I will be to him a Father, and he shall be to me a Son?

[6]And again, when he bringeth in the firstbegotten into the world, he saith,

And let all the angels of God worship him.

[7]And of the angels he saith,

Who maketh his angels spirits, and his ministers a flame of fire.

[8]But unto the Son *he saith,*

Thy throne, O God, *is* for ever and ever: a sceptre of righteousness *is* the sceptre of thy kingdom. [9]Thou hast loved righteousness, and hated iniquity; therefore God, *even* thy God, hath anointed thee with the oil of gladness above thy fellows.

[10]And, Thou, Lord, in the beginning hast laid the foundation of the earth; and the heavens are the works of thine hands: [11]They shall perish; but thou remainest; and they all shall wax old as doth a garment; [12]And as a vesture shalt thou fold them up, and they shall be changed: but thou art the same, and thy years shall not fail.

[13]But to which of the angels said he at any times,

Sit on my right hand, until I make thine enemies thy footstool?

[14]Are they not all ministering spirits, sent forth to minister for them who shall be heirs of salvation?

2 Therefore we ought to give the more earnest heed to the things which we have heard, lest at any time we should let *them* slip. [2]For if the word spoken by angels was stedfast, and every transgression and disobedience received a just recompence of reward; [3]How shall we escape, if we neglect so great salvation; which at the first began to be spoken by the Lord, and was confirmed unto us by them that heard *him;* [4]God also bearing *them* witness, both with signs and wonders, and with divers miracles, and gifts of the Holy Ghost, according to his own will?

[5]For unto the angels hath he not put in subjection the world to come, whereof we speak. [6]But one in a certain place testified, saying,

What is man, that thou art mindful of him? or the son of man, that thou visitest him? [7]Thou madest him a little lower than the angels; thou crownedst him with glory and honour, and didst set him over the works of thy hands: [8]Thou hast put all things in subjection under his feet.

For in that he put all in subjection under him, he left nothing *that is* not put under him. But now we see not yet all things put under him. [9]But we see Jesus, who was made a little lower than the angels for the suffering of death, crowned with glory and honour; that he by the grace of God should taste death for every man. [10]For it became him, for whom *are* all things, and by whom *are* all things, in bringing many sons unto glory, to make the captain of their salvation perfect through sufferings. [11]For both he that sanctifieth and they who are sanctified *are* all of one: for which cause he is not ashamed to call them brethren, [12]Saying,

I will declare thy name unto my brethren, in the midst of the church will I sing praise unto thee.

¹³And again,

I will put my trust in him.

And again,

Behold I and the children which God hath given me.

¹⁴Forasmuch then as the children are partakers of flesh and blood, he also himself likewise took part of the same; that through death he might destroy him that had the power of death, that is, the devil; ¹⁵And deliver them who through fear of death were all their lifetime subject to bondage. ¹⁶For verily he took not on *him the nature of* angels; but he took on *him* the seed of Abraham. ¹⁷Wherefore in all things it behoved him to be made like unto *his* brethren, that he might be a merciful and faithful high priest in things *pertaining* to God, to make reconciliation for the sins of the people. ¹⁸For in that he himself hath suffered being tempted, he is able to succour them that are tempted.

3 Wherefore, holy brethren, partakers of the heavenly calling, consider the Apostle and High Priest of our profession, Christ Jesus; ²Who was faithful to him that appointed him, as also Moses *was faithful* in all his house. ³For this *man* was counted worthy of more glory than Moses, inasmuch as he who hath builded the house hath more honour than the house. ⁴For every house is builded by some *man;* but he that built all things *is* God. ⁵And Moses verily *was* faithful in all his house, as a servant, for a testimony of those things which were to be spoken after; ⁶But Christ as a son over his own house; whose house are we, if we hold fast the confidence and the rejoicing of the hope firm unto the end. ⁷Wherefore (as the Holy Ghost saith,

To day if ye will hear his voice, ⁸Harden not your hearts, as in the provocation, in the day of temptation in the wilderness: ⁹When your fathers tempted me, proved me, and saw my works forty years. ¹⁰Wherefore I was grieved with that generation, and said, They do alway err in *their* heart; and they have not known my ways. ¹¹So I sware in my wrath, They shall not enter into my rest.)

¹²Take heed, brethren, lest there be in any of you an evil heart of unbelief, in departing from the living God. ¹³But exhort one another daily, while it is called To day; lest any of you be hardened through the deceitfulness of sin. ¹⁴For we are made partakers of Christ, if we hold the beginning of our confidence stedfast unto the end; ¹⁵While it is said,

To day if ye will hear his voice, harden not your hearts, as in the provocation.

¹⁶For some, when they had heard, did provoke: howbeit not all that came out of Egypt by Moses. ¹⁷But with whom was he grieved forty years? *was it* not with them that had sinned, whose carcases fell in the wilderness? ¹⁸And to whom sware he that they should not enter into his rest, but to them that believed not? ¹⁹So we see that they could not enter in because of unbelief.

4 Let us therefore fear, lest, a promise being left *us* of entering into his rest, any of you should seem to come short of it. ²For unto us was the gospel preached, as well as unto them: but the word preached did not profit them, not being mixed with faith in them that heard *it.* ³For we which have believed do enter into rest, as he said,

As I have sworn in my wrath, if they shall enter into my rest:

although the works were finished from the foundation of the world. ⁴For he spake in a certain place of the seventh *day* on this wise, And God did rest the seventh day from all his works. ⁵And in this *place* again, If they shall enter into my rest. ⁶Seeing therefore it remaineth that some must enter therein, and they to whom it was first preached entered not in because of unbelief: ⁷Again, he limiteth a certain day, saying in David,

To day, after so long a time; as it is said, To day if ye will hear his voice, harden not your hearts.

⁸For if Jesus had given them rest, then would he not afterward have spoken of another day. ⁹There remaineth therefore a rest to the people of God. ¹⁰For he that is entered into his rest, he also hath ceased

from his own works, as God *did* from his. ¹¹Let us labour therefore to enter into that rest, lest any man fall after the same example of unbelief. ¹²For the word of God *is* quick, and powerful, and sharper than any twoedged sword, piercing even to the dividing asunder of soul and spirit, and of the joints and marrow, and *is* a discerner of the thoughts and intents of the heart. ¹³Neither is there any creature that is not manifest in his sight: but all things *are* naked and opened unto the eyes of him with whom we have to do.

¹⁴Seeing then that we have a great high priest, that is passed into the heavens, Jesus the Son of God, let us hold fast *our* profession. ¹⁵For we have not an high priest which cannot be touched with the feeling of our infirmities; but was in all points tempted like as *we are, yet* without sin. ¹⁶Let us therefore come boldly unto the throne of grace, that we may obtain mercy, and find grace to help in time of need.

5 For every high priest taken from among men is ordained for men in things *pertaining* to God, that he may offer both gifts and sacrifices for sins: ²Who can have compassion on the ignorant, and on them that are out of the way; for that he himself also is compassed with infirmity. ³And by reason hereof he ought, as for the people, so also for himself, to offer for sins. ⁴And no man taketh this honour unto himself, but he that is called of God, as *was* Aaron. ⁵So also Christ glorified not himself to be made an high priest; but he that said unto him,

Thou art my Son, to day have I begotten thee.

⁶As he saith also in another *place,*

Thou *art* a priest for ever after the order of Melchisedec.

⁷Who in the days of his flesh, when he had offered up prayers and supplications with strong crying and tears unto him that was able to save him from death, and was heard in that he feared; ⁸Though he were a Son, yet learned he obedience by the things which he suffered; ⁹And being made perfect, he became the author of eternal salva-

tion unto all them that obey him; ¹⁰Called of God an high priest after the order of Melchisedec.

¹¹Of whom we have many things to say, and hard to be uttered, seeing ye are dull of hearing. ¹²For when for the time ye ought to be teachers, ye have need that one teach you again which *be* the first principles of the oracles of God; and are become such as have need of milk, and not of strong meat. ¹³For every one that useth milk *is* unskilful in the word of righteousness: for he is a babe. ¹⁴But strong meat belongeth to them that are of full age, *even* those who by reason of use have their senses exercised to discern both good and evil.

6 Therefore leaving the principles of the doctrine of Christ, let us go on unto perfection; not laying again the foundation of repentance from dead works, and of faith toward God, ²Of the doctrine of baptisms, and of laying on of hands, and of resurrection of the dead, and of eternal judgment. ³And this will we do, if God permit. ⁴For *it is* impossible for those who were once enlightened, and have tasted of the heavenly gift, and were made partakers of the Holy Ghost, ⁵And have tasted the good word of God, and the powers of the world to come, ⁶If they shall fall away, to renew them again unto repentance; seeing they crucify to themselves the Son of God afresh, and put *him* to an open shame. ⁷For the earth which drinketh in the rain that cometh oft upon it, and bringeth forth herbs meet for them by whom it is dressed, receiveth blessing from God: ⁸But that which beareth thorns and briers *is* rejected, and *is* nigh unto cursing; whose end *is* to be burned. ⁹But, beloved, we are persuaded better things of you, and things that accompany salvation, though we thus speak. ¹⁰For God *is* not unrighteous to forget your work and labour of love, which ye have shewed toward his name, in that ye have ministered to the saints, and do minister. ¹¹And we desire that every one of you do shew the same diligence to the full assurance of hope unto the end: ¹²That ye be not slothful, but followers of them who through faith and patience inherit the promises. ¹³For when God made promise to Abraham, because he could swear by

no greater, he sware by himself, [14]Saying, Surely blessing I will bless thee, and multiplying I will multiply thee. [15]And so, after he had patiently endured, he obtained the promise. [16]For men verily swear by the greater: and an oath for confirmation *is* to them an end of all strife. [17]Wherein God, willing more abundantly to shew unto the heirs of promise the immutability of his counsel, confirmed *it* by an oath: [18]That by two immutable things, in which *it was* impossible for God to lie, we might have a strong consolation, who have fled for refuge to lay hold upon the hope set before us: [19]Which *hope* we have as an anchor of the soul, both sure and stedfast, and which entereth into that within the veil; [20]Whither the forerunner is for us entered, *even* Jesus, made an high priest for ever after the order of Melchisedec.

7 For this Melchisedec, king of Salem, priest of the most high God, who met Abraham returning from the slaughter of the kings, and blessed him; [2]To whom also Abraham gave a tenth part of all; first being by interpretation King of righteousness, and after that also King of Salem, which is, King of peace; [3]Without father, without mother, without descent, having neither beginning of days, nor end of life; but made like unto the Son of God; abideth a priest continually. [4]Now consider how great this man *was,* unto whom even the patriarch Abraham gave the tenth of the spoils. [5]And verily they that are of the sons of Levi, who receive the office of the priesthood, have a commandment to take tithes of the people according to the law, that is, of their brethren, though they come out of the loins of Abraham: [6]But he whose descent is not counted from them received tithes of Abraham, and blessed him that had the promises. [7]And without all contradiction the less is blessed of the better. [8]And here men that die receive tithes; but there he *receiveth them,* of whom it is witnessed that he liveth. [9]And as I may so say, Levi also, who receiveth tithes, payed tithes in Abraham. [10]For he was yet in the loins of his father, when Melchisedec met him. [11]If therefore perfection were by the Levitical priesthood, (for under it the people received the law,) what further need *was there* that

another priest should rise after the order of Melchisedec, and not be called after the order of Aaron? [12]For the priesthood being changed, there is made of necessity a change also of the law. [13]For he of whom these things are spoken pertaineth to another tribe, of which no man gave attendance at the altar. [14]For *it is* evident that our Lord sprang out of Juda; of which tribe Moses spake nothing concerning priesthood. [15]And it is yet far more evident: for that after the similitude of Melchisedec there ariseth another priest, [16]Who is made, not after the law of a carnal commandment, but after the power of an endless life. [17]For he testifieth,

Thou *art* a priest for ever after the order of Melchisedec.

[18]For there is verily a disannulling of the commandment going before for the weakness and unprofitableness thereof. [19]For the law made nothing perfect, but the bringing in of a better hope *did;* by the which we draw nigh unto God. [20]And inasmuch as not without an oath *he was made priest:* [21](For those priests were made without an oath; but this with an oath by him that said unto him,

The Lord sware and will not repent, Thou *art* a priest for ever after the order of Melchisedec:)

[22]By so much was Jesus made a surety of a better testament. [23]And they truly were many priests, because they were not suffered to continue by reason of death: [24]But this *man,* because he continueth ever, hath an unchangeable priesthood. [25]Wherefore he is able also to save them to the uttermost that come unto God by him, seeing he ever liveth to make intercession for them. [26]For such an high priest became us, *who is* holy, harmless, undefiled, separate from sinners, and made higher than the heavens; [27]Who needeth not daily, as those high priests, to offer up sacrifice, first for his own sins, and then for the people's: for this he did once, when he offered up himself. [28]For the law maketh men high priests which have infirmity; but the word of the oath, which was since the law, *maketh* the Son, who is consecrated for evermore.

8 Now of the things which we have spoken *this is* the sum: We have such an high priest, who is set on the right hand of the throne of the Majesty in the heavens; ²A minister of the sanctuary, and of the true tabernacle, which the Lord pitched, and not man. ³For every high priest is ordained to offer gifts and sacrifices: wherefore *it is* of necessity that this man have somewhat also to offer. ⁴For if he were on earth, he should not be a priest, seeing that there are priests that offer gifts according to the law: ⁵Who serve unto the example and shadow of heavenly things, as Moses was admonished of God when he was about to make the tabernacle: for, See, saith he, *that* thou make all things according to the pattern shewed to thee in the mount. ⁶But now hath he obtained a more excellent ministry, by how much also he is the mediator of a better covenant, which was established upon better promises. ⁷For if that first *covenant* had been faultless, then should no place have been sought for the second. ⁸For finding fault with them, he saith,

Behold, the days come, saith the Lord, when I will make a new covenant with the house of Israel and with the house of Judah: ⁹Not according to the covenant that I made with their fathers in the day when I took them by the hand to lead them out of the land of Egypt; because they continued not in my covenant, and I regarded them not, saith the Lord. ¹⁰For this *is* the covenant that I will make with the house of Israel after those days, saith the Lord; I will put my laws into their mind, and write them in their hearts: and I will be to them a God, and they shall be to me a people: ¹¹And they shall not teach every man his neighbour, and every man his brother, saying, Know the Lord: for all shall know me, from the least to the greatest. ¹²For I will be merciful to their unrighteousness, and their sins and their iniquities will I remember no more.

¹³In that he saith, A new *covenant,* he hath made the first old. Now that which decayeth and waxeth old *is* ready to vanish away.

9 Then verily the first *covenant* had also ordinances of divine service, and a worldly sanctuary. ²For there was a tabernacle made; the first, wherein *was* the candlestick, and the table, and the shewbread; which is called the sanctuary. ³And after the second veil, the tabernacle which is called the Holiest of all; ⁴Which had the golden censer, and the ark of the covenant overlaid round about with gold, wherein *was* the golden pot that had manna, and Aaron's rod that budded, and the tables of the covenant; ⁵And over it the cherubims of glory shadowing the mercyseat; of which we cannot now speak particularly. ⁶Now when these things were thus ordained, the priests went always into the first tabernacle, accomplishing the service *of God.* ⁷But into the second *went* the high priest alone once every year, not without blood, which he offered for himself, and *for* the errors of the people: ⁸The Holy Ghost this signifying, that the way into the holiest of all was not yet made manifest, while as the first tabernacle was yet standing: ⁹Which *was* a figure for the time then present, in which were offered both gifts and sacrifices, that could not make him that did the service perfect, as pertaining to the conscience; ¹⁰Which stood only in meats and drinks, and divers washings, and carnal ordinances, imposed *on them* until the time of reformation. ¹¹But Christ being come an high priest of good things to come, by a greater and more perfect tabernacle, not made with hands, that is to say, not of this building; ¹²Neither by the blood of goats and calves, but by his own blood he entered in once into the holy place, having obtained eternal redemption *for us.* ¹³For if the blood of bulls and of goats, and the ashes of an heifer sprinkling the unclean, sanctifieth to the purifying of the flesh: ¹⁴How much more shall the blood of Christ, who through the eternal Spirit offered himself without spot to God, purge your conscience from dead works to serve the living God? ¹⁵And for this cause he is the mediator of the new testament, that by means of death, for the redemption of the transgressions *that were* under the first testament, they which are called might receive the promise of eternal inheritance. ¹⁶For where a testament *is,* there must also of necessity be the death of the testator. ¹⁷For a testament *is* of force after men are dead: otherwise it is of no strength at all while the testator liveth. ¹⁸Whereupon neither the first *testament* was dedicated without blood. ¹⁹For when Moses had spoken every precept to all the people according to the law, he took the blood of calves and of goats, with water, and scarlet wool, and hyssop, and sprinkled both the book, and all the people, ²⁰Saying, This *is* the blood of the testament which God hath enjoined unto you. ²¹Moreover he sprinkled with blood both the tabernacle, and all the vessels of the ministry. ²²And almost all things are by the law purged with blood; and without shedding of blood is no remission. ²³*It was* therefore necessary that the patterns of things in the heavens should be purified with these; but the heavenly things themselves with better sacrifices than these. ²⁴For Christ is not entered into the holy places made with hands, *which are* the figures of the true; but into heaven itself, now to appear in the presence of God for us: ²⁵Nor yet that he should offer himself often, as the high priest entereth into the holy place every year with blood of others; ²⁶For then must he often have suffered since the foundation of the world: but now once in the end of the world hath he appeared to put away sin by the sacrifice of himself. ²⁷And as it is appointed unto men once to die, but after this the judgment: ²⁸So Christ was once offered to bear the sins of many; and unto them that look for him shall he appear the second time without sin unto salvation.

10 For the law having a shadow of good things to come, *and* not the very image of the things, can never with those sacrifices which they offered year by year continually make the comers thereunto perfect. ²For then would they not have ceased to be offered? because that the worshippers once purged should have had no more conscience of sins. ³But in those *sacrifices there is* a remembrance again *made* of sins every year. ⁴For *it is* not possible that the blood of bulls and of goats should take away sins. ⁵Wherefore when he cometh into the world, he saith,

Sacrifice and offering thou wouldest not, but a body hast thou prepared me: ⁶In

burnt offerings and *sacrifices* for sin thou hast had no pleasure. ⁷Then said I, Lo, I come (in the volume of the book it is written of me,) to do thy will, O God.

⁸Above when he said, Sacrifice and offering and burnt offerings and *offering* for sin thou wouldest not, neither hadst pleasure *therein;* which are offered by the law; ⁹Then said he, Lo, I come to do thy will, O God. He taketh away the first, that he may establish the second. ¹⁰By the which will we are sanctified through the offering of the body of Jesus Christ once *for all.* ¹¹And every priest standeth daily ministering and offering oftentimes the same sacrifices, which can never take away sins: ¹²But this man, after he had offered one sacrifice for sins for ever, sat down on the right hand of God; ¹³From henceforth expecting till his enemies be made his footstool. ¹⁴For by one offering he hath perfected for ever them that are sanctified. ¹⁵*Whereof* the Holy Ghost also is a witness to us: for after that he had said before,

¹⁶This *is* the covenant that I will make with them after those days, saith the Lord, I will put my laws into their hearts, and in their minds will I write them;

¹⁷And their sins and iniquities will I remember no more.

¹⁸Now where remission of these *is, there is* no more offering for sin.¹⁹Having therefore, brethren, boldness to enter into the holiest by the blood of Jesus, ²⁰By a new and living way, which he hath consecrated for us, through the veil, that is to say, his flesh; ²¹And *having* an high priest over the house of God; ²²Let us draw near with a true heart in full assurance of faith, having our hearts sprinkled from an evil conscience, and our bodies washed with pure water. ²³Let us hold fast the profession of *our* faith without wavering; (for he is faithful that promised;) ²⁴And let us consider one another to provoke unto love and to good works: ²⁵Not forsaking the assembling of ourselves together, as the manner of some *is;* but exhorting *one another:* and so much the more, as ye see the day approaching. ²⁶For if we sin wilfully after that we have received the knowledge of the

truth, there remaineth no more sacrifice for sins. ²⁷But a certain fearful looking for of judgment and fiery indignation, which shall devour the adversaries. ²⁸He that despised Moses' law died without mercy under two or three witnesses: ²⁹Of how much sorer punishment, suppose ye, shall he be thought worthy, who hath trodden under foot the Son of God, and hath counted the blood of the covenant, wherewith he was sanctified, an unholy thing, and hath done despite unto the Spirit of grace? ³⁰For we know him that hath said, Vengeance *belongeth* unto me, I will recompense, saith the Lord. And again, The Lord shall judge his people. ³¹*It is* a fearful thing to fall into the hands of the living God. ³²But call to remembrance the former days, in which, after ye were illuminated, ye endured a great fight of afflictions; ³³Partly, whilst ye were made a gazingstock both by reproaches and afflictions; and partly, whilst ye became companions of them that were so used. ³⁴For ye had compassion of me in my bonds, and took joyfully the spoiling of your goods, knowing in yourselves that ye have in heaven a better and an enduring substance. ³⁵Cast not away therefore your confidence, which hath great recompence of reward. ³⁶For ye have need of patience, that, after ye have done the will of God, ye might receive the promise. ³⁷For

yet a little while, and he that shall come will come, and will not tarry.

³⁸Now the just shall live by faith: but if *any man* draw back, my soul shall have no pleasure in him.

³⁹But we are not of them who draw back unto perdition; but of them that believe to the saving of the soul.

11 Now faith is the substance of things hoped for, the evidence of things not seen. ²For by it the elders obtained a good report. ³Through faith we understand that the worlds were framed by the word of God, so that things which are seen were not made of things which do appear. ⁴By faith Abel offered unto God a more excellent sacrifice than Cain, by which he obtained witness that he was righteous, God testify-

ing of his gifts: and by it he being dead yet speaketh. ⁵By faith Enoch was translated that he should not see death; and was not found, because God had translated him: for before his translation he had this testimony, that he pleased God. ⁶But without faith *it is* impossible to please *him:* for he that cometh to God must believe that he is, and *that* he is a rewarder of them that diligently seek him. ⁷By faith Noah, being warned of God of things not seen as yet, moved with fear, prepared an ark to the saving of his house; by the which he condemned the world, and became heir of the righteousness which is by faith. ⁸By faith Abraham, when he was called to go out into a place which he should after receive for an inheritance, obeyed; and he went out, not knowing whither he went. ⁹By faith he sojourned in the land of promise, as *in* a strange country, dwelling in tabernacles with Isaac and Jacob, the heirs with him of the same promise: ¹⁰For he looked for a city which hath foundations, whose builder and maker *is* God. ¹¹Through faith also Sara herself received strength to conceive seed, and was delivered of a child when she was past age, because she judged him faithful who had promised. ¹²Therefore sprang there even of one, and him as good as dead, *so many* as the stars of the sky in multitude, and as the sand which is by the sea shore innumerable. ¹³These all died in faith, not having received the promises, but having seen them afar off, and were persuaded of *them,* and embraced *them,* and confessed that they were strangers and pilgrims on the earth. ¹⁴For they that say such things declare plainly that they seek a country. ¹⁵And truly, if they had been mindful of that *country* from whence they came out, they might have had opportunity to have returned. ¹⁶But now they desire a better *country,* that is, an heavenly: wherefore God is not ashamed to be called their God: for he hath prepared for them a city. ¹⁷By faith Abraham, when he was tried, offered up Isaac: and he that had received the promises offered up his only begotten *son,* ¹⁸Of whom it was said, That in Isaac shall thy seed be called: ¹⁹Accounting that God *was* able to raise *him* up, even from the dead; from whence also he received him in a figure. [20]By faith Isaac blessed Jacob and Esau concerning things to come. [21]By faith Jacob, when he was a dying, blessed both the sons of Joseph; and worshipped, *leaning* upon the top of his staff. [22]By faith Joseph, when he died, made mention of the departing of the children of Israel; and gave commandment concerning his bones. [23]By faith Moses, when he was born, was hid three months of his parents, because they saw *he was* a proper child; and they were not afraid of the king's commandment. [24]By faith Moses, when he was come to years, refused to be called the son of Pharaoh's daughter; [25]Choosing rather to suffer affliction with the people of God, than to enjoy the pleasures of sin for a season; [26]Esteeming the reproach of Christ greater riches than the treasures in Egypt: for he had respect unto the recompence of the reward. [27]By faith he forsook Egypt, not fearing the wrath of the king: for he endured, as seeing him who is invisible. [28]Through faith he kept the passover, and the sprinkling of blood, lest he that destroyed the firstborn should touch them. [29]By faith they passed through the Red sea as by dry *land:* which the Egyptians assaying to do were drowned. [30]By faith the walls of Jericho fell down, after they were compassed about seven days. [31]By faith the harlot Rahab perished not with them that believed not, when she had received the spies with peace. [32]And what shall I more say? for the time would fail me to tell of Gedeon, and *of* Barak, and *of* Samson, and *of* Jephthae; *of* David also, and Samuel, and *of* the prophets: [33]Who through faith subdued kingdoms, wrought righteousness, obtained promises, stopped the mouths of lions, [34]Quenched the violence of fire, escaped the edge of the sword, out of weakness were made strong, waxed valiant in fight, turned to flight the armies of the aliens. [35]Women received their dead raised to life again: and others were tortured, not accepting deliverance; that they might obtain a better resurrection: [36]And others had trial of *cruel* mockings and scourgings, yea, moreover of bonds and imprisonment: [37]They were stoned, they were sawn asunder, were tempted, were slain with the sword: they wandered about in sheepskins and goatskins; being destitute,

afflicted, tormented; [38](Of whom the world was not worthy:) they wandered in deserts, and *in* mountains, and *in* dens and caves of the earth. [39]And these all, having obtained a good report through faith, received not the promise: [40]God having provided some better thing for us, that they without us should not be made perfect.

12 Wherefore seeing we also are compassed about with so great a cloud of witnesses, let us lay aside every weight, and the sin which doth so easily beset us, and let us run with patience the race that is set before us, [2]Looking unto Jesus the author and finisher of *our* faith; who for the joy that was set before him endured the cross, despising the shame, and is set down at the right hand of the throne of God. [3]For consider him that endured such contradiction of sinners against himself, lest ye be wearied and faint in your minds. [4]Ye have not yet resisted unto blood, striving against sin. [5]And ye have forgotten the exhortation which speaketh unto you as unto children,

My son, despise not thou the chastening of the Lord, nor faint when thou art rebuked of him: [6]For whom the Lord loveth he chasteneth, and scourgeth every son whom he receiveth.

[7]If ye endure chastening, God dealeth with you as with sons; for what son is he whom the father chasteneth not? [8]But if ye be without chastisement, whereof all are partakers, then are ye bastards, and not sons. [9]Furthermore we have had fathers of our flesh which corrected *us,* and we gave *them* reverence: shall we not much rather be in subjection unto the Father of spirits, and live? [10]For they verily for a few days chastened *us* after their own pleasure; but he for *our* profit, that *we* might be partakers of his holiness. [11]Now no chastening for the present seemeth to be joyous, but grievous: nevertheless afterward it yieldeth the peaceable fruit of righteousness unto them which are exercised thereby. [12]Wherefore lift up the hands which hang down, and the feeble knees; [13]And make straight paths for your feet, lest that which is lame be turned out of the way; but let it rather be healed. [14]Follow peace with all *men,* and holiness, without which no man

shall see the Lord: [15]Looking diligently lest any man fail of the grace of God; lest any root of bitterness springing up trouble *you*, and thereby many be defiled; [16]Lest there *be* any fornicator, or profane person, as Esau, who for one morsel of meat sold his birthright. [17]For ye know how that afterward, when he would have inherited the blessing, he was rejected: for he found no place of repentance, though he sought it carefully with tears. [18]For ye are not come unto the mount that might be touched, and that burned with fire, nor unto blackness, and darkness, and tempest, [19]And the sound of a trumpet, and the voice of words; *which* voice they that heard intreated that the word should not be spoken to them any more: [20](For they could not endure that which was commanded, And if so much as a beast touch the mountain, it shall be stoned, or thrust through with a dart: [21]And so terrible was the sight, *that* Moses said, I exceedingly fear and quake:) [22]But ye are come unto mount Sion, and unto the city of the living God, the heavenly Jerusalem, and to an innumerable company of angels, [23]To the general assembly and church of the firstborn, which are written in heaven, and to God the Judge of all, and to the spirits of just men made perfect, [24]And to Jesus the mediator of the new covenant, and to the blood of sprinkling, that speaketh better things than *that of* Abel. [25]See that ye refuse not him that speaketh. For if they escaped not who refused him that spake on earth, much more *shall not* we *escape*, if we turn away from him that *speaketh* from heaven: [26]Whose voice then shook the earth: but now he hath promised, saying, Yet once more I shake not the earth only, but also heaven. [27]And this *word*, Yet once more, signifieth the removing of those things that are shaken, as of things that are made, that those things which cannot be shaken may remain. [28]Wherefore we receiving a kingdom which cannot be moved, let us have grace, whereby we may serve God acceptably with reverence and godly fear: [29]For our God *is* a consuming fire.

13 Let brotherly love continue. [2]Be not forgetful to entertain strangers: for thereby some have entertained angels unawares. [3]Remember them that are in bonds, as bound with them; *and* them which suffer adversity, as being yourselves also in the body. [4]Marriage *is* honourable in all, and the bed undefiled: but whoremongers and adulterers God will judge. [5]*Let your* conversation *be* without covetousness; *and be* content with such things as ye have: for he hath said,

I will never leave thee, nor forsake thee.

[6]So that we may boldly say,

The Lord *is* my helper, and I will not fear what man shall do unto me.

[7]Remember them which have the rule over you, who have spoken unto you the word of God: whose faith follow, considering the end of *their* conversation. [8]Jesus Christ the same yesterday, and to day, and for ever. [9]Be not carried about with divers and strange doctrines. For *it is* a good thing that the heart be established with grace; not with meats, which have not profited them that have been occupied therein. [10]We have an altar, whereof they have no right to eat which serve the tabernacle. [11]For the bodies of those beasts, whose blood is brought into the sanctuary by the high priest for sin, are burned without the camp. [12]Wherefore Jesus also, that he might sanctify the people with his own blood, suffered without the gate. [13]Let us go forth therefore unto him without the camp, bearing his reproach. [14]For here have we no continuing city, but we seek one to come. [15]By him therefore let us offer the sacrifice of praise to God continually, that is, the fruit of *our* lips giving thanks to his name. [16]But to do good and to communicate forget not: for with such sacrifices God is well pleased. [17]Obey them that have the rule over you, and submit yourselves: for they watch for your souls, as they that must give account, that they may do it with joy, and not with grief: for that *is* unprofitable for you.

[18]Pray for us: for we trust we have a good conscience, in all things willing to live honestly. [19]But I beseech *you* the rather to do this, that I may be restored to you the sooner. [20]Now the God of peace, that brought again from the dead our Lord Jesus, that great shepherd of the sheep, through the blood of the everlasting covenant, [21]Make

you perfect in every good work to do his will, working in you that which is well-pleasing in his sight, through Jesus Christ; to whom *be* glory for ever and ever. Amen.

²²And I beseech you, brethren, suffer the word of exhortation: for I have written a letter unto you in few words. ²³Know ye that *our* brother Timothy is set at liberty; with whom, if he come shortly, I will see you.

²⁴Salute all them that have the rule over you, and all the saints. They of Italy salute you.

²⁵Grace *be* with you all. Amen.

The General Epistle of
JAMES

1 James, a servant of God and of the Lord Jesus Christ,

to the twelve tribes which are scattered abroad,

greeting.

[2] My brethren, count it all joy when ye fall into divers temptations; [3] Knowing *this,* that the trying of your faith worketh patience. [4] But let patience have *her* perfect work, that ye may be perfect and entire, wanting nothing. [5] If any of you lack wisdom, let him ask of God, that giveth to all *men* liberally, and upbraideth not; and it shall be given him. [6] But let him ask in faith, nothing wavering. For he that wavereth is like a wave of the sea driven with the wind and tossed. [7] For let not that man think that he shall receive any thing of the Lord. [8] A double minded man *is* unstable in all his ways. [9] Let the brother of low degree rejoice in that he is exalted: [10] But the rich, in that he is made low: because as the flower of the grass he shall pass away. [11] For the sun is no sooner risen with a burning heat, but it withereth the grass, and the flower thereof falleth, and the grace of the fashion of it perisheth: so also shall the rich man fade away in his ways. [12] Blessed *is* the man that endureth temptation: for when he is tried, he shall receive the crown of life, which the Lord hath promised to them that love him. [13] Let no man say when he is tempted, I am tempted of God: for God cannot be tempted with evil, neither tempteth he any man: [14] But every man is tempted, when he is drawn away of his own lust, and enticed. [15] Then when lust hath conceived, it bringeth forth sin: and sin, when it is finished, bringeth forth death. [16] Do not err, my beloved brethren. [17] Every good gift and every perfect gift is from above, and cometh down from the Father of lights, with whom is no variableness, neither shadow of turning. [18] Of his own will begat he us with the word of truth, that we should be a kind of firstfruits of his creatures.

[19] Wherefore, my beloved brethren, let every man be swift to hear, slow to speak, slow to wrath: [20] For the wrath of man worketh not the righteousness of God. [21] Wherefore lay apart all filthiness and superfluity of naughtiness, and receive with meekness the engrafted word, which is able to save your souls. [22] But be ye doers of the word, and not hearers only, deceiving your own selves. [23] For if any be a hearer of the word, and not a doer, he is like unto a man beholding his natural face in a glass: [24] For he beholdeth himself, and goeth his way, and straightway forgetteth what manner of man he was. [25] But whoso looketh into the perfect law of liberty, and continueth *therein,* he being not a forgetful hearer, but a doer of the work, this man shall be blessed in his deed. [26] If any man among you seem to be religious, and bridleth not his tongue, but deceiveth his own heart, this man's religion *is* vain. [27] Pure religion and undefiled before God and the Father is this, To visit the fatherless and widows in their affliction, *and* to keep himself unspotted from the world.

2 My brethren, have not the faith of our Lord Jesus Christ, *the Lord* of glory, with respect of persons. [2] For if there come unto your assembly a man with a gold ring, in goodly apparel, and there come in also a poor man in vile raiment; [3] And ye have respect to him that weareth the gay clothing, and say unto him, Sit thou here in a good place; and say to the poor, Stand thou there, or sit here under my footstool: [4] Are ye not then partial in yourselves, and are become judges of evil thoughts? [5] Hearken, my beloved brethren, Hath not God chosen the poor of this world rich in faith, and heirs of the kingdom which he hath promised to them that love him? [6] But ye have despised the poor. Do not rich men oppress you, and draw you before the judgment seats? [7] Do not they blaspheme that worthy name by the which ye are called? [8] If ye fulfil the royal law according to the scripture, Thou shalt love thy neighbour as thyself, ye do well: [9] But if ye have respect to persons, ye commit sin, and are convinced of the law as transgressors. [10] For whosoever shall keep the whole law, and yet offend in one point, he is guilty of all. [11]For he that said, Do not commit adultery, said also, Do not kill. Now if thou commit no adultery, yet if thou kill, thou art become a transgressor of the law. [12]So speak ye, and so do, as they that shall be judged by the law of liberty. [13]For he shall have judgment without mercy, that hath shewed no mercy; and mercy rejoiceth against judgment. [14]What *doth it* profit, my brethren, though a man say he hath faith, and have not works? can faith save him? [15]If a brother or sister be naked, and destitute of daily food, [16]And one of you say unto them, Depart in peace, be ye warmed and filled; notwithstanding ye give them not those things which are needful to the body; what *doth it* profit? [17]Even so faith, if it hath not works, is dead, being alone. [18]Yea, a man may say, Thou hast faith, and I have works: shew me thy faith without thy works, and I will shew thee my faith by my works. [19]Thou believest that there is one God; thou doest well: the devils also believe, and tremble. [20]But wilt thou know, O vain man, that faith without works is dead? [21]Was not Abraham our father justified by works, when he had offered Isaac his son upon the altar? [22]Seest thou how faith wrought with his works, and by works was faith made perfect? [23]And the scripture was fulfilled which saith, Abraham believed God, and it was imputed unto him for righteousness: and he was called the Friend of God. [24]Ye see then how that by works a man is justified, and not by faith only. [25]Likewise also was not Rahab the harlot justified by works, when she had received the messengers, and had sent *them* out another way? [26]For as the body without the spirit is dead, so faith without works is dead also.

3 My brethren, be not many masters, knowing that we shall receive the greater condemnation. [2]For in many things we offend all. If any man offend not in word, the same *is* a perfect man, *and* able also to bridle the whole body. [3]Behold, we put bits in the horses' mouths, that they may obey us; and we turn about their whole body. [4]Behold also the ships, which though *they be* so great, and *are* driven of fierce winds, yet are they turned about with a very small helm, whithersoever the governor listeth.

[5]Even so the tongue is a little member, and boasteth great things. Behold, how great a matter a little fire kindleth! [6]And the tongue *is* a fire, a world of iniquity: so is the tongue among our members, that it defileth the whole body, and setteth on fire the course of nature; and it is set on fire of hell. [7]For every kind of beasts, and of birds, and of serpents, and of things in the sea, is tamed, and hath been tamed of mankind: [8]But the tongue can no man tame; *it is* an unruly evil, full of deadly poison. [9]Therewith bless we God, even the Father; and therewith curse we men, which are made after the similitude of God. [10]Out of the same mouth proceedeth blessing and cursing. My brethren, these things ought not so to be. [11]Doth a fountain send forth at the same place sweet *water* and bitter? [12]Can the fig tree, my brethren, bear olive berries? either a vine, figs? so *can* no fountain both yield salt water and fresh. [13]Who *is* a wise man and endued with knowledge among you? let him shew out of a good conversation his works with meekness of wisdom. [14]But if ye have bitter envying and strife in your hearts, glory not, and lie not against the truth. [15]This wisdom descendeth not from above, but *is* earthly, sensual, devilish. [16]For where envying and strife *is,* there *is* confusion and every evil work. [17]But the wisdom that is from above is first pure, then peaceable, gentle, *and* easy to be intreated, full of mercy and good fruits, without partiality, and without hypocrisy. [18]And the fruit of righteousness is sown in peace of them that make peace.

4 From whence *come* wars and fightings among you? *come they* not hence, *even* of your lusts that war in your members? [2]Ye lust, and have not: ye kill, and desire to have, and cannot obtain: ye fight and war, yet ye have not, because ye ask not. [3]Ye ask, and receive not, because ye ask amiss, that ye may consume *it* upon your lusts. [4]Ye adulterers and adulteresses, know ye not that the friendship of the world is enmity with God? whosoever therefore will be a friend of the world is the enemy of God. [5]Do ye think that the scripture saith in vain, The spirit that dwelleth in us lusteth to envy? [6]But he giveth more grace. Wherefore he saith,

God resisteth the proud, but giveth grace unto the humble.

[7]Submit yourselves therefore to God. Resist the devil, and he will flee from you. [8]Draw nigh to God, and he will draw nigh to you. Cleanse *your* hands, *ye* sinners; and purify *your* hearts, *ye* double minded. [9]Be afflicted, and mourn, and weep: let your laughter be turned to mourning, and *your* joy to heaviness. [10]Humble yourselves in the sight of the Lord, and he shall lift you up. [11]Speak not evil one of another, brethren. He that speaketh evil of *his* brother, and judgeth his brother, speaketh evil of the law, and judgeth the law: but if thou judge the law, thou art not a doer of the law, but a judge. [12]There is one lawgiver, who is able to save and to destroy: who art thou that judgest another?

[13]Go to now, ye that say, To day or to morrow we will go into such a city, and continue there a year, and buy and sell, and get gain: [14]Whereas ye know not what *shall be* on the morrow. For what *is* your life? It is even a vapour, that appeareth for a little time, and then vanisheth away. [15]For that ye *ought* to say, If the Lord will, we shall live, and do this, or that. [16]But now ye rejoice in your boastings: all such rejoicing is evil. [17]Therefore to him that knoweth to do good, and doeth *it* not, to him it is sin.

5 Go to now, *ye* rich men, weep and howl for your miseries that shall come upon *you*. [2]Your riches are corrupted, and your garments are motheaten. [3]Your gold and silver is cankered; and the rust of them shall be a witness against you, and shall eat your flesh as it were fire. Ye have heaped treasure together for the last days. [4]Behold, the hire of the labourers who have reaped down your fields, which is of you kept back by fraud, crieth: and the cries of them which have reaped are entered into the ears of the Lord of sabaoth. [5]Ye have lived in pleasure on the earth, and been wanton; ye have nourished your hearts, as in a day of slaughter. [6]Ye have condemned *and* killed the just; *and* he doth not resist you.

[7]Be patient therefore, brethren, unto the coming of the Lord. Behold, the husbandman waiteth for the precious fruit of the earth, and hath long patience for it, until he receive the early and latter rain. [8]Be ye also patient; stablish your hearts: for the coming of the Lord draweth nigh. [9]Grudge not one against another, brethren, lest ye be condemned: behold, the judge standeth before the door. [10]Take, my brethren, the prophets, who have spoken in the name of the Lord, for an example of suffering affliction, and of patience. [11]Behold, we count them happy which endure. Ye have heard of the patience of Job, and have seen the end of the Lord; that the Lord is very pitiful, and of tender mercy. [12]But above all things, my brethren, swear not, neither by heaven, neither by the earth, neither by any other oath: but let your yea be yea; and *your* nay, nay; lest ye fall into condemnation. [13]Is any among you afflicted? let him pray. Is any merry? let him sing psalms. [14]Is any sick among you? let him call for the elders of the church; and let them pray over him, anointing him with oil in the name of the Lord: [15]And the prayer of faith shall save the sick, and the Lord shall raise him up; and if he have committed sins, they shall be forgiven him. [16]Confess *your* faults one to another, and pray one for another, that ye may be healed. The effectual fervent prayer of a righteous man availeth much. [17]Elias was a man subject to like passions as we are, and he prayed earnestly that it might not rain: and it rained not on the earth by the space of three years and six months. [18]And he prayed again, and the heaven gave rain, and the earth brought forth her fruit. [19]Brethren, if any of you do err from the truth, and one convert him; [20]Let him know, that he which converteth the sinner from the error of his way shall save a soul from death, and shall hide a multitude of sins.

PETER

1 Peter, an apostle of Jesus Christ,

to the strangers scattered throughout Pontus, Galatia, Cappadocia, Asia, and Bithynia, ²Elect according to the foreknowledge of God the Father, through sanctification of the Spirit, unto obedience and sprinkling of the blood of Jesus Christ:

Grace unto you, and peace, be multiplied.

³Blessed *be* the God and Father of our Lord Jesus Christ, which according to his abundant mercy hath begotten us again unto a lively hope by the resurrection of Jesus Christ from the dead, ⁴To an inheritance incorruptible, and undefiled, and that fadeth not away, reserved in heaven for you, ⁵Who are kept by the power of God through faith unto salvation ready to be revealed in the last time. ⁶Wherein ye greatly rejoice, though now for a season, if need be, ye are in heaviness through manifold temptations: ⁷That the trial of your faith, being much more precious than of gold that perisheth, though it be tried with fire, might be found unto praise and honour and glory at the appearing of Jesus Christ: ⁸Whom having not seen, ye love; in whom, though now ye see *him* not, yet believing, ye rejoice with joy unspeakable and full of glory: ⁹Receiving the end of your faith, *even* the salvation of *your* souls. ¹⁰Of which salvation the prophets have enquired and searched diligently, who prophesied of the grace *that should come* unto you: ¹¹Searching what, or what manner of time the Spirit of Christ which was in them did signify, when it testified beforehand the sufferings of Christ, and the glory that should follow. ¹²Unto whom it was revealed, that not unto themselves, but unto us they did minister the things, which are now reported unto you by them that have preached the gospel unto you with the Holy Ghost sent down from heaven; which things the angels desire to look into.

¹³Wherefore gird up the loins of your mind, be sober, and hope to the end for the grace that is to be brought unto you at the revelation of Jesus Christ; ¹⁴As obedient children, not fashioning yourselves according to the former lusts in your ignorance: ¹⁵But as he which hath called you is holy, so be ye holy in all manner of conversation; ¹⁶Because it is written, Be ye holy; for I am holy. ¹⁷And if ye call on the Father, who without respect of persons judgeth according to every man's work, pass the time of your sojourning *here* in fear: ¹⁸Forasmuch as ye know that ye were not redeemed with corruptible things, *as* silver and gold, from your vain conversation *received* by tradition from your fathers; ¹⁹But with the precious blood of Christ, as of a lamb without blemish and without spot: ²⁰Who verily was foreordained before the foundation of the world, but was manifest in these last times for you, ²¹Who by him do believe in God, that raised him up from the dead, and gave him glory; that your faith and hope might be in God. ²²Seeing ye have purified your souls in obeying the truth through the Spirit unto unfeigned love of the brethren, *see that ye* love one another with a pure heart fervently: ²³Being born again, not of corruptible seed, but of incorruptible, by the word of God, which liveth and abideth for ever. ²⁴For

all flesh *is* as grass, and all the glory of man as the flower of grass. The grass withereth, and the flower thereof falleth away: ²⁵But the word of the Lord endureth for ever.

And this is the word which by the gospel is preached unto you.

2 Wherefore laying aside all malice, and all guile, and hypocrisies, and envies, and all evil speakings, ²As newborn babes, desire the sincere milk of the word, that ye may grow thereby: ³If so be ye have tasted that the Lord *is* gracious. ⁴To whom coming, *as unto* a living stone, disallowed indeed of men, but chosen of God, *and* precious, ⁵Ye also, as lively stones, are built up a spiritual house, an holy priesthood, to offer up spiritual sacrifices, acceptable to God by Jesus Christ. ⁶Wherefore also it is contained in the scripture,

Behold, I lay in Sion a chief corner stone, elect, precious: and he that believeth on him shall not be confounded.

⁷Unto you therefore which believe *he is* precious: but unto them which be disobedient,

the stone which the builders disallowed, the same is made the head of the corner,

⁸And

a stone of stumbling, and a rock of offence,

even to them which stumble at the word, being disobedient: whereunto also they were appointed. ⁹But ye *are* a chosen generation, a royal priesthood, an holy nation, a peculiar people; that ye should shew forth the praises of him who hath called you out of darkness into his marvellous light: ¹⁰Which in time past *were* not a people, but *are* now the people of God: which had not obtained mercy, but now have obtained mercy.
¹¹Dearly beloved, I beseech *you* as strangers and pilgrims, abstain from fleshly lusts, which war against the soul; ¹²Having your conversation honest among the Gentiles: that, whereas they speak against you as evildoers, they may by *your* good works, which they shall behold, glorify God in the day of visitation.
¹³Submit yourselves to every ordinance of man for the Lord's sake: whether it be to the king, as supreme; ¹⁴Or unto governors, as unto them that are sent by him for the punishment of evildoers, and for the praise of them that do well. ¹⁵For so is the will of God, that with well doing ye may put to silence the ignorance of foolish men: ¹⁶As free, and not using *your* liberty for a cloke of maliciousness, but as the servants of God. ¹⁷Honour all *men.* Love the brotherhood. Fear God. Honour the king. ¹⁸Servants, *be* subject to *your* masters with all fear; not only to the good and gentle, but also to the froward. ¹⁹For this *is* thankworthy, if a man for conscience toward God endure grief, suffering wrongfully. ²⁰For what glory *is it,* if, when ye be buffeted for your faults, ye shall take it patiently? but if, when ye do well, and suffer *for it,* ye take it

patiently, this *is* acceptable with God. ²¹For even hereunto were ye called: because Christ also suffered for us, leaving us an example, that ye should follow his steps:

²²Who did no sin, neither was guile found in his mouth:

²³Who, when he was reviled, reviled not again; when he suffered, he threatened not; but committed *himself* to him that judgeth righteously: ²⁴Who his own self bare our sins in his own body on the tree, that we, being dead to sins, should live unto righteousness: by whose stripes ye were healed. ²⁵For ye were as sheep going astray; but are now returned unto the Shepherd and Bishop of your souls.

3 Likewise, ye wives, *be* in subjection to your own husbands; that, if any obey not the word, they also may without the word be won by the conversation of the wives; ²While they behold your chaste conversation *coupled* with fear. ³Whose adorning let it not be that outward *adorning* of plaiting the hair, and of wearing of gold, or of putting on of apparel; ⁴But *let it be* the hidden man of the heart, in that which is not corruptible, *even the ornament* of a meek and quiet spirit, which is in the sight of God of great price. ⁵For after this manner in the old time the holy women also, who trusted in God, adorned themselves, being in subjection unto their own husbands: ⁶Even as Sarah obeyed Abraham, calling him lord: whose daughters ye are, as long as ye do well, and are not afraid with any amazement. ⁷Likewise, ye husbands, dwell with *them* according to knowledge, giving honour unto the wife, as unto the weaker vessel, and as being heirs together of the grace of life; that your prayers be not hindered. ⁸Finally, *be ye* all of one mind, having compassion one of another, love as brethren, *be* pitiful, *be* courteous: ⁹Not rendering evil for evil, or railing for railing: but contrariwise blessing; knowing that ye are thereunto called, that ye should inherit a blessing. ¹⁰For

he that will love life, and see good days, let him refrain his tongue from evil, and his lips that they speak no guile: ¹¹Let him eschew evil, and do good; let him seek peace, and ensue it. ¹²For the eyes of the Lord *are* over the righteous, and his ears *are open* unto their prayers: but the face of the Lord *is* against them that do evil.

¹³And who *is* he that will harm you, if ye be followers of that which is good? ¹⁴But and if ye suffer for righteousness' sake, happy *are ye:* and be not afraid of their terror, neither be troubled; ¹⁵But sanctify the Lord God in your hearts: and *be* ready always to *give* an answer to every man that asketh you a reason of the hope that is in you with meekness and fear: ¹⁶Having a good conscience; that, whereas they speak evil of you, as of evildoers, they may be ashamed that falsely accuse your good conversation in Christ. ¹⁷For *it is* better, if the will of God be so, that ye suffer for well doing, than for evil doing. ¹⁸For Christ also hath once suffered for sins, the just for the unjust, that he might bring us to God, being put to death in the flesh, but quickened by the Spirit: ¹⁹By which also he went and preached unto the spirits in prison; ²⁰Which sometime were disobedient, when once the longsuffering of God waited in the days of Noah, while the ark was a preparing, wherein few, that is, eight souls were saved by water. ²¹The like figure whereunto *even* baptism doth also now save us (not the putting away of the filth of the flesh, but the answer of a good conscience toward God,) by the resurrection of Jesus Christ: ²²Who is gone into heaven, and is on the right hand of God; angels and authorities and powers being made subject unto him.

4 Forasmuch then as Christ hath suffered for us in the flesh, arm yourselves likewise with the same mind: for he that hath suffered in the flesh hath ceased from sin; ²That he no longer should live the rest of *his* time in the flesh to the lusts of men, but to the will of God. ³For the time past of *our* life may suffice us to have wrought the will of the Gentiles, when we walked in lasciviousness, lusts, excess of wine, revellings, banquetings, and abominable idolatries: ⁴Wherein they think it strange that ye run not with *them* to the same excess of riot, speaking evil of *you:* ⁵Who shall give account to him that is ready to judge the quick and the dead. ⁶For for this cause was

the gospel preached also to them that are dead, that they might be judged according to men in the flesh, but live according to God in the spirit.

⁷But the end of all things is at hand: be ye therefore sober, and watch unto prayer. ⁸And above all things have fervent charity among yourselves: for charity shall cover the multitude of sins. ⁹Use hospitality one to another without grudging. ¹⁰As every man hath received the gift, *even so* minister the same one to another, as good stewards of the manifold grace of God. ¹¹If any man speak, *let him speak* as the oracles of God; if any man minister, *let him do it* as of the ability which God giveth: that God in all things may be glorified through Jesus Christ, to whom be praise and dominion for ever and ever. Amen.

¹²Beloved, think it not strange concerning the fiery trial which is to try you, as though some strange thing happened unto you: ¹³But rejoice, inasmuch as ye are partakers of Christ's sufferings; that, when his glory shall be revealed, ye may be glad also with exceeding joy. ¹⁴If ye be reproached for the name of Christ, happy *are ye;* for the spirit of glory and of God resteth upon you: on their part he is evil spoken of, but on your part he is glorified. ¹⁵But let none of you suffer as a murderer, or *as* a thief, or *as* an evildoer, or as a busybody in other men's matters. ¹⁶Yet if *any man suffer* as a Christian, let him not be ashamed; but let him glorify God on this behalf. ¹⁷For the time *is come* that judgment must begin at the house of God: and if *it* first *begin* at us, what shall the end *be* of them that obey not the gospel of God? ¹⁸And

if the righteous scarcely be saved, where shall the ungodly and the sinner appear?

¹⁹Wherefore let them that suffer according to the will of God commit the keeping of their souls *to him* in well doing, as unto a faithful Creator.

5 The elders which are among you I exhort, who am also an elder, and a witness of the sufferings of Christ, and also a partaker of the glory that shall be revealed: ²Feed the flock of God which is among you, taking the oversight *thereof,* not by constraint, but willingly; not for filthy lu-

cre, but of a ready mind; [3]Neither as being lords over *God's* heritage, but being ensamples to the flock. [4]And when the chief Shepherd shall appear, ye shall receive a crown of glory that fadeth not away. [5]Likewise, ye younger, submit yourselves unto the elder. Yea, all *of you* be subject one to another, and be clothed with humility:

for God resisteth the proud, and giveth grace to the humble.

[6]Humble yourselves therefore under the mighty hand of God, that he may exalt you in due time: [7]Casting all your care upon him; for he careth for you. [8]Be sober, be vigilant; because your adversary the devil, as a roaring lion, walketh about, seeking whom he may devour: [9]Whom resist stedfast in the faith, knowing that the same afflictions are accomplished in your brethren that are in the world. [10]But the God of all grace, who hath called us unto his eternal glory by Christ Jesus, after that ye have suffered a while, make you perfect, stablish, strengthen, settle *you*. [11]To him *be* glory and dominion for ever and ever. Amen.

[12]By Silvanus, a faithful brother unto you, as I suppose, I have written briefly, exhorting, and testifying that this is the true grace of God wherein ye stand. [13]The *church that is* at Babylon, elected together with *you*, saluteth you; and *so doth* Marcus my son. [14]Greet ye one another with a kiss of charity. Peace *be* with you all that are in Christ Jesus. Amen.

PETER

1 Simon Peter, a servant and an apostle of Jesus Christ,

to them that have obtained like precious faith with us through the righteousness of God and our Saviour Jesus Christ:

[2]Grace and peace be multiplied unto you through the knowledge of God, and of Jesus our Lord,

[3]According as his divine power hath given unto us all things that *pertain* unto life and godliness, through the knowledge of him that hath called us to glory and virtue: [4]Whereby are given unto us exceeding great and precious promises: that by these ye might be partakers of the divine nature, having escaped the corruption that is in the world through lust. [5]And beside this, giving all diligence, add to your faith virtue; and to virtue knowledge; [6]And to knowledge temperance; and to temperance patience; and to patience godliness; [7]And to godliness brotherly kindness; and to brotherly kindness charity. [8]For if these things be in you, and abound, they make *you that ye shall* neither *be* barren nor unfruitful in the knowledge of our Lord Jesus Christ. [9]But he that lacketh these things is blind, and cannot see afar off, and hath forgotten that he was purged from his old sins. [10]Wherefore the rather, brethren, give diligence to make your calling and election sure: for if ye do these things, ye shall never fall: [11]For so an entrance shall be ministered unto you abundantly into the everlasting kingdom of our Lord and Saviour Jesus Christ.

[12]Wherefore I will not be negligent to put you always in remembrance of these things, though ye know *them*, and be established in the present truth. [13]Yea, I think it meet, as long as I am in this tabernacle, to stir you up by putting *you* in remembrance; [14]Knowing that shortly I must put off *this* my tabernacle, even as our Lord Jesus Christ hath shewed me. [15]Moreover I will endeavour that ye may be able after my decease to have these things always in remembrance. [16]For we have not followed cunningly devised fables, when we made known unto you the power and coming of our Lord Jesus Christ, but were eyewitnesses of his majesty. [17]For he received from God the Father honour and glory, when there came such a voice to him from the excellent glory, This is my beloved Son, in whom I am well pleased. [18]And this voice which came from heaven we heard, when we were with him in the holy mount. [19]We have also a more sure word of prophecy; whereunto ye do well that ye take heed, as unto a light that shineth in a dark place, until the day dawn, and the day star arise in your hearts: [20]Knowing this first, that no prophecy of the scripture is of any private interpretation. [21]For the prophecy came not in old time by the will of man: but holy men of God spake *as they were* moved by the Holy Ghost.

2 But there were false prophets also among the people, even as there shall be false teachers among you, who privily shall bring in damnable heresies, even denying the Lord that bought them, and bring upon themselves swift destruction. [2]And many shall follow their pernicious ways; by reason of whom the way of truth shall be evil spoken of. [3]And through covetousness shall they with feigned words make merchandise of you: whose judgment now of a long time lingereth not, and their damnation slumbereth not. [4]For if God spared not the angels that sinned, but cast *them* down to hell, and delivered *them* into chains of darkness, to be reserved unto judgment; [5]And spared not the old world, but saved Noah the eighth *person,* a preacher of righteousness, bringing in the flood upon the world of the ungodly; [6]And turning the cities of Sodom and Gomorrah into ashes condemned *them* with an overthrow, making *them* an ensample unto those that after should live ungodly; [7]And delivered just Lot, vexed with the filthy conversation of the wicked: [8](For that righteous man dwelling among them, in seeing and hearing, vexed *his* righteous soul from day to day with *their* unlawful deeds;) [9]The Lord knoweth how to deliver the godly out of temptations, and to reserve the unjust unto the day of judgment to be punished: ¹⁰But chiefly them that walk after the flesh in the lust of uncleanness, and despise government. Presumptuous *are they,* selfwilled, they are not afraid to speak evil of dignities. ¹¹Whereas angels, which are greater in power and might, bring not railing accusation against them before the Lord. ¹²But these, as natural brute beasts, made to be taken and destroyed, speak evil of the things that they understand not; and shall utterly perish in their own corruption; ¹³And shall receive the reward of unrighteousness, *as* they that count it pleasure to riot in the daytime. Spots *they are* and blemishes, sporting themselves with their own deceivings while they feast with you; ¹⁴Having eyes full of adultery, and that cannot cease from sin; beguiling unstable souls: an heart they have exercised with covetous practices; cursed children: ¹⁵Which have forsaken the right way, and are gone astray, following the way of Balaam *the son* of Bosor, who loved the wages of unrighteousness; ¹⁶But was rebuked for his iniquity: the dumb ass speaking with man's voice forbad the madness of the prophet. ¹⁷These are wells without water, clouds that are carried with a tempest; to whom the mist of darkness is reserved for ever. ¹⁸For when they speak great swelling *words* of vanity, they allure through the lusts of the flesh, *through much* wantonness, those that were clean escaped from them who live in error. ¹⁹While they promise them liberty, they themselves are the servants of corruption: for of whom a man is overcome, of the same is he brought in bondage. ²⁰For if after they have escaped the pollutions of the world through the knowledge of the Lord and Saviour Jesus Christ, they are again entangled therein, and overcome, the latter end is worse with them than the beginning. ²¹For it had been better for them not to have known the way of righteousness, than, after they have known *it,* to turn from the holy commandment delivered unto them. ²²But it is happened unto them according to the true proverb, The dog *is* turned to his own vomit again; and the sow that was washed to her wallowing in the mire.

3 This second epistle, beloved, I now write unto you; in *both* which I stir up your pure minds by way of remembrance: ²That ye may be mindful of the words which were spoken before by the holy prophets, and of the commandment of us the apostles of the Lord and Saviour: ³Knowing this first, that there shall come in the last days scoffers, walking after their own lusts, ⁴And saying, Where is the promise of his coming? for since the fathers fell asleep, all things continue as *they were* from the beginning of the creation. ⁵For this they willingly are ignorant of, that by the word of God the heavens were of old, and the earth standing out of the water and in the water: ⁶Whereby the world that then was, being overflowed with water, perished: ⁷But the heavens and the earth, which are now, by the same word are kept in store, reserved unto fire against the day of judgment and perdition of ungodly men. ⁸But, beloved, be not ignorant of this one thing, that one day *is* with the Lord as a thousand years, and a thousand years as one day. ⁹The Lord is not slack concerning his promise, as some men count slackness; but is longsuffering to us-ward, not willing that any should perish, but that all should come to repentance. ¹⁰But the day of the Lord will come as a thief in the night; in the which the heavens shall pass away with a great noise, and the elements shall melt with fervent heat, the earth also and the works that are therein shall be burned up. ¹¹*Seeing* then *that* all these things shall be dissolved, what manner *of persons* ought ye to be in *all* holy conversation and godliness, ¹²Looking for and hasting unto the coming of the day of God, wherein the heavens being on fire shall be dissolved, and the elements shall melt with fervent heat? ¹³Nevertheless we, according to his promise, look for new heavens and a new earth, wherein dwelleth righteousness. ¹⁴Wherefore, beloved, seeing that ye look for such things, be diligent that ye may be found of him in peace, without spot, and blameless. ¹⁵And account *that* the longsuffering of our Lord *is* salvation; even as our beloved brother Paul also according to the wisdom given unto him hath written unto you; ¹⁶As also in all *his* epistles, speaking in them of these things; in which are some things hard to be understood, which they that are unlearned and unstable wrest, as *they do* also the other scriptures, unto their own destruction. [17] Ye therefore, beloved, seeing ye know *these things* before, beware lest ye also, being led away with the error of the wicked, fall from your own stedfastness. [18] But grow in grace, and *in* the knowledge of our Lord and Saviour Jesus Christ. To him *be* glory both now and for ever. Amen.

The First Epistle General of
JOHN

1 That which was from the beginning, which we have heard, which we have seen with our eyes, which we have looked upon, and our hands have handled, of the Word of life; ²(For the life was manifested, and we have seen *it*, and bear witness, and shew unto you that eternal life, which was with the Father, and was manifested unto us;) ³That which we have seen and heard declare we unto you, that ye also may have fellowship with us: and truly our fellowship *is* with the Father, and with his Son Jesus Christ. ⁴And these things write we unto you, that your joy may be full.

⁵This then is the message which we have heard of him, and declare unto you, that God is light, and in him is no darkness at all. ⁶If we say that we have fellowship with him, and walk in darkness, we lie, and do not the truth: ⁷But if we walk in the light, as he is in the light, we have fellowship one with another, and the blood of Jesus Christ his Son cleanseth us from all sin. ⁸If we say that we have no sin, we deceive ourselves, and the truth is not in us. ⁹If we confess our sins, he is faithful and just to forgive us *our* sins, and to cleanse us from all unrighteousness. ¹⁰If we say that we have not sinned, we make him a liar, and his word is not in us.

2 My little children, these things write I unto you, that ye sin not. And if any man sin, we have an advocate with the Father, Jesus Christ the righteous: ²And he is the propitiation for our sins: and not for ours only, but also for *the sins of* the whole world. ³And hereby we do know that we know him, if we keep his commandments. ⁴He that saith, I know him, and keepeth not his commandments, is a liar, and the truth is not in him. ⁵But whoso keepeth his word, in him verily is the love of God perfected: hereby know we that we are in him. ⁶He that saith he abideth in him ought himself also so to walk, even as he walked.

⁷Brethren, I write no new commandment unto you, but an old commandment which ye had from the beginning. The old commandment is the word which ye have heard from the beginning. ⁸Again, a new commandment I write unto you, which thing is true in him and in you: because the darkness is past, and the true light now shineth. ⁹He that saith he is in the light, and hateth his brother, is in darkness even until now. ¹⁰He that loveth his brother abideth in the light, and there is none occasion of stumbling in him. ¹¹But he that hateth his brother is in darkness, and walketh in darkness, and knoweth not whither he goeth, because that darkness hath blinded his eyes.

¹²I write unto you, little children, because your sins are forgiven you for his name's sake. ¹³I write unto you, fathers, because ye have known him *that is* from the beginning. I write unto you, young men, because ye have overcome the wicked one. I write unto you, little children, because ye have known the Father.

¹⁴I have written unto you, fathers, because ye have known him *that is* from the beginning. I have written unto you, young men, because ye are strong, and the word of God abideth in you, and ye have overcome the wicked one.

¹⁵Love not the world, neither the things *that are* in the world. If any man love the world, the love of the Father is not in him. ¹⁶For all that *is* in the world, the lust of the flesh, and the lust of the eyes, and the pride of life, is not of the Father, but is of the world. ¹⁷And the world passeth away, and the lust thereof: but he that doeth the will of God abideth for ever.

¹⁸Little children, it is the last time: and as ye have heard that antichrist shall come, even now are there many antichrists; whereby we know that it is the last time. ¹⁹They went out from us, but they were not of us; for if they had been of us, they would *no doubt* have continued with us: but *they went out,* that they might be made manifest that they were not all of us. ²⁰But ye have an unction from the Holy One, and ye know all things. ²¹I have not written unto you because ye know not the truth, but because ye know it, and that no lie is of the truth.

²²Who is a liar but he that denieth that Jesus is the Christ? He is antichrist, that denieth the Father and the Son. ²³Whosoever denieth the Son, the same hath not the Father: (*but*) *he that acknowledgeth the Son hath the Father also.* ²⁴Let that therefore abide in you, which ye have heard from the beginning. If that which ye have heard from the beginning shall remain in you, ye also shall continue in the Son, and in the Father. ²⁵And this is the promise that he hath promised us, *even* eternal life. ²⁶These *things* have I written unto you concerning them that seduce you. ²⁷But the anointing which ye have received of him abideth in you, and ye need not that any man teach you: but as the same anointing teacheth you of all things, and is truth, and is no lie, and even as it hath taught you, ye shall abide in him. ²⁸And now, little children, abide in him; that, when he shall appear, we may have confidence, and not be ashamed before him at his coming. ²⁹If ye know that he is righteous, ye know that every one that doeth righteousness is born of him.

3 Behold, what manner of love the Father hath bestowed upon us, that we should be called the sons of God: therefore the world knoweth us not, because it knew him not. ²Beloved, now are we the sons of God, and it doth not yet appear what we shall be: but we know that, when he shall appear, we shall be like him; for we shall see him as he is. ³And every man that hath this hope in him purifieth himself, even as he is pure. ⁴Whosoever committeth sin transgresseth also the law: for sin is the transgression of the law. ⁵And ye know that he was manifested to take away our sins; and in him is no sin. ⁶Whosoever abideth in him sinneth not: whosoever sinneth hath not seen him, neither known him. ⁷Little children, let no man deceive you: he that doeth righteousness is righteous, even as he is righteous. ⁸He that committeth sin is of the devil; for the devil sinneth from the beginning. For this purpose the Son of God was manifested, that he might destroy the works of the devil. ⁹Whosoever is born of God doth not commit sin; for his seed remaineth in him: and he cannot sin, because he is born of God. ¹⁰In this the children of God are manifest, and the children of the devil: whoso-

ever doeth not righteousness is not of God, neither he that loveth not his brother. ¹¹For this is the message that ye heard from the beginning, that we should love one another. ¹²Not as Cain, *who* was of that wicked one, and slew his brother. And wherefore slew he him? Because his own works were evil, and his brother's righteous.

¹³Marvel not, my brethren, if the world hate you. ¹⁴We know that we have passed from death unto life, because we love the brethren. He that loveth not *his* brother abideth in death. ¹⁵Whosoever hateth his brother is a murderer: and ye know that no murderer hath eternal life abiding in him. ¹⁶Hereby perceive we the love *of God,* because he laid down his life for us: and we ought to lay down *our* lives for the brethren. ¹⁷But whoso hath this world's good, and seeth his brother have need, and shutteth up his bowels *of compassion* from him, how dwelleth the love of God in him? ¹⁸My little children, let us not love in word, neither in tongue; but in deed and in truth. ¹⁹And hereby we know that we are of the truth, and shall assure our hearts before him. ²⁰For if our heart condemn us, God is greater than our heart, and knoweth all things. ²¹Beloved, if our heart condemn us not, *then* have we confidence toward God. ²²And whatsoever we ask, we receive of him, because we keep his commandments, and do those things that are pleasing in his sight. ²³And this is his commandment, That we should believe on the name of his Son Jesus Christ, and love one another, as he gave us commandment. ²⁴And he that keepeth his commandments dwelleth in him, and he in him. And hereby we know that he abideth in us, by the Spirit which he hath given us.

4 Beloved, believe not every spirit, but try the spirits whether they are of God: because many false prophets are gone out into the world. ²Hereby know ye the Spirit of God: Every spirit that confesseth that Jesus Christ is come in the flesh is of God: ³And every spirit that confesseth not that Jesus Christ is come in the flesh is not of God: and this is that *spirit* of antichrist, whereof ye have heard that it should come; and even now already is it in the world. ⁴Ye are of God, little children, and have overcome them: because greater is he that is in you, than he that is in the world. [5]They are of the world: therefore speak they of the world, and the world heareth them. [6]We are of God: he that knoweth God heareth us; he that is not of God heareth not us. Hereby know we the spirit of truth, and the spirit of error.

[7]Beloved, let us love one another: for love is of God; and every one that loveth is born of God, and knoweth God. [8]He that loveth not knoweth not God; for God is love. [9]In this was manifested the love of God toward us, because that God sent his only begotten Son into the world, that we might live through him. [10]Herein is love, not that we loved God, but that he loved us, and sent his Son *to be* the propitiation for our sins. [11]Beloved, if God so loved us, we ought also to love one another. [12]No man hath seen God at any time. If we love one another, God dwelleth in us, and his love is perfected in us. [13]Hereby know we that we dwell in him, and he in us, because he hath given us of his Spirit. [14]And we have seen and do testify that the Father sent the Son *to be* the Saviour of the world. [15]Whosoever shall confess that Jesus is the Son of God, God dwelleth in him, and he in God. [16]And we have known and believed the love that God hath to us. God is love; and he that dwelleth in love dwelleth in God, and God in him. [17]Herein is our love made perfect, that we may have boldness in the day of judgment: because as he is, so are we in this world. [18]There is no fear in love; but perfect love casteth out fear: because fear hath torment. He that feareth is not made perfect in love. [19]We love him, because he first loved us. [20]If a man say, I love God, and hateth his brother, he is a liar: for he that loveth not his brother whom he hath seen, how can he love God whom he hath not seen? [21]And this commandment have we from him, That he who loveth God love his brother also.

[5] Whosoever believeth that Jesus is the Christ is born of God: and every one that loveth him that begat loveth him also that is begotten of him. [2]By this we know that we love the children of God, when we love God, and keep his commandments. [3]For this is the love of God, that we keep his commandments: and his com-

mandments are not grievous. [4]For whatsoever is born of God overcometh the world: and this is the victory that overcometh the world, *even* our faith. [5]Who is he that overcometh the world, but he that believeth that Jesus is the Son of God? [6]This is he that came by water and blood, *even* Jesus Christ; not by water only, but by water and blood. And it is the Spirit that beareth witness, because the Spirit is truth. [7]For there are three that bear record in heaven, the Father, the Word, and the Holy Ghost: and these three are one. [8]And there are three that bear witness in earth, the spirit, and the water, and the blood: and these three agree in one. [9]If we receive the witness of men, the witness of God is greater: for this is the witness of God which he hath testified of his Son. [10]He that believeth on the Son of God hath the witness in himself: he that believeth not God hath made him a liar; because he believeth not the record that God gave of his Son. [11]And this is the record, that God hath given to us eternal life, and this life is in his Son. [12]He that hath the Son hath life; *and* he that hath not the Son of God hath not life. [13]These things have I written unto you that believe on the name of the Son of God; that ye may know that ye have eternal life, and that ye may believe on the name of the Son of God. [14]And this is the confidence that we have in him, that, if we ask any thing according to his will, he heareth us: [15]And if we know that he hear us, whatsoever we ask, we know that we have the petitions that we desired of him. [16]If any man see his brother sin a sin *which is* not unto death, he shall ask, and he shall give him life for them that sin not unto death. There is a sin unto death: I do not say that he shall pray for it. [17]All unrighteousness is sin: and there is a sin not unto death. [18]We know that whosoever is born of God sinneth not; but he that is begotten of God keepeth himself, and that wicked one toucheth him not. [19]And we know that we are of God, and the whole world lieth in wickedness. [20]*And* we know that the Son of God is come, and hath given us an understanding, that we may know him that is true, and we are in him that is true, *even* in his Son Jesus Christ. This is the true God, and eternal life. [21]Little children, keep yourselves from idols. Amen.

The Second Epistle of
JOHN

¹The elder

unto the elect lady and her children, whom I love in the truth; and not I only, but also all they that have known the truth; ²For the truth's sake, which dwelleth in us, and shall be with us for ever.

³Grace be with you, mercy, *and* peace, from God the Father, and from the Lord Jesus Christ, the Son of the Father, in truth and love.

⁴I rejoiced greatly that I found of thy children walking in truth, as we have received a commandment from the Father. ⁵And now I beseech thee, lady, not as though I wrote a new commandment unto thee, but that which we had from the beginning, that we love one another. ⁶And this is love, that we walk after his commandments. This is the commandment, That, as ye have heard from the beginning, ye should walk in it.

⁷For many deceivers are entered into the world, who confess not that Jesus Christ is come in the flesh. This is a deceiver and an antichrist. ⁸Look to yourselves, that we lose not those things which we have wrought, but that we receive a full reward. ⁹Whosoever transgresseth, and abideth not in the doctrine of Christ, hath not God. He that abideth in the doctrine of Christ, he hath both the Father and the Son. ¹⁰If there come any unto you, and bring not this doctrine, receive him not into *your* house, neither bid him God speed: ¹¹For he that biddeth him God speed is partaker of his evil deeds.

¹²Having many things to write unto you, I would not *write* with paper and ink: but I trust to come unto you, and speak face to face, that our joy may be full.

¹³The children of thy elect sister greet thee. Amen.

The Third Epistle of
JOHN

¹The elder

unto the wellbeloved Gaius, whom I love in the truth.

²Beloved, I wish above all things that thou mayest prosper and be in health, even as thy soul prospereth.

³For I rejoiced greatly, when the brethren came and testified of the truth that is in thee, even as thou walkest in the truth.

⁴I have no greater joy than to hear that my children walk in truth. ⁵Beloved, thou doest faithfully whatsoever thou doest to the brethren, and to strangers; ⁶Which have borne witness of thy charity before the church: whom if thou bring forward on their journey after a godly sort, thou shalt do well: ⁷Because that for his name's sake they went forth, taking nothing of the Gentiles. ⁸We therefore ought to receive such, that we might be fellowhelpers to the truth.

⁹I wrote unto the church: but Diotrephes, who loveth to have the preeminence among them, receiveth us not. ¹⁰Wherefore, if I come, I will remember his deeds which he doeth, prating against us with malicious words: and not content therewith, neither doth he himself receive the brethren, and forbiddeth them that would, and casteth *them* out of the church. ¹¹Beloved, follow not that which is evil, but that which is good. He that doeth good is of God: but he that doeth evil hath not seen God. ¹²Demetrius hath good report of all *men,* and of the truth itself: yea, and we *also* bear record; and ye know that our record is true.

¹³I had many things to write, but I will not with ink and pen write unto thee: ¹⁴But I trust I shall shortly see thee, and we shall speak face to face. Peace *be* to thee. *Our* friends salute thee. Greet the friends by name.

The General Epistle of
JUDE

[1]Jude, the servant of Jesus Christ, and brother of James,

to them that are sanctified by God the Father, and preserved in Jesus Christ, *and* called:

[2]Mercy unto you, and peace, and love, be multiplied.

[3]Beloved, when I gave all diligence to write unto you of the common salvation, it was needful for me to write unto you, and exhort *you* that ye should earnestly contend for the faith which was once delivered unto the saints. [4]For there are certain men crept in unawares, who were before of old ordained to this condemnation, ungodly men, turning the grace of our God into lasciviousness, and denying the only Lord God, and our Lord Jesus Christ. [5]I will therefore put you in remembrance, though ye once knew this, how that the Lord, having saved the people out of the land of Egypt, afterward destroyed them that believed not. [6]And the angels which kept not their first estate, but left their own habitation, he hath reserved in everlasting chains under darkness unto the judgment of the great day. [7]Even as Sodom and Gomorrha, and the cities about them in like manner, giving themselves over to fornication, and going after strange flesh, are set forth for an example, suffering the vengeance of eternal fire. [8]Likewise also these *filthy* dreamers defile the flesh, despise dominion, and speak evil of dignities. [9]Yet Michael the archangel, when contending with the devil he disputed about the body of Moses, durst not bring against him a railing accusation, but said, The Lord rebuke thee. [10]But these speak evil of those things which they know not: but what they know naturally, as brute beasts, in those things they corrupt themselves. [11]Woe unto them! for they have gone in the way of Cain, and ran greedily after the error of Balaam for reward, and perished in the gainsaying of Core. [12]These are spots in your feasts of charity, when they feast with you, feeding themselves without fear: clouds *they are* without water, carried about of winds; trees whose fruit withereth, without fruit, twice dead, plucked up by the roots; [13]Raging waves of the sea, foaming out their own shame; wandering stars, to whom is reserved the blackness of darkness for ever. [14]And Enoch also, the seventh from Adam, prophesied of these, saying, Behold, the Lord cometh with ten thousands of his saints, [15]To execute judgment upon all, and to convince all that are ungodly among them of all their ungodly deeds which they have ungodly committed, and of all their hard *speeches* which ungodly sinners have spoken against him. [16]These are murmurers, complainers, walking after their own lusts; and their mouth speaketh great swelling *words,* having men's persons in admiration because of advantage.

[17]But, beloved, remember ye the words which were spoken before of the apostles of our Lord Jesus Christ; [18]How that they told you there should be mockers in the last time, who should walk after their own ungodly lusts. [19]These be they who separate themselves, sensual, having not the Spirit. [20]But ye, beloved, building up yourselves on your most holy faith, praying in the Holy Ghost, [21]Keep yourselves in the love of God, looking for the mercy of our Lord Jesus Christ unto eternal life. [22]And of some have compassion, making a difference: [23]And others save with fear, pulling *them* out of the fire; hating even the garment spotted by the flesh.

[24]Now unto him that is able to keep you from falling, and to present *you* faultless before the presence of his glory with exceeding joy, [25]To the only wise God our Saviour, *be* glory and majesty, dominion and power, both now and ever. Amen.

The
REVELATION
of St. John the Divine

1 The Revelation of Jesus Christ, which God gave unto him, to shew unto his servants things which must shortly come to pass; and he sent and signified *it* by his angel unto his servant John: ²Who bare record of the word of God, and of the testimony of Jesus Christ, and of all things that he saw. ³Blessed *is* he that readeth, and they that hear the words of this prophecy, and keep those things which are written therein: for the time *is* at hand.

⁴John

to the seven churches which are in Asia:

Grace *be* unto you, and peace, from him which is, and which was, and which is to come; and from the seven Spirits which are before his throne; ⁵And from Jesus Christ, *who is* the faithful witness, *and* the first begotten of the dead, and the prince of the kings of the earth.

Unto him that loved us, and washed us from our sins in his own blood, ⁶And hath made us kings and priests unto God and his Father; to him *be* glory and dominion for ever and ever. Amen.

⁷Behold, he cometh with clouds; and every eye shall see him, and they *also* which pierced him: and all kindreds of the earth shall wail because of him. Even so, Amen.

⁸I am Alpha and Omega, the beginning and the ending, saith the Lord, which is, and which was, and which is to come, the Almighty.

⁹I John, who also am your brother, and companion in tribulation, and in the kingdom and patience of Jesus Christ, was in the isle that is called Patmos, for the word of God, and for the testimony of Jesus Christ. ¹⁰I was in the Spirit on the Lord's day, and heard behind me a great voice, as of a trumpet, ¹¹Saying, I am Alpha and Omega, the first and the last: and, What thou seest, write in a book, and send *it* unto the seven churches which are in Asia; unto Ephesus, and unto Smyrna, and unto Pergamos, and

unto Thyatira, and unto Sardis, and unto Philadelphia, and unto Laodicea. ¹²And I turned to see the voice that spake with me. And being turned, I saw seven golden candlesticks; ¹³And in the midst of the seven candlesticks *one* like unto the Son of man, clothed with a garment down to the foot, and girt about the paps with a golden girdle. ¹⁴His head and *his* hairs *were* white like wool, as white as snow; and his eyes *were* as a flame of fire; ¹⁵And his feet like unto fine brass, as if they burned in a furnace; and his voice as the sound of many waters. ¹⁶And he had in his right hand seven stars: and out of his mouth went a sharp twoedged sword: and his countenance *was* as the sun shineth in his strength. ¹⁷And when I saw him, I fell at his feet as dead. And he laid his right hand upon me, saying unto me, Fear not; I am the first and the last: ¹⁸I *am* he that liveth, and was dead; and, behold, I am alive for evermore, Amen; and have the keys of hell and of death.

¹⁹Write the things which thou hast seen, and the things which are, and the things which shall be hereafter; ²⁰The mystery of the seven stars which thou sawest in my right hand, and the seven golden candlesticks. The seven stars are the angels of the seven churches: and the seven candlesticks which thou sawest are the seven churches.

2 Unto the angel of the church of Ephesus write;

These things saith he that holdeth the seven stars in his right hand, who walketh in the midst of the seven golden candlesticks; ²I know thy works, and thy labour, and thy patience, and how thou canst not bear them which are evil: and thou hast tried them which say they are apostles, and are not, and hast found them liars: ³And hast borne, and hast patience, and for my name's sake hast laboured, and hast not fainted. ⁴Nevertheless I have *somewhat* against thee, because thou hast left thy first love. ⁵Remember therefore from whence thou art fallen, and repent, and do the first works; or else I will come unto thee quickly, and will remove thy candlestick out of his place, except thou repent. ⁶But this thou hast, that thou hatest the deeds of the Nicolaitans, which I also hate. ⁷He that hath an ear, let him hear what the Spirit saith unto the churches; To him that overcometh will I give to eat of the tree of life, which is in the midst of the paradise of God.

⁸And unto the angel of the church in Smyrna write;

These things saith the first and the last, which was dead, and is alive; ⁹I know thy works, and tribulation, and poverty, (but thou art rich) and *I know* the blasphemy of them which say they are Jews, and are not, but *are* the synagogue of Satan. ¹⁰Fear none of those things which thou shalt suffer: behold, the devil shall cast *some* of you into prison, that ye may be tried; and ye shall have tribulation ten days: be thou faithful unto death, and I will give thee a crown of life. ¹¹He that hath an ear, let him hear what the Spirit saith unto the churches; He that overcometh shall not be hurt of the second death.

¹²And to the angel of the church in Pergamos write;

These things saith he which hath the sharp sword with two edges; ¹³I know thy works, and where thou dwellest, *even* where Satan's seat *is:* and thou holdest fast my name, and hast not denied my faith, even in those days wherein Antipas *was* my faithful martyr, who was slain among you, where Satan dwelleth. ¹⁴But I have a few things against thee, because thou hast there them that hold the doctrine of Balaam, who taught Balac to cast a stumblingblock before the children of Israel, to eat things sacrificed unto idols, and to commit fornication. ¹⁵So hast thou also them that hold the doctrine of the Nicolaitans, which thing I hate. ¹⁶Repent; or else I will come unto thee quickly, and will fight against them with the sword of my mouth. ¹⁷He that hath an ear, let him hear what the Spirit saith unto the churches; To him that overcometh will I give to eat of the hidden manna, and will give him a white stone, and in the stone a new name written, which no man knoweth saving he that receiveth *it.*

¹⁸And unto the angel of the church in Thyatira write;

·   These things saith the Son of God, who hath his eyes like unto a flame of fire, and his feet *are* like fine brass; ¹⁹I know thy works, and charity, and service, and faith, and thy patience, and thy works; and the last *to be* more than the first. ²⁰Notwithstanding I have a few things against thee, because thou sufferest that woman Jezebel, which calleth herself a prophetess, to teach and to seduce my servants to commit fornication, and to eat things sacrificed unto idols. ²¹And I gave her space to repent of her fornication; and she repented not. ²²Behold, I will cast her into a bed, and them that commit adultery with her into great tribulation, except they repent of their deeds. ²³And I will kill her children with death; and all the churches shall know that I am he which searcheth the reins and hearts: and I will give unto every one of you according to your works. ²⁴But unto you I say, and unto the rest in Thyatira, as many as have not this doctrine, and which have not known the depths of Satan, as they speak; I will put upon you none other burden. ²⁵But that which ye have *already* hold fast till I come. ²⁶And he that overcometh, and keepeth my works unto the end, to him will I give power over the nations: ²⁷And he shall rule them with a rod of iron; as the vessels of a potter shall they be broken to shivers: even as I received of my Father. ²⁸And I will give him the morning star. ²⁹He that hath an ear, let him hear what the Spirit saith unto the churches.

3 And unto the angel of the church in Sardis write;

These things saith he that hath the seven Spirits of God, and the seven stars; I know thy works, that thou hast a name that thou livest, and art dead. ²Be watchful, and strengthen the things which remain, that are ready to die: for I have not found thy works perfect before God. ³Remember therefore how thou hast received and heard, and hold fast, and repent. If therefore thou shalt not watch, I will come on thee as a thief, and thou shalt not know what hour I will come upon thee. ⁴Thou hast a few names even in Sardis which have not defiled their garments; and they shall walk with me in white: for they are worthy. [5]He that overcometh, the same shall be clothed in white raiment; and I will not blot out his name out of the book of life, but I will confess his name before my Father, and before his angels. [6]He that hath an ear, let him hear what the Spirit saith unto the churches.

[7]And to the angel of the church in Philadelphia write;

These things saith he that is holy, he that is true, he that hath the key of David, he that openeth, and no man shutteth; and shutteth, and no man openeth; [8]I know thy works: behold, I have set before thee an open door, and no man can shut it: for thou hast a little strength, and hast kept my word, and hast not denied my name. [9]Behold, I will make them of the synagogue of Satan, which say they are Jews, and are not, but do lie; behold, I will make them to come and worship before thy feet, and to know that I have loved thee. [10]Because thou hast kept the word of my patience, I also will keep thee from the hour of temptation, which shall come upon all the world, to try them that dwell upon the earth. [11]Behold, I come quickly: hold that fast which thou hast, that no man take thy crown. [12]Him that overcometh will I make a pillar in the temple of my God, and he shall go no more out: and I will write upon him the name of my God, and the name of the city of my God, *which is* new Jerusalem, which cometh down out of heaven from my God: and *I will write upon him* my new name. [13]He that hath an ear, let him hear what the Spirit saith unto the churches.

[14]And unto the angel of the church of the Laodiceans write;

These things saith the Amen, the faithful and true witness, the beginning of the creation of God; [15]I know thy works, that thou art neither cold nor hot: I would thou wert cold or hot. [16]So then because thou art lukewarm, and neither cold nor hot, I will spue thee out of my mouth. [17]Because thou sayest, I am rich, and increased with goods, and have need of nothing; and

knowest not that thou art wretched, and miserable, and poor, and blind, and naked: [18]I counsel thee to buy of me gold tried in the fire, that thou mayest be rich; and white raiment, that thou mayest be clothed, and *that* the shame of thy nakedness do not appear; and anoint thine eyes with eyesalve, that thou mayest see. [19]As many as I love, I rebuke and chasten: be zealous therefore, and repent. [20]Behold, I stand at the door, and knock: if any man hear my voice, and open the door, I will come in to him, and will sup with him, and he with me. [21]To him that overcometh will I grant to sit with me in my throne, even as I also overcame, and am set down with my Father in his throne. [22]He that hath an ear, let him hear what the Spirit saith unto the churches.

4 After this I looked, and, behold, a door *was* opened in heaven: and the first voice which I heard *was* as it were of a trumpet talking with me; which said, Come up hither, and I will shew thee things which must be hereafter. [2]And immediately I was in the spirit: and, behold, a throne was set in heaven, and *one* sat on the throne. [3]And he that sat was to look upon like a jasper and a sardine stone: and *there was* a rainbow round about the throne, in sight like unto an emerald. [4]And round about the throne *were* four and twenty seats: and upon the seats I saw four and twenty elders sitting, clothed in white raiment; and they had on their heads crowns of gold. [5]And out of the throne proceeded lightnings and thunderings and voices: and *there were* seven lamps of fire burning before the throne, which are the seven Spirits of God. [6]And before the throne *there was* a sea of glass like unto crystal: and in the midst of the throne, and round about the throne, *were* four beasts full of eyes before and behind. [7]And the first beast *was* like a lion, and the second beast like a calf, and the third beast had a face as a man, and the fourth beast *was* like a flying eagle. [8]And the four beasts had each of them six wings about *him;* and *they were* full of eyes within: and they rest not day and night, saying,

Holy, holy, holy, Lord God Almighty, which was, and is, and is to come.

⁹And when those beasts give glory and honour and thanks to him that sat on the throne, who liveth for ever and ever, ¹⁰The four and twenty elders fall down before him that sat on the throne, and worship him that liveth for ever and ever, and cast their crowns before the throne, saying,

¹¹Thou art worthy, O Lord, to receive glory and honour and power: for thou hast created all things, and for thy pleasure they are and were created.

5 And I saw in the right hand of him that sat on the throne a book written within and on the backside, sealed with seven seals. ²And I saw a strong angel proclaiming with a loud voice, Who is worthy to open the book, and to loose the seals thereof? ³And no man in heaven, nor in earth, neither under the earth, was able to open the book, neither to look thereon. ⁴And I wept much, because no man was found worthy to open and to read the book, neither to look thereon. ⁵And one of the elders saith unto me, Weep not: behold, the Lion of the tribe of Juda, the Root of David, hath prevailed to open the book, and to loose the seven seals thereof. ⁶And I beheld, and, lo, in the midst of the throne and of the four beasts, and in the midst of the elders, stood a Lamb as it had been slain, having seven horns and seven eyes, which are the seven Spirits of God sent forth into all the earth. ⁷And he came and took the book out of the right hand of him that sat upon the throne. ⁸And when he had taken the book, the four beasts and four *and* twenty elders fell down before the Lamb, having every one of them harps, and golden vials full of odours, which are the prayers of saints. ⁹And they sung a new song, saying,

Thou art worthy to take the book, and to open the seals thereof: for thou wast slain, and hast redeemed us to God by thy blood out of every kindred, and tongue, and people, and nation; ¹⁰And hast made us unto our God kings and priests: and we shall reign on the earth.

¹¹And I beheld, and I heard the voice of many angels round about the throne and the beasts and the elders: and the number of them was ten thousand times ten thousand, and thousands of thousands; ¹²Saying with a loud voice,

Worthy is the Lamb that was slain to receive power, and riches, and wisdom, and strength, and honour, and glory, and blessing.

¹³And every creature which is in heaven, and on the earth, and under the earth, and such as are in the sea, and all that are in them, heard I saying,

Blessing, and honour, and glory, and power, *be* unto him that sitteth upon the throne, and unto the Lamb for ever and ever.

¹⁴And the four beasts said, Amen. And the four *and* twenty elders fell down and worshipped him that liveth for ever and ever.

6 And I saw when the Lamb opened one of the seals, and I heard, as it were the noise of thunder, one of the four beasts saying, Come and see. ²And I saw, and behold a white horse: and he that sat on him had a bow; and a crown was given unto him: and he went forth conquering, and to conquer. ³And when he had opened the second seal, I heard the second beast say, Come and see. ⁴And there went out another horse *that was* red: and *power* was given to him that sat thereon to take peace from the earth, and that they should kill one another: and there was given unto him a great sword. ⁵And when he had opened the third seal, I heard the third beast say, Come and see. And I beheld, and lo a black horse; and he that sat on him had a pair of balances in his hand. ⁶And I heard a voice in the midst of the four beasts say, A measure of wheat for a penny, and three measures of barley for a penny; and *see* thou hurt not the oil and the wine. ⁷And when he had opened the fourth seal, I heard the voice of the fourth beast say, Come and see. ⁸And I looked, and behold a pale horse: and his name that sat on him was Death, and Hell followed with him. And power was given unto them over the fourth part of the earth, to kill with sword, and with hunger, and with death, and with the beasts of the earth. ⁹And when he had opened the fifth seal, I saw under the altar

the souls of them that were slain for the word of God, and for the testimony which they held: [10]And they cried with a loud voice, saying, How long, O Lord, holy and true, dost thou not judge and avenge our blood on them that dwell on the earth? [11]And white robes were given unto every one of them; and it was said unto them, that they should rest yet for a little season, until their fellowservants also and their brethren, that should be killed as they *were*, should be fulfilled. [12]And I beheld when he had opened the sixth seal, and, lo, there was a great earthquake; and the sun became black as sackcloth of hair, and the moon became as blood; [13]And the stars of heaven fell unto the earth, even as a fig tree casteth her untimely figs, when she is shaken of a mighty wind. [14]And the heaven departed as a scroll when it is rolled together; and every mountain and island were moved out of their places. [15]And the kings of the earth, and the great men, and the rich men, and the chief captains, and the mighty men, and every bondman, and every free man, hid themselves in the dens and in the rocks of the mountains; [16]And said to the mountains and rocks, Fall on us, and hide us from the face of him that sitteth on the throne, and from the wrath of the Lamb: [17]For the great day of his wrath is come; and who shall be able to stand?

7 And after these things I saw four angels standing on the four corners of the earth, holding the four winds of the earth, that the wind should not blow on the earth, nor on the sea, nor on any tree. [2]And I saw another angel ascending from the east, having the seal of the living God: and he cried with a loud voice to the four angels, to whom it was given to hurt the earth and the sea, [3]Saying, Hurt not the earth, neither the sea, nor the trees, till we have sealed the servants of our God in their foreheads. [4]And I heard the number of them which were sealed: *and there were* sealed an hundred *and* forty *and* four thousand of all the tribes of the children of Israel.

[5]Of the tribe of Juda *were* sealed twelve thousand. Of the tribe of Reuben *were* sealed twelve thousand. Of the tribe of Gad *were* sealed twelve thousand. [6]Of the tribe of Aser *were* sealed twelve thousand. Of the tribe of Nepthalim *were* sealed twelve thousand. Of the tribe of Manasses *were* sealed twelve thousand. [7]Of the tribe of Simeon *were* sealed twelve thousand. Of the tribe of Levi *were* sealed twelve thousand. Of the tribe of Issachar *were* sealed twelve thousand. [8]Of the tribe of Zabulon *were* sealed twelve thousand. Of the tribe of Joseph *were* sealed twelve thousand. Of the tribe of Benjamin *were* sealed twelve thousand.

[9]After this I beheld, and, lo, a great multitude, which no man could number, of all nations, and kindreds, and people, and tongues, stood before the throne, and before the Lamb, clothed with white robes, and palms in their hands; [10]And cried with a loud voice, saying,

Salvation to our God which sitteth upon the throne, and unto the Lamb.

[11]And all the angels stood round about the throne, and *about* the elders and the four beasts, and fell before the throne on their faces, and worshipped God, [12]Saying,

Amen: Blessing, and glory, and wisdom, and thanksgiving, and honour, and power, and might, *be* unto our God for ever and ever. Amen.

[13]And one of the elders answered, saying unto me, What are these which are arrayed in white robes? and whence came they? [14]And I said unto him, Sir, thou knowest. And he said to me, These are they which came out of great tribulation, and have washed their robes, and made them white in the blood of the Lamb. [15]Therefore are they before the throne of God, and serve him day and night in his temple: and he that sitteth on the throne shall dwell among them. [16]They shall hunger no more, neither thirst any more; neither shall the sun light on them, nor any heat. [17]For the Lamb which is in the midst of the throne shall feed them, and shall lead them unto living fountains of waters: and God shall wipe away all tears from their eyes.

8 And when he had opened the seventh seal, there was silence in heaven about the space of half an hour. [2]And I saw the

seven angels which stood before God; and to them were given seven trumpets. ³And another angel came and stood at the altar, having a golden censer; and there was given unto him much incense, that he should offer *it* with the prayers of all saints upon the golden altar which was before the throne. ⁴And the smoke of the incense, *which came* with the prayers of the saints, ascended up before God out of the angel's hand. ⁵And the angel took the censer, and filled it with fire of the altar, and cast *it* into the earth: and there were voices, and thunderings, and lightnings, and an earthquake. ⁶And the seven angels which had the seven trumpets prepared themselves to sound.

⁷The first angel sounded, and there followed hail and fire mingled with blood, and they were cast upon the earth: and the third part of trees was burnt up, and all green grass was burnt up. ⁸And the second angel sounded, and as it were a great mountain burning with fire was cast into the sea: and the third part of the sea became blood; ⁹And the third part of the creatures which were in the sea, and had life, died; and the third part of the ships were destroyed. ¹⁰And the third angel sounded, and there fell a great star from heaven, burning as it were a lamp, and it fell upon the third part of the rivers, and upon the fountains of waters; ¹¹And the name of the star is called Wormwood: and the third part of the waters became wormwood; and many men died of the waters, because they were made bitter. ¹²And the fourth angel sounded, and the third part of the sun was smitten, and the third part of the moon, and the third part of the stars; so as the third part of them was darkened, and the day shone not for a third part of it, and the night likewise.

¹³And I beheld, and heard an angel flying through the midst of heaven, saying with a loud voice, Woe, woe, woe, to the inhabiters of the earth by reason of the other voices of the trumpet of the three angels, which are yet to sound!

9 And the fifth angel sounded, and I saw a star fall from heaven unto the earth: and to him was given the key of the bottomless pit. ²And he opened the bottomless pit; and there arose a smoke out of the pit, as the smoke of a great furnace; and the sun and the air were darkened by reason of the smoke of the pit. ³And there came out of the smoke locusts upon the earth: and unto them was given power, as the scorpions of the earth have power. ⁴And it was commanded them that they should not hurt the grass of the earth, neither any green thing, neither any tree; but only those men which have not the seal of God in their foreheads. ⁵And to them it was given that they should not kill them, but that they should be tormented five months: and their torment *was* as the torment of a scorpion, when he striketh a man. ⁶And in those days shall men seek death, and shall not find it; and shall desire to die, and death shall flee from them. ⁷And the shapes of the locusts *were* like unto horses prepared unto battle; and on their heads *were* as it were crowns like gold, and their faces *were* as the faces of men. ⁸And they had hair as the hair of women, and their teeth were as *the teeth* of lions. ⁹And they had breastplates, as it were breastplates of iron; and the sound of their wings *was* as the sound of chariots of many horses running to battle. ¹⁰And they had tails like unto scorpions, and there were stings in their tails: and their power *was* to hurt men five months. ¹¹And they had a king over them, *which is* the angel of the bottomless pit, whose name in the Hebrew tongue *is* Abaddon, but in the Greek tongue hath *his* name Apollyon. ¹²One woe is past; *and,* behold, there come two woes more hereafter.

¹³And the sixth angel sounded, and I heard a voice from the four horns of the golden altar which is before God, ¹⁴Saying to the sixth angel which had the trumpet, Loose the four angels which are bound in the great river Euphrates. ¹⁵And the four angels were loosed, which were prepared for an hour, and a day, and a month, and a year, for to slay the third part of men. ¹⁶And the number of the army of the horsemen *were* two hundred thousand thousand: and I heard the number of them. ¹⁷And thus I saw the horses in the vision, and them that sat on them, having breastplates of fire, and of jacinth, and brimstone: and the heads of the horses *were* as the heads of lions; and out of their mouths issued fire and smoke

and brimstone. [18]By these three was the third part of men killed, by the fire, and by the smoke, and by the brimstone, which issued out of their mouths. [19]For their power is in their mouth, and in their tails: for their tails *were* like unto serpents, and had heads, and with them they do hurt. [20]And the rest of the men which were not killed by these plagues yet repented not of the works of their hands, that they should not worship devils, and idols of gold, and silver, and brass, and stone, and of wood: which neither can see, nor hear, nor walk: [21]Neither repented they of their murders, nor of their sorceries, nor of their fornication, nor of their thefts.

10 And I saw another mighty angel come down from heaven, clothed with a cloud: and a rainbow *was* upon his head, and his face *was* as it were the sun, and his feet as pillars of fire: [2]And he had in his hand a little book open: and he set his right foot upon the sea, and *his* left *foot* on the earth, [3]And cried with a loud voice, as *when* a lion roareth: and when he had cried, seven thunders uttered their voices. [4]And when the seven thunders had uttered their voices, I was about to write: and I heard a voice from heaven saying unto me, Seal up those things which the seven thunders uttered, and write them not. [5]And the angel which I saw stand upon the sea and upon the earth lifted up his hand to heaven, [6]And sware by him that liveth for ever and ever, who created heaven, and the things that therein are, and the earth, and the things that therein are, and the sea, and the things which are therein, that there should be time no longer: [7]But in the days of the voice of the seventh angel, when he shall begin to sound, the mystery of God should be finished, as he hath declared to his servants the prophets. [8]And the voice which I heard from heaven spake unto me again, and said, Go *and* take the little book which is open in the hand of the angel which standeth upon the sea and upon the earth. [9]And I went unto the angel, and said unto him, Give me the little book. And he said unto me, Take *it,* and eat it up; and it shall make thy belly bitter, but it shall be in thy mouth sweet as honey. [10]And I took the little book out of the angel's hand, and ate it

up; and it was in my mouth sweet as honey: and as soon as I had eaten it, my belly was bitter. [11]And he said unto me, Thou must prophesy again before many peoples, and nations, and tongues, and kings.

11 And there was given me a reed like unto a rod: and the angel stood, saying, Rise, and measure the temple of God, and the altar, and them that worship therein. [2]But the court which is without the temple leave out, and measure it not; for it is given unto the Gentiles: and the holy city shall they tread under foot forty *and* two months. [3]And I will give *power* unto my two witnesses, and they shall prophesy a thousand two hundred *and* threescore days, clothed in sackcloth. [4]These are the two olive trees, and the two candlesticks standing before the God of the earth. [5]And if any man will hurt them, fire proceedeth out of their mouth, and devoureth their enemies: and if any man will hurt them, he must in this manner be killed. [6]These have power to shut heaven, that it rain not in the days of their prophecy: and have power over waters to turn them to blood, and to smite the earth with all plagues, as often as they will. [7]And when they shall have finished their testimony, the beast that ascendeth out of the bottomless pit shall make war against them, and shall overcome them, and kill them. [8]And their dead bodies *shall lie* in the street of the great city, which spiritually is called Sodom and Egypt, where also our Lord was crucified. [9]And they of the people and kindreds and tongues and nations shall see their dead bodies three days and an half, and shall not suffer their dead bodies to be put in graves. [10]And they that dwell upon the earth shall rejoice over them, and make merry, and shall send gifts one to another; because these two prophets tormented them that dwelt on the earth. [11]And after three days and an half the Spirit of life from God entered into them, and they stood upon their feet; and great fear fell upon them which saw them. [12]And they heard a great voice from heaven saying unto them, Come up hither. And they ascended up to heaven in a cloud; and their enemies beheld them. [13]And the same hour was there a great earthquake, and the tenth part of the city fell, and in the

earthquake were slain of men seven thousand: and the remnant were affrighted, and gave glory to the God of heaven. ¹⁴The second woe is past; *and,* behold, the third woe cometh quickly. ¹⁵And the seventh angel sounded; and there were great voices in heaven, saying,

The kingdoms of this world are become *the kingdoms* of our Lord, and of his Christ; and he shall reign for ever and ever.

¹⁶And the four and twenty elders, which sat before God on their seats, fell upon their faces, and worshipped God, ¹⁷Saying,

We give thee thanks, O Lord God Almighty, which art, and wast, and art to come; because thou hast taken to thee thy great power, and hast reigned. ¹⁸And the nations were angry, and thy wrath is come, and the time of the dead, that they should be judged, and that thou shouldest give reward unto thy servants the prophets, and to the saints, and them that fear thy name, small and great; and shouldest destroy them which destroy the earth.

¹⁹And the temple of God was opened in heaven, and there was seen in his temple the ark of his testament: and there were lightnings, and voices, and thunderings, and an earthquake, and great hail.

12 And there appeared a great wonder in heaven; a woman clothed with the sun, and the moon under her feet, and upon her head a crown of twelve stars: ²And she being with child cried, travailing in birth, and pained to be delivered. ³And there appeared another wonder in heaven; and behold a great red dragon, having seven heads and ten horns, and seven crowns upon his heads. ⁴And his tail drew the third part of the stars of heaven, and did cast them to the earth: and the dragon stood before the woman which was ready to be delivered, for to devour her child as soon as it was born. ⁵And she brought forth a man child, who was to rule all nations with a rod of iron: and her child was caught up unto God, and *to* his throne. ⁶And the woman fled into the wilderness, where she hath a place prepared of God, that they should feed her there a thousand two hundred *and* threescore days. ⁷And there was war

in heaven: Michael and his angels fought against the dragon; and the dragon fought and his angels, ⁸And prevailed not; neither was their place found any more in heaven. ⁹And the great dragon was cast out, that old serpent, called the Devil, and Satan, which deceiveth the whole world: he was cast out into the earth, and his angels were cast out with him. ¹⁰And I heard a loud voice saying in heaven,

Now is come salvation, and strength, and the kingdom of our God, and the power of his Christ: for the accuser of our brethren is cast down, which accused them before our God day and night. ¹¹And they overcame him by the blood of the Lamb, and by the word of their testimony; and they loved not their lives unto the death. ¹²Therefore rejoice, *ye* heavens, and ye that dwell in them. Woe to the inhabiters of the earth and of the sea! for the devil is come down unto you, having great wrath, because he knoweth that he hath but a short time.

¹³And when the dragon saw that he was cast unto the earth, he persecuted the woman which brought forth the man *child.* ¹⁴And to the woman were given two wings of a great eagle, that she might fly into the wilderness, into her place, where she is nourished for a time, and times, and half a time, from the face of the serpent. ¹⁵And the serpent cast out of his mouth water as a flood after the woman, that he might cause her to be carried away of the flood. ¹⁶And the earth helped the woman, and the earth opened her mouth, and swallowed up the flood which the dragon cast out of his mouth. ¹⁷And the dragon was wroth with the woman, and went to make war with the remnant of her seed, which keep the commandments of God, and have the testimony of Jesus Christ.

13 And I stood upon the sand of the sea, and saw a beast rise up out of the sea, having seven heads and ten horns, and upon his horns ten crowns, and upon his heads the name of blasphemy. ²And the beast which I saw was like unto a leopard, and his feet were as *the feet* of a bear, and his mouth as the mouth of a lion: and the dragon gave him his power, and his seat, and great authority. ³And I saw one of his heads as it were wounded to death; and his deadly wound was healed: and all the world wondered after the beast. ⁴And they worshipped the dragon which gave power unto the beast: and they worshipped the beast, saying, Who *is* like unto the beast? who is able to make war with him? ⁵And there was given unto him a mouth speaking great things and blasphemies; and power was given unto him to continue forty *and* two months. ⁶And he opened his mouth in blasphemy against God, to blaspheme his name, and his tabernacle, and them that dwell in heaven. ⁷And it was given unto him to make war with the saints, and to overcome them: and power was given him over all kindreds, and tongues, and nations. ⁸And all that dwell upon the earth shall worship him, whose names are not written in the book of life of the Lamb slain from the foundation of the world. ⁹If any man have an ear, let him hear.

¹⁰He that leadeth into captivity shall go into captivity: he that killeth with the sword must be killed with the sword.

Here is the patience and the faith of the saints. ¹¹And I beheld another beast coming up out of the earth; and he had two horns like a lamb, and he spake as a dragon. ¹²And he exerciseth all the power of the first beast before him, and causeth the earth and them which dwell therein to worship the first beast, whose deadly wound was healed. ¹³And he doeth great wonders, so that he maketh fire come down from heaven on the earth in the sight of men, ¹⁴And deceiveth them that dwell on the earth by *the means of* those miracles which he had power to do in the sight of the beast; saying to them that dwell on the earth, that they should make an image to the beast, which had the wound by a sword, and did live. ¹⁵And he had power to give life unto the image of the beast, that the image of the beast should both speak, and cause that as many as would not worship the image of the beast should be killed. ¹⁶And he causeth all, both small and great, rich and poor, free and bond, to receive a mark in their right hand, or in their foreheads: ¹⁷And that no man might buy or sell, save

he that had the mark, or the name of the beast, or the number of his name. ¹⁸Here is wisdom. Let him that hath understanding count the number of the beast: for it is the number of a man; and his number *is* Six hundred threescore *and* six.

14 And I looked, and, lo, a Lamb stood on the mount Sion, and with him an hundred forty *and* four thousand, having his Father's name written in their foreheads. ²And I heard a voice from heaven, as the voice of many waters, and as the voice of a great thunder: and I heard the voice of harpers harping with their harps: ³And they sung as it were a new song before the throne, and before the four beasts, and the elders: and no man could learn that song but the hundred *and* forty *and* four thousand, which were redeemed from the earth. ⁴These are they which were not defiled with women; for they are virgins. These are they which follow the Lamb whithersoever he goeth. These were redeemed from among men, *being* the firstfruits unto God and to the Lamb. ⁵And in their mouth was found no guile: for they are without fault before the throne of God.

⁶And I saw another angel fly in the midst of heaven, having the everlasting gospel to preach unto them that dwell on the earth, and to every nation, and kindred, and tongue, and people, ⁷Saying with a loud voice, Fear God, and give glory to him; for the hour of his judgment is come: and worship him that made heaven, and earth, and the sea, and the fountains of waters. ⁸And there followed another angel, saying, Babylon is fallen, is fallen, that great city, because she made all nations drink of the wine of the wrath of her fornication. ⁹And the third angel followed them, saying with a loud voice, If any man worship the beast and his image, and receive *his* mark in his forehead, or in his hand, ¹⁰The same shall drink of the wine of the wrath of God, which is poured out without mixture into the cup of his indignation; and he shall be tormented with fire and brimstone in the presence of the holy angels, and in the presence of the Lamb: ¹¹And the smoke of their torment ascendeth up for ever and ever: and they have no rest day nor night, who worship the beast and his image, and

whosoever receiveth the mark of his name. ¹²Here is the patience of the saints: here *are* they that keep the commandments of God, and the faith of Jesus. ¹³And I heard a voice from heaven saying unto me, Write, Blessed *are* the dead which die in the Lord from henceforth: Yea, saith the Spirit, that they may rest from their labours; and their works do follow them.

¹⁴And I looked, and behold a white cloud, and upon the cloud *one* sat like unto the Son of man, having on his head a golden crown, and in his hand a sharp sickle. ¹⁵And another angel came out of the temple, crying with a loud voice to him that sat on the cloud, Thrust in thy sickle, and reap: for the time is come for thee to reap; for the harvest of the earth is ripe. ¹⁶And he that sat on the cloud thrust in his sickle on the earth; and the earth was reaped. ¹⁷And another angel came out of the temple which is in heaven, he also having a sharp sickle. ¹⁸And another angel came out from the altar, which had power over fire; and cried with a loud cry to him that had the sharp sickle, saying, Thrust in thy sharp sickle, and gather the clusters of the vine of the earth; for her grapes are fully ripe. ¹⁹And the angel thrust in his sickle into the earth, and gathered the vine of the earth, and cast *it* into the great winepress of the wrath of God. ²⁰And the winepress was trodden without the city, and blood came out of the winepress, even unto the horse bridles, by the space of a thousand *and* six hundred furlongs.

15 And I saw another sign in heaven, great and marvellous, seven angels having the seven last plagues; for in them is filled up the wrath of God. ²And I saw as it were a sea of glass mingled with fire: and them that had gotten the victory over the beast, and over his image, and over his mark, *and* over the number of his name, stand on the sea of glass, having the harps of God. ³And they sing the song of Moses the servant of God, and the song of the Lamb, saying,

Great and marvellous *are* thy works, Lord God Almighty; just and true *are* thy ways, thou King of saints. ⁴Who shall not fear thee, O Lord, and glorify thy name? for

thou only *art* holy: for all nations shall come and worship before thee; for thy judgments are made manifest.

⁵And after that I looked, and, behold, the temple of the tabernacle of the testimony in heaven was opened: ⁶And the seven angels came out of the temple, having the seven plagues, clothed in pure and white linen, and having their breasts girded with golden girdles. ⁷And one of the four beasts gave unto the seven angels seven golden vials full of the wrath of God, who liveth for ever and ever. ⁸And the temple was filled with smoke from the glory of God, and from his power; and no man was able to enter into the temple, till the seven plagues of the seven angels were fulfilled.

16 And I heard a great voice out of the temple saying to the seven angels, Go your ways, and pour out the vials of the wrath of God upon the earth. ²And the first went, and poured out his vial upon the earth; and there fell a noisome and grievous sore upon the men which had the mark of the beast, and *upon* them which worshipped his image. ³And the second angel poured out his vial upon the sea; and it became as the blood of a dead *man:* and every living soul died in the sea. ⁴And the third angel poured out his vial upon the rivers and fountains of waters; and they became blood. ⁵And I heard the angel of the waters say,

Thou art righteous, O Lord, which art, and wast, and shalt be, because thou hast judged thus. ⁶For they have shed the blood of saints and prophets, and thou hast given them blood to drink; for they are worthy.

⁷And I heard another out of the altar say,

Even so, Lord God Almighty, true and righteous *are* thy judgments.

⁸And the fourth angel poured out his vial upon the sun; and power was given unto him to scorch men with fire. ⁹And men were scorched with great heat, and blasphemed the name of God, which hath power over these plagues: and they repented not to give him glory. ¹⁰And the fifth angel poured out his vial upon the seat of the

beast; and his kingdom was full of darkness; and they gnawed their tongues for pain, [11]And blasphemed the God of heaven because of their pains and their sores, and repented not of their deeds. [12]And the sixth angel poured out his vial upon the great river Euphrates; and the water thereof was dried up, that the way of the kings of the east might be prepared. [13]And I saw three unclean spirits like frogs *come* out of the mouth of the dragon, and out of the mouth of the beast, and out of the mouth of the false prophet. [14]For they are the spirits of devils, working miracles, *which* go forth unto the kings of the earth and of the whole world, to gather them to the battle of that great day of God Almighty.

[15]Behold, I come as a thief. Blessed *is* he that watcheth, and keepeth his garments, lest he walk naked, and they see his shame.

[16]And he gathered them together into a place called in the Hebrew tongue Armageddon. [17]And the seventh angel poured out his vial into the air; and there came a great voice out of the temple of heaven, from the throne, saying, It is done. [18]And there were voices, and thunders, and lightnings; and there was a great earthquake, such as was not since men were upon the earth, so mighty an earthquake, *and* so great. [19]And the great city was divided into three parts, and the cities of the nations fell: and great Babylon came in remembrance before God, to give unto her the cup of the wine of the fierceness of his wrath. [20]And every island fled away, and the mountains were not found. [21]And there fell upon men a great hail out of heaven, *every stone* about the weight of a talent: and men blasphemed God because of the plague of the hail; for the plague thereof was exceeding great.

17 And there came one of the seven angels which had the seven vials, and talked with me, saying unto me, Come hither; I will shew unto thee the judgment of the great whore that sitteth upon many waters: [2]With whom the kings of the earth have committed fornication, and the inhabitants of the earth have been made

drunk with the wine of her fornication. [3]So he carried me away in the spirit into the wilderness: and I saw a woman sit upon a scarlet coloured beast, full of names of blasphemy, having seven heads and ten horns. [4]And the woman was arrayed in purple and scarlet colour, and decked with gold and precious stones and pearls, having a golden cup in her hand full of abominations and filthiness of her fornication: [5]And upon her forehead *was* a name written,

MYSTERY, BABYLON THE GREAT,

THE MOTHER OF HARLOTS

AND ABOMINATIONS OF THE EARTH.

[6]And I saw the woman drunken with the blood of the saints, and with the blood of the martyrs of Jesus: and when I saw her, I wondered with great admiration. [7]And the angel said unto me, Wherefore didst thou marvel? I will tell thee the mystery of the woman, and of the beast that carrieth her, which hath the seven heads and ten horns. [8]The beast that thou sawest was, and is not; and shall ascend out of the bottomless pit, and go into perdition: and they that dwell on the earth shall wonder, whose names were not written in the book of life from the foundation of the world, when they behold the beast that was, and is not, and yet is. [9]And here *is* the mind which hath wisdom. The seven heads are seven mountains, on which the woman sitteth. [10]And there are seven kings: five are fallen, and one is, *and* the other is not yet come; and when he cometh, he must continue a short space. [11]And the beast that was, and is not, even he is the eighth, and is of the seven, and goeth into perdition. [12]And the ten horns which thou sawest are ten kings, which have received no kingdom as yet; but receive power as kings one hour with the beast. [13]These have one mind, and shall give their power and strength unto the beast. [14]These shall make war with the Lamb, and the Lamb shall overcome them: for he is Lord of lords, and King of kings: and they that are with him *are* called, and chosen, and faithful. [15]And he saith unto me, The waters which thou sawest, where

the whore sitteth, are peoples, and multitudes, and nations, and tongues. ¹⁶And the ten horns which thou sawest upon the beast, these shall hate the whore, and shall make her desolate and naked, and shall eat her flesh, and burn her with fire. ¹⁷For God hath put in their hearts to fulfil his will, and to agree, and give their kingdom unto the beast, until the words of God shall be fulfilled. ¹⁸And the woman which thou sawest is that great city, which reigneth over the kings of the earth.

18 And after these things I saw another angel come down from heaven, having great power; and the earth was lightened with his glory. ²And he cried mightily with a strong voice, saying,

Babylon the great is fallen, is fallen, and is become the habitation of devils, and the hold of every foul spirit, and a cage of every unclean and hateful bird. ³For all nations have drunk of the wine of the wrath of her fornication, and the kings of the earth have committed fornication with her, and the merchants of the earth are waxed rich through the abundance of her delicacies.

⁴And I heard another voice from heaven, saying,

Come out of her, my people, that ye be not partakers of her sins, and that ye receive not of her plagues. ⁵For her sins have reached unto heaven, and God hath remembered her iniquities. ⁶Reward her even as she rewarded you, and double unto her double according to her works: in the cup which she hath filled fill to her double. ⁷How much she hath glorified herself, and lived deliciously, so much torment and sorrow give her: for she saith in her heart, I sit a queen, and am no widow, and shall see no sorrow. ⁸Therefore shall her plagues come in one day, death, and mourning, and famine; and she shall be utterly burned with fire: for strong *is* the Lord God who judgeth her.

⁹And the kings of the earth, who have committed fornication and lived deliciously with her, shall bewail her, and lament for her, when they shall see the smoke of her burning, ¹⁰Standing afar off for the fear of her torment, saying,

Alas, alas, that great city Babylon, that mighty city! for in one hour is thy judgment come.

¹¹And the merchants of the earth shall weep and mourn over her; for no man buyeth their merchandise any more: ¹²The merchandise of gold, and silver, and precious stones, and of pearls, and fine linen, and purple, and silk, and scarlet, and all thyine wood, and all manner vessels of ivory, and all manner vessels of most precious wood, and of brass, and iron, and marble, ¹³And cinnamon, and odours, and ointments, and frankincense, and wine, and oil, and fine flour, and wheat, and beasts, and sheep, and horses, and chariots, and slaves, and souls of men. ¹⁴And the fruits that thy soul lusted after are departed from thee, and all things which were dainty and goodly are departed from thee, and thou shalt find them no more at all. ¹⁵The merchants of these things, which were made rich by her, shall stand afar off for the fear of her torment, weeping and wailing, ¹⁶And saying,

Alas, alas, that great city, that was clothed in fine linen, and purple, and scarlet, and decked with gold, and precious stones, and pearls! ¹⁷For in one hour so great riches is come to nought.

And every shipmaster, and all the company in ships, and sailors, and as many as trade by sea, stood afar off, ¹⁸And cried when they saw the smoke of her burning, saying, What *city is* like unto this great city! ¹⁹And they cast dust on their heads, and cried, weeping and wailing, saying,

Alas, alas, that great city, wherein were made rich all that had ships in the sea by reason of her costliness! for in one hour is she made desolate.

²⁰Rejoice over her, *thou* heaven, and *ye* holy apostles and prophets; for God hath avenged you on her.

²¹And a mighty angel took up a stone like a great millstone, and cast *it* into the sea, saying,

Thus with violence shall that great city Babylon be thrown down, and shall be found no more at all. ²²And the voice of harpers, and musicians, and of pipers, and trumpeters, shall be heard no more at all in thee; and no craftsman, of whatsoever craft *he be,* shall be found any more in thee; and the sound of a millstone shall be heard no more at all in thee; [23]And the light of a candle shall shine no more at all in thee; and the voice of the bridegroom and of the bride shall be heard no more at all in thee: for thy merchants were the great men of the earth; for by thy sorceries were all nations deceived. [24]And in her was found the blood of prophets, and of saints, and of all that were slain upon the earth.

19 And after these things I heard a great voice of much people in heaven, saying,

Alleluia; Salvation, and glory, and honour, and power, unto the Lord our God: [2]For true and righteous *are* his judgments: for he hath judged the great whore, which did corrupt the earth with her fornication, and hath avenged the blood of his servants at her hand.

[3]And again they said,

Alleluia. And her smoke rose up for ever and ever.

[4]And the four and twenty elders and the four beasts fell down and worshipped God that sat on the throne, saying,

Amen; Alleluia.

[5]And a voice came out of the throne, saying,

Praise our God, all ye his servants, and ye that fear him, both small and great.

[6]And I heard as it were the voice of a great multitude, and as the voice of many waters, and as the voice of mighty thunderings, saying,

Alleluia: for the Lord God omnipotent reigneth. [7]Let us be glad and rejoice, and give honour to him: for the marriage of the Lamb is come, and his wife hath made herself ready. [8]And to her was granted that she should be arrayed in fine linen, clean and white: for the fine linen is the righteousness of saints.

[9]And he saith unto me, Write, Blessed *are* they which are called unto the marriage supper of the Lamb. And he saith unto me, These are the true sayings of God. [10]And I fell at his feet to worship him. And he said unto me, See *thou do it* not: I am thy fellowservant, and of thy brethren that have the testimony of Jesus: worship God: for the testimony of Jesus is the spirit of prophecy.

[11]And I saw heaven opened, and behold a white horse; and he that sat upon him *was* called Faithful and True, and in righteousness he doth judge and make war. [12]His eyes *were* as a flame of fire, and on his head *were* many crowns; and he had a name written, that no man knew, but he himself. [13]And he *was* clothed with a vesture dipped in blood: and his name is called The Word of God. [14]And the armies *which were* in heaven followed him upon white horses, clothed in fine linen, white and clean. [15]And out of his mouth goeth a sharp sword, that with it he should smite the nations: and he shall rule them with a rod of iron: and he treadeth the winepress of the fierceness and wrath of Almighty God. [16]And he hath on *his* vesture and on his thigh a name written,

KING OF KINGS, AND LORD OF LORDS.

[17]And I saw an angel standing in the sun; and he cried with a loud voice, saying to all the fowls that fly in the midst of heaven, Come and gather yourselves together unto the supper of the great God; [18]That ye may eat the flesh of kings, and the flesh of captains, and the flesh of mighty men, and the flesh of horses, and of them that sit on them, and the flesh of all *men,* *both* free and bond, both small and great. [19]And I saw the beast, and the kings of the earth, and their armies, gathered together to make war against him that sat on the horse, and against his army. [20]And the beast was taken, and with him the false prophet that wrought miracles before him, with which he deceived them that had received the mark of the beast, and them that worshipped his image. These both were cast alive into a lake of fire burning with brimstone. [21]And the remnant were

slain with the sword of him that sat upon the horse, which *sword* proceeded out of his mouth: and all the fowls were filled with their flesh.

20 And I saw an angel come down from heaven, having the key of the bottomless pit and a great chain in his hand. ²And he laid hold on the dragon, that old serpent, which is the Devil, and Satan, and bound him a thousand years, ³And cast him into the bottomless pit, and shut him up, and set a seal upon him, that he should deceive the nations no more, till the thousand years should be fulfilled: and after that he must be loosed a little season. ⁴And I saw thrones, and they sat upon them, and judgment was given unto them: and *I saw* the souls of them that were beheaded for the witness of Jesus, and for the word of God, and which had not worshipped the beast, neither his image, neither had received *his* mark upon their foreheads, or in their hands; and they lived and reigned with Christ a thousand years. ⁵But the rest of the dead lived not again until the thousand years were finished. This *is* the first resurrection. ⁶Blessed and holy *is* he that hath part in the first resurrection: on such the second death hath no power, but they shall be priests of God and of Christ, and shall reign with him a thousand years. ⁷And when the thousand years are expired, Satan shall be loosed out of his prison, ⁸And shall go out to deceive the nations which are in the four quarters of the earth, Gog and Magog, to gather them together to battle: the number of whom *is* as the sand of the sea. ⁹And they went up on the breadth of the earth, and compassed the camp of the saints about, and the beloved city: and fire came down from God out of heaven, and devoured them. ¹⁰And the devil that deceived them was cast into the lake of fire and brimstone, where the beast and the false prophet *are,* and shall be tormented day and night for ever and ever.

¹¹And I saw a great white throne, and him that sat on it, from whose face the earth and the heaven fled away; and there was found no place for them. ¹²And I saw the dead, small and great, stand before God; and the books were opened: and another book was opened, which is *the book* of life: and the dead were judged out of those things which were written in the books, according to their works. ¹³And the sea gave up the dead which were in it; and death and hell delivered up the dead which were in them: and they were judged every man according to their works. ¹⁴And death and hell were cast into the lake of fire. This is the second death. ¹⁵And whosoever was not found written in the book of life was cast into the lake of fire.

21 And I saw a new heaven and a new earth: for the first heaven and the first earth were passed away; and there was no more sea. ²And I John saw the holy city, new Jerusalem, coming down from God out of heaven, prepared as a bride adorned for her husband. ³And I heard a great voice out of heaven saying, Behold, the tabernacle of God *is* with men, and he will dwell with them, and they shall be his people, and God himself shall be with them, *and be* their God. ⁴And God shall wipe away all tears from their eyes; and there shall be no more death, neither sorrow, nor crying, neither shall there be any more pain: for the former things are passed away. ⁵And he that sat upon the throne said, Behold, I make all things new. And he said unto me, Write: for these words are true and faithful. ⁶And he said unto me, It is done. I am Alpha and Omega, the beginning and the end. I will give unto him that is athirst of the fountain of the water of life freely. ⁷He that overcometh shall inherit all things; and I will be his God, and he shall be my son. ⁸But the fearful, and unbelieving, and the abominable, and murderers, and whoremongers, and sorcerers, and idolaters, and all liars, shall have their part in the lake which burneth with fire and brimstone: which is the second death.

⁹And there came unto me one of the seven angels which had the seven vials full of the seven last plagues, and talked with me, saying, Come hither, I will shew thee the bride, the Lamb's wife. ¹⁰And he carried me away in the spirit to a great and high mountain, and shewed me that great city, the holy Jerusalem, descending out of heaven from God, ¹¹Having the glory of

God: and her light *was* like unto a stone most precious, even like a jasper stone, clear as crystal; [12]And had a wall great and high, *and* had twelve gates, and at the gates twelve angels, and names written thereon, which are *the names* of the twelve tribes of the children of Israel: [13]On the east three gates; on the north three gates; on the south three gates; and on the west three gates. [14]And the wall of the city had twelve foundations, and in them the names of the twelve apostles of the Lamb. [15]And he that talked with me had a golden reed to measure the city, and the gates thereof, and the wall thereof. [16]And the city lieth foursquare, and the length is as large as the breadth: and he measured the city with the reed, twelve thousand furlongs. The length and the breadth and the height of it are equal. [17]And he measured the wall thereof, an hundred *and* forty *and* four cubits, *according to* the measure of a man, that is, of the angel. [18]And the building of the wall of it was *of* jasper: and the city *was* pure gold, like unto clear glass. [19]And the foundations of the wall of the city *were* garnished with all manner of precious stones. The first foundation *was* jasper; the second, sapphire; the third, a chalcedony; the fourth, an emerald; [20]The fifth, sardonyx; the sixth, sardius; the seventh, chrysolite; the eighth, beryl; the ninth, a topaz; the tenth, a chrysoprasus; the eleventh, a jacinth; the twelfth, an amethyst. [21]And the twelve gates *were* twelve pearls; every several gate was of one pearl: and the street of the city *was* pure gold, as it were transparent glass. [22]And I saw no temple therein: for the Lord God Almighty and the Lamb are the temple of it. [23]And the city had no need of the sun, neither of the moon, to shine in it: for the glory of God did lighten it, and the Lamb *is* the light thereof. [24]And the nations of them which are saved shall walk in the light of it: and the kings of the earth do bring their glory and honour into it. [25]And the gates of it shall not be shut at all by day: for there shall be no night there. [26]And they shall bring the glory and honour of the nations into it. [27]And there shall in no wise enter into it any thing that defileth, neither *whatsoever* worketh abomination, or *mak-*

eth a lie: but they which are written in the Lamb's book of life.

22 And he shewed me a pure river of water of life, clear as crystal, proceeding out of the throne of God and of the Lamb. [2]In the midst of the street of it, and on either side of the river, *was there* the tree of life, which bare twelve *manner* of fruits, *and* yielded her fruit every month: and the leaves of the tree *were* for the healing of the nations. [3]And there shall be no more curse: but the throne of God and of the Lamb shall be in it; and his servants shall serve him: [4]And they shall see his face; and his name *shall be* in their foreheads. [5]And there shall be no night there; and they need no candle, neither light of the sun; for the Lord God giveth them light: and they shall reign for ever and ever.

[6]And he said unto me, These sayings *are* faithful and true: and the Lord God of the holy prophets sent his angel to shew unto his servants the things which must shortly be done.

[7]Behold, I come quickly: blessed is he that keepeth the sayings of the prophecy of this book.

[8]And I John saw these things, and heard *them.* And when I had heard and seen, I fell down to worship before the feet of the angel which shewed me these things. [9]Then saith he unto me, See *thou do it* not: for I am thy fellowservant, and of thy brethren the prophets, and of them which keep the sayings of this book: worship God. [10]And he saith unto me, Seal not the sayings of the prophecy of this book: for the time is at hand. [11]He that is unjust, let him be unjust still: and he which is filthy, let him be filthy still: and he that is righteous, let him be righteous still: and he that is holy, let him be holy still. [12]And, behold, I come quickly; and my reward *is* with me, to give every man according as his work shall be. [13]I am Alpha and Omega, the beginning and the end, the first and the last. [14]Blessed *are* they that do his commandments, that they may have right to the tree of life, and may enter in through the gates into the city. [15]For without *are* dogs, and sorcerers, and whoremongers, and murderers, and

idolaters, and whosoever loveth and maketh a lie.

[16]I Jesus have sent mine angel to testify unto you these things in the churches. I am the root and the offspring of David, *and* the bright and morning star.

[17]And the Spirit and the bride say, Come. And let him that heareth say, Come. And let him that is athirst come. And whosoever will, let him take the water of life freely.

[18]For I testify unto every man that heareth the words of the prophecy of this book, If any man shall add unto these things, God shall add unto him the plagues that are written in this book: [19]And if any man shall take away from the words of the book of this prophecy, God shall take away his part out of the book of life, and out of the holy city, and *from* the things which are written in this book.

[20]He which testifieth these things saith, Surely I come quickly. Amen. Even so, come, Lord Jesus.

[21]The grace of our Lord Jesus Christ *be* with you all. Amen.

As you've seen, the Bible is a powerful drama telling us God's story of the world. Our prayer for you is that you will continue to explore this drama. As we said at the beginning, we believe the best strategy with the Bible is to go deep, and read big. Take in whole books, not just isolated bits here and there.

But it's also true that we all need help to read and absorb the Bible well. We need help to understand what these books meant when they were first written. We need help to live out the drama of the Bible today, to find the right way to carry the story of Jesus forward into our world.

For this reason we've developed a website so you can continue your journey deep into the Scriptures. We're committed to continually adding more features, insights, links and other follow-up resources. You can check it out on-line at:

BIBLICA.COM/LIVINGTHESCRIPT

We hope this resource will help you make deeper and deeper connections with the Bible. The process of being transformed by God's Word never stops. Of course, we can't give you all the help you need at a website. We also hope you'll seek out other people to read and discuss the Bible with, so you can engage the Bible together. The Bible was meant to be experienced in community. This is key for discovering what it means to live the story today. But perhaps the most crucial thing of all is for God himself to guide you into good understanding. We pray that you will stop and ask him to do just that. In the end, it is his drama that we're all invited into.

To find out how you can begin to experience the Bible in community, go to: Biblica.com/cbe.